THE CONTROL FREAK CHRONICLES

An award-winning broadcaster and journalist, Sarah Tucker was a presenter on the BBC1 *Holiday* programme and, more recently, anchored *I Want That House Revisited* on ITV1. She is the family travel columnist for *Wexas Traveller Magazine* and travel columnist for *The Richmond Magazine*. She regularly contributes to women's magazines, the *Sunday Times Travel Magazine* and *The Guardian*. Sarah Tucker is the author of the *Playground Mafia*, *The Battle for Big School*, *School's Out* and three romantic comedies published by Harlequin.

Praise for Sarah Tucker

'Scandal, backstabbing, illicit affairs . . . a fab, girlie read!' *New Woman*

'Mums will be able to see the truth behind this fun novel' *In The Know*

'A real laugh-out-loud tale' *OK!*

Also available by Sarah Tucker

The Playground Mafia
Battle for Big School
School's Out

Sarah Tucker

THE
CONTROL
FREAK
CHRONICLES

arrow books

Published in the United Kingdom by Arrow Books in 2009

1 3 5 7 9 10 8 6 4 2

First published in Great Britain in 2009 by
Arrow Books
Random House, 20 Vauxhall Bridge Road,
London, SW1V 2SA

www.rbooks.co.uk

Addresses for companies within The Random House Group Limited can be
found at: www.randomhouse.co.uk/offices.htm

The Random House Group Limited Reg. No. 954009

A CIP catalogue record for this book
is available from the British Library

ISBN 9780099519805

The Random House Group Limited makes every effort to ensure that
the papers used in its books are made from trees that have been
legally sourced from well-managed and credibly certified forests.
Our paper procurement policy can be found at:
www.rbooks.co.uk/environment

Typeset by SX Composing DTP, Rayleigh, Essex
Printed and bound in Great Britain by
CPI Bookmarque, Croydon, CR0 4TD

Always for Tom
And Caroline. And Helen T.

Author's Note

The idea behind this book came as a result of an interview I asked to do with a celebrity who shall be nameless and who is not in any way featured in the book. When I asked for the interview to be granted, their reply was concise.

I'd love to talk to you, but I would need to specify the exact moment, the time and place, where you sit and what you would be wearing. I will also give you the questions to ask and the order in which to do it in.

In researching this book and talking to psychologists about control freaks, I realised control freakery is nothing more than emotional abuse which our so-called civilised society finds increasingly acceptable, commendable and in some cases even celebrates. I began to feel I was surrounded by control freaks and that, indeed, through chance and circumstance, I may have become one myself. The nurturing a mother gives to her child, the barriers and goals set by teachers in the classroom, are totally different from the insidious forms of control that have grown in this country in the guise of what is good for us, the voter and the punter. Even Orwell could not have imagined 'Big Brother' would have been quite as surreptitiously realised as it has been, able to make lives and break with complete lack of guile, all for our entertainment. The media, the politicians, the law, the City, the church, all like to think they are in control of our minds and morals and motives and money, but ultimately no one has any control over anyone else. The only one who has control over you is you. Remember that the next time you are in the presence of a control freak, be it your partner, your ex-partner, your boss, or any establishment for that matter, emotionally lording it over you.

A woman in her mid-forties is at my doorstep. It's not a good time for visitors. It's a week before Christmas and I have ten guests to prepare for and a soon-to-be ex-husband who I've just found out is on holiday in the Caribbean with his girlfriend. I've got to make this the best Christmas ever, as it's the last time that Freddie, my two-year-old, will have his mum and dad together with him on Christmas Day. I've been playing my Dido CD for the past two hours and I'm having trouble breathing.

The woman has dark hair, dark eyes, a wide-open face and looks shocked by my appearance – I must look wired and manic, but I don't care how distressed and dreadful I seem. I've got other things on my mind. I haven't slept in days and I've been in the process of tearing up my wedding album, which was extremely difficult to do for practical as well as emotional reasons, as the binder was particularly strong. I've also just opened a card from one of Leonard's friends, who has rather unkindly addressed it to him and Freddie. I don't even get a look-in any more; I'm already out of the equation. His friends knew about the girlfriend a long time before I did, it seems.

I've been signing all our Christmas cards to friends as 'Leonard and Helena (the current wife)', because for some psychotic reason my soon-to-be-ex has chosen a girl with the same name as me, presumably so he won't accidentally call out the wrong name in the middle of a passionate embrace. Leonard preplans his life with anal precision down to the last irrelevant detail, but this time he's surpassed himself. I feel like my family is falling apart and there's a stranger at the door.

'Yes?' I say, wanting to close the door as soon as I've opened it. My words resonate with a 'no, go away' quality that makes the woman take a step back.

'Hello,' she replies, looking hesitant and alarmed.

'I'm looking for Helena Treadwell?' she says, her voice firm but soft.

'I'm Helena Treadwell,' I reply, although I'm not feeling myself at this moment in time.

She looks at me for a while without saying anything while I look back, rapidly losing patience.

'I'm your sister,' she says. Or I think that's what she says. It could have been 'I'm your solicitor,' but even in my fraught state I realise that's ridiculous. Charles Rushbrook is my solicitor.

'You're my what?' I ask, looking at her as though she's speaking in a foreign language.

'I'm your sister,' she repeats.

'Yeah right, of course you fucking are,' I snap and slam the door in her face.

2

Prologue

'I want ideas that make me wet with excitement!'

Elliott Sterling, award-winning senior executive producer of High Light Productions, one of the UK's largest independent TV production companies, bangs his pen on the table and grimaces at his production team of thirty-something attractive young men, all hungry for his approval and eye contact.

He has been tapping the nib of his Mont Blanc ball-point so hard it's started to make deep random pock marks on the highly varnished Canadian imported maplewood tabletop, but Elliott appears oblivious to the damage he's causing.

The group of five sit equidistantly around a table: Simon, Samuel, Luca, Jarred and Elliott. Each has an Orlando Bloom-style effeminate smoothness about him. They've been in the office for two hours now, slurping numerous cups of instant black coffee and fresh green tea, brainstorming ideas to present to the commissioning editors at ITV.

'We've all seen the commissioning letter from ITV and they want to fill the seven to eight weekday-evening slots. They want to encourage more forty-somethings to watch, and as all the forty-somethings I know are neurotic, self-obsessed baby boomers who want to be younger, live longer, don't want long-term commitment of any sort, and are fixated on the Ds – divorce, dating, debt and death (in short, delaying and denying) – they should be pretty easy to target. Don't you agree, guys?'

He looks round at his team like an agitated cobra who isn't quite sure which one he'll attack first, just knowing he will attack – eyeballing his team as they earnestly eyeball him back, nodding furiously but offering no further suggestions.

Elliott looks down at his papers and shakes his head slowly, inhales long, deep, and audibly for effect and spits, 'Then why the fuck can't you come up with any fucking good ideas?' Everyone jumps at the first particularly venomous 'fuck', with the exception of Jarred Collins, a seasoned producer who's used to Elliott's dramatic outbursts.

Elliott sighs and crosses his arms, this time speaking in a sinister slow hiss.

'This commission is important to us. Ed Hardings, the ITV commissioning editor, says he's looking for something new, but I've looked at what he's asking for and it doesn't look new to me. It's just a hybrid of stuff that's worked in the past,' he says, standing up and walking round the table, throwing bits of paper on to it with each step he takes.

'Hardings wants jeopardy, but ironically he doesn't look as though he's willing to take any risks himself. He wants formatted fly-on-the-wall documentaries of punters getting it wrong and our experts putting them right, preferably with as much humiliation, tears, tits and bums as possible. In other words, nothing different at all, just the usual fatuous crap, although don't quote me on that last bit.' Elliott laughs at himself, and everyone in the room, except Jarred, starts to laugh along in a sleep-deprived, coke- and caffeine-infused hysterics.

'You've said nothing, Jarred,' Elliott says, obviously annoyed that his colleague didn't find his unamusing comment funny. 'Do you have anything to contribute? Do you have any tiny gem of wondrous wisdom, Mr Collins? Do you have anything that will get my juices flowing?'

Jarred winces at the thought of getting anywhere near Elliott's juices, but stands up and starts walking round the table ready to hand out some papers of his own.

Thirty-three, producer of creative TV gems such as *Abandoned in the Wilderness*, *Celebrity Abandoned in the Wilderness*, and *Who Do You Want to Be Abandoned with in the Wilderness?*, single, ambitious Essex-born Jarred has been aching to produce something with meaning, substance, integrity and the ability to win a BAFTA for a long time now. He grew up watching *The World at War* narrated by Sir Laurence Olivier in the hope he'd produce something similar, and now he has to work with Ant and Dec in an Australian jungle. Although his shows get good ratings, they don't inspire him and he's been totally bored with the industry he's idealised since childhood ever since he realised it's actually run by children, albeit precocious ones.

Jarred left college wanting to do something creative, unlike his friends, who chose the City and who now see him only as a creative, interesting and colourful guest to invite to their dinner parties to prove they know creative, interesting people, even if they're incapable of being any of these things themselves.

These days he feels just as boring and sold-out as his former classmates, but without the cash cushion they enjoy. His last assignment for Elliott was to produce the top hundred best dying scenes on TV, and in doing so he almost lost the will to live himself.

Unlike the others in the room, Jarred has worked with Elliott for over five years, hasn't been sacked or seduced by anyone in the office and has bounced back from the bullying and rumour-mongering about his sexuality, or lack of it. He's managed to stay focused, professional and come up with excellent ideas, most of which Elliott has stolen the credit for, but because of his talent he's kept his job and a year-on-year salary increase which bought him his first yellow Spitfire and a repossessed three-bedroom flat in Pimlico.

He's also gained the confidence of Heather, Elliott's efficient but brittle PA, having listened to her maudlin tales of bastard ex-boyfriends who all deserve to eat shit and die, preferably slow, agonising deaths. As a result, Jarred isn't fazed by Elliott's bullying antics, mainly because he has more shit on Elliott than

Elliott has on him – and Elliott knows it.

'I've got a different take on this, Elliott,' he says, dropping photocopied newspaper articles about education standards; stabbings; teenage suicides; teachers, parents, nannies and children striking in front of them all.

'Oh, education has been done to death, Jarred,' Elliott says, looking at the headlines. 'Who gives a fuck if people are thick or not. Most of the stuff you've worked on over the past few years has only been watched because the audience are stupid.'

Jarred laughs at this comment, more out of exasperation than because he finds it genuinely funny.

'Good to know, Elliott, but keeping to the point, education has not been, as you say, done to death and it hasn't been done in this way,' he says, continuing to hand the last batch of photocopies to Simon, who looks up at him and winks.

'The school system in this country is in a complete mess, do we all agree on that?' Jarred asks.

'That depends on what newspaper you read or politician you listen to,' Elliott says, 'and who gives a fuck if it is? The TV commissioning editors certainly don't.'

'If I can just finish, I'll explain,' says Jarred, taking a breath and realising – because Heather has told him about Elliott's latest squeeze – why her boss is in such a rush to leave. 'How many people do you know – let's put this more succinctly – how many men do you know that you consider to be real men?' he asks.

'What do you mean by *real*?' Luca counters,

managing to look both confused and defensive. 'Do you mean straight?'

'No, nothing to do with sexual preferences,' replies Jarred, 'I'm talking about maturity. What turns a boy into a man? What is it that makes a man out of a boy? You know that old chestnut, a boy asks his mum what he'll be like when he grows up and she tells him not to be so silly because he's a bloke and he'll never grow up. Why are so many men in their forties cracking up, saying they're feeling emasculated by women, turning to quicksand when they should be dependable rocks?'

'I blame the mother,' says Simon, sighing. 'Smothering rather than mothering.'

'I blame the father,' says Luca. 'Fathers are increasingly absent, emotionally abusive, infantile and self-absorbed when they are there, behaving like juveniles themselves.' He looks as though he's speaking from personal experience.

'I blame *the blame culture*,' adds Samuel, trying to cover all bases.

'Yes, yes, yes, we could get a psychologist to talk the hind legs off that one,' says Elliott, swivelling on his chair to the right then to the left, then to the right again, making the men around him go quite dizzy. 'My personal take on it is boys have too good a time of it when they're young because their mothers spoil them; they get used to the treatment, probably.'

'Interviewing a psychologist as a talking head is dull and doesn't make good TV, which wouldn't please Hardings. What I suggest is this,' Jarred says, taking a breath. 'There's a place called Castleford on the south coast which boasts the most successful schools in the country, as well as the lowest crime rates, so much so that they're de-manning the local police station by two because head office consider it a non-effective use of resources.' Jarred sweeps his arm dramatically along the table, knocking off a few of the photocopied sheets in the process and pointing to a recent article in the *Daily Echo* headlined CASTLEFORD COMES TOP OF THE CLASS, amongst the other tabloid and broadsheet headlines. SCHOOL COULD SAVE YOUR LIFE, WHAT IS CASTLEFORD DOING RIGHT WHERE OTHERS ARE FAILING?, FECKLESS PARENTS FAIL TO PASS ON LIFE SKILLS, SCHOOLS FACE GROWING PROBLEM OF HOSTILE PARENTS, EVERY SCHOOL HAS AT LEAST ONE BAD TEACHER, PICKING UP YOUR CHILDREN: WE NEED YOUR FINGERPRINTS and ROBOTS ARE THE NEW CHILDMINDERS.

Elliott picks up and scans the Castleford article. 'So what you telling me? You're telling me this place produced men where men are men, and women are grateful. Well, there's a change. But it's already been done by these papers, so it's not news,' he argues sniffily.

'It hasn't been done by the papers,' Jarred interrupts, 'it's been touched upon in brief, as all papers do with any story. It's up to us to delve deeper. They've opened the door for us, now we need to walk in and see what we find.'

'There's no celebrity connection here,' Elliott says, scanning the papers again. 'Didn't anyone famous live in Castleford or at least go to one of these super schools?' he asks.

'Joey Whittaker, the crime writer; Michael Frost, the jazz musician; John Tremble, the sculptor; Dominic Field, the theatrical impresario; Jeremy Bishop, the Hollywood director; Tom O'Reilly, the millionaire philanthropist. We've even got a few women, Chantal Cooke, the eco-warrior who's married to Trent Hawes the actor who went to school there . . .' Jarred says, reading from a list.

'And could we get any of these guys on?' says Elliott, looking slightly more interested.

'I don't know,' replies Jarred, shrugging his shoulders. 'It's early days yet, but I can easily find out. And I'm sure there'll be lots of natural talent on the ground – we could shadow some key figures in the community. If everyone thinks they'll be shown in a good light, they should be happy to let us in.'

'But what's this got to do with boys becoming men?' Elliott says, starting to scribble notes. 'Are we saying if you live in Castleford, or are educated at a school there, your son will grow up to be a man and you won't have to nursemaid him for the rest of his life?'

'I don't know, but all the research shows is that whatever it is, they're doing something right in this community. These ex-pupils are not just successful financially, they're rounded people. I've looked at their profiles and they're decent as well as successful. They are philanthropists on a huge scale, and they don't shout about it and they command respect and trust from those they work with. Plus they're all family men. They debunk that old adage that you have be ruthless and manipulative to get on in life.'

'That's just a smokescreen. They're not decent. They just have great PR. They'll have skeletons in their cupboards,' sneers Simon, who's suddenly become interested, possibly because he's just split up with his partner, who's a teacher, and is therefore anti-schools for the foreseeable future.

'Joey Whittaker's books are great,' says Samuel. 'Hasn't his latest just been made into a film?' He looks around the table.

'I think so, the one about the—' starts Luca, but Elliott interrupts. His mistress is waiting and his bladder is full.

'Oh will you all shut the fuck up and let Jarred finish his pitch.'

Jarred continues. 'I've read their biographies. These guys are not money-driven, and they all talk about the passion they discovered when they were at school – at one school in particular, a boys' school, a state school – Castleford School. Why don't we produce a programme that people can actually learn from for a change, something positive and insightful, rather than one where we just sneer at people,' he sighs.

'Oh Christ!' bellows Elliott, throwing some of the press cuttings at him. 'You know why! Because that's what the punters want. That's what the advertisers want. That's what the likes of Hardings want. They want gladiatorial battles. They want to see people taken down a peg or two. They want to see them suffer, really suffer. The crap the characters get up to in soap operas makes them feel better about their own inane little lives and petty little issues. Real-life documentaries are one better than that because the issues are for real. The crap is real. The plus side to a documentary like this is that it may well leave them feeling worse, feeling jealous, wanting more for themselves and their kids than they've got, and that's where the advertisers will come in, telling them how they can get all this stuff and giving them another short cut to happiness.' Elliott is looking at his watch and getting really agitated.

'That wasn't exactly my intention,' smiles Jarred, realising his idea may appeal to Elliott now, but for all the wrong reasons. 'The documentary would show them how it could be done rather than saying, this is how the other half lives and yah boo sucks to you. What's wrong with wanting more? If it's more of the right stuff. And this school, this place, these people, have obviously done something right. Perhaps it's being by the sea or something in the air, but there are other coastal towns with good schools that don't have these great results or these low crime rates. This place is special, I tell you, I'll stake my job on it.'

Jarred sits down and gathers together his papers, shrugging his shoulders, feeling at least he's tried.

Elliott says nothing, just staring into the air for a few moments – which seems like an eternity to the rest of the team. Then he speaks. 'OK, Jarred. I am going to put it forward because there's enough there to make it work. There's celebrity, or we could turn the local talent into celebrity. I know Harding is looking for soft documentaries again, and you're right, Jarred, there's a real concern for our kids, although nothing seems to have changed. I like the story about Londoners moving into the area and bringing their money with them. Promising to soak the rich is always a crowd-pleaser, and public resentment towards the wealthy is verging on pure hatred. Rich rage has become a fire that I would personally very much like to stoke. The wealthy upping the local house prices in these rural communities so teachers can no longer afford to live in the area where they work – just like they've done in London. We might even get some bankers and City types pitching to this Castleford to spend their conspicuous bonuses, and making them even more conspicuous by putting them on TV. Yes, yes, I like it. This documentary could highlight that, too. We can never get to the underbelly of the seriously rich – they're always too well connected and closed – but this might give us a chance.

'Castleford as a place sounds pretty enough, sort of Sonning-by-the-Sea, and the summer term is a good peg. It could be *Bonfire of the Vanities* meets *Dead Poets Society* meets *Goodbye Mr Chips* meets *Looking for Mr Goodbar*. Love that dynamic. Lots of tension, possibility of tears and sacrifice, verbal and even physical violence. Like it, like it,' he says, getting quite excited as he visualises the potential of blood-letting on sports day as parents argue about who's doped their nine-year-old up with Mars Bars.

'The London high-flyers moving into the community could really shoot themselves in the foot with their self-serving platitudes, and we'd be there to record them doing it, which I like and Hardings will like too. I'm gonna put this to Hardings as a revolutionary idea, ground-breaking, something it will take guts to produce, which will appeal to his ego and sense of adventure. And what's more,' he says, surveying the others, who are now looking uncomfortable, 'none of you fuckers have come up with anything better. So, Jarred, if we do go ahead with this, you're in charge of production. This is your baby all the way. What are you going to call it, *The Castleford Cure?*'

'I don't know yet,' Jarred says, still in a state of shock that Elliott's bought into the idea. 'I'll see how it develops and what themes emerge. I know this has gold in it somewhere. I can feel it. But I'll need a really experienced film crew, perhaps two. There's a guy called Will Stafford who's sharp and may be available for at least six weeks,' he says, expecting Elliott to flinch. He doesn't. 'And I know the camera and sound I would like on the job.'

Elliott gets up and grimaces. 'Yeah, I know, I know,' he says, picking up his coffee cup and slurping the last cold dregs as he imagines his mistress on her knees, half naked, tied up and gagged, in suspenders and stockings purely for his pleasure. He allows himself a furtive smile and says, 'Now if that's all you've got for me, guys, I'm going for a piss.'

Chapter One

'I'm afraid we've got to let you go, Helena.'

Peter Bonham, my boss, is firing me. I know he dislikes doing this, as he is looking down at the desk and biting his bottom lip so hard it's starting to bleed. In the past when he's had to 'let go of senior people' as he puts it, he usually rings me up (he's not supposed to but he does) and tells me how difficult it is to fire someone, so I'm sitting in his office on the executive floor of Passion for the Planet's building momentarily feeling more sorry for him than I am for myself, but inside I'm crying.

I'm the fifth person Peter has fired today in the Passion for the Planet station cuts. He's been the MD of Passion for the Planet for the past decade, increasing the profile, revenue and audience figures year on year, a tall attractive man in his early fifties with an enigmatic smile

'This is very difficult for me,' he says, nodding all the while as if desperately wanting me to nod back and empathise, 'because you have been a protégée of mine since you started four years ago, but due to cutbacks and refocus of the station, we've got to let you go.'

I'm torn between wanting to make this as difficult for him as possible but also realising he's been put in a position he can't escape from. I know well that feeling of hands being tied and being helpless, but I'm still going to put up a fight and pull every emotional and financial string I can.

This job has been a lifeline to me over the past years. It's not only given me new-found confidence and focus – it's given me a necessary and independent source of income separate from the sporadic maintenance provided by my ex. It's offered me a voice to express opinions on everything from Gordon Brown's handling of the economy to Angelina Jolie's handling of Brad Pitt. I don't have an overwhelming interest in either subject, but the variety and pace of this place, the vibrancy and dynamism of the people I work with and meet, beats in every way the insularity and number-crunching monotony of my former job. I had been working as a PA for a director of a bank, meeting and greeting people who were even greyer and more homogeneous than the skirt suits I was forced to wear each day in the glass and chrome offices of NYW Banking Corporation. It took courage to leave a regular soul-destroying source of income five years ago, just like it took courage to leave a regular soul-destroying marriage two years before , but I took the plunge, did my journalism diploma by correspondence course, and got a job as a reporter. I worked hard, and made my way up the promotional ladder until I got the plum position of presenter on the mid-morning show. And now I'm being given the push.

Being a presenter at Passion for the Planet, at a time when I most needed it, all at once liberated me from my fears about the future and brightened my spirit, a spirit I thought had been all but crushed a decade ago. Not only did it give me courage to release myself almost entirely from what remaining financial control my ex had over me, but this job has helped so much in bringing back the old Helena I knew pre-marriage, I can hardly recognise the woman I was eight years ago. My self-esteem has gone up in leaps and bounds as I've met people I relate to, rather than those I have to relate to because I'm being paid to.

And then there's Freddie – my nine-year-old son and love of my life. A couple of years after he was born I divorced his dad, Leonard Wallis. For the past seven years I've been trying to remove Leonard from my life, and keep him in my son's.

I've loved the creativity of my job, initially researching on the morning programmes, finding guests to come on the shows, then learning to edit my interviews and sending in news reports for the bulletins, and eventually beating hefty competition (including much younger and better-known talent), ending up presenting the morning show when the effervescent and opinionated Victoria Stock left to take up a job as features editor of the *Daily Echo*. Victoria likes to appear as hard as nails, but she's a complete softie when you get to know her, as I have over the years. I remember the first time we met in a studio she looked me up and down and said, 'You look intelligent. We don't usually get intelligent here,' then introduced herself and asked what books I'd read recently. I hadn't read anything for years, but talked with knowledge and passion about the books I'd read for A level French literature: *L'Étranger* by Camus, *Eugénie Grandet* by Balzac and *La Symphonie Pastorale* by Gide. I then rambled on about Keats's odes and Jane Austen's greatest novels. She looked at me for a moment and laughed out loud. 'So you haven't read anything since your A levels either,' she replied, grinning widely at me. 'We'll get on fine.'

It was her job on the station I took when she decided to move on. Peter championed me in the selection process, arguing that I had a perfect broadcasting voice, an easy accessible manner, and listeners could relate to me, trust me. I've had the best of life coaches in Victoria, and Peter has always taken an interest in what I'm doing because Victoria has always had his ear, and I know, for a time, was also his mistress, until his wife found out. Victoria decided to put an end to the affair immediately, although Peter didn't want to, and I know she left her job and the station for that very reason. To this day Victoria says the position at the *Daily Echo* was a career move she had wanted to make for a long time, but I didn't believe that was her reason then and still don't now.

Since then, I've thrived and grown stronger on the discipline of the job, learning about the technicalities of presenting a show. I've come to appreciate more and more that my producer, George Tucker, is the one who makes the show happen – I'm merely a cog. For the past four years I've gone into the Passion for the Planet building in the early hours, kissing Freddie briefly on the forehead before he gets up for school, leaving my hard-working mum to do the school run, and have travelled up to London on the train and then the Tube. On my brisk ten-minute walk from Sloane Square Tube station where the wind whips round so violently at times I've seen grown men go flying like Mary Poppins, holding on to their executive brollies for dear life. I've always had a smile on my face when I've entered and left this building, but today will be different.

'I thought I would be one of the ones you would keep, Peter,' I tell him. 'The show is popular, one of the most popular on the station. I get excellent PR coverage for Passion for the Planet. We have great guests. Yes, I realise I'm not irreplaceable, but I've been adaptable, innovative about ideas for the show, and the station for that matter. I've doubled revenue to the business as well as doubling listeners. How can you let me go when I've done so much for the reputation as well as the bottom line of the station? This decision to get rid of me doesn't make business sense, let alone common sense!' I feel if I speak any more at this point, I will burst into tears, which will be embarrassing for Peter and for me, and getting emotional will not help matters. I've got to stay focused and stick to the facts.

'We've got to adapt to the present climate, and we're going to give someone else a chance,' Peter replies, his bottom lip now visibly bleeding. I get out a hanky from my pocket.

'Your lip is bleeding,' I say, handing it over.

He smiles, takes it and thanks me.

'It's not my decision to let you go. It's the board's decision. I was outvoted on this and I have to abide by the majority decision, no matter what my personal views are. Sandra Fellowes and Shane Whittaker will be replacing you,' he says, looking down at his papers.

'That couple! They're not even journalists! One's a footballer has-been and the other's a WAG – well, his wife, anyway. Haven't they just been on one of those celebrity reality shows? Don't think either of them even won it, despite getting their kit off, so why do we want them here at Passion, let alone taking my show?'

'Because their agent is also Tom Hardwick's agent, and as you know Tom is our main drive-time presenter and the star of the station. It seems Hardwick has been approached by our rival, and his agent has told our board in no uncertain terms Hardwick will only stay if we take on Shane and Sandra, and they want the morning slot.'

'Well tell them they can't have it then!' I shout. 'It would be bad enough losing my dream job to professionals with more ability than me, but it's an insult to lose out to people who possess fewer brain cells than Freddie's pet gerbils.'

Peter breaks into a smile, but I'm so annoyed I want to throw something.

'You have become an extremely accomplished presenter and reporter while you've been at Passion, and you've always been the consummate professional,' he says, although I don't feel I'm reacting to the news particularly professionally. 'I know there are a lot of opportunities out there for you, in all areas of the media.'

'I don't want any other area of the media, I love radio and I love my job. And what's more, everyone is being made redundant, everyone is cutting back on even the really high-profile celebrities, let alone people like me,' I say, realising by the look on Peter's face, no matter how much I try to reason with him, his hands are tied.

Peter gets up from behind his desk and walks round to me. 'I'm so sorry,' he says, starting to get all teary-eyed. This sets me off and we end up hugging each other and blubbing like a couple of flaky luvvies who've been nominated for Oscars and both lost. Then we start to laugh as we realise that's probably what we look like.

'Well, I give them a few months, six months max, and we'll be begging you to come back,' he says, drying his eyes with my hanky. 'One thing with radio is that the audience actually listens to what is being said. They can spot a dud a mile off. On TV they only care about what you look like. I personally think these two are going to do more damage to the station than losing Hardwick ever would, but it's a gamble the rest of the board are not prepared to take.'

'I realise that,' I say, 'and thank you for everything you've done for me. If I'm really pushed I can go back into working as a personal assistant to some corporate suit.'

'Oh God, don't get that desperate. You fought hard for this job. Don't take a step backward. Build on what you've done here and I'll keep my eyes and ears open for you. I have a lot of contacts in the business and you're too good to be wasted,' he says, looking at me as though he genuinely means it.

'Thanks, Peter,' I say, trying to smile through the tears, but they're still flowing. 'It's like a bereavement leaving this place.'

'Think of it as a trial separation. Don't worry, we'll come back to haunt you in six months – you just wait. Now you've got about a month's contract left, so there's plenty of time to think about what you want to do. I'll always be here for a chat if you want to discuss anything, and as I've said, I will put feelers out. Have you thought about what you want to do? Continue radio-presenting? Go into TV? Or do what Victoria did,' he blushes as he mentions her name, 'and move to a job on a paper?'

'I've hardly had time to think, Peter. You've only just fired me.'

'Let go of sounds better.'

'You've only just let go of me, then. But getting involved with TV would just drive me nuts. I can't think of anything worse, and there's so much crap on-screen as it is. At least radio was a cut above that. As for papers, I might give Victoria a call. I've kept in touch with her since she left a year ago.'

'Think it was eleven months ago actually,' Peter corrects, obviously keeping track of time better than I.

'And she may have some contacts and ideas as well, but I suppose at least in the meantime I can spend more time with Freddie and my parents.'

'That will be a plus. I know I should spend more time with my family,' he says, looking pensive. 'You know I love the station, apart from this bit,' he goes on, looking down at what presumably are redundancy notes on his desk, 'but I try to not forget why I'm really here, for my family. I try not to lose perspective about what's important. That's something I don't think you have ever been guilty of. You have always put family first, and I know you'll enjoy doing the school run with Freddie in the mornings now.'

'Yes I will, and I owe my parents a lot,' I say and smile, thinking about how I kissed Freddie this morning and he gently stirred before rolling over and going back to sleep. I wouldn't have been able to do this job if it hadn't been for my mum coming in each morning for the past year, like clockwork, never late, while I've had the presenter's job and needed help with Freddie. Now Mum will be able to have a lie-in. And my dad has been great too – helping me when I made the move to a cottage round the corner from them, finding out the property was for sale before the vendors put it on the market. He also helped me to strike a deal and pay for a deposit on a mortgage I wouldn't have been able to afford or negotiate by myself. My parents have been there for me, and I've been there for them.

Freddie has been able to spend loads of time with his grandparents, and until last year used to walk with both of them at least once a week after school, to the beach at Castleford Point, skimming pebbles and playing tag, which he invariably won – my father being in his early seventies, my mother early sixties. My parents have been kept young by their grandchild and their active outdoor lifestyle, and look and behave ten years younger than their respective ages. On their walks together, they always laughed a lot at Freddie's stories. My son would delight in recounting tales about sharks and a man-eating octopus that he'd caught sight of, with such conviction I know he'll make a great actor one day. Or politician. And over tea back at their cottage, Dad would tell Freddie about his days in the army, and about being a tennis coach to the boys at the school Freddie now attends, Castleford School. Dad would boast about how he could 'thrash them' at tennis, which Mum had to explain to a much-concerned Freddie had nothing to do with caning or hitting or any form of punishment, but was simply Grandad's turn of phrase. Dad had been headmaster at Castleford, and had many happy memories of the school.

Mum would make her cakes, chocolate marble cake being her speciality, crammed with Smarties and Jelly Tots in the middle. That was and still is Freddie's favourite, and although I make my own version it's never as good as Grandma's because Grandma says so.

If I was late getting back from work, Mum would take Freddie to his clubs, football, rugby, tennis, swimming, karate and now drama, usually driven by Dad in their automatic green Civic. Mum had never taken her driving test, although I was always suggesting it to her, but she said she was happy to be the navigator as Dad made the best driver. But that all dramatically changed when my father had an operation on his knee less than a year ago and anaesthetic got into his bloodstream. He hasn't been the same since.

'And is your father still poorly?' Peter asks, as though he can read my mind.

'Yes he is.' I nod. 'He can't walk properly any more or drive for that matter, so they're a bit housebound. But he's still got his sparkle, and the fact I moved back to Castleford when I got divorced has helped.'

'Is that why you moved there, to be closer to them?'

'Yes, that and I wanted Freddie to see more of them, as well. I've always wanted to make my own way in the world, be independent, never felt the need to keep close to them, which I suppose means they did their job right. I felt strong enough to go out on my own, which I did until I got married, then I lost that spark. I feel, over the past few years, I've started to get it back again. I'm settled, Freddie's settled, I've got great friends and a great job – well, I did have a great job.' I smile. 'I think moving to Castleford was the best decision I could ever have made at that time.'

'Victoria lives in Castleford too now, doesn't she?' he says, this time managing not to blush as he mentions her name.

'Yes, she moved there about a year ago, when she left here. She'd visited me on many occasions. She often said how much she loved the place, how calm and beautiful it is, how she always wanted to live by the sea, and how reasonable house prices were compared to where she was in London, And, well, she was at a time in her life when she felt she wanted to move on, you know . . .' I say, realising all too well Peter knows why Victoria left her job and her home – to try to forget him, something she admits to me in moments of (usually drunken) candour that she hasn't really been able to do.

'Yes, well,' he says, clearing his throat, 'you'll be able to see more of everyone until you decide where to go next. All I can say is, don't worry.'

'Easy to say, not so easy to do,' I reply, looking down at my hanky as he offers it back to me, bloodstained and slightly soggy. 'No, keep it. I'm meeting Victoria today for lunch, with a friend. As you say, she may be able to give me some advice.'

'Say hello from me,' he says, suddenly looking sad and wistful.

'I will.' I nod, not sure if I should, or that I will pass on the message. By the expression on Peter's face, it doesn't look as though he's got over Victoria either.

'Of course Nicola will be on the lookout for you as well.'

'Yes, but I usually let her talk the money rather than find the jobs. She's very good at that side of the business,' I reply, remembering the heated conversation my agent had with Peter four years ago, to get me more money for my contract. Nicola used to be a City trader, but left because she wanted to work with celebrities, thinking that having dealt with huge egos and huge sums of money for so long, she would find her new job required similar abilities, but with more interesting clients. Her negotiating skills are just as useful these days as they were on the trading floor.

'Yes, I remember speaking to her about your deal here. I wouldn't want to get on the wrong side of her.'

'Well, you might just do that when she finds you are giving me the push,' I say, smiling at him.

'It's not goodbye, Helena, because I know we'll see each other before you go, but I just wanted to say thank you for everything.'

I feel as though I'm losing a friend, but perhaps, being no longer constrained by the workplace, I'm really gaining a genuine one, with whom I can behave more honestly. But it's a small world and I don't want to be too honest just yet. If Peter doesn't like what he hears he may not recommend me to someone else, and he does, as he claims, know everyone in the business. He wouldn't have let me go without a fight, so perhaps he's personally got something in exchange, a quid pro quo – I just hope it's worth it.

As I walk out of his office towards the stairs I pass by the studio and see George, forty-something, grey and always grinning, doing his stuff, being the perfectionist that he is and needs to be, working with Mike Matthews who presents the show after me. He waves and smiles warmly at me through the glass. Perhaps he doesn't know what's happened, so I wave back and smile. I expect he'll find out soon enough. Or perhaps George is just grateful he's still employed, and is one of those who is, at work at least, genuinely irreplaceable.

Chapter Two

'What do you mean you've been fired?'

I'm sitting in bright spring sunshine outside the Oriel restaurant and café in Sloane Square. Victoria, who's off to interview some celebrity living off the King's Road, has made time to meet me in her hectic everything-must-be-done-yesterday schedule.

'Peter fired me after the show this morning,' I tell her, at the same time trying to fish out a cinnamon biscuit that has disintegrated in my cup. I've dunked it for too long. I go on to outline what happened.

'Do you want me to have a word with him?' she asks, noticing my dilemma with the biscuit and handing me a teaspoon. 'I'm sure I can change his mind.'

'I don't think even you could, with all your influence over him. The decision has been made and I could tell Peter wasn't pleased about the news nor being the one to have to tell me, but he suggested there would be other things in the pipeline and doors wouldn't be permanently closed for me there,' I say, managing to scoop the soggy remains out of my cup and pile them into a napkin without making too much of a mess. 'Being dictatorial was never his style. He's always managed to motivate and empower his team by getting people to pull together, but he's got some very stubborn know-it-alls on the board.'

Victoria is turning forty this June. She's over five foot nine, Oxford-educated (got a 2:1 in English which means, she tells me, that she's naturally bright, but had managed to have loads of fun while there), elegantly slim but not anorexically so, with long straight dark hair, large brown eyes, high razor-sharp cheekbones and a natural pout. In short, she turns heads on the street and I like being with her, because as well as being funny and vivacious and extremely good company, when men ogle her, it's nice to think they're also glancing over my way too.

But despite the pout and poise, Victoria has remained unmarried. She has been proposed to many times – at the last count, seven – by various boyfriends of various ages, professions and marital status (divorced, going through divorced, will get divorced if she commits to them, and single) in various countries. Each man has fallen hopefully in love with her, realising only at the bended knee/presenting-of-ring stage that she's not going to commit to marriage, or anything else for that matter. Ever since I've known her, she has claimed her decision not to walk down the aisle or live with a man has been based on the fact she's a career woman eager to break through the glass ceiling of a male-monopolised industry, and having a man about the house would distract and tire her. She says she wants control of her life, and does not want any man to dictate to her what she should and shouldn't do with her time. That argument held water in her thirties, but as she's already made it to the top in journalism on a national newspaper, I feel being ruthlessly career-focused is not a viable excuse any more. Her other excuse for not settling down is that she claims she attracts men who want her to support them, rather than it being a match of equals.

Victoria has several mantras, one being 'there is no room for compromise in my life' and another, 'if you want something done well always do it yourself'. These suggest she's tried to share responsibility in relation-ships, but had chosen men she either couldn't or wouldn't trust, and has therefore had to take charge. As she regularly tells me at the end of each relationship, 'If I wanted to be a mother, I would have had a baby.'

But Peter Bonham, as she told me when they were dating, was different. He was a grown-up, her equal in life experience and attitude. She may have felt he was her equal, but he was also married. Victoria admits she was foolish to allow herself to fall in love with him. She got hurt, and over a year down the line her heart is taking a long time to heal. She's determined never to allow herself to fall in love again. She hasn't said as much, but that's what I believe, because I feel the same way. It's been over eight years and my heart is still mending.

'Have you spoken to Nicola? She'll get on the case, you know she will.'

'I will do, but I want to really think hard about what I do next. You left Passion for professional and personal reasons, Victoria, and moved on to something you really enjoy. I don't want to put a foot wrong. I feel since I got divorced I've been on this path, and I've loved every minute of it. Meeting you and moving back to Castleford, and working for the radio station, well, I couldn't have aspired to any of it all those years ago, and to be blunt, I don't want to screw it up. So I want to think about my situation and make the right decision, based on the options I have.'

'That makes sense.' Victoria nods, taking a sip of coffee and realising she's done the same thing with her biscuit that I have with mine. 'But don't wait too long. You're only as good as your last broadcast, just like I'm only as good as my last byline.'

'Hullo girls!' Esther rushes to our table and pulls up a chair, nearly knocking a well-groomed emaciated lady with a well-groomed emaciated rat of a dog off her feet. 'I'm so sorry, love,' she says, turning round to the woman, who looks as though Esther has just slapped her hard. The woman and the dog walk on, both noses in the air as though they've smelt something they don't like.

'It's a bitch getting here from the City,' she moans, looking for a menu and realising neither of us have ordered yet. 'The Circle line is so bloody slow and Mansion House is a trek from my building. But it's good to see you both,' she says leaning over and giving me and then Victoria a hug and peck on the cheek.

I first met Esther Bullions when I was twenty-one and worked for a travel company who organised escorted trips round some of the most beautiful parts of Europe – the road to Assisi, the Cinque Terre, through the Dordogne, Provence and beyond. The trips would last anything from ten to twenty days, with groups of eight to twelve people at a time. I was one of the guides and Esther was the other on some of the trips. I said I could speak Italian (which I can't), and I said I had a full driving licence (which I didn't). I wanted to travel, do something more interesting than work in an office, and somehow managed to bluff my way through the interview with my enthusiasm and personality. I also had the attitude to risk that lemmings have to cliff edges – I ran into everything blindly and completely gung-ho. And I wanted to find love, overwhelming, passionate, all-consuming love. I couldn't live without passion, spontaneity and romance in my life, I would tell Esther, and she would laugh and, ever the pragmatist, would reply that I couldn't live without financial security and independence, which was sadly true.

Esther, unlike me, spoke fluent Italian at twenty-one, having lived in Rome for the first fifteen years of her life until her parents divorced (her father Italian, her mother Brazilian, the arguments monumental), and had passed her driving test as soon as she could take it. Even then her life was so organised that she had decided at what age she would be married and have children (two, one boy one girl, in that order). She booked a church and reception venue three years in advance and she hadn't even met her husband-to-be by then. Of course it didn't happen as planned (two girls, and she met Edward four years later), but I admired her spirit. We were complete opposites physically and emotionally when we met all those years ago. I was tall, gangly, insecure despite all the bravado. She was feisty, down to earth, short and very curvy. What would happen on each trip was that one girl would take the luggage of the guests in a four-wheel drive from one hotel to the next, while the other girl led the group through vineyards and olive groves to a picnic (previously prepared by the four-wheel-drive girl) and then on to the next hotel. The four-wheel-drive girl should have been me, but as Esther discovered my driving was worse than even the local Italians, she decided I should do the guiding on these trips.

It did not go as planned on the first trip, as I got the group lost and we ended up in someone's back garden. The guests only gave a ten-pound tip between us for that trip, but I gave her the lot; it was my fault the tip had been so meagre. I managed to get everyone in the second group to the right destination on time, *and* led them safely through a forest fire. This time the tip came to over £200, which Esther told me was more how it should be. I didn't initially think she liked me, but she told me halfway through the second trip that I was wonderful company, despite my laissez-faire attitude, and she found me totally different from all the other girls who were stuck-up, double-barrelled and utterly two-faced. We lost touch after she returned home, but met again when she moved to Castleford with her husband Edward, who's a successful novelist (acclaimed but not wealthy), and two daughters, Charlotte and Constance. I got a job temping at the bank where she worked, and still does, as a PA to a high-powered marketing executive called Digby.

Esther absolutely detests the job and the man and does it purely for the money, because Edward, who's handsome, interesting and talented, doesn't earn as much as she can. Esther is still as short and curvy and vivacious as she was when I first met her in Italy, albeit with a few more wrinkles and a lot more issues.

'Helena's been sacked from her job,' Victoria says, getting straight to the point before Esther's even sat down.

'Did you say something scandalous about someone on air you shouldn't have?' she says looking over at me more suspiciously than sympathetically.

'No I didn't,' I reply. 'It's cuts at the station and also they've taken on Shane Whittaker or is it Sandra Whittaker, anyway Shane and Sandra, you know that couple that did the reality TV show recently?'

Esther looks blank.

'Well anyway, they are celebrities, B-listers but celebrities, and they are taking my slot and I've been moved out, so as from next month I will be looking for more work.'

'Can you sue?' she asks. 'Can't you ask Charles Rushbrook for advice?'

'No, my solicitor specialises in divorce law,' I explain, beckoning a hovering waiter to provide us with a menu. The meeting this morning has not only heightened my emotions, but also my appetite. 'My contract runs out at the end of the month in any case, so they are not doing anything they are not entitled to do. Anyway, the last thing I want to do is sue. It would burn bridges, and I can't do that at this stage. I've worked too hard to build them. Mind you, at forty-four I think I'm getting on a bit, even for radio,' I say, deciding on a salad Niçoise which is made with fresh tuna at this restaurant, and is one of the more reasonably priced dishes. I've got to look after the pennies now. 'And to be fair, a lot of the other stations have moved to presenters in their twenties and thirties, so I should have known it was coming.'

'Perhaps that goes for TV, but not radio. The voice of enthusiasm and experience is surely more potent than the one of naivety and self-absorption,' Esther replies, taking hold of the menu and ordering a salmon dish.

'Perhaps they think younger is sexier,' Victoria says, taking the menu from Esther and pointing to something to the waiter, who nods and asks us if we want anything to drink with our meal, 'but I don't think it would matter on radio. TV, yes, but not radio. You're a voice, not a face.'

'Whatever,' I say, 'but I don't want to talk about it any more. How's things with you, Esther?'

'The usual. My boss has got a pile of stuff for me to do when I get back. He always dumps work on my desk at quarter to five that must be done that day. I'm sure he saves it up because it gives him a little power kick. I feel like his wife without any of the benefits, not that I can think there must be many benefits from being married to that horrid little man. I have to organise his laundry regularly, not only for his clothes at his home in the country but also for his pied-à-terre, which the wife doesn't know about. He's got several mistresses on the go and I have to organise the changing of sheets on the bed and go round the flat every day, sometimes twice a day, to make sure one never finds out about the other. His sex life is a bit like Clapham Junction – one wrong connection and everything will blow up in his face. I even organise the dirty weekends and have to make sure I get the right first names. They call him Mr Hoppy in the emails they send him. Sometimes I get them on my computer when they should go straight to him. If I wasn't so busy and didn't utterly detest the man it would actually be quite entertaining, but I have better things to do with my life.'

'Well that's what high-powered PAs are expected to do for their bosses these days, isn't it?' Victoria says. 'According to research we've just done there's more infidelity in the corporate world than in any other industry, or perhaps there's just more people admitting to it. We've just done a spread on four women who've been in relationships with corporate high-flyers and are spilling the beans on their affairs, and very sexy it is too.

It seems there's as much power play in the bedroom as there is in the boardroom, but the tables are completely turned.'

'Didn't you go out with a City man only recently?' asks Esther.

'Yes I did,' she nods, 'but it's very difficult nowadays to love a banker. It's sort of like loving a slave owner in the eighteenth century or a Nazi in the 1930s. The man might actually be nice but he represents something reprehensible, odious and dangerous. I didn't really give him a chance.'

'I don't think you give any man a chance these days,' I say as our food arrives.

'I do, I'm just fussy,' Victoria replies irritated by my remark and looking down at her meal which she doesn't appear to remember ordering.

'I think Helena has a point, but I understand your quandary,' says Esther, 'I think you'd be happier with a beta male. They may not be as challenging and stimulating for you, alpha female that you are, but they age well, there is that. Anyway, bankers are usually alpha males, which doesn't make them better than everyone else, just makes them think they are.'

'So what are you going to do about Digby?' I ask Esther. 'And if you hate it so much why don't you leave?'

'You know the answer to the latter, we need the money. Edward sells hundreds of thousands of books but doesn't make hundreds of thousands of pounds. It's just the way it works. And as for Digby, I had to sign a privacy agreement for him when I got this job. Not that that makes it any easier. I just think of some of the lies I've had to tell his wife about where he is and what he's doing, when he should have been at a sports day watching his children or taking them to football training, are despicable. I know he's playing Mr Hoppy with one of his girlfriends in his pied-à-terre and I just want to out him. It's immoral what he's doing and I'm an accomplice and I hate it.'

'You would have stood by your principles years ago,' I say, remembering our long philosophical discussions at the end of each day in Italy, after we had bid goodnight to the guests and crawled into bed, moralising about life, love and music and how Joni Mitchell was the best singer in the world, ever.

'I know, well, experience and material needs change you, don't they? They changed me. I was full of dreams once and one reason why I didn't want to have a proper career like you guys, I don't like the politics or the pressure my boss is continually under and I don't feel the rewards he gets, though high, are worth what it's done to him as a person. He's lost sight of what's important – his family and friends – and lost the plot in the process. I really think he's forgotten why he goes to work. He has more than enough money, he's just stuck in this greedy rut where there's no such thing as enough. I've been there for nearly two years and he's aged ten in that time. He's a changed man. If wealth does that to you, I don't want any part of it. And as for putting myself out there on the front cover, so to speak,

I couldn't do that either. I'm not ambitious that way. You're both in the limelight and need to have thick skins, which I don't believe either of you have, but over time you might lose that sensitivity. I don't need to be in the public eye. As long as I can make my voice heard with my family and friends and those who are important to me in my life, that's all that matters to me. I'm working to live, not living to work.'

'If both of us hated what we did, you'd have a point, Esther,' Victoria snaps back, 'but both Helena and I do,' she looks briefly over at me, 'well, Helena did, something we enjoy, which is more than you can say. Who's really selling out?'

Esther's just about to respond when the waiter comes over to ask us if our food is fine.

'Yes thank you,' says Victoria, 'although I'm not sure I ordered French onion soup, but it's great.'

'By the way, Peter says hello,' I tell Victoria, as the waiter leaves. I didn't want to mention this, but it seems wise to change the subject so Esther and Victoria don't start to bicker. I want everyone to be happy today. I need everyone to be happy today. The last thing I want is my friends niggling at each other.

'That's nice,' she says, giving me one of those fixed I-don't-really-mean-it-smiles. 'Is he still with the wife?'

'As far as I know, yes,' I reply, picking up a fork and poking through my salad.

'Just as well,' she says, 'with the children, it would have been messy if he'd left. And as you say, Esther, about your boss, people in power tend to lose the plot.

They think they're invincible and can do anything and get away with it, treating everyone around them like chess pieces, to be manoeuvred about at will.'

'You can only be controlled that way if you allow yourself to be,' I say. 'You did the right thing by moving on and away from the station and from Peter when you did. It was the sensible thing to do.'

'I know, I know,' she says, popping a crouton into her mouth, 'but well, you know I can't control the way I feel, only the way I react to a situation, and I tried to react to it the best way I could. Doesn't mean I didn't get hurt.'

'We both know you did,' says Esther. 'Remember we both were there for you when you made the decision to move on, so we know what you went through. But you've got a great job now, and all you need is for a man to distract you from the past so you can live for your future.'

'I don't need any more male distractions, thank you very much. That's what messed up my career at Passion. And as for the past and the future, I'd be happy with having a good time NOW,' Victoria replies. 'The woman I'm interviewing this afternoon is talking to me about the latest thing – living in the present, not in the past or for the future, but appreciating what you've got, and identifying what's important and what's not.'

'That's easy – sex and money,' replies Esther prodding her poached salmon and scowling at it.

'In the City perhaps,' Victoria says, 'and at your boss's level, but not everyone has that agenda.'

'They do, but they don't admit to it. At least you know why people work in the City. They are there for the money. And money means power and power means sex. You are in the media because it's creative and you can use your imagination, but you also like the attention, the acclaim, the fame, and fame means power and power means money and money means sex. All boils down to the same thing whatever way you look at it, and whatever profession you're in.'

'You're getting cynical in your old age, Esther,' I say, looking at her and remembering the feisty girl I met in Italy all those years ago who had dreams of becoming an author and actor and political activist, preferably all at the same time.

'Yeah well,' she shrugs her shoulders heavily, 'there's redundancies going around today and I don't think I or the boss will be amongst them, not that I'll get a good pay-off, but well, I do have those moments when I think it would be nice to do something more imaginative, just as you two have done. I suppose for all my talk about not wanting to be in the spotlight, put myself out there, I admire both of you for taking a risk in your lives that I never did.'

'Oh don't be like this!' I reply, leaning over to Esther and giving her a hug. 'You've done good with your life. You're one of life's winners. You're married to a wonderful man, you have great children and brilliant friends. Victoria will die a lonely old spinster.'

'Speak for yourself!' Victoria snaps.

'And so will I, probably. Plus, I've just got the sack,

you've got to cheer me up!'

'OK, I'll cheer you both up and tell you something very funny and indiscreet,' Esther says, drawing her chair closer to the table and beckoning us to come nearer so she can speak more quietly.

'I've recently been given a list of things to buy for Digby. This often happens, but this latest list is really spicy. I had to go into Ann Summers and get a nurse's outfit and a maid's outfit, size small, yesterday, and a whip and handcuffs.'

'I thought he would have got those himself,' Victoria says. 'Did he put it on corporate expenses?'

'Oh no, but it's my time and that's corporate time, isn't it. Just thought you might be able to do a feature on it or something in the *Echo*. I suspect he isn't the only one getting his PA to do errands like this.'

'Yes, but like you, no one wants to jeopardise their job, so they won't speak up.'

'Not only that, but one of the new mistresses sent him a very icky email which came to my computer. It seems he likes to stick sausages up her bottom.'

'Ugh,' I say, thankful that I didn't order the Toulouse sausage on the menu.

'Did you send the message on to Digby?' Victoria asks.

'No, I just deleted it. If I had sent it on, he would have known that I knew, which would make things difficult. He wouldn't have been able to look me in the eye, and at the moment he can.'

'You should have printed the email out and started a

file on him. That way you have information on him should you ever need it later when he wants to fire you, or intimidate you, or blame you for something. The *Echo* has files on all the celebrities and people in the public eye that they will use as and when they need to, within limits. The celebrity agents these days spend more time getting news out of the papers than they do trying to put it in. Next time something like that happens, print it out and file it away and keep it at home so he doesn't find it, otherwise he'll know what you're up to. Information is power. And with power you have control of the situation, should you choose to use it. Any other emails sent?'

'None like the sausage one, but I'll start a file as you suggest. Perhaps I should file them under "foodstuffs", "kinky outfits", "dirty weekend hotels",' Esther says, looking a little more positive, and for the first time sitting back and letting the warm sunshine flood over her face.

'You should entitle the file "The Control Freak Chronicles", something like that – he sounds like a complete control freak and, well, it would be good to keep a record of his antics and proof of the way he uses his influence to bully others, including emails he sends to you. Sounds like a case of the hubris syndrome.'

'What's the hubris syndrome?' I ask.

Victoria is full of gems of obscure knowledge, thanks to her work on the *Echo*, through which she has encountered numerous experts on various personality disorders suffered by both men and women. I suspect this syndrome is one of the many she's investigated since she's been there.

'In ancient Greek drama, a hubristic career proceeds something like this,' she says, taking the condiments and cups on the table and using them as illustrations of what she's about to explain.

'The hero,' she moves thc half-empty coffee cup, 'wins glory and acclamation by achieving success against the odds. The experience then goes to his head and he starts to think he's capable of anything. This leads him to misinterpret the reality around him and make mistakes. Eventually he gets his comeuppance and meets his nemesis, which destroys him.' She uses the salt cellar to push the cup over, not realising it still had coffee in it. It spills across the table, dripping on to the pavement.

'That's not hubris syndrome,' says Esther, 'you're describing every Catholic male. Take it from me, I was brought up a Catholic, and the level of self-righteousness is inbred in every male. That's why I didn't marry one, I married a good atheist. Edward believes in himself,' she says, trying to mop up the coffee on the table.

'Every man I've ever met is guilty of hubris as well. Most men, whatever their faith, think they're right all the time, especially wealthy men. Their money insulates them from the truth, everyone knows that,' says Victoria. 'All you've got to do is look at Helena's ex-husband to realise that's the case.'

'Don't get Leonard involved in this conversation. I

want to think happy thoughts about him and send them out to him, wherever he is, in the hope that I'll get happy ones back,' I say, determined to change the subject again, even if it is back to Digby and the rather tacky sausage story.

'Do you think he's happy?' Victoria asks me, finishing off her soup.

'Who's happy?'

'You know who. Leonard.'

'I expect so. He's got everything he always wanted. He's wealthy, with a girlfriend who cooks and cleans for him, and he sees his son when he wants without the day-to-day responsibilities of being a full-time dad, so what's not to be happy about?'

'A lot, actually,' interrupts Victoria. 'That's probably why you haven't got back any of that karma you've been sending out to him over all these years. Have you heard from him recently?'

'No, so no news is good news. I'm applying for a one-off alimony payment, so he should be very happy about that. Once I do that, he won't be obliged legally to pay me any more money. He's got to pay for Freddie, of course, but I don't have claim on any of his assets, earnings or bonuses from then on.'

'Isn't that shooting yourself in the foot financially, especially as you've just lost your job Helena?' asks Esther, looking concerned.

'Financially it's the wrong thing to do. Psychologically it's totally the right thing to do. It cuts me off from the money, his money, and as you've been saying, girls, money is power and power is control. I don't want him to have control over me any more, and money has always been a bone of contention between us, even when we were married. I'm hoping, by doing this, everything is settled and we will both be able to get on with our lives, get on with the past and move on and enjoy our respective futures.'

'Surely he must be jumping at the opportunity?' suggests Victoria.

'I would have thought so too,' I reply, 'but perhaps you're right about that hubris thing. Perhaps he'd rather keep the control over me and continue with the present financial situation. Some things are more important than money, when you've made enough of it, and perhaps having this control over me is what Leonard gets off on.'

'Well, at least you don't have to live with him any more,' says Esther, 'and see him every day. I have to see Digby every day and take all his crap. Which reminds me,' she says, looking at her watch, 'I've got to dash. Got to run a few more errands to his tailors, collecting a suit and waistcoat, and then off to the butcher.'

'Sausages?' asks Victoria.

'Yes actually, but for tea tonight thank you,' Esther replies, grimacing at her friend.

'I need to see Leonard, not every day but I will always need to see him – because of Freddie,' I say, 'but I know what you mean, Esther.'

I get up and give her another big hug. I do feel she should be doing something else with her life, going for the goals she set herself when we were in Italy together, but it seems she's living vicariously through Edward, who's the author she wants to be, and through her friends, who have the spotlight she wanted as an actress all those years ago. Instead she spends the day with Digby, metaphorically washing his dirty linen in private. But who am I to talk – it took the trauma of a divorce to change my life around; perhaps she needs something huge in her life to make her change the way she looks at herself.

'And I'd better dash as well,' says Victoria, realising what the time is herself, 'got those psychos to interview. Very good to see you, darling, and I will see if there's anything going at the *Echo* if you're interested. Are you interested?'

'I don't know at the moment, Victoria, but thank you. If I do get the one-off payment I won't have to worry about money the way I do at the moment. You know, the will he/won't he pay the money into my account this month, but so far this year he's been great. But I'm always concerned something will happen, and for some reason he'll delay it or reduce it, and we'll be back to not speaking, which is lousy for Freddie. Perhaps the contract ending at Passion is another shake-up that I need to put me into action, just like when I got divorced. I'm a great believer that good comes out of bad things, and when one door closes another opens.'

'You are so positive and upbeat,' says Victoria, laughing at me, 'and full of such bullshit platitudes, but

I love you anyway. Now must dash. After this interview I'm doing something on anorexia and how it's going out of fashion.'

'Never knew it was in,' I reply, but Victoria has already gone into work mode and moved off, both of my friends leaving me with the bill. And I'm the one that's out of work.

'Good luck with the job-hunting, Helena. You'll find something soon, and in the meantime, enjoy your break,' Victoria calls out as she wafts away, a group of men stopping to stare at her as she walks past them. She hasn't lost her touch.

As the bill arrives, my mobile rings and I answer it as I watch my friends head off in opposite directions.

I notice the call is from Peter Bonham, probably hoping I'm still with Victoria so he can speak to her directly. Unfortunately he's just missed her, but I answer it anyway.

'Hello, Helena,' says Peter. 'I may have already found something for you.'

Chapter Three

'You can open the door now,' I hear a voice say as I wait outside the boardroom of High Light Productions. My feet haven't touched the ground since I met Victoria and Esther at Oriel yesterday. Peter's call was to tell me about a documentary that was being made about Castleford. As luck would have it, he knew someone in radio who knew someone in TV called Elliott Sterling. This man, an executive producer, had just had a commission for a fly-on-the-wall documentary about my home town being one of the best places to live in the UK, and needed someone to co-produce the show, do the narration and perhaps appear in it as well. Peter had immediately thought of me. I'd been called by a guy named Jarred, who had asked me to meet him the following day at eleven sharp, so at eleven exactly I find myself sitting outside the boardroom of High Light Productions for my first-ever interview in TV.

A small, dark-haired, utterly miserable-looking woman opens the door.

'Would you follow me, please?' she says, smiling in the same scary, unnatural way Wednesday Addams smiled at her peers in *Addams Family Values*.

I get up and follow, wearing my designer stripy skirt and simple cream blouse, expensive remnants of the designer wardrobe I had when I was with Leonard, survivors of the ravages of my coloureds and whites mix-and-match washing disaster and pathetic attempts at ironing. On radio I could present dressed in sackcloth, but in TV, appearances, even if you're behind the camera, matter. At media parties I always tended to mix with the radio lot more, because although they said less than the TV lot, what they said was so much more interesting and intelligent. I'm not at all sure I'm going to fit in, but Peter suggested I at least give it a chance, and as it's on my home territory I could theoretically work from home. All in all, it seems like an ideal solution until I find something in radio again.

I also think that at forty-four, I must be an OAP in TV terms. The short, miserable woman leading the way looks no more than twenty-one. I thought everyone who worked in TV was supposed to be manically happy and irritatingly cheerful and jolly – perhaps she missed that memo.

I follow her into a large room with white walls containing large prints of people laughing uncontrollably and severe but beautiful models pouting. One wall is completely covered in top-to-toe mirrors, which is a little disconcerting, but as my back is towards it when I sit down, it doesn't put me off my stride. There's a white screen on the other wall, and around the table are three people, two of whom are sitting and one – Jarred, I presume – is standing and offering his hand for me to shake.

'Hello, Helena,' he says, 'thank you so much for coming to see us at such short notice.' He shakes my hand and offers me the seat nearest him.

The short, miserable woman leaves the room, returning a few seconds later with a tray of coffee cups and a Bodum cafetière, which she places on the table. Everyone is silent as they watch her push down the plunger on the coffee maker; her facial expression is so intense and angry that the plunger may as well be a pillow she's pushing down on someone she's determined to suffocate. I let out an inadvertent nervous laugh when she does the final push to the bottom, because it's so aggressive, and she looks up at me, shocked, as though I've read her thoughts. She smiles again. She's got to stop doing that. It's scary.

'Thank you, Heather, if you can just take notes now that would be great,' Jarred says, smiling at Heather, who looks at him as though he's just killed her cat and she's thinking of ways to kill his.

She turns to a small table that's in the corner of the room and sits behind it, picking up a notepad and pen. I don't know why, but despite her miserable demeanour I like her. She reminds me a little of my agent Nicola in the way she looks. I think that if I were in a street fight for any reason, I'd want Heather on my side.

'Firstly, let me introduce you to my two colleagues,' says Jarred, who's wearing a slim-fitting Paul Smith suit. I know it's Paul Smith because Leonard use to wear the same suits and they have a certain finish I recognise, but the style suits Jarred better. He's in his early thirties, I would say, has dark brown hair and striking green eyes that are made more vivid by the bright green shirt he's wearing under his brown suit. Esther would think him cute, Victoria would think him power-crazed, I just think he may present a solution to my imminent employment problems, so he could look like Johnny Depp or Johnny Rotten for all I care.

'These are my colleagues, Simon Thorpe and Samuel Allison,' he says, gesturing to the blonds on either side of him. They are also wearing fitted suits, but somehow they don't pull it off with the same flair as Jarred and just look gay, perhaps because they are.

'Please take a seat and I'll talk you through this programme,' he continues, as I sit down and help myself to a cup of coffee. 'In the next couple of months we're planning to film in Castleford for an as-yet untitled documentary, though it'll probably be called *The Castleford Cure*, in light of the fact that the country is going down the drain but Castleford seems to be doing something right. You have low crime, excellent schools and house prices have gone up at a time when they're going down or remaining stagnant everywhere else. We have a camera crew in place, but we need some research on the ground and we're also looking for people to take part in the programme who we can shadow. Ideally we'd like to film in Castleford School, which I believe your son currently attends?' he says, looking down at his notes.

'How did you know that?' I ask, confused.

'You talked about it on your radio show,' Simon says, 'so my researchers tell me. And I listen as well, of course.'

'Oh, right,' I say, looking at him more closely, not quite able to visualise him as one of my listeners. I wonder if he'll still listen to Shane and Sandra when they take over from me.

'Not only would we like you to help us with the production, we'd also like you to feature in and possibly narrate the story,' Jarred continues. 'We would need to ask for permission to film in the school, and also identify key characters in the community who we can shadow for a period of no more than six weeks.'

'What, continuously?' I say, unable to think of anyone I know in Castleford who'd allow that degree of invasion of privacy.

'It wouldn't be all the time, just for key occasions like, for example, the school play, where you'd get some interesting social interaction. Of course, the locals would have complete control over the final product, or at least be given a chance to view the programme before it went out,' Samuel says, although I don't believe a word of it.

'Really?' I say, 'that's the first time I've heard that. The subjects usually have to sign release forms, don't they? We don't even give them final say in radio.' I don't believe for one moment that these men would change anything that would make their programme less controversial, given the opportunity.

'We feel that if you came on board, the people we'd want to film would trust the credibility and integrity of the programme. I can understand how they might feel, as many documentaries just make fun of the characters they film and edit them so they come across as idiots or criminals, but with you on board, producing and helping to edit the final product, we know it will manage to fulfil both our remits. It will show everyone in an honest, accurate light,' Jarred says dogmatically.

'Will you sign something to that effect?' I ask, expecting a no and getting one.

'Well, no, we don't have a contract like that,' says Samuel, 'but you'll be able to see and edit everything.'

'You realise I have no TV experience. All my experience is in radio,' I say.

'Radio deals in sound bites, and so increasingly does television. You're a journalist and we need a good storyteller as well as story-getter, and according to Peter at Passion you do both extremely well.'

'When are you hoping to start filming?' I ask.

'In the next couple of weeks,' he snaps back.

'I'm not out of contract with Passion. I've got a month to run,' I reply.

'We can work that one out with Peter and your agent.'

'What will you do if there's a problem?'

'There won't be. If there is we will find someone else,

but your name was mentioned by more than one person and we thought you'd be ideal. As for money, we will need to talk to your agent about that as well,' he adds.

'Good, I'll give you her details. Her name is Nicola at Fairwell Agency,' I say, realising I haven't even told her I've been given the push from Passion yet, everything has happened so quickly. 'She's on holiday at the moment, but her colleague Julia is expecting your call.' I have briefed Julia about this potential project and she says she knows the company and Elliott well, but not Jarred.

'Heather,' says Jarred, looking at the woman in the corner, 'will you get Julia at Fairwell on the phone after the meeting and ask if she'll accept a call later today about Helena? Many thanks.' She looks up briefly from writing notes in what looks like shorthand. I didn't know anyone still did that.

I turn round as Heather gets up to leave the room. As she passes me I catch her eye, and I'm not certain, but I think there is a glint of a smile on her face. She returns with more coffee.

For the next two hours Jarred, Simon and I talk through what they want to achieve with the documentary and how they'll pull it together. They briefly mention some of the team I may be working with, actually they just talk amongst themselves about it, I suspect because they don't have crew finalised yet, but I catch the name Will Stafford and a Becca somebody or another.

'We want to be given permission to film in the school

and at the key events. We need to identify three to four key players in the community who we can film. We believe your father used to be the former headmaster of Castleford, so perhaps he'll be willing . . .' says Jarred.

'I don't think so,' I interrupt, 'he's not very well at the moment, so I don't think he'd be up to it, but I know Miss Compton-Batt, the current headmistress, and many of the teachers quite well, as well as a few others in the community who I think would be happy to allow you to film them. There's the local builder Anthony Flindell and his wife Agetha, who are both self-made and I'm sure would appreciate the exposure. And there's Victoria Stock, features editor at the *Daily Echo* who lives near me and is a good friend. My friend Esther Bullions is married to a novelist called Edward who could be willing to be interviewed, as he was born there. Esther works in the City and is a strong character, half-Italian and half-Brazilian, so you could get an interesting perspective on why she's chosen to live there. As far as filming the children is concerned, that would be up to the school and the parents, but I'm sure that if we promised to show the school in a good light they wouldn't see the harm in it. There are enough local events going on to make it visually interesting, although I still can't see how you'll find out why this place produces happy, healthy, successful people in only six weeks. You'd need a year at least, I'd think, which would be out of the question both financially and logistically.'

'Correct,' nods Jarred, 'and we don't have the luxury

of funds or time. So will you speak to these people?' He sounds as though he wants to wrap up the meeting and get an agreement on the table before I go.

'I haven't said I'd agree to come on board yet,' I say, taking a sip of coffee.

'Will you?' Jarred asks.

'Yes, as long as I receive the payments half up front and half at the end, and you negotiate direct with Nicola,' I reply, knowing full well she will strike a superb deal, and although Julia is lovely she may not be as tough.

'We don't usually do that,' says Jarred.

'If you want me you will,' I reply.

'OK, I'll see what we can do,' says Jarred, looking as though he's bitten off more than he can chew. 'Good, good. Well, I'll get in touch with those I think would work well on something like this, and I've got a director in mind. I'm sorry it's such short notice, but we've only just got approval for the commission. It's always like this in TV, I suspect it's like this in radio as well sometimes,' he says, smiling at me.

'No,' I reply. 'Never.'

I'm about to catch the train back to Castleford and I'm still buzzing with the thought that I've got my first job in TV. It's ironic, at the age of forty-four, to get a break like this long after I'd thought the opportunity had disappeared. Just like every other child, I'd wanted to be on TV at some stage, but as the years went by and my mother and husband told me not to be so impractical,

I put the thought to one side. It was only my dad who suggested I follow my dreams – to be a dancer, travel the world, or be on TV – but my mother silenced him as quickly as she silenced me. But now I've actually managed to do it, and just at the moment when I needed to find work. And it's stimulating work, too. I find myself looking upwards before getting on the train at Waterloo and mouthing 'Thank you' to a God I thought had forsaken me a few times in the past decade.

The train carriage is half empty as it's just after lunchtime, free of the suited men smelling of BO and tight-skirted women who should have bought a size larger. I'm quietly delighted to be out of the rat race now, but my mind and BlackBerry are full of plans, people I must see over the next days before Freddie returns from his holiday with his dad. He's been away just over a week now and I've missed him, especially in the evenings when I've got home to an empty house. I occasionally go into his bedroom and smell the duvet and his clothes, like some love-sick puppy, and check if his gerbils, Tom and Jerry, need food. They always look at me with their little black eyes, eager to be let out. They have a large yellow ball that they can be put in and can roll about the house in. But Freddie once put Tom in the ball on the landing and the little animal was nearly concussed when he bounced down the stairs.

Leonard wasn't going to tell me where he was taking Freddie for holiday until I threatened to sue him with kidnapping. He grudgingly told me they were going to France. I'm going to see Mum and Dad today, to see how Dad is coping and how Mum is coping with Dad, and Dad with Mum. I love them both dearly, but Dad has always been so active up to now, and Mum has had to take a role she's not used to, being the one in charge, and I don't think she likes it. I feel she was very happy to have Dad as the driving force in their relationship, in every way, and now, since his operation, she's become a carer and she's having to support him. I think that makes her short-tempered sometimes, so I hope she's in a good mood today. At least I can tell her about the new job. I haven't told either of them I've been sacked from Passion, simply because I know they would worry and they've got enough on their plates. And I've got to tell them a film crew are going to be in town, something I know they won't like. They both hate those reality shows. I tell myself I'm not going to screw up. I must have said it out loud, because a kindly-looking old lady sitting opposite me leans over and taps me on the knee. 'Of course you won't, my dear,' she says, smiling warmly at me, 'of course you won't.'

When I arrive home I open the door to find a pile of post waiting for me, as I left before Herbie the postman arrived. With my early starts while working in radio, I have only met him a few times during the seven years I've lived here, but Mum, Dad and Esther tell me he's very nice.

As well as Tom and Jerry, we have a ginger cat called Dillon, whom we adopted from Victoria. She was given him by one of her potential fiancés as a present, and when they split she didn't want to be reminded of him, so Dillon came to us. He's fluffy, meows loudly and is a very rakish cat. He likes to be stroked while sitting on Freddie's lap, watching anything to do with wildlife on the TV. He also has a particular penchant for *America's Next Top Model*, which is my candyfloss TV these days, so much so that I've managed to get Freddie hooked on it, too.

There are the usual bills waiting, and two letters – one that looks as though it's from Charles Rushbrook my solicitor, which hopefully contains an agreement about my alimony settlement, but more likely brings another stalling tactic from Leonard's lawyer, Felicity Matthews, who can write such incendiary letters I'm amazed they don't catch light in the post. I open the envelope in the hope of good news, but, as predicted, it's a request by Felicity to have mediation. Mediation about what? The word is not in Leonard's vocabulary, nor is the word compromise. It's his way or no way as far as he's concerned. I go cold and sit down abruptly. I can't negotiate to save my life, that's why I hire Nicola to do all the negotiating for me at work. Unfortunately she can't take my place this time around, but I really wish she could. The thought of being in the same room as Leonard for even a minute makes me feel quite ill. He intensely dislikes me, so why does he want mediation? I read on.

'My client is distressed that relations between your client and himself have become so bad . . .'

He's not distressed at all. He's enjoying it all immensely. And relations have become so bad because he's continually tried to intimidate me by sending me notes about Freddie having nits and warts and not having sufficient clothes when he stays with him each weekend.

'. . . and my client would like to address the situation.'

Leonard Wallis has never addressed anything in his life, that's why he still gets a buzz out of bullying me despite the fact we've been divorced for years. And he's never fought his own battles, either. Felicity is just the latest of his cronies, but admittedly a necessary one. He's surrounded himself with people who validate his lies, so much so that he probably doesn't have a clue what the truth is any more, but he works in property, so perhaps that's not surprising. He even got his mum to dump a former girlfriend when he couldn't do it himself. He's evidently planning to use mediation as a chance to say something to me when someone else is in the room, so I can't shout at him.

'Please could you ask your client when she is available to attend mediation with my client . . .'

Never. That's when I'm available. Never.

'. . . at a mutually convenient time. Yours sincerely . . .'

Inside, there's a covering note from Charles, asking me to call him and let him know about dates. He thinks the mediation will look good if we ever go to court about the divorce, as it will show that I'm willing to co-operate. He also thinks it might help with the money situation and getting a one-off payment. I personally think it's a delaying tactic. Leonard doesn't give a toss about getting on better with me. He would have tried harder and earlier if it was genuine. Now I've got to sit in a room with him while he shocks or tries to humiliate and upset me, although I can't imagine what he's got up his sleeve after all this time.

I walk into the kitchen, where Dillon is meowing loudly at me, and put the letter on the table. I love our home, but the room I love the most is my kitchen, not because I'm an amazing cook – I'm not – but because a radiance floods the room in the mornings, as though the angels have popped in for breakfast. It's the place where everyone seems to want to sit, stand and talk. In our sitting room, even the most chatterboxy people shut up, watch TV, listen to music or just muse and contemplate life while gazing out of the window, but in the kitchen, everyone opens up. It's as though there's an energy there that turns them into philosophers spouting platitudes and worldly truths about love, life and the meaning of the universe. I feed Dillon, sit down, make myself some green tea and open the other letter.

I've got so much to do and so much to look forward to. I don't want to go to this mediation thing or meet up with Leonard, but there are only so many things he can do to delay coming to an agreement about the settlement now. And though I may not have my radio job any more, I've got a new challenge with this TV show, so I find myself positively skipping upstairs to my bedroom to change out of my smart clothes and into some loose ones. Then I can get down to work and start making lists of who would be good to have on the show, who might be willing to co-operate and the best way to proceed.

Sitting on my bed, I take a quick look at my diary. It's Tuesday, which leaves me five days to organise as much as possible before Freddie gets back. I know Miss Compton-Batt isn't taking a holiday over the break, so I'll contact her. Then I need to meet up with the Flindells, a power couple if ever there were one. They're both so focused on money I'm amazed they got round to having children. And I've got a few other names in mind who might be interested in appearing on the programme.

I text Peter a brief thank-you message, because his phone is engaged when I try to call him.

'Thank you for suggesting me to High Light, Peter. If it goes well, I will owe you. If it goes badly, you will owe me!' I pause briefly before adding, 'And Victoria says hello back.'

Chapter Four

'Fab news about the TV!'

Victoria is shouting at the top of her voice down the phone. In the background I hear a few of her colleagues in what sounds like a screaming match, and she's got to make herself heard over the noise. I don't know how she can work in that environment. It was all rather civilised and ordered at Passion, even when things didn't go to plan, and at the *Echo* it sounds as though she's on a stock market trading floor. 'Could you hold two ticks?' She asks, and before I can tell her that's fine, I realise she's put me on hold and I'm suddenly listening to the latest single by Lily Allen. I don't mind Lily Allen, but I'd prefer Victoria Stock.

I'm calling from the studio, having broken the news to George about my leaving the station. I told him an hour ago just after the show finished, and he still looks utterly fed up, not only because we got on really well as mates but because, as he told me in front of Peter Bonham and some of the other presenters, I'm the most professional unpretentious colleague he's ever had. Now he's got to somehow work with two anodyne yet arrogant amateurs who have nothing to offer the station other than the fact they will make listeners feel they can do the job better than Shane and Sandra can. Peter, of course, was extremely diplomatic, as is his way with everything that goes on at Passion, and asked George to come to his office for a quick pep talk about why the move had to happen. I've just seen George exit Peter's office and although he looks slightly calmer, he still has the expression of someone about to kick something, preferably the footballer and his wife.

'Sorry about that, I'm back,' says Victoria, as Lily Allen clicks off mid-verse. The screaming in the background has calmed down, so she's not shouting any more. 'Now where were we? Oh yes, the TV.'

'Yes well, it's a new challenge for me and that's probably what I need at the moment,' I enthuse, smiling at George as he walks past me mouthing, 'Let me take you to lunch.'

'I agree. Did you give Peter my regards?' asks Victoria as I nod back to George about the lunch date.

'I did,' I reply.

There's a pause on the other end of the line as though Victoria expects me to elaborate in some way, but I have nothing else to say.

'Are you OK?' I ask.

'Oh yes, yes, just hectic at the moment. Just had the weekly morning meeting with Dena Benson that usually takes till lunchtime. We're trying to agree on what we're doing over the next month. We've got a lot of different potential feature ideas in the pipeline, some of which I like, you know, women-entrepreneur profiles, positive upbeat inspirational stories of success through adversity and stuff like that, and all Dena, our resolutely downbeat editor, wants is stuff about women being portrayed as victims, losers, downtrodden. She says readers will feel better about themselves because it'll make them think, hey, at least my life is better than theirs. I don't agree with her. I just think articles like that will make readers complacent with their lot and not try harder. They will, what's that buzzword . . .' She pauses briefly. 'It will disempower them and that's what I said in the meeting, and Dena said I was talking bollocks and told me to shut the fuck up. I didn't, of course, because that's not my style, so I went on about how we should be writing features about strong women, who have done well through hard work and ingenuity, who have real talent rather than just raw ambition and big tits. Their success stories are more likely to make readers feel they could do the same, rather than feel inadequate, but hey, two different ways of looking at an issue I suppose, and I have to accept that her management style is dictatorial with a touch of fascist thrown in for good measure.'

'So what are you working on at the moment?' I ask.

'Oh, several things. There's a reporter assigned to a story on the growing trend of swinging parties in London and that's another one I don't think is right for the *Echo*, but Dena wants the piece to feature. But that's not due for another couple of months now, until we've got enough quotes and proof to back up what we'll be writing. Plus, of course, we've got to get the legal department involved with that one, because as you can imagine, there's lots of sensitivity. But hey, as Dena says, "sex sells", and more papers are bought when they have sex in the headline, so what do I know?'

'For what it's worth I think you're right, and hopefully I can produce something half decent on Castleford. If High Light want any locals with sexual peccadilloes in Castleford I think they're going to be sorely disappointed.'

Victoria laughs. 'Do people have sex in Castleford? It's such a wholesome place to live, it's a bit like the first time I visited Canada, I had the same feeling. Everything was so wonderfully virtuous and, well, for want of a better word, uncontaminated, and I felt the same way about Castleford the first time I visited you.'

'You make it sound like a Stepford town, like something out of Walt Disney', I reply, feeling suddenly quite defensive about the place I was brought up in.

'No, I don't mean that. I don't mean Castleford is sterile, shallow and synthetic. In fact it's quite the opposite. It's a place full of genuine people, with strong values and healthy lifestyles, so I'm not surprised High Light want to do a documentary on it. It would be great if the *Echo* would do something like that, but Benson would be more interested in featuring the worst town in England rather than the best, because that's her style. And even if she did suggest we wrote something on Castleford, she'd probably search out the fly in the ointment, the dirty secrets people would prefer to keep hidden, because that's an easier story to write and to sell, or so she believes. And I don't.'

'Good on yer, girl. Nice to know there's a modicum of integrity still left in our tabloid press. Try not to get sucked in like the rest of them. Now would you like to come round for supper tonight? I'm inviting Esther over as well, if she's got cover for the girls. It depends if Edward is at home. Could you make it about seven or is that too early, with your deadlines?'

'That's fine. Anyway, better go now, another deadline looms and if I don't make this, I won't make that dinner. Love you,' she says and clicks off before I can answer.

After texting George that lunch would be lovely today if he's available in an hour's time, or tomorrow, I go next door to the café and sit down to make notes about who I should approach for interviews for the documentary. I need to call Esther, to not only ask her if she and Edward would be willing to appear but also what she thinks of my other choices, in particular Agetha and Anthony Flindell. I know she knows them, because they've been to a few dinner parties at her house.

'Hello Helena, what can I do you for?' Esther answers her phone quickly. It's a complete contrast to speaking to Victoria at work. Esther sounds as though she's in a soundproof studio.

'Quiet in the office today?' I ask before I tell her about my programme ideas.

'Yes, Digby is out shagging his latest squeeze. I've been ferrying calls all morning and doing as Victoria suggested, you know, printing up the emails she's sent him and he's sent her and making notes of when he's asked me to do things. I could have quite a thick file by the end of the month.'

'Just be careful Digby doesn't find it, or you'll be out of a job.'

'I'm taking it all home, so no worries there.'

I quickly run through how I've been asked to co-produce a documentary on Castleford and then start to tell Esther my plans about the people I think should appear in the programme. She doesn't interrupt my flow until I mention the Flindells.

'God, you're not thinking of putting Agetha and Anthony on-screen are you? They'll completely take over. They'd be producing the show if they had their way. You've got to be strong with them.'

'Well, I'll leave all the heavy-handed stuff to the other producer and director. He's a guy called Will Stafford. He's supposed to be very instinctive about what works and is able to deal with even the most stroppy punters, having worked mainly with A-list celebrities in the past, so he's used to strong egos and ridiculous demands.' A telephone call from Jarred after I returned home had given me this information.

'But including Agetha and Anthony could create totally the wrong impression of the town, and they're not even locals. OK, Anthony was born here, but he moved away, and Agetha comes from Essex. How about asking John Tremble, the local sculptor? I don't know him very well, but I have been told he's done the greats, like Olivier and Mandela. Mind you, he can be dreadfully indiscreet and very direct. He called Tony Blair a prat when he appeared on the morning breakfast show several years ago, and they had to apologise afterwards because he wouldn't. He could be quite controversial.'

'That's just what High Light are looking for – a degree of controversy, something they can market and make a good story out of, which other media can pick up on,' I say, making a note of John Tremble's name.

'Are you going to be in it?'

'Well, as a producer I don't think I can, and it would seem odd. If Dad were better I would have got him involved, him being the former headmaster at Castleford School and all that, but I think it would be too sad in his present state. He used to be so strong, confident and articulate, now he can hardly walk. He's changed so much and his memory isn't what it was. It wouldn't be how he would want to be remembered.' After a brief pause I ask, 'Would you two like to appear in it? You and Edward are both colourful characters, good talking heads with plenty to say about Castleford, yourselves and why this place works for you both; you'd be ideal.'

'Edward's publisher would be very happy if you covered his book launch. The publishing world is going through tough times at the moment, and anything to get his books into the supermarkets would be great. Anything that increases his profile will make him very happy, if it's the right sort of publicity. I'll ask him tonight.'

'Are you about for supper this evening? I've invited Victoria round as well.'

'I'll let you know. If Edward can look after the girls, you're on. If not, perhaps another night. Anyway, better go now. I'm expecting Digby back soon.'

After a lovely lunch with George, who tells me he'll keep in touch and try to sabotage Shane and Sandra as much as possible, although he doesn't think he'll have to do much because they will do it themselves, I catch the train back home to prepare supper for the girls, having heard that Esther can come.

Sitting on the train, I close my notebook and put it back in my bag, seeing Charles Rushbrook's letter. I wonder what the real reason behind the mediation is. I don't know whether I should text or call Leonard but remember he's in France with Freddie. I doubt he would tell me the truth anyway. And then the weirdest thing happens. As if he's read my thoughts I get a text asking me to call him. I ponder ignoring it, but call back, just in case it's urgent and Freddie is unwell. As soon as the phone picks up I recognise a voice I love.

'Hello Mummy.'

I might have known. It wasn't Leonard wanting to speak to me. It was Freddie wanting to speak to me and he's using his dad's phone, and Leonard doesn't want to be charged for the call. That's very Leonard.

'Are you having a good time?' I ask.

'Yes Mummy,' he says.

'And are you doing anything nice?'

'Yes Mummy.'

'That's good. Are you somewhere nice?' I ask, trying to elicit more than a 'yes Mummy' answer. I know boys are monosyllabic on the phone, but Freddie is naturally quite chatty and I sense his father is hovering nearby just in case Freddie lets out a 'get me out of here quick' before he can get to the phone and cut him off. I remember the times I was still with Leonard and that was what I always wanted to say to friends when I spoke to them, but couldn't, because he was lurking around. And as Freddie is so much like me, and Leonard and I never communicated well when we were married, and even less so now we're divorced, I get the feeling Freddie has the same problems with his father.

'And what are the things you've been doing?'

'We went swimming and the swimming pool was reeeeally cold Mummy.'

'Was it?'

'Yes.'

'And did you do anything else?'

'We went walking.'

'That's nice.'

'Yes.'

There's a pause.

'How is Grandad?'

'Grandad is fine and says he wants to give you a big cuddle when you get back,' I reply. Freddie is close to my father. Dad doesn't spoil him like Mum does, but he has that quiet, gentle authority and strong way with him, despite his recent troubles, that Freddie respects. I find it upsetting when Freddie asks about Dad, as I know he's really quite unwell.

'That's good.' Another pause.

'I love you very much, Freddie, and miss you loads and loads.'

'I love you very much Mummy, too. Very, very much. Now I've got to go.'

'Bye then. Love you.'

'Bye Mummy, bye bye.'

I've still got some of the voicemails Freddie has left on my phone from months back. He's at that age where he comes out with the most grown-up phrases and then goes back into boy speak, all in that unbroken voice of innocence that I bottle up as voicemails. Just thinking about Freddie makes me smile and lifts my spirits, and even makes all the rubbish with Leonard worthwhile.

As we're coming into my station I make use of the time by leaving messages with Jessica Compton-Batt, John Tremble and the Flindells, none of whom answer their phones, to call me back. I might as well get on with things, if only to find out that they don't want to appear in the programme and we have to start from scratch.

I arrive back home. Our cottage is nothing like the place Leonard and I had in London when we were married, which was small but central, just south of Primrose Hill. Our cottage hallway still has the original flagstones, and there's a large fireplace on the right-hand side as you walk in. To the left is the kitchen, which has an island in the middle, and to the right is the sitting room, which has yellow, red and lime-green sofas, which somehow work, thanks to suggestions from Victoria, who knows which colours clash and which complement each other. There are photos of Freddie and me on our travels, as well as snaps of me, Victoria, Esther, Mum and Dad scattered on the walls going up the stairs. I've also hung some paintings I did, and a few by my favourite artist, Maggie Thompson; her wild and wonderful flower paintings are on the walls in the sitting room and study as well as my bedroom. The bathroom has a large roll-top bath, in which Freddie and I sit to have our discussions before bedtime, although I think this may have to stop soon, mainly because he's getting too big, but also because it's no longer politically correct to do such things, which personally I think is utter nonsense and rather sad.

Freddie loves to run into my bedroom, which is simply furnished (a bed, a wardrobe, a chest of drawers – what else do I need?), and bound on to the bed, sometimes so violently I'm amazed it doesn't go straight through the floorboards. He broke it slightly once and I had to get the local carpenter in to fix it. He obviously thought the damage had been caused by some frenzied lovemaking – I didn't put him right – as he couldn't wipe the smile off his face. The strange thing is that I bought the bed for my flat in town, but it fits in this bedroom even better; it's as if it belongs here.

My bedroom is also confetti'd with hearts, as Esther

observed when she came up to go to the bathroom and poked her nose round my door. I hadn't noticed before, but I suppose it is all hearts. Wooden ones hang from the wardrobe and chest of drawers, felt and silk ones from the window, and they even dangle from the bedside lamps. I've got heart-shaped dishes for my rings, crystals hanging by the window, which rainbow the room on sunny days, and some edgy paintings of nude lovers, including one of a naked woman playing the violin, which I picked up on my last trip to Australia, where I met an artist in the Rocks in Sydney. Hopefully one day it will be a collectable.

Freddie's bedroom is all boy. He hasn't reached the Britney-Spears-poster stage, so it's more Arsenal players and a map of the world, where he puts silver stars against all the places he's visited, which thanks to the fact that I love travelling are far and wide across Europe, America, Africa and the Far East. His favourite holiday, he says, was skiing this year in Switzerland, when he accompanied me on a Club Med holiday. He managed to ski off-piste, but twisted his ankle and then had to ski down with the rest of the group in a snowstorm. The conditions were bad, but as the story's progressed the storm has become worse and worse, and his sprained ankle evolved into a broken leg and probable broken ribcage!

Freddie's bedroom is also a mess of the game cards he's collected, loved, played with and forgotten about, found and loved again. There are Warhammer painted and half-painted figures; paintings and drawings on the wall and ceiling above his bed and numerous ones on the floor, which I try to preserve before he or Dillon trample on them and ruin them for ever. His wonderful – well, I think they're wonderful – attempts at pottery are lined up on his windowsill, together with football trophies and karate belts he's won, and photos of him collecting his awards. And there's Tom and Jerry the gerbils who have to be kept out of Dillon's way. Mum thinks it was a stupid decision to have both a cat and the gerbils in the house, with the inevitable happening at some stage, but at the moment I think Tom and Jerry intimidate Dillon more than the other way round.

Freddie's bed is covered in spaceships and about twenty soft toys, including some that belonged to me as a child and even ones that belonged to Mum and Dad. The only faintly feminine touch is a large fluffy cat that he chose when we were skiing in Mont Tremblant three years ago, and which he decked out in biker gear and roller blades, which makes the unfortunate cat – named Eagle because he has an Eagle on his jacket – look camp.

I need to do the cleaning and a pile of ironing that's in the kitchen, but it can wait. I remember one time when I was still married to Leonard he got so angry about me not doing his ironing correctly that he pushed me down the stairs. I told Esther about it and she said I should have filed for divorce then, but I didn't. If Leonard could see the amount of ironing I've got piled up now, he'd have a fit. Perhaps that's what the mediation is about, after all – the legacy of me not doing the ironing.

I rush into the kitchen and get out some chicken breasts I've left marinating in wine, garlic, olive oil, soy sauce and herbs. I've sliced onions and button mushrooms already, so chuck everything into the pot and put it in the oven and forget about it until the girls arrive this evening. I haven't done dessert but I've got chocolate (Green and Black's), so that will be fine. I'm sure they'll bring wine and Esther usually has really good stuff, as she belongs to some sort of wine society in town and does wine tastings. I can't tell my Bordeaux from my Beaujolais, but she's very knowledgeable.

I'm just about to run a bath. The luxury of a bath alone at six o'clock on what could be a school night if it wasn't for the holidays is a rare experience, and I'm so looking forward to it. I should drizzle the fragrant oil and light the scented candles, but I've been looking through cupboards and I've run out of one and can't find the other, so it'll have to be water and soap tonight, with the lights dimmed.

Just as I get in, the phone goes – not my mobile but the house phone. I want to let it ring until it clicks off. The answer machine doesn't work (think Dillon did something to it – or so Freddie says) so I just lie in the bath, listening to the sound and expecting the caller to give up any moment. After ten rings, this has still not happened, and I'm starting to worry. Mum would give up and ring me on my mobile, so would Esther and Victoria, and even Leonard would try an alternative, although he could be playing games. I don't know why he would, but neither I think does Leonard sometimes.

I'm just about to get out of the bath because I'm not relaxing any more, when the ringing suddenly stops. I'm expecting my mobile to start buzzing now, but it doesn't. I get out and dry myself, still wondering about the call as I get dressed and make my way to the kitchen, where the casserole is smelling wonderful. I go to the phone, almost expecting it to start ringing again as I pass by and can't resist picking up the receiver and dialling 1471 to see who it was. I don't recognise the number. It's a mobile, so I press recall and wait to see who the persistent caller is.

'Hello.' A male voice answers abruptly, not introducing himself but expecting me to do so immediately.

'Hello, did you just call me?'

'I don't know. Did I?' the voice says. 'Who are you?'

'I asked you first.'

'You didn't actually, but my name is Will Stafford. I've called a number of people over the past half-hour, none of whom are in, and so you could be any one of them, but you don't sound like my mother or my builder. So you could be Becca or Helena. Which one are you?'

'Helena Treadwell,' I say.'

'Oh great. I'm the director you're working with on the documentary. I'm just calling to introduce myself to you. A girl called Becca Kite will be calling you tomorrow, hopefully, or sometime soon, to arrange for us to meet up. She's the production assistant on the show and she'll be helping you and me to make sure it all goes smoothly. We've got an experienced camera-man and soundman, so things are looking good. You haven't done TV before I understand?'

'No. How do you feel about working with an amateur?'

'I've worked with them before, and anyway you're not an amateur. You've done radio and you're a journalist and Jarred says you know Castleford, so you sound ideal for the job. And coming from radio you don't have an ego the size of a house, so we should get on fine.'

'Yes, I'm sure we will,' I reply.

'So I'll be in touch over the next few days, hopefully in person, to go over the schedule, but if you want to get moving on meeting those you think will be good to appear, start working on that. I'll get Becca to set up a schedule for next week, and we can start filming the week after that. How does that sound to you?'

'Well, that all depends. I'm due to be at the radio station for the next month as that's when my contract ends, but I know Jarred said he was going to have a word with my boss and my agent, but I haven't heard anything yet. As soon as I do, I'll let you know,' I reply, feeling slightly flustered.

'Oh right,' he says, sounding confused himself. 'I'll call Jarred and try to find out what's up. He should have let me know by now. This sort of thing happens all the time in TV. I'm sure it's the same with radio.'

'No.'

He laughs. 'Well, you'll have to get used to that, I'm afraid. There's a lot of go-with-the-flow in this job, and especially on something like this programme where we've got to be there to film just in case something interesting happens. But you're with experienced people and in good hands, Helena.'

'That's good to know.'

'Well, nice talking to you and I look forward to working with you.'

'Likewise,' I reply, suddenly realising I'm not being particularly friendly and that I've got to work with this person for the next couple of months or so, so it's important to make the right impression and not come across as some stuck-up cow. 'I very much look forward to working with you too, Will.'

As I put the phone down there's a knock on my door. Taking a quick look at the clock in the hall, I realise it's now almost seven. I open the door to find both Victoria and Esther standing there, with big smiles on their faces and bottles of champagne in their hands.

For the next hour, while eating dinner and drinking wine and champagne, I update them on the programme, the request for mediation, and how Will Stafford sounds very pleasant and professional.

'Could be some romance there?' asks Victoria, helping herself to more chicken.

'No,' I shake my head, 'you know from personal experience work and pleasure don't mix, and I've no intention of getting involved with anyone at the moment.'

'You've got to be open to new relationships, Helena. You can't live your life in a cocoon just because you've been burnt by a bad marriage.'

'Hark who's talking. You haven't exactly flung yourself into anything since you were with Peter, have you?' I snap back.

'I know, pot calling kettle black, but well, I'm more cautious, just like you are, now. I've made a single life for myself that is comfortable and orderly. I'm in control and I don't want to relinquish that again. I suppose you feel the same way.'

'Of course I do.'

'That's an excuse,' says Esther, looking at both of us. 'You know what your problem is, you have difficulty overcoming the past.'

'I don't need you to tell me that,' I say, 'but at least it allows us to live more in the present and appreciate things that are happening now. I think that's the right way to be. I'm doing what I wanted to do when I was married to Leonard. I'm building a life for myself, focusing on the things that are important to me, my family and friends, rather than the things he allowed me to do. And I think I'm managing just fine. Anyway, how's your diary on Digby coming along?'

'Very well. I'm getting to grips with his various women. There was a Tricksy, which I doubt is her real name, and another one called Alison something. Her last name began with an L. I've printed these emails up as you suggested, Victoria, and put them all in that file. I should have a nice set of notes in a few months' time.

Don't know what I'll do with it, mind you, but it could make interesting reading in my old age. Digby's such a smelly old fart. I really don't know what these women see in him apart from money and power. He isn't even funny. Plus I had to go into one of those sex shops and get a dildo and some other stuff. It's all very tacky and I come home and tell Edward about it and all he can do is laugh and say that we should be doing something like that. So I got a maid's outfit for myself and he seemed to like that. Mind you, I'm never doing the cleaning again if that's what he's trying to get me to do more of. Edward can do that,' she says sniffily, which makes Victoria and me laugh.

'I don't think that's why he suggested it,' I say.

I'm just about to take the plates into the kitchen when the phone goes again.

'Sorry, I'd better answer that. I bet it's something to do with the TV thing. Could be my agent telling me I can't get out of contract or Peter telling me he won't let me out of contract.'

'Well answer the bloody thing and find out,' snaps Victoria, probably because she likes the idea of it being Peter and she would have an excuse to say hello again via me. I wish she'd just call him herself and chat, but I understand the situation. She's doing the right thing, but it must be difficult for them both. Peter and Victoria must have been seeing each other for a year before his wife found out. I never agreed with the affair, but they seemed very much in love and he told her he would never leave his wife because of the children, and that his wife was happy with her life and her marriage. And then when the wife found out and understandably wasn't happy about anything, Victoria lost her job and her man – but it was her choice. She hasn't really opened up to either Esther or me about the affair, how it was, how it ended, because she's very self-contained. Although it's been over a year since she left the station, I sense her feelings for him have not diminished, and neither have Peter's feelings for her. And I have every sympathy for Peter's wife, who has done nothing wrong (no affairs, bad cooking, BO, drugs, late nights) apart from bore her husband, probably. I was in a similar situation myself, although in my case the husband didn't hang around.

'Hello,' I say, walking out of the room with my portable phone and making my way to the kitchen.

'Oh hello, Helena, it is Helena isn't it?' a voice asks. I recognise it as Jessica Compton-Batt, Freddie's headmistress.

'Yes it is,' I say, putting the plates down before I drop them.

'I'm returning your call about the TV programme. I'm intrigued. Can you tell me more?' she asks.

'In short, Miss Compton-Batt,' I start.

'Jessica, please. Only the children call me that,' she says.

'In short, Jessica,' I start again, 'I've been asked to produce a documentary about Castleford and the people who live here. It seems that this town has been identified as a place where other people want to live.

We've got low crime rates, excellent schools, a lovely location, and house prices are on the increase. Property is sought after even despite the credit crunch,' I say, listing all the things Jarred had mentioned.

'I don't think the house-price increase is a good thing,' she interrupts. 'It's only because we've got Londoners coming in and upping the prices, and the likes of the Flindells building here. But that's just a personal view, so don't quote me on it,' she adds quickly.

'I won't, Jessica,' I say, 'but that's why it's good that I'm producing the show, because I will have some control over what is finally broadcast. I was concerned that they'd do one of those fly-on-the-wall documentaries and make everyone look stupid, but as I'm on the inside I can prevent that happening. The last thing I want them to do is make us look like the people from *The Vicar of Dibley*.'

'Good God no. Although,' she laughs, 'I know some parents who aren't far off some of those characters. Anyway, yes I am happy to see you tomorrow to talk about it. We don't start term until next Tuesday as you know, as we've got a study day on Monday for the teachers, but you're welcome to come round to my house, or I can come to you. About nine o'clock is good for me if that suits you?'

Nine o'clock and on the week I don't have Freddie! I thought I'd be able to have a lie-in, but obviously not.

'Nine o'clock is fine,' I say, 'and I can come to you. Are you still at The Chestnuts in Lady Lane?'

'That's it, the house with the large yellow door,' she says. 'See you at nine.'

No sooner have I put the phone down than it rings again, making me jump out of my skin.

'It's Agetha Flindell, got your message. Very interested. Can you meet at the Mansions tomorrow?' she barks.

'Thank you for getting back to me so promptly,' I reply, managing to get a word in edgeways. 'I can come over around midday,' I say, realising that I might need some time to persuade Jessica that the show is a good idea, while Agetha and Anthony will just see it as a cost-effective way of promoting their business, which I suppose it will be.

'I've got a meeting at midday, but I can move it to later. I'll get Davina to sort it all out.' Davina is her beleaguered PA. 'If you come to the show house at the Mansions you can get an idea of the decor, and it might be a good idea to film the new properties. What do you think? Yes, that would be excellent!'

'Yes, I'd love to come and see the show home,' I reply, not wanting to commit myself in any way and aware that Esther is right – I might have a problem with Agetha wanting to take charge of everything. 'See you tomorrow then.'

I walk back into the room carrying the phone tentatively, half expecting it to ring again, but it doesn't.

'I wonder if I've got myself involved in something beyond my control. With radio, I knew what I was doing, where I was due to be, and had George there to hold my hand. Guests would arrive on time, and if they didn't, well we'd have a standby, and everyone was unseen so they could all be themselves and not try to be anything they were not. I'm already getting the impression with TV that it goes at a completely different pace, the agenda is completely different and I'm going to hit the ground running. I hope I know what I've let myself in for,' I say, sitting down with the girls.

'That's the fun of something like this,' says Esther. 'It's not knowing what you're going into but doing it anyway. Going out of your comfort zone. You may not think it now, but this is exactly what you need, Helena.'

Chapter Five

I find myself at Jessica's yellow door at five to nine sharp.

Freddie is currently in Year Four at Castleford School, where Jessica Compton-Batt's been head for over ten years, having replaced my dad when he retired. She's got two more or less grown-up children, and she lives in a large cottage overlooking the village green with her husband, Desmond, and her dog, Bertie.

When I see her at parents' evenings, she's always immaculately dressed in what looks like Aquascutum, with her glasses balanced on the end of her nose. She looks at parents and pupils over the top of her specs when she's talking, and I'm not sure if she needs them or wears them for effect. Victoria thinks women who wear glasses want to look sexy and intelligent, but I don't think that's the impression Jessica is trying to make, though I could be wrong.

When I moved back to Castleford and asked Dad if

there was a place at the school for Freddie, he said he'd find out. There was, but Freddie had to do an entrance exam (unusual for a state school but that was the policy at Castleford), and although my son is bright, I was worried he wouldn't pass.

I remember receiving the phone call from Caroline Belamy, the school secretary, and crying down the phone when I heard he'd got a place. That was the penultimate hurdle crossed. Freddie had looked round the school and liked it, he'd taken the exam and been offered a place, now all we needed was for Leonard to agree to the school. I rang him up and said I'd found a good school for Freddie and would he like to have a look around. I must have caught him on a good day, or maybe he'd just got laid the night before, but anyway he said that if Freddie liked it, he was happy for him to go there. On the day Freddie was due to start, Leonard came down and took us to school in his latest Porsche. Freddie looked so smart in his uniform and stripy blue blazer. Leonard took a photograph of him and I took a photograph of Leonard and Freddie – for Leonard's use, not mine, I might add.

I was so happy that day – Leonard even kissed me on the cheek, which shocked me so much I nearly fell over. I even told Freddie about it, which was something I came to regret later when Leonard accused me of manipulating Freddie by doing this. I suspect Leonard's annoyance was caused by Freddie saying this in front of his father's girlfriend. Perhaps the control is more evenly balanced in that relationship than it was in ours.

'Hello, Helena,' Jessica says, opening the door and allowing Bertie to jump out and lick my ankles, making me laugh. 'Having a good holiday?'

'Yes, very good, although it's not holiday for me as I'm working. Freddie is with his dad this week,' I say, overwhelmed by Bertie's welcome as he jumps up and attempts to lick my face. He's a friendly old dog, but has dreadful halitosis, and in his enthusiasm to welcome you he leaves a trail of ornaments and awards in his wake.

'How are you?' I ask.

'I've been preparing for next term. It's a big one in our calendar, with the staff play, the school play, school trips and sports day, and then of course we have reports to write, so it's busy, busy, busy,' she says, ushering me into her cottage.

'What a lovely home you have,' I remark, admiring the high ceilings and beautiful stairway.

'Thank you. It is nice, isn't it. It's lovely to come back here after a long day. It dates from the seventeenth century and we've tried to keep most of the original features, or at least the ones that weren't rotten with Capricorn beetle.' She laughs, and leads me through to the sitting room and a large apricot-coloured sofa. There's a lot of African and South American art on the walls, and some unusual, rather phallic ornaments on the side table, which look slightly out of place in the room.

'I've made some tea. I'll just get it,' she says and walks out.

I smile. My dad was always very organised and planned everything down to the final minute. He was an excellent time manager, and my own time management has improved significantly since having Freddic, although my mother disagrees. Jessica returns in a few minutes with a pot of tea, two cups and some chocolate biscuits.

'I don't know if you've managed to have breakfast yet,' she says. 'Let me know if you'd like some eggs or cereal. I didn't make anything just in case.'

'Thank you very much, but I've already had breakfast,' I say. 'I love all your paintings and ornaments.'

'Oh, thank you. They're presents from Henry, my son, who's been building mud huts in Paraguay for charity. He's just gone off to Africa to do something else for another charity. He travels so much it makes me dizzy, but he's on a gap year before he starts university and he wanted to do something constructive. I suppose building huts is as constructive as it gets,' she says, smiling. 'Now I could talk all day about my son and I'm sure you could talk about Freddie all day as well, but you are busy and so am I, so if you'd like to tell me a bit more about this documentary that would be good.' She produces an A4 pad of lined paper and writes on the front 'TV documentary – to discuss.'

I have also prepared for the meeting and start by describing how I became involved, why Castleford was chosen, and why I personally think it's a good idea. She listens without interrupting, just making the odd note.

After I've finished, she picks up her cup and takes a sip of tea.

'I like the idea of the documentary and the premise behind it. I must admit, I would have said no if anyone else had approached me about the school being included, but as you have a child here, it's in your interest to make us look good.' She takes another sip. 'I don't see there being any problem with filming in the school, as long as it doesn't disrupt things too much and you give us ample warning of when and where filming will take place. The parents will have to give permission for their children to be filmed, of course. In my opinion, if you want to know what makes the school as successful as it is, you should interview some of the staff, record the school play, perhaps even the staff play – our drama teacher, Mr Gates, has persuaded them to perform *'Allo, 'Allo* to parents and pupils. Mr Gates is also organising the boys to produce *Lord of the Rings*,' she says, grimacing slightly.

'Wow! That's rather ambitious, isn't it?'

'Yes, extremely. Some of our boys are born hobbits, although we're finding that everyone wants to be an Orc. Mr Gates is quite a teacher and quite a man, so if you're looking for inspirational role models to film, you couldn't get much better than him,' she says, making a note. 'There's also sports day, and perhaps you can film in some of the classrooms. I think you'll find filming a PTA meeting entertaining. We have a nice balance of proactive parents who, despite being very full on, recognise that teachers need to be allowed to do their job. They let us teach and we let them parent, if you know what I mean.'

I smile. 'Yes I do,' I say. 'I hope I do a good job with Freddie.'

'Freddie is a lovely boy, Helena, absolutely lovely. He needs to speak up more and improve his organisational skills and spelling, but apart from that he's fine. Well, I think the next thing to do is speak to the staff and liaise with the PTA,' Jessica concludes. 'Then we can announce it to the boys and think about timescales. If it shows the school in a good light, the project has my full approval.' She looks at her watch.

'Gosh, it's already quarter to ten, and I've still got to walk the dog, so unless you want to join me, I'll have to take my leave,' she says, standing up.

'No, thank you very much,' I say, 'I have another appointment as well.'

'Oh, I almost forgot to ask,' she says. 'I hope your dad is feeling better these days. I know he's been very poorly, so do send him my best wishes, and those of the school, won't you?' Then she holds my hand, which I find quite affecting.

'He's getting old,' I say. 'He's been younger than his years for such a long time, but since the operation he hasn't been himself. Mum is there to help him and at least we only live up the road, so I can see him regularly, but he's always been such an active man.' I tell her, thinking about the sport he played until only a couple of years ago. 'He's seventy-three, but a young seventy-three, and if it hadn't been for that operation going wrong I'm sure he'd still be active now.'

We bid our goodbyes and I walk back down the lane to my cottage, which is only a fifteen-minute stroll away if I'm walking fast. As always, my surroundings lift my spirits. I feel proud that so little has changed here for thousands of years. Castleford has managed to retain a lot of its original higgledy-piggledy buildings and charm, with its cobbled alleyways, small shops and a farmers' market where they sell the most delicious sausages, fresh pastries and herb breads. With both the sea and the countryside on its doorstep, Castleford has everything I could wish for, although I do occasionally miss Ocado, which doesn't come out this far.

Castleford itself will be the real star of the documentary, and I owe it to the town and the people who live here to make the programme great. Above all, Castleford has soul, but as I step into my lane, I remember my next port of call that day, a place with a distinct lack of soul, Flindell Mansions, the new-build that's the pride of Agetha and Anthony Flindell.

Agetha Flindell walks and looks as though someone has stuck a red-hot poker up her bottom. She has a permanently pinched appearance, with a nose, eyes and mouth that are all small, tight and neat. She has long brown wavy hair, a size-ten figure and a piercing gaze, and neither Esther nor Victoria particularly like her, but she invites both of them to her occasional dinner parties because, as Victoria comments, Agetha likes to invite guests who have more to talk about than money and property. If you don't have either, she writes you off as a nobody immediately. I think she's like an onion, multi-layered, and each time I meet her I try to see the good in her, although I've yet to find it. Esther and Victoria agree about my onion analogy, only they think every layer is as bitter and slimy as the one before.

Agetha Flindell is forty. I know this because she had two enormous birthday parties to celebrate the fact, at her mock Queen Anne home on the edge of Castleford, and her holiday home in Spain. She even managed to get the local papers and Spanish glossies to cover the events. She talks quickly, twittering like a bird, and she asks really personal questions while refusing to give anything away about herself. Even the articles featuring her birthday focused on the superficial – the dresses and guests – rather than the nitty-gritty of her background.

I have little to do with Agetha or her husband Anthony, a short corpulent man who reminds me of the puppet mayor in *Trumpton*. He's been in the building trade for the past thirty years, having taken over from his father, who passed away a few years ago, and has amassed a fortune selling multimillion-pound houses to multimillionaires. He drives a Porsche 911 turbo, while Agetha has a BMW, and they have three children, all of whom attend the nearby boarding school, Letchbury. Agetha dotes more on her designer handbags than she does her children, although when taking them out in public she shows them off in exactly the same manner.

I drive to Flindell Mansions with very mixed views about whether it's a good thing to have her in the programme. Both Flindells are obnoxious, but they'll contrast nicely with the rest of Castleford, where the locals are anything but.

I stop at the large black wrought-iron gates to the private estate, get out of the car and press the shiny gold intercom. Everything looks and smells so new.

'Hello, this is Helena Treadwell for Agetha Flindell,' I say when a tinny voice asks me who I am.

There's a brief pause, followed by, 'Come in, please, and go to house number seven, the show house, where Mrs Flindell will be waiting for you.'

The doors magically open and I rush back to the car – I've always had a fear of being caught out and the doors opening and closing before I've managed to drive through. I told Esther about my fear and she analysed it as me getting overanxious about missing opportunities when they present themselves. I just think I'm a bit nuts sometimes.

I make it through the gates before they close and journey along a tarmac drive, from which various other roads branch off. Each one is marked by a number, and when I get to number seven I turn off and drive for another three minutes towards a very large, square, red-brick modern-looking mansion, with a fountain at the front and a double garage to the left.

I park beside the fountain, get out and walk towards

the house, which reminds me of the buildings I used to make out of Lego when I was a child – very red, very square, very symmetrical and with no character whatsoever. But then again, I only had Lego bricks to build with and I was very young.

I walk up the three steps to an open veranda and knock on one of the two large double doors that make up the front entrance. While I wait for the door to open I turn to look at the garden, which is mainly laid to lawn with a few newly planted young trees. I start to giggle to myself, because it looks similar to the plain green Lego base I used to build my houses on.

Castleford has such wonderful views, lovely buildings overlooking the sea and green, and charming lanes, but these large, characterless houses have been built in the middle of nowhere and benefit from none of the town's character. On the plus side, though, at least we don't have to look at them. It's just a different side to Castleford and therefore, I rationalise to myself, it's a good idea to include it in the show.

The door opens and I turn around to be greeted by Agetha. She smiles at me, but it's still in that pinched way of hers, as though it pains her to do so. I hope she looks better on camera than she does in real life.

'Hello, Helena,' she twitters like a demented starling, lunging to give me a kiss on the cheek. I kiss her back.

'Hello, Agetha, thank you for seeing me at such short notice,' I say.

'No problem. Anything that's good for Castleford is

good for the Flindells and Flindells Mansions,' she says. 'Now come in and we can sit down and have a chat.' She turns and leads me through a hallway into a kitchen which opens in to a sitting area that goes onto a dining area and another lounge area. In fact, the entire downstairs, with the exception of the hallway and cloakroom, is open plan. For some reason, there's a bowl of chicken to the right of the front door, which I almost trip over.

'This is our show home, so please excuse the proliferation of magnolia,' she says, laughing at herself.

'It's very nice,' I lie. 'Very modern and I love natural light,' I add.

'Yes, well, natural light is important and we've used the feng shui principle of design. The wealth area,' she points to the far corner where there's a large flat-screen Bang & Olufsen TV, 'is very strong and extended, and the relationship area is also very strong, as are the career and health areas,' she says, pointing rapidly in so many different directions that I get confused. 'We have some very happy customers,' she tells me, nodding to herself.

'Who are now wealthy and healthy, I suppose. And is that why you have the bowl of chicken by the front door as well – because it's good for something?'

'No,' she laughs, 'that's for the cat.'

'Have you sold all of the properties?' I ask, feeling rather silly, but then I'm not the one who has a feng shui-designed house, so how the hell should I know about the chicken?

'We've got some provisional offers, and three have been sold to people who live in London, Primrose Hill I believe. I think they want them as holiday homes, but some may want them for their principal residence and then have a pied-à-terre in town. You used to live in London, didn't you?'

'Erm, yes,' I say, 'ironically in Primrose Hill.'

'So tell me about your documentary,' she asks, pouring tea from a pot that I thought was just for show, but has evidently been prepared for my visit. I go through the same spiel I gave Jessica, Agetha listening to my every word.

'It's still early stages, but I would like to know if you and Anthony would be interested in appearing in the documentary, and if we would be able to shadow you at some stage, perhaps showing a prospective buyer around one of the mansions and talking up the selling points of the area and the house?' I conclude.

Agetha looks delighted, well, as delighted she can look. Perhaps it's physically impossible for her to deliver a broad grin, but I can tell she's happy as there's a twinkle in those tiny green eyes of hers.

'That's an excellent idea, but I have an even better one. I could suggest to one of the new buyers that they hold a welcome party for the other new residents and some of the other characters you'll be featuring in the show. It could be a nice conclusion to the programme. You know, clinking glasses of champagne and everyone looking happy living in Castleford,' she says, taking a sip of tea.

'Mmm.' I try to be diplomatic. 'That's a technique often used in daytime TV property programmes when couples or families have just bought a house, but it's perhaps a bit clichéd for this documentary. But thank you for the suggestion.' I try to sound positive without committing myself.

'How is your father?' she asks, having taken another sip of tea and looking at me as I drink mine, which tastes as insipid as the house's decor.

'He's not very well at the moment,' I say. 'I'm going to see him later on today, so I'll send your regards.'

'I'm sure your mother will be at a loss when he passes away,' she says tactlessly.

'Yes, I'm sure she will, as will I.' I put the cup down, wanting to cut the conversation short as quickly as possible. I'm worried about what state Dad is going to be in when I see him. Every time I've visited he's become visibly worse; he seems to be going downhill very quickly. And the last person I want to talk to about it is Agetha Flindell, because then it'll get it round the town faster than if I'd broadcast it on the documentary.

'Well I'd better go now, but I'll be in touch about timings and when we'd like to film, so if you can give us details about when the first residents are moving in that would be great,' I say, standing up and thanking her for the tea.

'My pleasure,' she says, 'just let me know about your dad. That's a very nice property they have and I'm sure your mother won't want to live in such a large cottage after he's gone. Tell her if she's thinking of selling, I would always be interested to hear from her.' She offers me her hand and I manage to restrain myself from punching her, and shake it.

'Would you like to see round the rest of the house?' she asks as I head back to the main doorway.

'I don't have time right now, unfortunately, but when we return to film, which will probably be in about two to three weeks' time, I would love to,' I say.

'Are you paying your contributors?' she asks, as she opens the door.

'No,' I say, 'we're not. Goodbye Agetha.' I smile, turn away and don't look back, deciding that she will definitely provide an alternative side of Castleford life.

Next stop is the sculptor John Tremble, whom I don't know at all, but Esther suggested he'd be a colourful person to include, as well as a good talking head. His mother was German and his father was an army major, apparently, and Esther tells me he's extremely well travelled, thanks to an earlier career as a diplomat, which seems incongruous for someone who, Esther claims, is wonderfully indiscreet. She warned me that he probably wouldn't stop talking, either, and that my main problem would be editing for sound bites.

John is married to Edwina and they have two grown-up sons, who are both academics working for the Foreign Office. He lives in a farmhouse called Hedgerow Lodge on the outskirts of town, on the opposite side to the Flindells' Mansions, so it takes me about half an hour to drive there. Talking to Agetha about my dad has made me feel guilty that I haven't visited for the past few days, but as soon as I've seen John I'll go round with one of his favourite cakes, a Battenberg.

Hedgerow Lodge is at the end of a lane that isn't far from the estuary. I had wanted to interview John on my radio show, but sculptors weren't really right for our demographic, I was told. If he'd produced a bust of Madonna rather than *the* Madonna, it would have been different. The large red-brick house looks snug amongst the towering oaks that line the gravel drive up to the main entrance. I knock on the door, but there's no answer, and just as I'm about to return to the car and leave a message, thinking I've got the time wrong, I hear a voice calling out.

'Can I help you?'

I turn to see a fiftyish, slim-built, slightly stooped man with a large nose and dark wavy hair. He reminds me of the actor Alastair Sim, who played the head-mistress in the best of the St Trinian's films, only he's younger and more handsome.

'Hello, are you John Tremble?' I ask.

'Yes, that's me,' he says, looking me up and down inquisitively, as though I'm a new species, which makes me smile.

I introduce myself quickly.

'Ah yes, *Big Brother* comes to Castleford,' he says, smiling at me like a wise wizard. 'Please come in.'

I follow him round the side of the house and through another door, which leads to the kitchen. It's a small room with a table in the middle, an old fridge-freezer in one corner, an old sink and shelves containing lots of herbs and spices in assorted jars. There's a large pan of something wonderful-smelling on the hob, and there are loads of books, some about cookery, others on politics, art, Russian history and linguistics. There's a large walk-in larder at the far end, and a dog basket on the floor in the corner, from which two dogs look up at me. One is the size of a Labrador, though I don't know what breed it is, and the other is slightly larger than my hand and pitch black. They're an unlikely couple, but they seem very happy in each other's company.

'We keep pigs here as well. I like to know where my bacon has come from, don't you?' he says as he leads me into the sitting room.

'I don't eat bacon.'

'Pity. I'll take you out to the pigs after our chat. I always buy four piglets at a time, and then keep them for three to four months. These four I've called after banks. Lloyds, Coutts, Barclays and RBS. I tell you, these pigs give considerably more pleasure than their namesakes, although I do have a fondness for Coutts. He's not as greedy as the others,' he says, nodding to himself. 'Would you like some lunch?' he asks, looking at me as though I need a good meal.

'I am a little hungry, but don't trouble yourself,' I say, feeling peckish. I notice the wall clock says two and I have had nothing since breakfast; I've been on the go non-stop.

'No trouble at all, as I've made some chicken soup. From our own chickens and our own vegetables from the garden,' he says. 'Now, you sit down, and while I'm dishing up you tell me all about this programme of yours and I'll tell you if I'm interested in appearing in it.'

So I sit and outline the show for him, and he occasionally nods and smiles, and when I've finished he turns round with a bowl of soup and plops it down in front of me.

'There you are,' he says, 'you'll enjoy that.'

He gets one for himself and two spoons, and we sit for a few moments and eat. For the first time in a very long time I feel as though I'm being looked after, as if I'm being mothered, and it's by someone I've only just met. It feels very comforting and slightly odd.

'Thank you for this,' I say, 'it's delicious.'

'My pleasure, you looked tired and hungry. Let me top you up before I tell you what I think,' he says, getting up, taking my bowl and pouring some more soup into it. 'Right, first of all I don't trust TV. I never have. They make promises they don't keep and invariably they make everyone look stupid, even when it's not intentional, although it usually is. I would say that it's never a good idea to agree to be filmed even for a five-minute interview, let alone be shadowed for days by a film crew who may edit out every wise word and include only the stupid ones.' He puts my bowl back in front of me and sits down again.

'However, I need some more work in the coming

months, and from this programme other publicity will undoubtedly follow. The papers and magazines will contact me to do interviews, and that I don't mind. You have much more control over live interviews,' he asserts, sounding as though he's been through a media minefield before and probably suffered. 'So I'll think about it and give you my answer as soon as I can. I've just got to make sure I can afford the time, and that I won't be away – I have a possible commission coming up, which means following some people who are very short of time and temper, but very big on ego, I'll need to make some enquiries, but in principle I agree.' With this he finishes his second bowl of soup. 'I'll also find out if any of the subjects I'm sculpting at the moment will agree to be in the film, because that could make an interesting part of the documentary, seeing me on the job, as it were,' he says, smiling at me.

'You sound as though you've done a lot of TV before.'

'I have,' he replies, 'but hopefully that will make me easier to work with. I don't know – it depends on your director. If they want me to do something stupid that I wouldn't normally do, I'm going to say no. I'll tell you that now, but if you genuinely want me to be natural, that's OK. I am not a performer, and I will not perform.'

I give him a wide smile. 'I think you're just right as you are,' I reply honestly.

'My wife Edwina would disagree with you. She thinks I'm very difficult to live with, and will probably say that on camera, so I suggest you don't feature her as she might use it as a way to get back at me.' I'm not sure if he's joking or not, but I laugh anyway.

'Well, I have a painting class to organise,' he says. 'I teach art as well, which makes some pennies. So if you'll excuse me, Ms Treadwell, I'll be off.'

'Thank you very much for the soup.'

'If you want to take a quick look round the studio you can,' he offers as we walk to the car. 'It's just over there,' he says, pointing to a barn-like building.

'Thank you,' I reply, looking at my watch and realising I have enough time before I see Mum and Dad. I follow him into a room that's bare apart from some very large paintings, which appear to be oil or acrylic.

'They're of the wife,' he says. The paintings are of a nude woman in various positions, some of which are semi-pornographic but quite tasteful. Edwina, if he's painted her true to form, is a very beautiful, sensuous and curvy woman, probably in her fifties.

'Edwina doesn't like them,' he says, 'but I do.'

'I like them as well, and I can tell you like your subject,' I say. 'It's a very sexy thing to do, paint your wife.'

He looks at me as though I've said something surprising, something he wouldn't have expected me to say. 'I think so too, Ms Treadwell. I think so too.'

He leads me through to another room, where there are some sculptures of horses and dogs and a few heads of babies, which all look like cross versions of Winston Churchill. Some of them are half finished. 'I get asked to do a lot of babies and pets,' he says, sounding bored. 'I get more expression from the animals than I do the children, that's why they all look like . . .'

'Winston Churchill,' I suggest, smiling.

He looks at me with a twinkle in his eye.

'Why can't they see that?'

'For the same reason they see a mother in the street with her screaming toddler and think their baby will be different. It never is; it's just nature's little joke on us.'

'Do you have children?' he asks, walking out of the studio.

'Yes, a boy. His name's Freddie and he's nine,' I reply, following behind. 'He's with his dad this week. We're divorced.'

'Yes, well, everyone in your generation is either divorced or should be. I think us post-war lot messed up somewhere down the line, breeding such inadequate, restless human beings. Either that or it's all Maggie Thatcher's fault,' he says, showing his political colours. 'Hope my sons divorce their wives – bloody boring women.'

I don't think he expects me to comment, so I don't, but I thank him again for his hospitality and tell him I hope it will be possible for him to be filmed.

'You would be a very colourful addition to the programme,' I say.

Driving away from John Tremble, I feel strangely uplifted. It's as though just being in his presence has given me a positive creative energy of some sort. I like him: he's lively, mischievous and slightly eccentric, the sort of person who adds something to the world just by being in it. In fact, he reminds me a bit of how my dad used to be before the accident. I look in the wing mirror as I turn the corner of his lane and realise I'm smiling broadly. I like John Tremble, I think to myself, he's one of the good guys.

Chapter Six

'Lovely to see you, Mum,' I say, smiling as I hand her some red, orange and yellow roses I picked up after my meeting with John.

'Thank you, Helena,' she says, looking at me. She seems cheerful and not too tired, so perhaps she's had a few good days with Dad. She's a handsome woman, my mother, and she was stunning in her twenties and thirties (I've seen photos). She still has large, clear brown eyes and lovely thick brown hair cut into a neat wavy bob, and she has excellent skin for someone in her sixties. She could easily pass for many years younger, having avoided the sun all her life by wearing the largest of sun hats and insisting on smothering herself in moisturiser before she went to bed each night, so much so that Dad used to joke he could never get hold of her to give her a cuddle because she'd slither out from between his arms. (I guess that's why they only had one child – me.) All this is in total contrast to me, a dedicated sun worshipper who will probably look like a wrinkled prune by the time I'm fifty.

'You really look tired, darling. You've got dark rings under your eyes. You must be overdoing it,' my mother tells me.

My visits to Mum and Dad's have become increasingly painful lately. Don't get me wrong, I love seeing them, but with each visit I notice my father deteriorating, fading away like a ghost. Occasionally there's a glimmer of light and hope but then the next visit, it goes again, and I realise it's just a matter of time. I steel myself not to cry because it isn't helpful for him or my mother. He was such a fit man, a laughing, proud, gentle giant. Then he had the operation, and everything fell apart. My mother copes admirably, but she manages by being so pragmatic that I sometimes wonder if she has steel in her backbone, because I know inside she must be screaming. My mother has a sharp tongue and finds fault with petty things, like the way I dress or parent Freddie, but I know this is only a defence mechanism for suppressing the pain that comes from watching the love of her life be taken from her.

'Really, Mum, I'm fine.' I can feel all the energy from my visit to John Tremble slowly draining away.

'No, you're overdoing it,' she persists. 'You must be feeling depressed to look this dreadful, and you've got to keep your looks if you're to get another man, you know.' Which of course makes me feel like a million dollars.

I would normally argue the point, and a few years ago I'd have said, 'Don't tell me how I feel because I *know* how I feel,' or replied with a sarcastic 'Thanks for the compliment, Mum!' but it's easier to just let it go and move on to something else. She'll never change or mellow, and my only concern is that she and Dad are happy, even if every time I visit she finds fault with her only daughter.

'Dad's his usual self.' She sighs deeply. 'He's been talking gibberish,' she continues, 'and I've had to change the bed again,' she says, leading me into the sitting room.

Dad is sitting in the large cream armchair in the corner of the room. He looks like a huge daddy bear with his thick brown sweater and a blanket over his legs. As I walk in I can see him staring vacantly out the window, but as he hears our steps he looks around and smiles. His broad, open face looks up at me and beams, his wide mouth creasing his cheeks, his green glassy eyes sparkling at me with recognition and love. For some reason I think of being a child and watching *Doctor Who* with him, snuggled under his jumper, peeking up at the Cybermen beating the crap out of the human race.

I'm so pleased he recognises me today. It's not always the case; sometimes I'm a complete stranger to him. He is still handsome, despite all the pain he's gone through in the past year.

'You wet the bed again, didn't you, Norman?' Mum says, talking to him like he's a child, although I'd never have spoken to Freddie like that, even when he was younger and did wet the bed.

I walk over to Dad, kneel down at his feet and squeeze his hand, reaching up to give him a hug. He leans over slightly to hug me back.

'Don't be stupid, Helena,' Mum says. 'You don't want Dad falling out of the chair. Just give him a kiss; much better.' But I ignore her.

He used to have such a strong hug, but now I can just about feel his arms around me. I remember as a little girl, coming back from school and waiting for him to come in from work. When I heard his key in the front door, even if I was sitting at the dinner table, I would rush to give him a hug. 'How's my little princess?' he would ask, giving me a kiss.

'How's my little princess?' he says now, giving me a kiss.

'I'm fine, Dad,' I reply. 'I'm just fine. And how are you?' I ask, looking into his eyes, and thinking he doesn't look too bad today. A little tired, but not too bad.

'Oh, mustn't grumble,' he says. 'I don't grumble, do I, Sheila?' He looks up at Mum.

'I do enough grumbling for both of us,' replies Mum in a brief moment of self-awareness. 'Honestly, I don't know how I manage, but I seem to somehow, don't I Norman?' she says, biting her bottom lip, which she always does when she's stressed.

'You're great, Sheila.' Dad smiles at her.

'Hmm,' she says. 'I'll get some tea.' And with that she walks out.

I'm so pleased I returned to Castleford to be close to

my parents. Although I'd rather it hadn't happened the way it did – coming after a divorce – I suppose there's an upside to everything, and being able to see more of them, and Freddie being able to see his grand-parents more often, has helped.

Dad was never quite sure about Leonard, but I think he felt I'd be well provided for and that the man I married seemed to be kind to me, but then again, he never knew the whole story, although sometimes I think he guessed at it. On one particular occasion, when Leonard and I were going out, we'd had a row and Leonard pushed me and I ended up with a black eye. He was apologetic about it, although he blamed me for making him angry. Soon after the incident Mum phoned up.

'Darling,' she said, sounding half irritated and half anxious, 'sorry to bother you, and I feel utterly silly saying this, but Dad made me call you. He says that he felt, yes that's the word, *felt*, that you'd been hit, or hurt or something. And he wanted me to call to make sure you were OK. I told him it was utterly ridiculous and that you would have called if anything was wrong, but he insisted. So are you OK, Helena?' I know she wanted a 'yes I'm fine' back, so she could put the phone down and say to Dad, 'I told you so.' But I paused, possibly a little too long, because Mum said, 'Helena?'

'Yes I'm fine, Mum. Leonard and I had a play fight last night and I've got a bit of a black eye, but it's nothing, so tell Dad not to worry because it was just an accident. Tell him he's a witch, or warlock, or whatever the male equivalent is, and that I'm fine. And tell him I love him, and I love you, too,' I said.

There was a prolonged silence at the other end of the line, then, 'No more play fights again, Helena, please.' There was a tinge of controlled anger, a hint of fury in her voice that made me feel as young as Freddie. 'Or I'll tell your father what's going on. No more play fights.'

I know my mother always saw Leonard as someone who would never do anything spontaneously. Everything was premeditated in his life, she would say to me, which was a good thing, because she said I needed someone who was 'sensible', who thought before they acted. Perhaps that was why she was particularly angry about my black eye, and angry when I told her about his behaviour during the six months prior to the divorce, when Leonard tried to wear me down emotionally, suggesting I was an unfit mother as well as an unfit wife. Mum always thought Leonard intended to be cruel towards the end. She told me men like him would never mellow, never learn, never change, and that I must always watch my back where he was concerned, because he would never take responsibility for his own actions, always blaming his own failings on others.

The next time Leonard and I visited my parents for Sunday lunch, a few weeks after the 'play fight', my mother spent some time alone with him in the kitchen. I will never know what she said to him, and Leonard never spoke of it, although he emerged from the kitchen visibly shaking and ashen-faced.

On the way home in the car he said, 'I completely understand why you don't want to tell your mother anything. If I had a mother like that I wouldn't tell her anything either.'

I was never sure what he meant by that, nor did he offer any explanation when I asked, but now I think about it, perhaps Leonard had met his match in my mother. She understood him completely, even then, and in a war of words she would win, probably even now. Mum didn't say anything to me because she knew I'd ignore her. I'm every bit as strong-willed as she is.

'I have loads to tell you, Dad,' I whisper, knowing anything I tell him will stay with him, and if he does mention it to Mum, she'll just think he's delirious. 'I'm working on a TV programme about Castleford. They want to film the town to show what a wonderful place it is,' I say, stroking his hand.

'TV, eh?' he says. 'You always wanted to be on TV, didn't you, Helena?' He smiles.

'I wanted to be a dancer, Dad,' I say. 'I wanted to be on the stage and dance.'

'But there's no money in it, Helena. Besides, all dancers are self-obsessed and anorexic,' Mum says in her usual dogmatic fashion as she returns with tea and the Battenberg cake I've brought.

'Not *every* dancer is anorexic. I'm sure you get some emotionally and nutritionally balanced ones,' Dad says, looking up at me and winking mischievously.

'Well, you would know, wouldn't you?' Mum says,

which confuses me as I didn't know Dad was interested in dancing or dancers, but she continues before I can ask what she meant. 'Honestly, it's all go for me.' She sighs. 'All go.'

'Why don't you get some help?' I suggest, realising what's going to follow as soon as I've said it.

'Where would we get the money from?' she asks, putting the tray down. 'Neither the nursing home or the hospital looked after him well, and social services are so understaffed, which just leaves me. It's very hard,' she says, 'but I cope, I manage.' She looks at Dad, on the verge of tears.

I want to hug her, but I won't allow myself to. I've reached out to her so many times before, and every time she's slammed me down with a snipe about not asking me for help because I'm so impractical. If I was impractical I'd never have coped as a single mother, but she doesn't see me that way. Just as Dad still sees me as his little princess, so my mum still sees me as an awkward little girl who was never allowed to do anything for herself because she always made a mess of it. It made me feel inadequate in my twenties, as if I couldn't achieve anything through my own efforts and would have to depend on everyone else for success. It took having Freddie and getting divorced to make me realise that the only one I can really count on and trust is myself. Nowadays Mum's criticisms, which used to hurt so deeply, only skim the surface. But to be fair, when the chips are down, as they were when I was divorcing Leonard, she is always there for me.

'You're doing a great job,' I say, 'and Dad really appreciates it.'

'I know I am,' she says. 'I'm Superwoman, aren't I Norman?'

Dad nods at her. 'I'd rather you be Wonder Woman, Sheila, can you do the spin for me and wear those tight leotards?'

Mum laughs at him and I can't help but laugh too. 'You'd have a heart attack if I did that,' she says.

I sit there for an hour or so, holding Dad's hand, looking at him and smiling while Mum talks all the time. 'Well after I cleaned up the bed, then I had to get the shopping and honestly, I can't leave Norman alone for one moment. He fell out of the chair and got such a bruise, and he's still so heavy. He's still keeping that weight on. I ask him to help me by moving himself, but he can't. It's just the same as it was when he was all there. I did everything for him even then. He was awful in the kitchen, weren't you, Norman?'

Dad just smiles at Mum. 'Yes, I was awful, darling. You should put me down, you know.' He looks back at me and gives me another little wink; he's still got a glint in his eye.

'I left him once with something to put in the oven, a nice chicken casserole. It was in a plastic container and I thought he'd have the sense to put it in a Pyrex dish, but he didn't and the container melted. Absolutely no common sense – that's where you get it from, your father.' I say nothing.

Mum continues relentlessly. 'I'd never allow you in

the kitchen, either, you always used to make such a mess when you attempted to cook. Not that you ate much. You went through that funny stage of not eating anything and throwing food down the toilet, didn't you, Helena? Thank goodness you never became a dancer, you'd have been vomiting all over the place! God, the food that must have gone down that toilet, what a waste. What a waste of money.' She shakes her head at me. 'And you don't feed Freddie enough. He's looking very pasty these days, Helena. I know you don't cook properly for him. But he likes my roast dinners, doesn't he?' she says, not waiting for me to answer. 'Yes, he likes my cooking,' she assures us.

'Looking after Dad is just like looking after you when you were a baby. I have to do everything for him, although thank goodness I never have to go through the pain of childbirth again. I was left all by myself and I was in agony. I wasn't going to go through that again, not for anyone. And of course I had to look after Dad's father as well, which was so tiring, it really was.' She sighs deeply.

As neither Dad nor I comment, she changes the subject.

'So how is Freddie?' she asks.

'Freddie's fine; he's back from his dad's at the end of the week and everything is fine.' I say 'fine', because 'good' causes her to comment that at least it's good for someone, while 'very good' brings forth a lament about how tough her life is these days. I've offered to take her out, to look after Dad for a few days while she has a break, but she refuses, saying she'd never forgive herself if anything happened to him while she was away, and that I'd never forgive myself if Dad died while he was in my care, which of course makes me feel like a million dollars. If I say things are not so good, I get asked why, then she starts telling me about the bad day she's had and how life is much tougher for her, and that we don't realise how good we have it. But somehow every time I leave my parents' cottage I don't feel lucky, and I know Dad doesn't feel lucky. I know that no matter what I say to my mother, even if I sat her down and told her exactly what I thought of her, she still wouldn't get it. Perhaps one day I'll tell her, just not today. Not today.

After I leave them I head back home in the car. While I drive, tears run down my face: tears of guilt at leaving my dad there and not being able to help Mum enough financially or emotionally. I'm angry because I disapprove of the way she talks to and treats Dad, but I know it's her way of coping and that underneath it all she loves him dearly, she just has difficulty showing it.

I get back to my cottage and go into the kitchen, where I find myself sobbing hard tears into the sink. As I gradually calm down and catch my breath, I think of Dad and the fact that he can still smile, and that, despite my mum chipping away the remains of his self-esteem, at least he's at home, among the people and objects he loves and knows. She's still looking after him and her chicken casserole is admittedly very good – that's why he's still the weight he is.

I'm just about to pour myself a glass of wine before I log on to the computer and type out my notes for the day, when the phone goes.

'Hello, it's Esther, can I come round? I need to speak to someone.' She sounds agitated and very unlike Esther.

'Yes, of course you can,' I say. 'Do you want anything to eat?'

'No, no,' she says. 'It won't take long. I just need to talk to someone. Someone who'll understand.'

The phone clicks off before I have time to say anything else, and I get another wine glass out of the cupboard. It sounds as though she may need it.

Chapter Seven

'I have a sister.'

'Of course you have a sister,' I reply as Esther storms through the doorway and into my kitchen.

'I need a drink,' she says, seeing the wine bottle and marching over to it with intent.

'You sounded as though you might, so I've got you one,' I reply, picking up the glass and handing it to her. Esther drinks it down in one as though it were water.

'What's the matter?' I ask. 'What about your sister?'

She sits down and looks at me. 'Edward and I went round to Mum and Dad's for an early supper today and we took the girls. It's Dad's birthday so we'd bought him a nice present; he's into shooting, and Edward has a friend who was able to get him membership of a rifle club.'

'Wow, he must have been happy with that.'

'No, he's still an ungrateful bugger. He didn't even say thank you, just commented that he'd get more use out of it than the last thing we bought him for Christmas. I hope he bloody well shoots himself!'

'You don't mean that,' I say, looking at Esther, whom I've never seen this angry before.

'This time he has excelled himself.'

'What's he done?' I say, knowing how difficult Esther finds her dad, he's a bit like her boss Digby sounds, a bit of a control freak, but then so is everyone in their own way, I'm starting to think – my mum, Leonard, even John Tremble seems to have a very controlled way of life.

'He has announced to the family that he has another child. A child that was conceived three months after I was. So I have a half-sister – in fact, we all have a half-sister. Her name is Claire and she works for a bank and he told us it would be appropriate for us to meet her. Apparently she's far more successful than us and we could learn a thing or two from her.'

I look at Esther and laugh nervously. 'What did you say?' I ask.

'I didn't say anything at first, mainly because he kept on talking. He told us he'd met this very nice woman when he was married to Mum and that they'd had a relationship but that there was nothing tacky about it. He said he'd just fallen in love and it was one of those things. He said he decided not to leave Mum because it was the right thing to do and she wouldn't have been able to cope by herself. Claire's mother couldn't afford to look after the child and didn't want to keep her, either,' Esther continues, pouring some more wine into her glass and taking a swig. 'That's not all of it.

He'd asked my mother if she'd take in Claire and bring her up as her own, but Mum said no, so she was adopted by another family.'

Esther takes another swig while I take this in.

'Why did he decide to tell you now?' I ask after a pause.

'Only because this Claire decided after all this time to find out who her real dad was, and managed to do so. She met Dad, and when he told her about me, her half-sister, she was going to contact me, because guess which bank she works for?'

'Your bank.'

'Correct. So he pre-empted Claire turning up at my desk and decided to tell the family about her formally over supper. There's something about all this that remind's me of Digby's manipulative behaviour. Both men are totally oblivious of anyone else's feelings. At least I can resign from my job, but my dad will always be my dad.'

'I feel the same way about Leonard frequently but you can only change your behaviour, not theirs,' I reply, suddenly remembering something that happened to me over seven years ago. A woman coming to my door and telling me I was her sister. I'd completely forgotten about it until this moment. I don't want to mention it to Esther because I want to focus on her problem, but for a brief moment I'm back standing at that door, torn sheets of wedding album in my hand, angry and upset, wondering if it's another cruel practical joke Leonard's trying to play on me.

'Did your mum say anything at this stage?' I ask.

'She just nodded in agreement, but said nothing. He then told us he was arranging a lunch next week so that we could meet her. And that was it really,' she says, taking another gulp.

'So how do you feel about all of this?' I enquire, not wanting to express my opinion before I'm asked.

'What do I feel about it?' she shouts. 'The man is an arsehole. He's my father and he's an arsehole. He betrayed my mother and screwed around with another woman when Mum was pregnant. Claire is only three months younger than me. And now he has the nerve to bring his family together and tell us he spawned a child with his bit on the side, and that we're expected to meet her next week. He didn't ask us if we *want* to meet this woman, he told us we've *got* to meet her. There was no apology to Mum or to us. No "I did this dreadful thing and I'm really sorry" or any of the other stuff men come out with when they've been unfaithful and want forgiveness so they can go off and do it again. It was just a statement of fact; we were to take it as such and that was that.'

'Are you going to meet her?' I ask.

'Of course I'm not going to meet her!' shouts Esther, standing up and starting to pace. 'It would be like saying, Dad, what you did was OK, when it wasn't.'

'It's not her fault,' I say. 'It's your dad's fault. She couldn't help being born. You should feel sorry for her. She's got your dad as a father.'

'That's exactly what Edward said. He said that my

dad has always been a pompous, arrogant, shitty little man and that this is just another thing he's done to prove the point. Edward thinks my dad actually has loads of illegitimate children, he just hasn't been forced to admit to all of them yet. He's a sanctimonious git and he's still getting away with it after all these years. I'm an intelligent woman, aren't I?' she asks, looking at me.

'You are,' I say.

'Then why the fuck do I allow this horror of a man to get away with behaviour like this? Why do I allow it?'

'It's not normal,' I say, realising there's nothing constructive I can say to Esther at the moment, she's too angry.

'I agree, it's far from normal. And I blame Mum for not saying anything, for letting him do this to us all.' She sits down and looks tearful. 'I'm not going to cry. I'm not going to cry. I'm upset and angry but I'm not going to let him get to me,' she says, allowing him to do exactly that.

'You can let him get to you, you just mustn't do it in front of him,' I say. I take her hands. 'You have Edward and two beautiful girls, who are old enough and perceptive enough to know what your father and mother are like. You have a right to be angry and resentful and shocked, Esther. Your mother's reaction is her own concern. She made her choice and stayed with your father, but you should bear in mind that she was unable to leave your dad for financial reasons. At least she put her foot down about taking in Claire, so don't be too harsh on her. You may change your mind, so keep the door ajar. Attitudes were different then. Divorce was still a dirty word and it was very much a man's world.'

We sit in silence for a few minutes and stare into our empty glasses.

'Do you want some more?' I ask, going to the wine rack.

'No, I'd better not,' she says. 'Thank you for listening.'

'That's what friends are for,' I say. 'Actually, that's what parents are for, or so I thought when I was a child, but that's not the case. That's why we have counsellors, I suppose. If parents try to screw you up when you're a child, they continue to when you're an adult.'

'If you let them,' interjects Esther. 'I remember my mum and dad telling me I was very selfish not to give them grandchildren in my early twenties. Having kids in my early thirties was good enough for me.'

'You have to stand up to this sort of thing – moral blackmail allied to bullying. Eventually it will stop, but it will take time.'

'Is that what will happen between you and Leonard? He'll stop trying to play cat and mouse with you?'

'Yeah, I suppose so. That's why I'm trying for the one-off payment, because once that's through, well, if I'm the mouse, I'm out of the cage and in the hole and a little more difficult for the cat to get to. Then if he swipes at me, he'll be hitting out directly at Freddie too.'

'That's never bothered him in the past, Helena, so

don't hold your breath with that one. Anyway, let's not waste thinking time on bullies and control freaks,' Esther says, raising her empty wine glass and looking as though she's about to toast me. 'I asked Edward, and he has agreed to be in your TV programme. He's spoken to his publisher and they think it's a great idea if you can film at the book launch next month. He even wants to read out sections of the book. We're having it in a bar in Soho, I think, don't ask me where. They suggest asking some local celebrities as well, so you could get some other interviews of Castleford people all in one go. What do you think?'

'That's a brilliant idea. I'll mention it to Will Stafford. What with John Tremble a definite possibility, and Edward, and hopefully Jessica getting approval from the PTA and governors at the school, everything seems to be going smoothly.'

'Never say that too soon. In my experience things have a way of going wrong as soon as you think they're not,' Esther says, shaking her head.

'Well I'm thinking positive these days,' I reply. 'Positive thinking can lead to positive reality, right?'

Esther smiles and shakes her head as though she thinks I'm totally naive.

I pick up our glasses. 'Now I don't mean to rush you, but I want to get things ready for when Freddie returns, so if . . .'

'Oh God, sorry Helena, yes of course. I just wanted someone to talk to who knows what I'm on about. My dad always comes across as very courteous and lovely to everyone and if it wasn't for Edward being able to see right through him as well, I'd think I'm being totally unreasonable, but I'm not. Just like you're not with Leonard.' She hugs me, turns and goes, leaving me to contemplate my own private battles.

My last week at Passion is emotional and eventful. George takes me out to lunch and says if Shane and Sandra are at all problematic he will hand in his notice immediately. I get a huge bunch of flowers from the guys in the studio and a large lemon tree (because I asked for one) delivered to the cottage from Peter, who gets all teary-eyed when he takes me to the Lafitte restaurant for my goodbye lunch. It's not the sort of place I go to usually – expensive, itsy-bitsy very rich food, and very fine wines, but it's a lovely gesture from Peter and it's nice to be treated. We talk about my first interview at the station and how I've grown and learned so much, and changed so much. We laugh at some of the funny things that have happened over the years, and the guests who've not turned up and those who did and probably shouldn't have, because they were high on drugs, drink or life. I don't mention Victoria, although he can't help mentioning her when I give details of who is due to appear in the Castleford programme.

'Is she happy?' he asks.

'Yes, I think so,' I reply. 'How are things with your family?'

'Fine. People stay together for love, don't they?' he replies, which startles me a bit.

'Well, for a lot of reasons these days, but love is the best one, I always like to think.'

'Me too, Helena. Just that sometimes it's for the love of your children, not the love of your partner.'

I'm just about to change the subject, when who should walk in but Leonard with a lady. I don't know if she is his girlfriend, as I've never met Helena in all the seven years he's lived with her, but she sort of fits the vague description given by Freddie. She's short, curvy and pretty, although Freddie doesn't say she's pretty, but then he wouldn't to protect me. Leonard sees me immediately and freezes, looking awkward for a split second, then recovers. The waiter leads them to a table and they sit with the girl facing my way and Leonard with his back to me. I guess from her expression that he is talking about me, and that what he's saying is very amusing, and probably derogatory.

'My ex has just walked in with who I think is his girlfriend,' I explain to Peter, who is still in a world of his own, inhabited probably just by Victoria and himself.

'Oh, do you want to say hello?' he asks.

'Good God no. I try to keep contact to a minimum. I thought he'd be taking Freddie out to lunch today as he's still got him for the holidays, but perhaps he's left him with his parents. If I go over, he'll make some snide comment about me being on his territory and not expecting to see me in such a lovely restaurant. Actually, no he won't, because you're here,' I say, realising that that is not Leonard's style.

'He could think I am your latest boyfriend, in which case I think he probably would want to say hello,' Peter replies, looking round at Leonard, who immediately turns his attention to the menu.

'I don't want to speak to him. I'd prefer it if we ignored him, is that OK? He hates to be ignored.'

'If you know that, why don't you just say hello? He's expecting you to ignore him, so that's all the more reason to go over. I'll come with you if you like.'

'No you won't,' I say. 'He'll ask questions about who you are and what we're doing here and I don't want him to know I've lost my job at Passion and am starting on TV. He'll just make a quip about it. If you come he'll be as charming as anything, and you'll think it's all in my head that he's the psycho I've described all these years. If I go by myself he'll tell me to fuck off in a whisper. It's easier to pretend he's not there.'

'You're going and I'm coming with you, Helena,' says Peter, suddenly standing up. 'This is silly. You are the mother of his child and he's the father of yours, and you need to get on for Freddie's sake. If I can stay in a loveless sexless marriage for the sake of my children, you can be civil to an ex you have little or nothing to do with, for the sake of your son. Be nice and say hello and say you hope they enjoy their meal. Don't ask to be introduced to the girl. If he doesn't introduce her, he is rude. By going up to him and saying hi, it will show that you're cool about him being here.'

I get up and tell Peter to sit down, and walk over to

their table, wondering what the hell I'm going to say. I can't say, 'It's lovely to see you,' because it never is. I can't say, 'I hope you enjoy your meal,' when I'd like him to choke on it. As I walk up to the table I have an overwhelming urge to pour the large jug of water over his head. But I don't.

'Hello Leonard,' I simply say. Leonard looks up at me briefly, not saying a word, and gives one of his upside-down smiles, and the girl doesn't look up at all. Wow, I made an impression there then, but it was silly of me to approach him. With any other person it would be normal and natural to go up and say hello, and ask how Freddie is, and if he's enjoyed his holiday. Or make some comment about fancy meeting you in this restaurant and is this your usual haunt, but it's like talking to a stranger. No, worse than that. It's like talking to someone you wish was a stranger, but isn't. I turn back to my table and take my seat.

'Did he say hello?' Peter asks, leaning over to me and smiling.

'No, he said nothing and she didn't even look up.'

'Well, he's a rude git and she's stupid, and you did the right thing.'

'Did I?'

'Yes you did. And what's more we've almost finished our meal and they've just arrived, so you've probably given them indigestion as well.'

I smile and we order coffee and sit and talk for a further ten minutes or so. I don't glance over at Leonard's table again and soon forget they are there at all. It's only when the bill comes and Peter pays it that it occus to me I may have annoyed Leonard by my action, and he'll find a way of hitting back. He always does.

Chapter Eight

Leonard returns with Freddie today, Sunday, at six thirty prompt. Before I have a quick shower, I mentally rn through where I am with the programme. I'm still waiting to see if John Tremble will agree to be filmed. As to the Flindells, they're probably planning the documentary for me at this very moment. I thought it would be good if Victoria could appear in the programme as well, but haven't run this past her yet. Victoria at the *Echo*, in the aggressive environment of a news desk, Dena Benson bellowing at everyone, would contrast brilliantly with the serenity of life in Castleford.

Another idea I've had is to interview some of the people who regularly go down to the beach so we can have the crew there for a day, filming what they get up to. In contrast, some of the locals haven't been down to the beach for over a year now, despite the fact that it's on our doorstep. But then again, I was like that when I lived in London. I was only a short taxi ride away from the West End but I rarely went to the theatre.

I'm in the shower when I think I hear my front door bell go. It's still only about six o'clock, so it can't be Leonard, can it? Maybe he's decided to drop Freddie off early, but he's never done that before. I quickly get two towels, wrap one round my hair in a turban and the other round my body, as my dressing gown's in the washing machine.

There's another peal on the bell. It must be Freddie. I shout, 'Wait a minute,' as I quickly put on the first dress that comes to hand, an old M&S number that I must have got over ten years ago and thankfully still fits me – just.

'Hello, darling,' I say as I open the door and look down to where I know he's going to be waiting for me, eyes and arms wide open, grinning at me, unless Leonard has told him off, in which case he walks straight past me, shouting, 'Bye, Dad,' behind him.

But as I reach out for Freddie I find I'm looking at a man's crotch. It doesn't look like Leonard's crotch, either, or not the sort of weekend trousers Leonard would wear – beige and Gant – and Leonard has short stubby legs while these are long and encased in grey, worn trousers that look as if they belong to an explorer.

I quickly look further up his body, briefly noting a checked shirt, and find a face smiling at me, amused by my unorthodox greeting.

'Were you expecting someone shorter than me, or do you always greet people that way?' he says with a smile in his voice. I'm so used to hearing Leonard's low, supercilious tone, if he speaks to me at all during the handover, that it's a refreshing change.

'Only my nine-year-old son,' I explain, blushing, which I haven't done in years.

I look at the man's face. It's a nice open face, with a broad forehead and defined chin. He has quite a large nose – not hooked or squashy, just large – and wavy brown shoulder-length hair that doesn't look as though it's been brushed today, or for a few days actually, but it seems to work for him.

'Hello, my name is Will Stafford,' he says, offering his hand, 'we spoke on the phone.'

I momentarily look blank, not making the connection, probably because I've been thinking about what Esther told me about her sister, and it's been bugging me since I saw her about the woman who came to my door seven years ago. Right now the name 'Will Stafford' doesn't mean anything to me. He can tell.

'I'm from High Light. I'm the director for the documentary. We spoke earlier this week on the phone,' he repeats, looking slightly bemused.

'Oh yes. Oh God, what are you doing here?' I say, confused.

'Oh, I apologise,' he replies, looking distinctly annoyed. 'Becca should have made contact with you, but evidently she hasn't. I've obviously come at a bad time,' he says, taking a few steps back.

I take a closer look at Will Stafford. He's about six foot four, so a good five inches taller than me, and broad across the chest. He has striking blue eyes, brown hair, and is wearing a larger version of the biker's jacket

I've got, though his looks slightly more worn than mine. There's a presence about him which would come in useful when trying to get the best out of actors and crew, and a face that looks as though it could tell a thousand tales, all of them adventurous.

He's also very masculine, which I hadn't expected. I'm not suggesting men in TV are all gay or effeminate, in fact I've met more men of ambiguous sexuality in my corporate life than I ever have during my time in the media, but there's something almost caveman about him, that leaves me, well, a bit breathless.

'No worries,' I reply, feeling suddenly very unprofessional in the way I've behaved since I opened the door. 'Can we meet here tomorrow morning, say about ten o'clock? I should be back from dropping off Freddie at school by then.'

'That would be great, and I'll bring the production assistant, Becca, the girl I'll be killing when I see her. She should have contacted you about our meeting today, but anyway, she will be helping you coordinate meetings with the various personalities we're following in Castleford. Although the fact she's managed to screw up today doesn't bode well, does it?' he smiles.

'I'm sure she'll be fine,' I reply.

'Well, it's very good to meet you,' he says, offering his hand. I take it. He has a firm handshake and, although he's not smiling, his eyes are. He smells good and before I engage my brain I ask him what he's wearing.

He laughs – I think at me. 'What am I wearing?' he replies, looking at me as though I'm mad. 'Well, the shirt is by Gap and the . . .'

'No.' I laugh, feeling embarrassed. 'Sorry, I meant your aftershave.'

'Oh, that's just mc, and soap,' he replies. 'Why, does it do something for you?'

I laugh again, this time nervously, realizing my question was silly and personal and is getting the response it deserves from a man who's used to being surrounded by people who either try to browbeat him or suck up to him. As I want to do neither, I simply shake my head and say nothing.

'See you tomorrow, then,' he says, turning to walk back down the pathway, past my attempts at topiary – a squirrel that looks more like a snake and a dog that looks like a rabbit.

As I watch him start up his motorbike, I stand in the doorway, leaning slightly against it. If he likes me he'll look back before he drives off, I think. I'll give him five seconds to turn and look at me. If he doesn't look back by then, I'll close the door. I count, five, four, three, two, one. He doesn't look back, not even a hint of it, and I admit to myself with genuine disappointment that I'm obviously past my sell-by date. I've lost my touch.

'Hello, Mummy!' shouts Freddie as I open the door a little later.

I don't make the mistake of looking at crotch level this time, just in case it's not Freddie, so I end up looking Leonard full in the face, which I haven't done for ages. He is fat, tanned and grey-haired. He also seems shocked, possibly because I look him straight in the eye, but almost instantly he glazes over into his usual smug self and the expression on my face freezes into a smile that isn't one – it's a behavioural pattern we've got stuck in over the years. I smile and say hello when we initially meet, then he responds aggressively (perhaps thinking I'm having a good time and good life on what he considers to be his money with his son), and I respond defensively and stop smiling (trying to look as though I'm not having a good time and a good life. Point is, I'm not sure I am any more). I won't give up, though, on trying to smooth relations between us. I will always try, however briefly, to break the ice, but so far it hasn't happened.

Leonard is wearing a stripy coloured shirt even Victoria would approve of, and sporting a large shiny watch, which looks like a designer brand. As he usually turns up in shades of brown, grey, taupe and beige, I deduce he's either been somewhere where he needs to impress or has a new relationship running concurrently with his present girlfriend Helena, both of which are possibilities.

I give Freddie a huge hug and close my eyes, breathing him in as he squeezes me tight, though I don't want to prolong it as that means Leonard will hang around longer, waiting to say goodbye to his son. I expect Leonard to leave Freddie's bag at the door and ask him for a cuddle, which always lasts a long time, as he takes the opportunity to give me a snide look (Leonard, that is, not Freddie) as if to say, 'See, he loves me,' although these days it comes across more as 'He's mine.' Leonard has never been able to differentiate between love and possessiveness, and only over time have I managed to do this. However, today Freddie doesn't hug his dad, he just races in, quickly turning to say goodbye. I'm just about to close the door when I realise Leonard is lingering.

If it was anyone one else lingering – my mother or even Agetha Flindell – I wouldn't mind, but since it's Leonard, I'd prefer him to drive off in his Porsche as soon as possible, which he usually does as noisily as possible. The last few times Leonard has lingered, it's been to tell me a lie – either about when the maintenance is due to be paid or that he'll take Freddie to football and karate practice on his weekends. It's a total waste of time listening to him, as far as I'm concerned. And that voice. That 'low-voice thingy', as Freddie calls it. For some reason Leonard has lowered his voice a few octaves since I split up from him – at the moment he'd give Barry White a run for his money. On another man it would be funny, like a little boy trying to be a grown-up, and I try to think of 'the voice' that way, but on Leonard, with his continual lies and snide looks, it just comes across as sinister.

'Have you received details about the mediation?' he says, looking at me as though I'm a business colleague of a lesser grade.

'Yes I have, thank you,' I reply simply. I want to ask him why he has suggested we meet. Why now? I want to talk to him about Freddie's progress at school, and about the fact that his latest report says there's an anomaly between his ability to verbalise and his reading and writing, meaning he could be dyslexic. I suspected this two years ago and got him tested, despite the fact that Leonard said it was all nonsense and Freddie was just lazy. Thankfully the school are keeping an eye on it and his lovely form teacher, Caroline King, is a specialist in things like that, so I'm more reassured these days.

He looks at me as though he expects me to say something else, but I don't.

'Oh,' he says, 'I've given Freddie a trophy I won for rally driving. He can put it in his bedroom.'

'See you at mediation,' I reply, acknowledging the comment with a nod, but annoyed that he refuses to take Freddie to football and karate so that Freddie could win and show off his own trophies, but is quite happy for his son to show off his father's awards.

The last time I suggested Leonard take Freddie to a football game, he refused. I said that just because he had no interest in football himself, he shouldn't deprive his son of taking part in a sport that he obviously enjoys. Leonard sent me a text reply along the lines of 'I was head of the rowing team at school whereas you are an idiot', which I'm not sure, even to this day, I fully understand. He looks as though he wants to say more, but I'm now closing the door and he turns and goes.

Freddie is already looking for food as I enter the

kitchen. My blond, wavy-haired, blue-eyed boy, who's the spitting image of me and my dad, is foraging through our fridge like a young fox, as if he hasn't eaten in days, which is ridiculous because I know Leonard feeds him, albeit at swanky restaurants with fine wines and snotty service, where he has to behave impeccably. Already he comes up to just below my shoulder. With his long, slim body, long arms and long legs, he looks like a leggy, handsome spider. His voice is soft and full of emotion, questioning even when he isn't. He's always so full of energy and smiles, his moments of mischief more entertaining than annoying, and his observations about people and the meaning of life – which we've discussed in detail before bedtime on occasion – so honest and wonderful that I find myself writing them down and suggesting Esther asks Edward to put them in his next novel . . . if he ever writes about a little boy who just happens to be nine and gorgeous. His latest comment was about money and why we need it; he said the person who invented it was irresponsible.

'Did you have a nice time with Daddy?' I ask.

'Yes, OK,' he says. 'We went to France to be with those friends of his. You know, the ones you don't like.'

I smile to myself, because there are so many of Leonard's friends I don't like I'm spoilt for choice. I think he means the Ronson family, who have six children and two dogs. They also had a stinking great mortgage before the credit crunch got hold of their assets and sent them into exile in France, where they have a larger house but lower outgoings, better climate and vastly better food.

'Did you have fun?' I ask, starting to unpack his bag and finding a huge garish gold trophy with a golf ball on a plinth, and a gold-embossed LEONARD WALLIS – WINNER emblazoned across it. I'll let Freddie choose where he wants to put that one, although I know where I'd like to.

'It was OK. We went for walks. All the children can speak French now,' he says, taking a bite out of a Nutri-Grain bar he's found in the cupboard.

'I should hope so,' I say, looking at Freddie, who seems taller than ever. He's only been gone for a week and I've missed him so much.

'And Daddy's brother Uncle Richard got married as well, and I was a pageboy at the wedding,' he says.

'Oh,' I say, 'that's nice.' It would have been thoughtful of Leonard to tell me his brother was getting married, but then Leonard isn't thoughtful.

'I wore a suit and everything and Daddy even mentioned you in his speech,' he says, finishing off the bar and looking for something else to eat.

'Did he?' I reply, surprised but trying not to sound curious.

'Yes. He made a joke. He said that before the wedding I'd asked him how much it cost to get married. The thing is, Mummy, I hadn't asked him at all, but it was a joke, you see, so he made it up,' he says, nodding at me intensely. 'And well, the joke was,' he says, sitting down and pausing, 'I asked him how much a wedding cost, and he said that he didn't know because he was still paying for his. Everyone found it very funny, but I was a bit confused. But you know, I laughed. It was good he mentioned you, sort of, isn't it?' He smiles innocently. 'You were sort of there with us.'

'Yes, I suppose I was sort of there with you, and I'm sure the wedding was lovely.' I'm a little sad that I couldn't be there to see Richard get married. He was a nice brother-in-law, the rebel of the Wallis family, who couldn't wait to leave the nest. The other two boys were stuck to home for years by some sort of invisible super-glue. Richard was much more normal than the rest of them. I hope he's married someone who will make him happy and whom he will make happy. From what Freddie says about her, he has.

'Can we see Grandad?' Freddie asks, suddenly giving up on the food search. 'I want to see how he is and hear his stories.' Dad is very good with Freddie, telling him endlessly about his time in India when he was in the army. Stories about the time he ate a duck egg and was as sick as a parrot, or when he was on 'latrine duty' and had to clean all the army loos; he made the seats so wet that none of the soldiers wanted to sit down on them. My dad has told Freddie these stories so many times, but he never tires of them, although he's never seen a parrot being sick and I was called in once to school when he tried soaking the boys' loos and managed to flood them.

'It's a bit late now, Freddie.' I think of Mum's tight regime that no one's allowed to interrupt. 'You can visit after school tomorrow, although you've got karate, so I'll take you after that, all right?' I say, giving him a kiss on the cheek.

'All right, Mum,' he says, resigned to the fact that he's only got me this evening to read the latest *Great Glass Elevator* instalment, a book he enjoys listening to as much as I enjoy reading it.

'And by the way, I've got a lot to tell you, Freddie, so go upstairs and I'll get tea ready, then we can sit and chat.' Half an hour later, when Freddie still hasn't come down, I go to his bedroom and realise he's exhausted. Lying fully clothed, sprawled out on his bed, my not-so-little boy is fast asleep.

I gently sit him up and try to undress him, which is much more difficult than it used to be, as he's so tall now. I prepare his school clothes for the next morning, and sports and book bags, making sure he's got everything he needs. I've signed all the forms I need to sign for clubs and badges and have written in his homework diary, which he always leaves at school, especially when Miss King has written in it that he must remember to give it to me. Luckily it came home at the end of last term. As he snuggles into bed, naked except for his underpants, too tired for Roald Dahl and his wonderful stories, I stroke his forehead and kiss him on the cheek. Yes I do have full responsibility for this little boy, and for his sake I will go to this ruddy mediation and try to make it work with Leonard and me. I will try. And I will listen. And learn.

Next morning and Freddie is up and dressed and

ready for breakfast – cornflakes today, although it's usually toast and a banana. As we drive off to school, I'm aware that I still haven't told him about losing my radio job, and my new TV job, but Freddie is buzzing with excitement and longing to see his schoolfriends again.

His life is very full, and although I know he craves family, I think he's starting to enjoy having two lives – one with his dad and one with his mum. My only concern is that he seems to be bottling up so much – probably because he realises it's best not to tell me what he does with his dad, and vice versa, for fear of repercussions, judgement, jealousy or a heady cocktail of all three.

By the time I get to the school gates he's told me everything he wants to do today, this week, this term, this lifetime, but I haven't mentioned any of my news. I just hope Jessica will mention the TV programme to the boys at assembly.

I wave at some of the other mothers, some of whom have come on foot, some by bike and some non-eco-friendly mums like me who've driven. The boys look smart in their dark and light blue striped blazers, some with new haircuts, some with ties askew. There are the too cool for school Year Fives with their baggy trousers, and the younger boys trying, and failing, to emulate the look and tripping up and falling over with every other step. Freddie's best friend Henry tried it last year and lost his trousers completely one playtime; he has yet to recover from the shame.

*

Back at the house, at ten o'clock sharp, there's a knock at my door.

'Hi, Helena,' says Esther, looking flushed, 'just thought I'd pop over for a chat, and also to apologise for my outburst about Dad, and to thank you for the advice.' She smiles broadly. 'You look nice, anyone coming?'

'The programme director and his assistant. I've got my first production meeting this morning so I want to look as professional as I can. I'll call you when it's finished, OK?'

'Yes, no problem.'

As she turns and walks down the path, I see Will walking towards her, dressed in jeans and light blue shirt undone with a dark blue T-shirt underneath, and small dark glasses. He looks like a clean-shaven Jim Morrison this morning. The girl next to him has long blonde hair, large blue eyes, long eyelashes and a pout to outdo Angelina Jolie's. She looks like his groupie. She's a short, slim girl in a short, slim skirt and is wearing trainers. She's also wearing the same small round dark glasses as Will. They stop and I can see Esther introducing herself, though I can't hear what they're saying, but as Will turns back towards me, Esther winks behind his back and mouths, 'VERY SEXY.'

I presume she's referring to Will, but she could be talking about both of them, and as she waves goodbye Will walks towards me with a faint smile, as though he knows what she has just said.

'Please come in,' I say, smiling at them both.

'This is Becca Kite,' Will says, sounding very formal. Becca beams at me and offers me her hand, giving me an almost manic 'Hello there!'.

'Very nice to meet you,' I say, realising I'm about ten to twenty years too old for TV, and my skirt should be considerably shorter. They look a bit like ultra cool rock stars – elegantly wasted, easily stylish – and I can't help smiling at myself, dressed in what I think is bohemian and realising it's just my attempt at it. These two characters are the real thing.

I follow Will and Becca through to the kitchen.

'Oh sorry, I thought this was the sitting room,' he says, looking round at me.

'The kitchen is fine,' I smile, 'in fact it's tidier than the sitting room, and there's a large table and stools here, so it will be easier. Plus there's food here, too.'

Will perches himself on the nearest stool, looking around him at the brightly coloured cupboards. Becca sits next to him like some mini-me, doing the same.

'You like your purples, reds and oranges, don't you?' he observes.

'I like colour.'

'Quite,' he replies. 'My ex-wife wasn't into colour. She was a fan of beige. With two girls who were tomboys from the day they were born, and a very boyish boy, the house has always had much more colour than she bargained for. They scrawled over everything in crayon and paint – purple, red and orange being their favourite colours, oddly enough,' he says, taking in every detail of

147

my kitchen including Freddie's vivid, abstract Dali-esque contributions, which are emblazoned across the walls and fridge door.

'How old are your children?' I ask, not wanting to pry, but trying to be polite.

'Oh, they're all in their late teens now. We had them very young, and they live with their mother and her boyfriend in the States.'

'That must mean you don't see them much.'

'I go when I can. Being in TV isn't conducive to being a parent or having a social life, but it's not impossible,' he says, getting a large A4 file out of his bag and opening it up on the table. I'm a little taken aback that Will seems to have abruptly ended the conversation, but I realise we're on a tight schedule so perhaps I should just shut up and get on with it.

'Do *you* manage to balance your family life with your work?' he asks, still looking through his notes, while I make coffee.

'Well, I did until I lost my radio slot,' I say, 'and I've taken this opportunity because it's on my doorstep and I know the place and the people, so hopefully for the few months I'm working on this project, it should work out fine.'

'I don't know what you've been told by Jarred, but the show is going out on ITV later this year, so we've got a tight deadline for editing which means the schedule is tight too. It will be "An hour-long documentary – title yet to be decided – on why Castleford is producing well-balanced successful happy healthy people and what the rest of the country is doing wrong. The tone will be light but thought-provoking. If the programme were a tree it would be an oak, if it were a car it would be a Mini Cooper S . . ." I'm reading from the brief here,' he says, looking up at me, 'just so you know I am not a complete wet blanket, these are not my words, but Jarred's.' He looks down again and continues, ' ". . . with narration interspersed with live coverage following key characters in the Castleford community. Soft fly-on-the-wall over a two-month period." ' He looks up at me and asks, 'Any questions?'

'Does it say if the programme were a food what it would be?' I ask.

He looks down at his notes. 'A turkey,' he says, looking up at me again.

'Really?' I say, putting my hand to my mouth.

'No, only joking,' he replies and looks down at his notes again.

I can't help laughing, but realise Becca is now also sitting looking at notes and has a pen in her hand, ready perhaps to record what I have to say. I clear my throat and hand them each a mug of coffee, immediately realising I haven't asked if they want any, but they both take it gratefully and thank me.

'No. I don't have any questions. All those involved have been told what you'll need from them, although with the exception of Victoria Stock, and possibly John Tremble the sculptor, I don't think any of them have worked with the media before, so they won't realise how intrusive it will be,' I add, thinking especially of

Jessica Compton-Batt, who has been wavering about the whole idea.

'We will follow your lead on where to go and when to film. I'll introduce you to the film crew, Aled on camera, Richard on sound – both nice, experienced, laid-back guys – and we'll have to give regular updates to Jarred at High Light, so if you can make yourself available for some of those trips that would be great. Are you happy for us to film your son?' Will adds, looking up at me again.

'It's not just my decision, it's his dad's as well,' I explain, not wanting to go into the fact that getting any agreement out of Leonard will be nigh-on impossible, especially if I suggest I'm happy for Freddie to appear, so the answer is likely to be a resounding and resolute no. Even if I called him and was ambivalent about the idea he'd probably smell a rat and still say no.

'Right,' he says, staring at me quizzically, almost seeming to read my mind and detect I don't want to ask anything of my ex. 'If you like, Becca will have a word with him. She's very persuasive, is our Becca.' He looks at her and smiles knowingly.

'I'm very lucky. I've got a good relationship with my ex,' he says, 'but then, we are an ocean apart, so it's hard not to get on when there's so much distance between you. I can't throw a brick that far and neither can she.' I'm just about to ask more about his children when he switches back into business mode, talking through the schedule and dates, and making sure Becca has all the contact details of everyone involved, and confirming the main events we're going to cover.

I'm not sure what I make of Will Stafford, apart from the fact that when he leaves my house, again being very businesslike in shaking hands with me at the end of the meeting, I feel myself fizzing and I am out of breath. I reason that it's the excitement and sudden realisation that I'm actually working in TV. 'It must be that,' I say to myself out loud, 'or the coffee I've half drunk.' Yes, it must be that.

Chapter Nine

It's eight thirty in the morning. I've fed Dillon, got Freddie to feed the gerbils, made myself half decent in smart shirt and skirt (although not as short as Becca's) and dropped Freddie off at school, waving at some of the mums whom I'm due to see later this afternoon at the PTA meeting, which, if we keep to schedule, we're due to film.

I'm heading towards Edward and Esther's cottage to make sure the interview, the first shoot of the documentary, is going smoothly. I'm not needed at this one, but Esther has asked me to be there to put Edward at his ease with a friendly face. I don't have to be at every shoot, but I want to be at this one and a few of the others, just to ensure everyone is happy, both crew and interviewee.

We're scheduled to film a football match for the under tens after this, and hopefully some mums and dads will turn up to watch, as our school team is playing against Letchbury under tens, the neighbouring boarding school which the Flindell children attend. Castleford doesn't ever play private schools as they have their own leagues in the area, but for some reason, Jarred (so Will tells me) wants to use the football game as a symbol indicating money can't buy success, and has already contacted the Letchbury headmaster to ask if on this one occasion the two schools could play each other. He has agreed, and to the filming. Of course it could all backfire horribly and Letchbury could completely wipe the floor with our boys, suggesting that money does matter.

Freddie's playing, so I've got a personal vested interest in Castleford winning. The final shoot of the day is the committee meeting of the PTA to discuss the preparations for the school play. It's a full-on schedule, but I'm confident in Will. He has the experience I lack, and hopefully I've made sure everyone who needs to know about times and places will be there when we need them.

We've scheduled John Tremble to be interviewed tomorrow, preferably working on his latest project; then we've got Edward's book launch, held at a club in Soho, which sounds sleazy but I'm sure it will be fine; something at the Flindell Mansions – still to be confirmed by Anthony and Agetha who will probably organise something completely over the top which will doubtless make great TV; then there's Mr Gates's masterpiece, the school play, the school production itself and some of the preparation meetings and auditions, as well as filming inside some of the classrooms and possibly a field trip, but that has yet to be confirmed with Jessica Compton-Batt.

I've also managed to schedule in some of the local shopkeepers, including Mr Farnsworth, the fishmonger, and Mrs Dawson, the busybody who works in the post office. We'll even interview Herbie – my postman, whose father and grandfather both delivered post in Castleford – while he's on his rounds. I would have liked Dad to have appeared, but he's not good at the moment, so don't want to disturb him. Peter Bonham called me this morning to wish me luck with my first job in TV, and to say that if there's anything he can do, just call, which is sweet of him, and to send Victoria his best regards. Also to tell me that Sandra and Shane are already being prima donnas and that George has threatened to resign, which pleased me even more.

There's a notice on the door of the cottage saying FILMING IN PROGRESS, PLEASE DO NOT ENTER. Then in smaller letters, 'Unless part of the film crew'. As I consider myself a member of the film crew, I walk in the door of the cottage. I can see that the crew have already made themselves at home and that lights and wires fill Edward's usually pristine study.

Edward's a tall, handsome man, in his early fifties, with light brown hair; he looks like Mickey Rourke before the facelift. He's like a lovable, slightly ruffled cocker spaniel, with large come-to-bed eyes and a relaxed manner that puts me at ease immediately I see him. I can understand why Esther and he have been married so long. He's very easy-going, kind, thoughtful and (according to Esther) very sexy when he wants to be. She did recently confess to buying him some Horney Goat Weed to increase his libido and his ability to write sexy stuff rather than adapting the anecdotes she tells him about Victoria's life. Edward met Esther when they were both travelling in Vienna, at the Belvedere where they were looking at Schiele, or was it Klimt. He was working for a marketing company, but was bored with promoting products he didn't believe in to those he didn't respect. So he left and did what thousands dream of doing – he wrote a book, and then another. Fifteen books down the line, he earns a comfortable living, although without Esther's money I don't think it would be quite as comfortable as it is now. He pays for the basics, Esther pays for the luxuries and they both hope one day a book will be made into a film.

'Do you have make-up?' Will calls out to Becca, who's wearing an even shorter skirt than yesterday. Neither of them have seen me enter the room. 'Edward's shiny. Can you get rid of his shiny nose and cheeks, please. No shine,' he insists.

Becca bustles past me, saying a quick, 'hello there', and returns before I've taken another step, compact in hand.

I want to wave to Edward, but I don't want to distract him. There are two other men in the room, dressed uniformly in jeans and black sweaters; I presume they must be Aled and Richard. Aled has a camera perched nonchalantly on his shoulder – as if it's as light as a feather – and looks like he's just got out of bed and would prefer to still be there. Richard wears large head-phones and is looking intently at a little black box with loads of knobs on it, which he's busy tweaking.

'Now, Edward,' says Will when Becca has stopped powdering Edward's nose and cheeks, 'this morning we're here to listen to you talk about your childhood in Castleford, and about being a father and an author. It's basically a preamble and setting up shot for when we film you at your book launch later, so you could either just talk to camera or I'll ask you questions, whatever you're comfortable with.' I like his manner and I can tell he's immediately put Edward at ease. Edward is the first to notice me.

'Hello, Helena,' he calls out loudly – too loud for Richard, who has to take off his headphones. 'Oh, sorry about that, Richard,' says Edward, realising what he's done. 'How long have you been there?' he asks me, ignoring the fact that the team are ready to roll.

'Only just arrived,' I tell him. 'Ignore me, Edward, just focus on what you have to say, or answer Will's questions, and you'll enjoy it,' I say, realising that Becca, Aled and Richard are all looking at me as if to say, 'Go away.' Will turns round and smiles at me.

'Hello,' he says drily. 'Get up late?'

I'm a little taken aback. 'No, I had to drop off my son at school. It's one of the things mothers do,' I reply curtly.

'Not when they work in TV, it's not,' replies Aled,

giving me a wink and a grin.

Will turns back to Edward. 'Now, if we can have some quiet, Edward, would you please tell me – looking at me, not at the camera – who you are, starting with "my name is"; how long you've lived in Castleford and why you still live here and never moved away.'

'OK. Am I still shiny?' Edward asks, looking over at Becca.

'No, you're fine,' Becca nods.

'Is everyone ready?' Will asks. 'Richard, Aled, everyone?'

Everyone grunts.

'Action,' says Will, nodding to Edward to start.

'My name is . . .'

The doorbell rings.

'Who forgot to put a notice on the door asking people not to call?' asks Will.

'I did put a notice up,' complains Becca.

'She did,' I say. 'I saw it when I came in.'

Will looks at both of us. 'Then who can't read?' he asks, looking towards the study door.

'I should have guessed it,' Edward sighs as his father-in-law appears.

'What's happening here then?' he booms. 'What are you doing?'

Esther's dad is a short, stout man in his sixties, overbearing and egotistical. I look at him and wonder what his wife Monica sees in him and how on earth he was able to seduce another woman, too. He owns a large property on the outskirts of town, with a heated indoor swimming pool. Seeing him, pompous and red-faced, uncharacteristically well dressed today in a suit and tie, I sense that he has the potential to screw up our shooting schedule for the day if he doesn't bugger off soon.

Will turns round and offers his hand, but Mr Farina takes one look at him and refuses.

'Who may I ask are you?' he demands.

'I'm Will, and we're filming a documentary on Castleford, about why it's such a great place to live,' he explains briefly.

'Then why aren't you interviewing me?' he replies indignantly. 'My name is Louis Farina and I've lived in this town all my life and I'm very successful in the hotel business. I had a very profitable business in South Africa some years ago. I've made millions in the industry. I would have thought you'd want successful businessmen to appear on the show, not just writers and such,' he says, waving at Edward.

'I'm afraid you weren't on the list,' replies Will. 'We already have the Flindells and a broad cross-section of residents, but if we have the time we can add you on,' he says, looking over at Becca. 'Can you add Mr Farina to our list of possible interviewees? Get his details, including telephone number, please, Becca,' he says.

Becca takes one look at the little man and smiles, understanding that this is a ruse to get him to leave. 'If you'd like to follow me?' she says, leading him out of the room.

'Right,' says Will, 'Becca will keep him occupied

while we film you, Edward. Please continue. You look great, no shine,' he encourages. 'And action.'

Before Edward has time to speak, though, Richard raises his hand.

'Sorry, Edward, can I move your mic because there's something rustling against it.' He walks towards Edward and removes his microphone, which is attached to his shirt collar. Richard fiddles about with it, tapping and blowing, then attaches it on the other side, looking up at Edward. 'Try that.'

'Hello, my name is Edward.'

'Can you say that again?' Richard asks, putting the headphones on.

'My name is Edward,' he repeats more softly.

'Yes, that's fine. Right, carry on,' Richard says, nodding at Will and Aled, who are now deep in conversation.

'Great, great, so is everyone ready?' asks Will.

Everyone nods as Becca returns to the room minus Mr Farina, then Will turns to Edward and says, 'Action.'

Edward talks about how long he's lived in Castleford and how it inspires his writing. How the people he knows and the places he loves help him to write his novels. He says that he walks along the coastline in the mornings, as he used to do when the girls were babies and toddlers in buggies, to gather his ideas together. He talks them through with his little inquisitors, as he calls Constance, Charlotte and even Esther, who help to give him a female perspective. 'Very important even when writing a novel aimed at a male readership,' he explains.

'Your latest book, is it different from the others?' Will asks.

'It's sexier.' He smiles. 'Sometimes I get so turned on by what I write these days I want to wake Esther up, but I work late and she's always so tired when she gets in from work, so sometimes I have to, er . . . you know,' he says, looking round to see if he should finish his sentence.

I can't believe Edward has just said that. I should imagine Esther will be mortified. But Will doesn't stop the cameras rolling, and continues to ask questions as though the answer was nothing special. I can't wait to read Edward's next novel. They have always been so action-packed, with many deaths, usually accompanied by a lot of gore, and they have no sex in them – not even a kiss. This new book sounds like a complete departure for him. Esther never really talks about his books because she confesses she finds them quite dull, but then as Edward tells her, they are for men. This next novel sounds as though women might find it of interest as well.

'Your study is full of photos and paintings,' Will comments when Edward finishes. 'Can you tell me a little about them? Is there a story behind any of them?'

'Oh, they're photographs of when I was a young boy, and shots of the girls and Esther and me. We used to travel a lot, but we don't so much now. I had a real passion for travelling when I was younger and when the girls were toddlers. We went all over the place – South America, the Far East, Africa – to all the places everyone avoids with young children. It's a wonderful way to broaden the mind,' he adds wistfully. 'Perhaps one day I'll do it again, but at the moment writing takes up a lot of my time, as do my family and friends.'

'Thank you, Edward,' Will says. He turns round to Aled and Richard. 'That's it for this one, guys. Can you film some cutaways of the photos and paintings, Aled, and do some atmos, Richard? Our next appointment is the football match, at four o'clock. Aled, I'll go with you down to the beach meanwhile, and we can film some scenic stuff down there and general shots of the town, around the fishmonger's and post office. You OK with that?'

Aled nods while Richard asks everyone to be quiet for about thirty seconds while he records background noise that can be used to help the editor mix the final programme. While we're sitting in silence I notice Will is looking at me, saying nothing, just staring, so I smile at him, as if to say, 'What are you looking at?' He doesn't smile back, though, so perhaps he's miles away, just thinking.

When Richard gives the nod everyone starts to pack up and I turn to walk over to Edward, who's attempting to get the microphone off his collar with little success. 'Can I help you with that?' I ask.

'Yes please, Helena,' he says. 'How did I do? And be honest with me, I know these types will say I'm wonderful when I'm not. People who agree to be on TV wouldn't look as stupid and pathetic as they do if those producing the shows were honest with them.'

161

'Well, I liked that story about you having to finish yourself off when you wrote sexy scenes.' I giggle. 'I imagine that will make the final cut, although I'm not sure how Esther will feel about it.'

'Well, it does happen,' he says, grinning. 'I can't help being a good writer.'

'In answer to your original question, Edward, you were great, very evocative and positive about the place, and very passionate about your work. And "these types" can hear what you're saying because you've still got your mic on, so I suggest you leave your thoughts till later, eh.'

'Oh,' he says, looking up at Richard and mouthing, 'Sorry.'

Richard smiles at him. 'No worries, Edward.'

'Can I tempt you to a sausage sandwich?' Edward asks. 'Got them from the local butcher. They're lamb merguez and they're quite spicy. I've got some for all the crew.'

Will comes over to thank Edward. 'Your answers were very interesting and insightful,' he tells him.

'I hope they sell Castleford – and my next book,' Edward replies with a glint in his eye. 'Fancy a bite to eat before you go?' he asks. Will looks at the food and smiles. 'I'm fine, but I know two guys who would. Becca's a veggie, so she'll pass, but Aled and Richard have been up since six and I'm sure they're starving.'

Ten minutes later the crew are tucking into sandwiches and Edward has prepared some hummus and crudités for Becca. I get a text from Esther asking how Edward did and I text back that he did brilliantly and was very sexy. Perhaps I shouldn't have said that last bit, as I get a call from her immediately.

'What do you mean he was sexy?' she says, before I have time to say hello.

'He just told us how when he writes sexy scenes he gets very excited himself. It's a nice piece. Oh and your dad turned up and wants to be in the show.'

'He what!'

'It's unlikely we'll use him, but ultimately it's not my decision.'

'Great,' she says, sounding despondent.

'How's the control freak diary going with Digby? Is he in today?'

'Yes he is, so I've got to be quick. He's just finished a round of redundancies in the bank and it's all getting quite nasty. He's such a deceitful git, being nice to their face and then sending emails to our human resources director, who I'm getting to know quite well by phone because of all this. She's doing all his firing for him, the coward. I don't think for all his bullying he can deal with people fighting back and showing their emotions. They'd be honest about him for the first time and I think he knows it.'

'Do his women still call him Mr Hoppy?'

'Yes, Hoppy is still up to his tricks. I've had to book Blakes for tomorrow lunchtime. I've booked a room for an overnight stay but he's supposed to fly to Geneva tomorrow, so I know it's only going to be used for an hour.'

'Pity you can't ask if you and Edward can use it for the night.'

'Yes, that would go down like a brick. I've got to go, Helena, but hope all goes well and tell Edward I'll call him later and that I love him.'

'Why don't you tell him yourself?'

'I will later, but I've got to go now.'

Chapter Ten

At the football ground the boys are on the pitch. Freddie is there with the rest of Castleford team, and Tony, their young, earnest coach, is giving them a pep talk. Usually there's a maximum of ten spectators, but today there must be fifty, including some faces I've only ever seen at parents' evenings. Even Agetha and Anthony Flindell are there. Perhaps their son, I think he's called Tristan, is playing for Letchbury. The cynical side of me thinks perhaps it's just because the cameras are there, as I'm sure Tristan is twelve and therefore too old to play in this match. Word must have spread among the spectators that there's a TV crew in town. Mind you, if you tell the Flindells anything, it's guaranteed to spread like wildfire.

The other side of the pitch where the Letchbury parents are to stand is empty. I suppose the Letchbury children are put into boarding school because the parents are overseas or work long hours, and consequently wouldn't be able to come to a football match. I know, from my experience with Freddie, how important it is for him that Leonard watches him play. He wants to show his dad what he can do, and Leonard is very seldom there to see it. Perhaps, when he is ready to be more active in Freddie's life, Freddie won't want or need it. He'll want to be with his mates or other men, like his football coach, who has been there for him, encouraging him and teaching him, just as Leonard should have been. And knowing these things, I can't help but feel very sorry for the opposition today, who've grown used to parents never being there. These children aren't even ten yet. I'd love to get into a conversation about the whole boarding-school issue with one of those absent parents.

The Castleford supporters are to not only out in full force but are all dressed in smart country gear, as though they're posing for a Gant catalogue. Even the child spectators are dressed like mini versions of their parents. They all look ridiculous, especially Anthony Flindell, a rather portly man. He is wearing plus fours and looks like something out of a P. G. Wodehouse novel, ready for hunting, shooting or fishing, but certainly not for watching under-tens football. The scene is bizarre and I seriously consider advising Will not to film the crowd, as I don't want the viewers to think the people of Castleford are a bunch of eccentric nutters.

'We don't usually get this many spectators,' I say as I walk towards the crowd with Will and the crew. 'And they're never this oddly dressed, either.'

'This always happens when they know there's TV

around,' says Will. 'Everyone wants to be in the final edit. Turns sane people silly. Even celebrities get desperate, and they should know better.'

'Surely not everyone?'

'Yes, everyone,' he says. 'I've been in the business long enough to know that even the people I thought would brush it off as nonsense get all silly and formal in front of a camera, talking in platitudes and using words they don't understand. They also tend to dress totally inappropriately,' he adds, taking a look at Anthony's plus fours, 'just so they can appear on camera, even if they look utterly foolish. Just think of the motley bunch that put themselves forward for *The X Factor.*'

'But this isn't *The X Factor.*'

'No it isn't, and we're going to edit it accordingly,' Will says, scratching his cheek.

As predicted, as soon as the spectators notice Aled and the camera, they all start cheering and laughing at nothing.

'We may not be able to use this,' I whisper to Will. 'It looks so silly and incongruous with how I envisage the rest of the show. Viewers will think Castleford is a cross between *Village of the Damned* and *The Stepford Wives.* Why don't we just focus on the boys playing?'

'We'll do some of the crowd as well, and an interview with the coach,' Will replies. 'Do you want to do that one?' he asks, looking at Tony, who's now ushered the boys in to position after his pep talk. 'He looks like your type.'

'I don't have a type,' I reply, 'and he's already with someone,' I add dismissively, a little annoyed at the suggestion. Will stares at me again in the way that he does, without saying anything, which I'm starting to think is just a ploy to intimidate me.

'Don't stare at me like that,' I tell him.

'When I said your type, I didn't mean the type of man you sleep with, I meant the type of person you want to feature in the programme,' he replies, looking at me as though I've had a blonde moment. 'And I didn't realise my staring at you upset you. I tend to look at people and observe them because of what I do. It's an occupational hazard.'

'I could use that excuse as a journalist, Aled could use that excuse as a cameraman, but he doesn't stare at me the way you stare, and I don't stare at you the way you look at me. It's rude, so please don't do it,' I say firmly, and walk towards Aled and Richard, who are setting up at the side of the pitch, ready for the whistle to be blown.

Tony sees me and waves, walking over.

'Hello, Helena, how are you?' he asks.

'Very well, thank you,' I reply as he gives me a kiss on both cheeks, which is the way he normally greets me. Tony has been absolutely great with Freddie over the past couple of years; he's a brilliant role model for him.

'Is it still OK to film here today?' I ask.

'Yes, that's fine as long as they don't distract the boys too much. I've told the boys to try to just focus on the game. I must admit I've never seen this much support for the team, so perhaps you should come more often.' He laughs, looking over at the crowd, who are repositioning themselves in line with Aled's camera. Aled is obviously used to this kind of thing and just smiles at them, asking politely if they'll move so that he has a clear view of the game. Becca is helping him, but her manner is far pushier and she actually tries to shoo them into a corner like sheep. I'm sure if there were a pen available, she'd try to get them in it.

People do behave differently in front of the camera, I muse. There will be people like Edward and Tony, who will just be themselves, and others who will freeze and others, like Anthony and Agetha, who will milk it for all it's worth. But I suppose that's the fun of this industry, making that chemistry work.

'And can we interview you?' I ask Tony as he's about to join the boys on the pitch. 'I'll be the one doing it, if you're happy with that.'

'Yes, of course,' he replies, one eye on the boys, aware that they're getting restless and want to start. 'If we can do it after the game that would be great, as I want to keep the guys motivated. If they see me distracted, they'll get distracted too.'

The Letchbury boys arrive in a gleaming white coach, with two teachers, both a few inches taller than Tony. They usher the boys, who also look about an inch taller than all our boys, on to the pitch, their smart green and black tops and shorts contrasting with Castleford's blue and white. They all look happy and healthy enough so perhaps they don't miss their parents, not that they have an option one way or another.

For the next half an hour we watch the boys play, and it's a good game. Letchbury has some great players and they nearly score a few times, hitting the post, and we have a strong goalkeeper in Oliver, who manages to save one. Freddie almost scores as do a few of our other boys, but at half-time it's still nil—nil. Tony allows Freddie to come up to me to say hi, something he doesn't usually permit. Freddie wants something to eat.

I'm feeling utterly guilty as I forgot to bring anything when Will saves the day by producing some Kit Kats.

'Would you like one of these?' Will says. 'My name is Will and I'm working with your mum on a TV programme about Castleford.'

Freddie looks at him like he does everyone he first meets. He's very protective of me, and consequently weighs up every man I introduce him to as a potential friend or foe. He's witnessed some wild extremes in behaviour from my male friends and from his father.

'If I score a goal, will you film that?' he asks, still looking at Will, unbelievably managing to stare him out.

'Of course we will, but you've got to score first,' Will replies with a smile.

Freddie looks at me again, his mouth half full of Kit Kat. 'Can I play with Jack after this, Mummy?' he asks.

'I've arranged for you to go over to Grandma and Grandad's,' I tell him.

He looks disappointed. 'Can't I do both?' he asks.

'I'll ask Jack's mum if I see her,' I say, looking for her in the crowd who are now hovering around Richard, asking questions.

'Thank you, Mummy,' he says. 'And thank you for the Kit Kat,' he says to Will, handing him the wrapper. 'Got to go now.' And with that he bounds off in the direction of his team and Tony, who's readying them for another pep talk before the second half.

'Very nice and polite boy,' comments Will, looking after him. 'I liked that age. They change a lot you know, over the next two years. My girls were so mature even at four. I remember thinking, I don't know how boys stood a chance.'

'Perhaps that's why girls tend to go for older men, because they show more maturity, although my dad, who was headmaster at Castleford years ago, would tell you that boys reach the age of eight and continue to grow physically but not emotionally. And that's from someone who likes teaching boys and is a man himself. He may have been joking, of course.'

'Are we interviewing your dad?' Will asks. 'I didn't see him on the list, and an ex-headmaster of Castleford School would be a notable addition.'

'He's very ill,' I explain quickly, 'and I don't want to put him through that.'

'I'm sorry to hear that. No worries,' he says, and squeezes the top of my arm. As he does so I feel a surge of energy, like an electric shock running through my body. I look at him because I sense he feels it, too. We're just standing there and I'm only half aware that his hand is still on my arm when Aled comes over.

'Hi there,' he says, looking at us innocently. 'Do you want me to film some of the crowd now, set up for the interview with the coach or film more of the football? I got a lot of footage during the first half,' he says, lighting a cigarette.

'Focus on the game, Aled, would you?' says Will, turning to look at him. 'Get an occasional shot of the crowd, and Helena says she'll interview Tony at the end. Then we've got to head for the school and set up for the PTA shoot.'

'Right-oh,' Aled says, smiling at us both and walking back to the crowd, who now focus on him, having exhausted Richard's technical knowledge of sound equipment – and patience, by the look of him.

'I don't think I'll have to ask much of Tony, he's a good talker,' I say, 'and he knows the kids and grew up here as well. He'll give another perspective on the place – what it's like for young people in the town.' I am suddenly aware that Will is still holding my arm. He suddenly becomes aware of it too, and lets go, staring at me in that intense way of his and nodding. 'Yes, that'll be fine.'

I walk to the side of the pitch. I'm not used to people being so touchy-feely, not even my radio colleagues, so was on edge when Will held my arm – but I suppose that's how they are in TV. I've spotted Jack's mum and need to ask if she'd mind having Freddie for an hour or so and then dropping him round to Mum and Dad's. She's a nice lady, so I'm sure she'll agree.

The game starts again and within minutes the other team have scored, but then Harry passes to Jack, who passes back to Harry, who makes a pass to a boy whose name I can never remember, who passes back to Freddie, who scores. I scream my head off as Aled records it for posterity. I don't know if it will end up on the cutting-room floor, but I'll keep it whatever happens.

At the end of the game, which Castleford won 2–1 – one goal from Freddie, the other from Harry – I rush up to Freddie to congratulate him. The Letchbury boys shake hands with our team and don't look too unhappy, as though they're used to it, or they have learned to be good losers. Dad always said it was important to be a good loser, but not too often. Then I wait until Tony has given our boys their final pep talk and they have headed back to their parents.

Aled sets up the camera and Richard puts a mic on Tony. Then Becca walks over to introduce herself, fluttering her eyelashes and her legs, which seem to get longer every time I see her, or is it just her skirt that gets shorter? Tony grins back broadly, like a Cheshire cat, looking Becca up and down and raising his eyebrows, happy with the attention, but taking it all in his stride, just as I thought he would. He's a hot-blooded male, after all.

I quickly explain that I'll be asking some questions about how long he's lived in Castleford and why he chose to stay here, then I ask him to introduce himself. It's my first TV interview, and although I won't be on camera, I'm still hoping it will go smoothly. It's quite a breezy day and I'm a little cold, but I need to focus, and try to remember how Will questioned Edward. I ask Tony to look at me and not at the camera, and when Richard and Aled are ready, and Becca has managed to keep the lingering spectators away, Will nods. 'Action.'

Tony talks about himself, how he's lived in Castleford all his life and has a passion for football and the boys he teaches. He feels kids need outdoor activity and good role models as they don't get enough of them from their busy absent fathers, which obviously hits a nerve with me. 'Although,' he says, looking around, 'a lot more parents than usual seem to have turned up today.'

'Why do you think the crime rate is so low in Castleford?' I ask when he's finished.

'That's not rocket science. The kids here have a lot to do. It's not too built up and there's plenty of space. There are lots of sports on offer, and there's the beach, so the kids don't get bored. Kids who are bored mentally and physically, who don't have the stimulation and discipline, boundaries and freedom provided by their parents, they're the ones who have issues. They don't have to get all that from their parents, but they need it from someone. That's just my view. Could be bollocks for all I know.' Then he laughs at himself.

'That was great,' I say, smiling at him.

'Sorry about the swearing,' he says, looking a bit

shamefaced. 'Will that last bit have to be cut?' He glances at Will and Aled.

Before Will can answer, Aled does it for him. 'Nah,' he says, putting down his camera and shaking his head. 'They allow bollocks on TV all the time, don't they, Richard?' He turns to his colleague, who doesn't reply and just grins widely at him.

Having seen Freddie drive off with Jack and his mum, I head back to the car to go to Castleford School for the PTA meeting.

Chapter Eleven

Castleford School looks more like a large mansion house on four floors; it even has a turret classroom, where Year Six reside for their final year. Year Six is the best year to be in, Freddie tells me, because Mr Howe is the form teacher and he teaches science; according to Freddie, Mr Howe is the best scientist in the world.

In Year Four, Freddie has Miss King, whom I love. Freddie has come on by leaps and bounds with her encouragement and guidance.

My involvement with the school has been kept to a minimum. I've helped occasionally with the PTA fetes and Mr Gates's school productions – Freddie was an Oompa-Loompa in last year's fabulous rendition of *Charlie and the Chocolate Factory*, and I was given the job of making ten Oompa-Loompa costumes. The PTA is full of ball-busters, according to Miss King, who can be hilariously indiscreet sometimes. The last time I spoke to her when I was picking up Freddie, she commented that the boys all spent a lot of their time holding their willies. 'I tell the boys, "I'm not going to steal your willy, so you don't have to hold on to it." But they don't ever stop playing with their willies, do they, Miss Treadwell?'

I nodded and laughed as I had to agree with her. She's a lovely, funny lady, and although I don't know much about her background, I believe she was once a classical violinist, not that she ever plays to the boys, which is a pity.

As I approach the school gates with Will and the crew, I feel as though I'm leading them into the dragon's den, but then I remember that these guys have worked in war zones, so this lot should be a doddle.

Thankfully, Miss King is waiting for us at the entrance, and I make the introductions.

She smiles and shakes hands with everyone, looking quizzically at each of them in turn. 'Are you ready to do battle?' she asks.

'Well, I've worked in Afghanistan,' says Aled, 'is it worse than that?' He smiles.

'Far worse. The Taliban have nothing on this lot. You won't even see it coming, so make sure your lens is pointing in all directions as you don't know when the first shot is going to occur. Got that?' she says, turning round and leading the way in.

Aled mouths, 'Nutter,' to Richard, but I scowl at him. She's not nutty, just mildly eccentric, and Aled hasn't met these women yet, so he can't comment. As we're walking in, she starts to brief us. She looks jolly in her yellow cardigan, green skirt and long brown boots, like a sort of hippy-chick Miss Pepperpot.

'Now, as you perhaps know, Penny Vernon is head of the PTA. Penny is a barrister, specialising in child law, very thin with a pointy chin, pointy nose and clipped manner. She is married to someone in the City who she doesn't see very often as he's always working late, and they have a pied-à-terre in Kensington, which he stays at regularly. She takes notes about everything and has a photographic memory, which can be great, but also incredibly annoying,' she says, sighing.

'Next is Alicia Harris. Alicia takes the minutes and is married to a celebrity chef, and she also doesn't see much of her husband as he works late. He appears in lots of the glossy magazines. He hasn't reached the dizzy heights of Gordon Ramsay and Marco Pierre White, but Alicia says he's getting there and feels that he wants to spend more time with his family, although there's a rumour going round that he spends more time with Penny Vernon's family and that he and Penny are having an affair, but I didn't tell you that.

'And then there is Sonya Cardigan, an ex-City trader who's given up working to look after her children, although she spends more time with her horses than with them. As well as riding – they have their own stables – she enjoys skiing and climbing and has run the London Marathon several times. The first time she threw up halfway round but still managed to finish. I always get the feeling she's uncomfortable with her boy, and her boy looks just as uncomfortable with her, but I could be wrong.

'Sonya, Penny and Alicia are all ball-busters. They

raise lots of money for the school and for charity, and they're very active about promoting the school, so it will be interesting to see what they have to say about the documentary. Anyway, they've agreed for the meeting to be filmed, so they can't be that against it, can they? Jessica – the headmistress – can be very persuasive when she wants to be. In our assembly this morning she mentioned that you'd be coming round and filming everyone, and that we should all be on our best behaviour – no swearing, spitting or mooning from the boys or the staff, which all the boys laughed at.'

I'm aware of the time and look at my watch. 'Shouldn't we go in now, Miss King?' I suggest.

'Not yet,' she says, 'I haven't finished and you need to know this.' She takes me aside, speaking quietly, so only I can hear her words. 'Barbara Jacobs, on the other hand, is vivacious, loud, always smiling, but does very little for the school. She tries to contribute where she can, but is largely ignored by Penny's army and bullied by some of the other mums. I'm sure she is on some sort of happy pill because she always looks glazed, as if she's just had an orgasm or a bottle of vodka. She's a secretary for an advertising company, so is the most normal of the bunch, which is also perhaps why she doesn't get on with the rest of them – she sees straight through them, but that's just my take on it, you may see it differently. Plus,' she says, lowering her voice even more, 'she's pretty, which may be why Alicia, Penny and Sonya have taken against her; they probably think she's after their husbands.'

When she's finished we rejoin the group. 'There are others, but they are the main protagonists to watch out for,' she tells everyone. 'Now, we'd better go in.' And with that she turns to open the door to the room where the meeting is being held.

The women are already sitting around a large table on chairs fit for small boys, so everyone looks over-sized.

Mr Gates is walking round the table handing out papers, and looks up and grins when he sees me. He is the drama teacher, a tall handsome man in his forties who also appears in commercials, famous for shaking beans in a coffee ad, for which he gets teased in the staffroom. Fortunately that was over six years ago, so none of the boys remember it, though most of the parents do. He still performs in local rep, as well as doing voice-overs for toilet tissue and car insurance, but his most recent personal triumph came when he was the voice of a chipmunk in a successful Disney film, the name of which escapes me.

John Gates has produced some amazing plays for the school, all of which can be purchased on DVD for £8 a copy. He's been in several soaps, including *EastEnders* as a shop owner – they all seem to own shops in *EastEnders* – and he even had a part as an extra in *Extras*, which he found slightly disconcerting. He always wears T-shirts with jackets, even in winter, which makes him look like a thespian. He is not, to my knowledge, gay, although he remains resolutely single. Whenever I bump into him in the playground while dropping off or picking up Freddie we have a chat. He's never 'rested' in his life, he tells me, and has no intention of doing so.

Miss King goes to sit at the head of the table, with Penny Vernon on one side of her and Alicia Harris on the other.

'Hello, ladies and gentleman,' I say, coming forward, 'can I introduce the film crew to you?'

'Yes, you can,' replies Penny, 'but you're late; you've kept us waiting for ten minutes.' She looks annoyed.

'We were delayed at the football,' Will says, stepping forward. 'I'm sure you'll all be pleased to hear your boys won.'

'Harry scored a goal,' I add, hoping that will mellow her.

She smiles sarcastically. 'He usually does.'

'I'm Will Stafford the director,' Will says, realising the frosty reception isn't a good start, and shaking their hands one by one in a bid to charm them into submission. His ploy obviously works, as Penny no longer looks annoyed and giggles girlishly.

'Honestly, aren't women silly,' I say under my breath, but I think Richard, who's standing right beside me, hears me and smiles.

'Will can charm the knickers off anyone,' he says, which makes me laugh.

Mr Gates grins at me and winks. He's got a lot of charisma, and I know there are single mums at school who've invited him to dinner or lunch parties. He's always gone, but he's never got off with anyone. I've always got on with him well, and I wink back. Will notices, looking round at me as if to say, 'Don't flirt with the punters.' Which makes me smart because that's what Becca seems to be doing all the time when she wants to get something done.

'I would like to briefly introduce you to my crew,' Will continues. 'This is Aled, our cameraman, who'll make you all look even lovelier than you are.' Aled comes forward and does a little bow.

'I thought he was the cameraman because he was holding the camera,' Alicia says sarcastically.

'And this is Richard,' Will continues, ignoring Alicia, 'who will be clipping small microphones on your tops, if possible, so we can all hear what you're saying. Now before we start, can you please turn off your mobile phones. We don't want any of them going off in the middle of the filming. And that includes the crew,' he says, looking pointedly at Aled.

Before the other ladies have a chance to speak, Penny answers for them. 'Oh no, that's perfectly fine,' she says. 'I've done this before, you know,' she adds, nodding at everyone. 'I was on *Richard and Judy* once, being interviewed about child abuse. The sound man had very cold hands. Do you have cold hands, Richard?' she asks, looking at him flirtatiously.

'My fingers are like long icicles running up and down your spine,' he says, grinning at her mischievously, and she laughs nervously, which in turn makes me laugh. This is all becoming so silly. Penny is usually quite stern and sensible; today she's anything but.

'This lot have dressed up,' whispers Becca in my ear.

'No, this lot, as you put it,' I whisper back, 'always dress smart, even when they go to the supermarket. This is their casual,' I say, looking at the trouser- and skirt-suited ladies round the table.

Richard quickly applies everyone's mics, but finds he's one short.

'I've only got enough to mic five, Will,' he shouts over the table. 'Do you want a boom instead?'

'That won't be necessary,' says Penny, 'Barbara won't need to say anything. As long as everyone else has a mic, that's fine.'

There's a deathly silence in the room.

'I have a voice and I may want to use it,' Barbara comments, looking daggers at Penny.

'You could sit next to me, Barbara,' suggests Miss King, 'and shout down my cleavage. That might work. That's what the boys do sometimes when they want my attention.'

I smile at this, and thankfully a few of the other mums, and Aled and Richard, find it funny, too.

'I've got a few spares,' says Becca, coming to the rescue. 'They're in the car. Give me five, can you, Richard.'

Richard nods. 'Pity. I was looking forward to seeing that,' he says.

Ten minutes later, when Barbara's microphone is properly installed, Aled's positioned on Penny and everyone's looking as though they're about to go into battle or answer a quick-fire round of *The Weakest Link*,

Will calls out, 'Action,' and Penny stands up, clears her throat and begins.

'Thank you, everyone, for coming this evening. Four mums have sent their apologies for not being able to make it: Melina Hibbert, who's working on a house in South Ken at the moment, putting the finishing touches to some interior design; Amanda Ross, who's having her hair straightened at Harrods and it's taking a little longer than expected; and Deborah Jones, who hasn't given a reason but sends her apologies anyway. Jo Barr has sent her apologies because she's in Milan looking at next season's collections.'

'I bet they'd have been here if they knew we were going to be filmed,' says Barbara.

'Cut!' shouts Penny. A mobile phone goes off and everyone looks round to see whose it is.

'Sorry. I forgot to turn it off,' says an ashen-faced Aled from behind the camera.

Richard, Aled, Becca and Will all look at Penny, stunned at her instruction to cut.

'You can't mention there are cameras here, Barbara,' explains Penny, looking straight ahead of her, not even at Barbara. 'This is supposed to be a fly-on-the-wall documentary, as if the camera isn't there, don't you understand?'

'Oh don't be so stupid. There's a bloke with a bloody great camera walking around – as the viewers will know – so are we supposed to make believe we're blind?' Barbara replies looking straight at her.

'And no swearing either, Barbara, thank you. We

don't want viewers to think we're slovenly now, do we?'

Penny reminds me a little of my mother, with the patronising way she talks sometimes, and she's clearly getting up Barbara's nose, which doesn't surprise me.

Will intervenes. 'Thank you for that, Penny. And you're right, of course, to make the comment about ignoring the cameras if possible, but please don't shout "Cut" in future. The only person who does that in TV is the director, mainly because if everyone did poor Aled here wouldn't know whether he was coming or going.' Aled looks as though he doesn't care and is amused by the whole thing. 'And if everyone can check their mobiles to make sure they are definitely switched off, that would be great,' Will adds, giving Aled a quick glance over his shoulder.

'Right, I just thought I was helping,' Penny says sulkily, 'but I'll mind myself in future. Now, where were we?' She looks down at her notes. 'Do you want me to start from the top, Will? Or do you want me to just continue?' she asks pointedly.

'If you could start from the top that would be great, and let me know when you're ready, then I'll say "action" and we can start. Everyone is doing great, just great,' he says, sounding extraordinarily genuine, although I'm sure in this case it's unlikely.

Everyone waits for Will to say 'Action', then Penny stands up again.

'There's a lot to get through in an hour, and I know we all have things to do afterwards, so I'll start straight away,' she says, looking round at us as though she's speaking in court and we are her judge and jury. 'Miss King, as the teacher representative on our committee, is welcome,' she adds, suddenly turning to Miss King as if she'd appeared out of thin air like the shopkeeper in *Mr Benn*. Penny gives her a broad, warm smile, quite unlike the crocodile lady I've seen so far this evening, and continues. 'Now first things first, primarily we're here to discuss the organisation of the school play, *Lord of the Rings*, through which we hope to raise funds for the school charity, and the extra computer room we need, plus our float for the five-hundredth anniversary. For the details I'll hand you over to Mr Gates,' she says, gesturing exaggeratedly to the drama teacher, who smiles and stands up. Somehow I think he's not the only actor in this room this evening.

'I'd like to talk through the main issues with the play, including the dates of the auditions, rehearsals, performances, props, costumes and scenery needed,' he says, looking around. 'I've put papers in front of you with all the details and these will also be on the sports notice board outside the secretary's office.'

'How are you going to get all three films into an hour and a half?' asks Barbara, putting her hand up and shaking her head at the same time. 'I know you did wonders with *Charlie and the Chocolate Factory* last year, but condensing everything into a couple of hours and stage-managing the battle scenes, that's a lot even by your standards.'

'I've decided to film the battle scenes beforehand outside on the green and in the park – I know some people in the business who'll do that for us for free,' he explains, 'and I've pre-selected which parts we'll use. Esther Bullions's daughter Constance will be playing the character of Arwen, so it's all the other roles that need filling. It's a challenge, but it's not impossible, and the boys will love being in it. It'll help bring the books to life for them, the ones who haven't read them already.'

'Why does it have to be Esther Bullions's daughter?' asks Penny pointedly. 'Why didn't anyone else get a look-in?'

'Mainly because Constance has already performed the part at her school last year, which will cut out the need for lots of rehearsing – time is tight enough as it is. If you feel very strongly about it we could hold auditions for that role as well, but I thought we'd have enough on our plates just with the boys.'

'I think we should audition for this role, too,' Penny says, 'otherwise it's not fair.'

To my knowledge Penny Vernon doesn't have a daughter, but perhaps she knows someone who does. Esther won't be too miffed, but I expect Constance will be disappointed if she's already been told she's got the part. She's a grounded girl, though, and will take it in her stride, I'm sure. In this instance, Penny does have a point: some other girls should be given a chance.

'For the boys, first auditions will be held next Monday at 4 p.m., before the start of the drama club that's usually held for the senior school, and on Thursdays and Fridays, when it's held for the junior school. I would also ask the PTA to support our efforts by finding and making props, which will include a giant spider,' he says.

'You're doing that scene!' exclaims Sonya, evidently shocked at the memory of it in the film, when Frodo gets speared by the monster spider and wound into his web.

'It will be toned down considerably,' reassures Mr Gates. 'For the spider, we'll need lots of papier mâché and black paint. Perhaps we can ask for Mr Ware's input again, our art teacher is always very helpful.'

'Everyone will want to be Aragorn,' says Barbara. 'I know Harry will, and my son David will, I'm sure. Your son Freddie will as well, Helena,' she says, turning to me off camera.

'Cut,' says Penny again, then, 'Oh sorry, Will,' when she realises what she's done.

'Carry on, Aled,' Will countermands.

'I have, Will, I'm still rolling,' he replies.

'Great. Barbara, don't refer to Helena or anyone outside the circle if you can, and Penny, don't shout "Cut",' Will says, only more firmly this time, though he still manages a smile.

'The boys will be notified about audition times. If you could find volunteers from the parents in your classes and allocate them props to supply from my list, that would be great. We'll also need some all-important costume makers,' continues Mr Gates, who's obviously finding the whole thing amusing.

After Mr Gates's speech, the women take turns to

talk about what their year is doing for the school's chosen charity, which is something to do with saving endangered species like whales and polar bears, though personally I think 'juggling mums' should be added to the list. Aled moves around the table while they talk, his lens spying on them in turn. As I watch him I start to feel that perhaps it's cameras that are the genuine weapons of mass destruction. A camera's focus can make these women look exactly as it wishes – good, bad or ugly. It's all in the power of the person pointing the lens and, even more so, the person editing the footage.

After the charity work's been dealt with, the women move on to anti-bullying issues and walk-to-school week. They don't want a repeat of last year, when a child nearly got run over by a four-wheel-drive car. Its owner was racing to park half a mile away so that her son could walk back to the school. There's then lots of discussion about how some parents can't possibly hope to walk to school as they live too far away, which means their boys won't get the reward – a badge in the shape of a foot. This is a much-prized possession, especially for the younger children, most of whom seem to live in their parents' enormous four-by-fours. I suppose we do live in the countryside, though, so at least there's an excuse for having such a vehicle in case you get stuck in the mud. In London, the only thing you'd get stuck with is a parking ticket.

'Well, if no one has anything else to add, I think that's it,' says Penny, putting her papers in her handbag, which I think is Timberland, though I can't be sure – I didn't know Timberland did handbags.

'Cut,' shouts Will, and the women let out a small round of applause, happy to get it over and done with.

'Very good, ladies,' says Will, going round to Penny and making a point of thanking her personally. 'That was great, very good,' he says.

'That wasn't too bad. They all behaved themselves much better than they normally do,' Miss King says quietly to me, 'almost as well as their boys.'

'I'm missing one mic,' says Richard, coming up to Will, Becca and me. 'Has everyone had their mic taken from them?' he shouts out to the women, who are now chatting to each other with slightly less clipped accents than the ones they used in the meeting. 'Anyone eaten a mic?'

'Sonya's gone to the ladies with Penny,' says Alicia. 'I don't think you took hers.'

'Oh right, I'll make sure I don't listen in for the next ten minutes then,' says Richard, 'some things should be kept private.'

Chapter Twelve

The next morning, John Tremble and the crew arrive at my cottage.

'I thought we were coming to your house?' I ask, confused at the sight of everyone on my doorstep.

'I've been given a commission to make a bust of you, and when I told Will, he thought it would be a good thing to film, so we've come round here. It's all a bit last-minute, but I didn't think you'd mind,' John says, grinning.

'Er, right,' I say, disorientated, 'but I didn't think I was going to be in the film. I thought I was just doing the narration and some of the interviews,' I say, looking at Will.

'I've had a word with Jarred and he says that on this occasion it works. And you're a local, so you fit in perfectly. And the commission is genuine,' Will claims.

'Who commissioned you?' I ask John.

'I can't tell you. They want it to be a surprise.'

'It's not the film company, is it?' I look around, thinking it's a set-up.

'No, I promise you, Helena, it's no one here, but I've been sworn to secrecy as they want to tell you themselves. Now, will you let me in as this clay is getting very heavy,' he says, looking down at the large bucket of some green substance in his hand.

'Where do you want to do it?' I ask as the crew brush past me and head for the kitchen.

'The kitchen then,' I say resignedly, following on behind.

John asks me to sit and read while he sits the other side of the table and Will asks him questions about himself and his life in Castleford. He answers in much the same way as Edward did yesterday, with passion and attitude, saying how he gets much inspiration from the local area and his garden. He also repeats his earlier comment to me about every baby he's ever sculpted looking like a mini Winston Churchill, and regales us with a flow of indiscretions about the famous people he's sculpted. His answers are candid, colourful and humorous, and he name-drops continuously.

'Nelson Mandela was a gentleman and had a great way with people,' John says. 'He managed to balance the common-man approach with the aristocratic air that none of the British royals achieve – with the exception of Diana.' He also sculpted her, incidentally.

'Laurence Olivier was someone who wanted to come across as someone he was not,' he continues. 'The whole thing took four or five sittings, and I found him a lot like one of the characters he played – Archie Rice – quite a nasty, spiteful piece of work, and that came out in his face. I had a difficult decision there: either to portray him as the actor, with his mask intact, coming across as the public see him; or as the real man, which was altogether more unattractive. It was like meeting a real-life Dorian Gray,' he says, continuing to sketch me.

'Can you tell the true person by studying their face?' Will asks.

'You can tell a lot about them from the way they *use* their face and their facial expressions. I suppose actors become well versed in how to use their voice and face, but most of us betray ourselves without even knowing it. A look here, a glance there, a frown, that sort of thing. I have to spend quite a few sessions with them to see how they move and walk, even if I'm not doing a full-body sculpture,' he explains. 'For example, some people want just a bust, but if they're creative they're usually expressive with their hands, like a politician or an artist. I tend to include their upper torso as well, because it's very much part of their persona and who they are, their being, if you like.'

'Does that make you one of life's great observers?' I ask, forgetting that I'm not the one supposed to be asking the questions, but as I'm mic'd up and Will doesn't shout 'Cut', John is allowed to answer.

'I observe people,' he says, 'just like you do in your work. I observe them, but it's hard not to make judgements about people; it's just important that those opinions don't distort the final product.'

'You'll make me look good, then.'

'I'll make you look good,' he says, smiling back and winking at me.

Will lets the camera roll for five more minutes as Aled goes in front of and behind John and myself, looking at the sketch and watching him get out the clay. He asks him to do it three times so he can film it from different angles, which makes poor John's arms very tired.

'Long process, this filming business,' John comments after the third time of lifting the bucket of clay on to the table and emptying out some of its contents.

After Will has said 'Cut', I turn my mobile on. After what happened at the PTA meeting with Aled's mobile, I didn't want to make the same mistake. As soon as it's switched back on my mobile immediately goes off.

'Hello, Helena, how are you?' says a clipped, plummy voice. Charles Rushbrook, my solicitor, is an Oxford graduate with loads of enthusiasm and a dry sense of humour. If he wasn't charging £6 a minute excluding VAT, I would happily chat to him all day, but he is, so I won't.

'Hello. I got your letter about the mediation. What do you suggest and when?' I say, trying to be as brief as possible without sounding rude.

'Well, Leonard's solicitor has suggested tomorrow if that's not too short notice, but it's the one time both the mediator and Leonard can make, and I thought you'd be more flexible. She suggested ten at her offices in the City. They have suggested a Mr Dennis Greenman, a mediator who's attached to their firm, though don't worry, he's completely impartial.'

'How can he be impartial if he is attached to their firm?' I ask, immediately regretting doing so as I know Charles will spend the next ten minutes explaining the intricacies of legal practice, which hold no interest for me, except to find out if I'm being set up by Leonard and his lawyer. Charles begins to speak.

'No worries,' I interject. 'Don't bother to explain, but I do think this is a ruse for something else. How are we going with the one-off payment? His it been lodged at court for approval?'

I'm hoping Charles will say it's been approved and I can have the money tomorrow, but all he says is, 'The consent order has been lodged, Helena, but it's still waiting for approval. The process is itself quick, but there is a queue of papers waiting for approval first, which means the process takes about three weeks to a month to complete.'

'But it's been over two years this has been going on,' I say, trying not to sound too anxious. 'I've found this whole process extremely draining.' I realise the crew are still hanging around in my kitchen and I haven't even offered them tea or anything to eat. I walk into the hall.

'I know, Helena, that's why Leonard is doing it. He's trying to wear you down emotionally as he doesn't want to pay you anything. You're probably right and he probably does have money squirrelled away somewhere, but it's not in your interest – or Freddie's – to waste money pursuing something you don't even know exists. Let's see what happens with the consent order. If he wants to hide his money he will know how to do it. That is his business.' He pauses. 'For a long time he thought you were going to get married again, and if you do remarry, or live with someone, he is entitled to reduce his maintenance payments.'

'Yes, I know, I know,' I say, 'although how I would fit in someone else to look after I don't know.' I walk back into the kitchen, signalling to everyone that I'll make tea and coffee, and opening the cupboard to get out some M&S carrot cake, which makes Aled and Richard smile and nod 'thank you'.

'I think the idea is that they would look after you,' Charles replies.

I laugh. 'Charles, I don't know a single man who looks after his woman in the way they're supposed to do in romantic fiction. I have no intention of getting married or living with anyone,' I reply, suddenly realising my every word is being listened to, and that Will is doing his usual intense stare, which I still find most disconcerting.

'You say that, but you may meet someone else,' Charles suggests.

'No way. I wouldn't want to go through another divorce. Too expensive and too emotionally exhausting, not to mention a complete waste of time.' I put the cake on the table, point Aled to where the coffee cups are and manage to fill up the kettle at the same time – who says I'm not an efficient, multitasking woman?

'Yes, well, Leonard's solicitor has stated in her letter that he's not concerned about you remarrying.'

'Yes, I remember his wording,' I say, recalling the brittle letters sent by his solicitor, basically telling me that he wanted rid of me with as little cost as possible. Although it's taken so long and been so difficult that it's made me wonder. Does he really want to be rid of me, or is he enjoying continuing to play the cat and mouse game until I lie down, give up and die? Or remarry – whichever comes first. Since I've done none of these things and he's kept me hanging on for as long as he possibly can, accumulating interest on the amount I've asked for, which is a lot to me but a pittance to him, perhaps he has run out of time, though obviously not ideas, hence my concern about mediation. I says goodbye to Charles and sigh deeply.

The crew all sit down around the table and ask John more questions about the people he's met. I'm more than happy to listen to him, and for a moment forget about Leonard and money and the other stuff going on in my life. I think about the good things, like Freddie, my lovely cottage, my great friends and what a bunch of interesting people I'm working with. Aled talks about his time working in various war zones, about watching a man dying and how he could film that but couldn't do hospitals as he kept collapsing when filming operations, which is obviously something of a health hazard, especially if you fall towards the body.

Richard has been in the business for over a decade and mainly does daytime programmes, so he lets out all the secrets about the daytime presenters he's met who are nowhere near as nice and friendly as they appear on-screen.

'It's a bit like your Laurence Olivier story,' he says to John while tucking into carrot cake. 'They like to keep up this front – something they can control, an image – but in my experience the true them is as far from the public persona as you can get. And even though they're supposed to be pros, they often forget the mic is on and that I can still hear them. There was one newsreader who was presenting a BAFTA Awards evening and forgot the mic was on while she let rip about one of the actresses' dresses. Everyone in the studio heard it.'

'Have you still got the tape?' Will asks, smiling.

'Of course we bloody have,' he replies. 'Don't know when you're going to need it, do you?'

After everyone has had something to eat and drink they start packing up.

'What have you got to do this afternoon?' I ask.

'We're seeing the Flindells, then the postman Herbie, and if we've got time, Mr Farnsworth the fish-monger,' says Becca, looking at her call sheet, 'so we'd better get a move on.'

'I can't join you,' I say, slightly relieved that I won't be in on the Flindells' interview

'We've scheduled in extra time for the Flindells,' says Becca, 'but I won't go over on this. I want an early wrap today as we had a long day yesterday. If you don't give the boys a bit of a break, they're going to revolt.' She looks at Will warningly.

'Yeah, we're going to revolt,' shouts Aled, grinning at Will.

'We'll have a lunch break and I'll try to wrap early,' he says, nodding at them.

'Herbie is a sweetie and full of local gossip, and Mr Farnsworth can give you lots of seafaring stories. His father and grandfather were fishermen, and you'll get a really different perspective of Castleford from him. It's easy to forget we're by the sea,' I say.

'Do you go down to the sea much?' Will asks as I walk them to the door.

'Never by myself, but I take Freddie to the beach every opportunity I can. He loves it, especially when his friends come to stay and we all go down together. And on Freddie-free weekends I try to jog on the beach on Saturday mornings with my friend Victoria,' I say, thinking that I must start up that ritual again, because it's good fun.

'I love the sea air,' Will says, 'very invigorating.' He follows on behind the others, giving me a quick peck on the cheek as he leaves, as do Richard and Aled. John Tremble says his farewells and tells me he needs to see me at least three or four more times. Then, and only then, will he tell me who commissioned the sculpture.

I'm looking forward to a quiet afternoon. Freddie is out, Esther and Victoria working, and so are the crew. So I'm not expecting the knock on the door. For some reason I think back again to that time all those years ago when that woman told me she was my sister, and how I initially thought she said solicitor. I never asked Mum about it, or Dad for that matter. And now Dad is ill, so it's not appropriate and probably never will be. It was one of those things that happens, like an unsolved jigsaw puzzle. But every time there's an unexpected knock on my door, I get a sense it's that woman again. I sort of hope it is, because I wouldn't slam the door on her this time. I suppose I could look up my family tree, something I know I can do over the Internet now, but I haven't had the time. Perhaps it's something I should do, take time to do. I'm thinking all these things as I open the door. A woman about my age stands there. For a moment I freeze, thinking it's my alleged sister coming to visit me again, but as soon as she beams at me I know exactly who she is.

'Hello my dear friend. You are Helena Treadwell, yes? Eliana. Eliana Cescutti? Remember me?'

Chapter Thirteen

I remember Eliana Cescutti as a bright, bubbly girl who had just turned twenty when I met her. I was twenty-one, and we hit it off from the moment we met, working at the travel company where I met Esther. When Esther had to go back home, Eliana took over. I wasn't particularly good at languages and could only manage my mother tongue and a bit of schoolgirl French, whereas she had mastered five languages fluently, including English spoken with a lyrical Italian accent at breakneck speed, increasing in pace the more excited she grew.

Eliana and I would talk about authors as she had studied English and French as well, and while we were preparing the lunchtime picnics we would discuss each book as though it were a person. When our jobs ended after six months we promised to keep in touch, and it worked for a while, but then she got married and I met Leonard and our correspondence dwindled into Christmas cards and the occasional email about our children, our life, our respective marriages – both of which were unhappy at the time as I remember – until it became nothing.

The Eliana I see before me has ballooned as wide as she is tall. She still has the wonderful sparkling eyes, clear complexion and wide, open smile I remember, and her hair is still long and wavy, but she's obviously not rowing any more, not the fit person she once was. I'm so happy to see her I burst into tears.

'Eliana!' I shout, rushing to hug her tight. She hugs me back, her eyes watery as well. 'How wonderful to see you! What are you doing here?'

'I am in England visiting friends and wanted to find you and where you lived and found out you were working in radio. I contacted the radio station and a man called Peter told me you had moved and told me you were now in TV and then I found your address and now I am here to say hello. Just to say hello.' She pauses for breath.

'It is lovely to see you!' I tell her again. I don't usually like unexpected visitors. I'm not as bad as my mother, who would have a near heart attack if anyone came around unannounced, but I would have liked to have been better prepared. I might not have been in. I might have been working or in London, or indeed anywhere else, and yet I'm here and she's here, so it's meant to be. Fate is smiling on us both.

'My Gord, Helena, you're steel so skeeny!' she says after a few minutes, looking me up and down.

'I'm not,' I say. 'If I am, it's nervous energy more

than anything else. Freddie is still at school, but I know he'd love to meet you. Perhaps you can come with me when I collect him this afternoon.'

'How old is he now?'

'Nine,' I reply.

'Well, I 'ave some presents for you both, but first I 'ave my daughter Isabella in the car, and she is sleeping, so I want to check on 'er before coming in. Then, my dear, I would like to come in and 'ave something to drink,' she says, looking around her. 'You 'ave a nice place 'ere. I knew you 'ave good taste.'

Eliana disappears and I follow her. I'm fascinated to see her daughter and suspect that if she's as bright as her mother, she'll be a handful.

We peer through the car window at the little girl, who's no more than two, I guess, and fast asleep. Her dark curly hair, long black eyelashes and chubby face make her the spitting image of her mother.

'They look lovely when they are sleeping, yes?' Eliana says, smiling at me knowingly.

'She looks like you,' I comment.

'She is like me in temper as well. She likes to be centre of attention, but she listens and learns very quickly about people. Be careful what you say in front of 'er. She is like a parrot. She repeats things all the time.'

Isabella seems in no hurry to awake, so we leave her sleeping in the car. Eliana seems to think the entire population of Castleford will know when her daughter wakes, as her cry is 'magnificent', as she eloquently puts it

'I like your mirrors,' she says as we walk through the hallway and into the sitting room. 'Gord, I am a big girl now,' she says, laughing at herself in the mirror. 'Just shows you what divorce can do, huh?'

'And ze paintings, did you do these paintings, Helena?' she says, walking up to the ones by my friend Maggie.

'No, one of my friends in Yorkshire did those for me. They've got lots of colour and light, haven't they? I love them,' I say, admiring the one she's looking at of spring lilies.

'They are very dramatic, very feminine, very you,' she says, looking back and forth at me and then at the painting.

'So would you like coffee, tea, I even have herbal stuff,' I offer, remembering she wanted a drink. She looks horrified.

'No, Helena, you know me,' she says, and out of her bright red carpet bag she pulls a bottle of Tattinger.

In the kitchen I get out some glasses and Eliana cracks open the champagne, and for the next ten minutes we reminisce about the adventures we had in Italy, with Eliana jogging my mind about loads of things I'd forgotten.

'You couldn't drive and you said you could,' she laughs, reminding me that I'd told the tour operator I could drive even though I had yet to pass my driving test, which meant poor Eliana had to do all the ferrying around of suitcases from hotel to hotel while I led – or misled – the groups through vineyards and lavender-filled meadows to photo-opps in picturesque locations that we had previously selected.

'And do you remember that cow from LA?' she says, looking at me while we clink glasses.

'Oh yes,' I say, thinking of the tall skinny woman who used the word 'totally' all the time, as in 'totally happy' and 'totally all right'. She was 'totally' besotted with her daughter, whom we never met but who evidently could do no wrong. By the sound of it she was not only the most beautiful girl in the world, but also the brainiest. In comparison, Eliana and I were 'totally' stupid and ill-equipped to lead a group of ten like-minded professionals around Tuscan hilltop villages. She is one guest I wish I'd lost for good.

'And that woman from the newspaper who thought she knew everyting? Do you remember 'er?'

'Yes, I do,' I say. 'Mind you, journalists do think they know everything.' She wrote a snotty letter to the tour operator telling him she knew more about the area than I did, and consequently I was given precisely a week to get my local knowledge up to speed. And then there was the culture. There were so many churches and Byzantine this and Renaissance that, but I hadn't studied history of art like all the other trustafarian, double-barrelled plummy young things leading the other groups. I didn't really fit into the 'nice young gal' ethos of the company as I didn't come from SW1, and neither did my parents, but I was good with people and Eliana and I got on because, as she told me on our last evening together, 'The other girls are so snotty,

Helena, they know nothing because they think they know everything.'

'But we 'ad some lovely guests, too. All the lawyers? They all knew each other. They were very funny and very naughty, do you remember? They kept throwing water everywhere.'

I'm straining to remember the lawyers, but then . . . yes, on the second trip with Eliana there were three couples. All the men were judges and the wives were lawyers, and rather than being stuffy they were all very laid-back and funny and made each day fun for me, too, even when one afternoon I got us lost on a hilltop and it took us several hours to find our next destination. They loved water fights so much that at the end of each day, all of which were supposed to be spent enjoying relaxed cultural events, everyone ended up soaked to the skin. They'd purchased huge water guns and they couldn't give a toss about what church originated from what Byzantine period or where a town got its name.

Eliana then reminds me about the time I bought tins and tins of tuna for a trip and no one liked fish apart from me. She also reminded me of the young men she introduced me to in Levanto, saying I was 'very rich, very sexy and very Engleesh'. I'd thought myself so cosmopolitan, an English girl French-kissing an Italian in a picturesque village in the Cinque Terre. Not that it went any further, as I was still a virgin at the time and terrified of boys. I didn't realise then that I held all the power and they were far more terrified of me.

'I 'ave had an interesting life,' she says as we sit in the kitchen. 'Since we worked together, I was at the Olympics in Australia in the women's rowing. We got the bronze and I was very proud, then I got married to a man, and he was very nice but had been married before. He was four years younger than me, but with no children, and I had a daughter with him, Isabella. He was an entrepreneur, but he wasn't very good at eet. He had no ideas.' She shrugs her shoulders and laughs. 'The best one he ever had was to leave us, so 'ere we are.'

Suddenly we both hear a loud cry from Eliana's car.

'Madame awakes.' Eliana sighs. 'Now it is 'er time.'

Isabella Cescutti has brown eyes as large as saucers. You can tell she wants to cry, but she's so fascinated by all the new things around her that she tries to stop herself – she's so curious about everything she sees.

'What a sweetie,' I say, looking at her as she stifles her cries and rubs her eyes while Eliana takes her out of the car seat and gives her a hug.

'She is very bright and very inquisitive,' Eliana says, 'unlike her daddy who is a complete fucking wit, as you would say.'

I laugh. 'Yes, I'm sure he is. And what is your name?' I ask, Isabella not really expecting her to answer me or understand English.

Isabella looks at me and says nothing, just taking me in, a bit like Freddie used to when he was her age.

Eliana says something to her in Italian, encouraging her to answer, but the little girl is adamant about remaining silent.

'This is good. Isabella refuses to speak. We will have some peace for a few days,' Eliana says, giving me a wink.

'I can speak, Mamma,' says Isabella, looking slightly cross, which makes me smile. 'I can speak Engleesh.' Then, turning to me, 'My name is Isabella Cescutti. Isabella Cescutti,' she repeats, just in case I didn't hear it the first time.

'And what a lovely name,' I say. 'Would you like something to eat or drink?' Again no answer, so Eliana enters into a discussion in Italian with her. I don't understand what they're saying, but it sounds slightly argumentative. But then again, whenever I hear Italians talk it always sounds slightly argumentative, even when it's obviously not.

'She will have something to eat,' Eliana replies eventually. We go inside.

'And where are you staying?' I ask as I pop into the kitchen to prepare the sandwich that Isabella has requested.

'At a local bed and breakfast,' Eliana replies. 'I didn't know if you would be in, but thought I would try. We are very busy visiting loads of people, but I wanted to see my old friend.'

'Why don't you stay here and save yourself some money? I have space at the moment.'

'Well I suppose I could, but are you sure?' she asks.

'Yes, I'm sure, and it will allow us to catch up. I'll tell you what's been going on in my life and you can meet my friends and spend more time with Freddie, even if you are only here for a few days,' I say.

'Then we will stay, won't we Isabella?' But her daughter has fallen fast asleep again, looking perfect in every way.

After I have prepared the guest bedroom and checked to see what time I need to collect Freddie from school, I sit down with Eliana again and tell her all my news. She listens quietly, occasionally laughing, or hugging me when I talk about my dad or the divorce, and losing the radio job, but smiling when I talk of Freddie or the crazy world that is TV.

'Helena Treadwell, learning to let go of the hurt has never been easy for you. It was never easy for me, but it sounds as though you are doing it, step by step, and they are big steps you are taking. But what you say about Leonard, well I think he has not let go at all, and for it to be good for Freddie, you both need to learn to let go. I hope this will happen.'

And we sit and talk about the old times, carefree times before responsibility and children and marriage and men, when the journey through the Cinque Terre, though without signposts, was far simpler and more straightforward than the paths we have both chosen in later life. And it was exciting when we lost our way, because we knew we would always get back to the path again, and somehow, as we've got older, we've lost that courage to have faith in our own abilities to find our way home.

'But you have found your way home here to Castleford, to the womb, yes? Although you have problems like everyone, you need to be here, to gain strength. I know all this because I did it with my parents when I too divorced, but you find the parents need you more than you need them. You are the parent now. You have the control,' says Eliana. 'But from what you tell me, I do not think Leonard has found his way home, and that's the problem for you and for him and for Freddie. That is why he continues to want to hurt you and haunt you when the history between you is an old history, and the games should have long stopped and long been forgotten. When he finds his home he will find his happiness, and he will learn to forget and forgive himself. Have you thought perhaps it is the only thing that is real in his life, you and Freddie, have you thought of that?'

'We are a real thorn perhaps, or so he feels. But I've mediation with him tomorrow, so perhaps I should ask him.'

'You can't ask a man like that questions that deep. He would not understand. Men like that do not hear anything other than their own voice. He must ask them of himself. Some men never do. They are just left with nothing at the end of their lives. They have everything and nothing. They are worth so much and yet they go to their grave surrounded by nothing they feel is important, because it isn't. You have surrounded yourself with what is important – your family and your friends. And do you have a love in your life?'

'Apart from Freddie, no.'

'You will find it.'

'But that's it, I'm not looking for anyone. I don't

want to make the same mistake I made with Leonard and commit myself, because I'm still paying for what was a short-lived dream. I haven't really been with anyone for such a long time, I think I've forgotten how to flirt.'

'You meet the right man who fires your blood, you will remember very quickly, Helena. You did well with the Italian men we met in Cinque Terre, even though you pretended to not find them interesting. You had them on strings.'

'I cut them, though.'

'Yes, you cut them, but that was your choice, not theirs. They would have hung on if you hadn't told them to go. You were wary before you met Leonard and now you are even more so, because you think all men are like him. They are not. But I don't believe you know what you want from a lover. What *do* you want?' Eliana is so blunt, but she can get away with it.

'I haven't asked myself a question like that for ages. I've got so much practical stuff to think about, all the spiritual, emotional stuff in my life seems to have gone to the back of the list.'

'The practical stuff kills everything, passion, spontaneity, fun.'

'But without discipline even passion becomes chaos, so we need some to keep us from floating off into-mid air to our romantic dreams,' I reply, feeling I'm sounding like my mother, which makes me quite sad and annoyed at the same time. Please God, don't let me become as cynical as her. Eliana is right. One bad marriage doesn't mean all relationships should be a write-off. I should keep reminding myself of that. Perhaps Esther isn't the only one who's given up on the dreams she had in Italy.

'You still haven't answered my question of what you want in a lover, and I think it's because you don't know what you want and need yourself. I think that it is someone who is discreet, someone who listens to you, someone who makes love with a great intensity as if it was always the last time. Someone you have "in the blood" like a drug. Well, it's scary, don't you think, to have a lover, but so tempting! Like a dream.'

I laugh. 'You're not describing any Englishman I know, or have met for that matter. I think most women would be happy with someone who's sane, kind, caring, and financially secure, good with DIY. And if they're good in bed it's an added bonus.'

'Would you be happy with that?'

'I haven't asked myself that question for ages. I would say if I had a man in my life now he would need to have life experience. A man who is in his forties, without children, marriage and divorce, has baggage, but I would say a man who has none of these things and has reached that age probably has more. After experiencing what I did with Leonard, kindness comes top of my list. I don't think I could be with a man, however sexy, who would be unkind to me now. Not someone with the treat 'em mean, keep 'em keen philosophy. They would have to be great with Freddie, absolutely wonderful and financially sound and . . .'

'No, no, no!' Eliana interrupts. 'You are talking about the practical stuff. How about passion? How about being with a man who makes you feel happy to be a woman, his woman? Who makes you feel like a flower opening up in his arms every time you see him, touch him, kiss him. Who can, even when you are tired and cold and cross and distracted, melt you in his arms and his presence. Who makes you feel as an independent woman that you have met your match, your soulmate.'

'I don't believe in soulmates,' I shake my head, 'but the rest of what you say sounds wonderful and heady and yes, I wish for all those things. But I would spend my days dancing around the kitchen if I was on such an intoxicating high all the time, and wouldn't get anything done. I've been there, Eliana. It was lovely and wonderful and lifted my spirits, and I didn't care about work, career, family, friends, anything, only to be with this man, this match, this soulmate. And then I woke up and found him sleeping with someone else and I don't want to dance again, not only because I've forgotten how to do it, but because I just don't think I want to.'

'You are denying yourself a happiness all of us deserve,' she says, looking at me sadly.

'I'm happy. I have a wonderful son, a lovely home, great friends, my family are close. And I know you!' I say, trying to make light of the conversation.

'Yes,' she says looking at me shrewdly. 'You have filled your life with practical stuff, and it is full, but just because your time is full doesn't mean your heart is.

Freddie will leave after eight, perhaps ten years, and then you are by yourself. You will still have your work, your family, your friends, all these things. But you have a big heart and there will be a man out there to deserve it, somewhere, I know.'

'I don't believe in that any more,' I say, feeling quite tearful.

'I know,' she says, giving me a hug, 'but it doesn't stop you wanting to.'

I smile at my wise friend, remembering a happy-go-lucky past where I was brave enough to lead a group through a forest fire and come out the other side smiling.

'I'd better go now,' I say, looking at my watch, 'I've got to collect Freddie.'

Chapter Fourteen

'Another teenager was killed yesterday in a knife attack.'

My bedside radio has switched itself on automatically at 6 a.m., as it does every workday morning, and the newsreader's announcement is the first thing I hear. Eliana and Isabella are happily ensconced in the guest bedroom, having been introduced to Freddie when they came with me to collect him from school. He was squeezed almost to a pulp by Eliana's enthusiastic greeting at the school gates, an embarrassment he won't live down quickly. I got a phone call from Will last night to say that everything went well with the Flindells and Herbie, but they didn't have enough time to do Mr Farnsworth as the Flindells went on so long and insisted on them shooting the show house.

'They've also asked us to film a lunch party one of the new owners is having next week,' he says. 'They've bought the show home and I don't think that's a bad idea, because we can get to see some of the new blood coming into the area and see the house properly. Seeing it empty it looks cold, but with people it'll add some interest. Agetha insisted on us filming the house as though we were some sort of daytime property show. Aled did a tour of the house pretending to film, but he didn't turn the camera on as I told him we wouldn't use it. Filming the house in context, when there's a party going on and it's full of locals and new blood, will make much better TV. Did you have a good afternoon?'

'Yes,' I reply. 'A friend arrived unexpectedly from Italy. I've known her for ages, and it was lovely to see her again. We did a lot of reminiscing; it was good to talk over the old days,' I say, smiling at some of the things I did in my youth.

'Were you a different person then?'

'Less cautious, less wary, more trusting,'

'It's good to be wary,' Will replies enigmatically, then switches straight back into work mode, and gives me some more information about the next few days' shooting before he rings off.

I'm still pondering that comment when I hear the announcer on the radio.

'The stabbing of fourteen-year-old Hayley Carter in Hammersmith occurred yesterday as she was walking back from school. Education Minister Ernest Wiseman says parents and teachers should take more responsibility . . .' The voice continues but I turn it off. I don't want to hear any more: 'It's too much to digest first thing in the morning,' I say to myself.

'Too much of what to digest?' asks Freddie, walking

into my room, still half asleep and with severe bed head.

'Bad news on the radio, Freddie. A teenager has been killed,' I explain, realising that he will probably hear it from the other boys in the playground today anyway.

'That's very sad,' he says. 'Mrs Compton-Batt talked to us about teenagers killing themselves and each other last term, and said that we should always be very careful when we're out in strange places and stay close to our mum or dad.' He comes over to me and gets into bed beside me. 'She said if we had any problems we should always discuss them with our parents or our teachers.'

The most frequently used words on his school reports are 'enthusiastic and lively', which I would say is about right. He still comes into my bed in the morning and snuggles up, often demanding I tell him a funny story about when he was a baby or toddler, which seems to give him as much pleasure as it does me. I know I've only got a few more months of this innocent intimacy left, and perhaps only another two years, or maybe three, before he starts to feel he can't cuddle me any more – at least in public – so I'm relishing every moment of it. Freddie is so uncomplicated. I'm just happy being with him.

'Yes, it is very sad, Freddie,' I agree, cuddling up to him. 'And yes, you do have to be careful, especially about who you speak to, and never speak to strangers.' I think back to how I used to walk to school by myself when I was Freddie's age and how, even in Castleford, which I've always felt is one of the safest places in the world, I would never let him do this. I feel as though I'm always hovering about him, although I don't like to think of myself as one of those mothers who never lets her child out of her sight.

I go downstairs to find Eliana has prepared breakfast for all of us, and we sit and chat and I tell her more about how Dad is, and how Mum hasn't changed, and about the TV show, which she thinks sounds very exciting. I say that as I'll be at mediation with Leonard today I hope she'll be OK exploring the town by herself, then I suggest places she could visit, such as the the local café, St Agnes church, a restaurant that does very good fish and the playground by the green, which Isabella will love.

Later, when I'm on the train to the solicitors' offices, Esther calls me on my mobile.

'Where are you?' she asks. 'Sounds as though you're on a train.'

'I am, I'm on the way to mediation. My Italian friend Eliana has just arrived out of the blue, you know, I told you about her, the girl that replaced you after you had to go back home. You never met her but she's great. I've been so busy, Esther, I haven't had time yet to organise an evening to introduce her to everyone, but I'm going to try to get you and Victoria at least to meet her. Would you be free tonight?' I ask.

'Late afternoon would be better. Digby's in Geneva at a convention so I've taken a half-day. I'll give Victoria a call and see if she's free for a catch-up as well, but she's really busy at the moment, and still having problems with Dena Benson. I bet she wishes she'd stayed with radio now.'

'Well, perhaps,' I reply, thinking of how difficult it would have been for Victoria to continue to work with Peter, the chemistry between them being almost tangible when they were in the room together.

'Anyway, Victoria's a big girl. She can look after herself. Now remember, at mediation don't lose your temper, Leonard will only get off on that. Stay calm and focused, which will frustrate him. He won't expect you to be calm. He'll expect you to be emotional, something he can use to show the mediator how irrational you are. The only thing you should focus on is Freddie, and getting Leonard to think of Freddie more when he has him at weekends. That's all you want from this meeting. Leonard wants to make you look bad, mad and sad, while you just want to get what's best for Freddie. Keep to that agenda and you won't go wrong, OK, girl?'

'OK.'

'And be strong. Once you have the money he won't be able to hurt you any more, and that's all he wants to do.'

'He can still do it through Freddie.'

'The law will protect Freddie,' Esther replies. 'Leonard won't find hurting you through Freddie very satisfying. I always thought Freddie would be fine, and it would be you and Leonard who would have the issues, and I've been proved right. Just don't pass them on to Freddie. Let it end here.'

Leonard's solicitors are in a building in Holborn, an office block below which is a Starbucks and Pret A Manger. I go to the door, which has a buzzer, and press the pad marked 'Solicitors', hoping it's the right one. There's a small camera above the buzzer and a posh-sounding voice calls out, 'Hello, can I help you?'

'My name is Helena Treadwell. I have an appointment with Dennis Greenman,' I say, feeling as though I'm entering enemy territory, despite Charles's assurance that the mediator is entirely neutral.

'Ninth floor,' the voice instructs. 'You can use the lifts or the stairs,' it adds helpfully.

The door buzzes loudly and I push it and enter. I don't like these doors as I frequently push when I should pull or pull when I should push, or miss the buzz altogether and have to ring the bell again to be allowed in again. The voice always has a 'tut' in it the second time round, and by the time I get to reception I'm sure that the woman – and it nearly always is a woman – thinks I'm some kind of twit who can't even open a door properly.

As I walk up the stairs – the lift looked even less welcoming than the door – I feel as though I'm going to a headmaster's office to be told off. I've worn something basic for the occasion: my white skirt, a simple blouse and some boots, with a loose purple jacket.

I climb to the fourth, fifth, sixth floor, briefly stopping at the seventh to take breath, ponder life, love and the universe, then on to the eighth and ninth floor, where there's a large glass double door with yet another buzzer. Fort Knox is easier to get into than this place. I press the buzzer and through the glass I can see a woman sitting behind a desk lean over and talk into a microphone.

'Yes, can I help you?' she says.

I feel like saying, 'I'm Helena Treadwell and I still want what I wanted a few minutes ago, you idiot.' Perhaps they get a lot of people who change their mind halfway up the stairs. Instead I repeat, 'My name is Helena Treadwell. I have an appointment with Dennis Greenman.'

I can see her reflection pushing a button, then the door opens and I walk through.

The young woman, slim and attractive, looks as posh as her voice. She wears a smart Chanel-type suit, glasses, and her hair's in a loose bun. She looks me up and down before speaking. If she asks me who I am again I think I'll turn round and walk out.

'Would you like to go through to the waiting area as Mr Wallis hasn't arrived yet,' she says, pointing to a large room to my left.

'Could I possibly use the toilet?' I say, wanting to take a look at myself before the mediator and Leonard see me.

'It's the first door on the right,' she says efficiently, then looks back down at her desk.

I turn and walk towards the door, take the first right and walk into a small cubicle where I look in the mirror. This is weird. This is the building where Leonard used to meet his solicitor to discuss a plan of action when we were getting divorced; it's where he knew about the divorce before I did. I feel suddenly dizzy again; perhaps it's the stress of things. 'This is not a good time to pass out,' I tell myself as I leave the cubicle and head towards the waiting room.

There are two very large picture windows and a spacious meeting room to the left, which has two double doors that open and close as people in suits walk in and out of the room. There are sofas and chairs around the sides and lots of leaflets containing information on divorce, how to cope with separation, mediation and child welfare. There's also a book filled with press cuttings about the firm, which I skim through while I'm waiting. I read with interest the article on mediation, how the mediator is neutral and will see through falsity.

Dennis will have to be good to see through Leonard. I look out the window towards the City, watching the stallholders sell their jewellery, knitted hats and scarves, much as they do in Castleford at the Christmas fair. I remember visiting this area on dates years ago when I worked in town. Men would take me to bars, and sometimes to a restaurant, or we'd go dancing or to the cinema. Posher dates would take me to the theatre, or a party where I'd meet their friends.

That person who had no responsibilities apart from looking good, being on time for work and earning enough to afford the next pair of shoes, highlights and a season ticket, is a long way away from the Helena Treadwell who stands here today. I'm pleased I didn't know then what I know now; I'd have been less full of optimism if I'd realised what lay in store.

'Hello there,' says a male voice, and I turn towards a man who's offering me his hand, introducing himself as Dennis Greenman. I'm startled, because Leonard is sitting in the adjacent seat, watching me. I wonder how long he's been there, sitting watching and trying to read my face. Maybe he was hoping I'd take a call and give away some secret that might put him in a stronger position. Don't be silly, Helena, he's not that calculating. Well, he is that calculating, but perhaps he has off days and this is one of them.

I turn to Dennis and shake his hand, 'Hello, I'm Helena Treadwell,' I say.

'Yes I know,' he says; unlike the receptionist he doesn't need to be told twice.

Leonard nods at me as he stands up and I say a quick hello.

Dennis leads us past the receptionist, who looks up briefly and smiles at Leonard, but seems to have forgotten who I am already.

Dennis opens a door opposite the one I went through to get to the toilet and we enter a small room that's about the size of my bathroom, with a round table in the middle and three chairs placed evenly around it.

I take the furthest chair, facing the door, and Leonard sits to my right, Dennis to my left.

'Now, we are here today to talk through some issues which may help you parent your son, Frederick. Is that the case?' Dennis asks.

'Yes,' replies Leonard, 'and to talk about some financial issues.'

I nod, although I don't have a clue what Leonard has to say.

'I am completely neutral and my role is to encourage both of you to communicate more effectively, so that you can be better parents to your son,' Dennis continues. 'Now, shall we get down to details?'

We both nod.

'How long were you married?' he asks.

I look at Leonard. I hadn't realised we'd have to go back to the start, going over old ground again. I've done so much of this via counselling, and now I'd rather forget it all, so I let Leonard do the talking.

'We were married for five years and went out for a few before then,' he says.

'And when did you have Freddie?' Dennis asks.

'Three years into the marriage,' I say.

'And may I ask, why did the relationship break up?'

I want to hear Leonard's version of this, so I stay silent.

'Helena had an affair and I had a relationship with the person I'm with still now with,' he says.

That's very Leonard. *He* has a relationship and I had an affair, as though his was somehow more understandable, dignified, an act of integrity almost, and more complete than mine – yet we both had relationships while we were married. I don't say anything. There's a bigger picture here, and I'm here for Freddie, so I don't want to get sidetracked by petty stuff, which is what Leonard is all about.

'Are both your parents still alive?' Dennis asks.

I think I'm going to cry. I mustn't. I don't want that arsehole to see me cry. 'Yes, but my dad is unwell at the moment,' I reply.

'Both my parents are still alive and well,' says Leonard, 'and I have two brothers, both of whom are married.'

'Do they have children?' Dennis asks.

'No, Freddie is the only grandchild, so he's quite spoilt when he sees us, as you can imagine,' Leonard says, smiling smugly.

'So what would you like to talk about in particular, as I would like to make the most of this time with you?' Dennis asks. He looks at me first, so I start.

'Well, I would like to ask Leonard to be more supportive about taking Freddie to football, and to pay for his school uniform,' I say, because they are the only two things I want to bring up. I'd love to ask why he's taken such a long time to agree to the one-off payment, but I'm letting Charles and Leonard's solicitor settle this.

'Let's start with those two things first then, shall we?' Dennis says, looking at both of us. I want to smile, as he has the same manner with us as I have with Freddie and his friends.

'Freddie has football practice every Saturday morning and it's important he goes. He is an only child and he needs to be more active in team sports, especially as he grows up,' I say. 'I'm an only child myself, so I realise how important that is.'

Dennis looks over at Leonard and asks for his thoughts.

'Well, as it happens I have just purchased a house near to Helena and will be moving in shortly,' he says, looking at me. 'I haven't mentioned this to Helena until now, and Freddie doesn't know yet.'

My mouth drops open. I try to stop it, but I genuinely hadn't thought he would spring something like this on me.

Like me, Dennis looks confused. 'So you're going to move to the area, but didn't want to tell Freddie about it?' he asks. 'Or Freddie's mother?'

'I wanted it to be a surprise,' he replies earnestly, although from the look on Dennis's face it doesn't wash.

'Don't you think it would have been good to prepare Freddie for the move?' he says. I notice Dennis is keeping me out of the equation as far as possible, which is the right thing to do. He's detected the hostility Leonard feels towards me, despite him trying to be all smiles. Dennis is focusing on the needs of the child, just as Esther told me to do. I keep repeating her words in my mind.

'Yes, probably,' he says, 'but Helena has an issue with my girlfriend,' he adds, looking at me for a response.

I say nothing; I just wait for Dennis to turn to me and

ask, 'Do you have an issue with Leonard's girlfriend?'

'Not at all,' I say, looking at Dennis and then at Leonard. 'I have never met Helena.'

Dennis looks confused again. 'Helena?' he asks.

'Helena is the name of my girlfriend,' explains Leonard.

Dennis nods. 'And how long have you been with Helena?' he asks. 'Your girlfriend Helena, that is, not your ex-wife Helena.' Now he's starting to confuse himself.

'Since Helena – this one here –' Leonard says, waving towards me and obviously realising how silly it sounds going from one Helena to another, 'and I split up.' He looks smug again. 'We are in a very steady, happy relationship.'

'Are you married?' Dennis asks him.

'No,' Leonard replies.

'And do you have children from this relationship?'

'No,' Leonard replies.

'Right,' says Dennis, realising Leonard isn't prepared to give anything else away, such as the reason why, despite having a 'steady, happy relationship' it hasn't gone beyond boyfriend and girlfriend, even after all these years.

'And how would you feel about meeting Leonard's girlfriend?' Dennis says, turning to me.

'Well, it's been years now. I don't have an issue with her. I have an issue with what happened at the separation. Many people get divorced, but it's best to always try to do it well, especially when you have children, and it didn't happen that way. But it's in the past,' I say philosophically.

'What happened?' Dennis asks.

'I think our versions would differ dramatically on that one,' I say. 'We were unhappy for a long time, we both had affairs. He asked for the divorce, but I filed for it. Things went from bad to worse after that, culminating in a Christmas I would never wish to remember or repeat. We have not communicated on any level since. This was an issue in our marriage, and even more so now that we are divorced and only need to communicate for Freddie's sake, and we fail to do even this effectively. I think the best way of putting it is that when Leonard says something, I hear something else – and when I say something, he hears something else. When Leonard and I talk it's a bit like having a one-way phone line. I can hear his voice, he can hear his voice, but he can't hear my voice.'

'How are the changeovers with Freddie?' Dennis asks.

'Brief and businesslike,' Leonard says, 'but she gets stroppy when money is mentioned.'

'And you don't?' I reply. 'Why won't you pay for Freddie's uniform? And why won't you take Freddie to football regularly? They're the only things I've asked of you in all the years we've been divorced.'

'You tried to get Freddie into a school without my permission,' he says accusingly.

'Freddie needed to be in a better school than the one he was in when we lived in London. He wasn't doing well at his school there, even though the school claimed he was, and you wouldn't listen to me.' I manage to keep my cool, while remembering the pain of trying to extricate Freddie from a school where he was getting lost in a system that didn't care about him.

'How did you resolve this issue in the end?' Dennis asks.

'We didn't resolve it,' I reply. 'I moved out of London and back to Castleford, where I was born, and got Freddie into Castleford School, which is very good, and he's now thriving and completely settled.'

'And how did you feel about this?' Dennis turns to Leonard. I remember exactly how Leonard felt about this, because he delayed maintenance payments for months. If it hadn't been for my work, numerous phone calls to my building society about the mortgage, and help from my parents, I wouldn't have been able to survive. I paid all the outgoings for those months until Leonard decided, probably after a huge bonus of some sort, or work colleagues suggesting it would be a magnanimous gesture, that it was a good thing to be seen to be contributing towards his only child, especially as he was now loaded.

'I was fine about it,' is all he says, droning in his deep voice as he does and sounding even more pompous than usual, 'although obviously I was disappointed that she was taking Freddie away from me.'

'You can see Freddie whenever you like – you just choose to see him when you like, which is four weekends a month. You could see him more, but you don't. You could have seen him more when we were living near you in London, but you didn't because, you explained, of the pressure of work.'

Leonard is now almost rigid with rage.

'You look very aggrieved,' says Dennis, staring at him.

'I am aggrieved. I would like a greater show of gratitude from both my ex-wife and my son,' he says, glaring at me as though he's about to hit me.

Wow, I hadn't expected that word. GRATITUDE. Gratitude for what? What should Freddie be grateful for? What should I be grateful for? If it hadn't been for Charles Rushbrook, Leonard wouldn't have given Freddie or me anything like enough. I distinctly remember Leonard sitting down with me while I was in tears and working out on a piece of yellow A4 paper that Freddie and I could live on £300 a month, including all utility bills. He told me, with the utmost sincerity, that spiritually, in the eyes of God – Leonard doesn't give two hoots about God and never has – we would always be married, whatever happened. I also remember how enraged he became when I contacted a solicitor and he realised he'd have to pay considerably more than that. Should I be grateful for him giving me Freddie, I wonder. Yes, I should, but then again, I gave him Freddie, too. Perhaps, as Esther suggests, he thought he could wear me down emotionally by giving me all that hassle, just like he's been trying to do over this final financial settlement, because he knows that after that's made there'll be no more ties to bind us, apart from Freddie. What he doesn't seem to understand, and never has, is that when he messes about with maintenance payments it's Freddie's money he's messing about with, not mine.

'What should Helena feel grateful for?' asks Dennis, picking up on the same word I did.

'For the money, for me giving her Freddie,' he says. 'She's terrible with money, that's why I don't want to give her any more for the uniform. I give her enough,' he says, looking at me as though I'm shit. 'And she didn't have to move to an expensive area like Castleford, she could have moved to Brixton.'

'Helena is able to move wherever she wants to in England and Wales, as I understand the law,' says Dennis, 'and that is not the point.'

'Other mothers live off far less than she does,' Leonard snaps back.

'That is also not the point,' Dennis replies calmly. 'Helena, as Freddie's mother, needs to maintain a standard of living similar to those of Freddie's peers. You would want that for your son, wouldn't you?' he asks.

'It's not fair,' Leonard grunts. 'I want that for my son, but not his mother.'

'So how do you feel towards Helena?' Dennis asks him.

There's a slight pause.

'She's taken my son, she's taken my money and she betrayed me,' Leonard says, 'How am I supposed to feel about someone who has done that to me?'

'And how do you feel about Leonard?' Dennis asks me.

I am determined not to tell him exactly what I think of Leonard's behaviour since our divorce. I just think of what Esther said to me before I came here: that whatever I say should be for Freddie's sake.

'I feel nothing towards Leonard. After we split up I went into counselling, I talked to friends honestly and openly about how I felt, and having Freddie to look after has been a grounding force for me. It's made me confront the fact that I will always be in contact with Leonard, but it's also made me realise I've got to think of myself and Freddie now. So to be honest, all things considered, I feel nothing. My concern as I look at my ex-husband is that he seems to feel as much, if not more, animosity towards me as he ever did. I'm concerned that he hasn't moved on at all,' I reply calmly.

'What sort of effect do you think this has on your son?' Dominic asks, looking at each of us in turn.

'Not a good one,' I say. 'I would say he very much prefers it when his mummy and daddy are getting on.' I turn to Leonard, almost as a last attempt to reach him and get him to focus on Freddie's feelings, not his own, which seem to be dominating the meeting. 'Freddie loves you very much. He needs you, Leonard. Especially at this age he needs you around so he'll know that you haven't rejected him. You know that, don't you?' I look him in the eye, but for some reason this fills him with even more rage. I'm sure that if he could get away with it, he'd stand up and kick me across the floor.

'Do you think that if Helena could show you how the money you give her is spent on Freddie, you would feel happier?' Dennis asks Leonard, sensing his anger.

I bloody well wouldn't, I think. The last thing I want is to be accountable to Leonard, as I was when we were married. That's why I want a one-off payment, to ensure he has no control over my finances, but to sound accommodating, I say, 'I'm happy to do that.'

I can tell from Leonard's face that he doesn't care two hoots if I show him a budget sheet or not; he just wants to get at me and this is an opportunity.

'I think, Leonard,' Dennis says, turning to him, 'the next time Helena drops Freddie off at your home, Helena, your girlfriend, should be there, so that Freddie can see you're all able to get along.' Leonard's jaw drops visibly.

He will hate that – absolutely hate it. He won't have expected any of this. He set mediation to trap me, but he's ended up trapping himself – and Helena – in the process, not that I really believe she'll be there if I do go to their apartment. Mind you, if he moves to Castleford I am bound to see her around.

Dennis looks at his watch. 'I think that's all we have time for,' he says. 'Now, I believe it's Leonard who's paying for the session,' he says, looking at an extremely irritable Leonard. Not only has this not turned out as he'd wanted, he's having to pay for the experience as well, although I'm sure he'll find a way to make me pay for it. He usually does.

I shake hands with Dennis, who gives me directions

to the nearest Tube station, which I find endearing. I leave the room and walk to reception. Leonard walks after me, but doesn't say anything. When I leave he's chatting to the receptionist, but I don't care. I walk down the stairs by myself, press the button to let myself out and breathe.

Thank goodness I don't have to see him every day. How is he going to tell Helena what the mediator has suggested? I don't care. It's not my problem.

I head home, wanting to get back to normality and some friendly faces.

'He's what!' shouts Esther after I tell her Leonard is moving to the area.

I've managed to get the girls together to meet Eliana, who's had a great time today walking around Castleford, going to the beach and visiting the local church, and I'm in need of some light relief after the mediation session.

Freddie is in bed, as is Isabella, so it's the just grown-ups. We're in my sitting room and I'm telling everyone about the day's events.

'He's invading your space, you can't let him do that,' Esther says. 'He's still as angry, smug and self-righteous as ever. He doesn't want to get close to Freddie, he just wants to mess with your mind, shitty little man. If he wanted to see more of Freddie he would have made more of an effort already. He would have moved here long before this. It's all to do with the money and a last-ditch attempt to hurt you. He's vindictive, always was and always will be.'

I put my head in my hands. 'Esther, if every nasty, vindictive thing Leonard did annoyed me, if I knew about every lie he told me, or told about me, I would be as angry as you, but I don't know about them. And as I have charge of Freddie it's just as well, because I can live in the belief that Leonard is a good man and a good father.'

'If you know deep down that he's not a good man, or a good father, Freddie will know it too. No matter what you say, he will know,' Esther replies. 'You can't hide stuff like that from kids.'

'When I actually speak to and see Leonard, the reality is quite different to the Leonard I make up in my head; his actions are those of someone who is totally selfish and angry. But I don't see him every day, and nor does Freddie. If he can be an OK father for four days a month – less than that, actually – then that's fine. It may not be enough for Freddie right now, but he's nine, and in a couple of years' time he'll be off with his peers. I'm sure Leonard will try harder in future to integrate Freddie into his life, if only so he can introduce him to his friends' children. But even if this move to Castleford is, as you suggest, to be spiteful, it doesn't matter. Even if the motive's bad, if the outcome's good for Freddie, that's what matters, and for the next few years I'll just grit my teeth, make the handovers as brief as possible and simply be pleased that Leonard's taking the time to see Freddie, so he can get to know his dad. That's all I can do.

'It's impossible to control a control freak, mainly

because they don't realise they are one. Leonard used to make me doubt my own judgement and even sanity sometimes. After half an hour with him I used to feel I wasn't thinking straight. I used to see him do it at dinner parties: argue against his own beliefs just to prove a point. To him, it's like a sport. He delights in making people validate their beliefs – often beliefs they're passionate about – to the point when they start to exaggerate, then he introduces stuff that's totally irrelevant, just to get the upper hand. He had one woman in tears once arguing about her belief in God, and this was at a dinner party! He revels in making other people miserable. That's not someone I want to know.'

'And this man is going to be a part of the Castleford community, nice,' says Victoria sarcastically.

'Perhaps he's heard about the TV show?' Esther says, clapping her hands and nearly making me jump out of my seat. 'That's why he's moving to the area.'

'What's that got to do with anything?' I ask, confused.

'He's somehow heard about your new job and the fact that TV cameras are coming to town, and perhaps he thinks you're going to make it big, and then he'll become known as your ex-husband. He won't be able to control gossip about him, which he'll hate. Perhaps, before this can happen, he wants to damage your standing in the community.'

'What do you suggest I do?' I say, confused.

Eliana, who has remained silent for most of the

conversation, finally speaks up: 'Kill 'im,' she says. 'Kill 'im. In Sardinia, we could arrange for 'im to be killed.'

'Not that simple,' I reply, 'and I don't look good in stripes.'

'You've got to kill his credibility and reputation,' says Victoria. 'For Leonard, what people think of him is paramount. All you need to do is find his weakness and believe me, every man has one.' She smiles knowingly. 'Now, enough sex talk, "Dancing Queen" is on and I want to boogie!'

With that, we all get up, I turn up the volume on the TV, and we dance around the room like children. I can't stop laughing, forgetting about everything that's happened during the day and thinking how lucky I am to have such wonderful, supportive, feisty friends.

Chapter Fifteen

It's Friday afternoon. I'm on the five-thirty train to London Waterloo, delivering Freddie to his dad for the weekend, then I'm heading straight off to Edward's book launch.

The filming has gone fine so far, and we're due to shoot the lunch party at the Flindells' Mansions next week. I haven't given much more thought to the mediation, but then I remember and realise that today for the first time I might get to meet Helena, a thought that fills me with, if I'm honest, total indifference.

Edward has kindly invited Eliana and Isabella to the book launch, and Victoria will also be there. Will, whom I haven't seen much of this week, has been busy filming Victoria about her work in town, comparing the pace of her London life with that of Castleford. He's also filmed Mr Farnsworth, who took them out on one of his father's boats, and Jessica Compton-Batt at the school, as well as some of the other classes. Will says he's got some nice stuff, but it may not be sexy enough for Elliott Sterling. Celebrities could be at the book launch, which would be great, but I know he wants scandal, and there's none of that, unless you count Penny's possible adultery with Alicia's husband.

'Are you enjoying working in TV?' Freddie asks, as we munch some flapjacks I've brought along for the journey.

'It's very different, Freddie. I prefer radio because there's more flexibility, and I don't like the fact that if you're on camera you always have to look good, but I like the creativity,' I explain.

He just smiles and takes another bite of flapjack.

'Do you know what Daddy's got planned for you this weekend?' I enquire.

He shakes his head. 'I don't know, Mum, but I'll tell you when I get back.'

'What do you think of Eliana?' I ask him.

'She's very nice,' replies Freddie. 'You've known her for a very long time, haven't you?'

'Yes. We don't see that much of each other any more, but we share a history.'

'Just like you and Daddy,' he says, which throws me a bit.

'Yes, just like me and Daddy,' I agree.

He doesn't like it that we're barely speaking at the moment, but I have to be so careful about what I say and do in case Leonard uses it against me, which means it's easier to put as much distance as possible between us.

'Will you ever chat to Daddy like you used to?' he asks, looking down.

'One day, hopefully,' I reply and leave it at that.

Freddie has his weekend bag packed with trousers, T-shirts, jumpers and pants – lots and lots of pants after the letter complaing I don't send enough – and as it's warm I've also packed goggles and swimming trunks, just in case they take him swimming in the lake, which he loves. Leonard's parents have a farm, so perhaps they'll take him there this weekend, which I know he enjoys, particularly collecting the eggs in the morning and finding the double-yolkers.

'Have you got your homework?' I ask as we head into Waterloo.

'Yes, Mum,' he nods.

'Great, and do you want a snack to eat or will they cook for you when you get there?'

'Daddy cooks,' he replies. 'Daddy always cooks.'

'That's good,' I say.

We walk across the railway concourse, under the clock and down the escalators to the Underground – it's quicker by cab, but I'm taking the Tube to save money. Looking at my watch, I see we're still OK for time – I have to be at Victoria's offices in an hour.

The Underground is full of unhappy commuters who look tired and pale. They don't speak or smile, just gaze vacantly at newspapers, the ads on the Tube walls, each other or the floor. It's moments like this when I don't miss London one little bit, with its pollution and litter, swearing and graffiti, lack of general good cheer.

Not to mention the lack of parking and the overload of traffic wardens, who swarm like hyenas and are universally loathed, even more so than estate agents and politicians, and only marginally less than four-wheel-drive owners. No one looks at anyone in London, or smiles or says hello, not even when you go into a shop, where you're lucky to be served, let alone chatted to. When I lived here, London had some joy and humour, and an infectious energy. But now I walk up the escalator with Freddie holding his hand tight, not wanting to let go. I'm an urban girl at heart, but this town has changed, or perhaps I have.

I walk into Leonard's apartment block, which is half a mile from Holborn Tube. It's a tall building with twenty floors, and he's on the fifteenth. It's not quite the penthouse, but almost. I've got to know the doorman, who knows Freddie well and says hello and gives me a smile. 'Hello, we've come for Leonard Wallis,' I say.

The man pushes the intercom and says, 'Freddie for you,' when Leonard answers.

Sometimes Leonard asks me to let Freddie take the lift alone, but I don't like doing that. I usually go up with him, make sure Leonard's door opens and leave only when he's gone in. Today, arrived outside Leonard's door, I hug Freddie and tell him to knock, then move away.

'Have a lovely weekend, Freddie,' I say.

'I will, Mum,' he replies.

He knocks and I watch the door open and hear Leonard.

'Hello, darling,' he says, 'is your mum still here?'

I'm just about to get in the lift when I see Leonard step out of the doorway and walk towards me.

'Hello,' he says, giving me a thin–lipped, upside-down smile, where the edges of the mouth turn down rather than up. He always gives me that smile, and I've realised his mother smiles in exactly the same way – perhaps she's aggrieved about something, too. He invites me in.

'It won't take long,' he says, and allows me to walk ahead of him. Freddie stands just inside the door, looking slightly horrified as I've never been invited in before, even to see his bedroom. Perhaps, like me, he thinks there's a sinister motive.

'Can I show Mummy my room, Dad?' Freddie says, looking up at him.

'Yes, Freddie, of course,' he replies, looking at me with a much warmer smile, so that his eyes smile too.

I've probably never been to Leonard's flat for the same reason I've never met Helena. It's very odd and I've asked on occasion, but he's always replied that it's Helena's home as well, so it would be unfair, although fairness has never been Leonard's strong point, except when he thinks someone's been unfair to him, of course.

I walk in and immediately see the most wonderful view of London. I imagine at night, with all the lights shining, it must look stunning.

Freddie leads me to his room, which is about the same size as the one he has at our cottage. It's painted blue and has a bed approached by a ladder, with a desk underneath it. It's quite similar to the one he has at home, which I think is a good thing. There are some photos on the side, but I don't recognise any of the faces in them. These are the memories I've missed, but then Leonard has missed so many more over the years. I don't want to ask questions or look too closely. Instead I look around for posters and toys, but everything seems to be neatly put away in drawers and cupboards.

'It's lovely, Freddie,' I say, beaming at him but feeling an overwhelming sense of sadness. There's only a little boy in it four times a month, though perhaps Leonard has friends round to stay sometimes who might use it. I wonder if he ever walks in here just to feel Freddie, as I do at home sometimes when Freddie is away. I wonder if he ever sits down among Freddie's things and sheds a tear. Or does he close the door, lock it and never go in from one visit to the next?

Leonard watches my face for some indication of envy, but I focus on Freddie's enjoyment at showing me his latest PSP and X box games, which I know Leonard likes to play as much as his son.

'Can I have a word?' he says, leading me out of the bedroom and leaving Freddie absorbed in his PSP game, looking up only briefly and smiling as if to say, that went well, didn't it? I smile back and wink.

I follow Leonard to a large open-plan/kitchen living area. I smile, because the kitchen looks exactly the same as the one in our old house in Primrose Hill, maplewood with dark granite tops. There's a sitting area to the right with dark brown leather sofas and a glass coffee table, and a few photographs, mostly of Freddie, on the sideboard. I'm surprised, because there are no photos of anyone who might be Helena, but I just presume he took them down before I arrived, although why I don't know. There are some photos of him and his brother Richard, perhaps at Richard's wedding. They're laughing in them, but somehow Leonard still looks tired. It's the eyes that give it away, or perhaps I'm seeing something that isn't there.

There are floor-to-ceiling glass windows and a large balcony overlooking another magnificent cityscape. A large dining table and separate area are further on, but Leonard stands by the sofas as if to say, you've seen it but you're not allowed any further. Or perhaps Helena is just round the corner and about to go 'Ah ha! I'm here.' Somehow, though, I don't think that's her style . . . by the looks of the furnishings in the apartment, I'm not sure she or Leonard have one.

'What a stunning view,' I say, smiling. 'It's wonderful. Where's Helena?' I ask, looking back at him.

'She's at the gym,' he explains, looking nervous. For some reason I think he's lying. It is possible she's at the gym on a Friday evening, after all I used to do that when I was with Leonard. I used to work out all the time, and the more unhappy I became in the relationship, the more I worked out. I wonder if Helena will look anything like the woman I saw at Lafitte when I was with Peter Bonham. I didn't get a good look at her but it's on the tip of my tongue to ask if the Lafitte lady was Helena.

'It would have been a good opportunity to meet her,' I say, 'seeing the flat as well, and Freddie's bedroom.'

'I said she's at the gym,' he replies curtly.

'OK. So what do you want?' I ask, folding my arms and aware that time is ticking by.

'Thank you for going to mediation,' he says. 'I wanted to say some things, but we didn't have the opportunity. I thought Dennis was rubbish, didn't you?'

'No,' I reply.

'Well, I've been looking at other schools in the Castleford area. I'll be viewing a school next week, and wanted to know if you had time to look round it with me?'

I'm stunned. I didn't expect this and I'm not prepared. I'm amazed he didn't mention something as important as this at mediation, but perhaps it only occurred to him afterwards, when he realised how happy I was that Freddie was at Castleford School. This is just another way to get at me – through Freddie.

'It's the Letchbury,' he continues. 'It's a very good school with excellent sports facilities, so I'm told.'

'It's a boarding school,' I blurt out, feeling myself flush.

'Yes, well, as Freddie gets older he will want to be with his peers more, and he's an only-child, and I've read that only-children do best at boarding schools, and the discipline is superb and Freddie needs discipline,' he says, as though he's swallowed a how-to-bring-up-boys manual.

'That's rubbish. All children are different,' I reply, feeling myself getting annoyed and red-faced, which is not what I wanted to do. 'You can't categorise only-children like that, and Freddie is thriving at Castleford, absolutely thriving. And it's not just me saying that, it's his teachers as well. You were there at the last parents' evening and that's what you were told,' I say, remembering the feedback we received. 'He really doesn't need to be uprooted again. It wouldn't be good for him.'

'The Letchbury takes boys right up to eighteen, so he won't need to move again,' Leonard replies dismissively.

'The Letchbury is very expensive,' I say, knowing Leonard doesn't like to spend money. 'And there'll be a new uniform to buy,' I remind him.

'Well, with your new role in TV you can help with the fees,' he says, 'and don't forget the budget breakdown you promised you'd give me,' he adds.

I try not to show my surprise. How the hell does he know about my new job in TV? Does he have my home bugged or something, or the cottage watched? This is getting ridiculous.

Suddenly Freddie appears, and I'm just about to hug him goodbye when Leonard asks, 'Could you play for a little bit longer, darling, I've got to speak to Mummy about something.'

Freddie looks at me nervously and I smile at him reassuringly, not knowing what more Leonard has to say, but just wanting to hug my son and go. If the energy I get from being in Will's company is a positive one, the energy I get from Leonard is as dark and cloying as tar. When Freddie has disappeared back into his room, Leonard turns to me.

'And as I mentioned at mediation, I have decided to move to Castleford to be closer to Freddie. I feel that I need to see more of him and be more supportive. As you said in mediation, Freddie loves me and needs me, and I think it's best that I keep a closer eye on him so that he becomes the boy both of us want him to be,' he says.

'But if you send Freddie to boarding school you'll see less of him, won't you?' I reply. My mind's buzzing with so many questions that I don't know where to start, so I begin with the obvious contradiction in what he's suggesting.

'I don't feel they are doing enough for him at Castleford, and the Letchbury is good; he'll get excellent care there. I know quite a few parents there who are pleased with it,' he replies. 'Freddie, if you want to hug your mum goodbye, she's going now,' he calls out.

Freddie rushes out and runs into my arms. All I want to do is pick him up and carry him out of this cold, soulless flat. How little Leonard knows Freddie. How can he possibly want to send him to boarding school? Letchbury is OK, but it's nothing special. When I tried to move Freddie from the state school where he was slipping through the cracks to a private school five minutes' walk from our house, Leonard refused, saying that I just wanted to move him so I could mix with the Gucci mothers and boast that my son went to private school. He knew that wasn't true and that I'm anything but a Gucci mum, but yet again it was just a control thing. Leonard wanted to make the decision and because it was my suggestion he didn't like it. After thousands of pounds' worth of solicitors' letters, Freddie stayed at the state school and I paid for extra tuition, which in the end Leonard grudgingly agreed to contribute towards. But then Freddie started coming home in tears, and I decided enough was enough and moved to Castleford, which in hindsight I should have done years earlier.

As I leave Leonard's flat and head out to meet Victoria, Esther and Eliana at Edward's book launch, I feel shell-shocked. I can't wait to ask them what they think. I'm going jogging along Castleford beach tomorrow, so hopefully that will wipe some of the cobwebs away.

The party for Edward's latest book, *Angels Under Glass*, has been organised by the publisher's PR and is being held in the basement of a restaurant-cum-nightclub. It reminds me of the absurdly pretentious places Leonard used to take me and his clients, and no one has ever heard of it – not even Victoria, who knows all the in places in town. Edward is due to do two readings from the book to an audience of invited friends, guests and hopefully some press as well. I haven't been to a London do for ages, and walking into the room reminds me how superficial these events are.

''Ow are you!' shouts Eliana, having spotted me. She is carrying Isabella in her arms. 'We didn't think you would make eet.' She comes up and gives me a big kiss on the cheek and Isabella holds out her arms for a cuddle. I oblige.

'I'm pissed off, actually. Not only is Leonard moving to Castleford, he's just told me he wants Freddie to go to boarding school, and it's left me rather stunned.'

'Helena,' she says, shaking her head, 'he is doing all this to make you miserable, but they are empty threats. He doesn't want to give you the money and this is his last attempts at power, then poooff! She throws her arms up in the air. 'He is gone. So don't you worry. He just takes pleasure in your misery. Aren't you happy you no longer have to live with a man like that, huh? All will be well. Now enjoy the evening. I am very excited. I have not been to a book launch before and there are famous people here, you know. I have not heard of any of them, but your friend Victoria says they are very famous so they must be, yes?' Eliana laughs, and she has such an infectious laugh that I join in, as does Isabella. I'm soon feeling in a much better mood than when I arrived.

I know Edward quite well, but I doubt many of the people present do, although Esther tells me Edward has tried to keep it as intimate as possible. As I'm people-watching, I notice Aled, Will, Becca and Richard doing the rounds, interviewing different people in the room. Elliott Sterling should be pleased, as Joey Whittaker, the crime writer; Michael Frost, the

jazz musician; Tom O'Reilly, the millionaire philanthropist, Hazel Coxley, the actress and artist, and
Dominic Field, the theatrical impresario have all
turned up, probably as the result of Becca's badgering.
I just hope they don't overshadow Edward's evening,
but I suppose it's all good publicity for the book. There
are a few journalists here, I see, although Victoria,
dressed in slinky black, has probably already negotiated
exclusive interviews with the celebrities, knowing her.

A woman claps her hands and ushers everyone into
an adjacent darkened corridor which is swathed in
velvet with mirror-covered walls so that we all end up
staring at ourselves.

We walk down some steps and turn left into a large
room with a bar and a dance floor. To the left is a door
through which I can see Esther talking to a group of
people I don't recognise. There are a few women
taking round nibbles, and two more serving trays of
drinks.

'It all looks very impressive,' I say, walking in and
being asked my name. 'Helena Treadwell. I'm a friend
of the author,' I reply.

We move through to the room where Esther is. It is
full of networking men and women. Some are so
blatantly working the room I can see them look at their
watch after a few minutes' conversation, getting ready
to move on speedily, while identifying the next space to
drop into.

'Could everyone be quiet, please,' says a voice at the
front of the room. To the right of a stool, a slight, very

beautiful lady stands in front of a large poster of the cover of Edward's new book.

'Ladies and gentlemen, and members of the press,' everyone giggles, as she seems to regard the press as some sort of subspecies, 'hello, my name is Barclay Adams and I'm Edward's publisher. And this is Angela Morris,' she says, pointing to a short, pretty, no-nonsense-looking lady. 'She is Edward's editor. Thank you for joining us to celebrate the launch of Edward's new book, *Angels under Glass.* Those of you who've read it will know that it's both wickedly honest and very funny. I won't say any more, apart from letting you know that Edward is available for interview after the readings, and should you wish to arrange an interview at a later date, please see me. I give you Edward Bullions,' she says, clapping and beckoning Edward, who is holding his book, forward.

Edward is wearing smart jeans, a smart pink shirt and loose-fitting jacket. He looks like a slightly ruffled version of George Clooney – very relaxed and very sexy. Esther is wearing a bright turquoise dress and boots and looks every inch the boho hippy. She winks at her husband before perching herself on the stool, crossing her legs so she shows her fishnets, and adjusting the microphone for Edward – it squeaked a few times during Barclay's introduction.

'Hello, everyone,' Edward says as Aled jostles for pole position at the front. 'This book doesn't have the ending I originally intended. My wife will tell you that I am a romantic at heart, but I don't write romantic books. And I'm not one for happy endings, because although I consider myself an optimist, I like to write books people can relate to. And people, and when I say people I mean predominantly the English, don't tend to believe in happy endings these days. They believe in the fly in the ointment, they believe in, excuse my French, Sod's law, they believe the glass is half empty. But in these times where life may seem unfair, where greed seems to be rewarded and the worthy are not, I wanted to write a book where the ending is a happy one and the good guys win out and the bad guys lose. I hope I haven't given too much away by saying this latest book has a happy ending, something I believe all of us can achieve in our lives. We can each write our own stories and our own happy endings. *Angels under Glass* is also different from my previous books because it's written from a woman's perspective rather than a man's and I'm hoping it will give an insight into how women see men.' He opens the book and starts to read.

I feel myself go scarlet as I listen. Edward is describing something that happened to me a lifetime ago. This person and her actions are not me any more, they were the me who was a shadow of the woman she is today. This scene is something I told Esther about in private – or thought I had. In the middle of the night once, I found myself calling my lover because Leonard hadn't come home, and I was hoping for perhaps a little . . . well, I'm hearing what happened next, and so is everyone else in the room.

I feel my blood boiling with embarrassment, as if

everyone is looking at me and pointing, saying, 'It's you!' but as I look around casually nobody's noticed my agitation, except Will, who's staring at me again, perhaps noticing I've gone bright red. He doesn't stop staring at me as Edward vividly describes the phone sex I had been hoping to have that night. Where's that black hole when you need it?

After what seems like an eternity, the reading ends and the audience clap.

'I'll be doing another reading in ten minutes,' he says, smiling at everyone as he looks over at me. I'm still in deep shock, but all he does is smile at me and wink. He *winks*. I've just heard a part of my life – a very painful part – being read out in public. What other secrets of mine has Esther told Edward that are included in his book, for goodness' sake?

I don't know whether to leave or stay and try to speak to her, but before I make my decision, Esther walks over to me.

'What have you done?' I whisper in her ear as she pecks me on the cheek. I'm not sure whether to hit her or hug her. 'You've told Edward secrets I've told you in private. He's written my life story.'

'It's fictionalised,' she replies, 'no one will recognise it as you.'

'I do! What else have you told Edward about me?'

'The heroine isn't only you. She's an amalgamation of you and me and loads of other people Edward knows. The heroine's discovered her soon-to-be ex-husband has been unfaithful after finding scratch marks on his back, and she's livid and hurt. He's admitted the affair and now she's met someone who makes her happy and she's trying to end her marriage, but she has a child, which makes it more problematic.'

'That sounds very much like my situation,' I say, annoyed. 'Dare I ask what happens to her?' I enquire nervously, but before she can reply Victoria walks over to us, glass in hand, looking slightly squiffy and thankfully Will has stopped staring at me and is directing some interviews with Joey Whittaker and Tom O'Reilly. Edward beckons Esther to join him.

'The room is buzzing,' Victoria says. 'Edward should be very pleased with how it's gone.'

'He should be. I just wish he hadn't pinched part of my life for the inspiration behind his book.'

'Why?' Victoria looks shocked. 'Wow! That was your story?! Your phone sex? Wow! I'm impressed,' she says, patting me on the back.

'Not exactly,' I look at Victoria. 'I didn't end up on the floor playing with myself with my lover on the other end of the phone. I only wish I had!'

'What did happen, then?' asks Victoria, looking disappointed.

'I got his voicemail so I finished the ironing at about three in the morning, turned on the TV and watched reruns of *The Jerry Springer Show*, so I could see people who were even more unhappy than me.'

'Oh dear! Poor you,' she says, giving me a sympathetic hug which, for some reason, makes me laugh.

'My life is so much better now,' I say, pulling away

and looking at her. 'I'm annoyed that Esther didn't have the grace to ask me if Edward could include that little titbit in his book, but at least it's made me remember how miserable I was, and why it's still so difficult to be friends with Leonard, despite him being Freddie's dad. I wouldn't tolerate that sort of behaviour from anyone these days, but then, well . . .'

'Then you were different; now you are stronger and among people who love and like you. And you're with Freddie,' she says, sounding very sensible for Victoria.

Barclay shushes everyone again for Edward's next reading, and I hope against hope that it's not another episode from the life and times of Helena Treadwell. I hold my breath as he starts to speak.

'He pushed her into the bicycle shed. He told her he liked it outdoors, Woody Allen-style. Spontaneous with a risk of being found out. He'd wanted to have sex with her on Brighton beach, when she wore the simple cotton dress that buttoned up the front. He'd wanted to touch her in front of everyone, just stroking her thighs and pushing her panties to the side, leaving her skirt in place, kissing her all the time as the tourists and locals sat and watched the sea, throwing pebbles to see who could get one the furthest or hit the person they least liked the look of. He pushed his fingers into her as she kissed him, pushing deep inside her, no one realising what they were doing. Lying half on top of her softness, pressing hard, he was turned on by the thought that someone might notice and it wouldn't matter. He wanted that same spontaneous moment now they were in the shed, although of course no one would know this time, amongst the bicycles and tins of paint and the lawnmower that didn't work any more. He pushed her up against the wall and lifted her skirt. She was scared that splinters would get in her knickers, but he pushed himself inside her anyway. She didn't know if he could hold her if she lifted her legs around him, but he pinned her to the wall. He was strong, but so was she. He was experienced, but so she was she. "You've never had an orgasm this way before, have you?" he said, kissing and biting her neck, sucking and nuzzling, but she couldn't answer. "Well, you will this time." '

Edward stops and everyone claps.

I turn to Victoria, who smiles broadly, proudly even, knowing full well that the shed scene is hers.

I walk up to Will and ask if they've managed to get all the celebrity interviews they needed, and which I know Jarred will like and want to include.

'Yes, we've got everything we need,' he says, looking at me strangely.

'Are you OK?' I ask.

'Yes, I'm fine,' he says, 'but I noticed you seemed upset a little while ago.'

I feel myself going red, despite my attempts to remain calm.

'We've done all we need to here,' he says, realising that I'm uncomfortable with the conversation, 'so I'm going to tell the team to wrap for today if that's OK with you?'

'Yes, that's fine.'

'By the way, what are you doing this weekend?'

'I haven't planned anything much. Jogging with Victoria tomorrow morning, that's about it.'

Will nods and I suddenly realise he may be asking me out on a date. It would be my first date for goodness knows how long, but with a work colleague, and that's not a good idea as Victoria found out to her cost. Plus it would be on home territory, which would make it even worse. I don't want to screw up at my first opportunity in TV by sleeping with the director – that would be very irresponsible of me, although potentially fun and just the tonic I need. Oh, what the heck. I cut to the chase.

'Are you asking me out on a date, Will?'

Will looks at me, utterly bemused.

'Erm, no, I just thought we could go over what we've filmed so far. We've got a meeting with Elliott Sterling and Jarred in the next few days and I want to make sure we can show them the range of footage we've filmed, and amend any plans if they think something won't work.'

I feel two inches tall, like a squished tomato. Where are Esther or Victoria when I need them to call me away from the mess I'm making of this?

'Yes, I should be available tomorrow, after the jog.

Just give me time to have a shower, then I can prepare some lunch for us, if you have time,' I say, regaining composure and a measure of professionalism.

'Good, see you about one then.' And with that he returns to Aled and Richard, who have downed tools and are looking chilled and happy, drinking beer and wine with the rest of the guests. Becca is flirting with Joey Whittaker, Victoria is chatting to Tom O'Reilly and Esther is with Dominic Field and Hazel Coxley. Edward is talking to his agent, who looks delighted with how things have gone. All my friends are schmoozing with the stars, but I don't feel in the mood. I've been on a roller-coaster of highs and lows today, and I'd thought I'd end on a high note with a date; but it seems I've completely misread the situation. I feel something when Will's around, but he obviously doesn't, and now he thinks I'm pathetic, or worse, a woman who doesn't put her work first, which is all TV people seem to do. Eliana comes up to me, holding a sleeping Isabella in her arms.

'Too much for the little one and too much for the big one,' she says, looking at her daughter and then at her own stomach. 'We are going now. Are you coming?'

'Yes,' I nod, 'just want to say my goodbyes.' Then I finish my wine and make my excuses, giving Edward a congratulatory hug.

'See you tomorrow!' Will shouts as I walk out the door.

'Yes,' I say, smiling even though I don't feel like it.

'Interesting man, that one,' comments Eliana as we head back up the stairs.

'What man?' I say, slightly distracted.

'That man who said goodbye to you just then. The director. I think he likes you.'

'No he doesn't. We just work well together.'

She shrugs. 'Perhaps I'm wrong. I 'ave been wrong before. But he looks at you across the room when you are not looking at him, and you look at him when he is not looking at you. But what do I know?'

Eliana leans over to me as if to say that she's here for me, just as she was when we were touring all those years ago in Italy and I was feeling bullied by the guests. I'm very pleased she is here to hold my hand.

Chapter Sixteen

'Did you know short women have larger, wetter fannies than tall women?' Victoria says as we jog along the beach the next morning.

'No, I didn't, and I'm not sure I want to. Dare I ask how you found that out?'

'Oh, Dena Benson told me,' she replies. 'We're doing this piece on what men want in women. And that's one of the things that turns them on.'

'What, being large-fannied or being wet?'

'Both. And did you know there's a section on blackhead squeezing, bottom picking and hot dinners on YouTube – and I'm not talking school dinners, either?'

'No I didn't. And what's that got to do with what men want in women? Do you mean they want women to squeeze their spots and . . . no, don't tell me any more. I'm not interested and I don't want to know.'

Thankfully Eliana didn't want to come jogging with us, as she says she has enough trouble walking at the moment. I'm sure Victoria's conversation would soon stop her in her tracks.

Eliana is leaving on Sunday evening, just after Freddie gets back, and I must admit I'll miss her and her chats. I know she's enjoyed her time here; she thinks Esther and Victoria are very congenial and interesting, and has been amused by the film crew and the locals she's met.

'I've been thinking,' says Victoria, slowing down slightly so I can catch up with her. She's much fitter than me as she goes to the gym most lunchtimes at work, and runs on Saturday and Sunday mornings, whatever the weather. She's also into army-style training routines. She took me through them once and I almost threw up afterwards. 'It's ridiculous that after all these years you've never met Leonard's girlfriend.'

'I was due to meet her at the flat, the mediator suggested it and Leonard agreed to it, but he told me when I arrived that she was at the gym.'

'She was probably hiding in the bedroom or something. Anyway, that was rude and cowardly of him and her,' she says as we puff down the causeway. It's a lovely morning and the sharp blue light in the sky creates patterns on the beach, which is about half a mile long. A few painters are out with their easels, and Victoria and I aren't the only people running. The seagulls are noisy today; perhaps they're hoping for the remnants of Mr Farnsworth's catch. I think I can make out Tony the football coach running with his girlfriend in the distance, but don't want to wave in case it isn't him.

'Leonard dropped another bombshell on me when I took Freddie there,' I tell Victoria. 'Not only is he moving to the area, he wants Freddie to board at the Letchbury.'

'Empty threats,' Victoria replies.

'That's what Eliana said when I told her.'

'Leonard is a city man and he'll look down on anyone who isn't impressed by the same things as him; that'll make him a fish out of water in Castleford. As for sending Freddie to boarding school, that's rubbish. He couldn't bear to part with his money. Don't worry about that, just focus on having a good life here yourself. Leonard will give up trying to bully you eventually,' she says, squeezing my hand.

We run for another twenty minutes, up the hill towards a group of old cottages that used to be owned by fishermen but which have long since been turned into souvenir shops. They're all painted pretty colours – pink, orange and yellow – and remind me of the children's TV *Balamory* programme . We look back over Castleford as we run, seeing the spire of St Agnes, the school and even the lane I live in.

My mind wanders back to last night, and the way Will stared at me at the book launch. I can't look at that man without my heart missing a beat. I've got a silly schoolgirl crush at forty-four; I thought I'd grown out of feelings like that. Those heart-missing-a-beat, fizzing emotions should be dead to me now.

'I've got it!' Victoria says suddenly, stopping in her tracks and almost making me trip up.

'You've got what?' I ask, alarmed, thinking she's about to tell me she's got some awful disease and has only just gathered enough courage to tell me about it.

'I know how you can meet Helena,' she replies.

'Oh don't be so silly,' I say, continuing to jog on the spot, knowing that if I don't I won't want to start again.

'What is silly is you not knowing what she looks like,' says Victoria. 'I'll tell you what you should do.' She starts jogging again while talking me through her cunning plan. 'You say she never gets out of the car when they drop Freddie off? Well, get someone to be in the house while you park up the road. 'Whoever it is can ring you on your mobile and tell you when they arrive, and when they do, you can drive up and peer into the car.'

'Never.'

'OK then, just go up to the car and look through the window. You don't have to say, "Have a nice day," or anything. Just take a good look.'

'Won't she be a bit bemused? Leonard's probably told her I'm horrible, so doing this will make me look a nutter as well.'

'You just want to find out what the woman your son spends every other weekend with looks like. That's not being a nutter, it's normal and natural. Leonard's the nutty one for allowing it to go on this long and for not being more of a . . .' she pauses, briefly trying to find the words, 'a man about it. It would be even better if you could have a conversation with her to find out more about her, but it doesn't sound as though Leonard would allow that. He wouldn't be able to control the conversation and he wouldn't know where it would lead.'

'You're right. He likes to keep everybody in boxes. As long as people don't talk to one another he feels in control because people will never cross-refer and realise they've been told different stories. That way he can tell his lies and nobody will ever find out,' I say. 'That's how he was when we were married. He hasn't changed.' By now we have almost reached my cottage.

'Let me know if you want me to come round to the house, because I'm free on Sunday evening, so I can help out if you need it,' she says, and gives me a kiss on the cheek, which makes me quite tearful.

As I turn the corner and walk up my path I realise there's a figure standing on the doorstep.

'Hello,' says Will, 'I got here early. Sorry about that, but I've got a lot to do today, and Elliott has scheduled our meeting for tomorrow. Is it OK if we have a quick chat now?' He looks me up and down in my sweaty, scruffy state.

'I just need to get out of these things,' I say, 'so if you can make some coffee that would save time. I made some sandwiches earlier.'

I have a quick shower and join him in the kitchen. We spend the next half-hour going through what we've filmed, and what we have yet to film. Edward's book launch provides us with the celebrity element Elliott wants, and Aled captured some good moments with the locals talking about Castleford, so it all ties in nicely. Victoria looks suitably glamorous in her office and talks up her life in Castleford compared to city life – she says she enjoys the later but finds it a little superficial.

Will puts his notes away and I make a few more suggestions about what we still need to shoot – the beach and coastline round Castleford, and St Agnes church being two areas we haven't covered yet.

'Well, thank you for taking time out at the weekend. I hope whatever you're doing it'll be a good one,' he says, looking me up and down.

'My pleasure. And how am I doing? This is all so new to me, so any feedback would be gratefully received.'

'You're doing just fine,' Will says, smiling at me. 'You're starting to really be one of the team.'

I laugh as I wave him goodbye. I'm doing just fine am I, I smile to myself. I obviously haven't recovered from the jog this morning, because I can feel my heart thumping away and my entire body fizzing. I am so out of condition, that's the problem.

At 6 p.m. on Sunday, against my better judgement, I'm waiting in my car around the corner from my cottage for Leonard and his girlfriend to turn up with Freddie. I feel utterly ridiculous, but I've been thinking about what Victoria said, and she's right. It's even more ridiculous that I haven't met Leonard's girlfriend after all this time, so I sit and wait for Esther to give me the all-clear. Victoria couldn't make it in the end, so roped in Esther. Eliana and Isabella are also there in my kitchen. I feel like the camera crew on those makeover programmes, who wait until the family have left before starting work on the house and garden. I'm just about to tell Esther I don't want to do this when she rings.

'They've arrived,' she says. 'They've parked at the end of the road and Leonard's getting out of the car . . .' She pauses. 'There's a young boy with him. It must be Freddie. But it doesn't look like Freddie. Perhaps he's brought a friend with him . . . No, no, oh my God . . . that must be her. She's a midget,' she says, half laughing. 'He left you for a midget.'

'Oh don't be silly,' I reply, 'she can't be that small. I know Freddie said she was short, but . . .'

'Well, to Freddie she would be short, but to a fully grown person she's a midget. Come quick, she's getting back in the car and Leonard is walking towards the cottage with Freddie and his bag. Come now!' she shouts.

I drive my car to the top of the road, park it in front of Leonard's car and get out. I can see a figure sitting in the passenger seat, but I can't see her face, and since I've gone to all this trouble I might as well get a proper look. I walk up to the car slowly and bend down, looking through the window. I'm going to take one quick look and if she looks at me, I'll smile, but how can I smile at her? I don't want to smile at her. I just want to see what she looks like.

My first impression is that she looks anxious. My next thought is that she's either slouching or, as Esther says, she's very short. She doesn't look at me, but I suppose that's to be expected, and I'm just about to stand up when, for some reason, I wave. I don't know why, I suppose it's to catch her attention, because all I can see is a side view of her. She turns and looks at me and I'm shocked. I expected someone special. Some beauty with presence and magnetism, some wow factor, and instead there's a very normal-looking girl, not woman, but girl, in front of me. I realise I'm seeing her when she least expected it and have caught her off guard, but at least this is the real her, and the real her is . . . well . . . ordinary, which is exactly what all the mutual friends Leonard and I used to have said about her all those years ago. I thought they were just being kind to save my feelings; I didn't think they were being accurate.

She glares at me, which takes me aback, but then I guess I have been staring at her. I stand up and continue walking down the street, only to find Leonard coming towards me, obviously aware of what I've just done. He looks furious but says nothing, just stalking straight past me as though I don't exist.

As I walk up my path I hear the Porsche roaring off, making even more noise than usual. I shouldn't have done that, but at least I know what she looks like now. And I realise it's not the woman I saw Leonard with in the Lafitte. That must have been a work colleague. Well, it might have been a work colleague.

I go into the cottage to find Esther, Eliana, Isabella and Freddie all waiting for me in the kitchen.

'So what's she like?' asks Esther, handing me a cup of tea.

'Normal,' I reply, shrugging my shoulders.

'What do you mean, normal?' Eliana says.

'I'm not quite sure,' I say, taking a sip of tea and still slightly shaking. 'If she had a large nose, eyes or any features that were distinctive in any way I could mention them. If she had lovely hair or stunning eyes or high cheekbones or anything like that, I could describe them. But you'd find her difficult to pick out in a line-up. She's . . . well . . . she's normal, common-place, anodyne, unremarkable, pedestrian.' And with that I burst into tears.

Freddie comes up and hugs me. 'I told you, Mummy, she's not as pretty as you,' he says, misunderstanding my tears.

'Thank you, darling, but she looks as though she'll be fine with you. She is fine with you, isn't she, Freddie?' I ask, brushing away the tears and looking down at him.

'She's all right,' he replies, 'she ignores me a lot of the time, but she's all right. Daddy mainly looks after me, and Grandma and Granddad.'

'Well at least I know what she looks like now, and it's a release of tension, these tears,' I say, 'a real release of tension.'

'And if she was a beauty,' says Eliana pragmatically, 'you would have met her a long time ago. Leonard would have flaunted her in front of you, but how can he when there's nothing to flaunt? You say she looks unexceptional, so Leonard figures perhaps he will look more substantial by her side. People will notice him, not her, when they walk into a room. They will speak to him and listen to him, not her. It's strange Helena, but when you talk about Leonard he always seems to me like a flat pack man, not much to him. Someone like that needs someone almost invisible by his side. Perhaps he has found someone ideal for him. Someone even more unexceptional than he is.'

'Or more controlling than he is.' Esther interrupts, 'have you ever thought of that? That he has the power outside the home but inside it, she rules the roost?'

'Like attracts like you mean? I don't know about that.' I say, 'I suspect Leonard has his own reasons for keeping us apart. He would probably have worried that I'd hit her, I expect, which I probably would have done back then,' I say. 'Still, at least I know I can put a face to the name now when Freddie talks about her.'

'A very ordinary face,' says Esther.

'Whatever. The point is, when I didn't know what she looked like, it mattered. Now that I've seen her, it doesn't.' I finish my tea and turn to talk to Freddie. 'Enough of Mummy's silliness,' I say, smiling at him. 'How was your weekend, Freddie?'

'We climbed a mountain,' he replies.

'Wow! That's different,' I say.

'The tallest in Wales. I almost fell off, and so did Daddy. Helena started climbing with us, but she stopped and told Daddy he was on a mission and was being crazy. I think he was, too.'

'Well, very well done, darling. Perhaps you should have done it when you were a little older, but at least you've done it,' I tell him, giving him another hug, more for my benefit than his.

It's Eliana's last evening and I wanted to make it special for her, so I've invited Esther and Victoria as well. We're all sitting round the table in my kitchen, and Esther and Eliana are chatting away about the time they were both touring the Cinque Terre. Eliana's making both of my friends laugh at some of the goofy things that happened.

As I'm about to dish out the casserole my mobile goes, and it's Will. I take a breath and answer it.

'The Flindells' luncheon is tomorrow, you do know that?' he says, sounding friendly but formal.

'Yes, at Flindell Mansions.'

'Agetha and Anthony have organised a welcome party for the new tenants of the show house. It'll be a big bash with lots of booze and City people, so we're taking the cameras along to see the new blood in Castleford. Why don't you join us?' he asks.

'Do you really need me?' I reply, feeling as though I've made enough of a fool of myself over the past twenty-four hours.

'You are the producer and I think you should be there.'

I say I'll come, put the phone down and continue serving Eliana, who's trying to make Isabella sit still and getting nowhere.

'It seems I'm going to a luncheon party at the Mansions tomorrow.'

'I've been invited to that,' says Esther. 'I can't go because I've got work on and the usual errands for Digby. I think John Tremble has been invited, but he doesn't want to go. They are not his sort of people. Make sure you remember everything, Helena, so you can tell the rest of us mere mortals what it's like to dine with masters of the universe.' She giggles.

'I've been invited, too,' says Victoria, 'but I can't go. Working on an infidelity story about how many married men and women stray at work.' She blushes slightly.

'Ooh, I wish I could stay,' says Eliana, clapping her hands in the air. 'I would so like to go to a posh party.'

'I don't really want to go, but Will says I should,' I say.

'He likes you, that man.' Eliana winks at me.

'No he doesn't.' I shake my head. 'He's just friendly, that's all.' I explain how silly I felt at the book launch, when I mistakenly thought he asking me out on a date.

'He was teasing,' says Esther. 'He's playing with you.'

'Why would he do that?' I ask.

'Because he can,' says Victoria. 'Why don't you play with him as well? It could be fun and you might as well have fun while you're working. You don't have to do anything. Just be as friendly with him as he is with you, nothing more. You've got to let him make the first move; that's the first rule of getting your man. You encourage him, but he has to make the first physical approach. That's what I did with Peter,' she says, helping herself to more of my casserole. 'And have you heard from Peter at all?' she asks managing to drop his name into the conversation, albeit not very subtly.

'The last time I saw him was when we went out to lunch. In fact, that reminds me, I saw Leonard there with who I thought was Helena, but it wasn't. She had different coloured hair, very dark. It was probably a work colleague.'

'Perhaps he's getting bored with the girlfriend and you caught him out. Not your problem any more,' says Esther.

Eliana looks at me. 'I really don't want to go now, Helena. I'm leaving just as it's getting interesting. You will write to me, won't you? It's like almost seeing the end of a film and the power goes off and I don't know what happens to all the characters. Email or phone, won't you please?' she asks imploringly.

Chapter Seventeen

'Who is it?' squeaks out an officious-sounding metallic voice from the intercom at the entrance to Flindells Mansions. Will, Becca and I are in one car, Richard and Aled behind. Becca has just pressed the intercom button.

'The High Light TV film crew for the launch party,' Becca replies, leaning out of the car and as close to the intercom so she can be heard clearly. After a minute of whizzing and whirring, the bright blue gates creak open, allowing us through. Aled has done a recce of the show house the day before with Becca, so we know there'll be sufficient light, and we don't expect to be there long.

'I don't know why we're bothering with this,' I say to Will as we pass by one of the houses, which still only looks partially built despite the large SOLD sign outside. 'These places remind me of the Lego houses I used to build when I was a child,' I remark.

'You had an excuse,' says Becca, 'you were a child.'

'And I'm sure yours were better made,' adds Will, winking at me as we drive up to the house at the end.

'Please come this way.' An unsmiling lady with a wide-open face, high cheekbones and a hint of Icelandic about her (she looks and sounds a bit like Björk) greets us clinically when we knock at the door.

We follow her through a large open hallway with a marble floor, magnolia walls and large line drawings of nudes and views, none of which I know but all of which look vaguely Italian. I can hear voices in front of me, and as a door opens, the echoes of braying laughter explode through it.

'OK, guys,' says Will to Aled and Richard. 'After we say our brief hellos, can you get the kit ready so we can start filming immediately and make this as painless as possible. Remember, we're after interesting banter. The sort of thing we want to capture is what they're going to do when they move here, and what they think of the place – not only the house but the town. We want a glimpse of how these people differ from the locals. So keep your eyes and ears open, and Becca, can you ask questions as well as me?' he says. 'If you walk among the guests and help Aled identify who he should film that would be good, too.'

'And what do you want me to do?' I say, already feeling like a spare part, and still not sure how I can add to the shoot.

'You may have some ideas I've missed,' he says.

As I enter the room I stop. There are only about ten people in there, but already I recognise some voices.

Voices I haven't heard in ages. Voices from the long-distant past I thought I'd never hear again, and never want to. As I walk in, all heads turn to stare at me and there's a deathly silence. Some mouths drop open and there's a high, nervous titter from a woman in a red dress whose face I know but whose name I don't.

'This always happens to me when I walk into rooms,' I say, looking at Will and the guys, smiling.

'Pity Aled didn't have the camera on as soon as we came in,' says Becca, 'this would have made a great opening shot and we could have used some Serge Leone from one of the spaghetti Westerns. Who's going to make first strike with an hors d'oeuvre?'

'Do these people know you?' asks Aled as Richard walks in front with Will, suddenly seeming quite protective of me, which I find rather sweet.

'They're friends and colleagues of my ex-husband, Freddie's dad,' I explain, looking round and seeing Christine and Kenneth, Leonard's best friend and his wife, whom I always got on with prior to the divorce. Then there's Lorraine and Henry, two more of his friends, and Marcus and Alison Lovett, a very odd couple who never seem to smile, even on their wedding day, when I presume they were happy. I couldn't put a name to the others, but some of the faces I know. They all have the expression of constipated hampsters.

'Is your ex here?' Aled asks, sorting out his camera.

'I can't see him,' I reply, feeling quite sick, 'but if this lot are here, I expect so.'

'I wonder if they're all buying properties here?'

suggests Becca, making me quail at the thought of all these ghosts from my past coming to haunt my home town.

'Castleford will change if they do,' says Aled, taking a look at the faces.

'It's a possibility,' says Will. 'Any one of the new owners could be the hosts, although I understand the Flindells have paid for this bash because they knew it would get them on the programme.'

'Hello,' says Agetha, coming up to me. 'It must be like walking back into old times,' she says, giving me a peck on my cheek which feels like a razor blade.

'I know most of these people,' I say, trying to keep my composure.

'I'm so sorry,' she replies, looking genuinely embarrassed. 'I've only just found out myself, but I understand the man who's bought this property is your ex-husband. The deal was done through an agent, so I didn't know who the buyer was. I've met him, though, and he seems charming, and it will be good for Freddie, don't you think?'

I don't want to explain everything to Agetha, so I just smile and nod.

'Yes it will,' I reply. 'We'd like to set up in here. This is going to be a sit-down luncheon, isn't it, so if Aled could wander round filming with Becca that would be great. We'll be as unobtrusive as possible, obviously. Everyone does know there's going to be a film crew here, I take it?' I ask, aware that people are still staring at me, but needing to focus on the programme.

'Yes, they all know,' she nods.

'I'll get everyone to sign a release form,' says Becca, going into her large brown satchel and bringing out a thick wodge of papers, 'while Aled sets up his camera.' Meanwhile Aled gets the usual awed reaction from the women, all of whom look elegant in expensive summer outfits, despite the fact that it's quite chilly out today.

'What is it with cameramen? Why do they get all the attention?' Richard smiles.

'Because women like someone who's strong and creative.' Aled grins. 'It's like having a big gun in my hands. They feel there's a man in the house,' he says, half joking. Or at least I think he's joking.

'Rubbish, they just want to be on TV,' replies Becca. 'They think that if they flirt with you you'll show them in a good light, but really it's the rest of us they should be nice to, because we're the ones who'll be in the editing suite, relegating them to the cutting-room floor if they piss us off. And Richard here,' she says, tapping him on the bottom, which he seems to rather enjoy, 'will make sure he records all the things they'd prefer not to be heard, as well as their rehearsed lines. Punters always get it wrong.' She grins at Aled, who tips an imaginary cap at her and asks Will where he'd like him to start.

While Will and Aled go off with Becca, I'm left with Richard, who's busy sorting out his sound equipment: a bag full of black boxes covered in silver knobs with wires poking out of them.

'That looks like something out of an *Alien* film,' I say,

looking at him as he untangles the wires. 'How on earth do you know which bit goes where?'

'You get used to it,' he replies. 'I think it's easier doing this than being a cameraman.'

'Well, having worked in radio, I know exactly what you mean. When someone puts a camera in their face people tend to clam up, but a microphone is less intimidating, so they usually relax more.'

'Exactly.' He nods and heads off in the direction of Aled and Will, who have begun introducing themselves to the guests.

Becca returns. 'I'll hand the forms out. Are you OK here?' she asks, looking a little concerned.

'Oh, I'm fine,' I reply, 'just obviously rather shocked to see all these people from my past.'

'That's why I asked. I should imagine it is a dreadful shock. I overheard Agetha Flindell saying your ex is charming, and I'm sure he is, but the mere fact that you didn't know he was buying this house says it all to me,' declares Becca. 'It's not a very polite or mature thing to do.'

I shrug. 'Well, he's here now, so perhaps it's time to turn over a new leaf, especially as it seems I'll be seeing a lot of his friends as well by the looks of it,' I say, taking a brief glance around the room and feeling relieved that all eyes are now on Aled and Will, who are schmoozing nicely.

Becca leans over and gives me a kiss on the cheek, which is as unexpected as it is welcome. 'Good luck,' she says.

Despite her flirtatious attitude, Becca has always seemed totally focused on work. She's evidently kind and thoughtful as well, I think, as I watch her five-foot-five frame, clad in leather miniskirt and long black boots, stride over to some of the male guests, turning heads as she goes. A bit like Jessica Rabbit, she can't help the way she's built.

Suddenly I'm standing alone in the room. The crew all seem to be fully engaged and, as expected, I'm extraneous to their needs. I'm annoyed that I wasn't more firm with Will about not joining them, because I knew this would happen. If I'd known this was going to be Leonard's new home, I definitely wouldn't have come.

'Why hello!'

I turn round and feel quite sick again. Leonard is standing in front of me, slick and besuited, with Agetha and Anthony on either side of him. 'Lovely to see you. I thought this would be a great surprise for you,' he says, leaning over and kissing me on the cheek. I usually deal with Darth Vader, but here's Uriah Heep. Personally I prefer Darth Vader – at least I know where I stand with him.

'Hello,' I reply, trying not to look too annoyed or shocked, or give any reaction that appears less than gracious, since I can feel Agetha and Anthony watching me intently. Anything I say will be spread around the town quicker than I can say Castleford. 'Good to see you.'

'What do you think of our new house?' he asks,

without waiting for an answer. 'It will make a lovely home for Freddie when he comes to stay, won't it? He's always going on about wanting a dog, and now we have the space to have one. I know it's a bit difficult in the cottage, but it's the ideal house for a dog here – a large one – well trained, of course,' he says, laughing and making plenty of eye contact with Agetha and Anthony. 'We're really pleased with the house, its size and dimensions,' he says, turning to Anthony, who seems to have fallen for Leonard's charms, or is it his money? 'And the furnishings, and the windows. I like to think the windows are the eyes of a house and the kitchen is its soul, and you've blessed us with the very best of both.' I want to giggle because he sounds so stupid, but Anthony seems to be totally taken in.

'I'm so pleased you understand the design of the houses. We like the clean lines and large spaces. Agetha deals with the furnishings and she's got a wonderful touch, even if I do say so myself,' he says, looking proudly at his wife.

'So these aren't your choice?' I say, looking round at the oversized mottled apricot sofas and large pot plants.

'No,' Leonard shakes his head, 'but we love what you've done, so we'll be keeping a lot of it because, well, how can perfection be perfected?'

At this stage I nearly throw up. Admittedly, having only had a brief glimpse of his flat in London, with its brown leather sofas and soulless atmosphere, I think he'd rather eat his own tongue than live in a place with apricot sofas, but I could be wrong. Perhaps Helena's had more of an influence in this home. Which reminds me, where is the lady of the house?

'Where's Helena?' I ask.

'Oh, she'll be down in a moment,' he says, still retaining a smile and without showing a hint of annoyance that I know what she looks like, so have taken the sting out of my first meeting with her.

'Your girlfriend is called Helena, too?' Agetha asks. 'That must be confusing for you.'

'Not really,' he replies, still smiling but unwilling to give any more away. He's probably tired of people commenting on it.

'Hello, Leonard!' Kenneth walks to my side and gives my ex a big hug, almost knocking Agetha sideways in the process. 'And how is my man?' he asks.

Kenneth was a City trader who started his own property business; after the crash I have no idea what state it's in. I liked him when Leonard and I were together, although Leonard always found him quite dull and straight, though not as dull and straight as his wife, Christine, whom I liked even more. I'm surprised Kenneth doesn't even give me a hello.

'I'm great,' replies Leonard, 'and you remember my ex, don't you?' he says, introducing me with the broadest of smiles. This is so infuriating. He's so snotty when it's just the two of us, but anyone looking on at this scene would think what a lovely man he is. Perhaps he has decided to turn over a new leaf and my instincts are wrong, though they rarely are. When I look at

Kenneth, though, he seems as surprised by Leonard's warm introduction as I am.

'Hello,' he says coldly, 'how are you?'

'I'm fine,' I reply, 'are you moving to Castleford, too?'

'We're looking at one of the other properties here,' he replies, 'but we want to get to know the place better before we make a decision, so we'll be visiting Leonard over the next few months.'

He looks me up and down as though he's trying to take me in. I'm upset by his coldness, because the last time I saw him was when Leonard and I met up with him in Cambridge for a weekend when our respective children were toddlers, and we had a great time. Things have obviously changed since, though, and he is Leonard's friend, so I guess it's to be expected. I should imagine Leonard's been telling him about the money situation and Kenneth, who went through an expensive divorce himself before he met Christine, probably feels sympathetic. However, I can't help feeling sad when he asks Leonard to join the other guests, ushering him away from me and the Flindells, who are too full of excitement to notice the slight, although Agetha squeezes my arm as she walks past to speak to the caterers, winking as if to say, 'I know it's difficult.'

For the second time in under half an hour I find myself standing alone. I wish Victoria, Esther and John Tremble had accepted the Flindells' invitation. Victoria would probably suggest doping the drinks and seducing the husbands, Esther would pump the guests for material for her husband's next book and her own diary on control freaks (she'd get a lot of material here), and John would see right through everyone – perhaps even Leonard; I'm sure he would. It would be even better if Freddie were here. But if Freddie were here, his loyalties would be split, which would make things difficult for him, and I wouldn't want to do that to him. It's better he's out of the equation, playing football with Harry and Jack.

'Good God,' says Will, walking up to me and whispering in my ear. 'You'll never guess what? I know the owner of this place.'

'What? You know Leonard?'

'Yes,' he nods.

'Leonard's my ex-husband,' I say, feeling shocked and seeing that Will's reaction mirrors mine.

'You're kidding! I would never have put you two together in a million years. He's so dark, whereas you are . . . well, you're . . .' He can't find the words, or perhaps he can but just can't say them.

'I'm what?' I ask.

'Well . . . let's just say I wouldn't have put you together at all. He was always quite dark as a person, never smiling much, and you, well, you're the opposite,' he says hesitantly.

'I don't remember meeting you when I was with Leonard,' I say, looking at him closely, although I've always had a slight sense of déjà vu with Will.

'I feel like I've met you before, but I don't think I have. I knew Leonard when we were at Norton School.

He was in my year and we were friends, well, more acquaintances really. We lost touch because I went into something creative and he went into something commercial.' He looks quickly at Leonard. 'I don't think he's recognised me, though, and if he doesn't say anything I won't either, OK?'

'OK,' I reply.

'So how do you feel about being here?' he asks.

'Well, it's a bit like walking into our wedding-day photos, not that I can remember them because I destroyed the album. I don't think I'm going to be of any help to you here, and I know it's dreadfully unprofessional, but I feel rather miserable.'

'It seems that Leonard has allocated you a place for lunch, together with the rest of us, so if I were you I'd take up the gauntlet and hold your head high. It would be easy to make your excuses and walk away, but I wouldn't give him the satisfaction. You have come here for a perfectly valid reason. You didn't know it was his home, but he obviously knew you would be here, he saw the guest list and Agetha and Anthony told him the names of the crew, so I expect he'll be on his best behaviour. Couldn't you just accept the situation and disguise your feelings?'

'Will,' I say, feeling myself getting smaller, 'I don't know if I want to. I don't know if I want to pretend to be something I'm not. I pretended to be something I'm not for most of my marriage, because that's what Leonard wanted me to be, and now he's moved here I don't want to start kowtowing again to a man I don't respect, like or trust. I know I have to try to be nice for Freddie's sake, and yes, if Leonard were always the charming, expansive, smiling man we see before us it would be different, but that isn't the real man,' I say, looking at my ex performing like some professional politician in front of his guests and the camera, making everyone laugh with the same effortless grace he used to make me miserable.

'Helena,' Will says softly, holding my arm and turning me so I'm facing him, 'you are a beautiful, bright woman, a wonderful mother and a talented producer – not as talented as me, I might add,' he says with a cheeky glint in his eye, 'but you *are* talented, and whatever happened in your old life, you are not the same woman who married Leonard all those years ago. I know from my own divorce that my wife is stronger and happier now, and I'm happy for her. You are probably stronger than you were then, too; I can sense it and I'm sure your ex can, too. He should be happy for you, but if he's not, well, that's his problem, not yours, and it's an issue he has to deal with. Just be yourself and stay here for lunch. I'll see if I can sit near or next to you for moral support, and if he says something smarmy, I'll get Aled to bonk him on the head with the camera, or even worse, shoot him in a bad light which will add years and a few chins.'

Will makes me laugh and I kiss him on the cheek, feeling that now familiar electricity run up and down my body. As we're standing there staring at each other, I gradually become aware that people are looking at us.

I blush and smile, raising my glass to Leonard, who's also looking, perhaps recognising Will from his Norton School days after all, though he doesn't say anything. Leonard briefly looks shocked, but soon regains his composure, smiling and raising a glass too.

'To your new home,' I call across to him. 'May you be very happy in it,'

'That's my girl,' says Will, tapping me lightly on the bottom. 'If he's genuine, he'll be touched by that gesture; if he's not, he'll hate it. Win, win.'

The drink seems to be flowing nicely and the braying voices are getting louder and shriller, but Leonard's girlfriend still hasn't appeared.

'Lunch is served in the conservatory. There a place list on the table, so you'll know where you're sitting,' says Agetha. 'If everyone could sit down now we can serve the first course,' she instructs us, still managing to flutter her eyelashes at Aled, whose lens is fixed on her as she makes the announcement.

I walk to the long white table, thinking the Flindells have done their guests proud.

It's beautifully laid with simple white cutlery, which looks slightly French, and lovely pink and cream sashes draped across the table, making it look like something out of a fairy tale.

I walk round, nodding at Christine, whom I haven't spoken to yet, and she gives me a warm, genuine smile. She was always a woman of few words, but that's probably because Kenneth is a man of so many.

Lorraine and Henry are sitting at the other end of

the table to me, which is a pity. Henry is one of Leonard's oldest friends. He owns his own business and, despite being short and Welsh and consequently the butt of every joke in the British Isles, he's a kind-hearted, lovely man, who was always very thoughtful to me and attentive to Lorraine. I remember her as extremely bubbly and delightfully indiscreet to the point of ostracising herself from several dinner parties, because she told the hosts what she thought of them and their cooking. Less a breath of fresh air among the Stepford Wives of my former corporate life as a corporate wife, more a Siberian wind blasting through the fakeries of their lifestyle. I'm rather surprised Leonard has invited them, mainly because if anyone is likely to say what they mean rather than what they've been told to say at this gathering, it's Lorraine.

However, I'm not sitting with the lovely, reticent Christine, vivacious Lorraine or kind-hearted Henry. No, I'm sitting next to Alison and opposite Marcus, the third couple I recognised on entering. They both look as though someone has just burgled their house. By the way they're looking at me, I'm the suspect.

I smile and hold their gaze, hoping for some sign of recognition, but it doesn't come. Will isn't sitting down, and when I look round for him I see he's on his mobile, and Becca, Aled and Richard are filming at the other end of the table where Leonard is sitting.

Suddenly Leonard turns and stands up, looking towards the door as everyone follows his gaze. Has the Queen arrived?

I turn around to see who's there, expecting a celebrity Agetha or Anthony have invited as a surprise guest for the programme.

'Hello, my darling,' says Leonard, walking towards Helena, who's wearing a long black dress that looks a little out of place, as it's more of an evening gown than anything. But what do I know, I'm dressed for an outdoor walk.

'Hello, sweetheart,' she replies, and comes up to him. He bends down – he has to as she's so much shorter than him – and gives her a long, passionate kiss. Six years ago it would have broken my heart and I would have felt even smaller than she is, still wanting my family intact, but now it just makes me realise how little I feel for Leonard that way. I just hope he really has changed and is prepared to be civil to me, put the past behind him – especially as he's going to move, as Esther put it, on to my territory – and most importantly, put Freddie's needs before his own.

Aled is, of course, getting this all on camera, and all eyes are focused on the couple, or so I think. Then I notice, after the first thirty seconds of their embrace, that people are quickly turning to see my reaction, so I do my best 'Ah, isn't that nice' look and nibble an olive.

After Leonard and Helena release each other from their clinch, Helena looks round the table.

'Welcome to our new home, everyone. It's lovely to have you all here today and we're so happy to see all these friendly faces,' she says, looking round the table and skimming past me as though I'm not there. 'We wanted to move to Castleford so that Leonard could be closer to Freddie, but now that so many of you are thinking of moving to the area, too, we'll never be far from our friends either.' She sounds quite posh – plummy rather than well spoken – and has a small mouth and straight brown hair that skims her shoulders. Although she's much younger than me, in her long black dress she looks much older than me – older than Leonard, even. It's as though he's the boy and she's the mother, but perhaps that's what he needed and wanted all along. Whatever, as long as they're happy, genuinely happy, then that's good for Freddie, and hopefully it will be easier between us now that Leonard's moved closer and can see more of his son. I know he's aggrieved about the money – in fact, that's the only thing I think he really is aggrieved about – that was made absolutely clear in mediation, but now that's coming to an end, maybe everything will change for the better.

The first course appears, presented by Polish girls who can't speak English. I know this because I try to chat to them. I smile as the plate is put in front of me. Parma ham and melon – Leonard's dinner-party starter of choice when we were together. It may have been Agetha's choice, but I should imagine she asked Leonard and Helena for their opinion. I'm not particularly hungry, so I try to make conversation instead.

'How are you, Marcus?' I ask, remembering that the last time we met we had a row about bankers, because I had the temerity to say they didn't deserve what they earned and countered every argument he made until he became speechless with fury.

'Fine,' he says, stuffing a forkful of ham into his big mouth.

'Are you still running?' I ask Alison. I remember her as being just as morose as Marcus, only quieter and therefore slightly more sinister.

There's no answer, so I ask again. Without looking at me, she replies in a monotone,

'I don't run.'

I'm just about to excuse myself to go to the toilet when Helena comes up beside me and looks down at me – which makes a change.

'It's so lovely to see you here,' she says, disarming me. 'It was a total surprise when I saw you that time in the car. You caught me completely off guard, so I'm sorry if I seemed rude. I know it must be difficult for you, but we're glad you're here.' And with that she kisses me on the cheek. You could have knocked me down with a feather. 'When we heard the film crew were coming over and that you were producing the show, we wanted to surprise you. I just hope it's been a pleasant surprise,' she says, looking at me as though I'm some long-lost friend. None of this adds up, though. If she's this warm and friendly, then why wasn't she at the flat to meet me when this had been suggested at mediation? And even if she was off guard, why did she glare at me from the car? And why hasn't she tried to make contact before? Looking more closely, she's definitely not the woman Leonard was with at the

Lafitte. Rather than answering questions, her approach has only raised more in my mind.

'I hope things can be good between us,' I reply, feeling it would be churlish to say anything else under the circumstances. 'I know it will be best for Freddie and all concerned. You have a beautiful home. A lot more feminine touches than the flat in London, so perhaps you have more say here,' I add. I can sense Helena getting a little tense at this comment, as though I've unintentionally hit a nerve.

'Yes.' She nods, her smile becoming fixed. 'It is more feminine, isn't it.' Then she moves on, giving the still unsmiling Alison a kiss on the cheek.

I excuse myself and make my way out, heading for the cloakroom. I'm hoping I'll have a chance to call Victoria or Esther and give them the news that my ex and his girlfriend have arrived and are entertaining me in their new home. It's worthy of one of Victoria's headlines.

'Hello there!'

I turn and see it's Lorraine skipping across the hallway towards me. 'I just wanted to say hello and ask you, what the fuck are you doing here?' She gives me a big hug and giggles. 'Are you telling me that Leonard has invited you to this bash? Bloody hell, what's changed? From what Henry's hinted to me, Leonard hates the air you breathe.'

'Well, he didn't exactly invite me. I'm with the film crew producing this documentary on Castleford, and he's one of the new residents, so it was organised without either him or me knowing. But he's being very gracious about it now. I was expecting him to march me off the premises.'

Lorraine can't stop laughing. 'That's not his style, you know that. Henry only knows Leonard hates you because he's been with him when he's drunk and off guard and then the truth comes out. When he's sober, you'd never know. And you'd never know what Leonard was planning until it had happened. And anyway, if he was planning to attack you, he wouldn't do it here, there would be too many witnesses. You look fabulous, I just wanted to tell you that, and Henry says hello and he's sorry we can't speak to you with the rest of that lot in there. I've been shunned by so many people recently and Henry says if I speak my mind any more he won't have any corporate friends left, and there will be absolutely fuck-all chance of promotion,' she says shrugging her shoulders.

'Pity you can't say what you want. I loved it when you came come out with devastating comments at dinner parties.'

'I know you did. You were the only one that laughed. I used to get a right bollocking from Henry, but all that ostentatious twaddle I couldn't deal with. Don't get me wrong. It's nice, all this money, but God, the pretensions of this lot sometimes. You are best out of it, girl. Hope you know that. It takes a hard woman to stay married to a man like Leonard, but it takes a strong woman to leave.'

'Yes, but it seems it's come and followed me. Leonard is moving here.'

'I don't know the fuck why. He hates the country and he hates the sea, as far as I can gather from Henry. He talks about Freddie but not really in a regular sort of way. You know, he's proud of him, but when I've asked more about him, what Freddie does and things, I can tell he doesn't know. Dads know things about their children, don't they? But Leonard, well, he doesn't. So I sort of guessed it was to get to know his son better when Henry told me they were moving here.'

'Perhaps it was his girlfriend's idea?'

'Not bloody likely. She doesn't want anything to do with you. You're *persona non grata* with most of the old set, but she seems to be tolerated. Well, I'd better get back now, otherwise I'll be missed. Henry will guess what I'm up to – there are only so many excuses about having constipation I can give him. Lovely to see you. Sorry I haven't been in touch but just wanted to let you know that I think you're OK, OK?'

'OK,' I reply, 'and thank you for risking the wrath of Henry and the others for speaking to me.'

'Oh fuck them. But don't say I said that. But, well, you know what I mean,' Lorraine says, giving me a kiss on the cheek and slipping furtively back to join the party. I can hear Leonard's voice above the others.

I find the cloakroom at the side of the hall. I'm tempted to go upstairs and snoop around, but it's rude and I wouldn't like anyone doing that in my home, so I go into the cloakroom and enjoy a little time to myself. If I didn't think I would get caught I would go up and explore, but it would be hugely embarrassing if they found me, especially with the cameras here. Perhaps that's what they were expecting me to do, so I won't do it.

I expect to find myself in a small bathroom, but the Flindells have done Leonard proud. The room is as large as my bedroom, with wall-to-wall mirrors, so I can watch myself going to the toilet, which is a little disconcerting. There's a stand not only for toilet rolls, but also for newspapers and magazines, as well as a bidet, which I haven't seen in ages, and a large stand-alone sink – marble bowl on a silvery pedestal. As I put the loo lid up, I notice a TV screen in front of me, and as soon as I put bum to seat, *Friends* starts to play.

What a wonderful invention – silly, totally unnecessary and wonderful. It's the episode where Phoebe sings about her jelly cat, and I can't help but laugh – perhaps it isn't going to be such a bad lunch party after all, though admittedly the best bit so far has been my visit to the toilet. I'd be happy to remain on the loo for the next five minutes, or even until the end of the programme, but then I hear a knock on the door. As I get up and pull the flush, I realise it doesn't work, and then it dawns on me: it's a new house and some things may not be working – this could be one of them. I pull the handle again . . . and again, but the water just keeps rising together with the sound of the TV – it's as though the volume is affected by the water level. I'm about to flood the cloakroom in Leonard's house. I have one last go before accepting that my attempts are useless, then I open the door. Thank goodness it's Will.

'What the hell?' he says, but before he can finish the sentence I pull him in.

'The toilet doesn't work. It's about to flood; this can't happen. Not in any house but especially not in Leonard's,' I say, wanting to laugh, because although I'm very concerned I can see the funny side of it.

'I know you wanted to leave your mark, Helena, and Leonard may deserve it, but isn't this is a bit much? Go back to the others and finish your meal while I sort this out,' he says, smiling at me.

I walk towards the conservatory, hearing Leonard laughing and joking with the others.

Someone has put on some background music, Gerry Rafferty's 'Baker Street', which I like. I look around for Aled and the crew. They're taking a break, sitting at a separate table eating what looks like a combination of starter and main course. I glance over to where I was sitting – Alison and Marcus look just as unhappy as when I left them – then join the crew to see how they're getting on.

'Are you happy with what you've got so far?' I ask, standing behind Becca and Richard, who turn and smile at me.

'Yeah,' replies Aled, who's stuffing what looks like pheasant into his mouth. 'Mind you, they don't seem to talk about much apart from money and property. That and themselves, but it's different to the other stuff we've filmed. Plus Will seems happy, so unless something big happens I think we've got everything we need – we did manage to film them discussing Castleford. It's all very positive stuff, which I suspect Elliott will find dull – he probably wanted them to let their hair down and slag it off, but everyone's been very complimentary about the house and the town, so if you were looking for some friction, you're not going to get it here.'

'Oh well, we've done our best and got a slice of what the new residents will be doing with their time here,' says Richard.

'Yeah, talking about themselves, money and property,' yawns Aled before cramming more food into his mouth.

'Where's Will?' asks Becca, looking round.

'He's gone to the toilet, I believe,' I say, feeling myself go red.

'And how are you coping?' she asks more pointedly.

'Oh fine,' I say. 'Leonard and his girlfriend have been utterly delightful to me, so perhaps it's not so bad that they're moving here after all.'

'I still think it's strange that he didn't tell you. It's sort of like getting one over on you,' says Becca, 'and there's nothing delightful about that. I think it's very odd behaviour.'

I'm about to explain to her that I don't see Leonard's behaviour as odd any more, I just accept it as the way he is, when Will returns.

'Houston, we have a problem,' he announces as he comes through the door. 'I'm afraid the downstairs cloakroom is flooded. I must admit I used it and there's water and, well, it's everywhere and I don't know if you need to evacuate, but I would suggest calling a plumber.' He looks around for Anthony and Agetha. 'It's totally my fault.'

Agetha looks mortified and Anthony gets straight on his mobile to the plumber, while Becca quietly tells Aled to turn on the camera as unobtrusively as possible to get some reactions.

The other guests don't look too perturbed. In fact, it's a little like the final scene in *Carry On Up the Khyber*, when the Burpers are bombing the Governor's residence headquarters and the dinner party continues regardless. Lorraine is the only one who's finding the whole thing very funny.

Water is seeping into the conservatory now, but everyone just goes on sitting there, eating their pheasant and talking about the latest fashions, what's happening in London, where they hope to holiday this year, the problems they're having with their nannies and the horrifying price of the tennis court they've just had laid. While Agetha and Anthony run around like headless chickens, Leonard and Helena seem oblivious to the situation. Water could be swishing round their ankles and they'd still be sitting there drinking.

'Thanks for letting me off the hook and taking the blame,' I say to Will as he walks over and nicks some food from Becca's plate.

'No worries,' he replies. 'Better for them to think it was my stuff they were swimming in than yours, eh?'

I laugh at him, not quite sure how to take this last statement, but then I see his point and suddenly feel very naughty.

'I didn't do it intentionally,' I tell him.

'I know you didn't, Miss Treadwell,' he says, 'and anyway, one person's accident is another person's opportunity to add some spice to a very dull lunch party. Now at least we've got something to film. And we get to see how they cope in a crisis, albeit a minor one: they ignore it. Stiff upper lip, what, what?' he says, mimicking an army type.

Leonard claps his hands and calls everyone to attention, playing the sergeant major. He tells us that the plumber has arrived, and it would be best if we were on our way before the cleaners begin to mop up.

'Well, thank you all for coming,' he says, waving everyone goodbye while retaining his composure beautifully, I have to admit. I would have got people out as soon as possible, but he just ignored it all; he must have changed. When we were together, he used to go ballistic if the slightest thing went wrong, especially at parties. I walk out the door with the crew, smiling at Leonard and Helena and even giving them both a goodbye peck on the cheek, something I never thought I'd do.

'I've got an appointment with the headmaster at Letchbury next Wednesday morning. I can't make any other time due to work commitments, and if you can come round the school with me then, that would be great,' Leonard says. I didn't expect this. I thought Victoria was right when she said his suggestion about sending Freddie to boarding school was an empty threat, but he's obviously serious about it. And what's more infuriating, he's said this to me when I don't have any witnesses. Will and the crew are already outside. No one has overheard what he said, and his slightly menacing tone, and I go cold. Every time I think things are going well, or on the mend with Leonard, something happens to make me realise nothing has changed. And I know I'm not deluding myself about Freddie doing well at his school. I know boarding school isn't right for him. I know Castleford is great: for goodness' sake, a programme is being made about how wonderful the kids are who come from the school. I feign indifference.

'Yes, give me a call and let me know the exact time and I'll come with you, Leonard. I don't believe Letchbury is the right school for Freddie and he's so happy at Castleford, but I'm happy to look around it with you.'

He expected me to react differently and I can see he's annoyed, but I turn and leave. I get in the car with Will and Becca, and Will drives out of the gates of Flindell Mansions. I want to cry but bite my lip, unable to join in the banter going on in the car.

'Are you OK?' says Becca, obviously realising I'm not.

I can't hold back any longer and burst into tears.

'What's the matter?' asks Becca, squeezing my shoulder. Will pulls over and stops the car after we turn the corner. He flashes Aled and Richard so that they stop as well.

'The filming didn't go that badly,' says Becca, believing I'm got emotional because we haven't got enough friction, as Aled put it.

'No,' I say, shaking my head but still too upset to explain why I'm crying.

'Don't worry about the toilet,' laughs Will, thinking that's the problem.

'What about the toilet?' asks Becca, bemused, looking at Will.

'Oh, Helena bunged up their toilet,' explains Will, making me really embarrassed as well as distraught. Then Aled and Richard get out of their car and walk over.

'What's the matter?' Aled asks, then, noticing me, says 'Did your ex upset you?'

I nod, still crying.

'When?' says Will, looking at Aled and then at me, and putting his arm around me.

'You see, I notice these things. A cameraman always does. He's all smiles and charm, that man, but I had my lens on him and he occasionally was giving you looks of, well, I can only describe it as hate. What did he say to you?' Aled asks.

I brush my tears away and rub my eyes. My mascara must now be all over my face, but I don't care. 'Oh, he mentioned that he's going to look around a nearby boarding school, that one we filmed playing Castleford this week, and he asked me to accompany him, and I don't want Freddie to go there. He's happy where he is, and he's doing so well. But it's the way Leonard said it, and told me. He still gets to me, and Freddie is the only way he'll be able to get to me in future.'

'Tell him to go fuck himself,' says Aled. 'I'll tell him to if you like.'

This makes me laugh. 'I have tried that in the past, and all that happens is he finds a way to hit back. He waits perhaps days, even months, and it's always when I least expect it, like just now. If it isn't withholding maintenance, it's getting to me through Freddie. Now he wants to take Freddie away from me, and all the time I was thinking he was moving here to be closer to his son when really it's only to bully me. I've started a new life without him but I can't completely cut him off, because of Freddie.'

'You could have him killed,' says Becca helpfully. 'I know some Hell's Angels who would give him a good going-over.'

'You know, you're the third person who's put forward that idea,' I say, remembering my mother and Eliana also suggested as much. 'I only wish it was possible. Leonard is highly manipulative, cunning, intimidating and skilled at debate. He is a master of distorting the truth in any given situation and I know will resort to anything to get his own way. His mother is the same. She told everyone when we split that I had an affair and that's why we divorced, but it wasn't as simple as that. He's learned the skills from her.'

'I know the type,' says Becca, still squeezing my shoulder, 'I went out with a guy who simply had to be in control to feel good about himself. He took it to such extremes, it was just like being with a spoilt child. He had never really grown up.'

'Sounds like Elliott in the office,' says Will drily which makes me smile.

'Point is, you can resign from a job and get away from the bullying boss. You can chuck the boyfriend and never see him again. But if you've got a child with a control freak, or if you're related to one as my friend Esther is with her dad, then you're stuck with them. I know the best thing is to be indifferent to the games Leonard plays, and always be polite, don't rise to the bait and get angry, don't give him any ammunition, but when it's to do with my son, how can I not be emotional? It's not natural to be indifferent to something like this.' I sigh deeply.

Will smiles at me. 'Do you know, I think Leonard is using your own emotions against you. Perhaps you still feel a little guilty about Freddie being brought up by a single mum and he plays on that. Maybe he thought he could take advantage of your good manners at the lunch party. You could have freaked out in there, and got really intimidated by being surrounded by faces from the past you would rather forget, but you didn't. And hey, you screwed up their toilet, so you did something unintentional that got them back.'

'You did that!' beams Richard, leaning into the car, 'good going, girl!'

'Not on purpose,' I say.

'Your ex has a hidden agenda and his aim is to control and manipulate,' says Will. 'But you know what, this man is basically dreadfully insecure. If he is secure as a man and a person, he wouldn't have to play these

games. Trust me, he'll try so hard to control his surroundings, and you and Freddie, that he will actually
end up having no control at all.'

'I don't know. He's very credible,' I say, thinking of
all the times I've felt I've made a breakthrough only to
find out he's got away with something again, and everyone has decided I'm the villain of the piece.

'Helena, as I said to you earlier, you are a good
mother and a good person. You have friends and family
who love you, and you have made a good home for
yourself and Freddie. Leonard has decided to move
here. Why, you don't know yet, but he's already sending out mixed messages, saying he wants to be close to
his son and then considering sending him to boarding
school. None of it makes sense, and if it doesn't make
sense to us it won't make sense to Freddie or his
school,' Will declares firmly.

I sniff, realising I'm rather snotty now, and Becca
hands me a tissue.

'Thank you,' I say, suddenly feeling very silly. 'Sorry
about this. I didn't realise it would affect me this much,
guys. I apologise for being so unprofessional.'

'Screw that,' says Becca, 'if it had been me I would
have ripped her bloody eyes out and kicked him in the
balls. You behaved impeccably, and aren't you pleased
you don't mix with such a boring load of tossers any
more?'

'They weren't all tossers,' I reply, thinking of
Lorraine and Henry, 'not all.'

As Will drives Becca and me back I suddenly feel very

calm and relieved. It was difficult going to the party without Victoria and Esther, but I did it and managed to leave without embarrassing myself; well not completely anyway.

Chapter Eighteen

'I am not happy.'

Elliott is surrounded by Simon, Samuel and Luca, while Heather sits in the background, still looking miserable, and I sit with Jarred and Will.

Elliott has just seen the rushes of what we've filmed so far: the interview with John Tremble; the school PTA meeting; the book launch; the interview with the Flindells, which is unintentionally hilarious as they're both so made-up they look like clowns, and finally Leonard's lunch, which looks like a cross between *Abigail's Party* and a *Carry On* film. Richard had managed to pick up a few barbed comments from the guests about the local area lacking style and a Prada, and the locals lacking class. Thankfully there's also a few hilarious off-the-cuff remarks from Lorraine. Marcus and Alison look particularly miserable and out of place.

'I like seeing the new lot who are moving into the area. That's good,' Elliott says. 'It's a nice contrast with the kooky sculptor and the eccentric author talking sex, but apart from that it's all fucking dull!' he shouts, freeze-framing the screen as Leonard is about to stuff a potato into his mouth. 'We're not showing the punters anything new, just that the folks of Castleford are decent and honest and consequently they bring up decent, honest kids. So fucking what? I knew this would happen. Jarred, your head is on the block here. What are you going to do about it?' he asks, turning to Jarred suddenly.

'We have another four weeks, Elliott. We've got the school play to cover and some more local shopkeepers to interview. Then that's about it,' he says.

'Then what the fuck am I going to give our guys at ITV?' Elliott shouts. 'We'll have to fabricate something so that it becomes a story, because at the moment there isn't one. And if there's no story, no repeat commission. Disappointment like this lingers like a bad smell; this is a small industry we work in, as you know, and the stench is not going to stick on me. We don't have enough sex,' he growls, getting up and pacing to and fro. 'Surely they must have sex in Castleford? That author writes about it, for goodness' sake. He even admitted to frigging off as a result of some of the stuff he writes.'

'Only behind closed doors,' I say, thinking that if Edward were here he'd be shouting at Elliott right now, or at least thinking about putting him in his next book and giving him a very small penis. 'And apart from Edward, they're not the sort to talk about it,' I add.

'This new lot might be hot,' Elliott says, 'have we tried them? Becca is good at getting people to open up and do stuff they don't want to. Have you let her at them yet?' he asks Will, who seems remarkably unsurprised by this.

'No, but I could speak to her about it. She got on well with them, but they're all very media-savy. They don't trust us. We had a hard enough time getting access to the lunch party, it was only due to Anthony Flindell agreeing to pay for the catering and everything else that we managed to get in at all. But I will ask Becca to try.' He puts a note on his BlackBerry.

'You do that,' Elliott replies. 'Ask her to try fucking hard. Come back in a couple of weeks and I'll see what you have for me. I need more than this, guys. I need scandal and danger, so get your fingers out your arses, get back there and start finding me a story!' he shouts as he storms out.

We all sit there, the room buzzing with Elliott's words, 'fingers out your arses'. Heather is the first one to break the silence and explain his volatile mood this morning.

'He hasn't got laid this week,' she says, 'or had a blow job. He's much more malleable when he's just had sex.'

Chapter Nineteen

I never enjoy parents' evenings, and usually Leonard can't make them, but he has no excuse now that he lives in Castleford. Ironically, this one is being held the day before we're due to visit Letchbury school, and I'm wondering whether to mention this to any of the teachers, or only to say something if Leonard does. I decide to say nothing unless he does, in which case I will say that I am very happy Freddie is at the school and don't wish him to move, and let Leonard give his own reasons – which I will be as interested to hear as I'm sure Freddie's teachers will. Thankfully, all the teachers at Castleford think very highly of our son.

I've just bid farewell to John after a final sitting for the bust he's doing of me. He still refuses to tell me who commissioned it, despite my guessing everyone under the sun, including at one point Leonard (so he can ceremoniously break it, probably). When I arrive, all the other parents are waiting in the playground, and Penny Vernon comes up to me.

'I think I've seen your ex in his Porsche waiting outside,' she says, smiling at me. 'Do you want me to ask him to come in, or are you happy for him to stay there?'

'He'll come in when he wants to,' I reply. 'If he doesn't I'll go and fetch him, but I'm sure he's just on the phone or something.'

As seven o'clock strikes, the first of my nine appointments begins. They are all five-minute ones, apart from a ten-minute slot with Miss King, Freddie's form teacher. Suddenly Leonard appears – with Helena.

I'm amazed he's brought her. He's still in charming mode, as he was at the lunch party, but the low-voice thingy has made an unwelcome return.

'Hello,' he says. 'I thought I'd bring Helena along as she's sort of a surrogate mother.'

I look at him, feeling my mouth open. I'm utterly gobsmacked; I didn't think he'd ever be that thoughtless, but we're standing in front of the teachers and as Leonard's smiling at me, too, I feel I have no alternative but to agree. I've been put on the spot and reduced to the role of biological mother and main carer. Thank goodness the cameras aren't here. My face would be a picture. 'I hope the house is OK now,' I say, amazed I've come out with anything remotely intelligible.

'Yes, still rather damp, but Anthony can fix that. That's what we pay for, isn't it, darling?' he says, turning to Helena and giving her a big kiss on the lips. I feel very much like the odd one out here, until I notice the other parents and teachers looking distinctly unimpressed by this public show of affection.

Mr Gates is first on the list, so I head over to his desk where he's waiting, smiling at me. We all sit down and he looks confused.

'I'm sorry, why are there three of you here?' asks Mr Gates.

'This is Helena, who wants to take a more active part in Freddie's upbringing, so I thought it would be a good idea for her to be here, too,' Leonard says.

'But Helena is here,' Mr Gates replies, looking confused. 'Freddie's mum is here.'

'No, my girlfriend Helena,' Leonard corrects.

'I don't know if you are confused, Mr Wallis, but I certainly am. I hope this doesn't sound rude, as it's not meant to be, but I feel that it's best if there is just yourself and Freddie's mother here for parents' evenings. I'm sure you'll be able to relate everything that goes on to, erm, your girlfriend, when you get home, but it will make things much simpler if there are only two of you on these occasions.' Mr Gates is courteous but firm. Leonard looks slightly perturbed and his charming exterior slips a bit; he's evidently annoyed about Mr Gates's decision. 'I would say the same thing to Freddie's mother if she turned up with her boyfriend,' Mr Gates adds, obviously thinking that if Leonard knows the rule applies both ways he might be appeased. He isn't.

Leonard and Helena remain firmly seated, so Mr Gates nods to Miss Compton-Batt, who is sitting with some other parents. She walks over and Mr Gates explains the situation.

'I'm sorry, Mr Wallis, you obviously don't understand. If we did this with every step-parent it would be horrendous, as there would simply be too many people to get through, so we have a rule: one or two parents only. And since Helena here is Freddie's mother, and has turned up to parents' evening on every other occasion, I am sure she and you will be more than able to support your son in his work.' Like Mr Gates, she talks in a firm but friendly voice.

Helena gets up and smiles. 'The last thing I want to do is create a scene if Freddie's mother feels insecure in any way,' she says graciously, before walking out of the hall.

'That is the one thing she did want to do,' I say under my breath. 'Create a scene.'

Jessica smiles at Leonard and me. 'The filming seems to be going very well around the school,' she says. 'I hope they're pleased with it.'

'I think they are,' I say. She returns to the parents she had been talking to, who have turned round to watch the small confrontation.

Mr Gates starts again as if nothing had happened. 'Hello there,' he says to us both, looking at Leonard and me in turn. 'Well, I wanted to say that Freddie is quite a star performer in the play, and he's made a lot of improvement this year. He really has talent. Real potential,' he says.

I don't answer, but look over at Leonard, who is smiling and nodding at Mr Gates's comments. I know he thinks very little of actors. I remember one dinner party before we were married, when he reduced an aspiring actress to tears by demeaning the profession and suggesting she was going into it because she didn't have any character of her own and had to hide behind someone else's. He warned her she'd find it difficult to form relationships because no one would ever believe they were seeing the real her, which was pretty rich coming from him. The poor girl was sobbing by the end of it. He apologised gracefully afterwards, but I had my doubts about him even then. He was capable of being a total fuckwit.

'Really, I think acting is a wonderful profession. I'm always so interest when Freddie tells me at the weekend about what happened in drama club, and how much he's enjoying being in the play. What is it again? *Lord of the Flies*?' Leonard asks.

I'm gobsmacked yet again, as I know this is total and utter bollocks, either that or Leonard really has changed, but I've misread him before and I've learned my lesson by now. I can't take him at face value any more. Freddie tells me his dad has absolutely no interest in what he's doing at school, and drama would be the very last thing Leonard would ask about. After he'd returned from his dad's one Sunday, Freddie told me Leonard had said not to concentrate on acting as it didn't earn money.

'No, *Lord of the Rings*,' corrects Mr Gates. 'We may tackle *Lord of the Flies* later. I'm very pleased you're supportive of Freddie as far as acting goes. It's very good for his confidence and self-esteem and sense of self-image. He's excelled in rehearsals – thank you for being so supportive, Helena,' he says, looking at me, 'and please pass on my thanks to Aled for filming the battle scenes. It was very kind of you to arrange it, and thank Will for allowing us the time. I know you're up against a tight schedule.'

'My pleasure,' I reply.

There's no response from Leonard, but he continues to smile and look supportive, even though that's the last thing he's been for the past seven years. And he hasn't mentioned yet that he is considering moving Freddie to Letchbury, so perhaps the Castleford magic is working on even him.

'Are you both going to come and watch the play?' Mr Gates asks.

I simply smile, as he knows I'm coming.

'Yes, I hope to.' Leonard nods enthusiastically. 'I've moved to the area now, so I should be able to attend a lot more events.'

'That's good,' replies Mr Gates. 'Freddie will benefit greatly from that.'

The bell goes and Leonard gets up and offers to shake hands with Mr Gates, who gives him a broad smile. Leonard certainly hasn't lost his ability to charm people.

After that we see Mr Harrison, Freddie's much-admired science teacher, and he tells us Freddie got 82 per cent in his most recent test and that he's extremely pleased with him. Then there's Mrs Lamp, his French teacher, who thinks Freddie might not like her, because although he did well in his test he doesn't concentrate in class. I don't tell her this, but Freddie doesn't like French, so his lack of concentration has nothing to do with her. I'll give Freddie the feedback, though, as he wouldn't want Mrs Lamp, who's a sweet fifty-something woman, to take it personally.

Mr Brighton, Freddie's maths teacher, says he needs to concentrate more in class and spend less time getting himself ready for work, as does his English teacher, Mr Connor, who says his comprehension is good but his spelling is atrocious. Mr Ware, who teaches art, tells us that Freddie has a natural talent and that we should nurture it, something Leonard nods at, claiming his side of the family is extremely artistic, although I'm not sure that's true.

We occasionally have gaps between appointments, when we stand in the middle of the assembly room while other parents chat to the teachers or stand and wait their turn. I feel I should say something to Leonard, since his attitude seems to have changed, and I make an effort to be pleasant.

'You've bought a lovely house, Leonard,' I say.

'Yes, it has space and, well, it will be good for Freddie to have space and a change. Neither the flat in London or your small cottage is totally suitable.'

I want to reply that my cottage isn't small, but Leonard says it in a way that would make contradiction seem wrong, as though I was overreacting, even though he's insulting my and Freddie's home. And besides, I don't agree with him.

Miss King is the last teacher we see, and as we sit down she leans over to me. 'I thought the PTA meeting went very well. I hope the crew were happy with what they filmed,' she says.

'I think they were,' I reply.

'Well, now to Freddie.' She looks down at her notes. 'Freddie is a very likeable little boy, who's very mature in some ways but not in others. When he's confident of his answer he speaks up loud and proud, but when he's not he tries to distract attention by playing the clown and asking lots of questions rather than admitting that he doesn't know the answer. This is quite typical of a boy his age, but he needs to be more confident and you may, as parents, think he's more confident than he is. Freddie's progress this year has been good, although I understand his spelling hasn't shown any improvement,' Miss King comments, looking down at the notes provided by Mr Connor.

'Yes, well, I do his spellings with him when I see him, and read to him regularly,' says Leonard.

Liar, liar, pants on fire, I want to say, and I know Freddie would say the same if he were here. I don't have a spy camera obviously, but Freddie tells me enough to put the pieces altogether. Leonard sometimes plays a little football with Freddie, but that's rare. Leonard only takes him to football practice at the weekend if he's in the mood and the wind is blowing in the right direction; it's a very irregular thing because Leonard is so unreliable, which is one of the reasons, if not *the* reason, why Tony won't make Freddie a full-time player next season.

'Then you must have had him last weekend,' Miss King says to me, knowing full well I didn't.

'Well no, Leonard had him last weekend,' I reply.

'Ah, so perhaps you didn't practise as much last weekend, Mr Wallis. If you could make this a priority I would be most grateful. After all, it's for the benefit of your son and I know you would always want to put him first,' she says, being firm but polite and turning to give me a brief, wry smile.

After her final comments, which are all positive, we get up and walk out. I nod to a few of the mums and dads, as does Leonard.

'Thank you for coming,' I say before he goes.

'My pleasure,' he replies, 'see you at ten tomorrow at Letchbury,' and heads towards his car as I make for mine. Nothing has changed.

The next morning I drop Freddie off at school. I'm due to go round to see Mum and Dad, which I will do after visiting Letchbury with Leonard, and I'm not scheduled to be with the film crew today. I also want to catch up with Victoria and Esther, to let them know about Leonard's lunch and what happened at the parents' evening and about today's visit. While driving to meet Leonard I talk on the hands-free to Esther.

'Hello stranger, how are things?'

I tell her about everything and there's a silence at the other end.

'Are you still there? Have I bored you?'

'No, no,' Esther replies. 'It's just one of the names you mentioned from the party. I know those people from somewhere. I know it's a small world, but perhaps Edward knows them or he's used their names in a book, God forbid, but I know that name, Alison Lovett.'

'Well, she's very morose and she doesn't run,' I say, remembering the limited conversation I had with her. 'Anyway, wish me luck with Leonard. I hope this is going to be as short and painless as possible, and hope all things are well with you. How's the Digby diary going?'

'That's it!'

'What's it?'

'That's how I know the name. It's one of the women he corresponds with by email. I'm sure it is.'

'Oh, there must be loads of Alison Lovetts about. I'm sure it's not the same one. It's a common enough name.'

'Well, yes, you may be right,' replies Esther, sounding a little disappointed, 'but wouldn't it be funny if it was the same woman?'

'I don't think Digby would go for someone like Alison, she's a bit mousy.'

'I should imagine he likes variety. Anyway, pity it isn't Leonard's girlfriend, then you could really put the cat among the pigeons for once.'

'I wouldn't do that, Esther, it would just make matters worse and I'm still trying to get on with Leonard, for Freddie's sake.'

'Well good luck, girl, and I'll let you know if I find

out more about this Lovett woman. From the sound of the emails, she certainly "loves it" with Digby.'

'Funny ha ha,' I say, 'now I've got to go.'

I call Victoria. As usual she shouts down the phone at me, with uproar in the background.

'Hello Helena, I meant to call you but I've been up to my ears in this swinging story. I've actually got one of the women who's taking part to talk, and I'm interviewing her today,' she says. I can hear what is presumably Dena Benson booming at some assistant to get her arse in gear. She reminds me of a female version of Elliott Sterling.

'Can you hold just a minute,' Victoria says, then I hear her shout out.

'Will you shut the fuck up Benson, I'm on the phone and I can't hear myself fucking think!' This is immediately followed by silence.

I'm stunned and rather proud of my friend. 'Did I hear right? Did you just tell the editor to shut the fuck up?' I ask.

'I did and she did,' says Victoria. 'I'll say you're the girl I'm meeting for the interview if that's all right, but I did.'

'Did it feel good?'

'It felt amazing! Mind you, I may be out of a job, but it was worth it just to see her face. I don't think anyone has spoken to her like that before. Anyway, she says I deliver the goods and she's very happy with how I've been working – she said that only yesterday, so I feel I've got some leverage.'

'You may have just used it up – no one is indispensable.'

'Well, I'll let you know if I'm still in a job after you come out of your tour of Letchbury. Good luck, and don't give way on anything. Stay cool and calm and collected.'

'Just like you did,' I reply, laughing.

'No, not like I just did. But you've got to handle this one differently. Benson is an overt bully; she's loud and aggressive and you can see and hear her coming a mile off. I do my job well and everyone knows what Benson is like to work with. Leonard is different, and don't you forget it.'

Chapter Twenty

Letchbury School wouldn't look out of place in a Jane Austen novel, albeit the residence of the sinister baddie rather than the wondrous good guy. The three-storey pristine white building with its large symmetrical windows looks down over acres of land, perfectly manicured as though no one has set foot on the grass, let alone boys between the ages of eight and eighteen. I know very little about the school, but managed to look at their website. According to league tables it does well academically and has excellent facilities, including a heated indoor swimming pool, fully equipped gym, sports hall, drama studio and music room. The headmaster is a Mr Tomas Roth, who is of German origin, and has been at the school for over ten years. The website has lots of photographs of happy, studious boys in their classrooms, in the science lab, out playing rugby on their own rugby pitch. It all looks very polished and immaculate, and, I sense instinctively, cold.

I drive up the long approach to the main building, oak trees on either side, positioned an exact distance apart, almost like one of those Tuscan or Provençal roads with plane trees on either side. Perhaps, if those in charge take such care with their first impressions, they will take as much care with their boys.

I can see Leonard's car is already there, and as I get out of mine I realise that Helena could also be there, and I've got to prepare my response accordingly when I see him. I'm starting to feel every meeting with this man is like a military operation where I'm going under-cover, second-guessing his every possible move, although I'm sure sometimes even he can't be bothered to trip me up. He must get bored of it eventually. I certainly am.

I walk towards the building, trying to take in the atmosphere, considering the possibility that Freddie could be happy here. I want to go in with an open mind, but there's a voice inside me screaming 'this place is all style, no substance, all manufactured, no soul'. I could be wrong, though.

I walk through the main doors into the entrance hall. A couple are already sitting waiting on one of the sofas, as is Leonard. His back is towards me.

'Hello,' I say, smiling at the other couple, who stand up and shake my hand, as does Leonard (although he doesn't shake my hand). Leonard is dressed as though he's just come from a City meeting. I presume after this he'll be on his way to one. No sign of Helena, thank God.

'I'm George Davis and this is my wife Mary Ann,' the man says. He looks in his mid forties, and is wearing what looks like a cashmere jumper, smart chinos and Church's shoes, which I recognise because Leonard used to wear them all the time. The woman shakes my hand warmly. She has a nice open smile and a faint twang of American in her voice when she says hello, but she could be Canadian.

'Hello, I'm Helena Treadwell, I'm here with Leonard,' I say, looking at him, 'but we're not married.'

I say that realising it may sound as though we have an illegitimate child and we are still together, but I don't wish to explain further and say we are divorced. And as Leonard hasn't said anything to correct me, I don't correct myself. It doesn't matter anyway, so I let it pass.

'Hello everyone, I'm Mr Roth,' says a tall slim man in his late fifties, walking up to us. He looks elegant and angular and reminds me a bit of Charles Rushbrook in his manner – friendly but missing nothing, and I suspect his time is just as expensive. 'Now let me show you round the school, and please don't hesitate to ask any questions you may have,' he smiles.

I suddenly have this overwhelming and mischievous urge to misbehave, like some stroppy adolescent who is being made to do something she doesn't want to. Boarding school is so wrong for Freddie. Perhaps I should have turned up today in a clown suit or ask if the rumours about drugs at the school are true. I'm sure Mr. Roth wouldn't like any pupil here with such rude parents. But it might all backfire and convince Leonard – and Mr Roth for that matter – that I'm an unsuitable mother and that boarding school is undoubtedly the best place for our son. So I grit my teeth, hold my tongue and smile back. We follow him through the narrow corridors lined with the photographs of past headmasters, all looking handsome and confident, half smiling like the Mona Lisa, but less enigmatically. I'm aware the Davis couple are walking holding hands, while the body language between Leonard and me couldn't be more distant.

'This is the science lab,' says Mr Roth, knocking and opening the door to a large room where there are about twenty boys, several peering at test tubes, some of which have steam emanating from them. The teacher, in a white coat, looks up at us and smiles nervously, like a Labrador who wants to be patted but is not quite sure if he's been good enough. The children all stand to attention so dramatically, I half expect them to salute.

'Good morning Mr Roth,' they say in broken-voiced unison.

'Good morning, boys. You may sit,' Mr Roth replies, smiling and waving his hand regally.

'And what are you doing today, Mr Winston?' Mr Roth asks, looking over at the Labrador.

'We are learning about the noble gases and the halogens and lanthanides and actinides,' he tells us, losing me on 'noble'.

'And can anyone explain what a noble gas is?' Mr Roth looks over at the boys, and at one in particular, who seems thoroughly unimpressed with both the lesson and the intrusion.

'You boy, you. What's your name?'

'Featherstone, John,' he replies.

'Featherstone, what is a noble gas?'

'A very honourable one,' he replies.

I laugh out loud, but none of the other adults think it's clever, and Mr Roth tells Featherstone John that he would like to see him at lunchtime.

We then proceed on to the art studio, which is full of ten-year-olds creating Gaudí-inspired tiles. It's the sort of thing Mr Ware would do at Castleford, and although I'm impressed I don't think the work is any better than Freddie's artistic efforts. Then come the metalwork and woodwork studios, followed by the maths block (where all heads are down) and English block, where we disturb one boy mid flow reciting Chaucer. We're whisked past history, geography, the language lab where German, French, Spanish, Portuguese and Mandarin are taught from the age of eight. Then we're shown the school library, which is kept stocked with up-to-date books by a very proactive PTA, Mr Roth explains. I don't ask why they're not more visible as supporters at away matches. I suppose by sponsoring the library, they make presence felt in other ways.

'We are extending our current library facilities with a kind donation by the Flindells, parents of one of our boys,' says Mr Roth as we pass by. I expect that means Anthony Flindell's company is building it for them.

We then are shown through the drama studio where

they're doing *Hamlet*, which seems an unimaginative choice, remote from boys this age. Mr Gates's *Lord of the Rings* is much more contemporary and funky, but I don't say anything. The music studio is empty, all the many instruments sitting forlorn, and then we go out side to a gym area, where boys who look about fifteen are being put through their paces in military fashion on a sort of army assault course. The sports master is shouting at them in what sounds a very brutal way, but perhaps that's just for our benefit, to show the boys are disciplined.

'We believe in strong discipline at Letchbury,' Mr Roth says. 'We believe children, and boys especially, need to be shown how to succeed. This success comes through perseverance and attaining high standards which they will be able to live by after they leave the school. Boys need discipline and we provide it. We seek to make them feel they should strive for excellence in life, in all things.'

'Do you think that is healthy?' I ask. 'After all, some boys aren't naturally good at some things and if you make them feel like failures even before they've left school, they're going to feel like failures all their lives. Surely it's best to encourage and nurture them, identify their strengths and focus on those, rather than suggest they can be excellent in all areas of life, which is realistically impossible.'

'Our records speak for themselves,' replies Mr Roth, unfazed by my questioning, although I can feel the hairs on the back of my neck prickle as Leonard stands behind me. 'By pushing the boys this hard, or encouraging if you want to use that more politically correct term, we have found that if you ask them to reach for the sun they may not get there, but they will get further than if you ask them to do their best.'

'So you tried the other way, telling them to do their best, before you tried this way?' I want to know how Mr Roth researched what brings out the best in boys. I know Dad would have loved to be in on this conversation. I would have liked to have heard his views.

'Well, not exactly, but we have been highly successful using this method to date. Our academic achievements are excellent and our sporting achievements are excellent.'

'Right. What happens if any boy doesn't come up to scratch?' I ask.

'Well, with those boys,' replies Mr Roth quickly, 'we send a letter to the parents if they are not doing as well as their peers. Sometimes extra tuition is needed. If then there is still no improvement we feel it is only right to ask the parents to send their child elsewhere, where they can get the special attention they need. We feel that if the child stays in the class, it will have an impact on the other children and distract them from learning as they should.'

It would also have an impact on your academic league tables, I think to myself.

'And are the boys happy? Do you feel they miss their parents?' I enquire, aware I'm the only one who seems to be asking any questions at all.

'We have strong pastoral care at the school,' replies Mr Roth. 'We make sure that each boy feels as though we are his family, not just his school.'

I nod, not utterly convinced Freddie would want to be part of Mr Roth's family, and totally convinced that I would not. We walk past a few more classrooms and peer in. Everything is immaculate, clean and smells of nothing. Everywhere looks newly painted, as though the place is lived in by nuns, not by boys who, if they're anything like Freddie, are noisy, smelly, and at any opportunity get as muddy and dirty as possible. Everything is neat, ordered, spotless, pristine. It's fit for purpose but doesn't feel lived in, a bit like Leonard's new home. We go to the blocks where the boys sleep and as I go into the two- or three-bedded rooms, despite the posters on the walls, the awards and cups on the windowsills, the overwhelming impression is one of loneliness.

I know loneliness. I grew up with it when my father was away and my mother looked after me and Grandad, resenting it because she was bright and wanted to do her own thing. She was born before her time. She would have thrived in a place like this, where you were told to reach for the sun. She was a romantic, but domestic drudgery made her a pragmatist. The resentment she felt positively bounced off the walls of our home some days. I couldn't wait to leave when I was old enough.

I don't want this for Freddie. I don't want him to have the same sense of abandonment and loneliness that I felt playing by myself in my room for hours on end, not wanting to be any trouble, being a good girl at school, a people-pleaser. I don't feel the boys are allowed to grow here, and their spirit is allowed to soar, despite Mr Roth's comment about reaching for the sun. I think he's talking about pushing the boys in a direction the staff want them to go, not the direction the boys themselves want to go, intimidating them into harder and faster efforts. Competition is good, I know that, and I see the healthy side of it when Freddie is taught by Tony at football and at his karate class. I see the discipline there, but it doesn't crush his spirit. This place, this building, these teachers I've seen and even the boys I've seen – with the notable exception of Featherstone John – lack spirit, or perhaps they've just had it crushed out of them.

This is no Hogwarts. I don't want Freddie to go here and I must not show this, because if I do, Leonard will fight as hard to get him in as I will to keep him out. I've got to be polite, and, as Will suggests, try to seem indifferent to something that is so close to my heart. If I show I don't care, neither will Leonard. If he feels this won't hurt me, he won't bother to pursue it. So I mustn't show my feelings one way or another, and just hope that the fees will be high enough to make him flinch, and the cost of hitting out at me for one last time will be unaffordable.

At the end of the tour we go to Mr Roth's office, past a secretary who looks in her mid thirties and flirts with Mr Davis and Leonard. I find it quite funny, but Mary

Ann gets visibly annoyed. We sit and take tea and biscuits, and Mr Roth talks us through the curriculum and the age groups and then the fees and fee structure and when payment is due. It amuses me that despite the amazing sports facilities they have, the juniors still don't manage to do as well at football as Castleford, which proves it's more to do with the teachers than the facilities. I don't say this. When I leave I thank Mr Roth and say goodbye to the Davises, who look happy with what they've seen, and I thank Leonard for asking me to join him.

'It was good to look around,' I say.

He looks bewildered by my response, but I remain impassive.

'I've got to go and see Dad now,' I explain, 'so I must dash, but I'll send him your good wishes. He's still poorly, as you may know.'

'Yes, Freddie did tell me,' he replies.

I turn without saying any more and walk back to my car, keeping my face emotionless because I'm aware he's looking at me, standing and watching until I drive away.

Chapter Twenty-one

'How's Dad?'

I'm on the doorstep with a large bunch of flowers, yellow roses, some oversized daisy-like flowers, and white lilies. I hand-picked them from the florist on the way from Letchbury. I've been so busy with the filming that I feel I've been neglecting Dad, so I'm over-whelmed with guilt when my mother opens the door and looks as though she's come face to face with a ghost from the past.

'Hello Helena,' she says. 'Dad is not good today. You know how he gets sometimes, not himself. I'm sure if you sat and talked to him it would do him the world of good.'

I walk in and give mum a hug. 'And how are you?' I ask, feeling I should have brought two bouquets, but perhaps this one is large enough for them both.

'Oh you know, mustn't grumble.' This always makes me smile because she always does, but that's what keeps her going, and when Dad is not himself, as she puts it, her life is very difficult.

I walk into the room knowing what to expect. A man who is nothing more than a shadow, an outline of what he once was, sits there and stares into nothing, not even as though he's searching for something, or waiting. He's just existing. His body is there, but his mind has disappeared. I know it will reappear, and perhaps hearing my voice will help him to come back. These days when he is not himself last longer and grow more frequent, but I know Mum wants to keep him at home, though it gets more difficult for her emotionally and physically to cope. Thank goodness Dad has never become aggressive and has always been able to walk, albeit slowly, even on his bad days. I go over to him and show him the flowers. Mum gets a vase and she and I arrange them.

'We need another vase,' she says, as I fill one and put it by his chair – not too close as he might tip it over by accident.

As Mum leaves I hold Dad's hand. It's cold, but he has such strong hands. I remember when Freddie was born his hands were miniature versions of Dad's, with their long fingers, wide palms. I kneel by Dad's feet, stroking his hand and kissing it gently.

'So Mum says you've had a difficult day today, Dad. Well, can I tell you what I did today?' I say, looking at him and smiling. I know he won't respond in any way, but I keep on talking. I tell him about the visit to Letchbury and about how the filming is going, and about the Flindells' lunch party and how the mediation went. Mum comes back into the room and sits and listens to everything I say without interrupting. I'm sure she's bursting with questions and opinions, but she looks tired today, almost as though she's been wrung out. I tell Dad about the parent's evening and how Freddie is doing really well at football, and how he'll be round to visit him later today after school and the clubs.

'I remember how you would take me into school when it was my school holidays but not yours, and I would sit in your office and your secretary would look after me when you weren't there. I remember being so nervous, Dad, about being the only girl in the school. And how when the boys came in, those who were to be praised or punished, I would sit and watch you. You were a very good teacher, so much better than those I saw today at Letchbury. You cared about the boys, just as the teachers do at Castleford today. You cared about them. And they knew it. Children are like animals, Dad, aren't they? They know if someone's a good egg or a bad one and they knew you were a good egg, even though you were the one who had to cane them when they were naughty. I remember the boys always used to ask if you caned me at home. You never did, of course. You never really needed to, did you?'

'You weren't any trouble, were you, Helena, that's why,' Mum interrupts. 'You were a good girl. Mind you, it all went wrong when you got older,' she laughs.

I talk about Eliana and how I first met her, and all the adventures we used to get up to in Italy. There's no response in his eyes, or movement, but I talk anyway. I tell him about seeing Helena in the car, which my mum laughs at and says she would have shouted yoo hoo, which I know would have freaked the woman out even more. I think waving at her was bad enough. And then I start talking about the films I've seen with Esther and Victoria, telling him about *Mamma Mia!*, and then all the others I loved watching with him. I ask him if he remembers *Cinema Paradiso*, and that last scene which always has me in floods of tears, about unrequited love, and *The Ghost and Mrs Muir*, which even as a little girl I knew was about loneliness. And then I talk to him about watching him playing tennis and how he always told me to be a fighter all my life, and to fight for what I believed in, and to never give in. And I tell him that I won't. I remember him telling me the only thing I should ever be afraid of is fear itself, and that I shouldn't fear anyone, least of all Leonard.

After I don't know how long of just being there with him, talking to him, talking to my mum and listening to her describing how tough it is to look after Dad, although she knows it's best for him, I hug him. He doesn't respond, but I look in his eyes and tell him I love him and miss him, just like I missed him when I was a little girl.

I give Mum a hug and tell that I love her, and ironically she doesn't respond either. I say I'll be back tomorrow. I can see she's not in the mood to talk more, so I don't stay. I get the feeling she wants me out of the way so she can get on with things, so I go.

The next time I see Leonard it's in Miss King's

classroom at a parents' briefing meeting before Freddie's class go on their Flatford Mill field trip. At four o'clock prompt, Freddie's classroom is filled with parents. Leonard has turned up with Helena again, this time resplendent in pink. The crew are there to film a few shots, as they will also be going on the field trip.

Some of the parents have sent their nannies with A5 lined pads and pens at the ready, but Miss King has already typed out and photocopied medical question-naires, requests for next of kin, special dietary needs, and location addresses, phone numbers and the details of where the boys will be each day, and what they'll be doing. She has placed these on each boy's desk where his parents or nanny are now sitting, looking like overgrown schoolchildren.

'This may be the first time your child has been away for any length of time without you, so it's as important an event for you as it is for them, and I'd like to talk through what they'll be doing at Flatford, as well as giving you contact details, just in case you're worried,' she says, looking round at the expectant faces.

For the next ten minutes she goes through the sheets she's just given out, which are self-explanatory, but perhaps she's used to going through things in such detail with the boys.

'Do you have any questions?' she asks after each section.

Sonya Cardigan puts up her hand. 'Otto has a birth-day while he's away, so can I send a birthday cake to you?' she says.

'Yes, that will be fine. You'll have the address, or you can give the cake to me or Mr Black and we'll take care of it while we're there,' Miss King replies. 'They will have to make their own beds in the mornings and sandwiches at lunchtime, so it's a good idea for them to practise now,' she continues, looking round at the parents, some of whom are laughing.

'Harry wouldn't know where to begin with either of those,' says Penny, and the others nod.

'Well, they can start now, and it's a good way for them to begin to be independent,' Miss King says.

At the end of the meeting Barbara Jacobs puts her hand up and offers her son David's old PE pants and vests, as he's already grown out of them. There are three potential takers, including Helena, which I find quite surprising – and annoying, because clothing Freddie is my responsibility – but apart from that there seem to be no other questions.

As soon as the last of the parents has left I head for the assembly hall, the film crew trailing after me.

For the next few days I don't see anything of Leonard and Helena, but I half expect to find them – or Christine, Kenneth, Henry or Lorraine – driving past, jogging along the beach, or even visiting the post office or grocery store, but they all seem to have vanished as if they were part of a bad dream. By the time of the school play I've almost forgotten that Leonard has moved to the area.

The three performances of *Lord of the Rings* go well,

with surprisingly few hitches. Leonard is not in the audience on any night. Thanks to the TV crew being in town, the sound system and film footage are superb, and the actors all remember their lines. Even poor Hugo says his 'r's correctly most of the time. The set design is colourful, as Mr Wolf's Year Sixes have worked really hard on forest and battlement backdrops. The spider is the star of the show, and thanks to the brilliant make-up artist, the Orcs are terrifying, especially Daniel Monty from Year Five, who makes Sonya Cardigan develop hiccups. The knights all look noble, if not very well co-ordinated with their swordplay, despite Mr Beard's best efforts to teach them how to parry and thrust. The Black Riders, who have non-speaking parts, are all suitably black and silent, and Freddie's performance is faultless. As I clap from the wings on the last night, I look at my son with such pride, and find myself wondering what on earth could be more important to Leonard than watching his son perform.

The sports day a few days later also goes brilliantly, mainly because the sun shines and the boys are happy their exams are over, so they all behave really well and compete in all the events with gusto. Freddie comes second in the javelin and 400 metres race, and afterwards there is a picnic. Leonard and Helena are there, with a large entourage of friends, including Christine, Kenneth, Lorraine and Henry, who all give me a smile and a nod, which is unexpected but welcome. None of them come over to talk, though, and I must admit I don't make much effort either, though I really must.

Things have obviously changed, and all my worries about Leonard coming to the area seem completely unfounded.

The four days at Flatford Mill are a great success, and when Freddie returns he tells me how they painted and drew, and made their own sandwiches and beds – very badly, it has to be said. By the sound of things they talked earnestly together about life and love and what they were going to do when they grow up, as well as about their parents, how much they earn and how important they are.

'Jack and I caught a vole in our mammal trap. Harry cried because he thought it was cruel and David caught a field mouse. My team won joint first with Harry's team in the waterproof tent competition, while David's team's tent leaked rather badly. Jack is the worst snorer, Harry grinds his teeth in his sleep and I am the latest riser,' Freddie says, grinning at me.

Everything seems to be going smoothly. I've seen Leonard and Helena about the town and have heard that they've befriended some of the locals. Herbie the postman says what a nice dad Freddie has, and Mr Farnsworth says they're some of his best customers. But most importantly, Freddie seems happy that his dad is close by. I'm sure things will work out fine. I've been in touch with Charles Rushbrook, and apparently it's only a matter of weeks before I get the money that will enable me to sever all financial ties with Leonard, so we can really start afresh.

The staff at Castleford are putting on a performance

of *'Allo, 'Allo* for one night only, and I hear that Miss King is to appear as Helga, and Mr Pearman, the rather stern but handsome sports master, will be Herr Flick. I'm taking Esther to see the teachers do their best to outperform their pupils.

As we walk into the assembly hall, I see Aled buzzing around with his camera while Will gives directions. Leonard is sitting with Kenneth and Christine, and as I start to walk towards our seats, Helena walks up to us. I smile at her, since relations between us have been nothing but cordial in the last few weeks.

She starts to speak, but it's almost in a whisper, so I crane my neck to hear to what she's saying.

'How dare you show your face here, Helena Treadwell?'

Or that's what I think she says.

'Sorry?' I say, not quite sure I heard right the first time.

'How dare you tell people in town,' she keeps her voice to a barely audible whisper and glowers at Esther, 'about Leonard? How dare you suggest Leonard is anything other than perfect, you stupid bitch?' She smiles as she says all this, positively hissing the last few syllables, but somehow the last word, which I suppose is meant to intimidate me, shocks me for all the wrong reasons. I feel like Minnie Mouse has just sworn at me. Leonard perfect? I don't know whether to feel sorry for her or laugh at her. Leonard anything but perfect indeed.

My first reaction is to apologise, carefully. I'm wrong to have confided in Esther and Victoria as much as I did and I naively assumed they would keep anything I said in confidence. But perhaps word had leaked around town that Leonard was a snake, so it's my fault as well.

'Leonard is furious. I suggest you keep as far away from him as possible tonight,' she snarls.

'If Leonard wants to confront me about anything,' I retort, 'I expect him to do it in person. I didn't expect him to send some nobody to do his talking for him.'

Helena looks briefly at Esther, and Esther gives her a withering stare. I notice a few of the other mums staring at us, more intrigued than concerned. I can see Becca and the film crew interviewing Mr Gates, so at least we're not on camera, but I can't help thinking this stand-off would have made brilliant TV. There could even be theme music from a spaghetti Western to accompany the action. Who'll have first strike? Will it be Helena or Helena? Or will Esther get in the way? I want to giggle, but instinct tells me this is the wrong thing to do, so I try to think of something inane or depressing, like Posh Spice or cellulite.

We stand like this for a few more seconds, then suddenly, as if the bell has gone to signify the end of round one, Helena turns on her heel and goes back to her seat beside Leonard.

'Shall we go?' I ask Esther, who watches Helena closely as she chats to Leonard, probably telling him how she's managed to shame us into not staying for the play.

'No we bloody well won't,' Esther replies. 'I've paid my money and so have you. You want to see the teachers perform as much as I do. Freddie is expecting us to come back with some great stories about the play, and Edward is happy babysitting him. I'm staying and so, my dear, are you,' she says, pulling me towards our seats as I spy from the corner of my eye Helena and Leonard looking at us, open-mouthed at our audacity.

As we take our seats, Becca and the crew get into position, blissfully unaware of the drama that would have made much better viewing than anything we are about to see.

As the lights go down and the curtain rises, I hear Becca say, 'Action,' and feel my heart beating hard and fast as Esther's hand clasps mine. A few minutes into the performance she leans over and whispers, 'Exciting, eh?'

'The staff's performance or Helena's?' I ask.

'Life,' she grins at me. 'Your life.'

When we arrive back home Edward is fast asleep. The two girls are having a sleepover at their friends, so he doesn't have to look after them as well.

'He must have dropped off after reading Freddie several hundred bedtime stories,' says Esther, smiling at her husband. We walk quietly into the kitchen and I pour us a glass of wine each.

'Well that was quite an evening,' I say, heading upstairs to check on Freddie and give him a kiss on the cheek. He's sleeping contentedly and looks as though he's dreaming about all things good as he cuddles a teddy, which sadly he won't do for much longer now that he's nine.

I return to find Esther has turned on the TV and is watching *Dangerous Liaisons*. It's the bit where John Malkovich tells Michelle Pfeiffer that his cruel behaviour towards her is beyond his control.

'I feel a bit like that at the moment,' I say, taking a sip of wine.

'Like what?' asks Esther, still watching the screen and not looking at me.

'That everything is out of control. I thought I had it all sorted: my home, my work, even that my relationship with Leonard would get better, and now everything seems to be slipping away again,' I say. 'Even Freddie's education is no longer guaranteed. Is it worth it? Is all this hassle worth it? And now I've not only got Leonard on my back, it seems his girlfriend is a complete psycho too. And it's out of my control.'

'Nonsense,' replies Esther, looking at me now. 'You are just as in control as you've always been. You took control when you left Leonard and made a new life for yourself. You lost your old job and found a new and better one. This is just another hurdle. You are going to survive this. What doesn't kill you makes you stronger, and having Leonard here will make you stronger, I promise. It will strengthen your resolve; you'll make it work with him, I know you will. This is a small hiccup, nothing more,' she says, turning back to the screen. 'And as for Valmont, the character played by John Malkovich in this film not being in control, that's rubbish. He's in complete control and so is old Michelle there, they just choose not to use it.

Ultimately it's all in the mind. These power games, control games, are all mind games and nothing more. Bullies back down if you stand up to them.'

'I just wish Leonard hadn't moved into town. Everything bad seems to stem from that,' I say, 'but I know what you mean about control. I've never wanted to control someone else. Yes, I tell Freddie what to do and discipline him, but that's different. I've tried to compromise in life without compromising myself, but that didn't work with Leonard.'

'There are thousands, tens of thousands of women who could say the same. Like many women you think you and your situation are unique. You go around in isolation not talking to anyone about issues, because you feel you have to deal with them yourself. And when you start to talk you realise others are having exactly the same problems with exactly the same type of person Leonard is, and my dad is, and my boss is, even. There are so many women like you and Helena, and thousands of men like Leonard for that matter.'

'Good God, I hope not.'

'Well, I'd better get my sleeping beauty to bed,' Esther says, finishing her wine and looking at her watch, realising how late it is now.

The phone rings.

'Who could be calling at this time?' I say, getting up and reaching for it. 'Hello?'

'Hello, is that Helena Treadwell?' asks a voice I don't recognise.

'Yes,' I reply, 'who's this?'

'This is Dr Hastings from Letchbury Hospital. I'm afraid your father has been taken ill and we suggest you come as soon as possible.'

'Do you mean now or in the morning?' I ask.

'I suggest now, Ms Treadwell, it's a matter of urgency.'

I put the phone down as the credits of the film start rolling.

'I hate it when the good guy dies,' Esther says, getting up from her chair. 'Don't you?'

Chapter Twenty-two

'I'm coming with you,' says Esther, getting her bag. She writes a note for Edward.

We head out into the clear night, and there's a full moon and stars so bright it looks like dusk, although it must be nearer midnight. Esther turns on the radio and it's Frank Sinatra.

'Dad likes Sinatra,' I say. 'Perhaps I can get him some to listen to in hospital. I remember as a child dancing to Frank Sinatra for Mum and Dad in our living room, although Andy Williams and Barbra Streisand had more beat. On one occasion I even did a striptease for them, not knowing what it meant and thinking myself terribly clever.' I laugh, and immediately feel guilty.

'You were lucky. I had Dusty Springfield and Johnny Mathis. Can you imagine dancing or doing a striptease to Johnny Mathis?' Esther laughs and holds my hand, understanding that I'm talking rubbish to distract myself from the worry, the fear that I won't get to the hospital in time.

'I was only nine at the time, what did I know?' I say. 'No wonder my mother never gave me any lectures on sex. She was probably worried it would awaken a desire to experiment as much as possible, and as a result I went through my teenage years terrified of boys, thinking they were going to do horrid things to me and not realising the least of these would be sexual.'

'I think my first orgasm was in the Dordogne with a boy called Duncan, who spent an inordinate amount of time under the duvet with me. I was thinking of what we were going to do the next day but then, pow! I felt myself float off the bed. I immediately leapt up and ran around the room yelling, "That was amazing," at the top of my voice. It's the only time I've ever done that, mind,' Esther says, smiling at me. 'But Duncan was pretty chuffed with himself, I can tell you, and so was I actually.'

I realise Esther's trying to stop me thinking about my dad, but suddenly I feel an overwhelming urge to drive faster and I'm already going as fast as I can without being dangerous. The country around Castleford is beautiful, and each curve of the road reveals a stunning vista over countryside or sea, but everything is in shades of grey as the full moon casts a haunting light and shadows, and the trees wave us on faster and further.

'We should reach the main road soon,' I say, reassuring myself that we'll make it. 'It's easy to park at the hospital. I know because I took Freddie there last year when he broke his arm while running for his tennis lesson.'

'Oh yes, wasn't that when he told everyone at school he'd fallen off a horse?' Esther replies.

'Yes. Somehow running to a tennis lesson didn't sound as courageous.'

I turn on to the main road and put my foot on the accelerator, my little car stepping up a gear. 'My dad gave me my first driving lesson, you know. I remember him practising emergency stops with me later, and I almost crashed the car in the process,' I babble.

Esther squeezes my hand again. 'It will be fine. It's just a scare, darling,' she says. 'You can talk about all this to your dad when you see him.'

'I can't remember the last thing I said to him. I think it was about Freddie or Leonard or something. Oh yes, it was about my TV job, so that was OK. He wasn't himself the last time I saw him but I like to think he took some of it in, you know, he actually heard me tell him I love him.' I feel tears trickling down my face now. 'I hope he's OK. I hope he's OK,' I keep repeating.

'He will be,' says Esther. 'They've called you at this hour because they're worried, but if it was really serious they would have said on the phone.'

'The time before last, he was happy when I last saw him, and aware,' I say.

'And he will be again,' Esther reassures me.

The hospital is a large single-storey building set back off the main road in Letchbury, and lit up like a beacon in the surrounding dark residential area. I look at my watch. It's one in the morning. Esther and I must have been talking at home for longer than I realised. I find a parking space easily, although the car park seems quite full for the time of night, and we quickly make our way inside. I push through the swing doors of Accident and Emergency, nearly sending Esther flying as the doors swing back into her.

'So sorry, darling,' I say, looking round and realising what I've done.

'Don't mind me.' She smiles. 'You just get to your dad.'

Inside the reception area, the fluorescent lights flicker so it's like some sort of warped attempt at disco, and there are two men, a woman and a little boy looking very sorry for themselves in the waiting area, although I can't see any blood or tears. A nurse in her twenties with tied-back dark hair stands behind the desk.

'Hello, I'm looking for Dr Hastings. He phoned to say my father has just been rushed in,' I say, feeling slightly nauseous.

She smiles at me, looks through her directory and makes a call.

'Dr Hastings? . . . Yes . . . I have someone here for you. A Miss . . .' She looks up at me questioningly.

'Helena Treadwell. I'm the daughter of Norman Treadwell.'

'Helena Treadwell, daughter of Norman Treadwell,' she repeats down the line.

'Right,' she says and puts down the phone, looking back up at me. 'Dr Hastings will be down to see you in a few moments,' she says. 'If you would like to wait here,' she points to the seats next to the people waiting, 'the doctor won't be long.'

I don't want to sit down and neither does Esther, so we just stand there.

'The play was good, wasn't it?' she says, trying to make small talk.

'Yes, I'll never think of Mr Pearman in the same way,' I reply, but I don't want to talk. I just want to see my dad.

'Hello, Miss Treadwell,' a man says, coming towards us, 'I'm Dr Hastings, if you would like to follow me, please.' He smiles at me and Esther as he turns, and we follow him at a quick, steady pace out of the reception area, through two more swing doors – this time I'm careful not to let them swing back into Esther's face – and turn a corner to the right and then left. I expect to see Dad sitting up in bed grinning at me, but instead the doctor leads me into a small office and closes the door behind us.

'Are you a relation?' he asks Esther as I sit down.

'No, I'm Helena's best friend,' she says. The doctor turns to me.

'I'm afraid . . .'

I don't hear the rest of the sentence. After 'afraid' I know what he's going to say. I pick up the occasional word as he talks: 'Heart attack, very sudden, mother arrived but wasn't there when he actually stopped breathing.'

'Can I see him?' I ask, as though he's still alive and I

want to have a quiet chat, just like I used to in their cottage.

'Yes.' He nods. 'Your mother is in the relatives' room. She's been waiting for you so that you could see him together.'

'Do you want me to come with you?' Esther asks.

'I'll be fine,' I say. 'Just wait here. I want to see Mum alone and we'll go and see Dad together. Thank you for being here.' I walk over to her and give her a hug. I wouldn't have wanted anyone else with me at this moment.

The doctor leads me to another room, where a nurse sits with her arm around my mother. Mum looks up, her eyes red and sore with tears, and she looks very tired, as if she hasn't slept in weeks. But she still manages to smile at me.

'Oh, Helena,' she says, getting up and rushing to give me a hug. 'We weren't here when he died,' she gulps, sobbing on my shoulder, which immediately starts me off. It's like a huge release of emotion. I'm shocked because my mother never cries, or rather, I've never seen her cry.

She pulls me back and looks me in the eyes. 'Always live your life to the full,' she says.

'I have always tried to,' I say, thinking perhaps she wishes someone had told her that when she was younger.

'Good,' she says and sniffs. 'Shall we go and see Dad?'

The doctor leads us into a room where a curtain is

pulled around a bed. He draws back the curtain and Dad is lying there, looking calm and peaceful. There are two chairs by the bed and Mum and I sit down beside him.

'He looks at peace, doesn't he?' Mum says, echoing my thoughts.

'Yes, he does,' I say, 'and I feel he's here, looking down on us, smiling and telling us not to worry.'

'He's telling us he wants his ashes scattered around our cherry tree, that's what he's saying.' She looks at me and smiles. Dad's death feels like a release, not only for him but for Mum as well. The longer we're there with him, the calmer I feel. It's as if his pain has lifted and the burden of looking after him has gone.

'Esther and I will take you home,' I say to Mum, 'and don't you worry yourself about the funeral. I'll make all the arrangements. Are you OK with that?' I half expect her to say I'll only make a mess of it, but to my surprise she agrees.

'Thank you,' she says. 'Thank you.'

I decide to let Mum sleep in my bed, so she's not alone in her cottage. I'll sleep in the guest bedroom. Three generations of Treadwells under one roof. When we get back Esther wakes Edward, who's snoring rather loudly on the sofa. I tell him the news.

'I guessed as much when I read Esther's note. I'm so sorry.'

'Thank you, Edward, and thank you for looking after Freddie.'

'My pleasure, no worries. I'll get Esther off home now, and if you want anything in the morning, you just call, OK?' he says.

With Mum settled in bed, I check on Freddie, who's still sleeping peacefully. I decide Mum and I will tell him the news in the morning: Grandad died in his sleep and is now with the angels, and he asked for his ashes to be scattered round the cherry tree. I think he'll like the idea of being able to talk to his grandad's spirit still, even if he can't see him, as if Grandad's a guardian angel watching over him.

As I turn the last of the lights out downstairs, I stand in the hallway for a brief second in the dark and listen to the silent house and my breathing. I feel strangely in control of my life. My mother and my son are both in my home, under my care. I feel I'm the mistress of the situation at the moment, even as far as Leonard is concerned. I didn't let Helena's outburst at the play faze me, admittedly because Esther was there for moral support, but I finally feel I can make the situation work. And I know that Dad, if he could see me now, would approve.

It's eight o'clock in the morning and I haven't slept at all. Instead, for the past two hours I've been writing an action list as long as my arm. I seem to come into my own when big things happen in my life, such as childbirth, divorce and death. It's the little things I can't get the hang of. At eight thirty I speak to the undertakers, and then I contact the vicar, the Reverend Arbuthnot at St Agnes, and suggest a date for the cremation, to be confirmed once I have Dad's death certificate.

'I'm so sorry to hear the news,' he says, 'but from what you say it was quick and painless, and your father had a good, full life. The world was a better place with him in it, and the legacy he has left is an overwhelmingly positive one.'

Dad discussed what sort of funeral he wanted with Mum and me, even down to the flowers. I'll make sure he gets it – not that he'd know if we missed the odd thing. He wanted yellow roses ideally, his favourite, although he never explained why they were to either Mum or me.

I check on Mum at about nine, and when Freddie stirs I go up to his room and gently stroke his forehead to wake him. I decided to let him sleep on today, although he will be late for school.

'Freddie, I've got something to tell you,' I say as he gradually opens his eyes and yawns at me.

'Hello, Mummy,' he says, pulling me towards him and gripping me so tightly with his arm that I'm locked in a vice-like cuddle.

'Freddie,' I say gently, 'I've got something to tell you about Grandad.'

'What about Grandad?'

'Grandad died last night of a heart attack. It was very quick and painless.'

'But he didn't say goodbye,' Freddie says, suddenly sitting up, his eyes filling with tears.

'No, darling,' I reply, 'it was so quick he didn't have

a chance to. But I know the last time you saw him you gave him a big hug and told him you loved him, didn't you?' Freddie is crying now and he nods yes through the tears. 'And he told you he loved you, and that he wished he could still bite your bottom, didn't he?' I say, trying to make him laugh, although it doesn't seem to be working.

'If I'd known he was going to die I wouldn't have let him,' he says, looking up at me, which makes me smile because I know Dad would have liked that.

'Will he be all right?' he asks.

'He's just fine. He's in heaven now.'

'Wow, that's quick. So Grandad doesn't stay as a ghost or anything, he just goes to heaven?'

'Well, I'll let you into a little secret. When I was at the hospital with Grandma and we sat with Grandad, who had just died, I felt him looking down on us as we watched him. I suppose that's a bit like a ghost.'

'A bit like Patrick Swayze then?' he says, referring to the film *Ghost*.

'Yes, a bit like Patrick Swayze.'

'Only no one killed Grandad.'

'No, no one killed Grandad.'

As we cuddle each other again I can sense Freddie's mind ticking over, thinking of more things to ask me. He makes a far more insightful journalist than I could ever be with all his questions, his mind unclouded by anything other than what he sees.

'You've lost your daddy, and that's very sad, so you

must be sad too. But you're not to worry, Mummy,' he reassures me.

'Thank you, Freddie,' I say.

We go downstairs and Freddie helps get the breakfast ready – something he never does usually – then I hear Mum waking up. Dillon meows, wanting to be fed, and brushing his little body around my ankles.

'Grandma stayed the night with us last night,' I tell Freddie, 'and she'll probably stay with us for a few days as it will be lonely for her in the cottage.'

'Yes, and when she goes back home I think we should all go together, so she doesn't feel lonely,' he says wisely. 'We can't have that, can we?'

'No, we can't have that,' I say, smiling at how grown-up he sounds.

'We can't have what?' asks Mum as she walks through the door, dressed and looking well rested in spite of everything.

'You being lonely in the cottage,' I say as Freddie rushes to his grandma and tells her she's not to worry as Grandad is in heaven and he's perfectly fine, which I can tell Mum finds quite touching as she swallows hard on a tear.

'Can I help with anything?' she asks.

'No, breakfast's made,' I say, 'but if you want to walk Freddie to school that would be useful. I usually drive, but I think it would be good for you both, don't you? He'll be late, but I'll write a note explaining why.'

'Right,' she says, smiling down at her grandson and giving his cheek a tweak.

After waving Mum and Freddie goodbye, I phone Will to let him know the situation.

'Hi, Will. Sorry to bother you as I know you had some more interviews on the beach scheduled in for today, but my father died last night and I'm afraid I'm going to be tied up for a bit, as I've got to organise his funeral.'

There's a brief pause.

'I'm very sorry to hear that, Helena. Was it sudden?'

'He had a heart attack, so thankfully it was quick, and he hadn't been well for a while. His funeral will be next week at St Agnes, and it will probably be quite well attended. My dad was the former headmaster of Castleford School, as you know, so I should imagine there will be a few old boys there, as well as many of the locals who knew him. If you need me I'm at home.'

There's another pause, this time a longer one.

'Is that OK?' I say, feeling that perhaps it isn't and wondering if TV doesn't stop for bereavement. Not that I care, as it's definitely going to stop for me.

'Yes, that's fine, but I've just had an idea. Would you be willing to have the funeral filmed as part of the programme? If it's a no, I completely understand, but I feel it would add another dimension to what we've already got. Your father was something special in Castleford, and it would show a real sense of community spirit – the soul of the place, if you like, and how people come together at times like this to commemorate one of their own. I completely understand if you don't want the cameras there, but we would be very discreet. It's just a thought.'

I'm shocked by Will's request. It's something Elliott would probably suggest, because that man would put work before anything, but I expected more of Will.

'Will, honestly, this is so the wrong time to ask me something like this. This is my dad we're talking about here, who's just died. It's not just another set piece, another part of the documentary that could add some depth and pathos to it. This is real for me. It's not TV. And to have the cameras there, the intrusion into something that is such a private moment, no, no I can't do that to Dad or to Mum. That would be unfair and rude and wrong.'

'I apologise and understand. It was thoughtless to ask. I know when my father died I videoed the ceremony, the people who came to the funeral and all the wonderful things they said about him. And I was able to show it to my children, so they knew a little more about their grandad, because they never met him. But I completely understand, and I'm sorry for asking.'

'Apology accepted.'

'Were you very close?' he asks.

'Yes, we were. I was a daddy's girl. Aren't most girls?'

'Most, but not all. One of mine is, the other one prefers her mother, you know, shopping for dresses, having her nails done. It's not my thing really.'

Despite myself, I can't help smiling. 'I used to tell him all my secrets. I knew he loved me and I loved him, so there was nothing left unsaid between us, which I think is what really hurts when you lose someone. It must be horrible when your last meeting was a bad one and you never get the chance to say sorry.'

'I know what you mean,' he says. 'I know my kids, even though they're the other side of the Atlantic, are aware I'm there for them if they want me, and my wallet.'

There is another pause.

'I think you need some fun in your life, Helena, although perhaps this is the wrong time to say this. When you burst into tears after Leonard's party, which you'll be pleased to hear comes across as tacky with boorish people and vulgar conversation, and that's even without editing, I realised how vulnerable you are. Leonard shouldn't be getting to you like this after all this time. He's nothing more than a not particularly adequate guy. He was nothing special at school; perhaps he got lucky at work, but the best thing he's ever done is have Freddie as a son, and you enabled him to do that. You should be calling the shots, not him. I know my ex does with me when she wants to. You have so much responsibility that is entirely and completely yours, or you feel is completely yours. Perhaps it's because you're an only child and aren't a natural team player, or you've learned not to trust anyone and to value independence very highly.'

I smile. 'My mum told me when I was about Freddie's age that I should never trust anyone ever, and always try to have financial independence.'

He laughs. 'And what did you say to that?'

'I said fine, and could I carry on playing with my Lego.'

'God, no wonder you clam up and hold stuff in. Bet you felt you had the weight of the world on your shoulders as a child. I expect you saw your dad as this shining white knight who was able to show you love and affection but just like your mum, only loved you conditionally. And that everyone would only love you conditionally. Bet you were a good girl.'

'I was.' I don't agree with what he says about Dad, but I don't want to discuss this, otherwise I'll cry.

'And you don't love conditionally. And you didn't love Leonard conditionally, he did love that way. Well, you're not like your mother and you're not like Leonard. From what I've observed you've learned from the mistakes other people made, rather than copied them. I remember Leonard came from a very strict family and his mother probably had to take full control, especially with three boys on her hands. He hasn't learned from his parents' mistakes, he's copied them.'

'I don't know about all that. It was up to Leonard to deal with it.'

'He wouldn't see it that way, Helena. But I don't want to talk about him, I want to talk about you. You've created a loving atmosphere in your home where Freddie feels mothered but not smothered, and you love your friends for who they are, not what you want them to be. But do you love yourself for who you are and not what you want to be?'

'Good question. I like who I am now. I liked who I was before Leonard. I didn't like what I was becoming when I was with him. And now he's in my space, I want things to be OK with him. I want Freddie to have parents who get on, is that so difficult?'

'You want my honest answer?'

'Of course I do.'

'With Leonard, it will always be hard. My ex-wife reminds me of his behaviour a bit. It's very difficult to turn your back on them, which is what they deserve, but at least my ex is the other side of the Atlantic. Such people have not conscience, since they see everything they do as a consequence of your actions. My ex fed off negative energy and was the eternal victim. Why this condition is not listed as a mental illness is a mystery to me, but Leonard sounds so similar when you talk about him.'

'I don't know why he's come here. It's not to see Freddie, and Castleford isn't really him. He's more a city person.'

'Leonard needs people around him he perceives to be his inferiors. Hate to say it, but he see you like this. He needs that to feel better about himself, so that he can appear normal and pleasant to others. You give him his fix and he obviously feels insecure at the moment, as he feels his fix won't be there for much longer. You're cutting the ties.'

'I'm not a puppet any more,' I say.

'Exactly. Scary, isn't it!'

'Exciting, too.'

'And I wanted to give you some feedback from the crew. They think you're great. Even Richard, who doesn't say much about anything unless you absolutely force him to, says you're a real brick.'

'A real what?'

'I said a brick.' He laughs. 'You may be an only child, but you can be a team player when you want to be, and you can learn to trust again.'

'I know.'

We say goodbye. I feel better having spoken to Will. He's managed to lift my spirits. Yes, Dad and I were very close and now I've got to ring round his long list of friends to tell them the news and ask if they would like to attend the funeral, but I feel in a stronger, more positive frame of mind to do it. Will Stafford is a good man and a wise one, too.

The people I phone are sad, but they all say the same thing, that Dad had a good life and loved his family, and of course they will attend his funeral and celebrate his life. I phone Ernie Forster, one of Dad's oldest friends. He lives in Letchbury and knew my dad in the army in India, and they have kept in touch ever since.

After a few rings a soft voice answers.

'Hello, is that Ernie?' I ask tentatively.

'Yes, it is.'

'This is Norman's daughter Helena.'

'Hello, Helena. How is your dad?' he asks.

I tell him the news and there's a brief silence.

'I'm so sorry to hear that, Helena, but he was in a lot of pain at the end, wasn't he? I'm sure Sheila will be relieved that he's at peace now; she was a very good wife to him. Does his first wife know?'

I'm not sure I heard that right.

'Sorry,' I say. 'Was Dad married before?'

There's another pause, and then, 'Oh, yes, well, no, sorry. I'm getting muddled up in my old age.' It's unconvincing.

'I don't think so, Ernie. I didn't know Dad was married before. Who was he married to?' I ask.

'Well, I don't know much about it, but I thought your mother would have told you.'

'No, she hasn't,' I say.

'I believe it wasn't for very long. Only about a year or two. She was a very glamorous lady, a model. I think her name was Louisa Hone; she was a Norman Hartnell model. From what your dad told me she wanted to go out and party all the time, while he didn't, but he was very private about it so I don't know the ins and outs. It was a long time ago and he met your mum soon afterwards,' he says.

I'm stunned. Why didn't Mum or Dad tell me about this? Perhaps they felt it would be too much to take in when I was younger, but surely not once I grew up.

'Why didn't my parents say anything to me?' I ask.

'Probably because they didn't think it was important,' he replies.

'Well, thank you for telling me,' I say.

'I'm sorry you had to find out this way,' he says, 'but it could be that your dad just didn't want you to know.'

'Perhaps,' I say. And then I go cold, as a face comes

back to me. A woman who stood on my doorstep seven years ago, looking hopeful, in search of a sister.

'Did they have a child?' I ask.

There's a pause.

'Did they have a child?' I repeat.

'They did,' he replies quietly, almost in a whisper, 'but it's your mum's prerogative to tell you these things. She and Norman didn't tell you for a reason that only they knew. All I know is that your dad was married before and that he had a child. You will have to fill in the other gaps yourself, my dear. I'm just sorry you found out this way.'

I put the phone down and sit there motionless for a few minutes. Dad was married before, and I didn't know. I feel as though I'm a character in a David Lynch movie, not quite sure what to do, or what will happen next. Why wasn't I told?

There's a knock on the door and I open it to find Esther, laden with a basket of fruit and a casserole.

'I thought you wouldn't have time to cook for yourself today, so I've prepared a little something,' she says. 'Now, how can I help? I've taken the day off.'

'I've just been told Dad was married before,' I blurt out.

'Good God. First I find out my dad has another daughter, and now you find out your dad had another wife. Who knows, you might have a half-sister like me, or a half-brother for that matter,' she says, walking through the door and into the kitchen.

'And that they had a child.'

'What the hell were they doing in our parents' generation? They call our generation the one which has lost the plot with families, and boast that they were the ones who stayed together and didn't stray. They were worse than us, they just kept it all secret and hidden and thought if they ignored it the truth would go away, and it never does. It never does. Does your mum know he was married before?' she asks, putting the casserole on the stove and turning on the oven.

'I presume so,' I say, sitting down, still dazed by the news.

'Do you know the dates? When they married and divorced? You can check on the register of births, marriages and deaths, you know. Wow! How do you feel about it?' she says, sounding like a counsellor now.

'How do I feel about it? I feel very odd, actually. I thought Dad told me everything, but that's a big part of his life that he kept secret, and it makes me wonder why,' I say.

'Divorce was a taboo subject in those days. He was probably ashamed,' she suggests.

'But I could have assured him it's nothing to be ashamed of. After all, I'm divorced.'

'I know, but it's different now, isn't it. Everyone gets divorced, so there's less stigma attached to it, but then . . . well. He had a child with this woman and maybe wanted to still see them. Did he ever disappear and not explain where he was going?'

'Oh don't be so silly,' I say. 'He was a headmaster, wasn't he? He coached tennis and he used to go fishing on Sunday mornings. Are you saying he somehow fitted in visits to his ex-wife and child and never told me?'

'It's a possibility. My father did.'

'Well, my dad is nothing like your dad,' I say, feeling suddenly defensive of him.

'I'm not saying he is, it's just a possibility. Are you going to say anything to your mum?'

'I will ask her at some stage, just not right now. She's got too much on her plate already and it's probably the last thing she wants to talk about. She's just lost her husband of forty-odd years. And don't you go let Edward put this in his next novel, do you hear?' I say, looking at Esther.

'I wouldn't dream of it,' she replies. 'Now, how can I help with the funeral organisation?'

Chapter Twenty-three

By midday I've ticked half the boxes on my action list, and start to think about the food and drink I need for the reception assuming, once I receive the death certificate, I'm able to confirm the date I suggested to the vicar.

By three o'clock, Esther and I have managed to tick off everything on the list, from the catering to the flowers, choosing the music and notifying people I haven't already told.

'Right,' I say to Esther, who was in the kitchen while I was trying to make my final choice of music. 'Dad had a sense of humour and he loved the soundtrack from *The Commitments*, so I've chosen "Keep A Knocking" and "Try a Little Tenderness". I know he wanted to be in a wicker coffin because he told me, but I still can't get my head round it. Surely it will look like an oversized picnic basket being carried up the aisle.' I chuckle, even though it feels a little irreverent. 'I'll let Leonard know out of courtesy, but I doubt if he'll bother to show up.'

'Your dad wouldn't want him there anyway,' Esther says. 'He didn't like Leonard, did he?'

'I wouldn't say he didn't like him. Dad wasn't the sort to say he didn't like anyone, ever. But he was never quite sure about him. Leonard said a few things that he thought didn't ring true.'

There's a knock on the door and I open it to find Jessica Compton-Batt standing on the doorstep, looking as smart as always.

'Hello,' I say, smiling at her as she walks forward and gives me a hug.

'I wanted to come round to say how sorry I am to hear the news,' she says, 'and to tell you that the whole school are thinking of you and your family. I thought I'd come in person rather than send a formal note and flowers. I thought this would be nicer. Freddie's class have all made cards this morning for you and Freddie,' she says, handing me a pile of cards, which makes me feel happy and sad at the same time.

'I didn't expect this,' I say. 'None of them even knew Dad.'

'No, but they know you and they don't like the idea of anyone losing their daddy.' Then she gives me a kiss on the cheek, which I find quite affecting, and heads back to school.

Five days later, I'm at the doors of the church waiting for the coffin to be brought in. Mum is settling Freddie next to the Bullions and Victoria, who's just been promoted to deputy editor, she tells me. It seems the assertiveness with Dena Benson paid off. Peter Bonham is also there, with George Tucker, bless them both. It's good to see them and although I don't know how much time I can spend with them, I'm really very chuffed that they're here. After all, I'm just a former work colleague – nothing more. They both spend time chatting to Victoria, who seems comfortable with it. Perhaps she and Peter have finally put their ghosts to rest.

Despite my initial reaction to Will's suggestion, Mum and I discussed the filming and in the end felt Dad would have liked it to happen as long as the crew were discreet. Aled and Richard said they would be, and I trust them. I had to ask the permission of Reverend Arbuthnot, who didn't mind, so Aled and Richard are here, both looking extremely smart in suits, which they tell me are on hire, as neither of them owns one.

'Thank you for letting us be here,' says Becca, who gives me and even Mum a hug. She's soberly and smartly dressed in a navy dress, which finishes well below the knee.

'That's fine,' I say. 'I'm sure Dad would have been chuffed to think he's up there with royalty and celebrities, since they're the only funerals that get covered on TV these days. Mind you, I doubt royalty would use a wicker coffin,' I add.

John Tremble comes up to me and says, 'I just wanted to pass on my sympathies and tell you that it was your dad who commissioned the piece. Unfortunately he never saw it, but at least he was able to spend time with the person who inspired it. When you want to see it, let me know and I'll drop it round.' He gives me a hug. I feel I should cry now, but I can't. I'm still holding back. I haven't cried since Dad died.

St Agnes church can hold up to 200 parishioners, but even so people are standing in the outer aisles. I recognise Trent Hawes, the actor, whom my dad taught; he smiles at me and Mum and comes up to greet us.

'Your dad was a great teacher and a great man,' he said. 'I just wanted to say that.'

'Yes,' I say, thanking him, 'you played a teacher in that children's series, didn't you?'

'Yes, I did.' He nods. 'The school inspired me. I also played a serial killer, so perhaps not always!' he jokes, making Mum and me laugh, which feels good.

I didn't realise Dad had so many friends. I ask Mum, who's wearing her Sunday best rather than black – just as Dad had requested – while I'm wearing a long pink and white floral number, 'Who are all these people?'

'Former pupils,' she answers. 'Your dad was very fair and very popular at his school, and his ex-pupils obviously wanted to come to show their respects. I hope this programme you're making emphasises the success of the school. Dad knew it is all to do with the quality of teaching and the quality of the parents. It's nothing more complicated than that.' Mum sounds very forthright. It's almost as though she's come into her own again, as if Dad's death has given her a new lease of life.

As the music blares out from the CD player, everyone laughs gently. When we walk down the aisle behind the coffin it's a very surreal moment, but I know Dad would have wanted people to celebrate his life rather than his death, remembering him the way he was before he got ill.

Reverend Arbuthnot welcomes everyone to St Agnes as I get to my seat, we sing a hymn, 'Lord of the Dance', and then it's my turn to get up and say a few words. The Reverend has told me that if I'm not feeling up to it I should nod and he'll do it, but my nerve doesn't fail me.

At the end of the service, 'Try a Little Tenderness' is played while the coffin is carried out, and everyone follows me back to the cottage, where food and drink are waiting. I let the film crew come back and interview some of Dad's old boys, who wax lyrical about what a good teacher he was. Castleford School sent a wonderful bouquet to the funeral, and all the cards Freddie's class made are displayed around the cottage.

I talk to Ernie Forster. I haven't seen him for several years. He, rather weirdly, doesn't look unlike Dad. He has the same soft eyes, wide cheekbones and silver-grey hair. I feel quite tearful.

'Have you mentioned anything to Sheila about our conversation?' he asks.

'No, I haven't,' I say. 'I didn't think it was appropriate.'

At the reception everyone mingles, and the camera crew take the odd shot until Becca tells Aled and Richard to down tools. I say goodbye to Esther and Edward before they go, and see Victoria and Peter heading off in the same direction. I must remember to call Victoria to find out how they got on. To my knowledge they haven't actually seen each other since she left the radio station.

'I could never work in an office,' says Aled, taking off his jacket. 'I hate bloody suits.'

Later that evening, after everyone's left, John turns up with the wonderful bust of me that Dad commissioned. It's lovely and I give it pride of place on the mantelpiece, over our large open fire.

I receive a call from Eliana, who has heard the news and says she'd love us to come out to Sardinia as soon as possible, and there's a call from Jarred sending his condolences. High Light sent a huge bouquet of flowers from 'Elliott, Jarred, Heather and the rest of the team'.

The PTA committee came round this morning with flowers, which is very sweet, and even Mr Farnsworth, Freddie's football coach Tony, and Herbie the postman have sent flowers.

By ten o'clock Mum is in bed, as is Freddie, and it's just me left tidying up the last few things before I head upstairs. It's been a full-on day, but a successful one, and I think Dad would have enjoyed it. Once I have his ashes, Mum and I have agreed to scatter them around the cherry tree in their garden later on that week or maybe month – when we both feel like it. I'm just about to go into the kitchen when there's a knock on the door.

My first instinct is not to open it, as I'm feeling tired and emotional, but I decide to in case it's urgent or someone's forgotten something. Dillon curls around my ankles, wanting a cuddle, but it's me that feels like a cuddle at the moment.

I open the door to find Will standing there, and I give a start of surprise.

'I'm sorry to disturb you, but I didn't get a chance to speak to you earlier. I just wanted to say that I think your dad would have been proud of you today.' He smiles at me.

'Thank you,' I say. 'Do you want to come in?'

'Are you sure you're up to it?' he says, staring at me intently, as he usually does. I must look as tired as I feel.

'Yes, come in. I'll put the kettle on.'

I lead him into the kitchen. He's still in the suit he wore at the church, but unlike Aled and Richard he looks comfortable in smarter clothes, and almost sexy. Even in my tired state I can feel butterflies in my stomach, though perhaps that's all the stress I've been through in the past few days.

Will sits down at the kitchen table as I fill the kettle. I'm not concentrating, and before I know it it's overflowing.

'I'm so silly!' I say. 'My mind's on other things, I guess.'

'As it would be,' he says simply.

There's a pause. The kettle boils and I make coffee.

'So do you think we got anything good today, you know, filming-wise?' I ask.

'Yes, we got a lot of good stuff. Your father was very well thought of, very well respected and obviously loved by those who knew him, especially the boys he taught. It reminded me of that scene in *Goodbye Mr Chips*. You're well respected and loved in the community as well, you know that, don't you?' He looks at me as he says this.

'My parents have lived here for many years,' I say. 'I feel this is my home. So many communities and homes are disparate these days, and there's a closeness about Castleford. No one knows everyone's business – it's not like that. But they care about each other. They're not just interested, they actually care and perhaps that's what makes this place special. I don't know if you can teach people to be caring, I suppose some naturally are and others just think of caring as interfering, or being nosy or, well, being controlling.'

'There's a chasm of difference between caring and loving, and being possessive. One makes you feel stronger inside, the other weaker. That's why you should always trust how you feel when you're around others. Trust your instinct about people.'

I nod and hand him a cup of coffee.

'I should have trusted my instinct about you when I first met you,' Will says, taking a sip of coffee.

'What was that?' I laugh.

'Let's just say I've learned more about you today than I have on the whole shoot. When I first heard about you, and then met you, I thought you'd be a bit of a liability.'

'That's what Leonard thought about me and still does,' I reply.

'I don't mean it like he means it, and I don't think he believes it really, but I don't want to talk about him. I want to talk about you. You knew nothing about the world of TV or how to make a programme, and you're a little here, there and everywhere with your busy life, so I didn't think you could organise a piss-up in a brewery, let alone co-produce a documentary.'

'Thanks a lot,' I say, feeling annoyed at the criticism.

'Let me finish. You had so much going on in your life at the same time, what with organising Freddie, and this new job, and keeping in touch with friends past and present. I thought you were going to be a handful.'

'Depends on how big the hands are,' I reply, smiling at him.

'But I was wrong and I should have trusted my instinct,' he says, putting down his coffee cup and walking towards me.

'And what was your instinct?'

I can feel his energy as though there's something magnetic drawing me to him, and it scares me. For some reason I can feel something in my feet. I want to laugh because it sounds so funny, why my feet for goodness' sake? Why not my heart or stomach? But it's almost as though I'm lifting off the ground.

Will stands in front of me, our bodies almost touching.

'Is something wrong with the tea?' I ask, trying to make light of a moment that's becoming increasingly intense.

'Nothing's wrong with the tea, only that it's coffee,' he replies, which makes me laugh.

'I see what you mean about being here, there and everywhere,' I say. 'I don't even know my tea from my coffee these days.'

Without saying anything, he cups his hands around the back of my neck, lifts my head up and kisses me firmly on the lips. He starts with short tender kisses that turn into deeper, longer ones, while gently stroking my neck. He moves his hands around my throat, holding it as though he could strangle me, but I trust him. I raise my arms to his head and pull him closer, kissing him back tenderly, then harder as he becomes more passionate, moving his hands down my back, pushing me into him. I can feel myself getting wet as he pushes me on to the kitchen table, then holds my arms above my head by the wrists as he kisses me.

And then he stops. He stops kissing me for a few moments and looks into my eyes. It's only for a few moments, perhaps just seconds, but I'm breathless, my heart is beating heavily and I feel on fire. It's as though a flame has been lit inside me. He says nothing, just hovers above me as if he's about to kiss me again at any moment, and then I know. I know when he looks at me and holds me that I like this man. I really like this man. And he is a man, not a boy dressed up as one. He's had life experience, a family, marriage, children, a divorce – just like me – and he's learned from it. He's been successful and chosen a career that's creative and commercial; he takes risks. He appears confident, like me, but underneath I sense there are insecurities. And when I look deep into his eyes, I feel that I've met my equal.

When he starts to kiss me again, I feel that he's just as overwhelmed, almost surprised by the moment as I am. It's as though he wanted to make me wait for the next kiss, as if anticipation would excite me and leave me wanting more, but he didn't realise it would have the same effect on him. I can see by his expression he feels the same as I do. I hardly know this man. I've only known him for the last few weeks, and yet I've known him for much longer. Perhaps we met in a past life, perhaps we're old souls who've met before, but whatever the reason I feel as though I'm meant to be with him, and I've never felt that way before, not even when I first met Leonard.

Eventually Will lifts me up from the table, holding me and stroking me so I feel like a cat. If I were a cat I'd purr loudly and proudly now. I feel myself melting into him and I go to kiss him again as he continues to hold me.

'Leonard was a fool,' he says simply. 'If I'd had you I would never have let you out of my sight.'

'Oh God, you're not another control freak, are you?' I say, looking at him nervously.

'No,' he says, 'I don't think Helena Treadwell would allow anyone to control her now, least of all a man.'

'Leonard certainly tried to.'

'And failed.'

'Yes, and failed,' I repeat.

I expect him to kiss me again, take me in his arms and carry me up the stairs, although my mum and Freddie are in bed, so perhaps that's not such a good idea. But he doesn't, he just takes my hand, kisses it and leads me to the front door.

'I'll see you tomorrow,' he says, cupping his hands around the back of my neck again, as he did when we first kissed. I don't want to let him go or stop kissing him, but I do, and he smiles, kisses my hand, turns and goes.

I close the door behind me and slide down to the floor in the hallway, aware that I have a huge large beaming smile on my face. If Dad could see me now I know he'd be extremely happy for me. I know I am.

Chapter Twenty-four

'I want to take you swimming,' says Will, knocking on my door the next morning at seven o'clock, 'you need some fun in your life.'

'I can't. I've just got out of bed, and feel a complete mess.'

'What? You mean you can't have fun?'

'No, I can't come out. Freddie and Mum are still asleep and the sea will freezing.'

'It's a beautiful morning and the cold water will wake you up.'

I look at him standing there, handsome in his grey jumper and jeans. I want to run my fingers through his hair then and there. Swimming's a crazy idea and totally impractical. It's summer, but the sea will still be freezing and I'll probably catch pneumonia. But despite all the reasons I shouldn't go swimming, all I can think is that I'd love to. And I haven't been to the sea for ages, apart from jogging. I haven't even taken Freddie there recently, which is very remiss of me.

'I'll get dressed,' I say, 'shall I ask Freddie and Mum if they want to come?'

'No, we can do that another time. I just want you.'

'I'd better leave a note for them. We won't be long, will we?'

'Half an hour max,' he replies. 'Be quick.'

I rush upstairs to the bathroom.

'Everything OK?' I hear Mum call out as I tiptoe past her room.

'I've just got to pop out. I'm going for a swim. I won't be long, Mum. I'll probably be back before Freddie's up, but if not, can you give him breakfast?'

'Yes, of course,' she says, 'but swimming? It will be—'

'Yes, I know, freezing, but I feel like washing away some of the cobwebs and clearing my mind, and swimming will do that.'

'Sometimes I really don't understand you. But I did tell you to live your life to the full, so why not start by swimming in a freezing-cold sea? Just be careful of the current. You know how strong it is. On second thoughts, I'm sure the handsome man standing at the door waiting for you will look after you,' she says. She obviously overheard our conversation.

'Exactly,' I reply as I find myself skipping to the bathroom.

I rush down the stairs and take the hand Will offers me before we walk down the path and along the road. My heart is beating fast. I feel excited and alived.

As we walk I see Herbie the postman, who nods hello. 'Off filming early?' he asks.

I'm just about to say yes when Will replies, 'No, we're off for a swim. Good thing to wake us up, don't you think?'

'Cup of coffee usually works for me,' he replies, looking at us as though we're both potty.

There's a cool breeze, but it's a warm day, and if it wasn't for the wind it would be perfect. The tide is out as we walk down the narrow cobbled pathway towards the beach.

'I've always wanted to live by the sea – it's where I feel most at home – but work has always led me back to London,' he says, quickening the pace slightly, as though he can't wait to get in the water. I walk by his side, holding his hand tightly. On the bridge some of the local boys are out crabbing, dangling pieces of fish on the ends of wires. We stop for a few moments to see if they have any success.

'This really is a lovely place to live,' says Will, looking down at the boys, who are totally oblivious to us watching them as they pull up their wires, delighted to find a couple of crabs clinging on to the bait.

'Not far now,' I say as I pull Will away and head through the tufts of grass on to the sand. 'If we leave our clothes here, I'm sure no one will pinch them,' I tell him, starting to take my coat off.

Will removes his trousers to reveal his swimming trunks and a pair of very defined, strong legs.

'You work out, don't you?' I comment, admiring his physique as he takes off his shirt and reveals the sort of six-pack I haven't seen on a man, since, well, never actually.

'I run and work out regularly. I just look after myself because I know no one else will.'

'Good answer. I used to teach aerobics when I was in my twenties. I wasn't properly qualified like you have to be now, but I was very fit. Sadly that's not the case now,' I say, pulling off my jumper and tapping my tummy.

'You look pretty fit to me.'

'Right answer!'

I smile at him. He takes my hand again and leads me across the sand and on to the pebbles. The sea, despite the clear blue sky, looks rough. The wind has stirred it up and the waves are crashing on to the shore.

'We're crazy,' I shout, shivering with the cold, aware that we're not the only ones on the beach. Some people are out walking their dogs, all of them in coats and jumpers, while I'm just in my bikini.

'No, we're not. We're having fun. Feels good, doesn't it!'

'Last one's in is a sissy!' I shout as I run into the water, jumping over the waves, my brain trying hard to convince my body it's not freezing.

'It's freezing!' I scream, but I make my way through the gentle shallow waves to the deeper darker water, allowing it to crash over me. Will is just behind, running at full steam and then daring to start swimming while I'm still standing, jumping from one leg to the other, dancing a sort of warped Scottish jig, desperately trying to keep warm and upright. Finally I literally take the plunge into the freezing water, jumping up almost immediately and screaming at the top of my voice.

'This is amazing! I haven't felt this alive for such a long time!' I laugh, looking at him.

'Good, isn't it, being alive?' Then he swims over to me.

'Is this our *From Here to Eternity* moment?' I ask as he takes me in his arms.

'I don't know that one. Which band?'

'No matter,' I laugh, allowing him to kiss me passionately, then tenderly.

'We'd better go in now. Are you cold?'

'Just a bit,' I say, my teeth chattering so violently now I think they're going to cut my tongue off any moment. I can't feel my fingers or my feet. I'm aware of Mr Farnsworth walking along the beach and Tony jogging from the opposite direction.

'You are complete loonies!' Tony shouts at us.

'I know!' I shout back. 'Isn't it absolutely amazing!'

It seems my little excursion with Will won't be as private as I'd hoped, but everyone gets to know everything in Castleford, so why should I think I can hide anything?

'I want to go in again,' I say, suddenly turning and leaping back into the water. 'I absolutely hate the cold but I'm loving this moment. I feel invigorated and alive. Thank you for suggesting we do this. It's wonderful. Thank you so much.'

Afterwards, as we dry ourselves and get dressed, Will

pulls me to him and kisses me again, in that way that melts me, cupping my face gently in his hands, slowly taking my breath away.

As we walk back to the house hand in hand, I realise that Mum has had to deal not only with getting Freddie up and fed, she's probably wondering if she should take him to school. But as I open the door I see a note in the hall saying, 'Hello darling. Thought I'd better take Freddie to school. Rang your friend Edward and we've all gone in his car this morning. Hope you enjoyed your nice swim. I did that with your dad when I was younger – we went skinny-dipping! Hope you did too! Love Mum xxx'

'Is everything all right?' Will asks.

'Yes.' I nod, smiling. 'Everything is fine. I'm not sure if my mother is trying to shock me or impress me.' I show him the note.

'Think she's just sharing,' he says.

After saying goodbye to Will in the hallway, which takes a good ten minutes of kissing, touching and stroking each other, I eventually close the door and head to the kitchen.

Then there's a knock, which I expect is either Mum returning or, if I'm lucky, Will coming back for seconds, and I find myself skipping to answer it.

I open the door to find a smartly dressed woman standing there. I stare at her, almost doing a double take; it's as though I've met her in a previous life and should know her well, only I can't remember how or why. Then suddenly I remember when I last saw her, and what she said. 'I am your sister,' she says now. 'My name is Leah Nelder and I am your sister.'

I stand there motionless and numb, as though I'm in that ice-cold water again. She must be wondering if I'm going to slam the door on her as I did all those years ago, but I want to look at her, take her in, before I say or do anything else. I feel it's almost like seeing Dad standing on the doorstep, someone I thought I would never see again. I realise I'm unnerving her, so I step aside.

'Hello Leah,' I say, 'I know you are.' I politely ask her if she would like to come in. She says she would.

I lead her into the sitting room and ask her if she wants some tea, but she says no. I sit opposite her and look at her, trying to see traces of my father or myself in her face. Perhaps there's a little of Dad around the eyes and forehead, but the rest is her own, or perhaps her mother's. She has an open, kind face, but sad eyes. I wait for her to say something, to tell me what I need to know. She takes a deep breath.

'I don't know how to say this really,' she looks down at her feet, 'but the best way, I suppose, is to just come out with it.'

I look at her in silence. So many odd things have happened over the past few days that I feel able to handle anything at the moment.

'Your father married Louisa Hone when he came back from India after the war. They had a child. Me. My mother had an affair before I was born with a man called Julian Kettner, and I only found out seven years ago that Jules wasn't my father, your dad, Norman Treadwell, was. I'm your sister.'

I sit and look at her, not sure what to ask first, so I start with, 'I'm sorry I slammed the door on you when you came that time before Christmas.'

'It's OK,' she replies.

'Why did you decide to come back now?' I ask.

'I don't know,' she says. 'My mother left Norman for Julian when I was still a baby, and Norman never forgave her for it. He didn't want anything to do with her, and I don't think he believed I was his child, so he didn't want anything to do with me, either. But I know I am his child. Julian told me seven years ago, just before I came to your house to make contact. I thought it might be time to try to meet my real dad again.'

'I'm afraid you're too late,' I say. 'Dad died last week.'

She looks more shocked than upset.

'I'm sorry,' I say, leaning over and holding her hands.

'When is the funeral?'

'I'm afraid it was yesterday.'

'Oh, I couldn't even say a proper goodbye to him,' she says, looking very sad.

'Are you married? Do you have children?' I ask tentatively.

'Yes, my husband Jim and I have a boy and a girl,' she says. 'Emily and Mark. I wish they could have know their grandfather. What was he like?'

'He was a kind, good and loving man,' I reply, 'but there was always a sadness about him. Perhaps it was regret that he'd turned his back on you; perhaps he always felt there was a chance that you were his. He was a good father, though, and I loved him so much.'

'Mmm, that's how I imagined him,' she says.

I make some tea, which Leah has decided she would like now, and we sit and sip it as we chat. She talks about her family and her two children – teenagers, about the same ages as Esther's Charlotte and Constance – who sound just as active as Freddie. I tell her about Freddie and how happy he will be to know he has cousins on my side of the family. After an hour or so, she says she must go. We exchange phone numbers. I hug her, not wanting to let her go in case I never see her again.

'Please keep in touch,' I say, 'I don't want to lose my family again. My welcomes, I promise, will always be warm in future.'

'It was lovely to meet my sister at last and get some answers to my questions.' Then she gives me a kiss on the cheek. We have both lost our father but at least I knew mine; Leah never got the chance to know hers.

Before she leaves, she goes to her handbag, takes out an envelope and hands it to me. 'I think you should have this,' she says. 'Before Mum died she asked me to track down Norman and give this to him. I was going to give it to you the first time I came to see you, but it never happened. I don't know what it says, but I still think you should have it.' I open the envelope. It's a poem, entitled 'Please forgive me.'

As I read, tears start to trickle down my face.
'Before I die be nice to me, be kind to me
And give me hope that you love me so I can love
    in return
And trust in human nature
Don't wait until my last breath when guilt and
    grief overwhelm
Your sense of place and person and you lose your
    dignity and logic
But it's OK because I can't answer back or see
    your pain or feel your tears
Before I die be my friend
Who makes me laugh and laughs with me
And finds my faults a joy as much as my strengths
Because when I'm dead I can't see your tears
Or feel your pain or share my joy or yours
Don't waste your grief over lost time and lost
    opportunity and memory
Your kind words are no good to me when I am
    dead
Although my ghost may watch over you and time
    may fade the sadness
Into a stain that won't go away
Before I die be nice to me, be kind to me
And love me so that I may learn to love
And trust while I am living. Please.'

'Wow!' I say, brushing away a tear. 'What a shame Dad never got to read it. She sounds as though she desperately needed to be forgiven. How sad when people don't say the things they should before it's too late. And that happens all the time,' I say, thinking about my situation with Leonard. 'It happens all the time.'

As I close the door I suddenly feel an overwhelming urge to get in the car and drive over to see Leonard and talk to him. To tell him how I feel about him moving here, about the boarding-school idea, and how I've just learned I have a sister. I want to tell him about the poem, and how it's so important to communicate properly, because when we're dead it will be too late. And how I'm sorry things have happened like this between us. I know I'm taking a risk. I know Esther would tell me not to do it because he will never change, and Victoria would say I'm giving my power away, but I've got to try. Great love and great achievements involve great risks, that was what Dad always taught me, and I'm taking a huge risk going over to see Leonard now, but I've got to make peace with him. If he's going to settle in Castleford then I've got to accept it and open my arms to change, but not let go of my values and what I believe to be right for Freddie, and boarding school for our son isn't right. What did Nixon say when he resigned? Something along the lines of 'your enemies may hate you, but don't hate them back, because if you do, you destroy yourself.' I agree with that.

I don't hate Leonard, nor do I think of him as a thorn in my flesh, as I did a few weeks ago. I've regarded him as a control freak, a narcissist, who enjoys bullying me, but he can only do it if I let him. Leonard may be a bit of a prick, but he's not a thorn. He's just a person who doesn't have any more power or control than the next man, or woman for that matter. And I know why he came to Castleford now. He wants and needs a proper home, and hasn't found it in London. He wasn't born here. He didn't like it here when he visited my parents, but thinking about it now, that was more about the journey than the destination.

Castleford is Freddie's home and my home, and perhaps that's where Leonard feels most wanted, most needed, most in control. Those friends at his luncheon party aren't true, loyal friends. And he doesn't love this woman he's with. If he did, he would have married her long ago. He needs to meet the right person, to let go, and move on and up. But will he listen and will he understand? I ask myself, as I slam the front door and get into my car. As I turn the ignition I realise I've got to do this, and there's no going back now.

Chapter Twenty-five

I stand at the front door, realising I have to press the entryphone button to be let in. What do I do if Helena is there and Leonard isn't? Do I go home and ask him to call me? I don't want Helena to be there, I just want to talk to Leonard. I feel this conversation should be just the two of us, without mediators or people taking sides, just the two of us because that's all it involves. I press the buzzer and decide if it's Helena who answers I will say I'm here to ask Leonard if he wants to take Freddie out this Wednesday after school. I'll make something up. Please let it be Leonard. Please let it be Leonard. Please let it . . .

'Hello,' a woman's voice replies.

Shit.

'Hello, is that Helena?' I ask, knowing full well it is.

There's a pause.

'Yes.'

'This is, erm, Helena. I've come to talk to Leonard.'

Another pause.

'About what?'

'About Freddie.'

Another pause, this time longer. So long, in fact, I think she's put the phone down on me.

'Hello?'

'What about Freddie?'

'About whether he would like to take Freddie out this Wednesday.'

'I can tell him that,' she replies abruptly.

'There are other things I need to discuss as well.'

'I don't see why it is so urgent, but if you must.'

The door clicks open. If it's going to be this difficult to get to speak to Leonard, let alone actually speak to him, I'm wondering how long this is going to take me. Helena has been in his life for a long time now, so I should try to keep her on side. I don't want to, especially after the way she overreacted at the school play, but I will let it pass. I've got to be strong. I'm doing this for Freddie and for me, and, if he did but realise it, for Leonard.

She's standing there, mouth tightly shut, glaring at me.

'Please come in,' she says, although I don't feel I'm in any way welcome. Even though I'm in their home, I don't feel it's a home. It's a base. This building is merely somewhere to put their stuff. I don't feel any warmth in the place.

I enter the sitting room. There are two large sofas opposite each other, with a large gap in between.

Leonard is sitting on one sofa and doesn't get up when I come in.

'Hello,' I say.

'How did your father's funeral go?' he asks, which I didn't expect.

'A lot of people were there. A lot of his ex-pupils and friends. He wanted a wicker coffin, and it looked a bit like a large picnic hamper. I think he would have found that funny, if he'd been there that is, if you know what I mean,' I say, feeling I'm waffling on and not getting to the point. I'm aware that Helena is still hovering by my side and is determined to stay.

'Yes, your dad was well respected in the community, wasn't he? I've spoken to quite a few people who've mentioned his name. And Freddie always spoke about him with affection. I remember when we used to go out with your parents here, we'd be stopping every ten minutes or so for them to speak to people. It would take us ages to get to the sea front.'

'Yes, I remember that,' I laugh.

'Freddie likes the sea. He talks about it a lot when he's with me at weekends. And how much he enjoys playing with Tom and Jerry. I hear they chew everything they find.'

'Yes they do,' I smile. I find myself feeling upset by all of this. I hadn't realised Freddie tells his dad these things, or that Leonard is interested. I thought he would just tell Freddie nasty things about me, but perhaps he leaves those comments for me.

'Anyway, I've come to talk to you about Letchbury.

We didn't really discuss it after we'd visited the school. I just wanted your views on it again, and if you still think it's right for Freddie to go there,' I say, sitting down on the same sofa as him, although I haven't been offered a seat. I think bugger it, I'm sitting down anyway.

'He seems happy at Castleford, doesn't he?' says Leonard.

'Yes.' I nod. I don't say anything else. I don't think 'I told you so' would be particularly constructive at the moment, so I keep silent.

'Yes, I was very impressed with what the teachers had to say about him.'

'Darling, can I have a word with you pleassse,' says Helena behind me, which makes me jump. I'd almost forgotten she was still there.

'Can it wait a while?' Leonard asks, turning round.

She says it can't.

Leonard gets up and smiles, telling me he'll be back in a moment.

'Would you like a coffee, tea?'

'No, I'm fine,' I reply. This conversation I'm having with him feels almost normal, almost nice and friendly. I haven't had this sort of chat with him since I don't know when. His usual method of communication is to send bickering letters about nits and pants and warts. If we speak, he says I'm hassling him, and I say he's intimidating me. There's none of that now. This is how it should be.

I wait, and then realise I'm desperate to go to the

toilet. I just hope their downstairs loo has been fixed by now.

As I tiptoe out towards the cloakroom I can hear voices from the kitchen. I should walk past these voices. It's rude to listen to private conversations. So I stop and listen.

'Darling, we talked about this, didn't we now, darling. We talked about this and the Freddie issue. And we have so much we want to do with our lives. And you know how I am with Mother. I need to be close to my mother.'

'You are close to your mother,' I hear Leonard reply. 'You call her three or four times every day, including three a.m. this morning to complain you had an itchy toe.'

'Don't mock me, darling'

'I'm not mocking you, it's true, you do. And Freddie can't even have ketchup on his chips because the sight of it upsets you.'

Wow. Is that why Freddie always puts so much ketchup on his chips these days? I thought he was just going through a phase, but it's because of her obsession. I must remember if I invite them round to have ketchup on the table. No, that's silly, Helena, but I can't help smiling to myself.

'I thought we agreed, darling, that Freddie would be better off in a boarding school. That we could convince her that she wouldn't be able to cope with her son and looking after her parents, as well as well as having a full-time job. Yes, I know our plan, well my plan actually, as

I'm the one who seems to make the decisions around here, went awry when she lost her job, and then her father had to go and die, but we can still make this happen. You can still convince her she can't cope, you can wear her down into believing she's an unfit mother. You can do it, darling, I know you can.'

I want to burst in and punch the woman in the mouth. Unfit mother, indeed. Who the hell does she think she is? She hasn't even got children of her own, unless she keeps them tidied away somewhere in a boarding school.

'You've got enough evidence on her to prove she's a bad mother,' she continues.

'Nits, warts, and petty things like that are not enough to prove she's a bad mother, darling. I think even my solicitor laughed at me when I asked her to write that letter, and it cost me money. I felt an utter fool.'

'Well, you will look an utter fool if you don't follow this through. And I don't see why we had to come here, we could have made this happen from where we were in London with all our friends,' she snarls.

'They are mainly your friends, not mine. I only see a few of my friends now and I miss my son and I want to have as much influence on him as his mother does.'

'I hate this house and I hate sharing the same town and breathing the same air as your ex-wife, so it's either her or me,' she says.

Please, Leonard. Please tell the cow to go away. You sound as though you desperately need some freedom yourself. You've found someone who is even more controlling than you tried to be. If you'd met the right woman when you left Freddie and me, we wouldn't be where we are now, in this tangled mess of a relationship that is no good for anyone.

I quickly walk back to the sitting room, regain my seat and my composure and wait for them to return. I look out the window to their flawless manicured garden with huge tubs of flowers on the patio. They look so perfect they could be plastic. Then I realise they are.

'Leonard has something to say to you.' Helena comes in looking triumphant. What has she done, promised him a blow job if he'll tell me it's boarding school for Freddie and the ghetto for me? I want to smile at her amateur dramatics. Freddie is a much more convincing actor and has considerably more presence than she does.

'Freddie would do much better at Letchbury and I feel if you want this one-off payment, it is in your interest to make sure he goes there,' he says.

'I don't care about the payment.'

He looks shocked. She looks pleased.

'You can have the payment. You can keep the money. I know Castleford is right for Freddie, and if you are going to bargain for his future with money dangled as a bait, I'm not playing that game, Leonard. I'm long past playing that game. We need to be flexible, both of us. We need to compromise. If we don't put Freddie first, he is the only one who will suffer in all this. You know his school is good, you admitted so yourself.'

Helena glares at me. 'Leonard has made his

decision. If we can have it in writing that you don't want the money, we can get our solicitor on to it straight away.'

'Can't Leonard speak for himself?' I reply, not looking at her, looking straight at him.

'No he can't!' she says.

I look at her aghast. So does Leonard.

'So Leonard doesn't have a voice?' I say.

'He does, of course he does,' she snaps, turning to Leonard. 'What I am saying is that we are in total agreement. Aren't we, darling?' She smiles at him seductively but he doesn't say anything.

'When you want to talk, Leonard, let me know. All this is such a pity because Freddie has settled so well into the school and the community and is so happy to be seeing more of you, and now it all seems to be going downhill. We have a fabulous son who loves us both and wants us to get on,' I say, standing up to go. 'And by the way, Tony mentioned he had a word with you about taking Freddie to football training and practice now you're here, and he says you are going to do it. Thank you for that. It is what a father should do. So, I'm taking note of what you said in mediation about needing more gratitude from Freddie and me.'

I walk towards the door, realising that I may have totally screwed everything up. I may have said goodbye to the money, which I need, but hey, I can get it another way. Money isn't everything, after all.

As I leave I can hear the door slam hard behind me. Charming. They've probably electrified the fence and got landmines hidden in the front lawn. I get in my car and drive away. I want to go to the sea and stand on the beach, feeling the wind on my face, listening to the sound of the waves and smelling the salt air. I think of Freddie playing there, and me and Will dancing in the waves. I should go home and see Mum, though.

I've tried everything now for Freddie's sake and feel I've done the right thing. Louisa Hone's words never reached my dad. She never forgave herself or learned that he forgave her, and I don't think he ever forgave himself, either. I just wanted Leonard to know that we, Freddie and I, still need him to be there for us, and that we will always be there for him. I wanted him to know those things before the chance is gone and the moment destroyed.

I drive home and give Mum a hug when she opens the door. It still doesn't come naturally to her, hugging, but perhaps that will change in time. I tell her what I've just done, which she thinks is very brave if not a little foolhardy, and says she knows why I've made the decision.

As she makes us both a sandwich and a cup of coffee, I decide to tell her about the visit from my sister.

'I want to tell you about something that happened to me after our swim,' I say.

'You have lots of things to tell me, all of a sudden,' she says, smiling at me.

'You had enough on your plate when Dad was alive, plus I used to feel you judged everything I said and took it out of context.'

'I suppose I probably did, but my priority was your father. It was always your father, because I felt he needed the most from me. You were always a very independent and determined little girl, and you've grown into an independent and determined woman.'

'That didn't mean I didn't need you to listen to me and support me. I was still vulnerable,' I say.

'I know that now. I've realised that over the years, and I've been angry with myself for not being there for you. I could cope with looking after your father, and his father before him, but now I know I should have spent more time with you. I should have got the balance right, like you do with Freddie,' she says. It's the first time I've ever heard her say anything remotely positive about my parenting skills, and I'm a little taken aback.

'So what is this thing you have to tell me?' Mum asks.

'Seven years ago a lady came to my door and told me she was my sister,' I reply. 'I was in the process of tearing up my wedding album at the time, so I wasn't in a fit state to speak to anyone, let alone someone claiming to be my sister. Then she reappeared on my doorstep this morning and told me her name is Leah Nelder; she's the daughter of Louise Hone, Dad's first wife. Ernie Forster told me about Louisa when I rang to tell him about Dad's funeral, and that she and Dad had a child, but I didn't want to say anything to you then. Leah had a poem written by her mother before she died. She wanted Leah to give it to Dad, but he never saw it,' I say, going to my pocket to show her. But the poem's not there.

'Well, I did have it.' I say, rummaging in my pocket again, then realising I must have dropped it or left it at Leonard's.

'I've lost it!' I say, feeling dreadful and starting to get quite weepy. 'I've lost this poem that was so important. I wanted Leonard to see it, and I didn't even show him, and now you can't see it.'

'Leah will have another copy, I'm sure,' says Mum, realising how upset I am. She hugs me, this time warmly, like Dad used to.

'I'm so sorry Mum, it was a lovely poem. I do hope she made a copy. It was so sad. I felt her sadness and loneliness.'

'I'm sure you did, Helena. I think that's your problem sometimes, my love, you feel other people's sadness so much you don't take thought for yourself. What is Leah like?' she asks.

'She's very nice, Mum. Do you feel strong enough to meet her?'

'I think so now,' she says, tears starting to stream down her face as well. We must look a right pair. 'I'm so sorry we didn't tell you. We were both so thrilled when you were born, and your father didn't want you to know about what he called his mistake. Men are such fickle characters, aren't they? When men divorce, they say that they never loved the woman in the first place. When women divorce, they always say they loved the man, even if it was only at the beginning. Your father was no different, but I know he felt the shame of it and made me promise never to tell you. He thought you would be ashamed of him. I said you wouldn't, but he disagreed. It was always a bone of contention between us. He regretted it in the end, of course, not telling you, but by then it was too late. He had lost touch with Louisa, and then he became ill.'

I pass her a tissue. She gives me a wobbly smile.

'You've always tried to do the right thing by me, Dad, Leonard and Freddie, so now you should start thinking about yourself. That's what I plan to do too now. Grab your happiness with both hands and hold on to it. Don't be afraid of life or worry that you're doing the wrong thing. The only wrong thing you can do is nothing, coasting along and playing safe. I was always the strong one, the one in control in our marriage, but it's never been natural to me. I would love to meet someone I could share the control with. Your dad wasn't the type, though, so I took on the role because I loved him. You don't have to do that. You're a good mum and you've always been successful in your work, so now it's time to have some fun before it's too late. And as for Leonard, what will be, will be.'

I hug Mum tight. 'I've met a man,' I say.

'I know you have, darling,' she says. 'I can see it in your eyes. It only happens once in a while, that sort of connection. Don't throw it away. Enjoy it, make the most of it. It's special. I know because I experienced it with your dad, and it never goes away.'

I look at her and smile.

'I know you've always thought me very controlling,' Mum acknowledges, 'but I've had to be, darling, to keep things together. Now let me have Leah's number and I'll arrange for her to come over for a visit.'

'She'd like that. Now I'd better go and pick up Freddie,' I say, looking at the kitchen clock.

As I drive, I think about what Mum said about having to be the one who leads, and I realise that's probably how Leonard felt when we were together. He had to do all the organising because he thought I wasn't capable of sharing it with him. Since I've had to go it alone, though, I've thrived, and it's shown me that I had it in me all along. Perhaps he's found more of an equal in his girlfriend. She certainly seems to call the shots in their home.

Chapter Twenty-six

'So what's so special about this place, huh?' says Elliott, swivelling his chair round at the rest of us. We're in the boardroom at High Light Productions – Elliott taking centre stage as usual, Jarred, Will and me to his right, Samuel, Simon and Luca to his left, and Heather in her usual place in the corner with that 'make my day, punk' look etched across her face.

'I don't know if I've missed something, but I don't see it yet. What is it about these people, this place that makes it different from anywhere else? Anyone? Anyone? Will, you've filmed a lot of fly-on-the-walls like this. What's different about this place?' He lets go of his pen and it flies across the room, almost hitting Will on the forehead. Will ducks and answers the question.

'They are behaving naturally,' he says calmly, but I sense he is becoming increasingly exasperated. 'They don't perform for the camera. They don't want to talk endlessly about their sex lives. They get on with life rather than moaning about it all the time. They have close family ties and care for each other. They appreciate what they've got and they live in the moment. They cherish what the past has given them and aren't afraid of what's round the corner. They are what I would call a normal community, although, to be blunt, in all my years working in TV I haven't seen what is allegedly a normal community, so in that sense Castleford is unique. They even accepted a TV crew into their lives, for goodness' sake. They accept strangers, no matter how vulgar and pretentious and grasping they may be, and accept them for what they are, not what they want them to be, and they're strong enough to hold their own against such newcomers. They don't think anyone is better or worse than they are. With a few exceptions they're not materialistic. They have a strong sense of who they are, and they like who they are. You may not feel their lives have purpose, but they do! Does that answer your question?'

'No no no! We don't want this. We wanted sex, swinging parties, conflict in the PTA meeting, slanging matches, rich rage. We wanted more sex. That's what Ed Hardings wanted. That's what I sold him. Don't people in Castleford have sex? The only sex I saw in the rushes was two dogs doing it by the seafront, and even then we only had it for a second,' Elliott says, looking utterly fed up.

'Elliott, if you did but know it, this is groundbreaking stuff,' says Jarred, who's been quiet for the past hour, watching the rushes and then listening to Elliott's ranting. 'You could have got the sex and swinging parties in any other community in the country, probably. What makes Castleford different is that it doesn't have those things – don't you get it? You've actually got an insight here into what makes a community work, and the people within it functional and happy and healthy and contented. Then you've got the lunch party, where everyone is talking property and money, and pretending to be what they are not – happy – and we are seeing how discontented they are compared to the locals, and how even more miserable they are when the locals don't treat them with due deference despite them taking up their positions as lords of the Flindells Mansions. You wanted the, what did you call it, *Bonfire of the Vanities* moment, and you've got it there. We can easily edit the lunch party, with all its cold affectation and false conversation, to contrast with the warmth and genuine friendships in and around the making of the Castleford School produc-tion. You've got the characters in John Tremble, Edward Bullions, the teachers at Castleford School and the local shopkeepers. You've got the funeral, where it was clear that although everyone respects the past and what one man had done for them, they are not maudlin. They get on with life. Nor do they live for the future, aspiring to what they want next or achieve next, like the rest of us do, they live for the moment and what they have they share. Perhaps it would have been different if you'd put pressure on them. Perhaps we should have put them under a spotlight just like we've done with all the other reality shows I've ever produced for you over the past years, and watched them, like ants under a magnifying glass, burning up under the pressure of publicity, but there's nothing real about that situation. Anyway, that wasn't the remit with this documentary. The remit was to find out what Castleford does right that other towns, villages, cities, places that are allegedly communities, don't do, and that's what we found out. We found out they behave like a community – not just in name, but they are one. Castleford is like an Italian or French village, where everyone looks after everyone else. It's how we think England used to be but never was. It goes at its own pace, not the pace that we in television, who think we're more powerful than anyone, dictate for it. We can't show something that isn't there. The camera never lies.'

'What utter bollocks. The camera lies all the bloody time!' screams Elliott, throwing some files at Jarred, missing him but hitting Heather so hard on the head she wakes up. 'We can create whatever we fucking well want in the editing room. I have the power to turn a sow's ear into a fucking sucking silk purse and a silk purse into a fucking sucking sow's ear if I want to. As far as you are concerned *I am God*!'

'You are not God, Elliott, and not everyone wants to bow down to TV these days. They are not all impressed,' Jarred tells him.

'You haven't been in the business as long as I have, Jarred. Everyone, without exception, is impressed with being on television. If you're not noticed, you're nobody; invisibility is the biggest sin of the twenty-first century. People are more than ready to pour their shit out in public, knowing full well it's the last place they should ever do it. People will sell their souls to be on TV, let alone work in it. They are prepared to go to any lengths to get their moment of fame. All you need to do is take a look at the talent shows, and you can see their desperation to crawl out of the gutter.'

I'm listening to all of this and realising it's got ridiculous. A few months ago I would have said nothing to this man, who has sort of given me my first break in television, but after dealing with all the stuff I've had recently, my dad dying, discovering I have a sister, confronting Leonard and his girlfriend, standing up to Elliott is a piece of cake.

'Well, Castleford doesn't feel it's in a gutter to crawl from, nor does it feel the need to sell its soul and be anything other that what it is. You wanted the real thing and you got it, but it's not what you wanted, and you can edit the final rushes all you like, but the place and the people will still come out on top,' I say, getting up and gathering my papers. 'I don't want to be a part of this project any more. You disgust me, Elliott Sterling. You're an odious shitty little man who makes even odious shitty little men look bad. Your values are corrupt, you have no ethics or integrity and you feed off others, making them feel inferior so you can feel better about yourself. You know why you don't like what you see in Castleford? Because you don't get it. You hide behind the pretence that it won't make good TV, but really it's just because you don't understand why these people are happy with their lot and success-ful and rounded. It would make good TV, it's just that they don't tick your boxes.'

'It's not that they don't tick my boxes, young lady,' Elliott spits, standing up, although he's still a few inches shorter than me. 'It's that it doesn't make good TV.'

'Just because you think it doesn't make good TV doesn't mean it doesn't make good sense to live this way,' I say. 'Anyway, you picked the director, you picked the producer and you chose to go with the subject matter. The only person who was in control here was you. You take the responsibility. Your head, your neck, and you know it.'

'I don't have to take this!' he shouts at me.

I laugh at him. I laugh at the little man telling me what he can and can't take.

'You will never work in this industry again!' he shouts as I go to the door.

'I will never work with you again, Elliott Sterling, that is a totally different matter.'

I walk out of the boardroom, believing I'm doing the right thing. What is the matter with me at the moment? First of all I've gone and told Leonard he can keep his money, and now I've gone and told Elliott Sterling, allegedly one of the most powerful people in TV, that he's an odious little man. He is an odious little man, but perhaps I shouldn't have told him to his face. After all, no one else does.

I walk out of High Light Productions and head

towards the café where I'm due to meet Victoria and Esther. I don't feel like a coffee, I feel like a Vodka Berocca or something with a punch. I am so fired up I could kick something.

'Helena! Helena!' a woman's voice calls behind me.

I turn, half expecting it to be a policewoman that Elliott's set on me to have me arrested for verbal abuse, which would, in the light of how he talks to everyone in his office, be highly hypocritical. It's Heather.

'You forgot your coat in your rush to leave our den of inequity,' she says, grinning at me.

'Thank you,' I say, taking the coat and smiling back at her.

'You were magnificent in there. Absolutely magnificent, and I can't stop now, but the shouting matches are going on!' she says clapping her hands in delight, her eyes sparkling like you wouldn't believe. 'You have put a match to an oil keg. I'm not joking, if there was a camera in there, that would make the sort of TV that that – what did you call him?'

'Odious little man.'

'That *odious little man* swoon with delight. They're all having a go at him now. Even Simon, and Simon's a mouse! I have to go because I don't want to miss anything, this is better than anything I've seen on the box ever, but just wanted to let you know,' she says, nodding and beaming. I've never seen Heather smile and laugh, and she looks very pretty. She just needs a different boss and job, methinks.

In a slightly better frame of mind I find myself at Oriel again, where I was before all this began, with my two friends, pondering my fate and feeling exactly the same way about everything, as though I've come round full circle. I'm out of a job, I have no money coming in. I still have the issue with Leonard and I don't have a man, although that wasn't an issue first time round. After my outburst I'm sure Will would have followed me if he'd wanted me to stay or wanted to show his support, and he didn't. But it was nice while it lasted. A few passionate kisses, a swim in the sea. Brief and sweet, but I had hoped for more . . .

I'm at Oriel slightly early. I sit at a table outside. My mobile rings – Charles.

'Before you say anything, Charles,' I say, 'I feel I've done the right thing.'

'Well you've done something. I've just had Leonard's solicitor on the phone and he wants to transfer the money to you this week. What did you say to Leonard to achieve this?' he asks.

I'm gobsmacked.

'You wouldn't believe me if I told you,' I say, thinking I'm in a parallel universe where people are behaving like aliens.

'Try me.'

'I told him he could keep the money,' I explain.

After a deep intake of breath he replies, 'reverse psychology, well, it worked. He's giving you the money, the sum you asked for, and it will be sent to us this week. Now do we have your bank details?'

'I can send them,' I say. And then, 'Did his solicitor explain why he decided to go ahead with it?'

'No,' replies Charles, 'and to be frank, I didn't want to pursue it, just in case he changed his mind.'

'Thank you, Charles,' I say, starting to realise what this means. I can pay off my mortgage, I can help Mum out now. Going round to Leonard's brought this about. It is the last thing I was expecting.

The waiter comes up to the table and asks me what I would like to drink. I feel like ordering a glass of champagne or a bottle even, but I'll wait for the girls to arrive, and share the good news.

'I'll have a coffee and the menu,' I say.

I want to call Will, or my mother, or speak to Leonard and thank him, but perhaps I should wait. I'm still worried about that poem, as well. I tried this morning to retrace my steps, after a thorough search in the car. I drove very slowly the route I took to Flindells Mansions, without actually going in there.

I haven't read the paper this morning. I picked up the *Daily Echo* which was in High Light's offices and didn't put it back, although it does say in clear felt tip on the front page PROPERTY OF HIGH LIGHT – NOT TO BE REMOVED. I flick through and see a mugshot of Victoria above an intriguing-looking article. This must be what she's been working on.

The headline reads AFTER-DINNER MINX, exclusive by Victoria Stock.

Forget the after-dinner mints, swinging parties are becoming all the rage, even in some of the UK's primmer coastal towns. In upmarket settings, furtive fumblings among highly respectable couples are taking place. Audrey Louche (not her real name) told me about her experiences.

'A few months ago I was invited by a man I'd met at a party to attend a dinner at the Metropole Hotel. Here I met eleven others for a delicious meal, followed by drinks upstairs in two hotel bedrooms with communicating doors.

'My partner, who I will call Mr Hoppy – for reasons that will become apparent in a minute – started kissing and undressing me. Other couples started to do the same, and after half an hour most of them were naked, and the waitress who'd been handing out drinks had disappeared, leaving everyone to it. One woman simply watched what was going on. There's no obligation to have sex with anyone else, some of the group simply want to be voyeurs, watching other couples make love. As the evening progressed, some couples swapped, although there wasn't any man-on-man or woman-on-woman action.

'At the end of the evening Mr Hoppy invited me to another dinner party, ironically in the town where I live, although he wasn't to know this. Swingers don't ask many personal questions.

'The party was to be for six people, none of whom I'd met before. The evening began with introductions to everyone by their first names only, and we sat down to a meal. Talk was of money, property and designer labels, rather than the creative arty chat at the London party. These people were different. After the main course Mr Hoppy suggested we go to a corner of the room for some role play. I suggested I undress him, which he agreed to, and tie him up. He seemed to enjoy that, and while I teased him the others continued their meal, half watching us, half chatting. I told Mr Hoppy to pretend to be a kangaroo, and he obliged by starting to hop, quite a feat while tied up.

'The other couples didn't choose to stay with their partners and proceeded to swap, although I made it clear I didn't want to partner anyone other than Mr Hoppy. It's a growing trend, this swinging business. I suggest that those curious enough to take part should be careful about their choice of partner. There are some who swing better than others . . .'

I laugh. It's a far cry from what Victoria used to do at the radio station, but at least she's got her promotion.

'Hello there!' Her voice rings out at me from the other side of the road. 'You reading my latest piece?'

'I am indeed,' I say, 'and very good it is too.'

'Why, thank you. And how did it go with the meeting this morning?' she says, plopping herself down on the chair next to me.

'Well, the good news is that Leonard has decided

after all this time to give me the money, and the good news is that I'm no longer involved with the TV programme. I called the boss an odious little man.'

She laughs. 'Hell, I've called Dena Benson far worse. What did he say and do and what's more, what have you done to Leonard to make him do what he's done?'

'Well, Elliott wants more sex and violence in the show, and Castleford's not really like that.'

'That wasn't the point of it, was it? The point was to show why it produces such successful well-rounded people. They are not dysfunctional and violent, but where's the story in that? That's the point, there is none. I'm writing about swinging parties because they're still seen as slightly unusual, but when it and if they become commonplace they won't be news any more. Funny thing is, the norm isn't the norm any more – the abnormal is the norm, if you get my drift.'

'I think so,' I say, 'anyway, I won't work in TV again, according to Elliott.'

'What bollocks,' she says. 'I'll send him this cutting and he can make a documentary about it. It sounds more his level. Great about the money though, tell me all about it.'

'Hello!' Esther rushes up, a large file in her hand, 'and how are you two today?'

'Lots to tell,' I say.

'Read my article while I get the gossip from Helena,' Victoria tells Esther.

'Oh my God!' Esther exclaims, looking up from the paper. 'Mr Hoppy! This is about Digby!'

Of course, I remember now about the infamous Digby's nickname.

'Look!' Esther says, thrusting the file into Victoria's arms.

Victoria opens the file and starts looking at the emails it contains.

'All this is highly illegal what you've done here, Esther, you do realise that don't you?' she says. 'Mind you, fabulous stuff. By the way, the real name of the girl in my article is Alison Lovett, in case you were wondering.'

'I know an Alison Lovett!' says Esther. 'She's one of Mr Hoppy's girls. Don't you remember, Helena, we talked about this when you told me about Leonard's lunch party?'

'Of course!' I say. 'Alison Lovett was there, but she couldn't have been the same one. Surely not. What are you going to do with all this information, Esther? You can't sell it to a newspaper. I suppose you could give it to Edward to make into a novel, but then you could be on dodgy ground if Digby recognises himself.'

'If it was me I'd give it to Digby's boss,' Victoria says, sounding very excited. 'Give it to him and the other directors, so that they can see what their man is doing on corporate time. Show them the whole file if need be, and tell them what he asks you to do as his assistant, and if it's part of the policy of the company to make you do such things. What do you think?'

'You'll be out of a job, Esther,' I say, 'but then join the club, so am I.' I realise Esther doesn't know about my row with Elliott, and quickly fill her in.

'My view is that your employers will give you a pay-off to keep you quiet, Esther, to stop you talking to people like me,' says Victoria, looking through the file and giggling at some of the contents. 'Banks like to look as though they are responsible even when they are not, and they need all the good press they can get. That's what I would do if I were in your shoes. Let them think they're in control, take the money and walk away.'

'But won't I be putting all these good emails to waste?' Esther says.

'They're not wasted, Esther. Stuff like this is never wasted. And at least you won't be walking on eggshells again when you're in the office, nor will I now I've stood up to Dena, and nor will Helena. We've all managed somehow to release ourselves from, well, from our own demons. If you genuinely feel you have nothing to lose, then no one else has anything to gain by making you feel you have, so they can't hurt you – not really,' Victoria says, smiling at us both.

'I saw you speak to Peter at Dad's funeral, how did that go?' I ask.

Victoria blushes. 'It went well. I don't think my feelings for him will ever change, and he still feels the same about me. But he's with his wife and family, and I respect that. Self-control is one form of control I agree with when it's at the right time. And I know it is, and he knows it is too.'

'It's a bit like *Brief Encounter*,' says Esther, looking sad.

'Not quite, Esther,' says Victoria, 'we did bonk each

other silly for quite some time, and I don't think Celia
Johnson and Trevor Howard even got to the foreplay
stage.'

'And what about your love life, Helena?' asks
Victoria. 'What's the latest with Will?' I'd managed to
update both her and Esther last night about what had
happened with Will. I also told them about Leah.

'Well, I left him about an hour ago in the offices at
High Light and he's probably among the rubble I
created. I thought he would come after me and tell me
I'd done the right thing and that he had walked out as
well, but it wasn't him who stopped me, it was Heather,
just to give me my coat and tell me I was magnificent.'

'God I wish I'd been there!' says Esther.

'So do I!' says Victoria.

'Well, we've all had our victories over ourselves. I feel
this is something to celebrate. Champagne, anyone?' I
smile at them both.

I'm feeling slightly tipsy, having drunk two glasses of
champagne at lunchtime which is unheard of for me,
so when my mobile goes and I see it's Peter Bonham, I
hesitate before answering. Could this be him reproach-
ing at me because Elliott's just called him about my
outburst, in which case I don't want to speak to him?
Or perhaps he wants to talk about Victoria, in which
case I still don't want to speak to him. But with my new-
found courage, I take the call.

'Hello, Helena, it's Peter Bonham, as your phone has
probably told you. How are you?'

'Hi, Peter. Very well thank you, and you?'

'I'm well, but I've got to get to the point.'

Here it comes.

'Shane and Sandra didn't work out. They were never on time and we had lots of complaints about their swearing and the fact that listeners couldn't understand most lot of the slang they used, and, well, we want you back,' he says, sounding very nervous.

'Er, right.'

'Now I know you love working in TV, but we need a professional presenter and, to be blunt, George has threatened to go if you don't return.'

I don't know what to say, but Peter interprets my silence as a no.

'Of course, we don't want to offer you your old job.'

I still don't say anything.

'We were thinking of offering you the mid-morning show. I know you always wanted that slot.'

I decide to break the silence and put Peter out of his misery. 'I am interested, Peter, but I don't want to come back immediately. I plan to fly out to Sardinia with Freddie to see my friend Eliana and her family, and I want to spend time with Mum, too.'

'It would be good to have you back, Helena, whenever you're ready.'

'On my terms.'

'On your terms,' he agrees. 'And lunch when you get back. Your choice of restaurant this time.'

'That would be good, Peter,' I say, thinking what a different boss this man is to Elliott. I know which one I respect more and would work harder for. I update the girls, who congratulate me, and we go our separate ways.

I'm at home, and just about to go over and see Mum, who's back in her cottage, when I get a call from Will.

'Sorry I haven't been in touch before. I think Heather told you all hell broke loose when you left. Nothing has ever happened like this before, and he can't believe it. It was hilarious.'

'I'm very pleased to hear it. What are you going to do with the programme?'

'Produce it our way, or not at all.'

'And Elliott is going to allow you to do that?'

'He doesn't really have a choice.'

'Great!'

There's a pause.

'I'm going to a party in Somerset this weekend, and if you don't have Freddie, would you like to join me? No strings attached, but I need to book a bed and breakfast. We can book two rooms if you like. Please come.'

'That sounds lovely,' I reply, thinking belatedly perhaps I should have played hard to get, or waited a little bit longer to say yes.

I'm leaving my house when I see Leonard approaching. He looks rather stressed and yet pleased to see me.

He calls out my name and walks towards me. The first thing I think is something is wrong with Freddie, and I have this sinking feel that I've got another trip to the hospital.

'Is it Freddie, is something wrong with Freddie?' I say.

'It's not Freddie,' He replies.

'Is Mum all right?' I say.

'As far as I know,' he replies.

'What's up then?' I ask, now standing face to face with him.

'I just wanted to see if you were all right.'

'Why?' I say, feeling perhaps I should step back as he may be able to smell the alcohol on my breath and I could expect a letter about being an alcoholic and all bets being off.

'I got your poem.'

My face lights up. 'You've found it!' I say and then suddenly realise he thinks I wrote it, for him.

'Your poem made me think. Actually it made me think you were going to commit suicide with all that talk of death, and then that made me realise this has all gone on for far too long. We're always going to wind each other up, Helena. We did when we lived together and we do now, but your poem and how you've been since I dropped the bombshell about moving here, and putting Freddie into boarding school, surprised me. Well, I expected you to get angry, just like you always do, and react and hit out. You didn't react and that made me think about how I react and have reacted in the past to things. And when your dad died it made me think about my behaviour towards you and how I've been. How I've been angry with you and myself. How it hasn't helped Freddie. How we haven't helped

Freddie. Your poem made me realise life is too short for this. I'm exhausted trying to hurt you, punish you for stuff that happened such a long time ago. And when you said what you did about the money and then left me this,' he says, handing me the poem, 'I though if it makes you feel this bad, this desperate, it's not worth it. Nothing is worth this. It took great courage to come over to my place and say what you did. Don't know if I could have done it. As for the boarding school, I think Freddie should stay where he is, and have you to come home to each day.'

I would like to think Leonard said this. I would like to think he had this eureka moment when he realised that working together and being kind to each other was the right way forward. I would like to think that his motives in making the payment were magnanimous and grown-up. But he didn't say these things to me. Instead he told me the truth and what he really felt.

'Yes I got your poem, and I've brought it back to you. Not that it changed my mind, of course. It was typical you, although you did talk about death a lot, and it crossed my mind you were considering suicide. I didn't want the hassle of having to look after Freddie if you did decide to end it all. Freddie needs a mother even if you're not a particularly good one, and the money I would consider as passing on my inheritance to my son, just earlier than I had anticipated. I will be able to invest and get interest on the money I don't have to pay you each month, so I'll be financially better off in the long run. As for the boarding school, I looked at the fees and they're too high, and his present school seems fine. The teachers are mildly eccentric, but it seems fine.'

I'd like to think the poem had had an impact on him, no matter how insignificant Leonard thinks it is at this moment, but that will always be the romantic in me. I would like to believe the legacy of Louisa's letter to my dad has helped to mend a rift a generation later, almost by accident. And that perhaps what goes around comes around – it's just that it may take a generation or so for the karma to be felt and the lesson learned.

'Well, thank you for the money and thank you for this. I'm glad we've been able to talk,' I reply, smiling at him. 'Will you stay here?'

'I don't know. Helena didn't really want to come here anyway because you were here, and Castleford isn't me – too small-minded, too parochial. My friends and colleagues and I are so much more open-minded and cosmopolitan than the people who live round here.'

I don't bother to disagree. It's a waste of breath. 'Freddie would like to see more of you,' I tell him.

'I know, and he will. Or I will try. You know how work is.'

'I know,' I say, realising Leonard will always see Freddie on his terms, and eventually there will be a time when Freddie won't want to see his father any more. Leonard will go to his grave thinking he has known best all his life. Perhaps he is the lucky one to have such conviction, such self-belief which it overrides logic and compassion. Being blind, at least you can't

see the pain you cause. Perhaps he'll meet some guide
dog of a woman who'll lead him into the middle of a
busy road and leave him there.

'Well that's all then,' he says and walks away, back to
his car and his house and his girlfriend.

Chapter Twenty-seven

I am expecting Will to pick me up at nine this evening. Freddie is with his dad this weekend and Mum has agreed to be here when Leonard drops him back on Sunday. It's almost dark outside and I've had butterflies all day. I haven't felt like this since I was eight and Colin Bastick – who was the older man at ten – said he loved me and wanted to give me a kiss on the lips, which meant we had to get married. It was the law. Why did I always choose men with funny names? After Colin it was Nicholas Krushevsky and then Abraham Sundayman. No wonder I never fantasised about taking someone else's name when I married. God, how shallow am I!

I must have checked my packing a million times: something pretty for the mornings – light, floaty and natural – something simple for the walking he has suggested, and something a bit dressier for the party. He also said we're going to go for a run, but he was probably joking about that. I've packed running gear just in case. After all, this is the man who suggested we go swimming in a freezing-cold sea. Lastly, I've packed some very sexy skimpy underwear, not that anyone will see it as he's booked separate rooms.

At nine o'clock I get a text message.

'I'll be shinning up your drainpipe any moment now. Are you ready for me?'

There's a different tone in his voice – if text messages have voices. It's rather cheeky and I like it.

'No, I'm sitting on the sofa,' I text back, although I'm not. 'It's very uncomfortable.'

A text comes back. 'Silly sofa. If I were it I would enclose you to keep you warm and rock you to sleep!'

I laugh and text back. 'If you were the sofa I would never get any sleep. Just thinking about you makes me wet.'

I press send. Shit! What have I done? That's too much. I can't get it back. I press buttons but I've sent it. Well that's blown it, then. No shinning up drainpipes tonight.

But a text comes back. 'If I were a sofa I would be a sofa bed. I go hard when I talk to you or even text you, like now. Shame to waste it. Will be there soon.'

I can feel my heart beating faster and I'm flushed and dizzy with excitement. If Freddie saw me now I know he'd suggest I go to see a doctor.

There's a knock on the door and as I rush towards it I almost trip over the mat. I open it and smile. Will is standing before me, looking handsome and chilled.

'Are you ready?' he asks. 'Or do you want to stay on the sofa for the weekend?'

I smile. 'No, thank you. I've been sitting on it for far

too long, and I'm not the sitting-around type,' I say, picking up my weekend bag. Will takes it from me and with his other hand takes mine. We walk down the path to where he's parked.

'Is this yours?' I say, standing back amazed, because the car door he opens belongs to a silver Aston Martin Vantage. 'Have you pinched it or borrowed it?' I ask.

'All of the above,' he says, putting my bag in the boot and ushering me into the passenger seat.

'I've got to practise. It's very low,' I say, realising I haven't been in a sports car for ages, and never in an Aston. 'Where can you hire these things for the weekend?' I ask as he gets in beside me.

'Haven't got a clue. This is mine.' He starts up the engine as I put on my seat belt, then he punches the address in Somerset into the satnav. The automated voice sounds like a dominatrix who'll get cross if we don't do as she says.

'That's an assertive satnav you have,' I laugh.

'Good, isn't she,' he says, leaning over and giving me a quick kiss on the lips. Then he starts up the engine, which growls, like a lion getting ready to roar. I can feel its power but I can't hear it yet. It's a bit like the energy I'm getting from Will, actually.

We zoom off as I enthuse, 'What a wonderful car! Is it really yours? I didn't know TV paid that well.'

'It doesn't pay that well, but I made some money elsewhere, and though I'm not the sort to show off, I wanted to show off to you. Perhaps I'm trying to impress you,' he says with a glint in his eye.

'Where did you make your money?' I ask.

'I made it in another lifetime, a corporate lifetime before I realised it wasn't a life and got out. Now I feel I'm alive, although I'm still working with twats like Sterling.'

'What's happened to the show, by the way?' I ask.

'Sterling had to back down because everyone stood up to him after you made your little speech, and it's going out probably just as you would like it. Everyone comes across well, apart from the luncheon-party set, who come across as themselves, so they'll probably think they look just fine. That's the thing about people like that – they don't see how they really are.'

As we head out of town into the darkness, Will turns on what must be his 'seduction tape'.

'Are you trying to seduce me, Will?' I ask.

'Yes,' he says, driving a little faster and taking the car from a purr to a roar.

As he drives he asks me lots of questions about myself, and in turn I ask about him and his life. My heart is racing faster than the car. He tells me about a time when Leonard and he had girlfriends who were friends. I find it a bit unnerving that they used to know each other and were in the same class, yet are so different. Will is confident, like Leonard, but he seems more mature, more of a man.

We chat merrily as he hits the motorway, breaking the speed limit, which is obviously very wrong and irresponsible, but very exciting too.

Eventually we leave the motorway and head down

some narrow lanes that lead to the bed and breakfast we're staying at. We park up, then walk inside. Will announces that our rooms are called Pincushion and Foxhole.

'I'll be Foxhole,' I say.

'Of course you will,' he replies and smiles mischievously.

The inn is old with uneven stone floors, narrow, creaky stairs and wonderful old beams everywhere – it's absolutely charming.

I open the door to Foxhole, which has a double bed, while Will's room has only a single. I thank him.

'I'll see you for a drink downstairs perhaps?' he says hopefully.

'Yes, that would be good,' I reply.

I walk into my room and close the door, feeling excited and worried at the same time. I haven't felt this way about anyone for ages. I unpack but stay in what I'm wearing, which is perfectly fine, then I go downstairs to find Will waiting at the bar.

'Would you like a drink?' he asks.

'Yes please. Wine will be fine. Anything red.'

We sit by the unlit fire and just stare at each other for a little while.

'It's wonderful when something like this happens, isn't it?' he says, and we stay there, slowly getting tipsy. We eventually go to our separate rooms at the end of the evening. I give him a little kiss on the lips but nothing more.

The next morning he knocks on my door.

'Fancy a run?' he says, standing there in his jogging gear.

'I thought you were joking when you said we'd go running, but I can always change,' I say, suddenly realising I've forgotten my trainers. 'I'll run in my boots,' I say, though it's dreadfully impractical. A few minutes later I'm running along a narrow lane with Will. We pass a house where he tells me some of his relatives used to live, then head off across a meadow where cows and a bull look at us curiously, then off down another narrow lane. I'm out of condition, and I say so.

'Can we stop?' I ask. 'I'm a bit puffed; I'm not as fit as you.'

'You are, you're just not used to running. Why don't we bimble for a bit?' he suggests.

'Bimble?'

'Walk, look, bumble, bimble.'

'I like the idea of that,' I say.

We walk along the lanes, enjoying the sunshine and holding hands as Will talks about his parents – who sound like mine; upbringing – very much like mine; and values – identical to mine. The more he talks the more we realise how much we have in common, which is rather wonderful and rather scary for both of us. He takes me to the local church, where some of his ancestors are buried, and tells me about his great-aunt, who was a lion tamer, which I find hilarious. He tells me how his parents fell in love and his father lost the family fortune because Will's grandfather disinherited him. It's all so unexpected and fascinating, like him really. My mobile goes off and I'm half tempted not to answer, but it's Esther, so I do.

'Never guess who Digby's boss is?' she says, without even saying hello.

'Is that what you've rung me up to tell me on my romantic weekend away?' I hint loudly into the phone.

'Oh bugger! Sorry Helena, shall I phone back?'

'No, no, you've got me interested now. Who is it?'

'My sister.'

'Surely you'd know if your sister was Digby's boss.'

'No, my half-sister. You know the sister Claire I didn't want to meet? She happens to be Digby's boss. Well, the HR director who is sort of Digby's boss. Her name is Claire Chapman. Dad said she'd done well in the bank, but didn't realise she'd done that well. I was looking at lower middle management, not the senior levels, to try and find her. So I went to see this Claire Chapman quite innocently with the control-freak file and all the emails. Suddenly I realised who she was, I'm not sure how. I told her we were half-sisters. She was gobsmacked! We chatted and I showed her the file, which she found very interesting, as you can imagine, and now she's going to sit on it. I don't know what she's going to do with it, but I know she will do something. She said she didn't think much of our father either, which made me laugh. She said when she was first introduced to him she thought what a stuffed shirt he was, only polite to her when he realised how well she'd done career-wise. We're going out for a drink next week and I'd love you to come along, but perhaps you'll be seeing Will?'

'Perhaps,' I reply, turning round and smiling at him, 'but I'd like to meet her and I'm very pleased you've got together at last, even though it wasn't intentional. Things work out in the end. It reminds me of a poem Dad's first wife wrote to him, which has helped me heal a rift and understand my mum, and perhaps mend something with Leonard. Your dad's selfishness has unintentionally released you from your boss's selfishness. You've not only learned from your father's mistake, you've potentially gained from it as well.'

'I'm not going to thank him for this,' Esther replies.

'I'm not telling you to, I'm just saying that it's amazing how things happen. When we think we have no influence to make things go our way, they come round in the end. I think that's what I'm trying to say. You must excuse me, I'm bimbling at the moment.'

'You're what?'

'Walking through country lanes in Somerset, and very nice it is too.'

'Well, I'll leave you to your bimbling and your bloke. Give me a call when you get back and I'll introduce you to Claire. She looks nothing like me, nor my dad for that matter.'

'And you can meet Leah when you have time, Esther.'

'Wow, who said life is dull?'

'I never said it was.'

'Your life has never been dull, Helena. Mine, I think,

has just had a kick-start.' She laughs, and we say goodbye.

After a bit more bimbling and dodging AWOL tractors, Will speaks. 'I want you to meet my friends tonight, because I want to prove I'm not a fake. I know you've been hurt by Leonard in the past. I could sense it when I first met you, and I suspect, no matter how strong you like to come across, that you're quite vulnerable underneath. I just want to show you that you can trust me. I know how difficult that can be, as I had to learn to trust again when my wife had an affair. I know you trusted Leonard and he let you down, but you can trust me,' he says, pulling me to him and kissing me, just like he did that first time, in my cottage. Once again I find myself lost in his arms and enjoying every moment.

That evening when I meet Will's friends at the party, they're delightful: funny, clever, welcoming and warm. I sit for ages talking to an eighty-something lady who's amazing, and has been married three times. She seems more sprightly than a lot of sixty-year-olds I know, and she reminds me a little of a female version of John Tremble. There's some dancing, and Will teaches, or tries to teach me, how to salsa, but I keep leading.

'The man always lead,' he says.

'I find it very difficult to let go and let a man do that, as you can understand.'

'It's a dance, not life,' he replies, and gradually, very slowly, I start to relax and let him lead, until the music stops and I kiss him.

We are some of the last to leave, and as we drive back to the B & B, Will leans over to me and says, 'Thank you for being so calm and warm with my friends.'

'It was easy. They're lovely people,' I reply.

At the inn Will comes up to my room. I can tell he wants to stay as he sits on the bed, but I don't want to sleep with him just yet. I want to wait and I want him to wait, so I ask him to go. When he does I fall asleep, feeling very restless but knowing it's the right thing to do. I'm taking Esther's advice and making the man wait.

In the morning Will knocks on my door. 'Run?' I ask, getting ready to change into my gear.

'No, I've already been,' he says. 'Do you want to join me for breakfast?' I nod, and he goes.

He's gone running without me and I'm slightly disappointed because I had energy to burn off, as did he, obviously. I go down to find him sitting alone, waiting. He looks up and smiles a warm open smile, and I lean down and kiss him lovingly and gently on the mouth. When I stop and draw back I can see in his eyes that he's as happy as I am. I sit and order eggs for breakfast, while he has a full English, but neither of us can eat anything.

'Shall we go upstairs and have a cuddle?' he suggests.

'That would be nice,' I say and we both get up and thank the waiter, who looks at our full plates of food and asks if anything is wrong. We reassure him that everything was fine, we're just not hungry, and walk upstairs to my room. I turn to him and he holds me the way I love, cupping the back of my neck in his hands, making me purr inside.

'We've been invited to bimble with a few of my friends,' Will says. 'Do you want to meet up with them again?'

'I'd love that,' I say, thinking with pleasure about holding hands and wandering along feeling the sun on our skin.

He starts to kiss me, stroking my neck and undoing my blouse, pushing himself towards me. I kiss him back, wanting to be as close as possible to him, entwining myself like ivy round his body. He holds me round the waist, picking me up as though I'm as light as a leaf (which I'm not, I'm nine and a half stone and gaining), and carrying me to the bed, still kissing me as he does so. He lays me down gently and undresses me quickly while undressing himself, which I would have thought was impossible, but somehow he does it. I must tell the girls about it. Then again, perhaps not. If I do, it will appear in Edward's next book. And if I tell Victoria, it may appear in her next article.

He pushes my legs aside and moves on to me, and into me, holding my hands down above my head, kissing me and pushing into me. I kiss him back, expecting the lovemaking to last minutes, but half an hour later, an hour later, two hours later, Will is still making love to me. I have never, ever told a man that I think he's an amazing lover, because most men are conceited enough anyway about their sexual prowess, but I can't help myself.

'You are brilliant. You are absolutely wonderful. Sorry, I know that sounds clichéd and naff, but this is amazing. I didn't think any man could go on for this long. I didn't think it was humanly possible.'

'If you're with the right woman, it is,' he says, smiling at me, continuing to kiss me and move me on top of him and then by the side of him, spooning me and stroking my back as he does so.

After an all day-all night lovemaking session, we realise we've missed the Bimble with Will's friends by about twelve hours. It's four o'clock in the morning and we finally take a break. Will decides that we should have a walk in the open air, and gaze at the stars. I've come twice, he hasn't come at all, and I'm feeling distinctly like an underachiever, not having been able to turn him on as much as he has me, but he says it's nothing to do with it, and that I'm gorgeous and wonderful and he'll come tomorrow, but tonight he didn't want to. And I think I've got another control freak on my hands and tell him so. He laughs.

'No, but I see what you mean. I'd rather be like you were tonight,' he says, opening my bath robe and kissing me on my belly button, which I find both ticklish and sexy.

We walk outside and hold each other and try to find the Plough and the North Star, feeling overwhelmed by the vastness of the night sky, I remember Eliana telling me that I should have more fun and make time for passion and love. About how I should feel with my whole being that I want to be with a man who makes me happy to be a woman, his woman. Who makes me feel like a flower opening up in his arms every time I see him, touch him, kiss him. Who can, even when I am tired and cold and cross and distracted, melt me in his arms and his presence. And as I look up at the stars I realise how lucky and happy and small I am, and hope I've found him.

'I wish my dad could see me now, and see how happy I am,' I say.

'He's probably looking down on you now.'

'I hope so. He taught me a lot when he was alive, but I think even in death he continues to teach me things, about the importance of making the most of my life and not being afraid, or, what's that phrase, "feeling the fear and doing it anyway". I don't think I would have had the courage to confront Leonard or my own fear if Dad hadn't died. Dealing with his death gave me the courage to live the way I want. Even being with you is a risk for me, you know that. I don't want my heart broken again. It's only just recovering after all this time. Not that there's any pressure or anything,' I say, smiling and glancing at Will, who's looking up at the stars but looks down at me when I say 'being with you'.

'Do you know what I mean?' I say, as he gazes at me.

'Yes. I suppose it's a bit like going down a black run, when you've only been used to doing reds. Once you've done the blacks the reds are a doddle. Best way of dealing with fear is to face it, and then everything else seems a piece of cake. Do you feel you're in control of your life more now?' he asks, taking my hand. 'I felt

when I first met you that you had the veneer of someone in control, but were still a bit lost.'

'I always had control, just never knew it. I just felt I
was dominated by a control freak, Leonard, when really
I had the power all along. It's not having control that
matters, it's knowing how to use it, and I've never seen
the point of manipulating others, especially when the
purpose is to make them unhappy. I'm too aware of the
pain it causes, and the consequences, and life is too
short. And anyway, as you've just shown me in bed, it
can be more fun losing control than keeping hold of it
sometimes, yes?'

Epilogue – Six months later

Elliott Sterling is in a good mood. Jarred Collins is in the boardroom briefing him, and the usual suspects, on the aftermath of *The Castleford Cure*, broadcast a few weeks ago to brilliant and extensive review across the media – applauded by the broadsheets as being insightful, intelligent and ground-breaking journalism, and by the tabloids as being fun to watch. The documentary has already been nominated for several awards. Elliott is taking all the credit.

'A follow-up to *The Castleford Cure* has been commissioned,' Jarred says, handing his boss the large file of glowing press cuttings about the documentary. 'We wanted Will on the programme, working with Helena Treadwell as with the first one, but they're both in Sardinia at the moment on holiday. They've floated an idea to me about a project on control freaks, which I like the sound of.'

Elliott ignores the attempt at a pitch, snapping back abruptly, 'They an item, then?'

'It looks that way. Anyway, they said they'd talk about logistics when they get back. They are not committing to anything yet, but they like the idea of the follow-up.'

'Yes yes yes. They're not irreplaceable,' Elliott sneers.

'I am not working with any other director and producer on this one,' Jarred replies quickly. 'So as far as I'm concerned, they are.'

'OK.' Elliott is swivelling on his chair so fast that it looks as though he's going to take off any moment, like a helicopter. 'This is all good, all extremely good. I'm pleased with how this programme turned out. So is Ed Hardings, who's moved on to pastures new, but no matter, I'm sure the next guy has buttons we can push. The viewing figures for *Castleford* will speak for themselves, and we didn't even have any sex or violence. Who says sex sells, huh?'

'You did,' says Simon.

'Did I? Well it does. Anyway, no sitting on laurels, now we've got this in the bag, what else do we have? What else do you have to get my juices flowing, and those of the commissioning editors? What else is new?' Elliott says, looking round and expecting someone to stand up and make a dramatic and startling presentation.

Luca takes up the gauntlet, and stands.

'Well, I've got this idea about schools in inner cities,' he starts, but before he can hand out his papers Elliott stops swivelling and bangs the table, making everyone jump, except Jarred who sits back in his seat and sighs, and Heather, who sits as usual in the corner of the room, fuming as her latest boyfriend has just dumped her.

'No,' Elliott growls. 'That is old fucking news. We've ticked the boxes and got full marks on *Castleford*, now I want something new, something different, something with jeopardy and celebrity, sex, yes, sex and violence, boys. Give me ideas that make me wet with excitement!'

Acknowledgements

I'd like to thank my wonderful editor Emma Rose, who I'm very fortunate to work with. Thank you for your guidance, Emma. To the excellent publicity and marketing team at Random, thank you so much guys for all your hard work. To Luigi and Amanda for all their support (please get one made into a film soon!) and my friends Caroline, Amanda, Karen, Helen D, Clare B, Carron P, Coline, Paul (thank you so much for your friendship and support over the years), John D, and always to Hazel and Doreen, none of whom I would call control freaks, (well, I'm sure they have their moments), but all of whom are far more organised than I will ever be. To Amy and Julio and 'Bear' at Number Seven, thank you Julio for finding my computer! And to Jeremy. And to Dominic. And to Gary C. You told me to write and I did.

And note to Tom, you can only read mummy's books when I say so, OK.

ted. ✓

BRITISH HISTORY 1760 – 1914

Accounting an C
Accounting and Costing: Problems and
Biology
Book-keeping and Accounts
British History 1760–1914
British History since 1914
Business Calculations
Chemistry
Commerce
Commerce: West African Edition
Communication
Economic Geography
Economics
Economics: West African Edition
Electronics
Elements of Banking
European History 1815–1941
Financial Accounting
Financial Accounting: Questions and Answers
Geography: Human and Regional
Geography: Physical and Mapwork
Information Processing
Insurance
Investment
Law
Management: Personnel
Mathematics
Nutrition
Office Practice
Organic Chemistry
Physics
Principles of Accounting
Principles of Accounting: Answer Book
Statistics
Twentieth Century World Affairs

Success in

BRITISH HISTORY 1760 – 1914

Peter Lane, B.A.

JOHN MURRAY

to Peter James Illtydd

First published 1978
Reprinted 1981 and 1984 (with revisions); 1988, 1991

Printed in England by Clays Ltd, St Ives plc

0 7195 3483 6

Foreword

In 1760 Britain was only one of a number of equally important countries. Her political, social and economic life was dominated by the landed aristocracy, and agriculture was her main industry. Her governments played little active part in the lives of the people, most of whom lived in villages or small towns.

From 1760 to 1870 governments continued to follow the policy of *laisser-faire*, which gave enterprising industrialists the freedom to lay the foundations of our modern industrial society. By 1870 Britain had gone through the initial stages of the Industrial Revolution, and was the first country to do so.

One result of this was the creation of a large middle class which became the most important group in the country's political and economic life. Another effect was the growth in the nation's wealth, which allowed foreign ministers such as Palmerston to extend British influence throughout the world.

Between 1870 and 1914 Britain lost her industrial lead to the USA and Germany. It also became increasingly clear that the policy of *laisser-faire* had equally failed to produce 'the greatest happiness for the greatest possible number' which had been one of its claims. For a large section of the working class, industrialization led to poverty, unemployment and ill-health. By 1914 the working class, a product of industrialization, had formed its own Labour Party and forced the Liberals to lay the foundations for the modern welfare state. Britain was also on the brink of a major war which would, in time, bring about even more changes.

1760–1914 is one of the most eventful and crucial periods in British history. It is one which must be studied by anyone who wishes to follow the social, political and historical developments that came after it. For an author, a book such as this presents the overwhelming problem of selecting and delineating main issues. No picture of a century-and-a-half so complex can be completed within the space of a comparatively short volume; one can only endeavour to disentangle the wood from the trees and in doing so may over-simplify in some places, or prune too heavily in others. Whether the result is a successful balance is for readers to judge, and views are bound to differ. Readers who seek fuller or wider knowledge of any aspect of study should consult the lists of further reading.

The period is one of the most popular with 16+ students, and is basic preparatory study for those working at A level I have therefore designed the present text so that it will be of maximum help to students, and have tried to recreate the period in as clear and immediate a way as possible. I have made extensive use of original documents and of pictures which include cartoons, engravings and maps.

As many events overlap in time, or run parallel to each other, the text has been cross-referenced throughout so that students can easily trace the connection between one development and another, and can quickly revise any given topic. The sets of questions at the end of each Unit are mostly taken from recent examination papers, so this will familiarize students with the kind of examination requirements they may expect to meet, and give them plenty of opportunity for preparation and practice. The independent student will find the questions excellent for self-testing.

An increasing number of examining boards include data-based questions in their examinations. Questions of this kind appear at the end of each Unit in this book and further examples can be found in *Documents and Questions: 1. British History 1760–1815* and *2. British History 1815–1914* (John Murray, 1981).

P.L.

Acknowledgments

Any teacher is indebted to his students for part, at least, of his own developing body of knowledge. I have to thank my former pupils at St. Boniface's College, Plymouth, and at Coloma College of Education for stimulating my already deep interest in this period, and in history in general. I have also been helped by other teacher-writers and, in particular, by those who have produced collections of documentary material for teachers and students. I have acknowledged my debt to individuals in the sections of Further Reading at the end of each Unit and here wish to thank them collectively.

The text was read and criticized by my colleagues, Joan Kennedy and John Addison, also by Sean Garrett and Michael St. John Parker. I am grateful for their pertinent and constructive comments. I am also indebted to Carolyn Nichols and Rosemarie Burston, whose work on the manuscript, and at all stages of the book, was invaluable, and well 'beyond the call of duty'.

I must also thank my wife and children for their patience and forbearance during the whole course of the writing.

P.L.

We are grateful to the following for their kind assistance in providing illustrations:
Australian News and Information Bureau, 17.4; B. T. Batsford Ltd., 3.2, 4.1, 4.3, 10.3, 12.1, 19.2, 19.3, 19.4, 21.1, 23.3, 24.4, 27.1, 28.2, 29.1; Central Press Photos Ltd., 27.4; County Record Office, Stafford, 13.4; Greater London Council Photographic Library, 31.5; *Illustrated London News*, 28.3; Imperial War Museum, 15.1; London Museum, 28.4; Mansell Collection, 1.1, 1.3, 2.1, 2.3, 3.3, 3.4, 6.1, 6.4, 6.5, 7.2, 7.3, 8.1, 8.3, 9.2, 10.2, 10.4, 11.2, 11.3, 11.4, 12.2, 13.2, 13.5, 14.2, 15.2, 16.1, 16.2, 16.4, 17.2, 17.3, 18.2, 19.1, 21.3, 23.2, 31.1, 31.2, 31.4; National Army Museum, 6.6; National Maritime Museum, Greenwich Hospital Collection, 5.3; National Portrait Gallery, 2.4, 4.4, 25.1; Radio Times Hulton Picture Library, 2.2, 3.5, 5.1, 5.2, 7.4, 8.2, 12.3, 12.5, 13.3, 14.1, 14.3, 16.3, 18.3, 18.4, 20.1, 20.2, 20.3, 20.4, 21.2, 22.2, 23.1, 23.4, 24.3, 25.3, 26.1, 26.3, 28.1, 29.2, 29.3, 29.4, 30.4, 31.3; Victoria and Albert Museum, 6.3, 8.4, 8.5.

Bibliography

Further reading has been suggested at the end of each Unit, but the following will be found useful for the period as a whole.

Documentary Collections
Aspinall, A. and Smith, E. A. (ed.): *English Historical Documents, Volume XI: 1783–1832*. Eyre and Spottiswoode (London, 1959).
Court, W. H. B.: *British Economic History 1870–1914, Commentary and Documents*. Cambridge University Press (Cambridge, 1965).
Dawson, K. and Wall, P.: *Society and Industry in the 19th Century*, books 1–6. Oxford University Press (Oxford, 1969).
Handcock, W. D. (ed.): *English Historical Documents, Volume XII (Part 2): 1874–1914*. Eyre and Spottiswoode (London, 1977).
Hobsbawm, E. J.: *Labour's Turning Point 1880–1900*. Harvester Press (London and New York, 1974).
Lane, P.: *Documents and Questions: 1. British History 1760–1815*. John Murray (London, 1981).
Lane, P.: *Documents and Questions: 2. British History 1815–1914*. John Murray (London, 1981).
Tremlett, T. D.: *British History 1815–1914*. Arnold (London, 1971).
Young, G. M. and Handcock, W. D. (ed.): *English Historical Documents, Volume XII (Part 1): 1833–1874*. Eyre and Spottiswoode (London, 1956).

Sketch Maps
Catchpole, B.: *A Map History of the British People since 1700*. Heinemann (London, 1978).
Perry, D. G. and Seaman, R. D. H.: *Sketch-Maps in Modern History 1789–1970*. John Murray (London, 1971).

Biographies
Chamberlain, M.: *Lord Aberdeen*. Longman (Harlow, 1983).
Finer, S. E.: *The Life and Times of Sir Edwin Chadwick*. Methuen (London, 1980).
Longford, E.: *Victoria R.I.* Weidenfeld and Nicolson (London, 1971).

Economic and Social Histories
Ashton, T. S.: *The Industrial Revolution 1760–1830*. Oxford University Press (Oxford, 1968).

Marshall, D.: *Industrial England 1776–1851.* Routledge and Kegan Paul (London, 1983).

Roebuck, J.: *The Making of Modern English Society from 1850.* Routledge and Kegan Paul (London, 1983).

General Histories

Clark, G. Kitson: *The Making of Victorian England.* Methuen (London, 1966).

Cole, G. D. H. and Postgate, R.: *The Common People 1746–1946.* Methuen (London, 1961).

Ensor, R. C. K.: *England 1870–1914.* Oxford University Press (Oxford, 1936).

Evans, E. J.: *The Forging of the Modern State: Early Industrial Britain 1783–1870.* Longman (Harlow, 1983).

Read, D.: *England 1868–1914: The Age of Urban Democracy.* Longman (Harlow, 1979).

Robbins, K.: *The Eclipse of a Great Power: Modern Britain 1870–1975.* Longman (Harlow, 1983).

Seaman, L. C. B.: *Victorian England: Aspects of English and Imperial History 1837–1901.* Methuen (London, 1973).

Watson, J. S.: *The Reign of George III 1760–1815.* Oxford University Press (Oxford, 1960).

Woodward, Sir Llewellyn: *The Age of Reform 1815–1870.* Oxford University Press and Book Club Associates (Oxford and Swindon, 1979).

Contents

The Economic Framework, 1760–1914

1.1 Britain in 1760

One of the main tasks of the student of history is to try to picture the people, the society and the country he or she is studying. In the case of Britain in 1760 this is very difficult. It is all too easy to imagine that Britain then was like modern Britain, only about 200 years younger. In fact, of course, it was totally different.

Britain in 1760 was very thinly populated, with a total population of about 6½ million. This is less than the population of modern London. Most people then lived in small villages, whereas the modern Britisher is likely to live in a fairly large town or city. London was considered a very overgrown place even in the eighteenth century, when its population was about 500 000. Bristol and Norwich were the next largest centres, with populations of about 30 000. Liverpool, Newcastle, Exeter and Plymouth were growing centres of trade and commerce with populations of about 15 000, while Manchester had been described by Daniel Defoe in 1724 as 'the largest mere village in England', with its population of about 10 000.

Most people made their living from farming, which was Britain's main industry in 1760. Using primitive tools and methods they could grow enough food to feed themselves and the people who lived in the small towns and worked in one of the other industries for which Britain was well-known (Section 1.3). But they produced very little compared with the amount produced by farmworkers at the end of the nineteenth century or compared with farmworkers today using modern machinery. This helps to explain the low standard of living which the majority of people had to endure, and is also the reason why most people were anxious to have another job in addition to their regular work on the farm. 'Every cottage had its spinning wheel,' said one writer and, as Fig. 1.1 shows, the women and children worked at these machines to produce the yarn and the cloth which formed the raw material for Britain's second main industry—wool. Again we should note that the machinery used was primitive, so that each working person could produce only a fraction of the goods which a worker in a nineteenth-century textile factory produced.

Many trades were carried on in the workers' cottages: blacksmiths, the metal trades, nail-making and others were *domestic* trades, some of them remaining so until late in the nineteenth century. Other trades, involving the carpenter, baker, brewer, candle and soap manufacturer, were carried on in most small towns, so local people had most of their wants satisfied by local tradesmen and craftsmen.

Fig. 1.1 Spinning in a Yorkshire cottage in 1814. The simple machines were housed in the cottage and driven by hand. The workers were paid about ½d (one fifth of one new penny) for each pound weight of yarn that was spun. They were too poor to be able to afford much furniture, flooring and clothing

One of the reasons for this localization was the absence of any speedy method of communication. Until the railways were developed in the 1840s and 1850s, it was not possible for a manufacturer to sell his goods throughout the country or for a Cornish dairy farmer to sell his milk in London.

1.2   Forces for Change

In 1760 the British economic and social pattern had remained fairly stable for over a hundred years. Professor Asa Briggs has suggested that, if a Rip Van Winkle had fallen asleep in 1660 and woken up in 1760 he would have found himself in a familiar world of villages, small towns, local craftsmen, landed gentry and so on. But, says Briggs, if he had fallen asleep in 1760 and woken up in 1860, Rip Van Winkle would have been amazed at the changes that had taken place.

We shall consider some of these changes in Section 1.3, but first we have to consider *why* changes took place. What were the forces which compelled the British to change their styles of production so radically as to warrant the title 'the Industrial Revolution'?

There are two main reasons for the dramatic changes which took place. The first force was a growth in the British population, as Fig. 1.2 shows. You will notice that there was a steady decline in the death rate so that more people

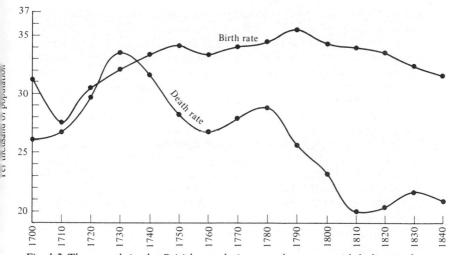

Fig. 1.2 The growth in the British population was due to a rapid decline in the death-rate after 1740. Although the birth-rate also declined after 1800 there was still a large increase in population so that there were more people to be fed, clothed and housed—and the agricultural, industrial and transport revolutions were the results

lived and more girls grew up (who previously would have died) to have families. The population of Great Britain grew as follows:

1801	10·9 million
1811	12·6 million
1821	14·4 million

All these extra mouths had to be fed, all those extra bodies had to be clothed.

The second force which produced great changes was an increased demand for British goods after 1760. Britain acquired, by conquest, a large Empire in India (Unit 17), the West Indies and Canada. British merchants were eager to trade with the new territories and peoples, and they began to demand goods which they could export. The old system of production was unable to meet this demand, and changes had to take place

1.3   The Changes, 1760–1830

(a) Agriculture

In 1760 there was a system of open fields throughout southern and eastern England. A village or estate would have three main fields, in each of which the individual farmer had a strip of land. There was also the common land which was not divided up but was used as grazing ground for each farmer's animals and as a source of firewood, fencing, pig food and so on. By 1760 this traditional system was unable to provide the food required by a growing population. Landowners wanted to introduce new root-crops and grasses to their farms, but this was impossible under the three-field system, in which each year two fields were tilled for wheat and barley and one was left fallow, as rough grazing, to recover its fertility. So some landowners applied to Parliament for an Enclosure Act which would allow the re-allocation of the separate strips into compact holdings, each holding (or farm) to be enclosed behind its own hedge. This led to the saving of time and land, and allowed farmers to experiment on their enclosed farms. By 1800 the face of the countryside had changed and the open fields had almost disappeared. New and varied machines had been invented to help make the farmer's work easier: Tull's drill enabled the farmer to sow a regular number of seeds in rows and so made hoeing, weeding and watering much easier. New crops had been introduced into British farming: new grasses, clover and swede were added to the already popular turnip crop with which the name of Townshend is often— and wrongly—associated. New methods of animal breeding were developed by Bakewell, the Collings brothers and Coke of Holkham (the Earl of Leicester), and this led to the production of more milk, cheese and meat, which were added to the British diet.

(b) Textiles

Another industry which underwent great changes was the textile industry, although it was not the traditional and long-established woollen industry, but the much newer cotton industry, which first experienced most of the changes. The older industry had a plentiful supply of workpeople, whereas there was no such workforce available for the newer industry. Merchants in the cotton industry were compelled to go in for machinery if they wished to expand. The supply of raw cotton could be increased easily. Owners of cotton plantations in the southern states of America, India or Egypt were able to extend their plantations and increase their output to meet the demand from British cotton-manufacturers. To increase the supply of wool was a much longer-term process. It was also found that wool was less suitable for use in the greasy machines whereas cotton did not suffer the same deterioration.

In the cotton industry the main changes occurred in:

(i) **Spinning.** Hargreaves' Spinning Jenny (patented in 1770) was a hand-driven machine which allowed one spinner to handle many spindles at once; Arkwright's Water Frame led to the development of the factory system since it was driven by water-power. In 1779 Samuel Crompton invented the mule, so called because it was a cross between the jenny and the water frame. At first this was used in the workers' homes, but by 1790 it had been converted into a power-operated machine, driven at first by water and later by steam, so that by the end of the century spinning had died out as a domestic industry and had been replaced by the factories of the spinning towns of Lancashire.

(*ii*) **Weaving.** Here change was much slower. Kay's shuttle (1733) was the first invention, but it was largely ignored. Between 1785 and 1787 Cartwright invented the power loom, but it was many years before it was adopted. Hand-loom weavers enjoyed high rates of pay for a long time, since there was plenty of yarn coming from the spinning factories and few machines in the weaving trade.

Fig. 1.3 Power-loom weaving, 1834. These machines were driven by a steam engine to which the machines were linked by driving belts

(*iii*) **Dyeing,** which was once a domestic chore, became factory centred.

(*iv*) **Cropping** was the name given to the process of putting the final finish to cloth by clipping it with shears. The invention of shears machines in the 1800s led to an outbreak of machine-breaking in Yorkshire, where former shearers found themselves displaced by machines. This was an example of the movement often described as Luddism (Section 7.3).

(*c*) **Iron**

There had been an iron industry in Britain for many centuries. By 1700 there were numbers of iron works and foundries where skilled men worked at blast furnaces and moulding plants, producing iron and steel which other skilled craftsmen turned into a variety of goods, from pots and pans to ploughshares and swords. Charcoal was used to smelt the iron, which explains why most ironworks were to be found in the well-forested regions of the Weald and Shropshire. In 1709 Abraham Darby succeeded in using coal as a fuel but it was another 50 years before this new method was widely adopted, and even in 1900 there was still at least one charcoal-fired blast furnace in operation, at Backbarrow in the Lake District.

In 1767 Darby's firm at Coalbrookdale built the first iron railroad and in 1779 the first iron bridge. Other firms took the pig-iron and cast-iron produced by Darby and others and turned it into wrought- or bar-iron. Henry Cort developed a puddling process by which the carbon was extracted from the pig-iron in a coke-fired reverberatory furnace; others invented new methods of rolling the hot iron into bars, which saved time and fuel in hammering.

The older iron works had been situated near forests, and near rivers which provided the power for the water wheels used in the blast furnaces. The invention of the steam engine (Section 1.4) enabled the ironfounders to build larger works away from the riverside. This led to the industry shifting away from its old centres into the coalfields of Scotland, Yorkshire and South Wales. The new, large foundries produced a wide range of iron goods including steam engines and textile machines. These, in turn, increased the demand for coal, another old industry which had to be developed if the industrial revolution was to proceed.

1.4   The Steam Engine

In 1698 Savery had invented a steam engine to pump water out of tin and copper mines. Thomas Newcomen, a Cornish engineer, had improved on Savery's work to produce a more efficient engine in 1708. It was this engine that was used by Darby at Coalbrookdale and, by 1770, there were over 170 of them in use in various industries. James Watt's first experiment with a steam engine was an attempt to mend a Newcomen engine; this led him to design a more efficient one (1765) and in 1769 he entered into partnership with Roebuck and then Matthew Boulton to manufacture his engine.

Up until 1780 all steam engines were simple pumps with a to-and-fro action. In 1781 Watt invented an engine which had a rotary movement and which could be used to drive a machine or a number of machines. By the end of the eighteenth century this engine was being used in textile factories, iron works, coal mines, breweries, flour mills, potteries and other industries. In one sense we can date the beginnings of the industrial revolution from the invention of this machine.

1.5   Factories and Towns

Increasingly the traditional industries changed from domestic businesses, with the workers' cottages as the workplace, to being factory-based. This change was accompanied by a shift of industrial centres from the south-east and south-west into the previously underpopulated areas of Yorkshire, Lancashire, Scotland and South Wales. Factory owners and mine developers had to build houses for their workers in each of these industrial areas, and so industrial towns grew up. By 1851 over half the population was living in towns of over 50 000 people and by 1900 three-quarters of the British people lived in such urban areas.

The massing together of large numbers of workers in these industrial centres helps to explain the growth of trade unionism (Units 18 and 29). But it was the new middle class which was the first and most immediate gainer from the industrial revolution. Industrialists and merchants, financiers and professional men such as engineers, doctors, accountants, surveyors, architects and designers became rich, built for themselves the large houses which can still be seen in older industrial areas and began to demand a share in the political system which had been dominated by the landed aristocracy. This demand for parliamentary reform (Unit 10) was led by the middle classes.

Once the middle classes had gained a share in the political system they used their political power to benefit themselves, by pushing through a policy of free trade (Unit 12). The success of the middle-class Anti-Corn Law League in 1846 (Unit 13) was the economic reflection of the political victory that the middle class had won in 1832 (Unit 10). This had been a victory over the landed aristocracy who resented the upsurge of this new, thrusting class. The clash between the old power and the new was finally resolved in favour of the new by the Parliament Act, 1911 (Unit 28); the industrial classes had finally overcome the landed gentry.

The working classes saw the victory of their industrial masters over the landed gentry and decided that they too wanted a share in the political system. They succeeded, in part at least, in this aim and then took the democratic process a stage further by forming a political party to represent the interests of the labouring classes (Unit 30). The birth of the Labour Party was a sign that the working classes had emerged as a mature and demanding group in society.

1.6 Increasing Wealth

We have seen that the eighteenth-century workman produced very little with his primitive tools and machines. The industrial revolution, with its new, busy and productive machines, allowed one workman to produce as much as dozens, or indeed hundreds, of workmen had once produced by hand. It is this which explains the vast increase in the annual value of the goods and services produced by British workmen. In 1688 the total had been £48 million; by 1801 this had increased to £232 million and in 1901 it had risen to £1642 million. British agriculture and industry were producing more wealth each year and each British workman was producing more than his father or grandfather had done.

The bulk of this increased wealth went at first to the middle class, who used part of it to finance new industrial development, part of it to raise their own living standards and part of it as loans to overseas borrowers who wanted to buy British goods and so industrialize their own countries. At first the working classes got a disproportionately small share of this wealth which they were helping to produce. But by 1914 they had learned how to use their new-won political power to compel politicians to take some part of that wealth—in increased taxation of the rich—to lay the foundations for the welfare state (Units 29–31). It is important to note that none of the housing, educational, health or other reforms could have taken place without the greatly increased wealth produced by Britain's industrial towns. The productivity of the British industrial system was, as it still is, the key to social progress.

It was also the key to foreign and imperial policies. It was Britain's industrial power which gave Britain the strength to defeat Napoleon (Unit 6) and permitted Palmerston to adopt a domineering attitude to world affairs (Unit 14). When other countries, such as Germany and the USA, became Britain's economic equals, Britain no longer had the ability to impose its will on the world (Unit 24). If it had been the founding of the Empire which had sparked off the industrial revolution, it was the power which was the result of that revolution which allowed British politicians to expand that Empire (Unit 17). And it was to try to maintain that economic power that Joseph Chamberlain and others sought to develop a more vigorous imperial policy when Britain began to lose its dominant position in world industry and commerce (Unit 24).

The rest of this book is concerned with the political, foreign and imperial policies followed by a succession of British governments between 1760 and 1914. We would do well to remember that, without the economic developments which 'took-off' in the late eighteenth century, this story would have been a different one.

Unit Two
George III's Government, 1760–82

2.1 The System of Government in 1760

(a) The King

In 1760 the twenty-two year old George III succeeded his grandfather George II as king of England, and inherited the powers which both George I and George II had possessed. A foreign observer who visited Britain during the reigns of George I and George II noted:

> England ... is governed by a King whose power is limited by wise ... laws, and by Parliament. ... The King cannot levy any new taxes, neither can he abolish privileges or make new laws, without the consent of Parliament. ... All civil and military posts are given away by the King. He also creates new peers ...
> Source: Saussure, C. de, *A Foreign View of England* (1725–30).

George I had been unable to speak English and much of the work of governing had been left to his chosen ministers, some of whom, notably Sir Robert Walpole, had exercised great power. George II, who succeeded to the throne in 1727, wanted to dismiss the powerful Walpole and to replace him with some minister of his own choice. It was Queen Caroline who persuaded her husband that if he was to govern the country wisely, he needed Walpole, who had a strong following in the Commons and was popular in the country as a whole. George II followed his wife's advice; Walpole remained in office and George II, who had begun his reign by wishing to get rid of him, soon 'took all occasions to declare him his first, or rather his sole, minister', as we read in Lord Hervey's *Memoirs of the Reign of George II*.

(b) The Ministers

There were 558 MPs in the House of Commons in 1760, but few of them were interested in holding political office. They were more involved in their other activities, as landowners, officers in the armed forces, lawyers, actors or writers. Those who were ambitious enough to want to hold office tended to come from one of a small group of powerful landowning families—the Pelhams, Carterets, Walpoles and Townshends—and it was these families which provided most, if not all, of the holders of the more important political offices. Each leading politician had the support of his own group of MPs, men who agreed with his policies, had received favours from him, or hoped to receive some in the future.

As de Saussure noted, the King and his ministers had to get parliamentary approval for their policies. This helps to explain why the Georges—I, II and III—were obliged to choose their ministers from among the ranks of those men who could command support in the House.

(c) The House of Commons

The Commons of 1760 was very different from the modern Commons. Many of the MPs were the sons of members of the House of Lords, filling in time until they inherited the family title. Another large group were officers in the armed forces. Nearly all MPs had got to Parliament by one corrupt method or another. Sir Samuel Romilly, later a leading campaigner for penal reform, wrote:

> I shall procure myself a seat in the new parliament, unless I find that it will cost too large a sum. . . . Tierney tells me that he has offered £10 000 for the two seats of Westbury, the property of the late Lord Abington. . . .
>
> This buying of seats is detestable, yet it is almost the only way in which one who is resolved to be an independent man, can get into parliament: to be placed there by some great lord, and to vote as he shall direct, is to be in a state of complete dependence.
>
> It is true that many men who do buy seats do it as . . . a political trade; they buy their seats and sell their votes. . . .
>
> *Source:* Romilly, Sir Samuel, *Memoirs*, Vol. II, pp. 200–2 in Cheyney, E. P., *Readings in English History* (1913).

Daniel Defoe noted:

> Old Sarum is an area of about one hundred yards in diameter taking in the whole crown of a hill. Near this is one farm house, which is all that remains of any town in

Fig. 2.1 Part of Hogarth's 'The Election' illustrating the bribery, flattery and violence that were associated with parliamentary elections in the eighteenth century

or near the place, for the encampment has no resemblance of a town; and yet this is called the borough of Old Sarum, and sends two members to parliament; who those members can justly say they represent, would be hard for them to answer.
Source: Defoe, D., *A Tour through the Whole Island of Great Britain* (1726).

The landowner in a place such as Old Sarum—and there were many such *pocket boroughs*—could pick two MPs. In other places a handful of voters decided the result of an election so that the majority of MPs were returned by a small number of people.

(d) Political Parties

The majority of the MPs sitting in this unrepresentative House of Commons were not members of political parties. They represented the interests of their own families or of the district from which they came, and they had little interest in national or international affairs. A small number had once supported the Stuart Kings and had opposed the accession of the Hanoverian George I in 1714. These were the *Tories*. Those who had opposed the Stuarts and had welcomed the accession of George I were known as *Whigs*. But there was little party loyalty as we understand it. Walpole organized the overthrow of Carteret, even though they were both Whigs, and was himself overthrown in 1742, after twenty-one years in power, by a combination of Whigs.

2.2   George III

George III had been brought up by his mother, who had been badly treated by King George II and his Whig ministers. She had persuaded her son that the Whigs had taken power away from George I and George II, and were using it for their own purposes. She was supposed to have advised him: 'George, be a King', suggesting that his Hanoverian predecessors had not really been kings except in name. In one sense this was true; as Thackeray noted, the first two Georges were more interested in Hanover than in Britain:

It was lucky for us that our first Georges were not more high-minded men; especially fortunate that they loved Hanover so much as to leave England to have her own way. Our chief troubles began when we got a King who gloried in the name of Briton, and, being born in the country, proposed to rule it.
Source: Thackeray, W. M., *The Four Georges* (1861).

But George III and his mother misunderstood what had really happened after 1714. As we have seen, the King had always exercised power—to choose and to dismiss ministers, to decide policy—always provided that Parliament approved of his actions. However, George III's misreading of history caused him to undertake a deliberate attempt to do without the Whigs, if that were possible, and to assert himself more than the first two Georges had done.

2.3   The Peace of Paris, 1763

When George III came to the throne Britain was engaged in a war with France, which had been going on since 1756. While Britain's ally, Prussia,

Fig. 2.2 'A connoisseur examining' by Cooper. George III examining a portrait of Oliver Cromwell—a reference to the belief that George was trying to set himself up as a dictator

kept France engaged in Europe, British troops were winning territory in India, Canada and the West Indies. But by 1760 the country was tired of the war, which was costing a lot of money and disrupting trade.

The two chief ministers at this time were Pitt, who ran the war, and the Duke of Newcastle, who ran the government. In 1761 George III appointed his former tutor, the Marquis of Bute, to office as one of the Secretaries of State, on an equal footing with Pitt. Bute was not an experienced politician but he had the support of the forty-five Scottish MPs, and the backing of the King, who could count upon the aid of many MPs.

Pitt wanted to declare war on Spain and when the Cabinet opposed this he resigned. In May 1762 Newcastle also resigned, because Bute wanted to stop paying a subsidy to Britain's ally, Prussia. These two resignations left Bute as head of the government, and by October 1762 he had arranged peace terms with France. However, there was some opposition to making peace with France and Pitt, a sick and bitter man, came to the Commons to lead it. Pitt did not challenge the King's right to make peace, but he did insist that this policy had to be approved by the Commons. The King and his advisers appreciated this last point. Henry Fox, previously a leading Whig, joined Bute in getting support for the peace proposals:

> Fox set himself to work at the root; he directly attacked the separate members of the House of Commons. A shop was publicly opened at the Pay Office, whither the members flocked, and received the bribes in bank-bills. Twenty-five thousand pounds, as Martin, Secretary of the Treasury, afterwards owned, were issued in one morning; and in a single fortnight a vast majority was purchased to approve the peace! . . .
>
> The Peace Bill was passed by 223 votes to 63. . . . Whomever, holding an official post, had voted against the preliminaries, was instantly dismissed.
>
> *Source:* Horace Walpole, *Memoirs of the Reign of King George III* (1798).

Bute had put forward the peace terms in a newspaper, *The Briton*, hoping to rally public support to his side. John Wilkes, MP for Aylesbury since 1757, published a newspaper which he called *The North Briton*, drawing attention in the title to Bute's Scottish background. In Number 45 of that newspaper he attacked the King's Speech of April 1763, in which reference had been made to the Peace of Paris:

> I am sure all foreigners, especially the King of Prussia, will hold the minister in contempt and abhorrence. He has made our Sovereign declare: 'My expectations have been fully answered by the happy effects which the several allies of my Crown have derived from this salutary measure of the definitive treaty. The powers at war with my good brother the King of Prussia have . . . been induced to agree to such terms of accommodation as that great Prince has approved; and the success which has attended my negotiations has necessarily and immediately diffused the blessings of peace throughout . . . every part of Europe.' The infamous fallacy of this whole sentence is apparent to all mankind. . . . No advantage has accrued to that magnanimous Prince from our negotiation, but he was basely deserted by the Scottish Prime Minister of England. . . .
>
> *Source:* Wilkes, J., *The North Briton*, Number 45 (1763).

2.4   Wilkes and Liberty

(a) The North Briton

John Wilkes had virtually called the King a liar, and the King and his ministers decided to take action against this outspoken opponent. A *general warrant* was issued for the arrest of the printers, publishers and authors of Number 45 of *The North Briton*, which was described as a seditious libel. The government had the right to issue a general warrant under an Act of 1695: it was a power which governments could easily abuse to stifle criticism.

Wilkes was arrested and imprisoned in the Tower of London. When he was brought before the Lord Chief Justice, in May 1763, he was discharged because, it was claimed, MPs were immune from arrest for anything except treason, felony or breach of the peace. During his trial, Wilkes had declared:

> My Lords, the liberty of all peers and gentlemen, and, what touches me more sensibly, that of all the middling and inferior set of people who stand most in need of protection, is in my case this day to be finally decided on a question of such importance as to determine at once whether English liberty shall be a reality or a shadow.

This was the origin of the popular slogan 'Wilkes and Liberty' which was taken up by the London mob.

While he was imprisoned, Wilkes' house had been searched and many of his papers removed. On his release Wilkes brought a court action against the ministers responsible for this and, in December 1763, he was awarded damages of £1 000 against one and £4 000 against another. The Chief Justice also decided that it was illegal for the government to issue general warrants, and in 1766 the Commons passed a motion outlawing them.

The King and his ministers, with their supporters in the Commons, were determined to continue their attack on Wilkes. They regarded him as a dangerous critic, all the more so because of his ability to rouse the London mob. In November 1763 Parliament voted that Number 45 was a seditious libel, whatever the courts decided, and the public burning of that paper was ordered. The Commons also decided that Wilkes was not entitled to claim immunity from arrest and ordered that he should appear to answer the charges against him. But he chose to seek refuge in Paris and, as he did not appear when Parliament re-assembled in January 1764, he was officially expelled from the Commons. In the following November the court decided that Wilkes was guilty of printing a scandalous *Essay on Woman* and of publishing Number 45 of *The North Briton*. When he did not appear before the court he was declared an outlaw and, wisely, he decided to remain abroad.

(b) The Return of Wilkes

In 1768 Wilkes, still an outlaw, returned from France and announced that he would be a candidate at the General Election. He was invited to stand for Middlesex, a constituency where many hundreds of people voted. This made it difficult for anyone to use the usual methods of bribing the voters; it also

Fig. 2.3 John Wilkes as drawn by Hogarth in May 1763. Hogarth hated Wilkes, who, he said, only pretended to be 'a saviour of the country'. Wilkes seems to be a devilish figure with his 'North Briton' papers and his dunce's cap of liberty almost covering his horned wig

meant that Wilkes could use his popularity with the mob to good effect. To guarantee that he won the mob's support, Wilkes forced the warden of the King's Bench prison to take him into gaol for publishing an obscene poem. The mob rioted, believing that he had been arrested by the unpopular government of George III. The troops were beaten and stoned, and during the riots outside the prison, on 10 May 1768, a young man, William Allen, was shot by Scottish soldiers. The affair was portrayed in cartoons and poems as an attempt by the Scottish Bute to attack the liberties of Englishmen; the magistrate who had given the order to fire on the mob was tried for murder. (This helps to explain why, at the time of the Gordon riots in 1780, the magistrates were unwilling to give such orders (Section 2.6(e)).)

Wilkes was duly elected MP for Middlesex, but the King persuaded Parliament to vote that he should not be allowed to take his seat since he was a traitor, a blasphemer and a writer of immoral poems. The election had to be held again, but Wilkes won on this and on a third occasion. However, Parliament decided to seat his opponent, Luttrell, even though Wilkes had gained 1143 votes to his 296. This led to agitation concerning the rights of electors to decide who their MP was to be. When Wilkes was finally allowed to take his seat in 1774, this issue had been decided in favour of the people and against the King.

2.5   George III and his Ministers

(a) The Fall of Bute

The King's government was, of course, carrying on with its many other affairs, while the Wilkes' incident was dragging on its way. Bute was forced to resign in April 1763, after his success in making peace with France. It was a combination of opinions which drove him from office. Popular opinion, particularly in London, was on Wilkes' side in condemning the peace treaty with France. Bute's relationship with George III's mother roused opinion against him and provided the material for many bawdy songs. His unpopularity was further increased by his decision to impose a tax on cider, which was to help pay for the late war.

Bute's fall illustrates the fact that the King, even one as able, ambitious and determined as George III, could not foist ministers on the people, unless the policies of these ministers were such as to win popular and parliamentary support.

(b) The Search for a Minister

The King was now anxious to have Pitt in the government, but the great man refused to serve with anyone who had had anything to do with the peace with France. The Duke of Newcastle was prepared to join the government only if his Whig friends were also allowed to join—something to which George III would not agree. And so from 1763 onwards the King had a succession of Prime Ministers, all of whom were involved with American affairs (Section 3.3(a)–(d)). *Grenville* (1763–5) was followed by *Rockingham* (1765–6) and by a government led by Pitt, now Lord *Chatham* (1766–8). Each of these governments was either overthrown or forced to resign because of failure to win support for its American policies.

Grafton (1768–70) led the last of the short-lived ministries, because in 1770 George III found the minister he was looking for in *Lord North*. North became Prime Minister at the age of thirty-seven and held the office until 1782, when the loss of the American colonies drove him from that position.

2.6 Lord North's Administration, 1770–82

This administration, like its many predecessors, was dominated by American affairs (Sections 3.3(e) and 3.6(a)–(d)). However, the government tackled many other problems and faced many other difficulties.

(a) Wilkes

Lord North refused to reopen the Wilkes' affair and in 1774 he allowed the former outlaw to take his seat as MP for Middlesex. This policy of doing nothing whenever possible was also followed in the field of taxation. North avoided increases in taxation by cutting expenses, particularly spending on the Royal Navy, which was to cost Britain dear in America.

(b) The King

North depended on the King's support for his continuing in office. The King could use his influence to get many MPs to vote for North's proposals. These 'King's Friends' ensured the survival of North's government. In return, North pleased the King whenever possible. In 1772 he persuaded parliament to pass the Royal Marriages Act which forbade members of the Royal Family to marry without the King's consent, unless they were over twenty-five years of age and had given a year's notice to the Privy Council. In this way North, and the King, hoped to avoid in the future the sort of problem posed by the Dukes of Cumberland and Gloucester, who had married commoners.

(c) India

See Section 17.1(b) for North's Regulating Act.

(d) Parliamentary Reform

The onset of the American War increased North's difficulties. The public became dissatisfied with the way in which the war was being conducted and

Fig. 2.4 Lord North, George III's long-serving Chief Minister

this encouraged some Radicals to demand parliamentary reform, an end to corruption and the reduction of the influence of the King over ministers and policies. In 1780 the case for reform was put to the Commons by an MP, Dunning, with a famous resolution that: 'The influence of the Crown has increased, is increasing, and ought to be diminished.' This movement came to nothing at this time because the Opposition was divided and the King still had sufficient influence in the Commons to ensure the defeat of such a critical motion.

(e) The Catholic Relief Bill, 1778

This bill was brought forward to abolish the severe laws which had once been passed against Catholics. The Protestants of Scotland formed the Protestant Association and the half-mad Lord George Gordon, an MP who hated North, became the President of the London Protestant Association. On 2 June 1780 Gordon led a mob to Parliament to petition for the repeal of the Relief Bill. From 4 June to 8 June the mob terrorized London, burnt chapels and houses, freed prisoners from Newgate and other jails, and tried to storm the Bank of England. Troops had to be brought in and by 9 June order had been restored.

(f) America

By March 1782, North had realized that the war had been lost and that the colonists would have to be given their independence. The King would not agree and so North resigned (Section 3.5(c)).

Test Yourself on Unit 2

(a) Document: Wilkes and Liberty

1763. The 3rd of December had been appointed for burning *The North Briton* at the Royal Exchange; but when the magistrates were assembled for that purpose, and the executioner began to perform the ceremony, a great riot ensued, the paper was forced from the hangman, the constables were pelted and beaten, and Mr Marley, one of the sheriffs, had the glass of his coach broken and himself was wounded in the face by a billet snatched from the fire that was lighted to burn the paper, and thrown at him. The cry was, 'Wilkes and Liberty'. A jackboot and a petticoat—the mob's symbols for Lord Bute and the Princess—were burned with great triumph and acclamation.

On the 6th the Duke of Bedford, who had moved that the Commons might be desired to permit Mr Harley, member for the City, to attend the House of Lords, called on him and Mr Blount, the other sheriff, to give an account of the late riot. They said the mob had been encouraged by gentlemen from windows and balconies, particularly from the Union coffee-house. One low man had been taken into custody; another had been rescued by the rioters. . . . The Duke of Bedford, spluttering with zeal and indiscretion, broke forth against Bridgen, the Lord Mayor, and the other magistrates, who, though within hearing, had taken no pains to quell the mob. 'Such behaviour', he said, 'in any smaller town would have forfeited their franchises. The Common Council had long been setting themselves up against Parliament.' . . . The Chancellor, alarmed at this injudicious attack on the City, said it would be right to proceed without delay against the acts and abettors of the riot; but without further proofs, he would not believe the magistrates of London guilty. . . .

Wilkes in the meantime, went on triumphantly with his prosecutions; and on the 6th of December obtained a verdict of £1 000 damages and costs of suit, against Mr Wood, the Under-Secretary of State. . . .

Source: Horace Walpole, *Memoirs of the Reign of King George III* (1798).

(b) Questions

1. What was *The North Briton*? Why was it so named? Who was its author?
2. Why was there to be a public burning at this time?
3. What was meant by 'Wilkes and Liberty'?
4. Why were Bute and the Princess of Wales so unpopular?

5. Why was Wilkes awarded damages?
6. Why was the London mob so difficult to control?
7. When and why did the London mob once again run wild during this period (1760–82)?

(c) **Further Reading**

Brewer, J. H.: *Party Ideology and Popular Politics at the Accession of George III*. Cambridge University Press (Cambridge, 1981).

Christie, I.: *Wars and Revolutions, Britain 1760–1815*. Arnold (London, 1983).

Evans, E. J.: *The Forging of the Modern State: Early Industrial Britain 1783–1870*. Longman (Harlow, 1983).

Marshall, D.: *Eighteenth Century England*. Longman (Harlow, 1975).

O'Gorman, F.: *The Emergence of the British Two-Party System 1760–1832*. Arnold (London, 1983).

Watson, J. S.: *The Reign of George III 1760–1815*. Oxford University Press (Oxford, 1960).

(d) **Exercises**

1. How far was it true that 'George III tried to turn back the clock'?
2. Explain George III's success in maintaining Lord North in power from 1770 until 1782.
3. What was the significance of the career of John Wilkes?
4. Write briefly on (i) the Peace of Paris, 1763, (ii) *The North Briton*, (iii) the Gordon Riots, (iv) eighteenth-century parliamentary elections.

Unit Three
The War of American Independence, 1763–83

3.1 The Old Colonies

By 1763 about two-and-a-half million settlers lived in thirteen separate colonies strung along the eastern seaboard of North America, from New Hampshire in the north to Georgia in the south (Fig. 3.1). These colonies had been established at different times and by widely differing groups of settlers. There were Quakers in Pennsylvania, Puritans in Massachusetts and a mainly Catholic settlement in Maryland. There was one colony, Georgia, founded mainly by debtors while another, New York, had been won from the Dutch. Many of the settlers in the southern colonies—from Virginia down to Georgia—were owners of large estates on which slaves worked in sight of the owners' lavishly-furnished and extensive houses. In other colonies, particularly the northern ones, most people owned small farms or lived in villages, and they were under constant threat of attack from the Indians, who had been pushed out to make way for the settlers.

The separate colonies were proud of their individual characteristics and there was no feeling of unity among them. If Indians attacked the colonists in New Hampshire, the settlers of Georgia felt little sympathy for the 'foreigners' in the north and no inclination to send help. Similarly, when the land-hungry colonists from Virginia moved into the Ohio valley and clashed with the French-Canadian fur traders and their Indian allies, the inhabitants of North or South Carolina did not regard this as an issue which affected them; they did not send armies to help the Virginians, nor did they raise their taxes to help the Virginians to fight an Indian war.

However, all thirteen colonies shared a number of common grievances against the Mother Country, Britain, in spite of their jealously guarded independence. Between 1763 and 1775 these grievances were deepened and inflamed until the colonies united to fight a long War of Independence, which ended with Britain signing a treaty and conceding independence to the recently-formed United States of America (Sections 3.5(a) and 3.7(a)).

3.2 Underlying Causes of the Revolution

(a) The Old Colonial System

Most of the colonies had been settled during the seventeenth century, when statesmen of all colonizing countries—Britain, France, Holland and Spain— had accepted the theories of *mercantilism*. These theories were based on the proposition that colonies, shipping, trade and the security of a country were very closely interwoven. Colonies were supposed to help their Mother Country by enabling her trade to expand. Gold would then flow into the national exchequer of the Mother Country, to be used to pay for the soldiers, arms and other material required to enable the Mother Country to engage successfully in foreign wars.

The colonies were encouraged to produce goods which could not be produced in Britain, such as timber, furs, tobacco and fish. In exchange for these goods they were to import manufactured goods from Britain. They were forbidden to produce goods which Britain already manufactured, so the Birmingham gunmakers, Dudley nailmakers and Staffordshire potters had substantial markets in America. The colonists were also restricted in their trade with foreign countries, so as to allow British merchants and companies the maximum advantage. Even the limited trade allowed to the colonies had to be carried on in British ships manned by British sailors.

This old colonial system was the subject of *Navigation Acts* passed in 1650, 1651 and 1660. Britain claimed that the system brought certain benefits to her colonies. They were assured of a market for their produce, and the Mother Country provided the armed forces required to defend the small and under-populated colonies from attack by the Indians or the French. But the colonists disliked the restrictions on their economic development and often ignored them: trade was carried on with the French West Indies and in French or Dutch ships. Goods were imported from France, Holland or Spain, and British governments tended to turn a blind eye to these violations of the Navigation Acts. Smuggling of foreign—and prohibited—goods was commonplace, and this brought the law into contempt and encouraged a feeling of resentment among the colonists. Why, they asked, did they have to resort to such illegal tactics?

(b) The Colonists 'Grow Up'

The first colonists had left Britain with feelings of grievance against the Old Country. The Puritans were driven to America because they were forbidden to practise their religion freely in the Anglican-dominated Britain of the Stuarts. Others went because they had failed in business or trade and had the alternatives of imprisonment or emigration. This feeling of resentment against the Old Country was one which they handed down to their children, who grew up in the small villages and ports of the new country and knew nothing of the Old Country, except what they were told by their parents and grandparents. Gradually, in the course of a century, the spirit of resentment grew fiercer, and the 'homesickness' of the first settlers gave way to a feeling of 'Americanism' among the second and third generations.

The first colonists had found life extremely difficult as they hacked out their farms from forests and suffered from attacks by Indians, fever and hunger whenever a crop failed. But by 1760 the third generation of Americans were living in relative comfort. They had built their own universities, splendid churches and houses, banks and warehouses, ports and business centres. The first colonists may have been relatively simple people, but some of their grandchildren became lawyers, scientists and philosophers, as well as plantation owners, bankers, merchants, industrialists and owners of large fishing fleets. These were not the people who had sailed in the *Mayflower*; they were able and willing to argue with British politicians on equal terms.

(c) The Political System

The political system under which they lived took no account of this development. Most colonies had a very democratic system of internal government; men and women shared the right to vote on equal terms, and elections were held to choose *legislative assemblies* (or state parliaments). In their small towns and villages men and women were accustomed to voting on issues which affected their own locality. Should they have a school or not? Should they collect a tax on incomes or one on property values?

But there was a *governor* in each colony appointed by the British government, who had the power to set aside decisions reached by the legislative assemblies and to impose his own decisions on colonists, without any discussion with them. Over and above the unpopular and seemingly dictatorial governors was the far-away British government which knew little, if anything, about conditions in America and yet had the power to legislate for the colonies.

(d) The Removal of the French Menace

In 1763 Britain signed the Peace of Paris, which brought to an end the Seven Years War with France. Under the terms of the Treaty, Britain gained Canada from France and more of the West Indies as well as parts of India. The Peace was also a major landmark for the colonies. In the past they had depended on the British army and the British navy to defend them against attacks from the French in Canada and New Orleans. After 1763 the threat from France was removed and thus the colonists' need for a British armed presence was also removed.

3.3 The Growth of the Revolutionary Movement

(a) The British National Debt

The British government had spent a great deal of money fighting the Seven Years War. Increased taxation—a cause of the downfall of the Marquis of Bute (Section 2.5(a))—had raised large sums, but not enough. It would also have been unfair to collect all the money in this way; taxation affected only people alive at the time, whereas the benefits of a successful war would be enjoyed by generations to come. So the governments of George II and

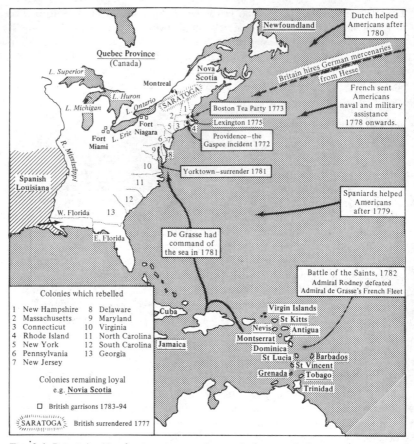

Fig. 3.1 Britain's North American colonies before and during the War of Independence

George III asked the nation to support the war effort by lending them money, to be repaid in future years.

In exchange for their loans, people received government bonds or *stock*. These were usually issued in units of £100, because the government expected only the wealthy to lend money. Each piece of stock was numbered, showed the date on which it was issued, and the rate of interest that the government would pay annually to the owner of the stock. Sometimes the government promised to repay the original loan on a given date, and this was known as *dated stock*. When there was no promise to repay the loan on a specific date, the lender received *undated stock*. So although the loans were made by people alive at the time of the war, the interest payments, and repayments of the original loans, would have to be borne by future generations.

The government's borrowing is known as the *National Debt*, since it is the nation, in the shape of its government, which owes the money—usually to other people in the country, although foreigners were, and are, free to buy government stock. The National Debt began in 1688 when William III and Mary II wanted money to finance the war against Louis XIV of France. Subsequent governments were compelled to borrow money to fight other wars—each more costly than the last:

Size of the National Debt

1697   £20 000 000
1713   £50 000 000 (at the end of the War of the Spanish Succession)
1748   £78 000 000 (at the end of the War of the Austrian Succession)
1763   £138 000 000 (at the end of the Seven Years War)
1784   £249 000 000 (at the end of the War of American Independence)

For later material on the National Debt, see Sections 4.5(*d*) and 7.1.

Part of the money that had been spent on fighting the Seven Years War had been devoted to the defence of the American colonies and to the defeat of the French in Canada. The British government accepted that this was its responsibility under the old colonial system, and did not ask the colonists to contribute to paying off the debt.

However, the Indians remained as a threat in North America, even though the French had gone. In 1763 a great union of Indian tribes under the leadership of a chief called Pontiac attacked the British-held forts in the Ohio valley, massacred the soldiers and for fourteen months waged a brutal war against the colonists. The colonists were reluctant to make any contribution—in men or money—to this war. They argued that the defence of the colonies was one of the duties of the Mother Country, which gained a great deal from her colonial possessions. However, when peace was signed with the Indians in 1766 the British government decided that the cost of the British army in America, which was about £350 000 a year, would in future have to be borne by the Americans.

The story of the next ten years is of the British government trying to find some way of collecting that money from the colonists, and of the increasing hostility of the colonists. They claimed that the British already had all the benefits of colonial trade but now wished to impose taxation on them as well.

(*b*) 1765: The Stamp Act

Grenville succeeded Bute as Prime Minister in 1763, and he tried to persuade the colonists to decide for themselves how they would raise the money needed to pay for the British army in America. The colonists resented this move and the presence of the army: they feared that the British army might one day be used against them. In any case, there was simply no way in which the separate colonies could agree on what each state should contribute to the total sum demanded by the British government.

In 1764 Grenville passed an Act which forbade the colonists to move any further westwards, hoping to cut down the danger of more costly Indian wars. He also tightened up the work of the customs officials in the colonies so as to limit evasions of the Navigation Acts. In 1765 he then passed the Stamp Act, part of which reads:

> Whereas it is just and necessary, that provision be made for raising a further revenue towards defraying the expenses of defending the British Colonies and Plantations in America, be it enacted that there shall be raised throughout the Colonies in America. . . . For every parchment or piece of paper on which shall be written or printed, any declaration, in any Court of Law within the British Colonies and Plantations in America, a Stamp Duty of three pence. . . . For any copy of any will a Stamp Duty of six pence. For any certificate of any degree taken in any University, Academy, College a Stamp Duty of two pounds. For every pack of playing cards, the sum of one shilling. And for every pair of dice, the sum of ten shillings.
> *Source: The Stamp Act* (1765).

This Act marked a major change in British policy towards the colonies. For the first time Britain was imposing an *internal tax* on the colonists, as distinct from the *external controls* previously exercised under the Navigation Acts. The colonists raised the cry of 'No Taxation without Representation', arguing that it was illegal for taxation to be raised by a government and approved by a parliament in which the taxpayers were not represented.

The Stamp Act hit at some of the most influential members of the separate colonies—lawyers, journalists, innkeepers, landowners—men who had the means of expressing their annoyance. Rioting broke out in Boston, Philadelphia and Virginia. Tax-collectors were forced to resign their posts, stamps were publicly burned and legal business came to a standstill. More significantly, representatives of nine of the colonies met in New York at a *Stamp Congress*, which sent a petition to the King and Parliament. In this the colonists declared their loyalty to the King but insisted that they ought not to be taxed by a foreign Parliament. While the Congress was meeting, extremists formed themselves into groups called 'Sons of Liberty', a sign of increasing hostility to the British government. Both the Stamp Congress and the formation of the extremist groups mark the beginnings of united action by hitherto jealously independent colonies.

(c) The Declaratory Act

The British Parliament was usually willing to support whichever minister the King had chosen, provided that the government's policy was successful. However, Grenville's policy towards America was obviously not succeeding and he was forced to resign to make way for another Whig minister, the Marquis of Rockingham. Rockingham repealed the Stamp Act—in the face of opposition from the King and his supporters in the Commons—but then, paradoxically, passed the Declaratory Act which claimed that Britain had the right to impose whatever taxes it wished. The King dismissed Rockingham following the passage of this Act.

(d) 1767: Townshend's Import Duties

Pitt, now the Earl of Chatham, became the King's chief minister in 1766, with Charles Townshend as Chancellor of the Exchequer. The British army in America was now costing over £400 000 a year and the question of paying for it became more urgent. Townshend, accepting the argument that the colonists ought not to pay *internal taxes* imposed by Britain, decided to impose taxes on imports entering American ports, such as tea, paper, glass, lead and paints. A Board of Customs Commissioners was set up in Boston to enforce the Navigation Acts.

The colonists had always admitted the right of the British to control America's external trade: they claimed it was Britain's benefit from the Old Colonial System, but also that it entitled the colonists to expect Britain to defend them. Townshend had caught them in a trap by imposing these import duties. The colonists now shifted their ground and argued that the *rights of man* forbade this imposition of taxes. Extremist groups were revived and troops had to be sent to Boston to support the Customs Commissioners.

The Massachusetts Assembly sent a circular letter to the Assemblies in the other colonies, inviting them to join in the protest against the new import duties. The British government retaliated by announcing that the Massachusetts Assembly was dissolved, thereby enraging the colonists in other colonies, who resented this interference with *internal* government. Disorder grew, especially in Boston, the capital of Massachusetts, and juries were unwilling to punish rioters. Meanwhile Townshend had died and Chatham resigned to make way for another Whig, the Duke of Grafton, who was succeeded in 1770 by Lord North.

(e) 1770: The Boston Massacre

The Americans had refused to import goods bearing the Townshend duties, so merchants and traders in both America and Britain were suffering. Lord North removed all the duties except the one on tea, which was maintained to show the colonists that the British government claimed the right to tax them. An ugly incident took place in Boston while this measure was going through Parliament. Troops had been sent there to guard the Customs Commissioners; the Bostonians were irritated by these troops. In the very cold March of 1770 a crowd gathered around a sentry guarding the Customs House and began to insult him. He called for help, snowballs were thrown, a soldier was knocked down, shots were fired and four Bostonians were killed. The soldiers were tried. Two were found guilty of manslaughter, but the Captain commanding the guard and six others were acquitted. This incident increased the tension between the British government and the colonists.

Fig. 3.2 'The Parricide' was drawn in 1776 and shows America as an Indian woman attacking Britannia. Wilkes, pointing towards Britannia, is directing the attack while Fox (represented by the fox in the background) looks on at this 'murder' of his country

(f) The Gaspée

In general, matters were fairly quiet in the remainder of 1770 and 1771. But in 1772 the British customs ship, *Gaspée*, ran aground off Rhode Island while chasing a ship suspected of smuggling. A group of Rhode Islanders boarded the *Gaspée*, burnt it and wounded the captain.

(g) 1773: The Boston Tea Party

Lord North's government maintained the tax on tea, but the Americans boycotted tea, which hit at the prosperity of the East India Company (Section 17.1(a), (b)). In 1773, therefore, North introduced a Tea Act which allowed the East India Company to ship its tea direct from India to America, without first coming to Britain. This brought down the price of tea, making it cheaper than that smuggled in from Britain, but the government still aimed to collect the tax if the Americans bought this cheaper tea. John Andrews was an inhabitant of Boston and he recalled:

> They mustered, I've told you, upon Fort Hill to the number of about two hundred, and proceeded, two by two, to Griffin's wharf, where Hall, Bruce and Coffin lay, each

Fig. 3.3 The Boston Tea Party as seen by a French artist of the time

with 114 chests of the ill-fated article on board, and before nine o'clock in the evening every chest from on board the three vessels was knocked to pieces and flung over the sides.

They say the actors were Indians from Narragansett. Whether they were or not, to a transient observer they appeared as such, being clothed in blankets with the heads muffled, and copper-coloured countenances, being each armed with a hatchet or axe and pair of pistols, nor was their dialect different from what I conceive these geniuses to speak, as their jargon was unintelligible to all but themselves.

Source: Letters of John Andrews, Esq., of Boston 1772–1776 (ed. 1866).

(h) 1774: The Quebec Act

The British government gave the Canadians the right to keep their own (French) laws and to practise their Roman Catholic religion freely. The Act also extended the area of Canada to include the area north of the river Ohio and east of the Mississippi. The Americans had hoped to expand into this area so they were annoyed by the far-away government's interference with their freedom of expansion. They were further annoyed by the concessions to Roman Catholicism.

3.4 Flashpoints, 1774–5

(a) The Intolerable Acts

Following the Boston Tea Party, the British government closed the port of Boston and removed the Customs House to Salem. They also insisted that the inhabitants of Boston had to provide barracks for the British troops in their town, forbade public meetings, increased the power of the governor of

Massachusetts and gave him the authority to send Bostonian prisoners to Britain for trial.

This attack on the political and economic power of Boston in particular, and Massachusetts in general, offended the remainder of the colonists. As a recent immigrant reported:

> Alexandria, Virginia—Wednesday, October 19th, 1774
> Everything here is in the utmost confusion. Committees are appointed to inspect into the characters and conduct of every tradesman, to prevent them selling Tea or buying British Manufactures. Some of them have been tarred and feathered, others had their property burnt and destroyed by the populace. Independent Companies are raising in every County on the Continent. A General Congress of the different Colonies met at Philadelphia on the 5th of last month are still sitting, but their business is a profound secret. Subscription is raising in every colony on the Continent for the relief of the people of Boston. In short, everything is ripe for rebellion. Independence is what the Massachusetts people aim at.
> Source: Journal of Nicholas Cresswell, 1774-1777 (ed. Thornely, 1925).

(b) The Philadelphia Congress

All the colonies except Georgia sent delegates to a Congress which met at Philadelphia in September 1774. After affirming its loyalty to the Crown, the Congress drew up a Declaration of Rights which demanded the repeal of all Acts passed since 1763. This would have meant the end of the old colonial system and Britain's control over her colonies. Some colonists thought that this was going too far, but many supported this move towards a demand for greater freedom.

(c) Lexington

General Gage had been sent from Britain with four regiments to close the port of Boston. In April 1775 he sent some troops from Boston to destroy a store of ammunition, which the colonists had collected illegally, at Concord, twenty miles from Boston. The soldiers met an armed force at Lexington, on their way to Concord: they scattered the rebels and went on to destroy the ammunition. But on the way back they were once again attacked: 273 soldiers were killed or wounded but the Americans lost less than 100. The news of this success caused colonists to enlist in an army to overthrow their British-appointed governors, and to set up provincial Congresses. The War of American Independence had begun.

3.5   The War, 1775-83

(a) 1775-6

The Massachusetts army tried to capture Boston; they occupied Bunker's Hill, overlooking the town, but the British drove them from this post. Later in 1775

Fig. 3.4 Signing the Declaration of Independence, 4 July 1776

the colonists attacked Montreal and Quebec in Canada, but they were defeated by General Burgoyne, who had arrived from Britain. George Washington was appointed commander-in-chief of the united colonial army and in 1776 he drove the British from Boston. General Howe withdrew his troops from Boston to Halifax. This success encouraged the colonists to issue their Declaration of Independence:

> We hold these truths to be self-evident, that all men are created equal, that they are endowed by their Creator with certain unalienable Rights, that among these are Life, Liberty and the pursuit of Happiness. That to secure these rights, Governments are instituted among Men, deriving their just powers from the consent of the governed. That whenever any Form of Government becomes destructive of these ends, it is the Right of the People to alter or to abolish it and to institute new government.
>
> *Source: Declaration of Independence* (1776).

(b) **Saratoga, 1777**

At the beginning of 1777 the British were in a strong position. Howe had captured New York and from there he controlled the sea approaches to the American colonies. Burgoyne, having repelled the colonists' attempts to conquer Canada, was preparing to march south along the routes of the Hudson and Champlain rivers. The plan was that Burgoyne would meet Howe and their joint forces would isolate the New England colonies. The defeat of these colonies would, they believed, lead to a speedy conclusion to the war.

However, Howe did not wait for Burgoyne. He defeated Washington's army at Brandywine Creek and then marched on to capture Philadelphia. This success was a very hollow one because Burgoyne, having reached Saratoga, found himself outnumbered by the rebels and was forced to surrender. This was a morale-booster for the rebels, particularly after their defeat at Brandywine Creek. It was also a great shock to the British who had thought it would be a simple matter to defeat the rebellious colonists.

(c) 1778–83

The French government welcomed the news of Saratoga. They realized that the American Revolution might well succeed and they joined the colonists in order to get revenge for their defeat in the Seven Years War. Spain joined France in 1779, and in 1780 Britain declared war on Holland for supplying the colonists with arms. The League of Armed Neutrality (Prussia, Russia, Denmark and Sweden) was formed to resist British claims to search neutral ships.

Fig. 3.5 George Washington (bareheaded in front of the flag) about to receive the surrender of Cornwallis (bareheaded on the right of the picture). Between them stands the Marquis de La Fayette (his sword in his left hand). He had played a part in this humiliation of the British in America, but he and his men took back to France some of the American ideas of liberty and equality,· and were to play a part in the overthrow of the French monarchy after 1789

Lord North had cut down expenditure on the navy (Section 2.6(a)), so it was not up to a standard fit to meet the demands made upon it. It was unable to blockade the French ports—to prevent French troops getting to America—and it could not ensure a sufficient supply of materials for the British troops.

In 1779 General Clinton succeeded Howe as commander. He took an army to Georgia where he captured Charlestown. He then returned to New York leaving Lord Cornwallis in charge of an army, with orders to complete the conquest of the South. By 1781 Cornwallis had reached the peninsula of Yorktown but he waited, in vain, for reinforcements to come from New York by sea. The French navy was in control of the sea here. Washington, marching south, attacked and forced Cornwallis to surrender at Yorktown, and this defeat marked the end of the war. Lord North resigned when the news reached Britain, and his Whig successors agreed to the Treaty of Versailles.

(d) The War Elsewhere

(i) **At sea.** The French and the Spanish captured Minorca in 1782, and tried to capture Gibraltar (1779–82) but, under the command of General Elliott, the fortress held out. In the West Indies the French fleet under De Grasse captured some of the British islands but in 1782 Admiral Rodney defeated De Grasse at the Battle of the Saints. This victory saved Jamaica and restored British power at sea.

(ii) **In India.** The French encouraged Hyder Ali, the King of Mysore, to rise against the British in the Carnatic, but Warren Hastings maintained British power, defeating Ali at Porto Novo in July 1781 (Section 17.1(b)).

3.6   Reasons for British Defeat

(a) Inefficient Leadership

Lord Sandwich, who was in charge of the navy, and Lord George Germain, the war minister, were both inefficient leaders. They did not appreciate the nature of the war, so too few troops were sent at the outset. The colonists were thus encouraged by initial successes which might have been avoided.

(b) The Navy

After 1780 Britain was also at war with three European countries and had to fight in many parts of the world. The navy had suffered from the economies of Lord North and was unable to meet all its commitments. In particular, it was loss of control of the sea that led to the British surrender at Yorktown.

(c) **Generals**

The British generals were not accustomed to the sort of war in which they found themselves engaged. They were unprepared for the guerrilla warfare waged by the Americans, who used small bands of relatively untrained men to ambush the British columns as they marched from place to place, and they lacked that intimate knowledge of the country which the colonists possessed. The red uniforms worn by the British also made them easy targets for the sharpshooting Americans.

The British generals suffered because they led a force consisting in the main of German mercenaries who had little enthusiasm for the fight and were more interested in looting and pillaging. This turned moderate colonists against the British. The Americans, on the other hand, enjoyed the leadership of Washington, who had none of the military training of his British rivals but his great force of character inspired the armies with a sense of victory, even during the most difficult periods.

(d) **Distance**

The British were hampered by the long sea journey which had to be undertaken by reinforcements and by ships carrying orders from the War Office. In America the British army found the vast distances between, for example, Charlestown and Halifax, a major problem, particularly when they lost control of the sea.

3.7 The Treaty of Versailles, 1783

(a) **Independence**

Great Britain recognized the independence of the states. Their territory was defined as lying between the Mississippi and the Great Lakes. Subsequent expansions led to disagreements about the border between Canada and the states (Section 12.8).

(b) **Territorial Changes**

The French regained the island of St Lucia, in the West Indies. Britain had taken this island from her at the Peace of Paris in 1763, but France had recaptured it when De Grasse attacked the West Indies. France retained the island of Tobago which she had captured in 1778, but Britain regained most of the other West Indian islands. France also gained Senegal in West Africa.

Spain retained Minorca and Florida but gave Louisiana to France, Britain retained control of Gibraltar.

Test Yourself on Unit 3

(a) Document: America's Burdens

Sir, they who are friends to the schemes of American revenue say that the commercial restraint is full as hard a law for America to live under. I think so, too. I think it, if uncompensated, to be a condition of as rigorous servitude as men can be subject to. But America bore it from the fundamental Act of Navigation until 1764. Why?

The Act of Navigation attended the colonies from their infancy, grew with their growth, and strengthened with their strength. Besides, they [the colonies] were indemnified for it by a pecuniary compensation. Their monopolist [Britain] happened to be one of the richest men in the world. By his immense capital (primarily employed not for their benefit but for his own) they were enabled to proceed with their fisheries, their agriculture, their ship-building (and their trade too, within the limits). This capital was a hot-bed to them. Nothing in the history of mankind is like their progress.

All this was done by England, whilst England pursued trade and forgot revenue. You not only acquired commerce but you actually created the very objects of trade in America; and by that creation you raised the trade of this kingdom at least fourfold. America had the compensation of your capital, which made her bear her servitude. She had, except for the commercial restraint, every characteristic mark of a free people in all her internal concerns. She had the image of the British constitution. She had the substance. She was taxed by her own representatives. She chose most of her own magistrates. She paid them all. She had in effect the sole disposal of her own internal government. This whole state of commercial servitude and civil liberty, taken together, is certainly not perfect freedom; but comparing it with the ordinary circumstances of human nature, it was a happy and liberal condition. To join together the restraints of a universal internal and external monopoly with a universal internal and external taxation is an unnatural union; perfect, uncompensated slavery.

Source: Edmund Burke, speech on American Taxation (1774).

(b) Questions

1. What were the aims of 'the Act of Navigation'? How many such Acts were there? When were they passed?
2. What was meant by 'commercial restraint'? Who benefited from this 'restraint'? Why was it a 'hard law for America to live with'?
3. What benefits did Burke believe the Americans gained from the old colonial system?
4. What did Burke mean by 'England . . . forgot revenue'? When and why did a British government remember revenue?
5. In what ways had America 'the image of the British constitution'?
6. Why did Burke make a point of naming the year 1764? Why might some Americans have named (i) 1763, (ii) 1767, and (iii) 1773 as significant dates in the development of the feeling of resentment?
7. Which of the Whig leaders did Burke serve? What was this leader's policy towards the taxation of Americans?

(c) Further Reading

Christie, I.: *Wars and Revolutions, Britain 1760–1815.* Arnold (London, 1983).
Mackessy, P.: *The War for America 1775–1783.* Longman (Harlow, 1964).

Watson, J. S.: *The Reign of George III 1760–1815*. Oxford University Press (Oxford, 1960).

(*d*) **Exercises**

1. What were the main causes of the War of American Independence?
2. Why did the British lose the War of American Independence?
3. Show the importance of sea power during the War of American Independence.
4. Write briefly on (i) the Stamp Act, (ii) the Boston Tea Party, (iii) Saratoga, (iv) Yorktown.
5. Imagine yourself to be an American colonist. Write a letter to a friend in England *either* (i) justifying *or* (ii) condemning the Declaration of Independence, by reference to past events.

The Younger Pitt as a Peace Minister, 1783–93

4.1 The Fox–North Coalition

(a) The War of American Independence

The surrender by Cornwallis at Yorktown in October 1781 virtually ended the American War of Independence. The surrender was a severe blow to Lord North's government which had been under attack both inside and outside the Commons for several years. After October, even some of his previously loyal supporters turned against him, joining the ranks of the critics of the war. They forced the King to form a new ministry under Lord Rockingham in March 1782. The King knew that Rockingham wanted to make peace with the rebellious colonists. He was also aware of Rockingham's support for proposals aimed at lessening the amount of royal patronage which enabled the monarch to control the voting behaviour of many MPs (Section 2.6(d)).

Rockingham appointed Charles James Fox as Foreign Secretary, another sign of the great change that had taken place in the political life of the nation. Fox, like Rockingham, was a supporter of proposals for political reform. He was also suspected of being a pro-French opponent of British power, trade and influence. When Lord Rodney won the notable battle of the Saints in the West Indies, in May 1782, the country rejoiced; but Fox recalled the victorious Rodney and replaced him by a less capable admiral, Pigot. The popular opinion was that Fox did not want Britain to take advantage of his victory, which she might have done by seizing all the West Indian islands claimed by France.

Rockingham died in July 1782 and was replaced by another Whig, Shelburne, who dismissed Fox and invited the Younger Pitt into his Cabinet as Chancellor of the Exchequer. The Shelburne government continued to try to make peace with the American colonists, who signed a truce in January 1783.

But in February 1783 Shelburne was driven from office when the Commons condemned the terms of the truce by sixteen votes. Shelburne's defeat was due to many causes; his own Cabinet colleagues disliked his domination of Cabinet proceedings; the Whigs disliked his close relationship with the King, suspecting that their Whig, Shelburne, was on the way to becoming a King's Friend. North's supporters disliked the terms of the truce, believing that it might have been possible to have obtained some sort of federal solution to the American problem, and resenting the way in which, they argued, the American Loyalists (Section 17.4) had been betrayed. Fox and his supporters were opposed to Shelburne, arguing that he ought not to have taken office in

Fig. 4.1 'Britannia's Assassination' by Gillray. An American Indian is running off with the head, pursued by an empty-handed France; Spain has a leg and Holland has taken the shield. Fox is represented by the animal biting Britannia's leg and Wilkes is hitting out with his 'North Briton'

July 1782, but ought to have forced the King to allow the Commons to choose the Chief, or Prime, Minister.

The resignation of Shelburne left the way open for one of a number of possible coalitions. Pitt and Fox might have come together, supporting a policy of reform and, perhaps, impeachment of North, the minister most to blame for the loss of America. In fact, Fox made a coalition with North, partly to keep Pitt from gaining office and partly to take revenge on Shelburne. They agreed to serve under the Duke of Portland—a worthy nonentity who became Chief Minister in March 1783. The government was not popular with the King because it had been imposed on him and was not one he would have chosen himself. Nor was the government popular in the country, where people remembered Fox's call for North's impeachment during the American War.

(b) The India Bill

In November 1783 Fox introduced his India Bill, to take power from the East India Company and transfer it to the government. Some sort of reform of the East India Company was needed: it had started off as a trading company but had conquered huge portions of Indian territory so that the company now ruled over Bengal, the Carnatic, Bombay and other parts of India (Section

17.1(*a*)–(*c*)). Merchants whose lives had been spent in trading were not trained to rule, and serious mistakes had been made in India. Reform was needed, but Fox's proposals were seen as an outrageous attempt to transfer the power of the Company to himself and his friends. This was contrary to the spirit of the 1688 Revolution, by which the policy of the government was supposed to be the policy of the monarch.

The King had never liked Fox—his long-time opponent—and he was anxious to get rid of this ministry. He could not persuade enough MPs to vote against the India Bill in November 1783, but when the bill went to the House of Lords, George III used his influence with the Lords, who threw the bill out on 17 December. The King then dismissed Fox and North and appointed Pitt as his Prime Minister.

4.2   The Schoolboy Prime Minister

William Pitt, the Younger, son of the famous William Pitt, Earl of Chatham, was born in 1759, his father's 'miracle year' when Britain had won several outstanding victories over France and taken control of Canada, India and several islands in the West Indies. The Younger Pitt was only fourteen years old when he went to Cambridge University and he had qualified as a barrister by the age of twenty-one. The following year he became MP for the rotten borough of Appleby.

The Younger Pitt supported Shelburne, a Whig who hoped to lead a ministry containing men of all parties. He had refused a post in Rockingham's government but became Chancellor of the Exchequer under Shelburne. He was only twenty-three, the youngest-ever Cabinet member. George III appointed him to lead a minority government in the following year, the youngest Prime Minister of all time. When Pitt took office in December 1783 he was mocked by Fox as 'a schoolboy' leading a 'mincepie administration' which, said Fox, would be dismissed once the mincepies of Christmas 1783 had been eaten.

4.3   The 1784 Election

At first Pitt faced a hostile Commons. Many MPs had opposed the Fox–North India Bill, but they also disliked the King's use of his influence to persuade the Lords to throw the Fox–North government out of office. However, Pitt's courage, honesty and determination soon persuaded many MPs that he was a great leader, who would not be easily controlled by the King nor be seeking his own gain, as Fox obviously had been in 1783, when he joined forces with his old opponent, North. John Robinson, a former Treasury secretary, helped Pitt to win the support of the many independent MPs in the House. This could be done by offering a job, a contract or a title to an MP who promised to support the government. The MPs who changed sides and began to support Pitt were called 'Robinson's Rats' by Fox, whose sup-

Fig. 4.2 William Pitt addressing the House of Commons in 1793. Fox, wearing his customary black hat, can be seen to the left of the Speaker's chair

port dwindled. Pitt also became more popular throughout the country. In March 1784, when he thought that he had won a sufficient following to form a majority government, he asked the King to dissolve Parliament and call an election.

Fox and his followers argued that the King had no right to do this, because Parliament had been elected in 1780 and should sit until 1787. They said that Pitt's government was not popular in the country, and Fox waved the 'loyal addresses' signed by his supporters as proof that what the country wanted was a change of government. By now many people had shown in cartoons, songs, poems and newspaper articles, that Fox was a self-seeking politician, comparable perhaps to Cromwell in his desire to limit the power of the King and not caring which argument he used so long as he advanced his own interest. In 1782 he had argued that Parliament had been corruptly elected and the country needed a new election to get rid of North. Now he was arguing that this same Parliament, in which he had a large following, was properly elected and should be allowed to choose its own ministers.

On 14 February 1784, at a meeting of his own Westminster electors, Fox was shouted down with cries of 'No grand mogul; no India tyrant; no turn-

Fig. 4.3 'The Mirror of Patriotism' by Sayers. Fox is looking into a mirror as he rehearses a speech, but his reflection is that of Oliver Cromwell. Fox's opposition to George III laid him open to the accusation that he wanted to be another dictator—but see Fig. 2.2 for another artist's view of George III

coat', indicating that he was no longer the darling of the crowd. The electorate understood that the real issue in the election was whether the King had to accept ministers and policies against his will. For the first twenty days of the election Fox seemed certain to lose his seat in the Westminster constituency, where electors were allowed to return two members. Admiral Hood, a popular, national hero, was expected to win one of the seats and he supported the campaign of another candidate, Wray. By the twenty-third day Fox had more votes than Wray, but fewer than Hood. Hood then called on sailors to form mobs to roam the streets in support of Wray, yelling insults about Fox and threatening anyone who appeared to support him. Fox invited the Irish to create another rival mob to act on his behalf. There were songs, poems, cartoons, posters, newspaper articles, all helping to create a great degree of excitement in the constituency.

The election ended when polling had lasted for forty days. Fox beat Wray by 246 votes, the figures being:

Hood 6 694

Fox   6 234

Wray 5 988

but elsewhere Fox's supporters lost heavily to their Pittite opponents. The youthful, honest and courageous Pitt had won that support which he needed and in the process had driven many former MPs—called 'Fox's martyrs'—out into the wilderness.

4.4   Pitt and Trade, 1784–93

(a) Commutation, 1784

Pitt owed a good deal to the support of the merchants of London, and he tried to help them by making it possible for trade to expand. Pitt was also influenced by the ideas expressed by Adam Smith in his book *The Wealth of Nations* (1776). He said that lower import duties and less government regulation of foreign trade were to be welcomed because lower import duties would lead to lower prices and more trade, while greater freedom would lead to an increase in the number of British merchants and traders employing their energies overseas. All this would make the country more prosperous and provide more employment for the working people. In 1783 a Parliamentary Committee showed clearly that high duties encouraged smuggling:

> It appears that the fraudulent importation of many articles without payment of duty has increased to a very alarming degree, and is carried on with the most open and daring violence, in every accessible part of the coast of this Kingdom. The landing of the cargo is regulated by signals, and secured by large gangs of men, armed chiefly with clubs and heavy whips, generally inflamed with liquor, and assembled in such numbers as to reduce the Revenue Officers to be quiet spectators of the proceeding. The total duties to be paid before the tea can legally come into the hands of the consumer, amount to more than 100%. It is well known that when ships are expected from the East Indies, smuggling vessels from every part of the coast, cruise for them in the British Channel, and carry on a constant traffic with them. Smuggling is managed with little risk, through the collusion and corrupt practices of the lower class of Revenue Officers. The quantity of tea supposed to be brought annually into Great Britain by the various methods of illicit importation amounts to near seven million pounds. . . .
> Source: *First Report of the Committee on Smuggling* (1783).

Accordingly, Pitt passed the Commutation Act, which removed much of the temptation to smuggle tea by reducing the duty from 119 per cent to 12 per cent. This was also a first step along the road to free trade which Adam Smith had advocated in *The Wealth of Nations*.

(b) Trade Treaties

In 1786, Pitt concluded a trade treaty with France, known as the Eden treaty. It was agreed that manufactured goods from both countries would be allowed in on easier terms than before, and duties on other goods (such as wine and silks) would be lowered. This enabled the British to enjoy the benefit of lower prices charged for French goods imported into Britain while also enjoying access to the French markets for their manufactured goods.

(c) The Anti-smuggling Campaign

Pitt was well aware of the vast amount of smuggling that went on. His reduction of tariffs and the trade treaty with France were undertaken as efforts to reduce the attractiveness of smuggling. He also passed the *Hovering Act* (1787) which said that foreign ships had to anchor at least twelve miles out to sea, unless they were intending to enter a British harbour in pursuit of normal trade. This, it was hoped, would make the task of the smuggler more difficult.

Pitt also extended the system of *bonded warehouses* which had first been proposed by Sir Robert Walpole in 1733. Before the setting up of this system the importer had had to pay any import duties immediately on the importing of the goods. With the setting up of bonded warehouses the importer put his goods into a bonded warehouse, where they were guarded by customs officers. If the goods were taken out of bond for re-exporting (as happened to many goods), the merchant signed a form and was exempted from paying import duties. If the goods were required for sale in Britain, the merchant would pay import duty only when he took out the goods and only on that quantity of goods which he took out at any one time. By 1803 this system had become a welcome part of Britain's trading arrangements.

4.5 Pitt and Finance, 1784–93

(a) New Taxes

The reduction in import duties charged on French goods led to a fall in the income which the government received from Customs and Excise. To make up this loss Pitt imposed a series of taxes on luxuries such as racehorses, carriages, clocks, hair-powder and servants. He also imposed a window tax which became an important source of government revenue. The tax was arranged so that the rate per window increased as the number of windows in a house increased. The rich thus paid more than the poor, an improvement on the import duties which fell equally on rich and poor alike.

(b) Old Taxes Tidied Up

(i) **Customs and Excise.** Until 1784 there was a complicated system of Customs and Excise whereby a separate duty was charged on each article imported. Pitt reorganized the Customs and Excise by introducing a single tax applicable to all imports.

(ii) **Consolidated Fund, 1786.** In the past the British suffered under a complicated system of tax-collecting and government spending. The revenue from each different tax—on candles, for example, or on cider—was put into a separate account, so that Treasury clerks had to contend with dozens of different accounts. When the government spent money, for example on the navy or on soldiers' pay, the charge was made against a particular tax-revenue account. There was ample room for corrupt politicians and civil servants to help themselves out of this complicated mess.

Pitt altered the system. All revenues, whatever their source, were put into one Consolidated Fund and all payments, for whatever purpose, were made from this one account. There was less scope for fraud, and fewer clerks were required, so that the cost of administration fell.

> That the several duties of Customs, Excise and Stamps, together with the duty on hackney coaches and chairs, the duty on house windows, and lights, the duties on male and female servants, the duties on salt, the duty of sixpence in the pound on pensions, the duties on shops, on coaches, and carriages, and waggons and carts and on horses shall be carried to, and constitute a Fund, to be called The Consolidated Fund. . . .
> Source: *Public General Acts, 27 George III c 13.*

(c) Sinecures (from two Latin words—*sine* (without) *cura* (care))

Edmund Burke had been responsible for the introduction of the Civil Establishment Act (1782), which is sometimes called the Economical Reform Act. This Act abolished dozens of official posts without the country suffering in any way, since these posts were sinecures (posts in which people were paid for doing nothing). Pitt carried on this process of weeding out people who held well-paid posts for which they did nothing, so further cutting down the costs of government administration.

(d) The Sinking Fund, 1786

The National Debt consists of money which the government has been forced to borrow, usually to pay for costly wars (Section 3.3(a)). The American War had increased the Debt by over £100 million, and by 1786 it totalled about

£249 million. The government had to pay annual interest to the people who had loaned the money, and this interest came from taxes which the government collected. If only the National Debt could be repaid, there would be no annual interest to pay and taxation could be lowered.

In 1786 Pitt found that the government had collected £1 million more in taxation than it needed to spend, as a result of the various economic reforms and the increase in overseas trade. Pitt therefore persuaded Parliament to pass an Act by which £1 million would be handed each year to a Board of Commissioners of the Sinking Fund. They were to use this money to buy back government stock which had been issued when money had been borrowed in times past; they would hold on to this stock, collect the interest on it in the usual way and use this interest to buy back more stock. Pitt believed that within twenty-eight years the National Debt could be repaid in full. Unfortunately, this policy depended for its success on the maintenance of peace, when the government could get a surplus of revenue over expenditure. In 1793 Britain went to war with France (Section 5.3) and government expenditure rose, so that there was no surplus. Pitt ordered the Commissioners of the Sinking Fund to carry on with their work, even though this meant borrowing money at very high rates of interest. Far from leading to a reduction in the National Debt, this only added to it.

4.6   Parliamentary Reform, 1785

Pitt was an MP for a rotten borough but he appreciated the strength of the demand for parliamentary reform, which had been started at the time of the Wilkes' affair (Section 2.4). In 1785 he proposed to abolish thirty-six rotten boroughs and to transfer these seats to London and the counties. He also proposed to enlarge the electorate by giving the vote to some copyholders and leaseholders, rather as was done later, in 1832 (Section 10.4). The Commons threw out this mild reform, however, and Pitt never tried to propose these much-needed changes again.

4.7   The Regency Bill, 1788

In 1788 King George III seemed to be on the point of death and the Prince of Wales, a friend of Pitt's great rival, Fox, was ghoulishly looking forward to inheriting the throne. With the King unable to carry out his official duties, such as signing Acts of Parliament, the Cabinet was forced to consider appointing the Prince to the post of Prince Regent. This would allow him to carry out his father's job although his father was still alive. Fox and his friends looked forward to being invited by the Prince to form a government if he became Prince Regent. But Pitt and his Cabinet wrote to the Prince:

> It is their [the Cabinet's] humble opinion that your Royal Highness should be empowered to exercise the royal authority during his Majesty's illness.

That the power to be exercised by your Royal Highness should not extend to the granting of any office whatever, except such as must by law be granted for life; nor to the granting any rank of the peerage to any person. . . .
Source: Huish, R., *Memoirs of George IV* (1830), i, pp. 209–10.

Fox protested that this was putting too many curbs on the powers of the Regent's position. Some of Pitt's colleagues, thinking of their own futures, sided with Fox. Fortunately for Pitt the King recovered and the Bill was dropped, but Pitt did not forgive those of his colleagues who had betrayed him and supported Fox. He insisted that Thurlow, the Lord Chancellor, should resign, so showing his power over the Cabinet. This was the beginning of the modern practice whereby members of the Cabinet agree, in public at least, with whatever decisions the Cabinet has reached.

Fig. 4.4 Charles James Fox, Pitt's great rival and an upholder of liberal views— on freedom of speech, religious toleration and parliamentary reform—when these views were unpopular

4.8   Foreign Policy, 1783–93

(a) The Triple Alliance, 1788

When the American War ended Britain found herself without a friend in the world, and with France, Spain, Denmark, Prussia and Russia as dangerous enemies. Pitt was anxious for a long period of peace during which his financial and trade policies would have a chance to restore British prosperity and repair the damage done by the costly and unsuccessful war. But almost immediately he found himself involved in the affairs of Holland and her neighbour, the Austrian Netherlands (modern Belgium).

The Emperor of Austria, Joseph II, planned to make the Netherlands into a great trading centre, and to develop the port of Antwerp as a rival to Holland's Rotterdam and Britain's London. In order to achieve this he had to try to force Holland to open the river Scheldt to foreign shipping, which Holland was unwilling to do. When Joseph II attacked Holland in 1784 the Dutch resisted, the Russians offered to help the Austrians and the French offered to help the Dutch.

Pitt was anxious that the Austrians should not succeed in opening the Scheldt and developing Antwerp; he was also anxious that France should not gain undue influence in neighbouring Holland. Pitt arranged an alliance with Frederick of Prussia and in 1787 Prussian troops, supported by Britain, went to the aid of the Dutch. In 1788 the Triple Alliance of Britain, Holland and Prussia was formed for the mutual defence of all three countries against France, or any other power which threatened to dominate European affairs. Britain was no longer friendless.

(b) Russia

Catherine the Great, the Czarina of Russia, was anxious to extend her country's influence both north and south. In the north this brought Russia into conflict with Sweden, whose neighbour and traditional enemy, Denmark, sided with Russia. The Triple Alliance forced Denmark to withdraw from this war and in 1790 Russia and Sweden made peace, agreeing to leave territorial arrangements as they had been before the war started. Pitt had prevented Russia from turning the Baltic into a Russian lake.

In the south the Russians were joined by the Austrians for an attack on Turkey, from whom Russia had recently taken the Crimea. In December 1788 Russia and Austria invaded Turkey, but the outbreak of the French Revolution in 1789 tended to overshadow events in this far-away country. In 1790 Austria, frightened at developments in France, withdrew from the Turkish War but Russia continued to win victories over the weak Turks. The Triple Alliance threatened to make war against Russia if she did not withdraw from Turkey, but Pitt changed his mind and agreed that Russia could keep her conquests. He realized that it would be difficult for Britain to attack Russia. This action disappointed Prussia and the Triple Alliance broke up, with Prussia turning to Russia as a possible ally. In 1792 Russia made peace with Turkey and, uniting with Prussia and Austria, attacked Poland. Pitt did not feel that British interests were involved in these matters.

(c) Nootka Sound

Nootka Sound was a harbour on the shores of Vancouver Island, where English fishermen had settled. The Spaniards claimed all the territory along the west coast of America. In 1789 a Spanish force was sent to capture Nootka Sound, in doing which it seized some British ships and ejected British settlers. Britain protested, prepared for war and received promises of help from her partners in the Triple Alliance. Spain agreed to discuss the dispute which was settled in October 1790, with the Sound being returned to Britain.

For information about the Empire in this period, see Unit 17.

4.9 Pitt the Politician

Pitt was a successful Prime Minister at that time, particularly with his forward-looking policies in finance and trade. Rosebery, Pitt's biographer, wrote:

> It is impossible to complete any sketch of his [the younger Pitt's] career, without setting him by the side of Chatham. Not merely are they father and son; not merely are they the most conspicuous English Ministers of the eighteenth century; but their characters illustrate each other. And yet it is impossible for men to be more different.
>
> Each Pitt possessed in an eminent degree the qualities which the other most lacked; one was formed by nature for peace, the other for war. Chatham could not have filled Pitt's place in the ten years which followed 1783; but, from the time that war was declared, the guidance of Chatham would have been worth an army. No country could have too many Pitts; the more she has the greater will she be. But no country could afford the costly and splendid luxury of many Chathams.
>
> *Source:* Rosebery, Earl of, *Pitt* (1891).

Test Yourself on Unit 4

(a) Document: a Tax on Candles

I should have enjoyed the first fine morning I have seen this month . . . if our new tax-maker had not put me out of temper. I am angry with him, not only for the matter but for the manner of his proposal. When he lays his impost upon horses, he is even jocular and laughs; though considering that wheels and miles and grooms were taxed before, a graver countenance upon the occasion would have been more decent. But he provokes me still more by reasoning as he does on the justification of the tax upon candles. Some families, he says, will suffer little by it. Why? Because they are so poor that they cannot afford themselves more than ten pounds in the year. Excellent! They can use but few, therefore they will pay but little, and consequently will be but little burthened, an argument which for its cruelty and effrontery seems worthy of a hero; but he does not avail himself of the whole force of it, nor with all his wisdom had sagacity enough to see that it contains, when pushed to its utmost extent, a free discharge and acquittal of the poor from the payment of any tax at all; a commodity, being once made too expensive for their pockets, will cost them nothing, for they will not buy it. . . . I wish he would visit the miserable huts of our lace-makers at Olney, and see them working in the winter months, by the light of a farthing candle, from four in the afternoon till midnight. I wish he had laid his tax upon the ten thousand lamps that illuminate the Pantheon, upon the flambeaux that wait upon ten thousand chariots and sedans in an evening, and upon the wax candles that give light to ten thousand card-tables. I wish, in short, that he would consider the pockets of the poor as sacred, and that to tax a people so necessitous is but to discourage the little industry that is left among us, by driving the laborious poor to despair.

Source: William Cowper, letter to the Revd William Union (July 1784).

(*b*) Questions

1. Whom did the writer attack as 'our new tax-maker'?
2. What was meant by an 'impost on horses'? What other forms of 'luxury taxes' did the Prime Minister impose about this time?
3. Why did the Prime Minister increase taxation in 1784? What steps did he take in 1786 and 1787 to reduce the level of taxation that would have to be paid in future?
4. Why did the tax on candles affect the poor as well as the rich? Why did (i) the rich pay more of this tax, (ii) the poor feel the burden of this tax more than did the rich?
5. What is the difference between a direct and an indirect tax? Were Pitt's taxes direct or indirect?
6. Which of the Prime Minister's new taxes did the poor avoid because the commodity was 'made too expensive for their pockets'?

(*c*) Cartoon

Fig. 4.5 'The Free Born Briton' drawn in 1786 to illustrate some people's opin-ions of Pitt's new taxes. Notice the absence of a tax on incomes

(*d*) **Questions**

1. Do you think that this was drawn by a supporter or by an opponent of the Younger Pitt?
2. Do you agree with the artist that the Englishman was weighed down by the burden of taxation between 1784 and 1793?
3. Why was the window tax opposed more by the rich than by the poor?
4. Which of the taxes named in the picture made the greatest impact on the poor?
5. Why does the artist not include income tax in the cartoon?
6. Which class paid most of (i) the land tax, (ii) the stamp duty?
7. Who paid the Customs and Excise duties (i) immediately, (ii) in the long run?
8. Why was the burden of taxation greater in 1784 than in 1774? Why was it greater in 1794 than in 1784?
9. How did Pitt try to (i) lower the level of government expenditure, (ii) lower the level of the National Debt?

(*e*) **Further Reading**

Christie, I.: *Wars and Revolutions, Britain 1760–1815*. Arnold (London, 1983).
Marshall, D.: *Eighteenth Century England*. Longman (Harlow, 1975).
O'Gorman, F.: *The Emergence of the British Two-Party System 1760–1832*. Arnold (London, 1983).
Watson, J. S.: *The Reign of George III 1760–1815*. Oxford University Press (Oxford, 1960).

(*f*) **Exercises**

1. Explain (i) the origin, (ii) the fall of the Fox–North Coalition.
2. Give an account of the work which the Younger Pitt did in the fields of (i) trade, (ii) finance, (iii) foreign affairs.
3. Do the Younger Pitt's achievements between 1783 and 1793 entitle him to the praise of Lord Rosebery (Section 4.9)?
4. Write briefly on (i) sinecures, (ii) the trade treaty with France, (iii) the Sinking Fund, (iv) Nootka Sound.
5. Show how the Younger Pitt restored the prestige and prosperity of Britain before 1793.

Pitt and the French Revolutionary Wars, 1793–1805

5.1 The French Revolution, 1789–93

In 1789 the French king, Louis XVI, was forced by circumstances to call a meeting of the *States-General*, which was something less, and at the same time more, than the British Parliament. Members of each of the three main social groups, the nobility, the Church and the ordinary people, elected delegates to meet the King at the Royal Palace at Versailles, in order to work out with him ways in which France might be made more prosperous. No French king had called such a meeting for 175 years, but France in 1789 was in a pitiful state. After a succession of costly and unsuccessful wars, the government had no money left in the Treasury, nor any new ideas on how it could increase its revenue from taxation. The harvests of 1787 and 1788 had failed, so many poor people were starving. And a growing number of middle-class people—merchants, lawyers, journalists, bankers and others—were being influenced by the political writings of such philosophers as Rousseau and Voltaire; they were beginning to demand that France ought to imitate Britain and become a more democratically run country.

(a) The Fall of the Bastille

The States-General met in May 1789. The hungry mobs of the Paris streets waited until July, growing angrier as they saw that the King, even with his States-General, was not quickly going to provide food for them. On 14 July they rioted and attacked the Bastille, a state prison which Parisians regarded as a symbol of the King's tyrannical government. The seven prisoners were released and, much more significantly, the Paris mob stole the guns and ammunition which had been stored there. In October they marched to Versailles and brought 'the baker and the baker's wife'—as they called the King and his Queen, Marie Antoinette—back to Paris. The royal couple were virtual prisoners of the Paris mob until June 1791, when they tried to flee from France to join their relations and friends in Austria. They were caught at Varennes and dragged back to Paris once again.

(b) The Assembly

In September 1791 new elections had resulted in extremists gaining control of the Assembly (as the States-General had become in 1789). This Assembly, which met in October 1791, announced that those French noblemen who had fled from France would be sentenced to death if they did not return im-

Fig. 5.1 'Storming the Bastille', 14 July 1789, painted by David. Notice the co-operation between soldiers and civilian men and women during this attack on the symbol of royal authority

mediately to their native land. When this did not lead to a mass return, the French felt a sense of grievance against the autocratic ruler of Austria. In August 1791 Leopold of Austria and Frederick William of Prussia had issued the *Declaration of Pillnitz* which said that the matter of the changes taking place in France was something which concerned all the rulers of Europe. This seemed, to the French, to indicate a will on the part of the autocrats to interfere in the internal affairs of France—perhaps to undo what had been achieved in France since 1789. The new government of France, controlled by the extremists, decided to invade the territory of Trier, where many of the French nobles were living. This brought France into conflict with Austria, since Trier was part of the Emperor of Austria's territory. Austria, aided by Prussia, refused to agree to the French demands for the return of the noblemen and in April 1792, Austria and Prussia were at war with France.

5.2   Britain and the Revolution

There was a variety of reactions among the British when they heard of the calling of the States-General, the fall of the Bastille and the setting up of a democratically-elected government in France.

(a) Pitt and His Followers

Pitt and most of the leading politicians welcomed the news that France had been thrown into confusion. If the French king was drawn into conflict with his people, if they were going to have to work out a new way of governing France together, then, so Pitt believed, there would be little danger of France trying to dominate European affairs, as she had done in the past. As late as 1792, Pitt said that Europe could look forward to at least fifteen years of peace, time in which Pitt's financial and trading policies would have a chance of bringing prosperity to Britain (Sections 4.4 and 4.5).

(b) Dissenters

Many people in Britain suffered because they were not Anglicans. Only Anglicans were allowed into Oxford and Cambridge Universities, and only Anglicans could sit on local councils, hold various official posts and enjoy full civil liberty. The Dissenters, or Nonconformists, welcomed the news of the French Revolution. They hoped that in the face of this gigantic upheaval Britain might be compelled to change its laws and allow Dissenters the same freedom as Anglicans enjoyed.

It was a Dissenter, Dr Price, who preached a famous sermon on 'The love of our country', in which he praised the French Revolution and started off the long debate on the merits and demerits of the Revolution. One consequence of this was the writing of *Reflections on the Revolution in France* in 1790, by Edmund Burke, and Tom Paine's reply to Burke, *The Rights of Man*, written in 1792.

(c) Burke

Burke had been a follower of Lord Rockingham (Section 2.5) and a supporter of the American colonists in their struggle with Britain. But in 1790 he wrote his detailed analysis of the French Revolution, prophesying that it would lead to great bloodshed and cruelty, the emergence of a dictator and a long war. Burke was a very influential writer, and many people in the upper class, who dominated Parliament, agreed with his views, which helps to explain their willingness to take action against British people who seemed to support the Revolution.

(d) Corresponding Societies

There had been a demand for parliamentary reform in the 1760s and 1770s, as we saw in Section 4.6. The news of the fall of the Bastille and the setting up of a democratically-elected form of government in France gave a spur to the activities of the Radicals, who were calling for parliamentary reform. It also inspired the setting up of a number of new societies. In 1791 some members of the upper class founded the *Society of the Friends of the People* which produced pamphlets calling for a variety of liberal reforms—of Parliament, the legal system, trade, taxation and other aspects of life. In 1792 the far more democratic and dangerous *London Corresponding Society* was formed among the skilled working class. Thomas Hardy, a shoemaker, was the founder of this Society which, like the others, took the name *Corresponding* because its members corresponded with members of the French Revolutionary Assembly and also with each other. (There was, after all, no other way in which people living in Yorkshire could share their ideas with people in London, since travel was slow and dangerous as well as expensive, and there were none of the modern, quick methods of communication, such as the telephone or the radio.)

5.3   Britain at War with France, 1793

Within a year of making his 'peace for fifteen years' prophecy, Pitt found himself leading the government into a war with Revolutionary France.

(a)   The Edict of Fraternity, November 1792

The French government, now dominated by the extremists, decided to spread the word of the Revolution throughout Europe—by force since it seemed that peoples in other countries were not making any move to follow the example which France had set in 1789. The French issued the *Edict of Fraternity*, in which they called on the lower classes everywhere to rise and join in the general revolution. The British government was frightened that some of the British lower classes might indeed listen to this propaganda. This increased the hostility between the French and the British government, which believed that the lower orders ought to stay in their 'proper stations'.

(b)   The Opening of the River Scheldt, November 1792

The French armies, having withstood invasion by Austria and Prussia, then invaded the Austrian Netherlands (modern Belgium). They threatened that they would open the river Scheldt to world trade and build up the port of Antwerp as a rival to Rotterdam and London. The British had already shown that they were not prepared to allow this to happen, as we saw in Section 4.8(*a*)).

(c)   General Disgust

The British public were horrified by reports of the way in which the French government of extremists had attacked members of the French upper classes who had remained in France. Thousands had been arrested in September and October 1792 and, after a mockery of a public trial, they were sentenced to death. The guillotine became a feature of every French town and city as the

September Massacres and *the Terror* swept through France. In January 1793, the French government ordered the execution of the French King, Louis XVI. This appalled the British people: they may have had no love for the King but they did not want to see a massacring government replacing him.

5.4   Pitt and the War

Pitt thought that the war with France, which began in 1793, would be a short-run affair. He believed that France would quickly become bankrupt and be unable to pay for a war, while its army, led as it was by 'a rabble' after the execution of most of its former officers, would be no match for the armies of the Allies.

(a) Subsidies

Pitt knew that the British army was too small and too ill-equipped to fight a continental war. He relied on Britain's Allies—Austria, Prussia, Russia and others—to do the greater part of the fighting. Britain would supply these Allies with the gold which they needed to buy equipment and pay their soldiers. Unfortunately, the Allies often used this money for their own purposes, such as feuding among themselves over Poland, instead of fighting the French.

(b) Colonial Wars

Like his father, Pitt thought that Britain's greatness depended upon an extension of the British Empire. He intended to use the small British army to attack the French colonies in the West Indies. Unhappily he made few plans when he ordered expeditions to undertake such attacks, and thousands of badly-fed and ill-clothed soldiers died of fever in the West Indies.

(c) The Navy

Again in imitation of his father, Pitt intended to use the navy to blockade French ports, cut off France from trade with her colonies and help British troops in their attacks on France and French colonies. But the navy was too small for these various purposes. Recruitment was by way of cruel press gangs, which roamed the ports of the country. The unwilling recruits had to suffer barbarous treatment from their officers, received little pay and were badly fed, so they were unwilling fighters.

5.5   The First Coalition, 1793–7

In 1793 Britain arranged the First Coalition against France in which Spain, Holland, Austria, Prussia, England and Sardinia (the 'Shapes' countries as they are sometimes called) were joined by Russia. Pitt must have hoped that the forces of such powerful Allies would easily defeat the much smaller forces of Revolutionary France. But there was little unity among these Allies. Britain was more concerned with developing her Empire than with actively engaging in fighting continental France. Russia, Prussia and Austria were more interested in dividing Poland among themselves, with Prussia and Austria in particular being traditional and longstanding enemies. The armies of these continental Allies were badly led and moved slowly across the vast distances which separated Russia from France.

The French, on the other hand, were fortunate in that a number of inspiring leaders emerged. Carnot organized supplies for the army and Danton inspired the French people with a slogan of *L'audace, l'audace, et toujours l'audace.* The armed forces, deprived of the leadership of most of their former officers— now condemned as Royalists—fought with great enthusiasm to defend their country against foreign invasion, rather as the Americans had fought against the British (Sections 3.5 and 3.6).

(a) Britain and the First Coalition

(i) **1793, Toulon.** Toulon was a naval base in southern France where Royalists rose in rebellion against the extremist government. The British hoped to take advantage of this civil war. A fleet was sent to help the Royalists and British troops landed to fight alongside the Royalist rebels. The expedition was a disaster and, under the leadership of a young Corsican, Napoleon Bonaparte, the French drove the British off.

(ii) **The West Indies.** In 1794 an expedition was sent to attack the French sugar islands. The campaign lasted until 1798 and during these four years over 100 000 soldiers and sailors died, mostly from yellow fever and dysentery. Some islands were captured in 1795 but most of them were recaptured by the French later on.

(iii) **The Cape of Good Hope.** In 1795 Britain seized the South African Cape— which had been part of the Dutch Empire—to protect her own trade routes to India.

(iv) **The Glorious First of June, 1794.** Admiral Howe commanded a fleet which was intended to blockade the French coast and cut France off from trade with the outside world. On 1 June 1794 some corn ships escaped the British blockade while the British fleet was engaged in a battle with French warships so that the glorious victory, as it was called, was a hollow victory in fact.

(v) **The Netherlands campaign.** Under the command of the Duke of York a small British army was sent to the Netherlands to try to drive the French back. The failure of this expedition is summed up in the nursery rhyme which commemorates the capacity of the Duke to take his men up and down hills without achieving anything.

(b) The Coalition Breaks Up

In 1795 Prussia, anxious to safeguard her interests in Poland, made peace with France. Sardinia followed in 1796 and in the next year Austria suffered a heavy defeat at the Battle of Rivoli and made her peace with the French at Campo Formio.

In 1796 Spain and Holland declared war on Britain, hoping to gain something for themselves out of the general conflagration in which Europe now found itself. Fortunately, the British navy, once again, rescued the fortunes of the country. At the Battle of Cape St Vincent (1797), Admiral Jervis, with Nelson as his second-in-command, defeated the Spanish and at the Battle of Camperdown (1797), Admiral Duncan defeated the Dutch fleet.

5.6 1797: the Year of Crisis

The break-up of the Coalition and the attempt by Spain and Holland to take advantage of the difficulties in which Britain now found herself marked 1795 and 1796 as dangerous years. But 1797 seemed to be even worse.

(a) Ireland

There was the danger of a French invasion of Ireland, which was on the threshold of revolution (Sections 16.1 and 16.2).

(b) Naval Mutinies

At the naval bases of the Nore and Spithead there were mutinies among the discontented sailors who had been press-ganged. They resented the poor food, lack of pay, infrequent leave and the cruelty of many officers, so in 1797 they rose in rebellion. As a young Lieutenant reported:

> On the 24th ult. I sailed for the Nore, having 122 new-raised men on board. In approaching Yarmouth Roads on the 19th I observed 3 sail of the line, one frigate and a sloop with red flags on the fore topmast head, which I conjectured was the signal of insurrection. Next morning I found the fleet in the utmost disorder. I was surrounded by armed vessels and told that if I did not hoist the red flag, the tender would be sunk. The contagion spread like fire among the volunteers. . . .
> Source: Lieutenant James Watson to Admiral Digby (June 1797).

Since Britain depended almost entirely on the navy, the danger presented by these mutinies was obvious. Fortunately the unrest was shortlived. The leaders were arrested and some were executed after a brief trial. Officers were told to take account of the men's complaints and conditions improved slowly, particularly in fleets led by humane commanders such as Nelson.

5.7 The Second Coalition, 1798

Britain, Austria, Russia and Turkey entered into another Coalition against France, but this one was even shorter lived than the First. In March 1799

Austrian and Russian armies drove the French from Italy but a Russian and British expedition failed in the mud of the Netherlands. This led to quarrelling among the Allies and the Russians withdrew from the Coalition. Indeed, in 1800 Russia joined Denmark and Sweden in the *Armed Neutrality*, which was aimed at limiting British trade and influence in the Baltic (the source of most of the timber required for shipbuilding), and which Napoleon hoped to use as a major alliance against Britain's naval power while he went on to win land battles. This left Austria to fight Napoleon and the other French generals. After a series of defeats the Austrians signed the Treaty of Luneville in 1801, and once again Britain faced France alone.

(a) British Naval Successes

Meanwhile the British navy had once again been successful. In May 1798 Napoleon had taken an army from France to conquer Egypt, which he saw as the gateway to India. On the way he captured the island of Malta. However, Nelson – who was commanding the British navy in the Mediterranean –

Fig. 5.2 The capture of Copenhagen, 1801

chased after and defeated the French fleet at Aboukir Bay, leaving Napoleon stranded in Egypt. His army was then defeated at the Battle of Acre by British troops supported by a fleet led by Sir Sidney Smith. Finally, the fleet recaptured Malta from the French in 1800.

In April 1801 a fleet under Admiral Hyde Parker sailed for Copenhagen where Nelson defied his commander's orders, sailed into the harbour and destroyed the Danish fleet.

(*b*) **The Peace of Amiens**

Meantime Pitt had resigned over the issue of Catholic Emancipation (Sections 8.5, 16.2 and 16.3) and was succeeded by Addington (1801), who was anxious to make peace with France. The Peace of Amiens was signed in March 1802. Britain returned all the colonial conquests she had made at the expense of France, Spain and Holland, with the exception of Trinidad (from Spain) and Ceylon (from Holland). The French on their part withdrew from Rome, Naples and Egypt, while Britain promised to hand back Malta to the Knights of St John. The Knights were one of the orders of Hospitallers, founded around 1070 to defend Christian pilgrims to the Holy Land. After the Turks had conquered the Holy Land, the Knights had made their headquarters first at Crete and then at Malta, from which they were driven by Napoleon in 1798.

5.8   War Again: The Third Coalition

The Peace of Amiens settled nothing; it was merely a breathing space. France, under Napoleon, wanted a chance to recoup her forces and to try to make arrangements with the various European Powers which would help her fight a war against Britain. Britain, for her part, could not stand by and watch Napoleon retain the stranglehold which he had over so much of Europe. But France continued to extend her influence, conquering northern Italy and interfering in Switzerland. Thousands of men along the French coast were engaged in building a fleet for the invasion of Britain.

On 17 May 1803 the British government again declared war on France, and Pitt came back to office in April 1804. He set about organizing yet another Coalition, in which Britain and Russia were joined by Austria. But the Austrian army suffered a series of crushing defeats, ending with the defeat at Ulm and Napoleon's triumphant entry into Vienna, the capital of Austria, in 1805. The combined Austrian and Russian armies were also defeated at the Battle of Austerlitz in 1805. This victory gave Napoleon a chance to redraw the map of Europe; he created new states in what had once been the Holy Roman Empire and new kingdoms for his various relatives to rule.

Napoleon now had an army ready for the invasion of southern England, but, once again, the British navy stood in the way of his complete success. This army waited, in ports along the northern French coast, for the arrival of the French navy under Admiral Villeneuve, which would protect them during the Channel crossing. But Villeneuve's fleet was in ports on the southern French coast, blockaded by Nelson and other admirals to ensure that it could not escape from the Mediterranean. When the French did try to break the blockade, the British gained a notable victory at the Battle of Trafalgar in 1805. They captured eighteen of the thirty-three French ships, while eleven more put into Cadiz and never sailed again. As Admiral Codrington noted: 'There never was so complete an annihilation of a fleet.' Nelson's death at the

Fig. 5.3 The death of Nelson at Trafalgar, painted by Devis

Battle marked the end of a great admiral's life, while his victory marked the end of Napoleonic hopes of invading Britain.

Shortly after this great victory, Pitt was guest at a banquet given by the Lord Mayor of London, where he made one of the shortest and most famous of his speeches:

> I return you many thanks for the honour you have done me; but Europe is not to be saved by any single man. England has saved herself by her exertions and will, I trust, save Europe by her example.

Within two months he was dead, worn out by his exertions on behalf of his country.

5.9   Pitt's Domestic Policy, 1793–1806

Between 1783 and 1793 Pitt had followed a reforming, forward-looking policy, as we saw in Unit 4. But once the French Wars began in 1793 he seemed to lose his touch, both as a war minister and as a politician of home affairs.

(a) The Corresponding Societies

Pitt feared the Corresponding Societies might produce so much unrest in Britain that a revolution on the French model might break out. There was no evidence for this but he ordered an attack on the Societies and their leaders, Horne Tooke, Thomas Hardy and others, were arrested in 1794. Tom Paine, fearing arrest, fled to France (where, as a member of the Convention, he was arrested for opposing the execution of Louis XVI). The government seized the papers of various Societies and persuaded Parliament to suspend the Habeas Corpus Act (1794) which meant that suspects could now be held in jail without trial.

The trials of the Societies' leaders ended with the acquittal of most of those who had been arrested, although two Scottish leaders, Muir and Palmer, were deported to Botany Bay in Australia. But the trials did frighten many people and deterred them from playing a part in the work of these and other reform movements. The movement for parliamentary reform, once led by Pitt himself, almost came to an end. Pitt himself led the way in seeming to link such demands for reform with the horrors of the Revolution in France.

(b) Public Meetings, 1795

To limit the influence of Hardy, Tooke and other radical leaders, Pitt's government passed an Act in 1795 which declared:

> Be it enacted that no meeting of any description of persons, exceeding the number of fifty persons, shall be holden, for the purpose or on the pretext of considering or of preparing any petition, complaint, remonstrance or declaration, or other address to the King, or to both houses, or either house of parliament, for alteration of matters established in church or state. . . .
>
> Source: The Seditious Meetings Act (1795), Statutes at Large, xl, p. 564.

(c) Seditious Practices Act, 1795

In October 1795 the King was attacked, on his way to open parliament. This, together with fear of the danger which might result from the spread of revolutionary fever from France, led the government to pass an Act which said:

> That if any persons intend bodily harm of the person of the King, or in order to put any force or constraint upon houses of parliament . . . shall express by publishing any printing or writing or by any overt act or deed; being legally convicted thereof, upon the oaths of two lawful and credible witnesses, shall be deemed to be a traitor and shall suffer pains of death as in cases of high treason.
>
> Source: The Treasonable and Seditious Practices Act (1795), Statutes at Large, xl, p. 561.

(d) Trade Unions

The government argued that the emergence of trade unionism was a sign that a revolutionary movement was developing. In 1799 and again in 1800 the government passed Combination Acts, making it illegal for men to form or to join trade unions (Sections 18.2 and 18.3).

(e) **Aliens' Act, 1794**

No foreigner was allowed to enter Britain without special permission. This, it was hoped, would make it harder for French people to bring into Britain the books, pamphlets and ideas current in France.

(f) **Income Tax, 1798**

Pitt introduced a 'temporary tax' on incomes from land, personal property, trade, professions, pensions and employment, to help pay for the costly war. The tax had to be paid by anyone earning more than £60 a year, and it was a graduated one on incomes of between £60 and £200 a year. People earning more than £200 a year had to pay a tax of 10 per cent on their incomes.

Test Yourself on Unit 5

(a) **Document: Resistance to Aggression**

To insist upon the opening of the river Scheldt is an act of itself in which the French nation had no right to interfere at all, unless she was sovereign of the Low Countries, or boldly professed herself the general arbitress of Europe. France can have no right to annul the stipulations [laws] relative to the Scheldt, unless she has also the right to set aside equally all the other treaties between the powers of Europe, and all the other rights of England or of her allies. England will never consent that France shall take the power of annulling at her pleasure . . . the political system of Europe established by solemn treaties and guaranteed by the consent of all the powers. . . . From the Treaty of Munster down to the year 1785, the exclusive navigation of the Scheldt has been one of the established rights of Holland. We are told it is to be said that no formal requisition [request] has been made by Holland for the support of this country. I beg gentlemen to consider whether ships going up the Scheldt, after a protest of the States General, was not such an act as to have justified them in calling upon this country for a contingent of men. . . . Are we to stand by as indifferent spectators and look at France trampling upon the ancient treaties of the allies of this country? Are we to view with indifference the progress of French ambition, and of French arms, by which our allies are exposed to the greatest danger? This is surely no reason for England to be inactive and slothful. If Holland has not immediately called upon us for our support and assistance, she may have been influenced by motives of policy, and her forbearance ought not to be supposed to arise from her indifference about the river Scheldt. If Holland had not applied to England when Antwerp was taken, the French might have overrun her territory. And unless we wish to stand by, and to suffer state after state to be subverted under the power of France, we must now declare our firm resolution effectually to oppose those principles of ambition and aggrandisement which have for their object the destruction of England, of Europe and of the world.
Source: William Pitt, speech to the Commons (February 1793).

(b) **Questions**

1. Which country was most interested in the future of the river Scheldt? Which ports along this river stood in (i) Dutch, (ii) Austrian territory?

2. Why was the possibility of the opening of the river of great importance to London merchants?
3. Why was *France* in a position to 'insist upon the opening of the river Scheldt' in 1793?
4. What dangers did Pitt foresee would follow the opening of the river by the French?
5. When had Holland become an ally of Britain? Against whom had this alliance been aimed?
6. What Edict issued by the French suggested that it was possible for 'state after state to be subverted under the power of France'?
7. What reasons, not offered in this extract, were there for British enmity to France in 1793?

(c) Further Reading

Briggs, A.: *The Age of Improvement 1783–1867.* Longman (Harlow, 1979).
Bryant, A.: *The Years of Endurance 1793–1802.* Collins (London, 1942).
Christie, I.: *Wars and Revolutions, Britain 1760–1815.* Arnold (London, 1983).
Evans, E. J.: *The Forging of the Modern State: Early Industrial Britain 1783–1870.* Longman (Harlow, 1983).
Hobsbawm, J. R.: *The Age of Revolution, Europe 1789–1848.* Sphere (London, 1977).
Marshall, D.: *Eighteenth Century England.* Longman (Harlow, 1975).
Perkins, H.: *Origins of Modern English Society 1780–1890.* Routledge and Kegan Paul (London, 1969).
Thompson, E. P.: *The Making of the English Working Class.* Penguin (Harmondsworth, 1968).

(d) Exercises

1. Why did Britain go to war with France in (i) 1793, (ii) 1803? Why was Britain unable to defeat France?
2. Give an account of Pitt's work as a war minister between 1793 and 1806.
3. Outline the work of the British navy between 1793 and 1805.
4. Explain, and give an account of, Pitt's domestic policies after 1793.
5. Write briefly on (i) Dissenters and the French Revolution, (ii) Corresponding Societies, (iii) the Peace of Amiens, (iv) Armed Neutrality.
6. Why was 1797 a 'year of crisis' for Britain?

The Defeat of Napoleon, 1806–15

6.1 Politics after Pitt's Death

In 1806 George III reluctantly invited Fox to form a ministry. The ageing Whig leader, lifetime rival of the dead Pitt, invited Whigs as well as followers of Pitt's supporters, Addington and Grenville, to join him. This so-called Ministry of All the Talents proposed to end the war. In September 1806 Fox died and was succeeded by Grenville. Pitt's more loyal followers, who refused to join a ministry containing so many men who had opposed their hero, followed George Canning in the Opposition. Canning described his followers as *Tories*, although Pitt had called himself a Whig.

In 1807 George III dismissed Grenville because the ministry supported Catholic Emancipation (Section 8.5 and Fig. 8.5) and the Whigs remained out of office until 1830. The support which Fox and his followers had given to the French Revolution and their opposition to British participation in the wars against France made them unpopular with the majority of the voters, who were mainly from the richer classes. Tory support grew in proportion to the voters' fears of the Revolution. Since it was Tory governments which led the fight against the Revolution and Napoleon, it was also the Tories who became increasingly popular—nothing, after all, succeeds like success.

The Tory Duke of Portland formed a government which lasted until 1809. He was succeeded by Spencer Perceval, who was assassinated in the Lobby of the House of Commons in May 1812. Lord Liverpool then became Prime Minister, a post which he held until his death in 1827. He appointed Castlereagh to the post of Foreign Secretary in 1812.

6.2 The Third Coalition, 1805

After Trafalgar Britain ruled the sea but was unable to defeat Napoleon, who remained master of Europe. Austria had been forced out of the Coalition after the defeat at Austerlitz, which left Britain and Russia in alliance. They were joined by Prussia until Napoleon defeated the Prussians at the Battle of Jena in 1806. In 1807 Napoleon met Czar Alexander I aboard a raft on the river Niemen where they agreed the Treaty of Tilsit, in which Russia joined Napoleon in an alliance against Britain. Russia promised to shut her ports to British ships, and so help Napoleon to carry out his economic war against Britain (Section 6.3). Alexander and Napoleon also agreed to force Denmark and Sweden to join them in this embargo, and arranged for France to use the Danish fleet against Britain. But the brilliant George Canning was in the Portland government. He learned of the Treaty of Tilsit and, to prevent the

Danish fleet falling into French hands, he sent the British fleet to Copenhagen to capture it.

6.3 Economic Warfare

If Britain was unable to defeat Napoleon on land, Napoleon was equally unable to defeat Britain at sea and so he could not invade the island fortress. He realized that Britain's continuing ability to oppose him was a result of her great wealth, the product of an ever-increasing foreign trade which carried British goods throughout the world and brought much-needed gold back into Britain, which could be used to finance the war effort.

Napoleon therefore decided to try to defeat Britain by waging an economic war. He planned to close all Europe's ports to British ships so that British goods could not be sold, nor could Britain get the French grain and Baltic timber which she needed. By this *Continental System* he hoped to produce such distress in Britain that she would be forced to make peace:

> Berlin, November 21st, 1806
> We have consequently decreed and do decree that which follows: Article I—The British Isles are declared to be in a state of blockade. Article II—All commerce and all correspondence with the British Isles is forbidden. Article V—Trade in English goods is prohibited, and all goods belonging to England or coming from her factories or her colonies are declared a lawful prize. Article VII—No vessel coming directly from England or from English colonies or which shall have visited these since the publication of the present decree shall be received in any port.
> *Source: Berlin Decree, 1806.*

Napoleon forced his allies and the governments of countries which he had conquered to obey these decrees. Britain replied with the *Orders in Council* (1807) in which she threatened to seize any ship trying to enter the ports of France or her allies. This led Napoleon to issue the *Milan Decrees* (1807), which ordered that any ship entering a British port would be seized by France when it came out again.

Napoleon almost succeeded in his purpose. British trade suffered, the price of bread rose sharply as the import of foreign grain fell away and there was a good deal of unemployment. However, France and her allies could not do without some of the goods which only Britain could produce in sufficient quantities. Smugglers prospered along the European coasts and Napoleon was finally forced to relax his system, even to allow French farmers to export their corn to Britain.

6.4 War with the USA, 1812–14

At first the Americans sympathized with the French Revolutionary government, in gratitude for the aid which the French had once given them in their war against the British (Section 3.5(c)). When the British insisted on stopping and searching neutral shipping after 1808, the Americans became annoyed. Finally, in 1812, the US government declared war on Britain.

The war took place mainly at sea and along the Canadian border. A US army invaded Canada and burnt down part of York (now Toronto). A British army led by General Ross invaded the USA in retaliation, and attacked Washington, setting fire to some important buildings, including the home of the US President. This house was whitewashed to hide the marks of the flames, and so became known as the White House.

Some US ships attacked British shipping in the English Channel, while British ships raided ports along the American sea-coast. In December 1814 both sides signed the Treaty of Ghent which ended this war although it ignored the question of the British claim to the right to search neutral vessels. Four boundary commissions were set up to examine the problem of the frontier between Canada and the USA.

6.5   The Peninsular War, 1808–12

(a) Causes of the War

(i) **Portugal and the Continental System.** Napoleon had to control the whole of the Iberian Peninsula (Spain and Portugal) in order to make himself master of Western Europe. Spain was his ally and supplied him with soldiers, but Portugal remained friendly with Britain, and Portuguese ports were used to break the Continental System. In 1807 Napoleon reached an agreement with the Spanish and sent his troops through Spain to attack Portugal, which caused the ruler of Portugal to flee the country.

(ii) **The Spanish throne.** Napoleon forced the Spanish Royal Family to abdicate in 1808, in order to guarantee a secure passage to Portugal for his troops, and he installed his brother Joseph as King of Spain. The Spanish people resented this interference with their freedom more than they resented the passage of French troops through their country. They rose in rebellion and Joseph was forced to leave Madrid.

(iii) **The British government** sent an army under Sir Arthur Wellesley (the Duke of Wellington, after 1809) to help the Portuguese and the Spaniards in their guerrilla rising. The Peninsular War had begun.

(b) British Advantages

(i) **Spanish nationalism.** The Spanish people refused to admit defeat, although the French had a much superior army and were able to defeat them in pitched battles. Spanish pride and patriotism led them to form guerrilla forces which harassed the French troops on their way to Portugal: they cut off supplies and prevented reinforcements from reaching their posts; they defended their towns from French attack and organized revolts wherever the French set up a garrison. This made life extremely difficult for the French, who had to leave many troops in Spain to guard the lines of communication with France. The success of the Spaniards also encouraged people elsewhere in Europe to think that they, too, might be able to rise against the hitherto unconquerable Napoleon.

(*ii*) **British command of the sea.** The French had to bring their supplies along poor roads where valleys and high mountain chains made their passage difficult. The British, with the control of the sea, were able to supply and reinforce their armies in Portugal and, later, in Spain, without much difficulty. When the British armies moved away from the coast and into the interior of Spain they also found life difficult and supplies very scarce, but they were never as badly off as the French, as Wellington reported:

> Pero Negro, 3 November 1810
>
> It is impossible to describe to your lordship the . . . distresses of the French armies in the Peninsula. All the troops are months in arrears of pay; they are in general very badly clothed; . . . their troops subsist solely upon plunder, whether acquired individually, or more regularly by way of requisition and contribution; they receive no money, or scarcely any, from France; and they realize but little from their pecuniary contributions in Spain. This state of things has very much weakened, and in some instances destroyed, the discipline of the army; and all the intercepted letters [tell of] acts of . . . corruption, and misapplication of stores, etc., by all the persons attached to the army.
>
> *Source:* Wellington, *Despatches* (1837), vi, p. 552.

(*iii*) **Wellington.** British success in the Peninsular War owed much to Wellington's patience, hard work and judgment. He waited behind the secure lines of Torres Vedras until he was sure that the French were sufficiently weakened for him to attack with some certainty of victory. A number of the most brilliant of Napoleon's generals were facing him, but there was little unity among them. Each one was jealous for his own reputation and more anxious to justify himself in the eyes of Napoleon than to come to the aid of a brother general in trouble.

(*iv*) **The British army.** Wellington had a poor opinion of the men that he led:

> Our army is composed of the scum of the earth—the mere scum of the earth. . . . The English soldiers are fellows who have all enlisted for drink—that is the plain fact— they have all enlisted for drink.
>
> *Source:* Wellington, *Despatches* (1838), x, p. 473.

But they were disciplined by an efficient leader until they became the best fighting force in Europe.

6.6   The Course of the War

(*a*) 1808

Sir Arthur Wellesley was sent to Portugal in June 1808, in command of a force of 10 000 men, to assist the Portuguese and Spanish against the French. After his army had won the battles of *Rolica* and *Vimiero* in August 1808, British diplomats signed the *Convention of Cintra*. The French agreed to give up their fight in Portugal but they were allowed to return to France with all their arms and equipment. This settlement roused a good deal of anger and the inept generals who had signed it used their authority to dismiss their junior, Wellesley, and send him back to Britain. This made it appear as though Wellesley were to blame for the lenient terms allowed to the defeated French.

Fig. 6.1 The popular commander, Sir John Moore, encouraging his men at the Battle of Corunna. His death and burial at Corunna were the subject of a popular poem by C. Wolfe (1791–1823)

Sir John Moore was appointed commander in his place. Following the defeat of the French, Napoleon himself arrived to take command of his forces. In November 1808 he captured Madrid and restored his brother Joseph to the throne. The British army under Moore was marching from Portugal to help the Spaniards when it heard of the fall of Madrid. Moore turned northwards in the hope that he could cut Napoleon's army off from his lines of communication with France. When this plan failed Moore led his army to Corunna where, in January 1809, he was killed in the defence of the city. Twenty-four thousand of his army of 30 000 were safely embarked by the British fleet, another example of the advantage enjoyed by Britain with its control of the sea.

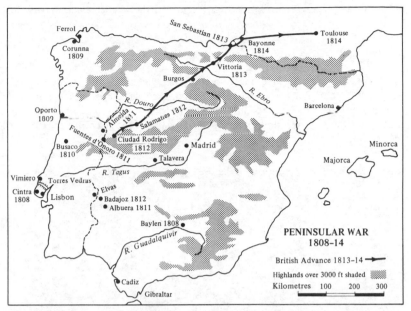

Fig. 6.2 The Peninsular War 1808–14

(b) The Freeing of Portugal: 1809–12

In April 1809 Wellesley returned to resume command of the army, after Moore's death. Napoleon had left Spain in January 1809 to deal with affairs in Austria. Wellesley won battles at Oporto (May 1809), where he defeated Marshal Soult, and Talavera (July 1809), after which he was given the title of Viscount Wellington of Talavera. Napoleon then appointed Marshal Masséna to command the French army in the Peninsula. The reinforcements which Masséna brought with him forced Wellington to retire to a position on the lines of Torres Vedras, three distinct ranges of defence. Masséna found these lines too strong to attack, while Wellington and his army enjoyed the plentiful supplies brought in by the British fleet. Masséna, running short of supplies, was forced to retire and he was pursued by Wellington, the French being defeated at a series of battles in 1811. In 1812 Wellington took Ciudad Rodrigo, Badajoz and Salamanca, after which he occupied Valladolid and, on 12 August, Madrid.

(c) 1813 and the Freeing of Spain

After the successes of 1812 Wellington had withdrawn to the frontiers of Portugal to prepare the British, Portuguese and Spanish troops for the campaign of 1813. In June of that year he won battles at Burgos, Vittoria, San

Sebastian and Pamplona, after which he pushed the French back across the Pyrenees.

6.7   The War Elsewhere, 1809–14

While Wellington was first harrying and then defeating the French in the Peninsula, Napoleon's star had risen and then fallen in other parts of Europe. In 1809 a British expedition was sent to seize the island of Walcheren in the river Scheldt, as a preliminary to the closing of the river and the capture of Antwerp.

Fig. 6.3 The Battle of Talavera 27–28 July 1809, where the French were commanded by Joseph Bonaparte and Marshal Jourdan. Following his victory here, Wellesley took the title of Viscount Wellington of Talavera when he was raised to the peerage by a grateful country on 26 August 1809

The expedition was badly planned, poorly led and ended in a disastrous withdrawal. At about the same time Napoleon's army defeated the Austrians at Wagram and the Austrians were forced to accept humiliating peace terms. In 1810 Napoleon still seemed to be at the height of his power. Austria had been defeated and an Austrian princess, Marie-Louise, became Napoleon's second wife. Spain and most of Portugal were under Napoleon's control, and so was the larger part of Western Europe. But at this high point, Napoleon's career started on its downward path.

(a) The Russian Campaign

In 1810 the Czar of Russia, so recently made a French ally, refused to co-operate further in the economic war on Britain and threw open his ports to British ships. To teach the Czar a lesson—and to win a route to that Indian Empire he had dreamt of since 1798 (Section 5.7(a))—Napoleon invaded Russia with an army of 700 000 men, half of them French, half of them from other parts of Europe. The Russians withdrew, fighting bloody battles as they went and destroying crops, animals and buildings, as part of what was called a 'scorched earth' policy. One

Fig. 6.4 The French Grand Army at the disastrous crossing of the river Berezina during the retreat from Moscow in 1812

result of this was that Napoleon's army found it difficult to get the food needed by men and animals. Over 100 000 men were killed at the Battle of Borodino, and although this victory left the road to Moscow open to Napoleon, both the victory and the entry into Moscow, in September 1812, were hollow successes.

For a few weeks Napoleon waited in Moscow for Alexander to appear and surrender. When nothing happened Napoleon, fearing the Russian winter, decided to retreat. There then took place one of the most terrible and costly marches in history, during which the Russian winter destroyed Napoleon's army: only about 20 000 of the Grand Army of 700 000 survived and returned to France.

(b) The Fourth Coalition

There was a brief lull during 1813. Napoleon used this opportunity to build up a new army, but it now contained many poorly trained men. Meanwhile, the Austrians, Prussians, Russians and Swedes joined Britain in the Fourth Coalition. The Allied armies closed in on Napoleon, who was defeated at the Battle of the Nations at Leipzig in October 1813. The Allies then entered Paris in March 1814: for the first time the Allies were fighting on French soil. When Wellington crossed from Spain into southern France, Napoleon felt his position to be hopeless and left for the island of Elba, having signed away the throne for himself and his son. King Louis XVIII, who had been living in exile in Britain, returned to the throne of France.

Fig. 6.5 The final assault by the British at the Battle of Waterloo, 18 June 1815

6.8   The Hundred Days, March–June 1815

After ten months in exile, Napoleon escaped from Elba and reached Paris in March 1815. The French king fled from Paris, and the Allies, busily engaged in discussing peace terms, had to defeat Napoleon once and for all. In June Napoleon left Paris to campaign in the Netherlands where he was heavily outnumbered by Allied forces, commanded by the Prussian, Blücher, and the Duke of Wellington. On 18 June the armies met at Waterloo and Napoleon's army was finally put to flight. Napoleon returned to Paris, gave up the throne again, and then travelled to the coast where he surrendered to the captain of a British ship, the *Bellerophon*. When the ship reached Plymouth, Napoleon heard that the allies had decided to exile him to the lonely island of St Helena, from which he would find it impossible to escape. He died there, on 5 May 1821.

Fig. 6.6 Napoleon on St Helena, a lonely figure on a small island

Test Yourself on Unit 6

(a) Further Reading

Briggs, A.: *The Age of Improvement 1783–1867*. Longman (Harlow, 1979).
Christie, I.: *Wars and Revolutions, Britain 1760–1815*. Arnold (London, 1983).
Hobsbawm, J. R.: *The Age of Revolution, Europe 1789–1848*. Sphere (London, 1977).
Lane, P.: *The Army*. Batsford (London, 1975).
Longford, E.: *Wellington: The Years of the Sword*. Weidenfeld and Nicolson (London, 1969).
Thompson, E. P.: *The Making of the English Working Class*. Penguin (Harmondsworth, 1968).

(b) Exercises

1. Give an account of the importance of the work of Wellington in the Peninsular War.
2. How do you account for British success in the Peninsular War?
3. What part was played in the defeat of Napoleon by (i) Nelson, (ii) Wellington, (iii) Castlereagh?
4. Write briefly on (i) the lines of Torres Vedras, (ii) guerrilla warfare, (iii) the Continental System, (iv) the Hundred Days.
5. State the main facts about *three* of the following, explaining their importance in the wars with France: (i) the Mutiny at the Nore, (ii) Aboukir Bay, (iii) the first battle of Copenhagen, (iv) Trafalgar, (v) the Orders in Council.

Unit Seven
Domestic Affairs, 1815–22

7.1 The Cost of the War

Wellington defeated Napoleon at the Battle of Waterloo on 18 June 1815. The long war was finally over and British prestige had never stood higher. Britain was the only European power not to have been defeated by Napoleon. It was British money which had sustained the fickle Allies during the periods of Coalition, the British navy had defeated Napoleon's attempts to win an Empire in Egypt and a path to India (Section 5.7(a)), as well as his attempt to invade Britain (Section 5.8), and it was the demand for British goods which had led to the break-up of Napoleon's Continental System (Section 6.3). And the underlying cause of this British supremacy at sea and finally on land was her industrial power (Unit 1).

However, Britain had to pay a price for having led the struggle against Napoleon. In 1793, on the eve of the outbreak of the French Revolutionary Wars, the British National Debt was just under £234 000 000 (Sections 3.3(a) and 4.5(d)). In 1815 the Debt had risen to the staggering figure of £834 000 000. The interest on that Debt had to be paid each year, and taxes would have to be imposed to pay for it.

7.2 Causes of Social Distress, 1815–22

(a) Industrial Change

As we saw in Unit 1, and Fig. 1.1 the textile industry was carried on in the cottages of domestic workers before the invention of steam-driven machinery. Steam-driven machinery led to a fall in the wages paid to hand-loom workers: power-driven looms required fewer workers so that there was a high level of unemployment and, for those fortunate enough to have work, a low wage level. As a Parliamentary Committee reported:

A very great number of the weavers are unable to provide for themselves and their families a sufficiency of food of the plainest and cheapest kind; that they are clothed in rags, ... that they have scarcely anything like furniture in their houses; that their beds and bedding are of the most wretched description, and that many of them sleep upon straw; that notwithstanding their want ... they ... have full employment; that their labour is excessive, not infrequently 16 hours a day. ...
Source: Report of Hand-loom Weavers Committee (1835), Parliamentary Papers, 1835, xii.

(b) Agricultural Change

The enclosure movement saw the disappearance of common land, the increasing use of new machinery on the larger farms and a decline in the number of agricultural workers. Many went to work in the new factories; those who remained on the land were forced to accept low wages.

(c) A Larger Workforce

In 1815 the government demobilized about 300 000 soldiers and sailors in an effort to reduce its expenditure. These ex-servicemen had to try to find work in a labour market which was already overcrowded. There were the thousands of Irishmen who had migrated to Lancashire and other industrial areas, and millions of children born in the first decade of the century. Child labour had been a feature of the domestic system, and the simple machines of the early industrial revolution could be worked by children as easily as by adults.

(d) Falling Demand

With the end of the war came the end of government contracts for clothing, food, armaments and other supplies. By late 1815 government expenditure had fallen by half. This created unemployment in industries which had relied on supplying the government and led to a fall in the demand for iron, coal and other raw materials.

Foreign countries, impoverished by the long war and anxious to develop their own industries, also reduced the volume of goods they imported from Britain. This fall in exports was not met by a rise in domestic demand: large-scale unemployment and low wages combined to ensure that the mass of the population were unable to afford the goods which British factories were capable of producing.

(e) Low Wages

British employers could now choose their workmen from an enlarged workforce, willing to accept whatever wage was offered because unemployment was rife. Juvenile labour was plentiful and cheap. The increased number of Irish immigrants came from a country where poverty was even worse than it was in Britain, and they were willing to work for very low wages. Even skilled workers were forced to accept cuts in wages until trade improved.

(f) Prices

In 1814 prices were about twice what they had been in 1793, before the French Wars had broken out; by 1816 they had fallen to a little above the 1793 level and they continued to fall until 1822. There were many reasons for this fall in prices: the government had been spending a great deal of money on war materials and on paying a vastly swollen army and navy. As soon as the war ended this spending was abruptly halted as the government cancelled orders from factories and workshops and demobilized the armed forces. There was thus a massive reduction in spending—by the government, by the families of men and women who had had work in munitions factories and by the families of servicemen. On the other hand, the war had seen an expansion of output: goods had been consumed by the government's war machine and by the prosperous workers and their families. When the war ended this capacity to produce remained, but the demand for goods fell. When supply exceeds demand there is normally a reduction in the price at which manufacturers can sell their goods. After 1815 there was a very great disproportion between the capacity to supply and the ability to buy (or demand) goods. Businessmen felt little confidence in the face of such deflation; many who had contracted debts at the old price levels were ruined by the sharp fall in prices, and their bankruptcies acted as a warning to others. Investment slowed down as industrialists were unwilling to borrow money: without investment, employment levels at best remain stagnant, and at worst, actually fall.

However, the fall in prices was not as sharp as the fall in wage levels. For the workers there was a fall in *real wages*, that is, the amount that their wages would buy when considered together with the prices of goods. The majority of working people experienced a fall in their standard of living.

(g) Corn Laws

In 1812 wheat prices had reached £6.35 a quarter (28 lb). The price fell to £3.27 a quarter after the Peace of Paris in 1814, as British ports were open once more to imports from the cornlands of France and Eastern Europe. Farmers and landowners had invested a good deal of capital in the development of inferior land for corn growing during the long wars, when they had been assured of high enough prices to pay the interest on their borrowed capital. A sharp fall in the price of corn would have led to ruin for these politically important sections of the population.

In a petition to Parliament the farmers of Cleveland noted:

> That the great . . . depreciation in the value of the produce of their farms has reduced many of the petitioners to a situation of great difficulty and that the expense which now attends the cultivation of poor . . . land exceeds the value of its produce; and . . . many of the petitioners will no longer be able to pay their rents and taxes. . . . The petitioners beg leave very respectfully to state, that they conceive the grievance under which they labour to arise from the . . . importation of foreign corn; and the petitioners humbly conceive it is unfair and impolitic to suffer these foreigners to have the command of the British market. . . .
> Source: *Petition of the Occupiers of Farms in Cleveland* (February 1815).

The majority of MPs were landowners and represented the interests of other landowners, so in 1815 Parliament passed the Corn Law. This said that there

Fig. 7.1 In spite of the hunger of the working class (to the right of the illustration) and the eagerness of the foreigners to sell their corn cheaply (to the left), the landowners in Parliament passed the Corn Law to maintain a high price for corn, and high incomes for farmers and landowners

was to be no importing of cheap foreign corn until the price of corn on the British market had reached 80 shillings (£4) a quarter. This measure was aimed at safeguarding the incomes of farmers and landowners, whose rent income depended on the ability of farmers to sell their corn at a high price.

However, high incomes for farmers and landowners led to high prices for bread, as the merchants and businessmen of Westminster noted in their petition to Parliament after the Corn Law had been introduced:

> That your petitioners have, however, noted with extreme concern and anxiety the introduction into your honourable House of a Bill relative to the importation of corn, which if passed into a law, must necessarily and directly produce, and in the judgement of your petitioners is intended to produce, a great permanent increase in the price of one of the first necessaries of life, for the sake of enabling the proprietors and cultivators of land to maintain undiminished a splendid and luxurious style of living, unknown to their fathers, in which they were tempted to indulge during the late war, so highly profitable to them, and so calamitous to their fellow-subjects.
>
> *Source: The Westminster Petition Against the Corn Law of 1815.*

Wheat prices rarely reached the £4 a quarter at which foreign imports would have been allowed, so many farmers were ruined and some landowners received a falling income from their diminished rent rolls. However, even at £3.50 a quarter, wheat prices were higher than they would have been in a free market so that bread prices remained higher than they ought to have been, especially in view of the low incomes offered to the working class. High prices for bread—a necessity of life—meant that people had less to spend on other less essential goods. This led to a falling demand for goods in shops and from factories, and so to further unemployment, and a fall in the standards of living of the less well-off members of British society.

(h) Government Policies

The social distress of the post-war period was due immediately to the factors we have mentioned above. But the government *added* to the distress by a series of unfortunate decisions made in 1815 and 1816. The Corn Law was one such decision. The abolition of income tax in 1816 was another government decision which was bound to add to the problems facing the country.

We saw in Section 7.1 that there was a huge increase in the National Debt, and therefore a huge increase in the annual interest that the government had to pay to the people who had lent this money. This interest was paid out of revenue which the government collected from taxes on incomes, imports and exports, and on goods sold at home. The abolition of income tax led inevitably to an increase in taxes on a wide range of household articles such as salt, candles, sugar and beer, which affected those less well-off more than the rich.

7.3   Evidence of Discontent

(a) The Luddites

In various parts of the country working men who found their jobs placed in danger by the development of machinery formed themselves into militant and destructive groups. Many of these groups were organized by men who used the fictitious name of Ned Ludd, and the machine-wreckers thus became known as Luddites. Their activities are illustrated by this letter, sent to a Huddersfield manufacturer in 1812:

> Sir, Information has just been given in, that you are a holder of those detestable Shearing Frames, and I was desired by my men to write to you, and to give you fair warning to pull them down. . . . If they are not taken down by the end of next week, I shall send one of my lieutenants with at least 300 men to destroy them, and further-more take notice that if you give us the trouble of coming thus far, we will increase your misfortune by burning your buildings down to ashes, and if you . . . fire at any of my men, they have orders to murder you and burn all your Housing. . . . Signed by the General of the Army of Redressers, NED LUDD, Clerk.
> *Source:* Letter sent to a Huddersfield manufacturer (1812).

The Luddite movement was a blind reaction by working people to what they saw as the cause of their economic and social problems. They wanted to halt industrial progress because they believed it would only bring unemployment in

Fig. 7.2 Henry Hunt, nicknamed 'Orator', addressing a crowd, some of whom carry placards demanding cheaper bread and more liberty. The government believed that Hunt and others might stimulate the mob to behave as the French had done in 1789 (Fig. 5.1)

its wake. They did not appreciate that there were many reasons for the depression, nor could they foresee that industrial progress would, in the long run, lead to more jobs, higher wages and an improvement in living standards for working people.

(b) Public Demonstrations

The years 1816–19 saw a series of public demonstrations arising from the social and economic problems facing the country.

(i) **Spa Fields, 1816.** In 1816 there was a meeting at Spa Fields, Islington, where a leading radical, Henry Hunt, addressed a crowd of workers. Here a resolution was passed which demanded parliamentary reform as a step towards the creation of a more just society. Some of the demonstrators broke into nearby gunsmiths' shops after this and marched on the Royal Exchange, where the riot ended in a confrontation with the Lord Mayor.

(ii) **The 'March of the Blanketeers', 1817.** In 1817 a group of cotton workers set out from Manchester to march to London, where they hoped to present a petition to the Prince Regent.

Fig. 7.3 The artist Cruikshank drew this in 1819 to rouse feelings against the Manchester magistrates and the Liverpool government. In this illustration Hunt (bareheaded on the platform) is shown in an unusually favourable light as compared with Fig. 7.2

(*iii*) **The Derbyshire Insurrection.** This 'March' was followed by the Derbyshire Insurrection of unemployed framework knitters. Three of them were hanged and eleven were transported for life.

(*iv*) **St Peter's Fields, 1819.** This unrest came to a climax in 1819, when Henry Hunt was addressing a meeting of many thousands at St Peter's Fields, Manchester, on the question of parliamentary and other reforms. The local magistrates were alarmed by the size of the crowd and frightened at the possibility of another Spa Fields riot. The Riot Act was read to the crowd, which was ordered to disperse. When it did not do so the magistrates ordered the local yeomanry to charge: eleven people were killed and hundreds injured. In mocking irony this event quickly became known as the Peterloo massacre.

7.4   The Government and the Unrest

The Corn Law typified the legislation of a government which represented, in the main, only the landowners. Another example of their narrow policy was the maintenance of the Game Laws, limiting the right to shoot or take game—pheasants, partridges, rabbits and hares—to the landowners. The enclosure movement had enabled many landowners to extend their parks to include what had once been common land, where labourers had had the right to take game. In the distressed years following 1815 they felt an increased need to catch a rabbit or two as a source of food and of income. But in 1816 the government strengthened the Game Laws: anyone found with a net was liable to seven years' imprisonment, no matter whether he was found poaching or not.

In 1817, following an attack on the Prince Regent's carriage, the government suspended the Habeas Corpus Act so that suspected troublemakers could be imprisoned without a trial.

The government than passed the Six Acts, in 1819, to try to stifle the movement for reform. These (*a*) prohibited the possession of arms; (*b*) forbade military training by private individuals; (*c*) confined attendance at political meetings to members of the parish where the meeting was held; (*d*) gave magistrates the right to search premises for seditious literature; (*e*) allowed magistrates to try cases previously only tried before a judge and a jury (in the hope that radical reformers would be convicted); (*f*) increased the stamp duty on pamphlets and newspapers, so that radical newspapers such as Cobbett's *Weekly Register* would become too expensive for people to buy.

7.5   The Radicals and their Supporters

(*a*) Who Were They?

The word 'radical' comes from the Latin *radex*, which means root. A radical is a person who wants to see very great changes in political, economic or social

Fig. 7.4 The Cato Street conspirators on the night of 23 February 1820, at the moment of arrest when a police officer, Smithers, was stabbed. This view of the interior was sketched on the spot and the scene 'faithfully represented from the description given by Mr Ruthven (another police officer)'

affairs; he wishes to go to the roots of things. There has never been an organized Radical Party in Britain, where there is a Liberal Party, a Labour Party and a Conservative Party. But at different periods we have had individuals who have tried to get others to follow a more radical policy; we will see that Joseph Chamberlain (Unit 24) and Lloyd George (Unit 27) both earned the title of radical.

From about 1780 onwards there was an increased interest in political affairs, following the loss of the American colonies (Unit 3). Wilkes (Section 2.4) was a radical—at least until he had won his place in the Commons. During the first years of the French Revolution there were a number of radical societies, which later governments tried to stamp out (Sections 5.2 and 5.9). After 1815 there were a number of men who deserved the title radical, although since they rarely—if ever—worked together, and generally wanted reforms in different spheres, we ought not to think of them as an organized political movement.

Henry Hunt, who earned the nickname 'Orator', was one of those who believed that parliamentary reform was essential if social, economic and other reforms were to be achieved. Nothing could be expected from a Parliament dominated by the landowning class; everything, on the other hand, was to be hoped for from a reformed, more democratic, parliament. Francis Place, once a breeches-maker, by 1815 the owner of a tailoring shop in Charing Cross, was active in the movement for the repeal of the Combination Acts (Sections 5.9(*d*), 18.2 and 18.3) and was also a leader in the agitation for parliamentary reform. In his shop, it was said, one might have met all the Radicals—Hume and Bentham, Roebuck and Burdett, Hobhouse and Attwood. Burdett and Hume were two of the small band of Radical MPs who raised the question of reform in the unreformed Parliament and campaigned for radical causes outside Parliament. Perhaps the best known of the Radicals was Cobbett, of whom the Chartist leader, William Lovett, wrote:

> How few of the politicians of the present day [1874] are able to estimate how much of their own views and opinions they owe to Mr Cobbett's long teaching of the multitude, and how many of the reforms that have been effected in England since the days of Castlereagh and Sidmouth, are justly to be attributed to the public opinion he helped to create. . . .
> *Source:* William Lovett, *Life and Struggles of William Lovett* (1876).

(*b*) Who Supported Them?

Many middle class industrialists became attracted to the cause of parliamentary reform, particularly after they had seen the bad effects of the Corn Law on people's real wages (which affected their demand for the industrialists' products). Some Humanitarians supported the demand for factory reform led by Radicals such as Robert Owen. But the mass demonstrations at Spa Fields and Peterloo were due to the following which the Radicals had gained among the working classes in the industrial towns. A novelist wrote in 1821:

> The cottonmill was built [in 1788]—nothing like it had been seen before in our generation—and, for the people that were brought to work in it, a new town was built in

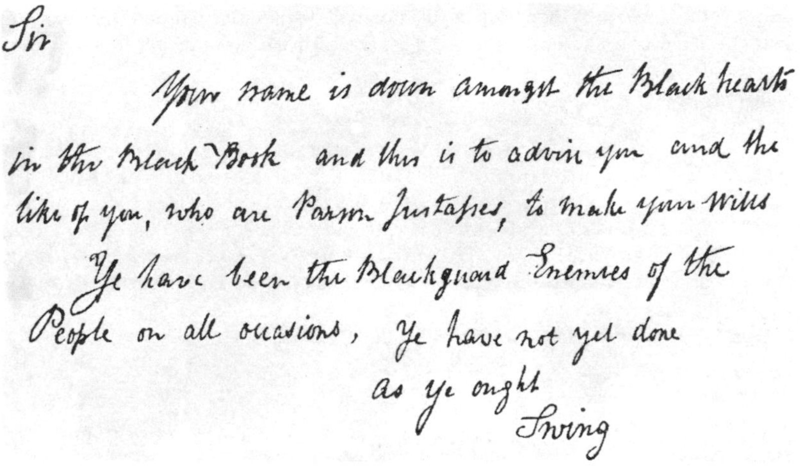

Sir

Your name is down amongst the Black hearts in the Black Book and this is to advise you and the like of you, who are Parson Justasses, to make your wills

Ye have been the Blackguard Enemies of the People on all occasions, Ye have not yet done as ye ought

Swing

Fig. 7.5 There was great distress in the countryside as well as in the industrial towns. In 1830–1 this distress boiled over into the 'Captain Swing' movement. This letter from a member of the movement illustrates its objects and methods

the vicinity. The minds of men were excited to new enterprises and there was an outlooking spirit that was not to be satisfied with the regularity of ancient affairs. . . . I began to discover signs of decay in the simplicity of our country ways. Among the spinners and weavers of Cayenneville were ambitious spirits, who clubbed together and got a London newspaper which, when I heard, I sent for them, to convince them of their error, but they confounded me with their objections. . . . So that I was troubled, fearing that some change would ensue to my people. . . .
Source: Galt, J., Annals of the Parish (1821).

This fictitious vicar understood that changes in the economy lead to changes in social behaviour, even if he regretted it. The development of a working class movement was foreseen by Galt, the perceptive novelist.

Test Yourself on Unit 7

(a) Documents

(i) It is a matter of history, that whilst the laurels were yet cool on the brows of our victorious soldiers on their second occupation of Paris, the elements of convulsion were at work amongst the masses of our labouring population; and that a series of disturbances commenced with the introduction of the Corn Bill in 1815, and continued, with short intervals, until the close of the year 1816. In London and Westminster riots ensued, and were continued for several days, whilst the bill was discussed; at Bridport there were riots on account of the high price of bread; at Bideford, there were similar disturbances to prevent the exportation of grain; at Bury, by the unemployed, to destroy machinery; at Ely, not suppressed without bloodshed; at Newcastle-on-Tyne, by colliers and others; at Glasgow, where blood was shed, on account of the soup kitchens; at Preston, by unemployed weavers; at Nottingham by Luddites, who destroyed 30 frames; at Merthyr Tydfil, on a reduction of wages; at Birmingham by the unemployed; at Walsall, by the distressed; and December 7th, 1816, at Dundee, where owing to the high price of meal, upwards of 100 shops were plundered.
Source: Bamford, S., Life of a Radical (1859).

(ii) March 1, 1820: Thistlewood was taken this morning after the affair. It was the intention of these men to have fired a rocket from Lord Harrowby's house as soon as they had completed their work of destruction; this was to have been the signal for the rising of their friends. An oil shop was to have been set on fire to increase the confusion and collect a mob; then the Bank was to have been attacked and the gates of Newgate thrown open. The heads of the Ministers were to have been cut off and put in a sack which was prepared for that purpose.
Source: Whitwell Wilson, P. (ed.), The Greville Diary (1927), i, p. 307.

(b) Questions

1. Why does Bamford refer to the second occupation of Paris? When had the first occupation taken place? Why did it end? When did the second occupation take place?
2. Who was Prime Minister in 1815? When did his Premiership come to an end?
3. List six reasons for unrest mentioned in item (i). Which of these can you attribute to the Industrial Revolution and which to the effects of the War?

4. Why was there a 'high price of bread' at this time? Why was this distressing for working people? Why were manufacturers anxious to have a lower price for bread?
5. How do you account for the unemployment of weavers in Preston? How different were the causes of unemployment in Birmingham and Preston?
6. What was 'the affair' in item (*ii*)?
7. Why did Thistlewood expect a mob to support him in 1820?
8. Why did this affair fail? What was the fate of its leader?

(c) Further Reading

Briggs, A.: *The Age of Improvement 1783–1867*. Longman (Harlow, 1979).

Cookson, J. E.: *Lord Liverpool's Administration: the Crucial Years*. Scottish Academic Press (Glasgow, 1975).

Evans, E. J.: *The Forging of the Modern State: Early Industrial Britain 1783–1870*. Longman (Harlow, 1983).

Gash, N.: *Aristocracy and People: Britain 1815–1865*. Arnold (London, 1983).

Hilton, B.: *Corn, Cash, Commerce: The Economic Policies of the Tory Government 1815–1830*. Oxford University Press (Oxford, 1980).

Hopkins, E.: *A Social History of the English Working Classes 1815–1945*. Arnold (London, 1979).

Lane, P.: *Radicals and Reformers*. Batsford (London, 1973).

O'Gorman, F.: *The Emergence of the British Two-Party System 1760–1832*. Arnold (London, 1983).

Thomis, M. I. and Holt, P.: *Threats of Revolution in Britain 1789–1848*. Macmillan (Basingstoke, 1977).

Thompson, E. P.: *The Making of the English Working Class*. Penguin (Harmondsworth, 1968).

(d) Exercises

1. Explain the unrest in Britain between 1815 and 1822.
2. How did the government deal with the social unrest after 1815?
3. Write a paragraph on each of the following: (i) the Corn Law, 1815, (ii) Spa Fields, 1816, (iii) the Six Acts, 1819, (iv) Peterloo, 1819, (v) the *Weekly Register*, (vi) income tax.

Unit Eight
Domestic Affairs, 1822–30

8.1 Changes in the Government

Lord Liverpool was Prime Minister from 1812 until his death in 1827. Between 1815 and 1822 he presided over a government whose more important members were Lord Sidmouth (Home Secretary), Lord Eldon (Lord Chancellor and leader of the House of Lords) and Viscount Castlereagh, second Marquis of Londonderry (Foreign Secretary). It was this government which carried out the repressive policies we outlined in Section 7.4.

In 1822 Castlereagh suffered a mental breakdown and on 12 August he committed suicide. Lord Liverpool had to appoint a new Foreign Secretary. A former Foreign Minister, George Canning (Section 6.2) had quarrelled with Castlereagh in 1809 and they had fought a duel on Wimbledon Common. The anger of the more respectable Tories with Canning, the son of an actress, had driven him from office. In 1822 he had just been appointed Governor-General of India when Lord Liverpool invited him to fill the vacancy left by Castlereagh's death. Several members of Liverpool's government, loyal to the memory of Castlereagh, resented this promotion of his former enemy and

Fig. 8.1 The Liverpool election, 1812. George Canning addressing the constituents

resigned, so that Liverpool was forced to reshuffle his Cabinet and bring in some new men, among them Sir Robert Peel, formerly the Chief Secretary of Ireland, and William Huskisson, a Liverpool MP like Canning. Canning, Peel and Huskisson followed policies which were, in many important ways, very different from the policies of the previous government, and they earned for themselves the flattering nickname of 'the Young Tories'.

8.2   A Changed Economic Scene

By 1822 the British economy had recovered from the effects of the Napoleonic Wars. Internal trade was in a healthier state than it had been in the depressed years following 1815, and European countries had recovered from the Wars so their volume of British imports was rising. British traders had extended their markets into South America and the United States. Trade with India had also expanded and, since 1815, British merchants had developed trading links with the new acquisitions of Ceylon, the Cape of Good Hope and Trinidad. Even Australia was becoming more than a penal settlement and while Bradford merchants bought Australian wool there was a growing volume of British exports to 'that land of convicts and kangaroos', as a contemporary writer described it.

With this growth in both exports and internal trade there was a demand for more labour, so unemployment was less of a problem than it had been between 1815 and 1819. Wage rates rose in some industries while prices stabilized or, in some cases, fell so that working people enjoyed a small rise in real wages and thus in their standards of living. In these more prosperous days there was a decline in the activities of the Radicals so that when Canning and his colleagues entered the government there was less fear of revolution than there had been in the dark post-war years.

This improvement in the social and economic situation allowed politicians a breathing space in which to consider the situation of the country. It had been argued that repression was essential in the years following 1815—the memory of the French Revolution was still fresh and British politicians believed that in the mobs at Spa Fields and 'Peterloo' they could see the British versions of the Paris mobs of 1789. But by 1822 the situation was different. The mobs no longer gathered and clamoured, the fears of revolution had diminished and the new breed of politicians had a chance to ask, 'Can repression be considered a suitable, long-term policy?' Fortunately they decided to adopt a set of new policies, more in keeping with the needs of a country which was becoming increasingly industrialized and urbanized.

8.3   Sir Robert Peel as Home Secretary

(a) The Death Penalty

In 1822 there were about 160 crimes which were punishable by death, but a campaign against the death penalty led by Sir Samuel Romilly (Section 2.1(c)) had won widespread support. In 1808 there had been a change in the law: in future pickpockets would not be hanged but would be transported for life instead. In 1810 Romilly proposed the abolition of the death penalty for several trivial crimes—stealing five shillings (25p) from a shop, for example—but his proposals were rejected by the House of Lords. After his suicide in 1818 the campaign was led by Sir James Mackintosh and was supported by lawyers and writers such as Jeremy Bentham. They argued that there was

Fig. 8.2 A public execution on 9 January 1824, a fairly common spectacle at the time

increasing evidence that juries were not prepared to administer the law as it stood: criminals were being found 'not guilty' by a jury which was unwilling to condemn a man to death for a minor offence. The law was thus being brought into disrepute. In 1823 Peel persuaded Parliament to abolish the death penalty for about a hundred crimes, and in the 1830s more crimes ceased to be punishable by death. Since 1838 no one has been executed in Britain except for the crimes of treason or murder.

(b) The Police Force

We saw in Sections 2.4(b) and 7.3(b) that riotous disturbances were a feature of British life in the early nineteenth century. Highwaymen terrorized travellers on the roads, smugglers flourished in coastal areas (Section 4.4(a)), rich men fought duels with swords or pistols, poorer men fought in the streets with clubs or bare fists. Violence was common—against individuals in the streets or shopkeepers suspected of overcharging, against election candidates or

Fig. 8.3 A Peeler, the symbol of a new approach to the problem of law and order

unpopular preachers; noblemen's coaches were attacked by the inhabitants of slums and alleys.

There was a pitiably poor system of watchmen and constables to counteract this violence. In country towns and villages local magistrates had control of constables who were elected but unpaid. Not surprisingly they did their job reluctantly and badly. In towns and cities the local authorities controlled the watchmen. One foreigner who visited London wrote:

> London does not possess any watchmen, either on foot or on horseback as in Paris, to prevent murder and robbery; the only watchman you see is a man in every street, carrying a stick and a lantern, who, every time the clock strikes, calls out the hour and the state of the weather. The first time this man goes on his rounds he pushes the doors of the shops and houses with his stick to ascertain if they are properly fastened. . . .
>
> Source: Saussure, C. de, *A Foreign View of England* (1725–30).

Peel determined to create a new, efficient police force for the metropolis of London for which, as Home Secretary, he was directly responsible. By 1829 he had formed this new force with its headquarters at Scotland Yard. In a letter to an MP he noted:

> Whitehall, October 10th, 1829
>
> My Dear Croker,
> No doubt three shillings a day will not give me all the virtues under heaven, but I do not want them. . . . I have good reasons for thinking that one of my police constables, if a single man, can find out of his pay of a guinea a week: (1) lodgings, (2) medical attendance, (3) very comfortable subsistence at his mess, (4) clothing; and can, after finding these, save out of his pay ten shillings a week . . .
>
> Ever most faithfully yours,
> ROBERT PEEL
>
> Source: Jennings, L. J. (ed.), *The Croker Papers* (1884).

8.4   William Huskisson at the Board of Trade

(a) Freer Trade

In 1822 Britain was well ahead of the rest of the world in industrial development; her manufacturers could produce goods more cheaply than could manufacturers elsewhere. It was in the interests of British manufacturers that restrictions against overseas trade should be abolished, if this were possible, or reduced to a minimum. Huskisson, MP for Liverpool, where trade was the reason for the port's development, appreciated this. He worked closely with the Chancellor of the Exchequer, 'Prosperity' Robinson, to encourage trade and free it from restrictions. Together they lowered customs duties on many raw materials used in the textile and metal industries, so that prices of finished products could be lowered and, hopefully, demand would be increased. They abolished all prohibitions on the import of manufactured goods as Britain had no need to fear that there would be a sudden inflow of foreign goods. (They also hoped to discourage smuggling, by making it less profitable.)

In 1823 Huskisson set up a Committee to look into the question of the emigration of skilled workmen. This was forbidden under a law designed to prevent skilled workers taking the secrets of British inventions in textiles and, particularly, in steam-engines abroad with them. It was to this Committee that the Radical, Francis Place, and his friend Joseph Hume MP, took their case for the Repeal of the Combination Acts (Sections 18.2 and 18.3).

(b) Reciprocity of Trade

In 1823 Huskisson persuaded Parliament to pass a Reciprocity of Duties Act so that ministers could make trade treaties with foreign countries which allowed for a mutual reduction of tariffs. Most European countries signed such treaties, so there was a fairly rapid growth in the volume of British exports to Europe. But Holland refused to sign such a treaty, which caused Canning to write:

> In matters of commerce the fault of the Dutch
> Is giving too little and asking too much.
> The French are with equal advantage content,
> So we clap on Dutch bottoms just twenty per cent.

Huskisson was one of the first politicians to realize that the British Empire was a valuable market for British manufactured goods as well as a rich source of raw materials. To help the colonies to develop he imposed a lower duty on goods coming from colonial territories than those imposed on similar goods from other countries.

(c) The Navigation Acts

During the seventeenth century a number of Navigation Acts had been passed to ensure that goods coming into Britain were carried in British-built and British-manned ships (Section 3.2(a)). The main aim of these Acts had been to exclude Holland from the carrying trade of the world. By 1823 Holland was no longer a serious rival to Britain, but Huskisson did not abolish the Acts altogether. Between 1823 and 1825 he modified them, restricting trade within the Empire to British ships but allowing more freedom for foreign ships to take part in Britain's foreign trade. The Acts were not entirely abolished until 1849.

(d) The Corn Question

Huskisson appreciated that Britain was becoming an industrialized country, depending on increasing its foreign trade if its people were to be employed and enjoy reasonable living standards. But even Huskisson had to take account of the fact that Parliament—both Lords and Commons—was dominated by landowners whose income came from rents, which in turn depended on the price of wheat. So although Huskisson was a believer in free trade, he did not support a free trade in corn; and although he was a friend of Liverpool merchants, he had to bow to the power of the landowners in Parliament. This explains his reluctance to do for the Corn Law (Section 7.2(g)) what he was prepared to do for customs duties on other raw materials.

Fig. 8.4 'Going to Downing Street' drawn in 1828 when the Duke of Wellington was Prime Minister. The Duke lived in Apsley House, with its address of Number 1, London, and each day made his way to Number 10 Downing Street to supervise the work of his government

Huskisson proposed that the Corn Law should be replaced by a sliding scale of duties on corn. If the price of British corn rose then the duty on foreign corn would fall, so encouraging imports and bringing the price of British corn down again. If the price of British corn fell, because of a good harvest, the duty on foreign imports would rise. This would discourage imports and drive up the price of British corn. But the landlords rejected this idea and in 1828 Huskisson resigned from the government.

8.5   Catholic Emancipation

(a) Repeal of the Test Acts

A series of Test Acts had been passed during the seventeenth century to ensure that only loyal Anglicans were appointed to positions of power in the civil service, local government and the legal profession. A campaign to abolish these restrictive Acts was mounted during the early part of the nineteenth century and in 1828 the campaign won a partial victory in the Repeal of the Test and Corporation Acts, part of which reads:

> It is just and fitting to repeal such parts of the said acts as impose the necessity of taking the sacrament of the Lord's Supper according to the rights or usages of the Church of England as a qualification for office.

But while the Anglican Parliament, under the influence of its leaders, Peel and Wellington, was prepared to concede this repeal to the mainly Nonconformist leaders of the campaign, it was unwilling—again because of the influence of Peel and Wellington—to concede legal freedom to Roman Catholics, who were still suspected of being members of a foreign and anti-British church.

(b) Canning

Between 1822 and 1827 Canning had spoken in favour of religious liberty for Nonconformists and Catholics alike. On Liverpool's death in 1827 Canning became Prime Minister, which was an acknowledgement of his power and influence in the Liverpool government. Wellington and Peel refused to serve under him fearing, probably correctly, that he would try to carry a bill giving freedom to Catholics. After Canning's death in August 1827 Robinson (Goderich) took office until January 1828. Wellington then became Prime Minister and Peel accepted office again, as Home Secretary and Leader of the House of Commons, assured that the Catholic question would not now be raised. Huskisson was a 'Canningite', and he resigned from the Wellington government over the Catholic question and, as we have seen, over the question of corn.

(c) O'Connell

In 1823 an Irish Catholic lawyer, Daniel O'Connell, formed the Catholic Association with the aim of persuading the British government to give Catholics equality with their Anglican fellow-citizens (Sections 16.1 and 16.4). In 1828 O'Connell decided to offer himself as a candidate in the by-election being fought in County Clare, Ireland. Not surprisingly, he won the seat: the majority of voters in the constituency were Catholics, and probably members of his Association. Wellington and Peel had come to power determined to resist the demands for Catholic Emancipation, but in so doing they had lost the support of such Canningites as Huskisson, Palmerston and William Lamb (later Lord Melbourne). As Peel recalled:

> The events of the Clare election, with the conviction that the same scenes would be enacted in nearly every county in Ireland if matters were to remain just as they have been for the last five or six years, convinced me that it was not safe for the Protestant interest in Ireland that they should remain so. . . .
> Source: The Speeches of the late Right Hon. Sir Robert Peel (ed. 1853).

At first Wellington and Peel attempted to halt the inevitable: they declared that O'Connell would not be allowed to take his seat in Parliament. This decision led to popular demonstrations in Ireland. But Wellington had seen what civil war meant during his Peninsular Campaign against Napoleon, and Peel was unwilling to turn Ireland into a battlefield for the sake of the principle of resisting Catholic advance. In 1829, therefore, Parliament passed the Roman Catholic Emancipation Act, part of which reads:

> And be it enacted, that it shall be lawful for any of his majesty's subjects professing the Roman Catholic religion to hold, exercise and enjoy, all civil and military offices and places of trust or profit under his majesty, his heirs or successors; and to exercise any other franchise or civil right, except as hereinafter excepted, upon taking and subscribing . . . the oath hereinbefore appointed. . . .

Peel's reluctant acceptance of Catholic Emancipation is one of the proofs of his political greatness, which he was to show again in 1846 over the issue of the Corn Laws (Sections 13.4 and 13.6). This acceptance of reality—of what the situation *is* rather than what one would wish it to be—was one of the legacies which Peel left to the Tory Party. Under his leadership the Tories lost their blind adherence to reaction and became a party of reform.

The wealthier Catholic voters had gained a victory in 1829 and the success of O'Connell's campaign was an encouragement to the leaders of other reform movements. The supporters of parliamentary reform immediately took fresh heart from O'Connell's success and, more significantly perhaps, the methods used by O'Connell were to be the ones which the leaders of the Anti-Corn Law League employed when they campaigned after 1839 (Sections 13.4 and 13.5).

8.6   The Divided Tories

In 1815 the Tory Party seemed 'the party of government'. It had provided the ministers who led the country in the successful war against Napoleon while the Whigs had split over the issue of the War. Some Whigs joined the Tories, a few retired from public life and only a handful remained to represent the party which had once dominated the political scene. After 1815 the Tory Party guided the country through the difficult post-war years and enjoyed the popularity arising from the more prosperous decade of the 1820s. It provided a glittering array of ministers, including Canning, Peel, Huskisson, Wellington, Robinson and many others.

But in 1829 the house came tumbling down, because of the Catholic question. Wellington and Peel, determined at first to oppose Emancipation, lost the support of the Canningites, many of whom joined the Whigs. Then, by giving in to the demands of O'Connell and his Association, Wellington and Peel earned the hatred of the Old Tories led by Lord Eldon and other staunch Anglicans. As Macaulay reported at the time:

> Who can forget in what a roar of obloquy their anger burst forth? All history, all fiction were ransacked by the old friends of the right honourable Baronet, for nicknames and allusions. That Ministry which, when it came into power at the close of 1828, was one of the strongest that the country ever saw, was, at the close of 1829, one of the weakest. It lingered another year, staggering between two parties, leaning now on one, now on the other, reeling sometimes under a blow from the right, sometimes under a blow from the left, and certain to fall as soon as the Tory opposition and the Whig opposition could find a question on which to unite.
>
> *Source:* Lord Macaulay, *Miscellaneous Writings* (1889).

This three-way split among the Tories was the main reason why King William IV had to ask the Whig leader, Earl Grey, to form a government in 1830. It was this government which introduced the Reform Bill in 1831 (Section 10.3). We may say that parliamentary reform owes its origins—in part at least—to divisions in the Tory Party. Once back in office, the Whigs tried to hold on to it, and the Tories, once the party of government, had to spend the 1830s as the party of opposition.

Test Yourself on Unit 8

(a) **Cartoon**

Fig. 8.5

(*b*) **Questions**

1. Who were represented by 'the Cabinet-maker' and 'his man Bob'?
2. When were they driven from office?
3. What attitude had they taken, when in office, towards the distress suffered by agricultural and industrial workers? How does the artist draw attention to this?
4. Which different groups of politicians combined to drive them out of office?
5. How did events of (i) 1829–30, (ii) 1832–4 indicate that leading politicians were prepared to change their attitude towards important issues? Is this a sign of strength or of weakness?
6. When did each of these ex-Ministers hold office in (i) the 1830s, (ii) the 1840s?

(*c*) **Further Reading**

Briggs, A.: *The Age of Improvement 1783–1867*. Longman (Harlow, 1979).
Cookson, J. E.: *Lord Liverpool's Administration: the Crucial Years*. Scottish Academic Press (Glasgow, 1975).
Evans, E. J.: *The Forging of the Modern State: Early Industrial Britain 1783–1870*. Longman (Harlow, 1983).
Gash, N.: *Aristocracy and People: Britain 1815–1865*. Arnold (London, 1983).
Hilton, B.: *Corn, Cash, Commerce: The Economic Policies of the Tory Government 1815–1830*. Oxford University Press (Oxford, 1980).
Hopkins, E.: *A Social History of the English Working Classes 1815–1945*. Arnold (London, 1979).
O'Gorman, F.: *The Emergence of the British Two-Party System 1760–1832*. Arnold (London, 1983).
Thomis, M. I. and Holt, P.: *Threats of Revolution in Britain 1789–1848*. Macmillan (Basingstoke, 1977).
Thompson, E. P.: *The Making of the English Working Class*. Penguin (Harmondsworth, 1968).

(*d*) **Exercises**

1. Give an account of the reforms introduced by the Young Tories between 1822 and 1830.
2. Account for the passage of the Catholic Emancipation Act, 1829. What was the effect of this on the Tory Party?
3. Write briefly on the work of (i) Peel, (ii) Huskisson, (iii) O'Connell between 1822 and 1830.
4. How far did 'Catholics and Corn' dominate the politics of the period 1815–27?
5. Do you think that the Tory reformers of the period 1822–30 deserve that title?
6. Discuss the government's attitude towards the working classes between 1815 and 1830.

Castlereagh and Canning: Foreign Affairs, 1815–30

9.1 Castlereagh—a Good European

Castlereagh was Secretary of State for War in 1805 and again between 1807 and 1809, and he was Foreign Secretary from 1812 until his suicide in 1822. From 1805 until 1815 he was closely involved in the struggle against Napoleon, trying to hold together the rickety Coalitions and being the leading member of the Congresses which met first at Paris (1814) and then at Vienna (1815) to arrange peace treaties with the French. It is not surprising that Castlereagh's experience of European affairs and his close contact with statesmen from other European countries should have given him a wider view than was common among the insular British, to many of whom 'abroad was a bloody place'. This helps to explain why so many of his contemporaries were suspicious of his policies and were ready to attribute to him ideas which, in fact, he did not hold or follow.

9.2 Castlereagh at Vienna, 1815

The treaties with France were arranged during 1814 and 1815. At the Congress of Vienna the arrangements made by previous treaties were amended and the outcome was the *Treaty of Vienna*, which aimed at ensuring that France would not again be the menace to European peace that she had been for almost thirty years. While Russia, Austria and Prussia were laying claim to extra territory for themselves, Castlereagh took a more detached view. He could afford to do so; during the wars Britain had made a number of important acquisitions, including the Cape of Good Hope, Ceylon, Malta, Trinidad, Tobago and St Lucia. These were well scattered over the earth's surface, making convenient ports of call for British merchant ships *en route* around the world. They were also sources of raw materials and might be exploited as markets for British goods. At Vienna Castlereagh followed a policy outlined in a letter written by his Prime Minister, Lord Liverpool, on 15 July 1815:

> We shall never be forgiven if we leave France without securing a sufficient frontier for the protection of the adjoining countries. The prevailing idea in this country is that we are fairly entitled to avail ourselves of the present moment to take back from France the principal conquests of Louis XIV.
>
> The French nation is at the mercy of the Allies, in consequence of a war occasioned by their violation of the most sacred Treaties. The Allies are fully entitled, under these circumstances, to indemnity and security.
>
> *Source: The Correspondence of the Second Marquis of Londonderry* (ed. 1851).

Fig. 9.1 On 24 January 1815 the Duke of Wellington replaced Castlereagh as British representative at the Congress of Vienna. The Duke is shown standing on the far left as he is being introduced to the statesmen by Metternich, who is standing in front of an empty chair

9.3   Castlereagh and the Congress System

Castlereagh was the main architect of the Quadruple Alliance which was signed at Paris on 20 November 1815. It confirmed the territorial arrangements of 1814 and 1815, excluded the Bonaparte family from holding power in France, and was the basis for the subsequent meetings or *congresses*, as Article VI declared:

> To secure the execution of the present Treaty, and to consolidate the connections which at the present so closely unite the Four Sovereigns, the Parties have agreed to renew Meetings at fixed periods, either of the Sovereigns themselves, or by their respective Ministers, for consulting upon their common interests, and for consideration of measures which at each of these periods shall be considered the most salutary for the prosperity of Nations, and for the Peace of Europe.
>
> *Source:* Hertslet, E. (ed.), *The Map of Europe by Treaty* (1875).

You will see from this extract that Castlereagh intended the meetings (or congresses) to have very limited functions. However, even he believed that 'the Sovereigns ... or ... their ... Ministers' had the right to take whatever actions they saw fit for 'the peace of Europe'. Castlereagh had played a major role at the Congress of Vienna where, among other things, it was agreed that Catholic, industrial and French-speaking Belgium was to be handed over to the rule of Protestant, agricultural and German-speaking Holland. The rulers of Russia, Prussia, Austria and Britain had little, if any, regard for the nationalist feelings of the Belgians.

9.4 Castlereagh and the Holy Alliance

While Castlereagh and Metternich of Austria were turning their attention to the practical details of boundaries and armies of occupation, the more flamboyant Czar Alexander I of Russia produced his Treaty of the Holy Alliance. The Treaty, by which the European powers agreed to live together in a spirit of Christian brotherhood, was signed by the Emperors of Russia, Austria and Prussia. Castlereagh sent a copy of it to Lord Liverpool on 28 September 1815; Castlereagh's opinion of the Alliance is evident from the letter which he wrote to his Prime Minister:

> As soon as the instrument was executed between the Sovereigns, the Emperor of Russia brought it to me, developed his whole plan of universal peace, and told me the three Sovereigns had agreed to address a letter to the Prince Regent, to invite him to accede. Foreseeing the awkwardness of this piece of sublime mysticism and nonsense, especially to a British Sovereign, I examined with Prince Metternich every practical expedient to stop it; but when it reached me the deed was done and no other course remained than to do homage to the sentiment upon which it was founded, and to the advantages Europe might hope to derive from three such powerful Sovereigns directing all their influence to the preservation of peace. . . .
>
> Source: Supplementary Despatches of the Duke of Wellington (1861).

However, his critics preferred to believe that Castlereagh was at best a supporter of the Holy Alliance, which was the expression of the anti-nationalist and anti-liberal sentiments of the rulers of Europe.

9.5 Castlereagh and Intervention

Castlereagh's critics were right to assume that he was sympathetic to the problems facing the European sovereigns in the aftermath of the French Revolution and the Napoleonic Wars. He had no sympathy with the revolutionary movements which had erupted in various states in Italy, had support among university staffs and students in Austria and had succeeded in overthrowing Turkish power in Greece (Section 15.2). We have to remember that the French Revolution was still a recent happening for Castlereagh and the rulers of Europe. Memories of the excesses of the Terror and the execution of the French king and his family were still fresh in the minds of the men who controlled the destinies of Europe after 1815. We ought not to be surprised that they adopted policies which were intended to prevent any similar outbreak anywhere in Europe. But Castlereagh's sympathy for the position of rulers in the face of revolutionary activity did not lead him to support the claims of Alexander I, who said that his Holy Alliance gave the rulers the right to interfere in the internal affairs of other countries.

(a) Austrian Intervention in Naples

In 1820 the Kingdom of Naples was the centre of a revolution led by the *Carbonari*, a secret society who hoped to establish a republican government in place of the cruel and oppressive government of the Bourbon kings. Austria had a special interest in Italian affairs: its Empire included most of northern Italy and it had also assumed the role of protector to some other Italian states. Castlereagh's friendship with the Austrian Chancellor, Metternich, his dislike of the revolutionaries and his appreciation of the particular and peculiar position of Austria in Italian affairs caused him to concede that Austria had the right to interfere in Naples. On 16 September 1820 he outlined his position in a letter to Lord Stewart:

> The revolution at Naples does not come within any of the stipulations of the alliance. It is, nevertheless, an event of such importance that it necessarily occupies our most anxious attention. I concur in regarding the change as pregnant with danger ... as having been the work of rebellious troops and of a secret sect whose object is to subvert all existing Governments in Italy. Austria may feel that it cannot hesitate in the adoption of immediate and active measures against this danger. ... The natural result of this seems to be that Austria must make the measure her own ... and ... receiving such acquiescence from the other Powers as they may be prepared to afford to her. You will see that engagements of such a nature, at least on our part, are out of the question. We desire to leave Austria unembarrassed in her course; but we must claim for ourselves the same freedom of action.
> *Source:* Temperley, H. W. and Penson, L. M. (ed.), *Foundations of British Foreign Policy 1792–1902* (1938).

(b) The State Paper, 1820

While conceding some rights to Austria in the affairs of Naples, Castlereagh was adamant that the same right did not apply to all powerful states at all times. Indeed, while he was writing the Stewart letter he was also at work upon a State Paper, part of which reads:

> The principle of one State interfering by force in the internal affairs of another is always a question of the greatest possible moral as well as political delicacy. To generalize such a principle and to think of reducing it to a System, is utterly impracticable and objectionable. We shall be found in our place when actual danger menaces the System of Europe but this Country cannot, and will not, act upon abstract and speculative Principles of Precaution: The Alliance which exists had no such purpose in view in its original formation.
> *Source: Foreign Office Papers, 7/148*, Public Records Office.

(c) The Troppau Protocol

Castlereagh's British critics failed to appreciate the distinction which he was capable of making between the principle of intervention in general and the application of that principle to a particular case, such as that of Austria and

Naples. But it seems that Metternich was equally incapable of appreciating the distinctions made by Castlereagh.

When the powers met at Troppau in 1820 Metternich persuaded the representatives of Russia, Prussia and France to agree to a declaration—the Troppau Protocol—that whenever and wherever a revolution broke out, the powers had the right to send in troops to support the legitimate ruler and to crush the rebellion. The State Paper had explained Castlereagh's opposition to this. He withdrew his delegates from the Troppau Congress to indicate his opposition, and on their return home sent a circular letter to all British Ambassadors so that they would be able to explain Britain's policy to whichever government they were accredited.

> The British Government is prepared to uphold the right of any state to interfere, where their security or essential interests are seriously endangered by the internal transactions of another state. But they cannot admit that this right can receive a general and indiscriminate application to all revolutionary movements. . . .
> Source: Hertslet, E. (ed.), *The Map of Europe by Treaty* (1875).

(d) Intervention in Piedmont

Metternich, however, decided to ignore Castlereagh's point of view and called another meeting of the powers at Laibach in January 1821. Here the other Allies agreed to invade Piedmont to put down a revolt there. As Metternich wrote:

> We shall finish the Piedmontese affair as we did the Neapolitan. Another French Revolution could alone interpose grave—perhaps insurmountable—obstacles to this second enterprise.
> All the venom is at present on the surface. The cure will be so much the more radical and what we began together in July 1819, can be finished with the help of God and for the salvation of the world in 1821.
> Source: Hertslet, E. (ed.), *The Map of Europe by Treaty* (1875).

9.6   Castlereagh's Death

Castlereagh had striven to obtain a wide measure of co-operation among the European powers. This had been the object of his work before Napoleon was defeated and again in the Quadruple Alliance (Section 9.3). He had given way to Metternich's appeal for special consideration in the case of Naples and then had seen his concession rewarded by the application of the principles of the Holy Alliance, which he had always opposed. The disappointment over the failure of his European policy was compounded by the continued attacks on him at home, where he was wrongly blamed for the repressive policy of the government (Section 7.4). The radical poet Shelley wrote a savage attack on him in *The Mask of Anarchy*, as a denunciation of the government after the Peterloo Massacre:

I met murder on the way—
He had a mask like Castlereagh—
Very smooth he looked, and grim;
Seven bloodhounds followed him. . . .

9.7   Canning as Foreign Secretary, 1822–7

Canning had been Foreign Secretary (Section 6.2) while Castlereagh was Secretary of State for War, but Tory anger with the non-aristocratic Canning drove him from office in 1809. In 1822 the East India Company appointed him Governor-General (Section 8.1), and he was on the point of sailing for India when he received Liverpool's summons to succeed Castlereagh as Foreign Secretary. He showed little inclination to follow a different policy from that of his predecessor. Indeed, as late as 1824, he wrote to his cousin, Stratford Canning, who was to become British Ambassador to Turkey:

> To preserve the peace is the leading object of the policy of England. For this purpose it is necessary in the first place to prevent the breaking out of new quarrels; in the second place, to compose existing differences; and thirdly, where that is hopeless, to narrow as much as possible their range; and fourthly to maintain for ourselves an imperturbable neutrality in all cases where nothing occurs to affect injuriously our interests or our honour.
> *Source:* quoted in Petrie, C., *George Canning* (1946), p. 226.

Castlereagh might have written something along the same lines.

(a) Canning—an Englishman first

But there was a major difference between the two men's attitudes towards foreign affairs. Castlereagh had been affected by his wartime experience, his frequent meetings with Metternich and other European leaders, and his concern—and theirs—with the danger of revolution again affecting Europe. Canning was much more directly concerned with the interests of Britain, as can be seen from a note he wrote in 1823:

> In the conduct of foreign affairs, the grand object of my work is the interest of England. Not, gentlemen, that the interest of England is an interest that stands isolated and alone. The situation that she holds forbids an exclusive selfishness; her prosperity must contribute to the prosperity of other nations, and her stability to the safety of the world.
> *Source:* quoted in *Britain in Brief*, Central Office of Information (1958).

Canning here shows an appreciation that Britain was a major industrial and trading power, and that her merchant class—increasingly important as taxpayers and employers—deserved to be the concern of the Foreign Office.

(b) More Forceful than Castlereagh

Canning was more fortunate than his predecessor had been. By 1822 Britain was experiencing a trade boom (Section 8.2). The optimism produced by expansion, rising living standards and a decline in popular discontent had its effects on the Foreign Office, where the Minister could afford to be more expansionist and more forceful in his attitudes.

(*i*) **Verona, 1822.** The Powers agreed that France should invade Spain to put down a liberal uprising, Canning wrote to Wellington, who was representing Britain at the Congress of Verona:

> If there be a project to interfere by force in the present struggle in Spain, so convinced are His Majesty's Government of the danger of any such interference, as well as utterly impracticable in execution, that when the opportunity offers I am to declare that to any such interference, His Majesty will not be a party.
>
> *Source:* Therrge, R., *Speeches of Rt. Honourable George Canning* (1828).

(*ii*) **Spanish colonies in South America.** In 1823 the French and the Holy Alliance Powers indicated that they intended to carry their attacks a little further by mounting invasions of the former Spanish colonies in South America. Here, since 1812, Bolivia and other countries had declared themselves independent. President Monroe of the USA announced that his government would resist any attempt by European powers to restore the old regime in South America. (This *Monroe Doctrine* was a sign of the emergence of the USA on to the world scene as a major power.)

Canning, who had felt unable to commit a British army to the defence of Spanish liberals, had no hesitation in threatening to use British naval power should the European Powers try to carry out their proposed attack on South America. In a speech to the House of Commons he said:

> If France occupied Spain, was it necessary, in order to avoid the consequences of that occupation, that we should blockade Cadiz? No, I looked another way: I sought materials for compensation in another hemisphere. Contemplating Spain, such as our ancestors had known her, I resolved that if France had Spain, it should not be Spain with the Indies. I called the New World into existence to redress the balance of the Old.
>
> *Source:* Therrge, R., *Speeches of Rt. Honourable George Canning* (1828).

Here we have the British Foreign Office flexing its muscles for a possible war with France and, maybe, Austria. These latter Powers decided to abandon whatever project they may have had in mind and the former Spanish colonies retained their independence—and acquired a real gratitude to Britain. British merchants and financiers found in these newly independent countries a fruitful area for investment. Later in the nineteenth century Britain acquired a stranglehold on South American trade, largely because of Canning's support for their newly-won independence.

9.8   The Eastern Question

(a) Russian Expansion

The Turkish Empire had extended into south-eastern Europe since the fifteenth century. From the beginning of the seventeenth century Russia had been trying to obtain a foothold in that area, hoping to gain access to the Mediterranean and an all the year round, warm water outlet for her exports. Britain had watched Russia's encroachment with some fear that this might be a danger to British trade in the eastern Mediterranean, which was the terminal of the important overland trade routes from Asia, and also a possible threat to British India. This fear grew steadily during the eighteenth century as Turkey became gradually too weak to control her widespread European possessions. Britain feared that Russia would take advantage of this weakness to extend her own influence. This apprehension had been increased by the Treaty of Kutchuk Kainardji (1774), when Russia, having defeated Turkey in war, obtained important territorial concessions.

(b) Greek Independence

By 1820 Turkey's ability to control the outposts of her Empire was increasingly weakening, and revolts against Turkey were frequent. These revolts were partly of Christians against their Turkish Moslem overlords, but they were also similar in nature to those in Naples and Piedmont (Section 9.5(a)). Czar Alexander I, a Christian monarch, felt some inclination to side with the Greek Christians—and so to further Russian long-term ambitions by acquiring a sphere of influence in the Balkans. But Czar Alexander, the author of the Holy Alliance, was persuaded by Metternich that to aid Greek rebels—even Christian ones—would be to further the cause of liberal revolutionaries elsewhere. So, under Alexander I, Russia remained neutral while the Greeks fought their Turkish masters.

Alexander was succeeded by Czar Nicholas I in 1825 and his government decided to play a more active role in aiding the Greeks. Canning did not want to see Russia gaining this influence in the Balkans and he persuaded the Czar to sign a Protocol:

> Greece should be a dependency of that Empire [Turkey] and the Greeks should pay to the Porte an annual tribute, the amount of which should be permanently fixed by common consent. . . . In this state the Greeks should enjoy a complete liberty of conscience, entire freedom of commerce, and should, exclusively, conduct their own internal government. . . . That His Britannic Majesty and His Imperial Majesty should reserve to themselves to adopt, hereafter, the measures necessary for the settlement of the details of the arrangements in question, as well as the limits of the territory. . . . That, moreover, His Britannic Majesty and His Imperial Majesty will not seek, in this arrangement, any increase in territory, nor any exclusive influence, nor advantage in commerce for their subjects. . . .
> Source: Hertslet, E. (ed.), The Map of Europe by Treaty (1875).

On 6 July 1827 England, France and Russia signed a treaty pledging themselves to carry out this Protocol, which would have given Greece virtual
independence while ensuring that no one power gained for itself a predominant position *vis-à-vis* Greece.

(c) **Mehemet Ali**

The Sultan of Turkey had called on his vassal, Mehemet Ali, Viceroy of
Egypt, to help him crush the rebellious Greeks. In return for this aid Mehemet

Fig. 9.2 The romantic poet Lord Byron, a lover of Greece and an enemy of
Castlereagh

Ali had been promised greater independence for his rule in Egypt and an extension of his territory to include Syria. Part of his assistance consisted of a naval force, which was at Navarino when the Note from the Three Powers was sent to the government of Turkey and the leaders of the Greek rebellion, asking them to cease fighting and agree to the decisions of the major Powers. Canning had sent a British naval squadron commanded by Admiral Codrington to ensure that these peace terms were obeyed.

Mehemet Ali's son, Ibrahim Pasha, commander of his father's forces in Greece, refused to accept the terms laid down by the outside powers and on 20 October 1827 Codrington led the navy into the harbour at Navarino, where they sank the Egyptian and Turkish fleets, and so ensured that Greece would become independent.

By this date Canning had died and it was left to Wellington, as Prime Minister, to apologize to the Turks for this action and so allow Russia to remain as guardian of Christian Greece in the final negotiations leading to Greek independence.

Test Yourself on Unit 9

(a) Document: Foreign Policy—Castlereagh and the Congresses

In short, the Grand Assembly of Crowned Heads and Ministers at the ill-starred Congress of Vienna, almost wholly occupied, as they were, in promoting their own aggrandizement, either entirely neglected to take measures for preserving the future tranquillity, or they betrayed the most lamentable ignorance of the public feeling. But civilized nations are not now in a humour to be transferred from sovereign to sovereign like the slaves of Africa. . . . Who is there that thinks the Poles can be satisfied with their country having been rendered a province of Russia? Have they derived any advantage from the downfall of Napoleon?

It was unfortunate for this country that our late Minister for Foreign Affairs had not a sufficient knowledge of the character of the Statesmen of modern Europe. Isolated as the British Cabinet was during so long a period of the war, it was not possible that the English Ministers should have an accurate knowledge of the principles and conduct of the Continental Statesmen.

The honourable character of Lord Londonderry [Castlereagh] himself tended still further to prevent him from even suspecting that his new friends could act in the manner which he afterwards witnessed with astonishment. And when in addition to these reasons, it is recollected that he suddenly entered into terms of personal intimacy and friendship with these men . . . no one can wonder that he should have been in some respects dazzled and deceived. . . .

I have already observed that the Allies had publicly proclaimed the restoration of the status quo in Europe, if its different nations assisted them in overthrowing Buonaparte. On the fulfilment of this pledge, the Marquis of Londonderry should have insisted. . . . We formerly traded with the States which were parcelled out at the Congress of Vienna; and if they had been placed on their ancient and independent footing, Great Britain would have immediately resumed her commercial relations with them. But, instead of this . . . the partitioned States are incorporated with Governments who have prohibited or restricted our commerce! . . .

The discerning mind of Mr Canning will, doubtless, draw the true and most useful conclusions from the scene which has passed before him. He is not personally connected with any of the Foreign Courts, nor personally pledged to their measures. The adoption of a new line of policy by him does not carry with it the painful acknowledgment that his former system had been wrong. . . .

Source: Goldsmith, Lewis, Observations on the Appointment of the Rt. Hon. Geo. Canning (1822).

(b) Questions

1. Which four powers dominated affairs at Vienna? Who were their representatives? Who represented France?
2. What criticism is levelled at the Treaty of Vienna in the first paragraph of this extract?
3. Do you think that the criticism of Castlereagh in paragraph 2 is justified?
4. How far does Castlereagh's policy after 1815 indicate that he had been 'dazzled and deceived'?
5. Did Canning carry out 'a new line of policy' with respect to (i) intervention by powers in other countries' affairs; (ii) the Holy Alliance as a principle?
6. What evidence is there in the extract that European powers extended their boundaries as a result of the Congress of Vienna? Which countries did so? Where? Can you suggest why Castlereagh agreed to this?

(c) Further Reading

Joll, J. (ed.): Britain and Europe: Pitt to Churchill 1789–1940. Oxford University Press (Oxford, 1967).
McManners, J.: Lectures on European History 1789–1914. Blackwell (Oxford, 1974).
Seaman, L. C. B.: From Vienna to Versailles. Methuen (London, 1972).
Watson, R. W. Seton: Britain in Europe 1789–1914. Cambridge University Press (Cambridge, 1937).

(d) Exercises

1. What were the aims of Castlereagh's policies (i) at Vienna, (ii) between 1815 and 1822?
2. Give an account of Canning's foreign policy.
3. Compare and contrast the foreign policies of Castlereagh and Canning between 1815 and 1827.
4. Explain British interests in Spanish America and Greece in the period 1815–27.
5. What problems confronted British Foreign secretaries between 1816 and 1827. How did they meet them?
6. Describe the part played by Britain in (i) the Congress System, (ii) the Greek War of Independence, (iii) the establishment of Belgian independence (Section 14.2).

Parliamentary Reform, 1830–2

10.1 The Old System

Corn (Section 8.4(*d*)) and Catholics (Section 8.5) may have dominated political life in the late 1820s, but increasing attention was being paid to the growing demand for a reform of Parliament. Hunt, Place, Cobbett and other Radicals led the demand, and they were supported by mass meetings such as that which took place at Peterloo (Section 7.3). They demanded a reform in each of three parts of the old system.

(a) The Constituencies

As Fig. 10.1 shows, the majority of MPs were elected for constituencies in the southern part of Britain, one-quarter of them for the four south-western counties. This arrangement had been suitable for Britain in the seventeenth century, when agriculture was the country's main industry and the majority of people lived in the more fertile south. But by 1830 an increasing number of people were living in industrial towns in the Midlands, South Wales, the north west and the north east. Towns such as Manchester, Leeds, Sheffield and Stoke were largely unrepresented in a Parliament which, nonetheless, passed laws, imposed taxes and otherwise governed them.

(b) The Voters (the Franchise)

Today we are accustomed to a uniform qualification for the franchise: every-one over the age of eighteen is entitled to vote in elections. In 1830 there was a uniform qualification for voters in county constituencies but, as a Report published in 1793 had indicated, there was a bewildering variety of qualifica-tions for voting in different boroughs:

> The members for the 52 counties are all elected by one uniform right. Every man throughout England, possessed of 40 shillings per annum freehold [land] is entitled to a vote for the County in which such freehold is situated. With respect to the different cities, towns, and boroughs, the right of voting shows an infinite diversity of peculiar customs. ... In some places the number of voters is limited to a select body not exceeding 30 or 40; in others it is extended to 8 or 10 000. In some places the freeman must be a resident inhabitant to entitle him to vote; in others his presence is only required at an election. ... Burgageholds, Leaseholds, and freeholds,—scot and lot inhabitants, householders, inhabitants at large, potwallopers, and commonalty, each in different boroughs prevail. In some the choice of two members lies with as many inhabitants as every house can contain; in others, to the possessor of a spot of ground where neither houses nor inhabitants have been seen for years. ...
> Source: *Report of the Society of the Friends of the People* (9 February 1793).

x Notorious boroughs

o Some of the large towns
unrepresented before 1832.

45 members
(Act of Union 1707)
4 000 electors in the
whole country

All English and Irish
counties 2 members each

All Welsh and most
Scottish counties
1 each

8 counties had
fewer than 30
electors each.

Sunderland

Yorkshire

100 members
(Act of Union 1800)

Equal
representation

Leeds

Bradford

Bolton o

Sheffield

Catholics could
not vote till 1793
and could not be
M.P.s till 1829.

Manchester

Co.
Clare

Stoke

Rutland

More than half of the 203 boroughs, which
were in the southern counties, elected 50% of the House of Commons.

24 members

Dunwich

These six counties elected
one quarter of the members
—more than Scotland and
Ireland combined.

Gatton

Old Sarum

London was
greatly
under-represented

Grampound
(disfranchised 1821)

Kilometres   100   200

Fig. 10.1 Parliamentary representation before 1832

The reformers hoped to persuade Parliament that a uniform voting qualification was desirable for boroughs as well as for counties.

(c) Corruption

(*i*) **Rotten boroughs.** Some boroughs were 'rotten' in that the owner of the
local estate, who was often a member of the House of Lords already, con-

trolled the election. Two MPs were returned to Parliament for a borough where few—sometimes no—voters lived (Section 2.1(c)). Some people believed that the dominant position of the landowners was desirable. In 1793 R. B. Jenkinson (later Lord Liverpool) had declared:

> [I] suppose every person would agree that the Landed interest ought to have the preponderant weight. The Landed interest [is], in fact, the stamina of the country.
> *Source:* R. B. Jenkinson in the House of Commons (6 May 1793).

(*ii*) **Bribery.** Although there were laws against bribery, few if any elections went by without open and ample evidence that men preferred 'sovereigns to principles' (Section 2.1(c)). As *The Extraordinary Black Book* noted in 1831:

> At Nottingham, one gentleman confessed to having paid away in the election of 1826, above £3000 in bribery in a single day. At Leicester, the voters, in anticipation of a contest, expressed their hope that [the] price of votes might rise to £10, as they said it commonly did, if the struggle was severe. At Hull, one of the sitting members dared not appear before his constituents—not for any defalcation of duty in Parliament, but because he had not paid 'the polling money' for the last election.
> *Source: The Extraordinary Black Book* (1831).

10.2   The Argument

(*a*) For Reform

(*i*) **The new middle class.** By 1830 a new middle class of industrialists, financiers, canal-owners, merchants and professional men had grown sufficiently large and sufficiently confident to want to challenge the political power of the landowners (Section 1.5). Some of these men formed political unions in various parts of the country, one of the most important of these being in Birmingham. In 1830 the Birmingham Political Union declared:

> The great aristocratical interests of all kinds are well represented in Parliament. But the interests of Industry and of Trade have scarcely any representatives at all! These, the most vital interests of the nation, the source of all its wealth and of all its strength, are comparatively unrepresented.

(*ii*) **The Whigs.** In the past some historians have made the mistake of assuming that the Whigs were eager for parliamentary reform. The evidence is that Grey and his colleagues were only slightly more willing to consider reform than the Tories, but the Whigs did resent their long exclusion from a share in the political spoils. Some of them believed that in parliamentary reform they had a catchword which might sweep them into power. Brougham, a leading Whig, said:

> We don't live in the days of Barons—we live in the days of Leeds, of Bradford, of Halifax and Huddersfield. We live in the days when men are industrious and desire to be free.

Fig. 10.2 *Scenes from an election with its open system of voting, bands supporting the candidates, the participation of the mob—none of whom had a vote—and
an air of excitement missing from modern elections*

But Grey was Prime Minister of the Whig government which came to power in 1830 (Section 8.6). Princess Lieven was a confidante of Grey and other ministers, and she wrote:

> London: 10/22 November 1830
> Yesterday Lord Grey told me—'In the composition of my Ministry I have had two essential objects in view: the first, to show that in these times of democracy it is possible to find real capacity in the aristocracy—not that I wish to exclude merit if I should meet with it in the commonalty; but, given an equal merit, I admit that I should select the aristocrat, for that class is a guarantee for the surety of the State and of the throne. . . .
> Source: Robinson, L. G. (ed.), *Letters of Princess Lieven, 1812–34* (1902).

This tepid attitude towards democracy augured badly for the cause of reform. Indeed there were many leading Whigs who took up the cause of parliamentary reform in the hope that a minor reform of the parliamentary system might be enough to win the support of the middle class radicals who were leading the working class in demanding sweeping reform. Lord Macaulay spoke for many Whigs when he argued that if only the middle class could be satisfied then the danger of a French-type revolution could be averted (Test Yourself on Unit 10(*c*)(i)).

(*iii*) **The working classes** supported the activities of radicals like Hunt and of the various political unions. They formed the masses at meetings called by the various reform associations. They hoped that a reformed, democratically elected Parliament would pass laws to improve the conditions in which they worked and lived. As we shall see, they were to be very disappointed.

(*b*) **Against Reform**

(*i*) **Wellington and the Tories.** Lord Liverpool had consistently opposed demands for reform, not surprisingly in view of his beliefs in the good influence of the landowner (Section 10.1(*c*)(i)). In 1830 Wellington was Prime Minister and in answer to a motion calling for reform, he was reported as having said:

> He had never heard of any measure up to the present moment which could in any degree satisfy his mind that the state of representation could be improved . . . the legislature and the system of representation possessed the full and entire confidence of the country.
> Source: Wellington in the House of Lords (15 November 1830).

Wellington had learned little, if anything, from the demands of the political unions, reform associations and popular demonstrations.

(*ii*) **Other supporters of the old system.** There were also those who argued that the old system worked well. It had produced politicians of genius, such as Pitt (Section 4.9), Burke (Section 5.2(*c*)), Fox (Section 4.1) and Huskisson

(Section 8.4), who had led the country through the dangerous period of the French Wars to a period of industrial and commercial greatness. Many of these leaders had entered Parliament as MPs for rotten, corrupt boroughs. Was there any guarantee that a more democratic system would allow the emergence of similarly gifted politicians? Or was it more likely that the mass voters of a democratic system would prefer the less intelligent but more promisingly wordy demagogue? No one could know the answers to these questions, and the more cautious wondered whether it was safe to change a well-tried system for a less assured one.

(*iii*) **King William IV** had come to the throne in 1830. In that year he had seen King Charles X of France overthrown by a Parisian rising led by the industrial middle class who wanted a share in political power (Section 14.2), and he was afraid that the British middle class might sweep him from power in a similar rising. He expressed his fear in a letter which he wrote to Prime Minister Grey:

> The King had felt willing to admit the necessity of engaging in this question [of reform]; His Majesty would deceive Earl Grey if he were to disguise that his anxiety was not free from uneasiness, that the innovations proposed at a period which other circumstances rendered so critical, did not greatly outweigh his expectations of advantage to the state and the country.
> *Source:* Earl Grey (ed.), *Correspondence of Earl Grey with William IV* (1867).

10.3   The Course of Events, 1831–2

(*a*) The First Bill

On 15 November 1830 Wellington's government was defeated over a proposal to appoint a Select Committee to investigate the Civil List accounts. The issue was unimportant—it merely served as an excuse for embittered Tories to unite with Whigs and force Wellington from office (Sections 8.5 and 8.6). Grey became Prime Minister and asked Lord John Russell to prepare a Reform Bill. On 1 March 1831 Russell's Bill was presented to the House of Commons, passing its second reading by only one vote (302–301) at the end of March.

(*b*) The Second Bill

The first bill had not passed through all the required stages of debate and vote, committee and discussion by the time the parliamentary session had reached its end in the summer of 1831. So when a new session opened in the autumn, Russell introduced a second bill. This passed the Commons but was defeated in the Lords on 8 October 1831. It is hardly surprising that the Lords should reject a bill whose intention was to curtail the power that they had previously exercised over the election of members of the lower House.

Fig. 10.3 The carrying of the second reading of the first Reform Bill in the House of Commons, 21 March 1831

(c) Whig Uncertainty and Popular Unrest

Grey was unwilling to ask Parliament to discuss the issue of reform yet again. Thomas Attwood and other leaders of local political unions now organized a National Political Union and on 8 October 1831 it issued a Charter demanding that the nation should unite to defeat this aristocratic attempt to deny reform in the face of popular demand. There were outbreaks of violence in Derby, Nottingham, London and Bristol.

Fig. 10.4 Bristol reform riots, 30 October 1831. The scene in Queen's Square

(*d*) **The Third Bill**

Grey tried to defuse the situation by finally agreeing to the introduction of a third bill, which was sent to the House of Lords on 26 March 1832. The Lords threatened to reject this as they had rejected the previous bill, so Grey resigned. Wellington tried to form a government but had to tell the King that he could not get enough support. A reluctant King then sent for Grey who agreed to become Prime Minister again, but only on condition that William IV would agree to create, if necessary, over one hundred new peers to ensure the passage of the bill through the Lords.

While the politicians in London parleyed and bargained, people in the country resorted, once again, to violence. The army was ordered to prepare to act against popular demonstrations. As one soldier wrote in his autobiography:

> It was rumoured that the Birmingham Political Union was to march for London that night (Sunday 13 May 1832); and that we were there to stop it on the road. . . . We had been daily booted and saddled, with ball cartridge in each man's possession for three days. . . . But until this day we had rough-sharpened no swords. The purpose of so roughening their edges was to make them inflict a ragged wound. Not since the Battle of Waterloo had the swords of the Greys undergone the same process. Old soldiers spoke of it and told the young ones. . . .
> Source: *The Autobiography of a Working Man* (1848).

The Lords gave way in the face of Grey's threat to enlarge the noble House with a lot of 'Johnny-come-lately' peers. On 7 June 1832 the bill became law and Parliament was reformed.

10.4   The Terms of the 1832 Reform Act

(a) The Constituencies

The Reform Act took away 143 seats from the south and distributed most of them among the towns where population was growing rapidly. As *The Times* dated 2 March 1831 reported:

> The boroughs to be totally disfranchised amount to 60 . . . all those which, by the census of 1821, had not a population of 2000 inhabitants, were not entitled to return members. The disfranchisement, however, did not stop there. It was thought that one member was sufficient to represent a borough which, by the same census, contained less than 4000 inhabitants. . . .

Sixty-five of the 143 seats were distributed among the larger counties, while 8 more were given to Scotland and 5 more to Ireland.

(b) The Franchise

The Act imposed a uniform qualification for the borough constituencies and extended the franchise for county constituencies. *The Times* dated 2 March 1831 reported:

> With regard to the qualification, [the government] thought that the possession of a house of the value of £10 a year, either as a renter or proprietor, was high enough. All the inhabitants of boroughs or towns with this qualification are therefore entitled to vote in towns. . . . No change is made with respect to the 40s freeholders; but new classes of electors are introduced into the constituencies of counties—copyholders having property of the value of £10 a year and leaseholders paying a rent of £50 a year.

10.5   Second Thoughts

(a) The Electorate

The Act whose passage had roused such controversy and passion was soon revealed to be the small thing that it was. Whereas before 1832 about 440 000 people were entitled to vote, after the great crusade only another 217 000 were added to the electoral roll. The total population of the United Kingdom and Ireland was 25 million. The Act thus gave electoral recognition to the new class of rich industrialists, who were now on more or less equal terms with the old aristocracy, but landed aristocrats still sat in the Lords and could set at naught the will of the Commons, and landowners still controlled many constituencies, for not all rotten boroughs had been swept away (Sections 19.1

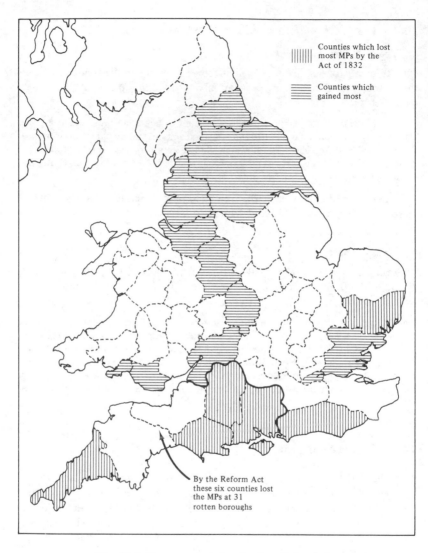

Counties which lost
most MPs by the
Act of 1832

Counties which
gained most

By the Reform Act
these six counties lost
the MPs at 31
rotten boroughs

Fig. 10.5 Changes made by the first Reform Act

and 20.1). The Act gave nothing to the working class, as the *Poor Man's Guardian* reported on 15 December 1832: 'We have often told you the Reform Bill would do you no good. The great majority of the new electors are middlemen who thrive by your degradation.' But the 1832 Act did make a hole in the dam which had held back the movement for parliamentary reform. In doing this it released forces which were eventually to lead to the democratic system under which we live now (Sections 28.1(*c*), (*d*) and 28.4).

(*b*) The Middle Class

The rich middle class now had the opportunity to use their new political power for their own ends. The aristocracy had always used power for their own ends—the Game Laws (Section 7.4) and the Corn Law (Section 7.2(*g*)), for example—so it is not surprising that the middle class did the same. The Act which repealed the Corn Laws in 1846 was the economic consequence of the political Reform Act in 1832 (Section 13.6).

This clash between the interests of the aristocracy and the middle class was to lead to a clash between the House of Lords (where the aristocracy sat) and the House of Commons (which increasingly became dominated by the middle class). This hostility between the two Houses of Parliament reached a climax in 1909 when the Lords tried to assert their authority over the Commons. The passing of the Parliament Act in 1911 was the sign that the Commons had won that struggle (Section 28.5).

(*c*) The Working Class

As we have seen, the working class gained nothing from the 1832 Act, and the new Parliament proved to be as unwilling to try to improve their working and living conditions as had the unreformed Commons. The Act can, therefore, be said to have been responsible for the emergence of the Chartist movement (Section 13.1).

(*d*) The Whigs

The Whigs had never intended to offer anything to the working class. Their hope was that the newly enfranchised middle class urban voters would vote solidly for them as the party of reform, so that there would always be a large number of Whig MPs being returned from the urban constituencies.

Test Yourself on Unit 10

(a) **Cartoon**

Fig. 10.6 King and Whigs drive Tories from office

(b) **Questions**

1. Who was the King represented in the cartoon? How did he help to get the Reform Bill through the Lords?

2. Who was the Prime Minister at this time? Do you think he deserved the title of 'Radical'?
3. Who introduced the Reform Bills? What office did he hold when the Chartists presented their petition in 1848? Do you think he deserved the title of 'democrat'? Why?
4. Which one of the following would have approved of this artist's representation of events—Wellington, Brougham, Huskisson, Thomas Attwood? Give reasons for your answer.
5. Which of the following would have condemned this artist's version of events— Cobbett, Grey, Durham, O'Connell? Give reasons for your answer.
6. How far did events in France at this time affect the fate of the Reform Bills?
7. Who or what, do you think, was represented by the serpent?
8. People can be seen rejoicing. Can you suggest which groups might have been rejoicing (i) at the fall of the Tories, (ii) at the passage of the Reform Act? Which groups might have been disappointed at the terms of the Reform Act?

(c) Documents

(i) Macaulay supports Reform, 1831

But, Sir, every argument which would induce me to oppose universal suffrage induces me to support the plan which is now before us. I am opposed to universal suffrage, because . . . it would produce a destructive revolution. I support this plan; I am sure it is our best security against a revolution.

That we may exclude those whom it is necessary to exclude, we must admit those whom it may be safe to admit. At present we oppose the schemes of revolutionaries . . . with only one quarter of our proper force. We say that it is not by mere numbers, but by property and intelligence, that the nation ought to be governed. Yet, saying this, we exclude great masses of property and intelligence. . . . We do more. We drive over to the side of revolution those whom we shut out from power.

History is full of revolutions, produced by causes similar to those which are now operating in England. A portion of the community which had been of no account expands, and becomes strong. It demands a place in the system, suited to its present power. If this is granted, all is well. If this is refused, then comes the struggle between the young energy of one class and the ancient privileges of another. Such is the struggle which the middle classes in England are maintaining against an aristocracy, or the owner of a ruined hovel, who have powers which are withheld from cities renowned for the marvels of their wealth and of their industry.

Source: Macaulay, Speech in the House of Commons (2 March 1831).

(ii)
                                                    Strathfieldsaye, March 6th, 1833

My dear Croker

I will endeavour to obtain for you the details which you require regarding the state of the representation in the House of Commons. I know none, excepting regarding this county. I have compared notes with others, and I think that all agree in the same story. The revolution is made, power is transferred from one class of society, the gentlemen of England, to another class of society, the shopkeepers.

I don't think that the influence of property in this country is diminished. That is to say that the gentry have as many followers and influence as many voters at elections as ever they did.

Wellington

Source: Jennings, L. J. (ed.), *The Croker Papers* (1884).

(d) Questions

1. What is the meaning of universal suffrage? How far, do you think, were Wellington and Macaulay united in their opposition to this?
2. Why was Macaulay against universal suffrage? How far was he influenced by events which had recently taken place in France?
3. Who, according to Macaulay, should be admitted to a share in the system? How far were these people revolutionaries—as Wellington describes them?
4. Why, do you think, would 'another class of society, the shopkeepers' be opposed to increased taxes or an extension of the franchise?
5. Give examples of cities 'renowned for their wealth and industry'. Why were many of them unrepresented in the 1831 Parliament? What was Wellington's opinion of this situation?
6. How and why did the aristocracy try to prevent the passage of the Reform Bills in (i) 1831, (ii) 1832?
7. What is the significance of 'the owner of a ruined hovel . . .'?

(e) Further Reading

Briggs, A.: *The Age of Improvement 1783–1867*. Longman (Harlow, 1979).
Brock, M.: *The Great Reform Act*. Hutchinson (London, 1973).
Evans, E. J.: *The Great Reform Act of 1832*. Methuen (London, 1983).
Gash, N.: *Aristocracy and People, Britain 1815–1865*. Arnold (London, 1983).
Hopkins, E.: *A Social History of the English Working Classes 1815–1945*. Arnold (Longman, 1979).
O'Gorman, F.: *The Emergence of the British Two-Party System 1760–1832*. Arnold (London, 1983).
Smiles, S.: *Self-Help*. John Murray (London, 1958). Centenary edition with Introduction by Professor Asa Briggs.
Thompson, E.P.: *The Making of the English Working Class*. Penguin (Harmondsworth, 1968).

(f) Exercises

1. Why was there a demand for parliamentary reform between 1815 and 1832?
2. Explain the point of view of those, such as Wellington, who defended the unreformed system.
3. Explain the defects of the unreformed parliamentary system. How far were these remedied by the 1832 Act?
4. Give an account of the passage of the Reform Bill. What were its main terms?
5. Describe how and explain why the House of Lords opposed the passage of the Reform Bill (1831–2) so strongly. Why was the Act a disappointment to the working classes?

Unit Eleven
The Whigs, 1833–41

11.1 The Politicians

Earl Grey retired in July 1834, and Melbourne became Prime Minister. The King dismissed the Whig government in November 1834, and asked Peel to form a Conservative government. Peel called an election, during which he issued his Tamworth Manifesto (Section 12.2). He failed to win a majority, which meant that his government suffered a series of defeats in the Commons. In April 1835 he resigned, and Melbourne became Prime Minister at the head of a Whig government. In some books this period has been called 'the era of great reforms', but we should note that the reforming zeal of the Whigs really ran out with the end of the Grey government.

By passing the Reform Act in 1832, the Whigs had won the support of the new middle class, whose wealth depended on industrial development and the expansion of British markets overseas. It is strange, therefore, that during this period the government did nothing to further middle-class interests. Huskisson had done so between 1822 and 1827, as we saw in Section 8.4 and Peel and Gladstone were to do so between 1841 and 1846 (Sections 12.3, 12.6 and 12.7); but the Whigs did nothing about tariffs or trade.

11.2 The Abolition of Slavery

(a) The Campaign Against Slavery

In 1807 the British government had made the slave *trade* illegal in the British Empire, and in 1815 the delegates at Vienna, under Castlereagh's influence, also passed a resolution condemning this horrible trade. But nothing had yet been done to change the lot of the millions of slaves throughout the world.

The campaign for the abolition of the slave trade had been led by Clarkson, who interviewed sailors to get the information he needed, and by the Quakers. Quakers could not sit in Parliament, however, so they invited William Wilberforce to speak on their behalf. Wilberforce and others held meetings all over the country to try to persuade people that the abolition of slavery should be supported. They discovered that many people were unaware of the horrors of slavery, and that others were uninterested in something which affected unknown people in faraway countries. They also met opposition from people representing the interests of slave-owners.

(b) Abolition of Slavery Act, 1834

In 1833 a dying Wilberforce heard that Parliament had finally agreed to pass

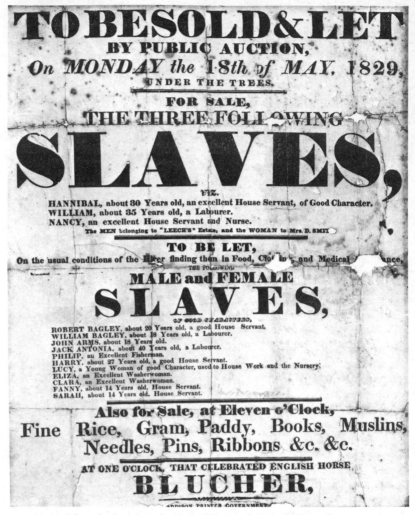

TO BE SOLD & LET

BY PUBLIC AUCTION,

On MONDAY the 18th of MAY, 1829,

UNDER THE TREES.

FOR SALE,

THE THREE FOLLOWING

SLAVES,

VIZ.

HANNIBAL, about 30 Years old, an excellent House Servant, of Good Character.
WILLIAM, about 35 Years old, a Labourer.
NANCY, an excellent House Servant and Nurse.

The MEN belonging to "LEECH'S" Estate, and the WOMAN to Mrs. D. SMIT

TO BE LET,

On the usual conditions of the Hirer finding them in Food, Clothing, and Medical   nce,

THE FOLLOWING

MALE and FEMALE

SLAVES,

OF GOOD CHARACTERS,

ROBERT BAGLEY, about 20 Years old, a good House Servant.
WILLIAM BAGLEY, about 18 Years old, a Labourer.
JOHN ARMS, about 18 Years old.
JACK ANTONIA, about 40 Years old, a Labourer.
PHILIP, an Excellent Fisherman.
HARRY, about 27 Years old, a good House Servant.
LUCY, a Young Woman of good Character, used to House Work and the Nursery;
ELIZA, an Excellent Washerwoman.
CLARA, an Excellent Washerwoman.
FANNY, about 14 Years old, House Servant.
SARAH, about 14 Years old, House Servant.

Also for Sale, at Eleven o'Clock,

Fine Rice, Gram, Paddy, Books, Muslins, Needles, Pins, Ribbons &c. &c.

AT ONE O'CLOCK, THAT CELEBRATED ENGLISH HORSE

BLUCHER,

ADDISON PRINTER GOVERNMENT

Fig. 11.1 Although the slave trade had been abolished throughout the British Empire in 1807 and had been made illegal by the Congress of Vienna, posters such as this still appeared in the West Indies and other parts of the Empire since slavery itself was not abolished until 1833

the bill outlawing slavery in the British Empire. The main terms of the Act, which became law on 1 August 1834, were:

(i) All slaves under the age of six years were to be freed immediately.

(ii) Other slaves, over the age of six, were to remain as part slave and part free for a further four years. In that time they would have to be paid a wage for the work they did in the one-quarter of the week when they were 'free'.

(iii) Since the slave-owners were to lose 'property' which they had bought, Parliament provided £20 million as compensation. This worked out at about £37.50 per slave.

(c) Effects

(*i*) **In the West Indies** the results of this Act were disastrous. The economy of the islands depended on the sugar trade, and the sugar trade had depended on slave labour. The freed slaves were unwilling to work for the wages offered by their former owners. The sugar-growing industry had already been damaged by a negro uprising during the French Wars and by the abolition of the slave trade (1807), which had cut off the supply of slave labour. Although the planters received £15 million of the £20 million paid in compensation by the British government, they were unable to make the islands of the West Indies the thriving centres of trade which they had been in the eighteenth century.

(*ii*) **South Africa.** Britain had acquired the Cape of Good Hope from the Dutch during the Napoleonic Wars (Section 9.2). The original Boer settlers resented the influx of British settlers after 1815, partly because of the imposition of British rule but largely because of the British treatment of the Africans. British missionaries tended to sympathize with the negro and, influenced by missionary opinion, the British government tended to favour the negro. In a court of law, for example, the word of an African had the same standing as that of a white man. The Dutch Boers had always treated the Africans as their inferiors, and they resented this 'new deal' bitterly. Emancipation was merely the straw that broke the camel's back. In 1836 the Boers undertook the Great Trek, leaving the Cape Colony for the less-populated lands of the north where they set up two states—the Orange Free State and the Transvaal. The anti-British feeling which they took with them was nurtured by their descendants and was to lead to the Boer War at the end of the century (Sections 24.2(*b*) and 25.7).

11.3   Factory Reform

(a) Children at Work

In the days before the Industrial Revolution children had always worked—on the farm, in the cottage or wherever there was work to be done. When the factory system was introduced it seemed natural that they should be employed, because the machinery could be worked by quite young children (Section 7.2(*c*)). As the poet Southey was told by one factory owner whose premises he visited:

> Mr — remarked that nothing could be so beneficial to a country as manufactures. 'You see these children, Sir,' said he. 'In most parts of England poor children are a burden to the parish; here the parish is rid of all expense; they get their bread almost as soon as they can run about, and by the time they are seven or eight years old bring in money. There is no

idleness among us: they come at five in the morning; they leave work at six, and another set relieves them for the night; the wheels never stand still.' I was looking, while he spoke, at the dexterity with which the fingers of these little creatures were playing with the machinery. . . .

Source: Southey, Robert, *Espriella's Letters from England* (1809).

(*b*) Humanitarian Campaign

It was the plight of pauper children which first roused the interest of factory-owners such as Peel's father in factory reform. In 1802, Robert Owen, factory-owner as well as radical reformer, supported the campaign launched by Sir Robert Peel who persuaded Parliament to pass a Factory Act which limited the working hours of pauper apprentices to twelve per day. In 1819 Sir Robert Peel, Sr., promoted an Act which extended the 1802 Factory Act to *all* children working in cotton mills: it stipulated that no child under the age of nine was to be employed.

These Acts were largely inoperative because the government did not appoint independent inspectors to see that they were obeyed. The government

Fig. 11.2 The hiring fair at Spitalfields, London, when parents handed over their children to employers for an agreed term of months or years in exchange for a few shillings, which many of them spent in the nearest ale house

relied on local magistrates—often themselves factory-owners or friends of factory-owners—to inspect factories and to summons anyone guilty of breaking the law.

(c) The Commission, 1830–2

In the late 1820s Michael Sadler MP took up the cause of factory reform. He persuaded Parliament to appoint a Commission to investigate conditions. This Commission heard from one child:

Q. At what time in the morning, in the busy time, did these girls go to the mills?
A. In the busy time, for about six weeks, they have gone at 3 o'clock in the morning, and ended at 10, or nearly half past, at night.
Q. What was the wage in the short hours?
A. Three shillings a week each.
Q. When they wrought those very long hours what did they get?
A. Three shillings and sevenpence halfpenny.
Source: Report of Committee on Factory Children's Labour (1831–2).

Michael Sadler lost his seat as a result of the Reform Act, but the cause of factory reform was taken up by Ashley Cooper, later Lord Shaftesbury. It is with his name that we associate the first effective Factory Act, which Parliament passed in August 1833.

(d) The Factory Act, 1833

We may not think that the Factory Act was a radical measure when we look at its terms, but it did lay down the principle that Parliament had the right to interfere with the way in which industry was run. This was a major blow to the believers in outright freedom for a man to do as he wanted with his own, whether it was machinery or workpeople. The Act was also important in that it appointed four inspectors who, as civil servants, would not be susceptible to local influences in their judgments of whether or not an owner should be prosecuted.

No person under eighteen years of age shall be allowed to work in the night between the hours of half past eight o'clock in the evening and half past five o'clock in the morning in any cotton, woollen, worsted, hemp, flax, tow, linen or silk mill or factory . . .
    No person under the age of eighteen years shall be employed more than twelve hours in any one day, nor more than sixty-nine hours in any one week . . .
    It shall not be lawful to employ any child who shall not have completed his ninth year . . .
    It shall not be lawful to employ for longer than forty-eight hours in any one week, nor for a longer time than nine hours in any one day any child who shall not have completed his eleventh year . . .
    That it shall be lawful for His Majesty to appoint four persons to be inspectors. . . .
Source: Factory Act (1833).

11.4   Poor Law Reform

(a)   The Poor Old Law

The Poor Law system operating in Britain until 1834 was based on a series of
Acts passed during the Elizabethan period (1558–1603) and slightly amended
in the succeeding centuries. Basically, each parish was responsible for its own
poor, and had to provide out of local rates for the unemployed, the sick, the
old, orphans, widows and other people unable to make a living. In 1795 the
magistrates at Speenhamland in Berkshire had added a new thread to the

*Fig. 11.3 A workman's home in Bethnal Green. The Whigs ignored the social
problems of the hardworking labouring classes*

tangled skein. They decided that many hardworking but low-paid workers
were suffering too many hardships, so they began to supplement wages out of
the poor rates with a cost-of-living bonus which would vary with the price of
bread. This drove up the level of the poor rate, first in the parish of
Speenhamland and then in most parishes in the agricultural south where the
system was copied. As the system spread farmers realized that they did not
need to increase wage rates to keep in step with rising prices of food and other
necessities because their workpeople were able to go along to the local magistrates and obtain the cost-of-living supplement from the Poor Rates.

(b)   The Poor Law Commission

This system alarmed the property-owning classes who paid the bulk of the
poor rate. The Whig government set up a Commission to investigate the

Fig. 11.4 Frustrated, unemployed and downtrodden workpeople sometimes resorted to violence, as the agricultural workers did in 1830–1 when machines were wrecked and ricks burned. One response to such activity was to send for the army (speaker standing on platform) while another was to call for more reform (speaker standing below platform). The Whigs favoured the former method

existing Poor Law system and, not surprisingly, it found that there was a wide variety of abuses:

> The most pressing of the evils are those connected with the relief of the able-bodied. Sometimes an individual will be exposed to the danger of perishing. The occurrence of extreme necessity is prevented by almsgiving; but the public is warranted in imposing conditions on the individual relieved.
>
> *Source: Report of the Commission for inquiring into the Administration of the Poor Laws (1834).*

The Commissioners were anxious to make conditions as harsh as possible for anyone who received aid from the Poor Rates. In particular they wanted to abolish the system of *outdoor relief* whereby a family received money from magistrates or other authorities and took the money away from the workhouse to spend as they saw fit. Outdoor relief was to be abolished for most applicants. In future people would have to undergo the *workhouse test*: the Poor Law authorities would only give aid to able-bodied people if they agreed to become inmates of the workhouse. And, as a final disincentive, the Commissioners proposed the principle of *less eligibility*:

> The first of all conditions is that his situation shall not be made as eligible as the situation of the independent labourer of the lowest class. ... We recommend that except as to medical attendance all relief to able-bodied persons or families, otherwise than in well-regulated workhouses, shall be declared unlawful, and shall cease.
>
> *Source: Report of the Commission for inquiring into the Administration of the Poor Laws (1834).*

The Commissioners also indicated the need for a new system of administration:

> We recommend the appointment of a Central Board to control the administration of the Poor Laws, with such Assistant Commissioners as may be found requisite; and that the Commissioners be empowered to enforce regulations for the government of workhouses, and the nature and amount of the relief to be given, and the labour to be exacted in them, and that such regulation shall be uniform throughout the country.
>
> *Source: Report of the Commission for inquiring into the Administration of the Poor Laws* (1834).

(c) The Poor Law Amendment Act, 1834

In 1834 the Whig government passed the Poor Law Amendment Act. Edwin Chadwick became Secretary to the three-man Poor Law Commission in London, which began to issue a series of directives to ensure uniformity. In 1836, for example, a diet sheet was drawn up:

> Breakfasts—6 oz. bread and $1\frac{1}{2}$ oz. cheese.
> Dinners—Sundays, 5 oz. meat and $\frac{1}{2}$ lb. potatoes.
> Tuesdays and Thursdays, ditto.
> Other days $1\frac{1}{2}$ pints soup.
> Supper—days on which there was meat for dinner, 6 oz. bread and $1\frac{1}{2}$ pints broth;
> Other days, 6 oz. bread and 2 oz. cheese.
>
> *Source:* Second Annual Report of the Poor Law Commission (1836).

The working classes, disappointed by the terms of the 1832 Reform Act (Sections 10.4 and 10.5) were outraged at the workings of the Poor Law Amendment Act. They were particularly angry at the sudden transition from the old system of outdoor relief to the new system with its workhouse test and the application of the principle of less eligibility. Many turned to Chartism in the hope that they might obtain social redress through political action (Sections 13.1 and 13.2).

11.5   Municipal Corporations Act, 1835

(a) The Local Government Commission

In 1835 a Commission was set up to investigate the working of local government in the 170 or so towns which had, at one time or another, received a Charter, allowing the townspeople to have their own council (or corporation). They found that power rested in the hands of a small number of people. The Mayor of Bath was questioned by the Commission:

> Q. Have the goodness to describe how that corporation is composed.
> A. It is composed of 10 aldermen and 20 common-councilmen.
> Q. How are they chosen?

A. The members of the corporation, that is, common-council, are elected out of the free citizens of the city, and the aldermen are elected out of the common council.

Q. Are the free citizens a numerous body?

A. Altogether about 110 (out of a population of 38 000). . . .

Source: *Minutes of the Select Committee on Municipal Corporations* (1833).

In many boroughs the Commission found evidence of corruption, with the council members enriching themselves at public expense:

Corporate funds are frequently expended in feasting and in paying the salaries of unimportant officers. In some cases, in which the funds are expended on public works, an expense has been incurred beyond what would be necessary if due care had been taken. These abuses often originate in negligence . . . in the opportunity afforded of obliging members of their own body, or the friends and relations of such members.

Source: Royal Commission on Municipal Corporations (1835), *Parliamentary Papers* (1835), xxiii.

(b) Reform, 1835

The Whigs had passed the 1832 Reform Act with its provision of a uniform system of qualification applying throughout every borough (Section 10.4). It was logical, therefore, that they should try to make the corporations of the old towns more democratic, with a uniform pattern of electoral qualifications and systems. The Municipal Corporations Act, 1835, said:

Every male person of full age who shall have occupied any house or shop within any Borough during that year shall be a burgess of such Borough: [if] he shall have been rated in respect of such premises so occupied by him.

In every Borough shall be elected one person, called 'The Mayor', a certain number of persons called 'Aldermen', a certain number of other persons called 'The Councillors'. The number to be elected Aldermen shall be one third of the number to be elected Councillors; the Council shall elect from the Councillors, or from the persons qualified to be Councillors, the Aldermen of such Borough.

Source: *Statutes of the Realm, 5 and 6 William IV, c. 76.*

But the Whigs were not great social reformers and the 'shopocracy' which they represented was not anxious to spend money on necessary social reforms. They were property owners, anxious that the riotous behaviour associated with the parliamentary reform movement should not break out again. This may help to explain their reluctance to compel the reformed Councils to concern themselves with such matters as the water supply, while they did compel the councils to organize police forces which would guard the properties of the wealthier ratepayers. These issues are reflected in the following extract from the Act:

It may be expedient that the powers now vested in the watching, regulating, supplying with water, and improving certain Boroughs, should be transferred to the Councils of such Boroughs respectively. . . . The Council shall immediately after their first election, appoint a sufficient number of their own Body, called the Watch Committee to appoint a sufficient number of men to act as Constables for preserving the peace by day and night.

The Whigs hoped that this Act would give them and their supporters control of local government, just as they hoped their 1832 Reform Act would give them control over the central government.

11.6   The Government and Popular Education, 1833 and 1839

Until 1833 the government made no contribution towards the provision of schools for working-class children. They had left this task to the Churches and to the supporters of Dr Bell, an Anglican vicar, and Joseph Lancaster, a Quaker (Section 31.2). Bell's monitorial schools replaced the former Charity Schools; they were Anglican institutions, supported by the National Society which insisted that the Anglican catechism should be taught in their schools. The British and Foreign Bible Society had taken over the work of providing funds and supervising Lancaster's schools, where children of all religious beliefs could be taught because there was no religious catechism. There was great rivalry between the two societies, one accusing the other of intolerance and the National Society accusing the Lancastrians of irreligious free-thinking.

By 1833 the government had become persuaded that the two Societies were doing a good job but that they did not have enough money to build as many schools as were needed. The government therefore allocated £20 000 to be divided between the Societies for the provision of new schools. Each Society would still have to collect subscriptions from well-wishers but in future they could approach the government and ask for a grant to supplement the fund established by their rich patrons.

In 1839 the government increased the grant to £30 000 and set up a Committee of the Privy Council to supervise the spending of this money. This was the first hesitant step along the road to the establishment of the Department of Education and Science and the provision of compulsory, full-time education for the nation's children.

11.7   Minor Reforms

After 1835 the Whigs seemed to run out of steam. There was an Act for the registration of Births, Marriages and Deaths (1836) and, under the influence of Rowland Hill, the establishment of a uniform rate of postage. Hill published his ideas in a pamphlet called *Post Office Reform* in 1837, and in 1839 he was attached to the Treasury. In 1840 his system was put into practice and the Anti-Corn Law League (Section 13.5) was one of the first to take advantage of this cheap, national and efficient system, which owed much to the development of a network of railways throughout the country. There were also measures affecting Ireland (Section 16.5) and Canada (Section 17.4).

11.8   The New Queen

King William IV (Sections 8.6 and 10.2(*b*) (*iii*)) died in 1837, and his eighteen-year-old niece, Victoria, came to the throne. During the early years of her reign the young Queen was very grateful for the devotion of her experienced Prime Minister, Lord Melbourne. In 1840 Queen Victoria married Prince Albert of Saxe-Coburg-Gotha, whom she treated as her 'permanent Minister' after Melbourne's defeat in the General Election of 1841, when Peel's Conservative–Tory Party gained a majority of 90. The Queen did not learn fully to trust a Prime Minister again until after Albert's death, when the ageing Disraeli became her new favourite (Sections 20.5(*c*) and 20.5(*e*)).

Test Yourself on Unit 11

(*a*) Document: The New Poor Law

In 1833, when the bourgeoisie had just come into power through the Reform Bill . . . the bourgeoisie began the reform of the Poor Law according to its own point of view. A commission was appointed, which investigated the administration of the Poor Laws and revealed a multitude of abuses. It was discovered that the whole working-class in the country was pauperized and more or less dependent upon the rates, from which they received relief when wages were low. . . . They accordingly brought in the New Poor Law, which was passed by Parliament in 1834, and continues in force down to the present day. All relief in money and provisions was abolished; the only relief allowed was admission to the workhouses immediately built. The regulations for these work-houses or as the people call them, Poor Law Bastilles, is such as to frighten away every one who has the slightest prospect of life without this form of public charity. To make sure that relief be applied for only in the most extreme cases and after every other effort had failed, the workhouse has been made the most repulsive residence which the refined ingenuity of [man] can invent. The food is worse than that of the most ill-paid working man while employed and the work harder, or they might prefer the workhouse to their wretched existence outside . . . the workhouse is a jail, too; he who does not finish his task gets nothing to eat; he who wishes to go out must ask permission. To prevent their labour from competing with that of outside concerns, they are set to rather useless tasks. To prevent the 'superfluous' from multiplying, and 'demoralized' parents from influencing their children, families are broken up. . . .

Source: Engels, F., *The Conditions of the Working Class in England in 1844.*

(*b*) Questions

1. What is meant by 'the bourgeoisie'? Which social class, according to the author, 'had just come to power'? Do you agree with this verdict?
2. How were 'the working class . . . pauperized'? Do you agree that this was true for 'the whole working class in the country'?
3. Why should students be suspicious of this document as a piece of historical evidence?
4. Why did the Whigs appoint a commission?
5. List the ways in which, according to Engels, the 1834 Act affected the operation of the Poor Law.

6. Why did people call the workhouses 'Poor Law Bastilles'? Why were these places so unpopular?
7. Why did Chadwick and his fellow-commissioners insist that conditions in workhouses should be worse than those enjoyed by 'the most ill-paid workers when employed'?
8. Why were families separated in the workhouses?
9. Engels saw the 1834 Act as a direct result of the 1832 Reform Act. In what ways did the Chartist campaign (Unit 13) indicate that the Chartists saw a link between political power and social reform?

(c) Further Reading

Adelman, P.: *The Middle-Class Experience 1830–1914*. Longman (Harlow, 1984).
Briggs, A.: *The Age of Improvement 1783–1867*. Longman (Harlow, 1979).
Finlayson, G. B. A. M.: *England in the Eighteen Thirties: Decade of Reform*. Arnold (London, 1969).
Gash, N.: *Aristocracy and People, Britain 1815–1865*. Arnold (London, 1893).
Marshall, J. D.: *The Old Poor Law 1795–1834*. Macmillan (Basingstoke, 1974).
Rose, M. E.: *The Relief of Poverty 1834–1914*. Macmillan (Basingstoke, 1972).

(d) Exercises

1. What were the main achievements of the Whig governments between 1833 and 1841?
2. Describe three of the major reforms passed by the Whigs after 1832.
3. How did the Whig reforms affect (i) factories, (ii) the Poor Law, (iii) Municipal Government?
4. Write briefly on (i) the Penny Post, 1840, (ii) Edwin Chadwick, (iii) Lord Melbourne.

Peel's Ministry, 1841–6

12.1 Sir Robert Peel

Sir Robert Peel differed from the majority of the leading members of the Tory Party in that his father was a prosperous cotton industrialist whereas they came from the traditionally landowning class. Peel was one of the few Tories who was familiar with life in an industrial town and so he appreciated the problems and outlook of the new class of industrialists. Like many other newly rich people, both then and now, Peel senior spent some of his money on providing for his son the sort of education which had previously always been the right of the sons of the aristocracy. He sent him to school at Harrow and to the University of Oxford. Young Robert Peel received a training which fitted him for the political life he hoped to follow.

Lord Liverpool recognized Peel's talents, appointing him Secretary for Ireland (1812–18) and then giving him the post of Home Secretary in 1822. He proved to be an able administrator with a willingness to press for the legal and penal reforms demanded by Romilly and others (Section 8.3). However, he had opposed Canning's plan for Catholic Emancipation in 1827, had served with Wellington and played a part in the disagreements in the Tory Party in 1829–30 (Sections 8.5 and 8.6). As leader of the Tory MPs in the Commons he had led the fight against Russell's Reform Bill (Sections 10.1, 10.2, 10.3) so winning back some of the support among the Tories which had been lost by his 'betrayal' over Emancipation.

12.2 A New Conservative Party

In November 1834 Melbourne was dismissed and the King asked Peel to form a government—just two years after the passage of the Reform Act which he had so vigorously opposed. This gave Peel a chance to make public his attitude towards that Act and towards the new political situation which it had created. He wrote to his constituents at Tamworth:

> The Reform Bill constitutes a new era, and it is the duty of a Minister to declare explicitly—first, whether he will maintain the bill itself,—and secondly, whether he will act upon the spirit in which it was conceived.
>
> I will repeat now the declaration which I made when I entered the House of Commons as a Member of the Reformed Parliament, that I consider the Reform Bill a final and irrevocable settlement of a great constitutional question which no friend to the peace of this country would attempt to disturb.
>
> Then, as to the spirit of the Reform Bill. If, by adopting the spirit of the Reform Bill, it be meant that we are to live in a perpetual vortex of agitation; that public men

can only support themselves in public estimation by promising the instant redress of any thing which any body may call an abuse—if this be the spirit of the Reform Bill, I will not undertake to adopt it. But if the spirit of the Reform Bill implies merely a careful review of institutions, civil and ecclesiastical, undertaken in a friendly temper, combining, with the firm maintenance of established rights, the correction of proved

Fig. 12.1 A Victorian middle-class family waiting in their suburban home for father to return from work in the city via the railway at which the mother is looking. Thousands of well-off middle-class families lived in this way—and Peel wanted to win their support for his Conservative Party

abuses, and the redress of real grievances,—in that case, I can for myself and colleagues undertake to act in such a spirit and with such intentions.
Source: The address of Peel to the Electors of Tamworth (London, 1835).

Here we have the foundations of a new philosophy for the Tory Party which had veered from repression (1815–22) to liberal reform (1822–7) and back again to opposition to much-needed change (1828–32). Here we have the charter for the new party which was prepared to reform—as Peel was to do in the fields of health, factories and mines—but was also anxious to conserve what was best in the existing system. Here, in fact, we can see the origins of the Conservative, as distinct from the Tory Party.

In putting forward such a policy Peel hoped to appeal to the traditional supporters of his party but he also hoped to attract the support of the moderates who had been given the vote in the 1832 Act. These new middle classes had grown in number and, as a result, in political importance; the probability was that this growth would continue. This class was also growing in economic importance, employing an increasing number of workpeople, contributing a great deal to the nation's Exchequer and being largely responsible for the steady growth of the nation's wealth. Peel realized that this class wanted the government to provide a political, economic and social framework in which they could best pursue their natural inclination of enriching themselves and, in so doing, enriching their workpeople and the nation as a whole.

12.3   The Economic Scene

By 1841 Britain had had almost three-quarters of a century of industrialization. One effect of this was that the country was becoming increasingly urbanized. A new society was being created, of people living in large numbers and in close proximity to each other. But the birth pangs of this new society were accompanied by a series of problems which compelled governments to try to provide some answers. What, for example, was to be done about the appalling social conditions in which so many people lived, and because of which so many died at an early age? What was to be done about the freedom of factory-owners and mine-owners in the matter of child-labour?

The Whigs, under Melbourne—who was Prime Minister from 1835 to 1841—had failed to consider these problems and the problem of the trade depression. They had failed to manage the nation's finances, collecting insufficient tax to meet the needs of the spending ministries, so that the country found itself in 1839 and 1840 with an inflationary budget, while trade was depressed. *The Sunday Times* noted:

The iron trade of South Staffordshire is depressed. Out of 111 blast furnaces fifty-three are blown out and are wholly unproductive, and as they would each produce full eighty tons of iron per week, the quantity withdrawn from the market is 220 480 tons, and yet the market is still overstocked, prices are receding, wages are being still

further reduced, while the sufferings of those usually employed at the iron works are, from want of employ, on the increase.
Source: The Sunday Times (30 April 1843).

Violence resulting from popular discontent was more likely during periods of economic depression (Section 7.3), so it is not surprising that the depression of the late 1830s led to an upsurge in the activities of the Chartists (Section 13.3). But, more immediately, the depression caused the downfall of the ineffective Melbourne government and the advent of power of the Conservatives led by Peel in 1841.

12.4   Peel and Social Reform

(a) The Mines

In 1842 the Report of the Commission which had examined the Employment of Children in Mines appeared. It presented a horrifying picture:

> The practice of employing children only six or seven years of age is all but universal. The children go down into the pit with the men usually at four o'clock in the morning, and remain in the pit between eleven and twelve hours each day. The use of a child up to six years of age is to open and shut the doors of the galleries when the coal trucks pass and re-pass. For this object a child is trained to sit by itself in a dark gallery for the number of hours described. . . .
> *Source:* Children's Employment Commission, *Report on Mines* (1842).

Peel, with Shaftesbury urging him on, passed the Coal Mines Regulation Act, 1842, part of which reads:

Fig. 12.2 Thousands of small boys were employed as trapper boys in Britain's expanding coal industry. They sat in the dark and dirt guarding the draught door which provided ventilation

I. From and after Three Calendar Months from the passing of this Act it shall not be lawful for any Owner of any Mine or Colliery to employ any Female Person who at the passing of this Act shall be under the Age of Eighteen Years within any Mine or Colliery.

II. It shall not be lawful for any Owner of any Mine or Colliery to employ any Male Person under the Age of Ten Years. . . .

Source: Coal Mines Regulating Act, 1842.

(b) Factories

In 1844 Parliament passed a Factory Act which compelled factory-owners to fence in dangerous machinery under the threat of a fine or imprisonment. The Act reduced the age at which children could be employed from nine to eight years, a compensation to manufacturers since the Act reduced the hours of work for children aged from eight to twelve years to $6\frac{1}{2}$ hours a day.

(c) Public Health

Peel appointed several Commissions to investigate the conditions in Britain's industrial towns. The picture they presented was appalling. This account of life in Merthyr was typical of conditions in all towns:

> This town is in a sad state of neglect. From the poorer inhabitants, who constitute the mass of the population, throwing all slops and refuse into the nearest open gutter before their houses . . . some parts of the town are complete networks of filth, emitting noxious exhalations. There is no local Act for drainage and cleansing. In some localities, a privy was found common to 40 or 50 persons, and even up to 100 persons and more.

Source: Health of Towns, Commission Report (1845).

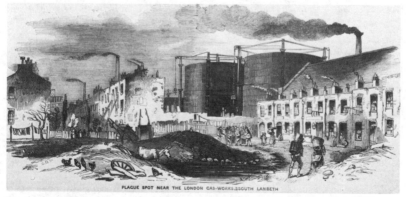

PLAGUE SPOT NEAR THE LONDON GAS-WORKS, SOUTH LAMBETH

Fig. 12.3 A plague spot near the London Gas-Works, South Lambeth. This was typical of the conditions found in working-class districts before the advent of systematic methods of refuse collection, street-cleansing, mains drainage and street-paving

Chadwick of the Poor Law Commission (Section 11.4) headed one Commission which reported in 1842. He showed that the death rate was much higher in industrial towns than in country districts, not because of accidents at work but because of the spread of disease in the unhealthy towns. Chadwick argued that these deaths were preventable. Decent water supplies, proper sanitary systems, and frequent, efficient street-cleansing and refuse-collection

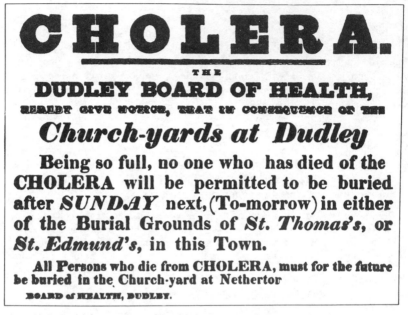

CHOLERA.

THE
DUDLEY BOARD OF HEALTH,

HEREBY GIVE NOTICE, THAT IN CONSEQUENCE OF THE

Church-yards at Dudley

Being so full, no one who has died of the CHOLERA will be permitted to be buried after *SUNDAY* next, (To-morrow) in either of the Burial Grounds of *St. Thomas's,* or *St. Edmund's,* in this Town.

All Persons who die from CHOLERA, must for the future be buried in the Church-yard at Nethertor

BOARD of HEALTH, DUDLEY.

Fig. 12.4 One of many notices published in the 1830s and 1840s when cholera and other diseases swept the country

would create healthier towns, lead to a decrease in the rate of sickness and death—and so lead to a fall in applications by the sick, orphaned and widowed to the Poor Law Guardians.

Peel was forced out of office in 1846 (Section 13.6), so he can claim only indirect responsibility for the passage of the first Public Health Act in 1848, part of which reads:

Whereas further and more effectual provision ought to be made for improving the sanitary conditions of towns and the populous places in England and Wales . . . be it therefore enacted . . .
IV. That 'The General Board of Health' . . . shall have and execute all the powers and duties vested in or imposed on each board by this act . . .
VIII. Upon the petition of not less than one-tenth of the inhabitants rated to the relief of the poor in any city, parish . . . or where it shall appear . . . that the number of deaths annually . . . have on an average (of seven years) exceeded the proportion of

twenty-three to a thousand of the population . . . the General Board of Health may . . . direct a Superintending Inspector to visit such city . . . and examine witnesses as to the sewerage, drainage, and supply of water, the state of the burial grounds, the number and sanitary condition of the inhabitants, and as to any local acts of Parliament in force . . . for paving, lighting, cleansing, watching, regulating, supplying with water or improving the same. . . .

Here we have further evidence of government attempts to come to grips with the problems created by the development of a new society. Local councils had been made more efficient (Section 11.5), the government was beginning to play a part in popular education (Sections 11.6 and 31.2), and an increasing number of civil servants were administering laws about factories, mines and the Poor Law. And now, in 1848, the first steps were taken along the road which would lead to the passing of a series of Acts dealing with the environment in which people lived and worked.

12.5   The Railway Act, 1844

The development of a railway network was one cause of the creation of the new society; without the railways there would have been no national markets for manufacturers, no national newspapers, chain stores or mass advertising; nor would there have been so many children travelling to boarding schools or families going away for a day's outing. Peel appreciated that this important new means of communication had to be controlled in the interests of the people as a whole. In 1844 a Railway Act was passed to regulate the activities of the railway companies, who realized that their greatest profit was to be made from carrying goods and not from providing a service for passengers. It was Peel's Act which compelled the companies to provide the passenger service that the Victorians and their heirs came to take for granted:

> VI. All passenger Railway Companies shall send one train at least along their railway from one end to the other . . . on every week day, except Christmas Day and Good Friday, to provide conveyance of Third Class passengers. The fare or charge shall not exceed one penny for each mile travelled.
> *Source:* Railway Act (1844).

Here we have a government which imposes rigid operating conditions on the previously unregulated railway companies.

12.6   Finance and Trade

The central part of Peel's policy between 1841 and 1846 was to restore business confidence and to create conditions in which businessmen would be prepared to invest money. If they were encouraged to expand their activities, this would create more employment and help to improve living standards for the people as a whole. Peel achieved these aims through the following measures and policies.

THE RAILWAY—FIRST CLASS.

SECOND CLASS.

Fig. 12.5   'God bless the squire and his relations,
                    And keep us in our proper stations—'
            and in railway carriages fitting to those social stations

(*a*) **Budgetary Policy**

Peel—with William Gladstone at the Board of Trade—continued the free trade policy favoured by Huskisson (Section 8.4). In 1842 import duties were reduced to (i) a maximum of 5 per cent on raw materials, (ii) 12 per cent on semi-manufactured goods, (iii) 20 per cent on manufactured goods. These reductions led to lower prices, increased the demand for cheaper products and so led to more employment. The policy was so obviously successful that in 1845 Peel reduced tariffs once again, until there was only a 10 per cent import duty on manufactured goods.

(*b*) **Income Tax**

Reducing tariffs led to a fall in government revenue, so to make good this loss, Peel imposed a tax on incomes which he claimed would be temporary, but which has never been dropped, and is, today, one of the main sources of government revenue. People earning more than £150 a year—equivalent to something like £4 000 a year today—had to pay 7d (3p) on each pound.

(*c*) **The Repeal of the Corn Law, 1846**

See Sections 13.4, 13.5 and 13.6 for this important but natural consequence of the adoption of a free trade policy. It was also the cause of yet another break-up of the Conservative Party, and of Peel's fall from office.

(*d*) **The 'Workshop of the World'**

By 1852 Britain had become the unchallenged 'workshop of the world'. One Parliamentary motion proposed:

> That it is the opinion of this House that the improved condition of the country, and especially of the industrious classes is mainly the result of recent legislation, which has established the principle of unrestricted competition and abolished taxes imposed for the purposes of protection, and has thereby diminished the cost and increased the abundance of the principal articles of food to the people. That it is the opinion of this House that that policy firmly maintained and prudently extended, will best enable the industry of the country to bear its burdens, and will thereby most surely promote the welfare and contentment of the people.
> *Source:* Parliamentary Debates, 3/cxiii/458,701.

Free trade played a major part in transforming the Britain of the 'Hungry Forties' into the booming, confident Britain of the Great Exhibition of 1851.

12.7 The Bank Charter Act, 1844

Until 1797 any bank which issued notes was obliged by law to exchange the notes for gold if a customer asked for this. This law was suspended during the

French Wars but cash payments were resumed in 1821. There were hundreds of small banks in the country. In 1820 Plymouth, with a population of about 30 000, had a dozen or more banks. These 'country' banks were free to issue notes as they saw fit, provided that they were willing to exchange notes for gold on demand. There was a great temptation for them to issue more notes than they had gold in their vaults. One result of over-issue was inflation; another was the failure of many banks, when customers presented notes and asked for cash, and the bank was unable to meet the demand.

Business confidence went down every time there was a banking failure, so in 1844 Parliament passed the Bank Charter Act. This had three main clauses.

(*a*) The Bank of England was divided into two separate sections, one dealing with the issue of notes and the other looking after ordinary banking business. The Issuing Department was allowed to make an issue of £14 million worth of notes without any gold backing, but apart from this 'fiduciary' issue, every note had to be backed by gold. In this way Peel hoped to limit the volume of paper money being printed by the country's most important Bank.

(*b*) The Act forbade the formation of any new note-issuing Bank and limited the note-issuing of existing banks to the limits reached prior to the passage of the Act.

(*c*) If a note-issuing bank went bankrupt or amalgamated with another bank it then lost the right to issue notes. As British business grew and industrial concerns became larger, there was a series of amalgamations as small banks tried to form larger units, which were better able to meet the needs of the owners of larger businesses. In this way the number of note-issuing banks declined (although the last did not disappear until 1921 when Fox, Fowler and Co. of Taunton amalgamated with Lloyds Bank).

12.8   Peel's Foreign Policy

Peel's Foreign Secretary, Lord Aberdeen, was much less forceful a minister than his predecessor, Palmerston (Section 14.2). Aberdeen negotiated the signing of the Treaty of Nanking (1842) which brought the Opium War to an end. It also brought Hong Kong into the British Empire and compelled China to open five other 'treaty' ports to foreign trade.

Aberdeen also handled the tricky question of the boundary between Canada and the USA. As the populations of both countries pushed further westwards there was the danger of friction between them over the border question. Aberdeen appointed Alexander Baring as special commissioner to the USA: Baring had been created Lord Ashburton in 1835 and it was the Ashburton Treaty of 1842 which settled the frontier between Canada and the USA on the eastern seaboard. In 1846 the Oregon Treaty settled the remainder of the boundary, naming the forty-ninth parallel as the frontier between the two expanding countries.

See Sections 16.4, 16.5 and 16.6 for information about Ireland during this period.

Test Yourself on Unit 12

(a) Cartoon: Father Thames

FATHER THAMES INTRODUCING HIS OFFSPRING TO THE FAIR CITY OF LONDON.
(A Design for a Fresco in the New Houses of Parliament.)

Fig. 12.6

(b) Questions

1. Why should the Thames and other rivers (i) have been so contaminated, (ii) been the means of spreading diseases among the population?
2. Why, according to Chadwick and others, were such diseases 'preventable'?
3. How does this illustration help you to understand (i) the high death rate in early Victorian Britain, (ii) the low expectation of life?
4. Did the artist approve of the state of affairs in London? Why was he advocating (i) more legislation, (ii) increased taxation?
5. Why did the demand for health reform lead to a demand for stronger and more efficient local government?
6. Why did Chadwick and the Poor Law Commission call for a Public Health Act?

(c) Further Reading

Adelman, P.: *The Middle-Class Experience 1830–1914.* Longman (Harlow, 1984).
Beckett, J. C.: *The Making of Modern Ireland 1603–1923.* Faber (London, 1981).

Blake, R.: *Disraeli*. Methuen (London, 1969).

Briggs, A.: *The Age of Improvement 1783–1867*. Longman (Harlow, 1979).

Chamberlain, M.: *Lord Aberdeen*. Longman (Harlow, 1983).

Gash, N.: *Peel*. Longman (Harlow, 1976).

Stewart, R. M.: *The Foundation of the Conservative Party 1830–67*. Longman (Harlow, 1978).

The Hungry Forties. Historical Association pamphlet.

(*d*) Documentary

Gash, N.: *The Age of Peel*. Arnold (London, 1968).

(*e*) Exercises

1. Give an account of the main achievements of Peel's ministry, 1841–6.
2. How did Peel try to help the working classes?
3. How did Peel try to promote national prosperity?
4. Show the importance of each of the following in the career of Sir Robert Peel: (i) penal reform and the creation of the Metropolitan Police, (ii) the Tamworth Manifesto, (iii) the repeal of the Corn Laws (Section 13.6).

Chartism and the Anti-Corn Law League

13.1 Working-class Discontent and the Origin of Chartism, 1832–1848

In the late 1830s and throughout the 1840s, there were two major movements pressing for reform: one was known as *Chartism*, because its leaders wrote out their demands in charters which were signed by their followers and then presented to Parliament or the press; the other was the Anti-Corn Law League (Section 13.4). The two movements existed side by side for about ten years, until the League succeeded in its aim and the Corn Laws were repealed. At first sight the two movements may seem to be very different; Chartism, with its *Six Points* (Fig. 13.1) appears to have political ends, and the League an economic end. However, both had their roots in the social conditions of the period, and were more alike than people sometimes think. The Anti-Corn Law League certainly had an economic end—the repeal of the Corn Laws and, as a result, cheaper bread. But the economic end was achieved by political means: the newly enfranchised middle-class voters (Sections 10.4 and 10.5) used their political power to force Parliament to pass the laws which suited them. In the past, Parliament had made laws which favoured the landowners (Section 7.4); with the passing of the 1832 Reform Act, the middle class demanded its economic benefits. On the other hand, the Chartist movement had a very obvious political aim; the Chartists demanded a series of reforms which, if they had been passed, would have created a more democratic society than the one in which we live today. They hoped that a reformed Parliament would pass the laws needed to improve the economic and social conditions of the mass of the people. The Chartists, like the supporters of the League, realized that if they had political power, they could make Parliament pass Acts which produced economic and social benefits.

(a) Living and Working Conditions

We have seen that Britain's industrial towns had developed without any planning, without any government interference with the freedom of factory-owners or builders to put up houses as and where they saw fit. One result of their freedom was that the majority of working-class families lived in over-crowded houses, jammed into overcrowded districts which were provided with the minimum of sanitary arrangements (Section 12.4). One of the hopes of the Chartist leaders was that a more democratically elected parliament would pass laws which would improve the conditions in Britain's towns.

It is important to note that the Chartists assumed that Parliament would pass laws which would satisfy the demands of the electorate. When the majority of MPs had represented only the landowning class, laws favouring that class were passed, as we saw in Section 7.4. As Parliament came to represent the interests of the middle class, legislation favouring that class had been passed (Sections 12.1, 12.2, 12.6 and 12.7). The Chartist leaders believed that if Parliament represented the majority of the people, laws would be passed in the interests of that majority. The saying, 'He who pays the piper calls the tune' had, for the Chartists, a political significance.

We have seen that there had been some attempts at factory reform in the 1830s and 1840s (Sections 11.3 and 12.4), but this reforming movement was very slow. It was also opposed by many MPs and factory-owners as being an interference with the freedom of the factory-owners to do as they wished with their plant and equipment, among which they numbered the workpeople. The Chartists hoped that a more democratically elected Parliament would speed up the reforming process, put an end to child-labour, shorten the working day and otherwise improve life for the workers.

(b) Disappointment with the 1832 Act

The middle-class radicals who had demanded reform in 1830 and 1831 had gained the support of the working classes by promising that parliamentary reform would lead to a new world. Cobbett in particular had spelt out the link between the reform campaign and the good, new life that would follow (Section 7.5). However, as we have seen, only the rich middle class actually obtained the franchise under the 1832 Act (Section 10.4). In a petition drawn up in 1837 the Chartists said:

> We dwell in a land where merchants are noted for enterprise, and whose workmen are proverbial for their industry. Yet we find ourselves overwhelmed with public and private suffering. It was the fond expectation of the people that a remedy for their grievances would be found in the Reform Act of 1832. They have been bitterly and basely deceived. The Reform Act has effected a transfer of power from one domineering faction to another, and left the people as helpless as before. . . .
> Source: The National Petition (1837).

One substantial piece of evidence that the working class was now as 'helpless as before' was the Poor Law Amendment Act (Section 11.4 and Test Yourself on Unit 11 (a)). This took no account of the workings of an economic system which depended so much on an industrialist's ability to sell the product made in his factory, mill or workshop. When a trade depression occurred, thousands of people might be laid off because the industrialist could no longer sell his goods. The Chartists believed that a Parliament in which working people were represented would be bound to repeal the hated 1834 Act, and pass legislation which would help relieve the misery of the poor.

Thomas Attwood, once the leader of the Birmingham Political Union and

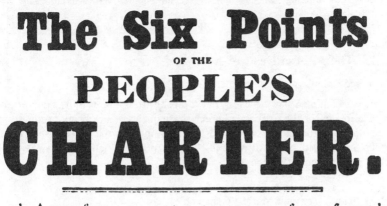

The Six Points
OF THE
PEOPLE'S
CHARTER.

1. A VOTE for every man twenty-one years of age, of sound mind, and not undergoing punishment for crime.

2. THE BALLOT.—To protect the elector in the exercise of his vote.

3. No PROPERTY QUALIFICATION for Members of Parliament —thus enabling the constituencies to return the man of their choice, be he rich or poor.

4. PAYMENT OF MEMBERS, thus enabling an honest trades-man, working man, or other person, to serve a constituency, when taken from his business to attend to the interests of the country.

5. EQUAL CONSTITUENCIES, securing the same amount of representation for the same number of electors, instead of allowing small constituencies to swamp the votes of large ones.

6. ANNUAL PARLIAMENTS, thus presenting the most effectual check to bribery and intimidation, since though a constituency might be bought once in seven years (even with the ballot), no purse could buy a constituency (under a system of universal suffrage) in each ensuing twelvemonth; and since members, when elected for a year only, would not be able to defy and betray their constituents as now.

Fig. 13.1 The Charter

in 1839 an MP, presented the People's Charter to Parliament. He was reported as saying:

> The petition originated in the town of Birmingham and it was now presented to that House with 1 280 000 signatures, the result of not less than 500 meetings. The men who signed the petition were honest and industrious. They had seen no attempt to

relieve their sufferings, whether they were hand-loom weavers, artisans, or agricultural labourers.

Source: Thomas Attwood speaking in the House of Commons (14 June 1839).

13.2   The Alternatives to Chartism

(a)   Trade Unionism

Some working men had believed that a strong trade union movement would be able to win for the workers a higher share of the wealth being produced in the nation's factories. The collapse of the movement in the 1830s dashed these hopes and turned men's attentions towards political action as a means of social improvement (Section 18.4).

(b)   William Lovett and Moral Persuasion

William Lovett was born in Cornwall in 1800 and had, at first, believed that the workers' hopes lay in a national trade union to which all workers would belong (Section 18.4). When this movement collapsed he helped to form the London Workingmen's Association, using it as a means of persuading the working class that they should seek political reform as a means to social improvement. Lovett believed that the middle classes could be persuaded that parliamentary reform was essential, and in this he was a forerunner of the Fabian Society (Section 30.3), which had an influence on the development of the British Labour Party. Lovett and the later Fabians were believers in the process of evolution—progressive change will come about slowly but inevitably.

(c)   Feargus O'Connor and Physical Force

Feargus O'Connor was an Irish Protestant who had supported the cause of the peasants in Ireland (Section 16.1). He was the editor of the Chartist newspaper, *The Northern Star*, which made a great deal of profit. O'Connor tried to use this profit to start a land settlement scheme at O'Connorville to the north-west of London but he was unable to manage the finance of the scheme, which collapsed.

O'Connor did not share Lovett's optimistic belief that the middle class could be persuaded to give up the political power which they had won in 1832 and hand it over to the working class. He wrote:

Shall it be said, fellow countrymen, that four millions of men, capable of bearing arms, and defending their country against every foreign assailant, allowed a few domestic oppressors to enslave and degrade them? . . . We have resolved to obtain our rights, 'peaceably if we may, forcibly if we must'; but woe to those who begin the warfare with the millions, or who forcibly restrain their peaceful agitation for justice. . . .

Source: Northern Star (3 July 1847).

Lovett appreciated the dangers of O'Connor's threatening behaviour. He wrote:

> The whole physical force agitation is harmful and injurious to the movement. Muskets are not what are wanted, but education and schooling of the working people. Stephens and O'Connor are shattering the movement. . . . Violent words do not slay the enemies but the friends of the movement. O'Connor wants to take everything by storm, and to pass the Charter into law within a year. All this hurry and haste, this bluster and menace of armed opposition can only lead to premature outbreaks and to the destruction of Chartism.
>
> Source: Lovett, W., *Life and Struggle of William Lovett* (1876).

13.3   The Cycle of Chartism

Chartism experienced a number of ups and downs in its short history. It won increasing support when trade was bad, unemployment high and the impact of the Poor Law at its greatest. So in the depressed years of 1837–9 (Sections 12.3 and 13.4(*b*)) there was an upswing in the movement. *The Northern Star* was founded in 1837; there were Chartist-led riots in Birmingham in 1838, and a rising by Welsh miners and ironworkers in 1839. The presentation of the first Charter to Parliament also took place in 1839. The movement then seemed to peter out as trade improved and there were more jobs and higher wages—the result of the boom in railway building coupled with the success of Peel's policy of freer trade (Sections 12.5 and 12.6). The depression of 1842–3 led to the Plug Riots at Preston, the Rebecca Riots in South Wales and the presentation of a second Charter to Parliament in 1842. But it was in 1848 that the Chartist

Fig. 13.2 The Chartist procession in Blackfriars in 1848. Notice the policeman with his truncheon (right foreground)

movement seemed to many to reach a peak and to be on the point of succeeding.

In 1848 there was a series of revolutions throughout Western Europe which toppled the rulers of France and Hungary from their thrones, and compelled former autocratic monarchs in Rome, Prussia, Austria and Spain (Section 14.3(a)) to give democratic forms of government to their rebellious peoples. Many people thought that the revolutionary fever might spread across the Channel to Britain. The Chartists decided to hold a mass rally on Kennington Common in April 1848 and then to march on the House of Commons where they would present their third Charter. Many middle-class people saw in this the beginnings of a British Revolution. We read:

> Great preparations were accordingly made. The inhabitants along the thoroughfare to Kennington Common kept doors and windows shut. The measures of government devised by the Duke of Wellington were on a large and complete scale. The Thames' bridges were the main points of concentration, bodies of horse police and masses of special constables being posted on either side . . . a strong force of military was kept ready for instant movement. . . .
>
> Source: *Annual Register* (1848).

The march went off peaceably in the rain, the Charter was presented—and then ridiculed by its opponents. A government spokesman got a great laugh from the Commons when he reported:

> It is evident to your Committee that on numerous consecutive sheets the signatures are in one and the same handwriting. Your Committee also observed the names of distinguished individuals, among which occurs the name of Her Majesty, as Victoria Rex, April 1st, F. M. Duke of Wellington, Sir Robert Peel [and a] . . . number of names which are obviously fictitious, such as 'No Cheese', 'Pug Nose', 'Flat Nose'.

So Chartism was laughed into defeat in 1848. O'Connor and a handful of other radicals tried to persuade Londoners to rise in rebellion, but they received no support. O'Connor became insane and in 1852 he was arrested and sent to Chiswick Asylum. Lovett, the evolutionist, left politics to become a teacher. Over the next hundred years Lovett's view was seen to be correct: parliamentary reform did come about, peaceably, and even more completely than he himself had hoped for.

In the short run, Chartism was a failure, since it achieved none of its aims and the organization withered away. The reasons for this decline in support, like the reasons for the origins of the movement, were both social and economic. In the years of depression, Chartism tended to be very active and gain wide support, but after 1850, Britain became more prosperous. This was due partly to Britain's early start in the industrial race (Section 24.1), and the boom which followed the building of her railway network (Section 12.5). It was also due to the long-term effects of Britain's policy of free trade (Sections 12.6 and 19.2(a)). The 1850s were years of plenty, with high levels of employment, falling prices and rising living standards for the vast majority of people. Chartism had no chance of attracting support in 'booming Britain'.

Fig. 13.3 Prime Minister John Russell portrayed by 'Punch' as the unwilling recipient of the 1848 Charter

However, its influence did not die out completely. The leaders of local Chartist clubs and societies continued to influence trade union leaders and other working-class people in their own areas. In some places Chartists still met for regular discussions; they formed debating societies and Chartist schools, to which adults and children went on Sundays to learn about their rights, the need for political reform and its link with social reform. When the next depression set in—around 1870 (Section 24.1)—there were many old Chartists and their younger disciples who were unwilling to accept a fall in their living standards. These people helped to generate an enthusiasm among the working class for the formation of an active working-class political movement (Sections 29.7–29.10 and 30.1–30.5).

13.4   The Origins of the Anti-Corn Law League

(a) Middle-class Demands

In 1832 the middle classes had been given the vote, which put them on an equal footing with their 'social superiors', the landowning upper class. But they were still on an unequal footing on economic laws, since the Corn Law existed to protect the economic interests of the upper class (Section 7.2). As Richard Cobden noted:

> I am a manufacturer of clothing, and I do not know why the making of clothes should not be as honourable as the manufacture of food. Did you ever hear any debates in the House to fix the price of my commodities in the market?
> *Source: Speeches of Richard Cobden, MP* (1870).

The Anti-Corn Law League was an attempt by the emancipated middle class to use their newly-won political power to serve their own economic interests.

(b) Depression, 1837–9

We have seen that in the later 1830s the country suffered from an economic depression and that there were masses of unemployed (Sections 12.1 and 12.3). One result of the depression was a fall in the profits of the middle class, whose factories began to close down. The middle class argued that if the Corn Law was abolished and foreigners were allowed to sell their cheap corn in Britain, this would give them the money to buy manufactured goods from Britain. This in turn would create employment for the working classes while restoring the profit-incomes of the middle class. A Dr Bowring spoke in Manchester in 1838, saying:

> When I went into Brittany and Normandy, what said the Normans and Bretons? 'Why,' said they, 'admit our corn and then we'll see whether anybody can prevent the importation of your manufactures into France.' (CHEERS!) 'We are millions,' said they, 'willing to clothe ourselves in the garments you send us, and you have millions of hungry mouths to take our corn.'
> *Source:* Prentice, A.: *History of the Anti-Corn Law League* (1853).

And Richard Cobden emphasized the point when he said:

> To pay for that corn, more manufacturers would be required from this country; this
> would lead to an increased demand for labour in the manufacturing districts, a rise of
> wages, and would clear your streets of the two millions of paupers which now exist in
> the land. . . .
> Source: Speeches of Richard Cobden, MP (1870).

(c) The Formation of the Anti-Corn Law League

There were already a number of local repeal associations in existence in 1838,
but the League as such was founded on 10 January 1839, at a meeting held at
the York Hotel, Manchester:

> To consider the proper mode of carrying forward the proceedings of the Anti-Corn
> Law Association, in a manner commensurate with the magnitude of the obstacles to
> be surmounted, and worthy of the object for which it has been established. Mr
> Cobden recommended to those present, an investment of part of their property . . .
> and subscriptions were at once put down in the room for £1800 and in the course of a
> month they had reached £6136.10.0d.
> Source: Ashworth, H., Recollections of Richard Cobden and the Anti-Corn Law
>   League (1877).

13.5 The Campaign

The League was fortunate, unlike the Chartists, in that the rich middle class
provided large sums of money to finance a national campaign. Some of this
money was used to produce pamphlets, notes for speakers and to finance three
newspapers, The League, The Economist and The Sun (a London newspaper
which supported the League's campaign in return for an annual payment of
£500). The League was able to distribute its pamphlets and other material
because of two recent developments. In 1840 Rowland Hill introduced the
penny post (Section 11.7) and by 1845 a network of railway lines had been
established. The League's cheap literature could thus be carried through the
post and its speakers transported throughout the country to address meetings.

One of the aims of these League speakers was the formation of local groups
which would support the national campaign. Such local groups would ensure
that their members were enrolled on the electoral register, if they were entitled
to vote, and that they gave their vote to a League sympathizer, if one stood in
an election. In this way the League managed to get some of its members into
Parliament, where they were led by Richard Cobden, a cotton manufacturer.
Cobden and his supporters backed Peel's policy of freeing British trade from
import duties (Section 12.6) and argued that the repeal of the Corn Law
would be the logical outcome of such a free trade policy. But it was events in
Ireland which really reinforced Cobden's arguments.

No Starvation Law!

In Poland there are millions half clothed, but who have an abundance of food to spare; and in England there are millions half fed, who have an abundance of clothing to spare. These millions in either country would gladly exchange with the other that which they do not want and have to spare, for that which they do want and have not. But the hard-hearted landowners of this country, deaf to the cries of the wretched, and heedless of the miseries which they inflict on their fellow-creatures, step in between the naked millions on the one hand and the starving millions on the other, and, by their food monopolies and trade restrictions, keep up their RENTS by preventing that mutual exchange which would give abundance and happiness to all.

ELECTORS OF WALSALL!
Aid the Starving Millions,
AND
VOTE FOR MR. SMITH
AND THE
ABOLITION of the BREAD TAX.

Fig. 13.4 *The Anti-Corn Law League used the electoral system to increase the number of MPs who would support the League's cause*

13.6   The Irish Famine, 1845

Living standards for the Irish peasants had always been poor. Their main diet was potatoes which they could grow on the small plots that they rented from absentee English landlords (Sections 15.1(*d*) and 16.6). In the 1840s the potato crop was affected by a blight which spread throughout the country and brought great hardship to millions of families (Section 16.6). Some people argued that the Irish peasants could be helped if the Corn Law was repealed, since cheaper foreign corn could then be imported into starving Ireland. Lord John Russell, the leader of the Whig Party, wrote to his constituents:

> To the Electors of the City of London
> Gentlemen—The present state of the country, in regard to its supply of food, cannot be viewed without apprehension. Two evils require your consideration. One of these is the disease in the potatoes, affecting very seriously parts of England and Scotland, and committing fearful ravages in Ireland. Another evil, however, under which we are suffering, is the Corn Law. By this law grain of all kinds has been made subject to very high duties on importation. This defect was pointed out many years ago by writers on the Corn Laws, and was urged upon the attention of the House of Commons. I used to be of [the] opinion that corn was an exception to the general

rules of political economy; but observation and experience have convinced me that we ought to abstain from all interference with the supply of food . . .

Let us, then, unite to put an end to this system. . . .

Edinburgh, November 22 1845

J. Russell.

Source: Walpole, S., *Life of Lord John Russell* (1891).

Some of Peel's supporters feared that, like Russell, he might undergo a conversion on this issue. One of them wrote to him at the end of November 1845:

An abandonment of your former opinions now would, I think, prejudice your character as a public man. . . . I do not see how the repeal of the Corn Law is to afford relief to the distress with which we are threatened. . . . I think it impossible to show that the abandonment of the law now could materially affect this year's supply.

In my opinion, the party of which you are the head is the only barrier which remains against the revolutionary effects of the Reform Bill. If it be broken in pieces by a destruction of confidence in its leaders (and I cannot but think that an abandonment of the Corn Law would produce that result), I see nothing before us but class animosities and the ultimate triumph of unrestrained democracy.

Source: Mr Goulburn's letter to Peel (30 November 1845).

Peel, however, was always open to conversion—as he had demonstrated in 1828–9 (Sections 8.5 and 8.6) and again in 1834 (Section 12.2). He had come to power as the leader of a party representing the landowning class but, since 1841, had followed a policy of free trade which was designed to please the middle class and to help develop the nation's economy. He was not a party man in a narrow sense, so it was not surprising that, faced with the Irish problem and having followed a free trade policy, he should have been prepared to ask Parliament to repeal the Corn Law. Speaking on 16 February 1846, he said:

I admit that a natural consequence of the course I have pursued, is to offend a great party. I know what would have conciliated temporary confidence. It would have been to underrate the danger in Ireland, to invite a united combination for the maintenance of the existing Corn Law . . . by such a course I should have been sure to animate and please a party, and to gain for a time their cordial approbation. . . .

Source: Sir Robert Peel's speech on the second reading of the bill for the repeal of the Corn Laws (16 February 1846).

Peel was honest enough to change his mind when he saw that a change was required. He was also honest enough to attribute his conversion to Cobden, whom he had once vigorously attacked. On 23 June 1846, with the Corn Law repealed, he declared:

A combination of parties, and the influence of the Government has led to the ultimate success of the measures. But, Sir, there is a name which ought to be associated with the success of these measures . . . the name of a man who has advocated their cause with untiring energy, and by appeals to reason. The name which will be associated with the success of these measures is the name of Richard Cobden.

Source: Sir Robert Peel's speech in the House of Commons (23 June 1846).

Fig. 13.5 Peel addressing the House of Commons on 22 January 1846

Benjamin Disraeli was a Conservative Party backbencher between 1841 and 1846 (Section 20.1). He believed that the landowning class had a traditional right to govern and that the Corn Law was essential if that class was to maintain its position. He considered repeal to be a betrayal, not a conversion (Section 20.2 and Test Yourself on Unit 13(c)). But when Disraeli became the leader of the handful of MPs who remained in opposition to the Whigs and the Peelites he noted: 'The Corn Laws are damned and dead.' He, too, had come to accept the inevitable.

Test Yourself on Unit 13

(*a*) **Cartoon**

PAPA COBDEN TAKING MASTER ROBERT A FREE TRADE WALK.

PAPA COBDEN.—" Come along, MASTER ROBERT, do step out."
MASTER ROBERT.—" That's all very well, but you know I cannot go so fast as you do."

Fig. 13.6

(b) Questions

1. Who was Papa? To which social class did he belong? Why was this class able in the 1840s to exercise political influence which it had not been able to use in the 1820s?
2. Who is represented by the smaller figure in the cartoon? What office had he held (i) in 1828, (ii) between 1841 and 1846?
3. Do you think that 'Master' went for this walk willingly? Why?
4. What steps had he taken along this road in 1842 and 1845?
5. Why was Master unwilling to go as fast as Papa?
6. In 1900 a cartoon appeared showing another tall man taking another smaller figure back along the Free Trade Road in the opposite direction. Can you say who (i) the taller figure was, (ii) who was represented by the smaller figure?

(c) Documents

(i) We trusted to one who obtained the greatest place in the country, and at this moment governs England. Well, Sir, what happens? The right hon. gentleman, the first minister, told his friends that he had given them very significant hints of the change of his opinions.

More than a year ago I said that it happened to me that Protection was in the same state as Protestantism was in 1828. I remember my friends were very indignant with me for that assertion. But I am bound to say that the right hon. baronet may congratulate himself on his complete success in having entirely deceived his party (loud and prolonged cheers) . . .

When the minister at last met the house and his party, he acted as if we had deserted him, instead of his having left us (great cheering). Who can forget that indignant glance? . . . which means to say, 'I, a protectionist minister, mean to govern England by the aid of the Anti-Corn-Law League (cheers). And, as for the country gentlemen, why, I snap my fingers in their face.' (continued cheers) . . .

I think great justice has been done to him throughout these debates. Sir, the right hon. gentleman has been accused of always having intended to abandon the opinions by which he rose to power. Sir, I entirely acquit the right hon. gentleman of any such intention. When I examine the career of this minister, which has now filled a great space in the parliamentary history of this country, I find that for between thirty and forty years that right hon. gentleman has traded on the ideas of others (loud cheering). He is a burglar of others' intellect. He is one of whom it may be said as Dean Swift said of another minister, that 'he is a gentleman who has the perpetual misfortune to be mistaken!' (great cheering and laughter).

Source: the Speech of Mr Disraeli, delivered in the House of Commons (May 15 1846).

(ii) The League

Who are that blustering, canting crew,
Who keep the cheap loaf in our view,
And would from us more profit screw?
The League.

Who wish to gull the working man,
And burk the Charter if they can,
With their self-aggrandising plan?
The League.

Who deal in sophistry and cant—
Of common sense evince the want—
And strive the Charter to supplant?
The League.

Source: Ryder, William, *The Northern Star* (3 April 1841).

(d) Questions

1. What was meant by 'Protection'? What was meant by 'a protectionist minister'? Were the official opposition for or against Protection: (i) when in office in the 1830s, (ii) in the early 1840s?
2. In what state had Protestantism found itself in 1828? How had Peel's decisions at that time affected his party?
3. Who were the 'country gentlemen'? Why were they so opposed to the Anti-Corn Law League?
4. There is frequent reference in the extract to 'cheering'. Which party, do you think, cheered this attack on Peel? What was the fate of this party in 1846? To which party did most Peelites belong in the 1850s and 1860s?
5. Do you think that it is a sign of weakness or of strength for a politician to be willing to admit that he has been mistaken? Why?
6. Why did Chartists attack the Anti-Corn Law League? Why did many working-class people support the activities of the League while they did not support the Chartists?
7. Why were the supporters of the Anti-Corn Law League opposed to the activities of the Chartists?

(e) Further Reading

Adelman, P.: *The Middle-Class Experience 1830–1914*. Longman (Harlow, 1984).

Briggs, A.: *The Age of Improvement 1783–1867*. Longman (Harlow, 1979).

Chartism. Historical Association pamphlet.

Evans, E. J.: *The Forging of the Modern State: Early Industrial Britain 1783–1870*. Longman (Harlow, 1983).

Gash, N.: *Aristocracy and People, Britain 1815–1865*. Arnold (London, 1983).

Hopkins, E.: *A Social History of the English Working Classes 1815–1945*. Arnold (London, 1979).

Royle, E.: *Chartism*. Longman (Harlow, 1980).

Thomis, M. I. and Holt, P.: *Threats of Revolution in Britain 1789–1848*. Macmillan (Basingstoke, 1977).

Thompson, E. P.: *The Making of the English Working Class*. Penguin (Harmondsworth, 1968).

(f) Documentary

Gash, N.: *The Age of Peel*. E. Arnold (London, 1968).

(g) Exercises

1. Trace the steps by which Britain adopted a policy of Free Trade.
2. What were the Corn Laws? Why were they repealed in 1846?
3. Give an account of the work of Richard Cobden.
4. What were the aims of the Chartists? Why did they fail?
5. Explain why the Anti-Corn Law League succeeded while the Chartists failed.

Unit Fourteen
Palmerston and Foreign Affairs, 1830–65

14.1 Palmerston's Early Career

Lord Palmerston entered the Commons as a Tory MP in 1807, and from 1809 until 1828 he was Secretary of State for War. He became a supporter of Canning (Section 6.2) and in 1828, along with Huskisson and the other Canningites, he resigned from Wellington's government because of its anti-Canningite policies (Sections 8.5(*a*), (*b*) and 8.6). In 1829 he joined the Whigs, becoming Foreign Secretary when Grey came to power in 1830 (Section 8.6). Speaking in the House of Commons in 1848 Palmerston declared:

> And if I might be allowed to express in one sentence the principle which I think ought to guide our English Ministers, I would adopt the expression of Canning, and say that with every British Minister the interests of England ought to be the aim of his policy.

This not only illustrates Palmerston's debt to Canning—dead for twenty years—but also the main object of his foreign policy throughout his long career, which was the upholding of British interests.

14.2 1830–41

(*a*) Belgian Independence, 1830

In 1815 Catholic Belgium had been joined to Protestant Holland by the peacemakers at Vienna (Section 9.3). The union was dominated by the Dutch. Dutch farmers were financially aided while the Belgian industrialists were heavily taxed, the Dutch language was forced on the unwilling Belgians and most of the posts in government service also went to the Dutch.

In 1830 the French revolted to get rid of the Bourbon King Charles X and replaced him with the more liberal Orleanist King, Louis Philippe. This revolution encouraged the Belgians to take up arms against their Dutch masters, a move which Austria, Prussia and Russia saw as entitling them to invoke the terms of the Troppau Protocol (Section 9.5(*c*)). They prepared to invade the Belgian provinces of the united country, and King William of Holland was glad to agree to this. The Belgians turned to the new King of the French for support and promised that if they gained their independence they would offer the crown to Louis' son.

Palmerston, the Canningite, had no love for the Holy Alliance (Section 9.4) and was willing to help Belgium in the event of a struggle. But he had no wish to see France extend her influence over Belgium, because this would have destroyed the idea of the Low Countries as a buffer zone against French aggression (Section 9.3). So he offered to help the French in their efforts to stop the Holy Alliance powers from interfering. He also used British naval power to compel the Dutch to concede Antwerp to the Belgians, and then he persuaded the Belgians to accept Prince Leopold of Saxe-Coburg-Gotha as their King. (Leopold was related to the British Royal Family.) In 1839 Palmerston persuaded the major powers to agree, in the Treaty of London, that Belgium would be permanently a neutral country: none of the powers would attack her, nor would they ask her to be an ally in the event of a war.

Palmerston's Belgian policy served British interests well. France was excluded, while British influence was extended. There would be no danger of any major power using Belgium as a base against Britain as Louis XIV and, more lately, Napoleon, had done.

(b) Spain and Portugal, 1834

In 1828 Dom Miguel had illegally seized the throne of Portugal during the infancy of the rightful Queen, Donna Maria. In Spain, Don Carlos was challenging the will of his brother, King Ferdinand, who had named his daughter Isabella as his successor. Palmerston sent British forces to help expel both the male claimants to these thrones and establish the young Queens on their thrones, hoping that this would lead to the establishment of democratic and liberal governments. He explained his policy in a letter to his brother:

> I have been very busy working out my quadruple alliance between England, France, Spain and Portugal, for the expulsion of Carlos and Miguel from the Portuguese dominions. I carried it through the Cabinet, taking them by surprise, and not leaving them time to make objections. I will settle Portugal, and go some way to settle Spain also. What is of more importance, it establishes a quadruple alliance among the states of the west, which will serve as a powerful counterpoise to the Holy Alliance of the east.
>
> Source: Palmerston's letter to his brother (21 April 1834).

(c) The Opium War, 1839–42

In the 1830s the British government had taken over the power once exercised by the East India Company (Section 17.1(d)), and one of its first actions was to make the opium trade illegal in India. Indian opium growers found a new market for their profitable crop in China, and British merchants set up warehouses and settlements in Chinese ports. By 1839 the Chinese had come to resent the British 'invasion' on two grounds. They did not see why they should be asked to buy opium which the British government considered too harmful to be sold in India. In addition, and more significantly, they refused to accept the Europeans' high opinions of themselves and their low opinions of the Chinese; on the contrary, the Chinese believed that they were 'the Sons of Heaven', while they referred to the Europeans as 'red-haired barbarians'.

There were clashes between British merchants and Chinese officials which led to the Chinese destroying British ships carrying opium. A brief war fol-

Fig. 14.1 The East India Company's steamer 'Nemesis' supported by boats from other ships owned by the company, destroying the Chinese war junks in Anson's Bay, 7 January 1841

lowed which was concluded when Peel's government and the Chinese signed the Treaty of Nanking in 1842 (Section 12.8). Some people believe that Palmerston was acting like a bullying warmonger in his Chinese policy; others believe that he was merely upholding the right of British merchants to sell their goods throughout the world. But even his supporters have to agree that he was compelling China to adopt a trade policy which suited Britain more than it suited China.

(d) The Eastern Question

We deal with the details of this part of Palmerston's policy in Section 15.2(b) and (c), *The Eastern Question*.

14.3   1846–51

(a) The 1848 Revolutions

In 1848 a series of revolutions shattered the peace of Europe, as we noted in Section 13.3. King Louis Philippe of France was deposed by a revolution which established a republican government, with Louis Napoleon as President. Many of the rulers of states in Italy either lost their thrones or were forced to give their peoples a democratic form of government. And upheavals in Prussia and Austria, the largest states in the German Confederation, had the effect of uniting students with workers, intellectuals with soldiers, and forcing the King of Prussia and the Emperor of Austria into handing over some of their power to constitutional assemblies.

Palmerston had tried to persuade these European autocrats to grant some form of democratic government, warning them that otherwise they faced revolution. In 1849 he reminded the House of Commons:

> For many years the Governments of Europe imagined that they could keep down opinion by force of arms, and [avoid the] revolution which was their constant dread. We gave an opinion to the contrary effect, and we have been blamed for it. We have been accused of meddling with matters that did not concern us. The result has proved that if our opinions had been acted upon, great calamities would have been avoided. . . .
> *Source:* Lord Palmerston, House of Commons (21 July 1849).

But if we believed that Palmerston was always and everywhere the champion of liberal movements, it might come as a shock to read:

> Austria is a most important element in the balance of European power, a barrier against encroachment on the one side, and against invasion on the other. The political

Fig. 14.2 The Austrian General Haynau had been active in repressing the nationalist risings in Italy and Hungary in 1848–9. He came on a visit to London during which he visited Barclay's Breweries. The workers recognized 'the hyena of Brescia' and attacked him. He was eventually rescued by 'bobbies', five of whom can be seen escorting him to the police galley, while another tries to hold back the crowd

independence and liberties of Europe are bound up with the maintenance and integrity of Austria as a great European power; and therefore anything which weakens Austria must be something which Englishmen ought to try to prevent.
Source: Palmerston in the Commons, *Parliamentary Debates* (Third Series), CVII, Col. 808.

Palmerston was anxious that peace should be maintained and that Russia should be held back. Austria played an important part in the achievement of these policies. Palmerston gave no help to the liberal revolutionaries and he was glad in 1849 and 1850 when the autocratic rulers regained their former power and dismissed their democratic assemblies. However, he did welcome the exiled liberals from France and Austria, Prussia and Hungary, and was less welcoming to General Haynau, whose army had crushed the Hungarian revolution.

(b) Don Pacifico

During some anti-government riots in Athens in 1847, the home and stores of a merchant, Don Pacifico, were destroyed by the mob. Don Pacifico applied to the Greek government for compensation, but the government had more important things to worry about and, anyhow, the Greeks believed that Don Pacifico was overestimating the value of the property that had been destroyed. The merchant was a Gibraltarian-born Jew and, claiming to be a British subject, he applied to the British government for help. In December 1849 Palmerston wrote to the British Minister in Athens:

> I have desired the Admiralty to instruct Sir William Parker to take Athens on his way back from the Dardanelles, and to support you in bringing at last to a satisfactory ending the settlement of our various claims upon the Greek Government. He should, of course, begin by reprisals; that is by taking possession of some Greek property. . . . The next thing would be a blockade of any or all of his ports. . . . Of course Pacifico's claim must be fully satisfied.
> *Source:* Palmerston's letter to Wyse, the minister in Athens (December 1849).

The British navy was too strong for the Greeks, who climbed down when it blockaded the port of Athens.

The Russians objected to this British interference in Greek affairs and British liberals, such as Cobden and Bright, challenged the Foreign Secretary and called him a bully. In the debate which took place over the Don Pacifico affair, Palmerston defended himself in a long speech, in which he said:

> The Roman in days of old held himself free from indignity when he could say, 'Civis Romanus sum', so also a British subject, in whatever land he may be, shall feel confident that the watchful eye on the strong arm of England will protect him against injustice and wrong.
> *Source:* Palmerston's speech to the Commons (June 1850).

Many patriotic Britishers supported this use of power to extend British influence in Greece, as in China. Others, taking a more moral line, agreed with Gladstone:

What then, Sir, was a Roman citizen? He was a member of a privileged caste; he belonged to a conquering race. . . . Let us recognize the equality of the weak and the strong; the principles of brotherhood among nations. . . . Let us refrain from meddling in the internal concerns of other States, even as we should resent the same interference.

Source: Gladstone's speech to the Commons (June 1850).

But it was Palmerston whose views were most widely supported, as Greville noted in his diary:

London, July 1, 1850 . . . I rode with Lord Grey yesterday in the Park. He said that it was remarkable that this discussion, which was intended to damage Palmerston, had left him the most popular man in the country; that of this there could be no doubt. Bright had said that his vote had given great offence at Manchester, and that Cobden's vote and speech would probably cost him the West Riding at the next election; that amongst all the middle classes Palmerston was immensely popular.

(c) Palmerston's French Policies, 1846–51

(*i*) **Louis Philippe.** In 1830 Palmerston and King Louis Philippe had co-operated over the question of Belgian independence (Section 14.2), but, between 1839 and 1841 they had quarrelled over the Eastern Question (Section 15.2(*c*)). However, there was not a complete breakdown between the two until 1846, when the French King broke an agreement which Britain and France had made in 1843 about marriage plans for the Queen of Spain and her younger sister, Luisa. It had been agreed that the French King's son would marry Princess Luisa, but only when the Queen herself had married and had an heir. Louis Philippe arranged a marriage for the Queen—with a very old Prince who would probably not be able to produce an heir for the Spanish throne. He then broke his agreement by having both the marriages celebrated on the same day which meant that, if all went as he expected, his son's child would one day become the ruler of Spain and so the influence of France would be extended. Palmerston could not forgive this deliberate attempt to break an agreement between the two countries.

(*ii*) **Louis Napoleon.** In 1848 Louis Philippe was driven from the throne of France, and a Republic was established with Louis Napoleon as President for four years. In 1851 Louis Napoleon used his power to persuade the French people to elect him President for ten years. Palmerston had watched events in France since the fall of Louis Philippe and was anxious that the rising tide of working-class demands for democracy and intellectual demands for a socialist form of government should be held back. He believed that Louis Napoleon could provide the strong government which France would need if radicalism, socialism and democracy were to be held in check. He informed Waldewsky, the French Ambassador in London, that he approved of Louis Napoleon's acquisition of additional powers. This brought to a head a conflict between Palmerston and the Queen.

In August 1850 Queen Victoria had told the Prime Minister, Russell, that she did not like Palmerston's way of conducting foreign affairs. She wrote:

> The Queen requires, first, that Lord Palmerston will state what he proposes in a given case, in order that the Queen may know to what she is giving her royal sanction.
> Source: Queen Victoria's letter to Lord John Russell (August 1850).

Palmerston's approval of Louis Napoleon's *coup d'état* annoyed the Queen and she compelled Russell to make Palmerston resign. Palmerston wrote to his brother:

> John Russell replied that the question was not whether the President was or was not justified in doing what he has done, but whether I was justified in expressing any opinion thereupon (to Walewsky) without having first taken the opinion of the Cabinet upon that matter. My letter left him no alternative but to advise the Queen to place the Foreign Office in other hands.
> Source: Palmerston's letter to his brother (22 January 1852).

14.4   1852–65

Palmerston was too powerful a politician to be so easily dismissed, however. Louis Napoleon had assumed the title of Emperor Napoleon III, and in Britain there was a revival of fears of French aggression. Russell proposed that a local militia be formed in each county, to prepare for a possible invasion by the new Napoleon. Palmerston argued that nothing less than a national militia would do, and Parliament agreed with him. Within two months of his own fall from office he persuaded a majority in the Commons to vote against Russell's proposals for a local militia, and Russell resigned. 'I have had my tit-for-tat,' Palmerston told his wife.

After the Conservatives had failed to form a government, the former Peelite, Lord Aberdeen (Section 12.8), became Prime Minister and appointed Palmerston Home Secretary. Within a short time this government was involved in the Crimean War (Sections 15.4 and 15.5), one effect of which was to make Aberdeen unpopular. He resigned in 1855 and the Queen was forced, reluctantly, to appoint 'the most popular Minister'—Palmerston—as her Prime Minister. He held this post until his death in 1865, apart from a brief period after his Conspiracy to Murder Bill was defeated. Palmerston's main interest in these years was, as always, foreign affairs. He supervised the signing of the Treaty of Paris in 1856, which concluded the Crimean War and seemed to bring to a halt Russian plans for increasing her power in the Balkans (Sections 15.6 and 15.7).

(a) Italian Unification

When Palmerston took office in 1855, there was no 'Italy' as we understand it. There were several separate states—some large (the Kingdom of Piedmont), some small (the Duchies of Parma and Modena), and some under Austrian rule (Venice) or the control of Austrian-dominated rulers (the Kingdom of Naples and Sicily (Section 9.5(a)). Cutting right across the centre of Europe were the Papal States, where the Pope ruled. The Austrian Chancellor, Metternich, had given the best description of Italy when he spoke of it as 'a geographical expression'. However, there were a number of societies and movements whose aim was to unite all the individual states into one Italy. Austria was opposed to all such movements; France, under Napoleon III, was anxious to try to follow two opposing policies—on the one hand Napoleon wanted to appear as the champion of Italian nationalism, but on the other he was anxious to keep the support of French Catholics by upholding the Pope's claims to his Papal States. Britain favoured Italian unification, providing it could be achieved without a general European war.

In 1858 an Italian patriot, Orsini, had tried to assassinate Napoleon III (as Louis Napoleon became in 1852). Orsini said that Napoleon III had not given enough support to the movement for Italian unification. Orsini escaped to Britain and Palmerston's *Conspiracy to Murder Bill* was introduced so that Britain could send him back to France to face trial. Palmerston was defeated on this issue and resigned. But after a short period of minority government led by Lord Derby and Disraeli, Palmerston was back in power in June 1859, when the Italian problem grew more urgent.

In May 1859 Napoleon III went to war against Austria, the main obstacle to the movement for Italian unification (Section 9.5). Palmerston and his Foreign Minister, Lord John Russell, had tried to persuade Napoleon not to go to war, fearing that what started off as an Italian campaign might blossom out into a general and widespread war against Austria. Napoleon ignored this British advice. In a short war French troops defeated the Austrians at the Battles of Magenta and Solferino, liberated most of northern Italy from Austrian domination and then, surprisingly, Napoleon made a peace treaty with the Austrians at Villafranca.

Although Palmerston had previously opposed French entry into a War of Italian Liberation, he was equally opposed to the Treaty of Villafranca, because this still left Austria in a powerful position in northern Italy. As Palmerston said:

> [England] might well deem it her duty to protest most emphatically against such an enslavement of the Italian peoples. Austria ought to be excluded from all interferences beyond her boundaries. If that is not done the whole business will, in a very short time, have to begin all over again.
> *Source:* quoted in Marriott, J. A. R., *The Makers of Modern Italy* (1931).

Palmerston and Russell supported the rebels in various states in northern and central Italy who refused to accept the decisions that had been reached at Villafranca. These rebels were united to Piedmont as a further move towards Italian unification. Palmerston wrote to the British Ambassador in Paris on 22 August 1859:

The peoples of these Duchies [in Northern and Central Italy] have as good a right to change their leaders as the people of England, France and Belgium. The annexation of these Duchies to Piedmont would be a blessing for Italy, France and Europe.
Source: quoted in Marriott, J. A. R., *The Makers of Modern Italy* (1931).

Napoleon took the hint, persuaded the Austrians to accept changes in the terms of the Treaty of Villafranca and the Duchies were merged with Piedmont. This left the Papal States and the Kingdom of Sicily and Naples yet to be brought into a similar merger, when Italy would be united.

The invasion of Sicily by Garibaldi and his thousand followers in their romantically-coloured red shirts was greeted with enthusiasm in England Some firms named a new biscuit after Garibaldi, while fashionable dress-makers produced Garibaldi-type blouses which were bought by the well-to-do ladies. More seriously, Palmerston and Russell gave their support—backed by the presence of the British fleet in the seas around Sicily and Naples—to the voyage of Garibaldi from Genoa to Sicily and from Sicily to the mainland in August 1860. By October, Sicily and Naples had been conquered and handed over to the King of Piedmont by the victorious Garibaldi. Once again Britain gave its support to Italian unification. Lord John Russell wrote:

His Majesty's government can see no ground for the censure with which Austria, France, Prussia and Russia have visited on the acts of the King of Piedmont. The British government will turn their eyes to the prospect of a people building up the edifice of their liberties and their independence.
Source: quoted in Marriott, J. A. R., *The Makers of Modern Italy* (1931).

The Italians appreciated this support in the face of the hostility shown by the rulers of the other Great Powers. Russell's nephew wrote to his uncle from Rome:

You are blessed night and morning by millions of Italians. The moment your letter was published thousands of people copied it from each other to carry it to their homes.

Shortly after this the first Italian Parliament met (January 1861) and the union of north and south was formally signed. Palmerston, with his liberal–nationalist views, had won a great success.

(b) The American Civil War

In 1861 the American Civil War broke out. Gladstone and many of his col-leagues symphatized with the government of Abraham Lincoln, which desired to bring slavery to an end. Palmerston, on the other hand, felt more sympathy for the aristocratic slave-owners of the southern states who were opposed to Lincoln. The Lincoln government tried to bring to a halt the exporting of raw cotton from the southern states to Britain. They also claimed the right to search ships trading with the South. One of their ships stopped a British ship, the *Trent*, which was carrying two delegates from the southern states to Britain.

Palmerston wrote a very angry note to President Lincoln, which might well have led Lincoln to declare war on Britain as a trading ally of the South. Fortunately the Prince Consort saw the letter and altered its contents. Lincoln chose to ignore the note and the danger of war was averted.

The British government allowed the southern states to pay a north-of-England dockyard at Birkenhead, to build a ship called the *Alabama*. Later this ship was used by the southern states to attack shipping making for northern ports. The Lincoln government claimed that this amounted to favouring the southern states and called for compensation for the damage that had been done to their shipping. It was left to Gladstone to sort out this problem (Section 19.5).

(c) China Again

In 1856 a Chinese ship, the *Arrow*, was seized by the Chinese Governor of Canton on a charge of piracy, and its Chinese crew were arrested. The *Arrow* had once been owned by a British merchant and had then flown the British flag. In 1856, however, it was the property of a Chinese merchant. This did not prevent Palmerston's being persuaded by British merchants trading in China that the Chinese government's action was part of an attack on British trading interests.

War was declared and Canton was bombarded. The French joined in and the war was concluded by the Treaty of Tientsin, which forced the Chinese to open more ports to trade with the West.

14.5   Palmerston's Bluff Called

Palmerston's success as a Foreign Minister was based on the power of Britain, 'the workshop of the world', which enabled her to stand up to and browbeat almost any country or combination of countries. But in the 1860s she could no longer do this. Bismarck was the Chancellor of Prussia, which was on its way to becoming a powerful industrialized country (Section 24.1), the basis for the powerful Germany that he created in 1870–1. In 1863 the Poles revolted against their Russian master and Palmerston was anxious to send help. Bismarck, who needed the support of Russia, refused to allow the passage of British help through Prussia, in spite of Palmerston's blustering. In 1864 Bismarck planned a war against Denmark as part of his long-term plans for the unification of Germany. Palmerston warned him that if he attacked Denmark he would have to deal with Britain. Such a warning might once have been sufficient to cause a country to change its policy, but Bismarck went ahead with his plans, the war did break out, Denmark stood alone and was defeated. Palmerston and Britain were forced to stand by. Britain was no longer so overwhelmingly powerful as she had been, and Palmerston's death in 1865 marked the end of an era.

Test Yourself on Unit 14

(*a*) **Cartoon:**

Fig. 14.3

(*b*) **Questions**

1. Who is the smaller of the two men shown in this cartoon? What office did he hold when this cartoon was drawn?
2. How had the taller of the two men brought about the dismissal of the smaller man?
3. When, and over what issue, had the Queen and the shorter man co-operated to dismiss the taller man? Which office had he held at that time?
4. Comment on the use by the Queen of the word 'servants' when describing her politicians.

5. What office did the taller man hold just after this cartoon was drawn? Which Prime Minister appointed him to that post?

(c) Document

Bowood, 26th December 1845

As to Peace, I succeeded, as the organ of Lord Grey's Government and yours, in preserving it unbroken during ten years. And, if now and then it happened that in pursuing a policy which seemed the best for British interests, we thwarted the views of this or that Foreign Power, and rendered them for the moment less friendly, I think I could prove that in every case the object which we were pursuing was of sufficient importance to make it worth our while to submit to such temporary inconvenience. There never was indeed, during those ten years, any real danger of war except on three occasions; and on each of those occasions the course pursued by the British Government prevented war. The first occasion was just after the accession of the King of the French, when Austria, Russia and Prussia were disposed and preparing to attack France, and when the attitude assumed by the British Government prevented a rupture. The second was when England and France united to wrest Antwerp from the Dutch, and to deliver it over to the King of the Belgians. The third occasion was when Mehemet Ali's army occupied Syria, and when he was constantly threatening to declare himself independent and to march on Constantinople. The Treaty of July 1840, proposed and brought about by the British Government, put an end to that danger.

Source: Benson, A. C. and Esher, Viscount (ed.), *The Letters of Queen Victoria* (1908), ii, pp. 67–8.

(d) Questions

1. To whom was this letter written? Of which ten years was Palmerston writing?
2. Which British interests did Palmerston claim to have furthered in this period?
3. Name three other important items which featured in his policy during this period.
4. Do you agree that there 'never was, indeed, during those ten years, any real danger of war except on three ... occasions' mentioned in the extract?
5. Who was the King of the French? Why was he in danger of being attacked by the rulers of Austria, Russia and Prussia?
6. Who had sided with the Dutch in the Belgian affair? When and how had the British aided the Belgians? Why? What benefit did Britain gain from Palmerston's policy towards Belgium?

(e) Further Reading

Chamberlain, M.: *Lord Aberdeen.* Longman (Harlow, 1983).
Chamberlain, M.: *British Foreign Policy in the Age of Palmerston.* Longman (Harlow, 1980).
Gash, N.: *Aristocracy and People, Britain 1815–1865.* Arnold (London, 1983).
Ridley, J.: *Lord Palmerston.* Constable (London, 1970).

(f) Documentary

Joll, J. (ed.): *Britain and Europe: Pitt to Churchill 1789–1940.* Oxford University Press (Oxford, 1967).

(g) Exercises

1. Describe Palmerston's foreign policy between 1830 and 1841.
2. What part did Britain play in the independence movements in Greece and Belgium?
3. What were the aims of Palmerston's policy after 1846? How successful was he?
4. Describe Palmerston's policy towards (i) China, (ii) Austria, (iii) Italy.
5. Do you agree with Palmerston's policies during (i) the Don Pacifico affair, (ii) the American Civil War? Give reasons for your answers.
6. How do you account for the popularity of Palmerston with the British public?
7. Show how each of the following illustrated the principles of Palmerston's foreign policy: (i) Belgium, (ii) the Revolutions of 1848, (iii) Don Pacifico.

Unit Fifteen
The Eastern Question, 1820–56

15.1 What Was the Eastern Question?

There were three facets to the Eastern Question.

(a) Turkish Weakness

In the fifteenth century the Turks had conquered most of what today is called south-eastern Europe, and part of north Africa. From the seventeenth century onwards there was a sharp decline in the ability of the Turks to control their vast Empire. By 1820 this decline had reached such a state that Turkey could already be called the 'sick man of Europe'.

(b) Nationalism

The Christian peoples of the various regions which had been conquered had, at first, submitted to the power of the Turkish sword. By the time that the French Revolution broke out, they already had less respect for their Muslim rulers. The Greeks and the Macedonians, the Slavs and the Bulgars developed the nationalist urge which drove them to rise against their Turkish rulers in an effort to establish their own nation states, free from Turkish control.

(c) The Interests of the Big Powers

If Turkey was the 'sick man of Europe' and if that man was to die, the question was, 'Who or what was going to take his place?' Russia looked at the Turkish Empire and saw a chance to gain economic, political and military advantages for herself in territories which belonged to Turkey. In particular Russia was anxious to gain an outlet to the Mediterranean Sea which required that she had freedom of movement through the Straits, for her navy as well as for her merchant shipping.

The British, who had begun to think of the Mediterranean as 'our sea', had a large volume of trade with the Turkish Empire. They saw a threat to that trade and to the Indian Empire, Britain's 'jewel in the crown', in the Russian advance, so it was British policy to thwart Russian ambitions in this area.

France was another of the Great Powers interested in the affairs of Turkey. Was there a chance that France might pick up an Empire in north Africa if the Turks were driven from power?

15.2 1820–41

(a) The Greek Revolt

From 1812 onwards there were uprisings among the Greek subjects of the Turkish Empire under the leadership of the Hypsilanti family. In the 1820s the Greek leaders had won support from the majority of the subject Greeks and the weak Turks were unable to contain the nationalist, Christian uprising. The Turkish Sultan turned to one of his subjects—Mehemet Ali, the Viceroy (administrator) of Egypt—for help against the Greeks. An ambitious and efficient ruler, Mehemet Ali had turned his part of the Turkish Empire into a prosperous and well-run province, hiring French advisers to help him organize his own Egyptian army and navy. It was a sign of the Sultan's weakness that he had to turn to Mehemet Ali. He promised Mehemet Ali that, once the Greek rebellion had been crushed, he could add the province of Syria to Egypt as part of his 'kingdom'.

Mehemet Ali sent part of his army and navy to help his Sultan-ruler to put down the Greek rebels, but the Egyptian fleet was sunk at Navarino (Section 9.8). The Greeks won their independence because Russia and Britain united to force the Turks to concede (Section 9.8). Mehemet Ali returned to Egypt having seen that his Sultan-master was unable to control the Christians in the Balkans, and having taken part in the first stage of the break-up of the once-powerful Turkish Empire.

(b) Unkiar Skelessi, 1833

The Turkish Sultan did not hand over Syria. In 1831 Mehemet Ali declared war on his master, took Syria, and proceeded to march north towards the Turkish capital at Constantinople. The Sultan appealed to the Great Powers for help. Britain was in the throes of the Reform Bill campaign (Section 10.3) and Palmerston did not offer any help. Louis Philippe of France was in no position to undertake foreign adventures so soon after his own accession (Sections 10.2 and 14.2). 'Like a drowning man clutching at a serpent', the Sultan appealed to Russia, knowing, as he must have done, that Russia's long-term aim was the break-up of the Turkish Empire. Russia responded by sending a fleet of warships through the Straits into the eastern Mediterranean, which forced Mehemet Ali to come to terms with Turkey.

In return for this assistance the Russians forced the weak Turks to sign the Treaty of Unkiar Skelessi, by which (i) Russia was acknowledged as the Protector of Turkey, (ii) Turkey agreed to allow Russian warships complete freedom to use the Dardanelles so that Russian ships could get from their bases in the Black Sea into the Mediterranean. But only Russian warships were given this right. The Straits remained closed to the warships of other nations, who would thus be prevented from attacking the Russian bases in the event of war.

(c)˙ The Straits Convention, 1841

The news of Unkiar Skelessi alarmed the British. For the first time they realized the threat posed by Russia. In 1839 the Sultan and his subject, Mehemet Ali, again went to war, and this time Palmerston acted quickly to uphold British interests in this vital area. He explained his policy in a letter which he wrote to the Prime Minister on 5 July 1840:

> I have been endeavouring for some months past, with the representatives of Austria, Russia and Prussia, to persuade the French to come in to some plan of arrangement between the Sultan and Mehemet Ali. . . . The British Government now has to decide whether the four Powers, having failed in persuading France to join them, will proceed to accomplish their purpose without the assistance of France. . . . If we decline to go on with the three Powers because France does not join us Russia will withdraw her offers to unit herself with the other Powers for a settlement of the affairs of Turkey; and she will again resume her separate position with respect to those affairs; and you will have the Treaty of Unkiar Skelessi renewed. . . . The result of such a decision will be the division of the Turkish Empire into two separate States, one a dependency of France, and the other a satellite of Russia.
> *Source:* Palmerston's letter to Melbourne (5 July 1840).

If France helped Mehemet Ali then she could expect to have some influence in a larger Egypt. This was one reason for Palmerston's hostility to Louis Philippe (Section 14.3(c)).

Palmerston failed to persuade France to act with the other powers but he did succeed at a London Conference in July 1840 in persuading Russia, Austria and Prussia to act with Britain to impose terms on Mehemet Ali and to help the Sultan to enforce those terms. But Mehemet Ali refused to accept the terms offered because he hoped for French help. As a consequence the British navy bombarded the port of Beirut and the Allied armies defeated Mehemet Ali's army, capturing Acre in November 1840. The prestige of France dropped since she had failed to act, and the danger of French influence was averted. But this still left Palmerston with the problem of Russia and the Treaty of Unkiar Skelessi. In July 1841 he arranged the drawing up of the Straits Convention which was signed by Britain, Austria, Prussia, France (now back in line with the other powers), Russia and the Sultan. In this most important Convention the powers affirmed their determination:

> To conform to the ancient rule of the Ottoman Empire, by which the passage of the Straits must always be closed to foreign warships, so long as Turkey is at peace.

Palmerston had undone the Treaty of Unkiar Skelessi and upheld British interests against the French, the Russians and Mehemet Ali.

15.3 Rumours of War, 1841–52

The British Ambassador at Constantinople was Stratford Canning (Viscount Stratford de Redcliffe), a cousin of the great George Canning (Sections 9.7 and 14.1). In the 1830s and 1840s there was no quick method of communication between London and a distant foreign capital such as Constantinople. The attitudes and policies of an Ambassador were therefore more important then than they are today, when he can check with London and be told what his government wishes him to do. In the 1830s and 1840s the Ambassador was, in practice, making British foreign policy.

Czar Nicholas I suggested to Stratford de Redcliffe, and later to the government in London, that they should recognize that Turkey was a sick man, on the verge of collapse. He also suggested that the powers should get together to parcel out the Turkish Empire peacefully, rather than allow it to disintegrate piece by piece as a result of a series of Greek-type revolts or Mehemet Ali-type wars, with the dangers which these had for relations between the powers. These 'sick-man talks' aroused great suspicion in the minds of de Redcliffe and the British government in London.

15.4   The Drift to War, 1853–4

The Turkish Empire contained many places which were of great religious significance to Christians, particularly the Holy Places in Jerusalem. The Turks had permitted Roman Catholic and Orthodox Christians to build churches and temples in Jerusalem and had allowed clergy to live there to minister to the needs of the pilgrims who visited these Holy Places. France, once the leading Catholic country, had acted as guardian to the pilgrims but had allowed this right to lapse; since 1774 Russia, as the leading Orthodox Power, had been allowed to act as protector or guardian of these Holy Places. When Napoleon III became Emperor of France in 1852 (Section 14.3(c)) he wanted to win French Catholic support for his regime (Section 14.4). He thought he could do this by renewing French guardianship of the Catholics in Jerusalem.

In February 1853 the Russians decided to try to clear up this dispute. They invited the Turks to agree that it was Russia who was to be recognized as guardian, not only of the Holy Places, but of all Christians throughout the Turkish Empire. The British government sent de Redcliffe to a meeting with the Turks:

> Your Excellency's Mission at this time is to counsel prudence to the Turks and forbearance to those Powers who are urging her compliance with their demands. You are instructed to use every effort to ward off a Turkish War, and to persuade the Powers interested to look to an amicable termination of existing disputes. . . .
> Source: Clarendon to Stratford de Redcliffe, No. 1 (25 February 1853), F.O. 195/396.

The Turks agreed to Russia's claims to the Holy Places but refused to agree to their wider claims. A British fleet, with a French fleet, was sent to the Dardanelles in June 1853 to indicate to the Russians that the British supported the Turks' position. Russia decided to take military action in pursuit of her claims, in spite of the British support for Turkey. She invaded the Danubian Provinces of Moldavia and Wallachia in June 1853. Palmerston wanted to send the British fleet into the Straits as a sign that Britain was prepared for war. The Cabinet was divided and merely agreed to a conference which, at Vienna, issued a Note inviting France, Russia and Turkey to compromise on the issues involved.

The Turks, influenced by de Redcliffe, refused to accept the terms of the Vienna Note and on 4 October 1853 they declared war on Russia. Still the British did not declare war. But at the end of November 1853 a Russian fleet attacked and destroyed a weak Turkish fleet at Sinope on the Black Sea. *The Times* noted:

> Sinope dispels the hopes we have been led to entertain of pacification. . . . We have thought it our duty to uphold and defend the cause of peace as long as peace was compatible with the honour and dignity of our country . . . but now war has begun in earnest.

Not until January 1854 did the divided Cabinet agree to send the British fleet into the Black Sea, and officially war was not declared until the end of March 1854.

15.5   The Crimean War

The British slipped unwillingly into the Crimean War. They also entered it unprepared for what was to come. On 14 September 1854 they invaded the Crimea with the intention of capturing the Russian naval base at Sebastopol. On 20 September they fought the Battle of the Alma, on 25 October the Battle of Balaclava and on 5 November 1854 the Battle of Inkerman. Not for the first, nor the last time the British army was led by incompetent commanders—'lions led by donkeys'. At the Battle of Balaclava the Charge of the Light

Fig. 15.1 The Battle of Balaclava, 1854: the Charge of the Light Brigade

Brigade took place, the result of a quarrel between two British commanders and a misunderstanding over the orders that had been given.

The army was not only badly led, it was badly supplied because of the lack of a proper and efficient administration. As one soldier wrote:

> December 9th 1854. Our supply of provisions is getting worse and worse all owing to the want of transport from Balaclava . . . our horses are literally starved. The Medical Department is disgracefully neglected . . . hundreds of poor devils died upon the road with no means whatever of assistance; men rolling on the ground with cholera, and not a drop of laudanum for them, nor any means of conveyance. . . .
>
> Source: Windham, Lieut.-General Sir C. A., The Crimean Diary and Letters (1897), pp. 86–7, 90, 98.

One result of this lack of efficient administration was that the army was taken by surprise when the Russian winter set in. The Times reported:

> Winter is setting in upon us. Our army is likely to suffer severely unless instant and most energetic measures be taken to place it in a position to resist the inclemency of the weather. We have no means of getting up the huts—all our army can do is to feed itself. Captain Keen is here in charge of the 4000 tons of wood for hutting, but he cannot get anyone to unload it. As to the 'warm clothing', the very words immediately suggest to us all some extraordinary fatality. Some went down with the ill-fated Prince, some of it has been lost, and now we hear that a ship with clothing has been burnt off Constantinople; that some of it has been saturated in water; and I had an opportunity of seeing several lighters full of warm greatcoats etc. lying in the harbour of Balaclava beneath a determined fall of rain and snow. There was no one to receive them when they were sent to the shore, or rather no one who would receive them without orders.
>
> Source: Russell, W. H., dispatch to The Times (2 January 1855).

Our knowledge of this war is greater than our knowledge of events in previous wars because of the activities of W. H. Russell, who had been sent to the Crimea to report the war for The Times. Russell was the first of a long line of war correspondents. His reports did a great deal to rouse public anger against the government and the army administration.

Florence Nightingale was another person who played a large part in forming public opinion. She had been appalled at the reports of the lack of medical services in the Crimea. She got together a group of nuns and other women who had nursing experience and went to Scutari where she challenged the army's attitude towards the sick and wounded. Her hospital at Scutari was the first efficient military hospital, in which men did not die of infected wounds or one of the many fevers which had swept through the insanitary and unorganized hospitals of the past.

15.6   The Peace of Paris, 1856

Russell's reports, Florence Nightingale's activities and the failure of the army to capture Sebastopol from the Russians—whom the British had both feared

Fig. 15.2 The British hospital at Scutari.

and despised—led to a demand for a change of government. In February 1855 the Queen was forced to send for Palmerston who had the support of a majority of MPs, a wide following in the country and was friendly towards Napoleon III (Section 14.3(*c*)). Palmerston was anxious to bring the war to an end once Sebastopol had been captured, in September 1855, and the accession of a new Czar, Alexander II, gave the Russians a chance to accept the offer of a peace.

In March 1856 the Treaty of Paris was signed between Britain, Russia, Turkey, France and the Italian state of Piedmont. (Piedmont had sent a small army to help the Allies, in order to draw British and French attention to her claims to be regarded as the centre of Italian nationalism.) The treaty had four main sections.

(*a*) The Black Sea Clauses

These revised the Straits Convention of 1841 'in the interests of the balance of power in Europe'. In effect these clauses neutralized the Black Sea since the Russians were forbidden to have any military or naval fortifications on it. Britain had achieved its main object, which was to hold back Russian advances in this area. However, when Russia—with German support—decided to ignore the Black Sea Clauses in 1870 and to erect fortifications there, Britain—under Gladstone—did nothing about it (Section 19.5).

(b) The Principalities

The treaty promised European guarantees to the independent principalities of Moldavia and Wallachia, which Russia had invaded in 1853 and which she might well have claimed if she had won the war. In 1861 the two principalities united to form the independent kingdom of Roumania, and Turkey had lost another part of its Empire.

(c) The Danube

The treaty decided that the River Danube should come under international control.

(d) Turkish Integrity

Russia had to give up her claim to be the Protector of the Christians living in Turkey. Turkey, on the other hand, promised that she would reform her government and administration to make it more efficient, and would treat her Christian subjects in a humane way. In fact, Turkey proved incapable of modernization and her weakness continued to pose a European problem. Turkey also proved unwilling to treat her Christian subjects other than barbarously, and in 1875 the Bulgarian atrocities led to the danger of a fresh Anglo-Russian–Turkish conflict (Sections 22.3 and 22.4).

15.7   The Results of the Crimean War

This costly and pointless war had several major effects on British life.

(a) It confirmed Palmerston as the idol of the nation. He had brought order out of chaos, victory out of stalemate and had halted the hated Russians.

(b) Army administration was submitted to investigation by a Parliamentary Committee, which found:

> The Administration which ordered that expedition had no adequate information as to the amount of force in the Crimea or Sebastopol. They did not foresee the probability of a protracted struggle, they made no provision for a winter campaign. The Administration was the chief cause of the calamities which befell our army.
> *Source:* 5th Report from the Select Committee on the Army before Sebastopol (1855), pp. 22–3.

Army reform followed shortly (Section 19.4).

(c) The Army Medical Service was investigated and condemned by a Select Committee. A more efficient hospital service was organized and Florence Nightingale carried the development of a good nursing service into civilian life.

(d) The British garrison in India was weakened by the withdrawal of troops to serve in the Crimea. This helps to explain why the Indian Mutiny started in 1857 (Section 17.2).

Test Yourself on Unit 15

(a) Document: Disraeli's opinion of Palmerston

Confidential CARLTON CLUB, S.W. Feb. 2, 1855—I was so annoyed and worn out yesterday that I could not send you two lines to say that our chief has again bolted! . . .

What is most annoying is that, this time, we had actually the Court with us, for the two Court favourites, Aberdeen (of the Queen) was extinct, and Newcastle (of the Prince) in a hopeless condition, and our rivals were Johnny in disgrace and Palmerston ever detested. The last, however, seems now the inevitable man; and although he is really an impostor, utterly exhausted, and at the best only ginger-beer, and not champagne, and now an old painted pantaloon, very deaf, very blind, and with false teeth, which would fall out of his mouth when speaking, if he did not hesitate and halt so in his talk, here is a man which the country resolves to associate with energy, wisdom and eloquence, and will until he has tried and failed.

(b) Questions

1. Who was 'our chief'? (Section 14.4(a))
2. What office had the writer held in 1852?
3. Why, in 1855, was Aberdeen 'extinct'?
4. Who was rival 'Johnny in disgrace'? What office had he held most recently?
5. When did the writer become Prime Minister?
6. When did Palmerston become Prime Minister again? When did he resign?

(c) Further Reading

Chamberlain, M.: *Lord Aberdeen*. Longman (Harlow, 1983).
Chamberlain, M.: *British Foreign Policy in the Age of Palmerston*. Longman (Harlow, 1980).
Grenville, J. A. S.: *Europe Reshaped 1848–1878*. Fontana (London, 1976).
Ridley, J.: *Lord Palmerston*. Constable (London, 1970).
Woodham-Smith, C.: *The Reason Why*. Penguin (Harmondsworth, 1958).

(d) Documentary

Joll, J. (ed.): *Britain and Europe: Pitt to Churchill 1789–1940*. Oxford University Press (Oxford, 1967).

(e) Exercises

1. What part did Britain play in the Eastern Question from 1830 to 1841?
2. What were the causes of the Crimean War? What were the main effects of this war for Britain?
3. Write briefly about: (i) Mehemet Ali, (ii) the Treaty of Unkiar Skelessi, (iii) the Straits Convention; (iv) the Battle of Sinope, (v) Russell of *The Times*.
4. 'Britain's entry into the Crimean War was forced on her by Russian aggression.' Is this an adequate explanation of Britain's action?

Ireland, 1760–1850

16.1   Irish Grievances

(a)   The Political Scene

While the British government was concentrating on the American War of Independence (Section 3.5), an Irish politician named Henry Grattan was leading a movement which forced the British Parliament to grant independence to the Irish Parliament in Dublin in 1782. Previously the Irish Parliament had been obliged to pass any laws which had already been passed through the London Parliament and, on the other hand, had to submit its own decisions for approval by the London Parliament. This, obviously, was a mockery of independence. Grattan's campaign ended with the removal of these limitations on the independence of the Irish Parliament.

For many Irishmen even this 'independence' was a mockery because no Catholic was allowed to stand for Parliament or vote in elections, even though about three-quarters of the Irish population were Catholic. Catholics resented this limitation on their freedom, this example of religious intolerance, and they had the support of some radical Protestants who believed in religious equality and tolerance.

Many Irish Protestants resented the way in which their Irish Parliament continued to be controlled by the English, even after 1782. The Queen's representative in Ireland was the Lord Lieutenant, who lived in Phoenix Park, Dublin, and had his administrative headquarters at Dublin Castle. From either or both of these centres he used his influence to persuade Irish MPs to vote as the British government wished. MPs would be invited to functions, awarded contracts, offered titles, promised posts for their relatives—provided they voted 'in the English way'.

(b)   The Economic Scene

Ireland was predominantly an agricultural country, as was England until the 1830s or 1840s. But the British government insisted that there should be no industrial development in Ireland which might provide a challenge to a similar development in England. Thus the Irish were forbidden to start up a woollen industry and even their native linen industry's development was controlled by a jealous London government. Protestant merchants resented this interference with their freedom to use their money and ingenuity as they wished.

(c) **The Religious Scene**

Three-quarters of the Irish people were Catholics. From the end of the seventeenth century Catholics had suffered from a set of Penal Laws described by the Protestant writer, Edmund Burke (Section 5.2), as 'well fitted for the oppression, impoverishment and degradation of a people as ever proceeded from the perverted ingenuity of man'. No Catholic could legally practise his faith, educate his children, vote, own land or get a job in the civil service or the army. Irish Catholics were obliged to hand over a portion of their produce as a tithe, or church tax, to the Protestant church.

(d) **The Agricultural Scene**

The land problem was even more serious. Ireland had been divided up into huge estates which had been handed over to English and Scottish supporters of the Protestant Kings of England in their struggles with the Catholic Church and Catholic monarchs in the sixteenth and seventeenth centuries. Most of these landlords did not live in Ireland. As absentee landlords they employed agents to rent their land to Irishmen who became 'tenants at will', that is, they had no security of tenure but could be legally evicted from their farms as soon

Fig. 16.1 The interior of an Irish peasant's cabin-home, a single-roomed hut shared by humans and animals

as they were in arrears with their rents. There was always a great demand for land after 1780 because of the population explosion. Landlords and their agents could push up rents, evict tenants who could not pay and allow others to try their luck on the farm of the now evicted, homeless, penniless and wandering peasant.

16.2   The French Revolution and Ireland

In 1790 a Belfast lawyer, Wolfe Tone, founded the Society of United Irishmen. He hoped that Irishmen would sink their religious differences and unite to force England to give Ireland complete freedom. Although Tone was a Protestant he declared that the repeal of all anti-Catholic laws was an essential part of his campaign. In 1792 the Irish Parliament softened some of the laws against Catholics. They were allowed to run their own schools, send their children abroad for higher education and become lawyers. One who benefited from this change was Daniel O'Connell, as we shall see in Section 16.4. In 1793 Catholics were allowed to vote in Parliamentary elections, but they could not stand as candidates in these elections.

All these concessions were too little and too late for Tone and his allies. In 1796 Tone went to Paris to ask the Revolutionary government to send help in the event of an Irish revolution. But there were divisions within Ireland too. In Ulster the Protestants formed gangs known as 'Peep o' Day boys' whose aim was to attack the Catholics as a means of safeguarding the Protestant cause. After one battle between the Protestants and a Catholic gang called the Defenders, the Protestants formed the Orange Society to help maintain the Protestant supremacy.

In December 1796 a French fleet commanded by General Hoche set out for Ireland, but only sixteen of the forty-three ships reached Bantry Bay: strong winds made a landing impossible so the French sailed away. The English government sent an army under General Lake to restore order in Ulster and to search out arms, leaders of gangs and other trouble-makers. In May 1798 the Irish rose in an abortive rebellion. They had some success in the south-east, capturing the towns of Wexford and Enniscorthy for a few weeks before General Lake defeated them at Vinegar Hill, near Enniscorthy. Shortly before the rising collapsed two French expeditions reached Ireland. One, under Humbert, landed at Killala Bay, County Mayo in August 1798, but it was soon forced to surrender to the army led by Lord Cornwallis. The second expedition arrived at Lough Swilly where an English naval squadron forced it to surrender. Among the prisoners was Tone, who committed suicide while awaiting execution.

16.3   The Act of Union

Pitt believed that Ireland could not be allowed the luxury of an independent Parliament because it might cut the ties with England and make Ireland a base

Fig. 16.2 Following the arrest of Lord Edward Fitzgerald, rebellion broke out in various places and without a central plan. The Cruikshank drawing illustrates the destructive nature of the Irish rebels and helped to rouse English fears

from which an enemy, such as Revolutionary France, might attack. By using various pressures, bribes and offers of peerages, Pitt, Cornwallis (the Lord Lieutenant) and Castlereagh (the Chief Secretary) persuaded the Irish Parliament to agree to its own abolition.

(a) Terms of the Act of Union

In August 1800 the King signed the Act of Union, which came into force on 1 January 1801. Its main terms were:

(i) Ireland was to be joined with Great Britain into a single kingdom, 'the United Kingdom of Great Britain and Ireland'.

(ii) The Dublin Parliament was to be abolished. Ireland was to be represented at Westminster by 100 Irish members in the House of Commons, and by 4 Spiritual and 28 Temporal Peers in the House of Lords.

(iii) The Anglican Church was to be recognized as the official Church of Ireland.

(iv) There was to be free trade between the two countries.

(v) Ireland was to keep a separate Exchequer and to be responsible for two-seventeenths of the general expenses of the United Kingdom.

Pitt had intended to grant Catholics their political freedom in the new

United Kingdom, where they would be a minority and not, as in an independent Ireland, a threat to Protestant supremacy. King George III refused to allow the passing of such a law, however. He wrote to Pitt:

> A sense of religious as well as political duty has made me consider the Oath that the wisdom of our forefathers has enjoined the Kings of this realm to take at their Coronation, and with taking the Sacrament, as so binding a religious obligation to me to maintain the maxims on which our Constitution is placed, namely the Church of England being the established one, and that those who hold employment in the State must be members of it, and consequently obliged not only to take oaths against Popery, but to receive the Holy Communion agreeably to the rites of the Church of England.
>
> *Source:* George III, in a communication to Pitt (February 1801).

Pitt had promised that the Catholics would be given their freedom once Ireland was joined to Great Britain to form the United Kingdom. He was unable to keep that promise because of George III's obstinacy and so, as he was a man of principle, Pitt resigned from office (Section 5.7(*b*)).

(*b*) Catholic Disappointment

Catholics were still not allowed to sit in Parliament and the English landlord still 'owned' Ireland: the Protestant supremacy was now firmer than ever. Grattan, a member of the London Parliament after 1805, demanded Catholic Emancipation, but the position had not changed when he died in 1820.

16.4   Daniel O'Connell and Catholic Emancipation

The Catholic cause was then taken up by a Catholic lawyer, Daniel O'Connell, who roused Catholic support with speeches such as this one, which he made at Limerick in 1812:

> The principles of Pitt's Administration was despotism—the principle of Perceval's Administration bigotry. The principle of the present Administration is still more obvious. It consists in Falsehood! Some of this Ministry pretend to be our friends. You know it is not true—they are only our worse enemies for the hypocrisy. They declare that the Catholic Question is no longer opposed by the Cabinet—the fact is otherwise—and their retainers are carefully advised to vote against us.
>
> The Minister, Lord Castlereagh, is reported to have said in the House of Commons, that in the years 1797 and 1798 there was no torture in Ireland. What—no torture! Great God! no torture!! Within the walls of your city, was there no torture? Could not Colonel Vereker have informed Lord Castlereagh, that the lash resounded in the streets, even of LIMERICK, and that the human groan assailed the wearied ear of humanity.
>
> In Dublin there were for weeks, three permanent triangles, constantly supplied with the victims of a promiscuous choice, made by the Army, the Yeomanry, the Police Constables, and the Orange Lodges—and that, along by the gate of the Castle yard a

human being, naked, tarred, feathered, with one ear cut off, and the blood streaming from his lacerated back, has been hunted by a troop of barbarians!!

Source: Counsellor O'Connell's speech at the Limerick Aggregate Catholic meeting on Friday, 24 July 1812 (Dublin 1812).

(a) The Catholic Association

O'Connell had seen that the English could not be beaten by an Irish rising; the failure of Tone had shown this. He decided to organize the Catholic peasantry into a peaceful force which, he believed, could be used to force the English to listen to Catholic demands. In 1823 he formed the Catholic Association to which people were invited to contribute 1d (½p) per month. O'Connell persuaded the Catholic clergy to side with him, to allow him to use the parish churches as centres where his agents could collect the Catholic Rent (as he called the 1d) and recruit new members for his Association. The Association was banned by Parliament in 1825.

(b) Catholic Emancipation

In 1828 O'Connell stood as a candidate in the County Clare by-election and, not surprisingly, he won—the majority of voters were Catholics and probably members of his Association—but, as the law stood, he could not enter

Fig. 16.3 *O'Connell (in lawyer's wig) and the Pope, taking their pickings from the pudding while Wellington and Peel wait on them*

Parliament. Feelings ran high in Ireland, as was shown in the letter which Lord Anglesey wrote:

> Such is the extraordinary power of the agitators, that I am quite certain they could lead on the people to open rebellion at a moment's notice, and their organization is such, that in the hands of desperate and intelligent leaders, they would be extremely formidable. . . . I believe their success inevitable—that no power under heaven can arrest its progress. There may be rebellion, you may put to death thousands, you may suppress it, but it will only put off the day of compromise.
>
> I see no possible solution but by depriving the demagogues of the power of directing people. By taking Messrs. O'Connell, Sheil and the rest of them from the Association, and placing them in the House of Commons, this desirable object would be at once accomplished.
>
> *Source:* Lord Anglesey to Lord Gower (2 July 1828).

There was a great deal of wisdom in the final lines of this letter. The Prime Minister, Wellington, and Peel, the Home Secretary, agreed with it and in 1829 they persuaded Parliament to repeal the seventeenth-century laws against Catholics and so emancipate them (Section 8.5).

16.5   The Repeal Movement, 1830–43

O'Connell had won only a partial victory with Catholic Emancipation. His main aim was the repeal of the Act of Union so that Ireland would have its own national, free Parliament. He is reported as having said in the House of Commons:

> The House must know that there was not a man in Ireland who did not know what benefits she would derive from her national independence. He prophesied not what might be the results of the continuance of the Union, but he believed them to be essentially dangerous. He valued highly the British connexion with Ireland: he could tell the advantages of an Irish Parliament; he could not tell any good which would arise from the separation of the two countries. No man could be an advocate for the separation of the two countries. He proposed the federal continuation of the connexion, so that the two countries should be a protection to each other—that as Ireland required to export linen, England should export manufactures to Ireland. He proposed, and it was one of his objects, the restoration of the Irish Parliament.
>
> *Source:* Repeal of the Union, Report of the Debate in the House of Commons on Mr O'Connell's motion April 1834 (London 1834).

(a) The Whigs and O'Connell

In November 1834 King William IV dismissed the Whig government led by Melbourne and invited Peel to form a government. In spite of the promises contained in the Tamworth Manifesto (Section 12.2), Peel failed to win a majority at the general election of December 1834 although he continued to head the government until April 1835 (Section 11.8). His fall was due, in part, to the Lichfield House Compact, the name given to an agreement which was

reached between Lord John Russell and the Whigs on the one hand, and
O'Connell and his followers on the other. The Irish promised to vote for the
Whigs in the Commons, hoping that a Whig government would do something
for Ireland.

The Whigs drove Peel from power in April 1835 and Melbourne became
Prime Minister (Section 11.1). To please their Nonconformist supporters, the
Whigs passed a series of Acts which were also welcomed by O'Connell and the
Irish. In 1836 they abolished the law which had compelled Catholics to
pay tithes to the Anglican Church, and passed the Marriage Act which
allowed Nonconformists and Catholics to be married in their own churches.
However, the Whigs did nothing to indicate that they were going to help
O'Connell achieve his great aim of Repeal.

(b) Peel and O'Connell, 1841–6

(i) **The Maynooth Grant.** Peel became Prime Minister in 1841. He had shown
a willingness to listen to an argument, to be persuaded to change his mind if
events showed that a change was required, so O'Connell hoped to show Peel
that the Union should be repealed. Peel, however, was the leader of a party in
which the Anglican Church was very influential. Indeed, the Anglican Church
has been described as 'the Tory Party at prayer'. Peel wanted to maintain the
Union of England and Ireland. He hoped that the Irish Catholics could be
bought off by less serious concessions than Repeal. One such concession was
an increased grant which he proposed for the Catholic College at Maynooth,
where the majority of Irish priests were trained. He hoped this would please
the Catholics, but he failed to see how such a move would anger the English.
The *Morning Chronicle* reported:

> The great body of the Roman Catholic priests have gone into the movement in the
> rebellious sense. Priests of the old school held out for a time but the young priests
> brought up at Maynooth have gone into it almost to a man. Some, more heady than
> the rest, even lead their flocks to battle. The priests have given to the repeal
> movement all the weight of a religious cause in the eyes of a superstitious people.
> *Source: The Morning Chronicle* (October 1843).

But Peel increased the grant from £9 000 to £26 000, in spite of this opposition,
and he also set up three university colleges in Ireland in 1845.

(ii) **O'Connell's arrest.** Meanwhile O'Connell toured Ireland addressing mass
meetings. At Mulingar he said:

> My first object is to get Ireland for the Irish (loud cheers). What numberless advan-
> tages would not the Irish enjoy if they possessed their own country? A domestic
> parliament would encourage Irish manufactures. The linen trade, and the woollen
> would be spreading amongst you. An Irish parliament would foster Irish commerce,
> and protect Irish agriculture. . . .
> *Source: The Nation* (20 May 1843).

But the Peel government arrested O'Connell, charging him with stirring up rebellion. At his trial O'Connell declared:

> There is another matter in my life—my opposition to the Chartists. When the repeal association was in full force the Chartists were in insurrection in England. I kept the Irish from joining them. The very moment a Chartist subscribed to the funds of the association his money was handed back to him, and his name struck off our list. Now, if my object was popular insurrection, good heaven! would not any man in my situation have wished to have strength?
>
> *Source:* The Liberator's Defence, in a Special Report of the Proceedings against Daniel O'Connell MP on an indictment for conspiracy (Dublin, 1844).

O'Connell was found guilty and sentenced to a year's imprisonment, although the House of Lords quashed the sentence. O'Connell was freed but he was a sick and broken man, and he died on his way to Rome on 15 May 1847.

(c) The Irish Radicals

Younger, more radical supporters of Irish freedom had already decided that O'Connell's peaceful approach was the wrong one. Lord Anglesey's advice might well have been followed by Peel in the 1840s (Section 16.4(b)). If O'Connell's moderate demands had been met, perhaps there would have been no Irish problem for Gladstone—and ourselves—to meet. But the rejection of the moderate allowed the emergence of the more violent.

O'Connell was denounced by the *Young Irelanders* such as John Mitchell, who believed that Ireland should have its 1848 revolution, like France and other countries (Section 14.3). When this rising failed and the leaders of Young Ireland had been shot or exiled, a new and even more violent movement arose. The *Fenians* had their origins in America where millions of Irish exiles made their homes after the famine of the 1840s. In the 1850s Irishmen joined the Fenians after swearing:

> I, A.B., do solemnly swear, in the presence of Almighty God, that I will do my utmost, at any risk, while life lasts, to make Ireland an Independent Democratic Republic; that I will yield implicit obedience, in all things not contrary to the law of God, to the commands of my superior officers; and that I shall preserve inviolable secrecy regarding all transactions of the secret society that may be confided to me. So help me God! Amen.
>
> *Source:* O'Leary, J., *Recollections of Fenians and Fenianism* (1896).

Perhaps Ireland was on the verge of a bloody uprising?

16.6   The Famine

The 1841 census stated that just under nine million people lived in Ireland, about half of whose homes were 'windowless mud cabins of a single room'. They scraped a living from the small plots which the agents of absentee landlords allowed them to rent. They paid the rent from the money they obtained selling potatoes, which was the easiest and most profitable crop to grow on their small plots.

In 1845 a fungus, which had previously appeared in England, attacked the Irish potato crop. Within six months the majority of the Irish peasants were starving and without money. They were unable to pay their rent and were evicted from their 'homes'. Landlords and their agents called in the army and police to help them enforce the law. Famine brought other epidemics, mainly cholera and typhus. By the time of the 1851 census over one million Irish people had died and another two million had emigrated—most of them to America—taking with them a bitter hatred of Britain.

Fig. 16.4 One of the many hundreds of ships which carried Irish emigrants to England, Australia and, above all, America

Peel's response to the famine was the Repeal of the Corn Laws (Section 13.6) which was ironic since there was no shortage of corn in Ireland at the time. Indeed, emigrants walking to the nearest port saw a stream of waggons and carts carrying Irish corn on its way to the English market. The starving Irish, who could not afford even the cheap potato and the rent of a hovel, were quite unable to buy the relatively expensive wheat and other grains that were grown on Irish estates by English landowners. So Irish corn was sold in the prosperous English market.

Test Yourself on Unit 16

(a) Documents

(i) An English view of O'Connell

The County of Carlow was in a state of profound tranquillity, until the month of May last [1841], when it was first announced that a dissolution of Parliament would take place without delay. Mr O'Connell put his beloved son Daniel in nomination as a candidate and he followed up the announcement by taking the field himself five weeks before the election, and in his train were Messrs. Thomas Steele, Thomas Reynolds, William John O'Connell, and other notorious agitators. Mr O'Connell proceeded to every village in the county, denouncing Colonel Bruen as a man 'unfit to live in such a country as Ireland', and exciting the people to madness by telling them that the struggle for their liberation was about to take place. ... The population could not at first be induced to proclaim war to the knife. He was obliged to resort to the population of other counties, which were organized by their priests at their respective chapels, and he obtained that force, consisting of thousands well armed with pikes, scythes, and bludgeons, that invaded the county Carlow, both by day and night, committing murderous outrages, breaking into houses, and forcibly carrying away voters, tied on cars like malefactors, and spreading terror throughout the country.
Source: The Reign of Terror in Carlow (1841).

(ii) An Irish view of O'Connell

But the noblest instance of his moderation is furnished by his constant denunciations of rebellion. O'Connell has uniformly warned the people against appealing to arms; he exhibited at all times an almost Quaker detestation of force. Perhaps no higher tribute has ever been paid him than that of Mr Mitchell, who declared that next to the British Government, he regarded O'Connell as the greatest enemy of Ireland; for it was altogether owing to his eloquence that the Irish people could not be induced to follow the revolutionary movement of 1848.
Source: Lecky, W. E. H., *The Leaders of Public Opinion in Ireland* (1861).

(b) Questions

1. Who was Prime Minister after the election referred to in the first extract? What did he do for Ireland between 1841 and 1846?
2. What was meant by 'their liberation'? Who led the struggle in (i) the 1790s, (ii) the 1880s, (iii) in 1910? Which English Prime Minister was the first to recognize the need for this liberation?
3. What evidence is there that O'Connell was supported by the Catholic Church? How had the Church helped him in the 1820s? Why had this caused some Protestants to oppose Peel's policy on Maynooth?
4. What is the main difference between the opinions of O'Connell expressed in these extracts? How do you account for the difference? Why is this difference a warning to students of history?
5. Where did 'revolutionary movements' break out in 1848? Why, according to Lecky, did Ireland not experience an 1848 Revolution? Who was Mitchell?

(c) Further Reading

Beckett, J. C.: *The Making of Modern Ireland 1603–1923.* Faber (London, 1981).

Gash, N.: *Peel*. Longman (Harlow, 1976).
O'Farrell, P.: *England and Ireland since 1800*. Oxford University Press (Oxford, 1975).
The Hungry Forties. Historical Association pamphlet.

(d) Exercises

1. What were the main grievances of the Irish in 1783? How far had these been removed by 1850?
2. Account for (i) the Irish rising of 1798 and (ii) its failure.
3. Give an account of the career of Daniel O'Connell.
4. Give an account of Peel's Irish policy in (i) the 1820s, (ii) the 1840s.
5. Write briefly about (i) the United Irishmen, (ii) the Act of Union, (iii) the Clare election, 1828, (iv) O'Connell's monster meetings 1842–3, (v) Young Ireland.

Unit Seventeen
The Empire, 1760–1860

17.1 India

(a) The East India Company

By 1700 a British company called the East India Company had set up a number of trading posts in India, where officials and clerks organized trade with the native population. Silk, ivory, spices and cotton were imported into Britain in the famous 'Indiamen' sailing vessels, and shareholders in the company made huge profits from this trade. A French East India Company had been formed in 1664 and from 1741 the British and French companies struggled for power in India.

Both the British and the French companies provided aid to various native princes who were anxious to set themselves up as independent rulers. Each of the rival companies hoped that their particular prince would give them the sole right to trade in his new kingdom. The British and French fought a series of wars between 1741 and 1763, and in the Treaty of Paris (1763) (Section 2.3), British supremacy was established. The defeated French were allowed to retain trading posts only at Pondicherry, Mahé and Chandernagore. The British company controlled the provinces of the Carnatic (with its capital at Madras) and Bengal (with its capital at Calcutta). In 1764 the native princes in Bengal and Oudh combined to try to throw the British out, but their revolt was crushed and the company extended its influence over the province of Oudh.

We have to remember that these large portions of India were acquired by a trading company and not by the British government. The clerks and other officials of the East India Company had been trained to buy and sell, to run warehouses and offices, to deal with the company's accounts and so on, but not to govern. The British government gradually, and almost reluctantly, took the right to govern vast provinces of India away from the company.

(b) Lord North's Regulating Act, 1773

In 1773 the British government took the first step along the road to government control of India, and decided to set up a system whereby it supervised or regulated the work of the East India Company, but did not take power for itself. The terms of the Regulating Act were:

(i) The company had to appoint an official who would be Governor-General of all the districts controlled by the company.

(ii) The British government appointed a council of four men who were to advise and control the Governor-General.

(iii) British judges were to be sent to India to administer the legal system.

Warren Hastings was the first Governor-General to be appointed. He had been employed by the company before this and in 1772 had become Governor of Bengal, so that he had a good deal of experience of Indian affairs. However, after 1774, he was in a very difficult position. His council of four came out to India convinced that all East India Company officials were dishonest and inefficient. They tried to undo all that Hastings had done and later they organized his impeachment. However, before that happened, and in spite of the council's opposition, Hastings had achieved a good deal. He established a civil service, dismissed native tax-collectors and appointed British collectors who were strictly forbidden to take bribes. He sent a British army across India to Bombay to fight the first Mahratta War against the Mahratta tribes of central India. These warlike tribes had been persuaded by the French that Britain would be unable to take firm action against them because of her involvement in the War of American Independence (Section 3.5). Hastings's firm action saved Bombay and extended the influence of the company in the western provinces. In 1780 the King of Mysore, Hyder Ali, attacked the Carnatic. Hastings sent Sir Eyre Coote and a British army to defend it and in 1781 Coote defeated Hyder Ali at Porto Novo, so saving Madras and the Carnatic.

(c) Hastings and the Expansion of British Influence

The ruler of Oudh had made a treaty with the company which, in return for the right to trade in his province, agreed to help him maintain law and order. He asked for Hastings's help when his female relations, the Begums of Oudh, refused to hand over the jewels and other treasure which they had seized and wished to hold on to. Hastings sent a force to invade the palaces where these princesses lived and to seize the treasure. When the treasure had been captured, it was handed over to the ruler of Oudh. One of the charges brought against Hastings at his impeachment trial in 1788 was that he accepted rewards for this and similar actions.

(d) Pitt's India Act, 1784

One of the council of four was Philip Francis, the leader of the campaign against Hastings. In 1780 he returned to Britain and persuaded politicians that the company and its officials were behaving dishonestly and tyrannically. In 1785 Hastings was recalled and tried before the House of Lords. The trial lasted from 1788 to 1795, and Hastings was finally found innocent of all the charges that were brought against him, a small consolation after such a long, expensive and bitter trial. However, Francis's campaign had one good effect in that it led to the passing of Pitt's India Act in 1784. In this the British government took another step along the road to control of India. The Act said that:

(i) The work of trading had to be separated from the work of ruling India.

(ii) To control the work of ruling India the government, via a Board of Control, should appoint a Governor-General and other important officials.

(iii) The Governor-General had the power to over-rule his council.

(e) The Marquess of Wellesley

The Marquess of Wellesley was Governor-General from 1798 to 1805, and he extended British power.

(i) He concluded alliances with the weaker native rulers; the company made itself responsible for the defence of the state, and gained control of the province's trade.

(ii) He attacked and defeated Tipoo of Mysore, annexing lands on both east and west coasts and appointing a puppet prince to rule the rest of Mysore.

(iii) He forced the Nizam (or ruler) of Hyderabad to dismiss his army and submit to an alliance with the British.

(iv) He conquered the whole of the Carnatic on the east coast and large areas around Bombay on the west coast.

(v) He attacked the Mahrattas. The future Duke of Wellington, Arthur Wellesley, brother of the Governor-General, led the British armies against the Mahrattas and won a notable victory at Assaye in 1803.

(f) Marquess of Hastings

The Marquess of Hastings was appointed Governor-General in 1813 and continued Wellesley's work of extending British power. He completed the destruction of the Mahrattas, annexed Poona and forced the Hindu chiefs to submit, and captured Nepal. By 1823 all India was directly or indirectly under British control. In 1823 Britain began her attack on Burma and in 1839 she tried to impose a puppet king on Afghanistan. In 1843 Britain conquered Sind and took control of the southern route to India, and in 1849 Britain annexed the Punjab, thereby controlling the northern route into India via the Khyber Pass.

(g) Bentinck, 1828–35

With British power firmly established over the whole of India, various Governors-General tried to introduce reforms into the vast sub-continent. Following Hastings's promise of 'enlightening her temporary subjects', Lord William Bentinck suppressed one religious sect called *thuggees* who, in the name of religion, robbed and murdered travellers along the long and dusty roads. He also abolished the practice of *suttee*, by which the widows of deceased Hindus burned themselves to death on the fire which was cremating their husband's body.

Bentinck also introduced the English educational system into India, so that the company and the government would be able to recruit Indians on to their staffs. He decided that Indians should be admitted into the lower ranks of the Indian civil service, where they could gain the experience they would need later on to govern themselves.

(h) Dalhousie

Lord Dalhousie was Governor-General from 1848 to 1856. He annoyed some of the native rulers by seizing their territories when he believed that they were being misgoverned. He also annoyed influential Indians by inventing *the doctrine of lapse* under which he took over a province if the ruler died without having left any blood heir to the throne. In this way Dalhousie succeeded in gaining seven states for the British, and he deposed the ruler of Oudh and seized that territory.

On 29 February 1856 he wrote to the Queen:

Government House 29th February 1856
Lord Dalhousie presents his most humble duty to your Majesty.

The guns are announcing from the ramparts of Fort William that Lord Canning has arrived. In an hour's time he will have assumed the Government of India. Lord Dalhousie will transfer it to him in a state of perfect tranquillity. There is peace, within and without. Lord Dalhousie is able to declare, within reservation, that he knows of no quarter in which it is probable that trouble will arise. . . .

Source: Benson, A. C. and Esher, Viscount (ed.), *The Letters of Queen Victoria* (1908), iii, p. 179.

17.2   The Indian Mutiny

Dalhousie's optimism was misplaced because, within a year, India was the centre of a mutiny in which native troops and civilians combined to slaughter thousands of Europeans. The British took a different view of their Indian subjects after this.

(a) Causes of the Mutiny

(i) **The Centenary of Plassey.** In 1757 Robert Clive had won a great victory over the forces of the ruler of Bengal, Surrajah Dowlah. Dowlah had been responsible for the infamous Black Hole of Calcutta in which 123 Europeans had died of suffocation. In 1856 and 1857 agitators went among the superstitious natives of India telling them that Dowlah would return in 1857 to lead another attack on the Europeans, who had deposed the Indian rulers, taken power for themselves, and were taking great wealth out of their country.

(ii) **The Indian Army.** There were few British troops in India, for the British government did not believe in spending money on a large army except in time of war. The result was that a large proportion of the British army in India

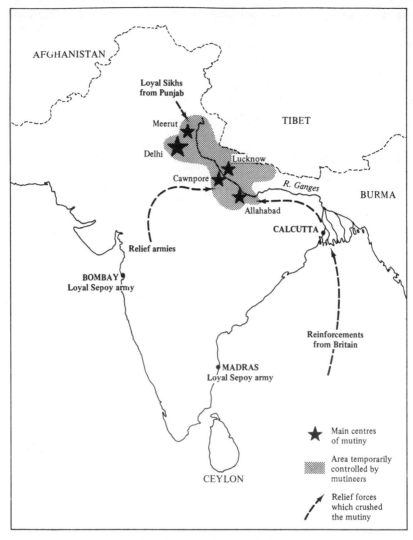

Fig. 17.1 The Indian Mutiny

consisted of native troops or *Sepoys*, who resented some of the reforms which had been brought in by westernizing Governors-General. They shared this resentment with many other Indians who were not in the army, but the Sepoys particularly resented the fact that they had been sent abroad to fight—in Burma, for example. Such travel offended against the caste system, so important to the Hindu majority of India, and they also objected to the way in which they were forced to travel by railway, where there was no provision for the different castes. Troops were simply bundled into carriages or wagons under the orders of British officers, who did not understand the religious significance of separation of the castes.

In 1856 the British government ordered thousands of British soldiers to travel from India to fight in the Crimea (Sections 15.5 and 15.7). This further depleted the strength of the British in the Indian army and increased the proportion of Indians. Under the leadership of political and religious agitators, some of the Sepoys rebelled.

(*iii*) **Religion.** The Sepoys received a good deal of support from a native population which had been led to believe that British rule would ultimately lead to the suppression of the Hindu and Muslim religions. The British had, said the propagandists, overthrown powerful rulers of other thrones and brought in new inventions, such as the telegraph and the railway. What was to stop them bringing in their own religion and forcing this on the native people? They had, said the agitators, gone ahead with the westernizing of India with an educational system, an army, a civil service and so on. What was to stop them continuing this process by forcing everyone into their Christian church?

(*iv*) **The cartridges.** Then the British gave the agitators their greatest provocation. A new Enfield rifle was introduced into the Indian army, and the user had to bite the ends off the cartridges before inserting them into the rifle. These cartridges were greased with animal fat. The agitators told the Hindus that the fat

Fig. 17.2 The destruction of a bungalow at Meerut during the Indian Mutiny, 1857

came from the cow—a sacred animal to them—while they told the Muslims that the fat came from the pig—which Muslims regard as an unclean animal.

(b) Centres of the Mutiny

The first uprising took place near Calcutta, but the major uprising broke out at Meerut. From there the Sepoys advanced on Delhi and proclaimed the restoration of their own Mogul Empire. Nana Sahib, a Mahratta chief, led a savage massacre of the English population at Cawnpore and captured Lucknow for a time. It was recaptured by General Havelock who, in turn, was besieged until he was saved by the advance of Sir Colin Campbell.

The worst outrages took place at Cawnpore from where one of Havelock's officers reported:

> I was directed to the house where all the poor miserable ladies had been murdered. I never was more horrified. The place was one mass of blood. I am not exaggerating when I tell you that the soles of my boots were more than covered with the blood of these poor wretched creatures. Portions of their dresses, collars, children's socks, and ladies' round hats lay about, saturated with their blood; and in the sword-cuts in the wooden pillars of the room long dark hair was carried by the edge of the weapon, and there hung their tresses—a most painful sight! I have often wished since that I had never been there, but sometimes wish that every soldier was taken there that he might witness the barbarities our poor countrywomen had suffered.
> *Source: Annual Register*, cix (History), p. 292.

Fig. 17.3 The Campbells come to the relief of Lucknow: a contemporary sketch by Watson

(c) Clemency Canning

While the mutiny still raged and Lucknow had not been retaken, the Governor-General, Canning, sent orders to the civil servants of the company that they were to refrain from taking revenge on the natives once the mutiny had been firmly put down. He wrote to Queen Victoria:

> One of the greatest difficulties which lie ahead will be the violent rancour of the English community against every Native Indian of every class. Not one man in ten seems to think that the hanging and shooting of forty or fifty thousand mutineers, besides other Rebels, can be otherwise than right; nor does it occur to those who talk and write most upon the matter that to govern India without employing natives, both in civil and military service, is simply impossible.
>
> *Source:* Benson, A. C. and Esher, Viscount (ed.), *The Letters of Queen Victoria* (1908).

(d) After the Mutiny

In 1858 the government passed a Government of India Act which abolished the East India Company and put India firmly under the control of the British government. The Act said:

> I. The Government of the Territories now in the Possession of the East India Company and all Powers in relation to the Government exercised by the said Company shall become vested in Her Majesty.
> III. One of Her Majesty's Principal Secretaries of State shall have such Powers as should have been exercised by the East India Company.
> VII. A Council shall be established to consist of Fifteen Members, and to be styled the Council of India.
> XXIV. The Appointments of Governor General of India shall be made by Her Majesty.
>
> *Source: Statutes at Large,* xxxiv, p. 228.

The government decided to slow up the pace at which reforms had been introduced and to send more British troops to India, and the European officers and officials who had once mixed freely with the Indians now cut themselves off. This helped to build up resentment later on.

17.3   South Africa

In 1815 Britain had acquired the Cape of Good Hope from the Dutch as part of the Treaty of Vienna (Section 9.2). British settlers emigrated to make a new home in territory where Dutch farmers (Boers) had settled in the seventeenth and eighteenth centuries. The Boers owned native slaves who worked their farms for them, and they resented the demands of British missionaries for equality between the races. They also resented the British government's decision that the word of a white man would carry the same weight as the word of a black one in a court of law.

In 1834 the British government passed the Act which abolished slavery in the Empire (Section 11.2(c)). This was, for the Boers, the final straw. In 1836 nearly 5 000 of them left the Cape Province and more followed in the next few years. This movement was known as 'the Great Trek'. They set up new states and eventually, in 1852 and 1854, two of them, the Transvaal and the Orange Free State, were recognized by the British as independent Boer Republics.

17.4 Canada

South Africa was one of the places where British settlers could make a new life. Australia, New Zealand and Canada were other places with climates suitable for British settlement. Canada had been acquired from the French in 1763 (Section 2.3) and after the War of American Independence many people (known as 'Empire Loyalists') had left the American colonies to seek a new life under the British flag in Canada. The English clashed with the older, French Canadians, and in 1791 Pitt passed his Canada Act, which declared:

> His Majesty has been pleased to divide his Province of Quebec into two separate Provinces, to be called Upper Canada and Lower Canada; there shall be within each of the said Provinces a Legislative Council and Assembly and in each of the Provinces His Majesty, His Heirs . . . shall have power with the advice and consent of the Legislative Council and Assembly to make laws.

In both Upper (or English) and Lower (or French) Canada there was a great deal of discontent with the workings of the 1791 Act. The English settlers resented the power of the Governor, who was appointed in London and allowed to over-rule the local assemblies. The Catholic French resented the fact that an English-speaking, Protestant Governor had the right to dictate to them. In 1837 there were rebellions in both provinces which led the Whig government to send Lord Durham to investigate conditions there.

Durham had Gibbon Wakefield and Charles Buller as his two assistants and in 1839, with their help, he produced his report which recommended (i) the union of the two provinces, and (ii) the grant to Canada of responsible government so that the ministers should be responsible to a Canadian Parliament, just as the British Cabinet is responsible to the British Parliament. Durham wrote:

> Perfectly aware of the value of our colonial possessions, and strongly impressed with the necessity of maintaining our connection with them, I know not in what respect it can be desirable that we should interfere with their internal legislation. . . . The colonists may not always know what laws are best for them, or which of their countrymen are the best fitted for conducting their affairs; but at least they have a greater interest in coming to a right judgment on these points . . . than those whose welfare is very slightly affected by the good or bad legislation of these portions of the Empire.
>
> Source: Earl of Durham, Report on the Affairs of British North America, presented to Parliament (31 January 1839).

In 1848 the Governor of Canada was Lord Elgin, Durham's son-in-law. He had been appointed after the passing of the Reunion Act (1840), which implemented one part of the Durham Report. He proceeded to implement the other part of the report, as is indicated in this letter from Lord Grey (Secretary for War and the Colonies) in 1848:

> I can have no doubt that you must accept such a council as the newly elected Parliament will support, and that however unwise their measures may be, they must be acquiesced in, until it shall pretty clearly appear that public opinion will support a resistance to them. There is no middle course between this line of policy, and that which involves in the last resort an appeal to Parliament to over-rule the wishes of the Canadians, and this I agree with both Gladstone and Stanley in thinking impracticable. If we over-rule the Local Legislature we must be prepared to support our authority by force, and in the present state of the world and of Canada, he must be in my opinion an insane politician who would think of doing so.
>
> Source: Lord Grey to Lord Elgin (22 February 1848).

The boundary between Canada and the USA was agreed by the Ashburton and Oregon Treaties (Section 12.8).

17.5 Australia

Captain Cook had explored the Australian coast between 1768 and 1779, taking possessions of the territory which he called New South Wales. How-

Fig. 17.4 Some aspects of emigration from England to Australia

ever, the British government was not interested in this far-away land until the loss of the American colonies forced the government to look for new homes for convicts. In 1788 Captain Phillip landed at Sydney with the first batch of convicts, the original British settlers of Australia. Other convict settlements were made at Hobart (1804), Brisbane and Melbourne. Each of these places was originally part of New South Wales, but the difficulties of communication made separate administration almost inevitable.

Free settlers were also encouraged to go to Australia to farm and by 1830 there were more free settlers than convicts in New South Wales. By this time the introduction of the Spanish merino sheep had established sheep farming as a profitable venture. In 1850 the British government, following the principles of the Durham Report, granted representative government to New South Wales, Tasmania, South Australia and Victoria, and in 1855 it granted responsible government to New South Wales.

17.6   New Zealand

Captain Cook had claimed New Zealand for Britain in 1769. The fertile islands attracted various groups of settlers, traders, whalers, seamen and run-away convicts. They came into contact with the native Maoris who lived in the islands and among whom British missionaries worked. The white settlers and Maoris fought numbers of battles, and many Maori tribes lost their lands to the settlers. This news disturbed the British government, which was even more alarmed by the report that the French were about to annex the South Island.

In 1840 the Governor of New South Wales, Captain Hobson, was told to take over New Zealand and he signed the Treaty of Waitangi with the native chiefs. This Treaty declared:

1. The chiefs of the confederation of United tribes and the separate and independent chiefs cede to Her Majesty absolutely all rights and powers of sovereignty.
2. Her Majesty confirms to the chiefs the full and undisturbed possession of their lands and estates.
3. In Consideration thereof, Her Majesty extends to the natives of New Zealand Her royal protection, and imparts to them all the rights and privileges of British subjects.

Shortly afterwards New Zealand was declared a separate colony with its capital at Auckland.

Test Yourself on Unit 17

(a) Document: the Indian Mutiny as seen by *The Times*, 8 June 1857

To bring high-caste Hindoos into contact with lard is, of course, a mistake, but we doubt if it would in itself lead to disaffection shared in more or less by an entire army. Those who know India well are not unprepared for the appearance of a restless, sullen feeling on the part of the millions whom we rule, and especially of the troops. By education, by a glimpse of history and natural science, by the spectacle of railways and telegraphs, and by the great events which have lately passed in Europe, the Hindoo has been roused from his sluggishness. In the old times when the Sepoy had no knowledge and no ambition, there was pretty nearly always something for him to do. An enemy was always on our frontier; there were tribes of robbers, tribes of murderers, or gangs of fanatics, to be put down. But now we have conquered all enemies within and without. A quarter of a million of native soldiers are now transformed into a vast police. There is no activity, there is no excitement. We cannot help thinking that this dull and aimless existence is too much even for the apathy of a Hindoo.

Whether it be not necessary to remodel the organization of the Indian force, to increase the number of white troops and the number of officers in the native corps, is a question which has for some time engaged the attention of some of the most experienced men in the country. The matter becomes one of surpassing interest when we are told that a mutinous spirit has shown itself, at Barrackpore and Meerut, at Dinapore, Lucknow, Agra, and Umballa. It may be that this ill-feeling is the last stand made by the Hindoo mind against the growing influence of European culture. It is not impossible that at a time when widows are marrying and men of all castes are sitting together in a railway carriage the last efforts of bigotry should be made. . . .
Source: The Times (8 June 1857).

(b) Questions

1. Which were the two major religious groups in India? Why did they object to coming into 'contact with lard'? When did they have to do so?
2. Which two Governors-General had helped to 'rouse the Hindoo from his sluggishness'?
3. What, in the opinion of the writer, had helped to keep the Sepoys occupied and out of mischief in the past?
4. Name (i) a gang of murderers, (ii) a warlike tribe of central India, (iii) a frontier province, each of which engaged the army in the early nineteenth century.
5. Why were there fewer white troops in India in 1857 than in 1850?
6. What is the significance of the clause 'when widows are marrying'?
7. Why were 'men of all castes . . . sitting together in a railway carriage'? What was the significance of this?
8. What is meant by 'bigotry'? On what grounds were Indian bigots able to make an appeal to Indians in 1856 and 1857?

(c) Further Reading

Hibbert, C.: *The Great Mutiny: India 1857*. Penguin (Harmondsworth, 1980).
Morris, J.: *Heaven's Command*. Penguin (Harmondsworth, 1979).
Seaman, L. C. B.: *Victorian England: Aspects of English and Imperial History 1837–1901*. Methuen (London, 1973).
Shaw, A. G. L.: *The Story of Australia*. Faber (London, 1983).
Woodruff, P.: *The Men Who Ruled India*. Cape (London, 1954).

(*d*) **Exercises**

1. What was the significance of the work of (i) Dalhousie, (ii) Bentinck?
2. How did the British government extend its control over Indian affairs in (i) 1773, (ii) 1784, (iii) 1858?
3. Write briefly on (i) the thugs, (ii) suttee, (iii) the caste system.
4. What were the main causes of the Indian Mutiny?
5. Why was Lord Durham sent to Canada? What were the main features of his report? Why is it important?
6. Explain briefly what is meant by (i) representative government, and (ii) responsible government.
7. Write about the importance of *three* of the following: (i) the transportation of convicts; (ii) the abolition of slavery; (iii) the Great Trek; (iv) Dalhousie's reforms in India.

Unit Eighteen
Trade Unions, 1760–1850

18.1 The Early Industrial Revolution

From 1760 onwards there was a slow but steady growth of industrial towns around coal mines, textile mills, engineering shops and other factories. Small towns such as Birmingham, Rochdale, Bury and Burnley came into being and bigger towns such as Liverpool, Manchester, Leeds and Sheffield grew even larger. In these and other towns, men, women and children worked in huge factories, built to house the new machinery which was too large to fit in the workers' cottages, and also needed water or steam-power to drive it (Section 1.3). The traditional method of wage fixing by the Justices of the Peace soon proved impossible to operate. The government realized this and in 1813 and 1814 repealed the laws which had once governed wage-fixing. Employers then claimed for themselves the freedom to fix wages in their own factories and workshops. But in the larger factories and growing towns, workers found a common strength in their common grievances—long hours, low wages, frequent unemployment, great poverty and so on. It is not surprising that they quickly learned that 'in unity is strength', and that they tried to form their own self-protection *societies*, *unions*, or *combinations*—all of which names were given to these first attempts by workers to help themselves.

18.2 Combination Acts

These first unions were generally *local* in character. The Durham miners, Sheffield file-grinders and Bury brush-makers each had their own union. It was almost impossible to form a *national* union until cheap and efficient communication was made possible by the development of the railway system. Each of these unions was a *craft* union. The Sheffield file-grinders did not join with the Sheffield carpenters in one union; each of these crafts—and every other craft—had its own union.

Employers regarded these unions as an interference with their freedom to run their factories as they wished, and they asked Parliament to stamp them out. After the outbreak of the French Revolution in 1789, policitians believed that unions could be the forerunners of a British Revolution, as can be seen in this extract from a report on a Parliamentary debate:

> 8 April. Sir John Anderson brought up a Report of a Select Committee to whom the Petition of the master millwrights was referred. The substance of the Report was that there existed among the journeymen millwrights, within certain districts in and about the metropolis, a combination which was dangerous to the public, and which the masters had not sufficient power to repress.

The Report being read, Sir John Anderson moved 'That leave be given to bring in a Bill to prevent unlawful combination of workmen employed in the millwright business, and to enable the magistrates to regulate their wages within certain limits.'

Mr Wilberforce said he did not object to the principle of this motion ... but he [asked] whether it might not be advisable to extend the principle of this motion, and make it general against combinations of all workmen. These combinations he regarded as a general disease in our society.

17 June: Mr Chancellor Pitt said it was his intention to endeavour to provide a remedy to an evil of very considerable magnitude; he meant that of unlawful combination among workmen in general—a practice which had become much too general and was likely, if not checked, to produce very serious mischief. . . .

Source: Debate in the House of Commons (1799), *Debrett*, vols. liii–liv.

Notice that Wilberforce, the enemy of slavery (Section 11.2), was one of the main opponents of trade unionism. Pitt was as good as his word and in 1799 produced the first of the Combination Acts, which said:

All contracts and agreements made by any workmen for obtaining an advance of wages or for altering their usual hours of working, or for preventing any person from employing whomsoever he shall think proper to employ in his business, are hereby declared to be illegal.

Source: Combination Act (1799), *Statutes at Large*, xviii, p. 164.

Many trade unionists were prosecuted under this Act, and employers used the threat of prosecution to compel workpeople to accept cuts in wages or to work longer hours. A number of cases were brought before magistrates. William Salt, a cotton spinner, told of his own experience:

Q. Have you suffered prosecution under the Combination Laws?
A. Yes, in 1822. We had not the same wages as the other factories, and we gave notice.
Q. In what way?
A. Singly, by ourselves.
Q. All the men in the factory or a limited number?
A. All of them.
Q. What followed?
A. As I was coming home, there was a large body of people on the road, my master and the constable were after me: and the constable, Mr Pickford, struck me over the forehead and took me off to gaol. On the next day I was taken up before Mr Phillips, the magistrate; he never asked me any questions.

Source: From the Report of the Select Committee on Artisans and Machinery (1824).

But in spite of this sort of treatment the number of unions grew after 1800.

18.3   Legalizing Trade Unions

We have already seen (Section 8.1) that after 1822 there was a change of government and the Liberal Tories came to power. Francis Place and Joseph Hume, a Radical MP, persuaded Huskisson (Section 8.4) to set up a Committee to consider, among other things, the position of workers and their trade unions. They were motivated by a strong attachment to *laissez-faire* economics and a belief that there should be as little interference as possible in the running of the economy, rather than by sympathy with trade unions. This Committee reported favourably and in 1824 the Combination Acts were repealed. Trade unions could not be formed without danger of legal action being taken against the members or officers. Not surprisingly there was a rash of strikes by workers enjoying their first taste of freedom. Employers persuaded the government to pass another Act in 1825 which permitted the formation of unions but limited their power and influence. This Act of 1825 said:

> If any person shall force any workman to depart from his work or endeavour to prevent any workman from accepting work, every person so offending shall be imprisoned to hard labour for three calendar months.
> *Source: Statutes at Large*, xx, p. 576.

But unions and strikes were still legal and this was a major breakthrough, although, as employers were generally from the same social class as JPs, they were able to persuade them to allow the use of police or some other group to break strikes and to evict striking workpeople from the employers' cottages.

18.4 Robert Owen and Trade Unionism in the 1830s

When the 1832 Reform Act failed to provide the working class with the vote (Sections 10.4, 10.5 and 13.1), the workers turned their attention once again to the development of trade unionism as a means of improving their lives. Robert Owen was the owner of some mills at New Lanark, and he provided his workpeople with good working and living conditions, built schools for their children and encouraged the workers to take an active part in political affairs. He believed that the wealth being produced in industrial Britain could be used to provide a better standard of living for everyone, instead of being devoted to providing great wealth for a minority and poor living conditions for the majority. Owen wanted to form a national union, so he helped to establish *the Grand National Consolidated Trades Union*. As its name suggests, this was a union to which workers of any and every craft were encouraged to belong. Owen sent out officials to found branches of his union throughout the country. Hundreds of branches (lodges) were formed and in 1834 Owen claimed that he had over half a million members.

Employers tried to stop their workmen joining this union. In some places— Derby, for example—employers simply locked out the workmen until they agreed not to join the union. Men who were known to have joined were not re-employed, while all those who were taken on had to sign *the document*, as was reported to a Parliamentary Committee:

> Immediately afterwards an agreement was offered by the masters; the operatives were to sign, or not to be employed . . .

Fig. 18.1 An artist's impression of the secrecy practised by trade unions in the early part of the nineteenth century

'We, the undersigned, agree with Messrs. . . . that we will work for them on the following terms.

'We declare that we do not belong to the "Union" or any other society which has for its object any interference with the rules laid down for the government of mills.

'We agree with our masters that we will not become members of any such society while in our present employ.

'We will not subscribe or contribute to any such society, or to any turn-out hands whatsoever.

'And if we are discovered to act contrary to the above agreement, each of us so offending will forfeit a sum equal to a fortnight's wages . . .'

Source: Evidence before a Select Committee, *Parliamentary Papers* (1831–2), xv, pp. 28–30.

Other employers persuaded their friends, the magistrates, to take action against local branches of the union. The most famous example of such a prosecution was that which involved a group of six farmworkers who formed a lodge at Tolpuddle in Dorset, in the hope that this would somehow enable them to resist the employers' attempts to cut their wages. They demanded a wage of ten shillings (50p) a week while the employers wanted to cut wages to 7 shillings (35p). The magistrates decided that the oath which members took when joining the lodge was forbidden by the Act passed at the time of the naval mutiny at the Nore in 1797 (Section 5.6), although this was only a pretext used by men anxious to stamp out trades unions. The men were sentenced to seven years' transportation by a Judge who told them:

I am not sentencing you for any crime you have committed, or that it could be proved that you were about to commit, but as an example to the working classes of this country.

Source: Judge John Williams, Dorchester Assizes (19 March 1834).

Robert Owen had claimed that his union, which hopefully would enrol all British workers as members, would be able to challenge the government. Owen claimed that a general strike would make employers and government realize that the workers had to be listened to, if not obeyed. But the weakness of Owen's claims was revealed by the Tolpuddle decision, which was confirmed by the Home Secretary, Lord Melbourne, who congratulated the magistrates on their decision. The *Tolpuddle Martyrs* were sent to Australia (Section 17.5) in spite of Owen's protests; his members did not manage to bring the government to its knees nor compel it to obey the union. The freeing of the 'Martyrs' in 1838 was due to political pressure and not to Owen's campaign. Owen's union had only a superficial strength; there were too many dishonest officials, too few members paying their subscriptions, too few willing to strike for anything which did not concern them personally, and the work of the union was hampered by the lack of an efficient communications network.

Fig. 18.2 A demonstration by trade unionists and their supporters against the sentences imposed on the Tolpuddle martyrs, 21 April 1834. St Paul's can be seen in the background and the limited expansion of London at this time (1834) can be seen in that this demonstration took place on a site later filled by Euston Station

And with this failure of an ambitious scheme the workers turned once again to politics as a means of obtaining access to the better life that they wanted. Chartism flourished after the failure of Owen's union (Section 13.2).

18.5   Model Unions

Chartism ebbed and flowed in the 1830s and 1840s (Sections 13.1 and 13.3) but after the fiasco of 1848 workers turned once again to trade unionism. Some tried to use peaceful means to persuade employers to listen to their unions, only to find that employers were unwilling to do so. One example of such an attempt and failure involved the miners of Northumbria:

> There was no eagerness for a strike, for there were no defensive resources. The tommy shops [owned by the mining company and the only shops where miners' families had been able to obtain food etc.] would close. There were no co-operative societies with little saved-up balances to the name of each member. The union had no reserve fund. So methods of conciliation were resorted to. . . . On March 20, 1844, the men sent a letter to the owners asking them to receive a deputation from the Miners' Association. There was no reply of any sort.
>
> In 1844 the men left their work in April; and immediate steps were taken to fill the

Fig. 18.3 Newcastle employers recruited Welsh and other 'foreign' workers to try to break an engineers' strike in 1871. Such use of blackleg labour often led to clashes between the strikers on one side and the police, army and blacklegs on the other

places left vacant. Men were brought from Wales under much better terms than those which had been refused to the men on the spot. Then came the evictions. The coal-owners are the proprietors of the cottages in which the pitmen live. Occupancy can be terminated with the cessation of employment, and eviction means the throwing out of the people into the village street. . . . The workhouses, too, were closed against the strikers. 'Starvation had to be endured', [for] twenty-six weeks, during which no word of any sort could be obtained from the employers.

Just as the cause might be, it was not at that time destined to prevail. The mine-owners won 'hands down' by treating the men as if they did not exist, except when their furniture was to be cast out of the cottages.

Source: Watson, Aaron, *The Life of Thomas Burt* (1908).

Other workers, modelling their behaviour on the writings and speeches of William Lovett (Section 13.2(*b*)), turned to education, to 'self-help' and to the formation of *friendly societies* as a means of improving their lives. The majority of those who followed this line were the skilled workers whom employers needed to build the new machinery, to operate the new railway system, or to build the new factories. These carpenters, bricklayers, plumbers and engineers were relatively few in number and received much higher wages than did the mass of unskilled workers. From their £2 a week they could afford to pay for insurance policies, to save in a savings bank, to contribute to the building of the mechanics institutes where they had libraries, classes, reading rooms and games rooms. These skilled workers formed their own craft unions to which they paid a subscription of about 1 shilling (5p) a week and from which

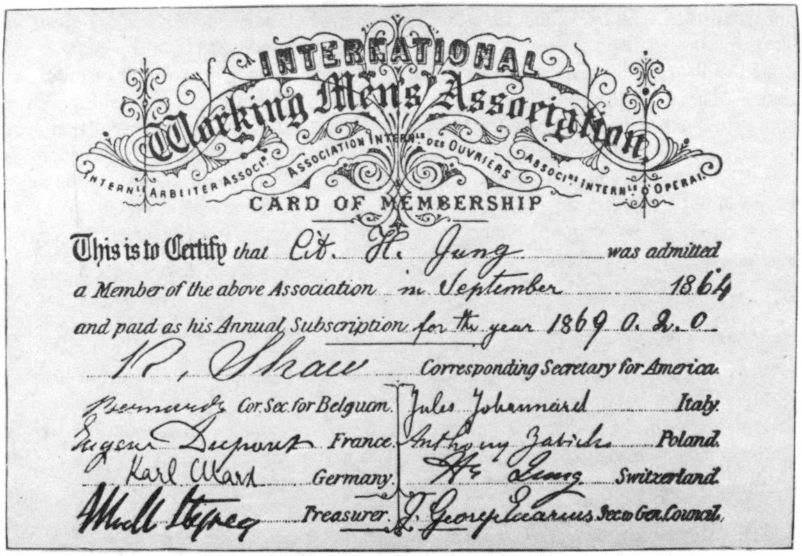
International Working Men's Association
Internle Arbeiter Associn. Association Internle des Ouvriers Associne Internle d'Operai
CARD OF MEMBERSHIP
This is to Certify that Cit. H. Jung was admitted
a Member of the above Association in September 1864
and paid as his Annual Subscription for the year 1869 0. 2. 0
R. Shaw Corresponding Secretary for America.
Bernard Cor. Sec. for Belgium. | Jules Johannard Italy.
Eugene Dupont France. | Anthony Zabicki Poland.
Karl Marx Germany. | H. Jung Switzerland.
Treasurer. | J. George Eccarius Sec. to Gen. Council.

Fig. 18.4 Membership card of a proud and confident union

they obtained welfare benefits. With high wages when they were at work and with welfare payments from their unions if they were sick, unemployed, injured or retired, these 'aristocrats of labour' enjoyed a relatively high standard of living.

Test Yourself on Unit 18

(a) Document: William Allen, General Secretary of the Amalgamated Society of Engineers Giving Evidence on his Model Union, 1867

The witness stated that the society was formed in 1851 of a number of societies which had previously existed, and it now numbered 33,000 members, with an annual increase of 2,000 or 3,000 a year. There were, he said, 308 branches. All these branches are governed by one code of rules. Each member pays 1s. [5p] a week and the society now has a fund in different banks, in round numbers, of £140,000. The annual income in 1865 was £86,885, made up, besides subscriptions, of entrance fees, each member having to pay an entrance fee varying from 15s. [75p] to £3.10s. [£3.50]. The expenditure in 1865 was £49,172, the heads under which it was distributed being—members out of employment, £14,076; to sick members £13,788; superannuated members (members who are 'too old to gain the ordinary rate of wages at the trade' being allowed 7s. [35p] to 9s. [45p] a week each), £5,184; on the death of members and members' wives, £4,887; and the sum of £1,800 among 18 members who met with accidents and were unable to follow the trade. Then there is a benevolent fund, made up of a compulsory levy on every member. It should here be remarked that a member, on ceasing for any reason to be a member, loses all these benefits, except those who have received the injury money, and they are entitled to the benefits on paying 6d. [2½p] a week. With respect to 'trade purposes' the secretary stated that the average annual payment for members out of work for the 15 years the society had been in existence was £18,000. On being questioned as to what percentage of this money had gone through strikes and disputes, he said: 'We have only had one dispute which you may call important in our trade since the commencement of the society, and that was in 1852. In the first six months of that year we expended £40,000 on a lock-out; it was not our fault we were out of employment: it was the fault of the employers who locked us out'. He added, on another question being put to him: 'We have not kept a separate account of the money spent under this head: but, leaving that £40,000 out, I should say it does not exceed 10 per cent, as far as any strikes with our employers are concerned'. . . .

(b) Questions

1. What, do you think, was meant by 'a number of societies'? Why did such a link-up take place in 1851 and not in, say, 1831?
2. How many members did this union have? What does this tell you about the size of the skilled working class? Why was this class a growing one?
3. Why could unskilled workers not afford to join unions such as this?
4. What benefits were paid to union members?
5. Why were union leaders reluctant to call strikes?
6. Why did evidence from Allen and the leaders of other Model Unions lead to a change in public opinion?

(c) Further Reading

Gash, N.: *Aristocracy and People, Britain 1815–1865*. Arnold (London, 1983).

Hopkins, E.: *A Social History of the English Working Classes 1815–1945*. Arnold (London, 1979).

Pelling, H.: *A History of British Trade Unionism*. Penguin (Harmondsworth, 1976).

Porter, R.: *English Society in the Eighteenth Century*. Penguin (Harmondsworth, 1982).

Thompson, E. P.: *The Making of the English Working Class*. Penguin (Harmondsworth, 1968).

(d) Documentary

Browne, H.: *The Rise of British Trade Unions 1825–1914*. Longman (Harlow, 1979).

Evans, L. W.: *British Trade Unionism*. Arnold (London, 1970).

(e) Exercises

1. Why did the government pass the Combination Act, 1799? When and why was it repealed?
2. What was the main purpose of the formation of the Grand National Consolidated Trades Union? Why did it fail?
3. Why were Model Unions formed after 1851? Why were these (i) small, (ii) able to change public opinion about trade unionism?
4. Give an account of the efforts made by the working classes to improve their economic and social position between 1780 and 1850.
5. Write briefly on (i) the Tolpuddle Martyrs, (ii) Robert Owen, (iii) Friendly Societies.

Gladstone, 1833–74

19.1 Gladstone's Early Career

Gladstone was the son of a wealthy merchant, one of the increasing number of rich members of the middle class who benefited from the growth of Britain's industry and overseas trade. Gladstone went to Eton, where he mixed with the sons of the aristocracy, then to Oxford, where he continued his classical education. He was an Anglican and was influenced by the writings and sermons of Anglican clergymen such as Newman, Keble and Pusey, the leaders of the Oxford Movement which led many of its members into the Roman Catholic church. Gladstone did not follow this path but he did remain a 'high' Anglican (a section of the Anglican church whose members follow many of the rituals of the Roman Catholic church).

In 1833, when he was twenty-four years old, Gladstone became Tory MP for the rotten borough of Newark (Section 10.5) and quickly made a good impression in the House of Commons. He also published several books on topics such as Ancient Greece, biblical studies and, in 1838, *The Church and its Relations with the State*. Macaulay, himself a famous writer and a leading Whig MP (Unit 10 and Test Yourself on Unit 10(*c*)), reviewed this book and drew attention to Gladstone's great promise:

> The author of this volume is a young man of unblemished character, and of distinguished parliamentary talents, *the rising hope of those stern and unbending Tories.* . . . We are much pleased to see a grave treatise on an important part of the Philosophy of Government proceed from the pen of a young man who is rising to eminence in the House of Commons. . . .
> *Source:* Lord Macaulay, *The Edinburgh Review* (April 1839).

No one thought of writing such praise for the novelist, Benjamin Disraeli, who was considered a very flippant and flamboyant MP (Section 20.1).

(*a*) President of the Board of Trade, 1843–5

Gladstone served in Peel's government as President of the Board of Trade. In this office he played a large part in developing the free trade policy followed by Peel (Section 12.6) and so won praise from the Cobdenites in the Whig–Liberal Party. In 1846 he supported Peel's decision to repeal the Corn Laws (Sections 13.5 and 13.6), which earned him the enmity of Disraeli who believed that repeal was a betrayal of the Tory Party's best interests (Unit 13 and Test Yourself on Unit 13(*c*)).

Fig. 19.1 The young Gladstone being chaired by his supporters after his electoral victory at Newark in 1832

(b) Chancellor of the Exchequer

Gladstone served as Chancellor of the Exchequer in Aberdeen's Whig–Peelite coalition from 1852 to 1855 (Section 14.4), and again in Palmerston's Whig ministries (1858–65). As Chancellor he lowered taxation, completed Britain's transition to free trade and declared that he would like to be the man who abolished income tax. This won him the support of the growing number of middle-class industrialists, merchants, financiers and others who were rapidly becoming the backbone of the Whig Party throughout the country. They also welcomed his policies on free trade and in particular the Cobden Treaty, which he arranged with France in 1860, and under which Britain and France agreed to reduce the tariffs on goods imported from each other.

(c) An Idealist

Palmerston and Russell both believed that Gladstone deserved his place in the government, but Gladstone himself was not a mere seeker after high office. He believed that a politician should do whatever he believed to be right, even if this made him unpopular with his colleagues and the electorate. Between 1860 and 1865 he consistently argued for a further reform of Parliament, though both Russell and Palmerston were opposed to this. He supported Palmerston's policy when this favoured Italian unification in 1859 (Section 14.4) but he had already shown his opposition to Palmerston's foreign policy, when he vigorously criticized him for the Don Pacifico affair (Section 14.3). When Britain became involved in the Crimean War (Sections 15.4 and 15.5) Gladstone resigned from office as a matter of principle.

19.2   Leader of the Whigs

In 1865 Palmerston died and Russell once again became Prime Minister. Gladstone was appointed leader of the Whigs in the House of Commons, and won praise from MPs of all sides for his skill as a parliamentarian and as an organizer of the affairs of the Commons. Russell was a sick man and it was obvious that soon the Whig Party would have to look for a new leader. When the time came, in 1867, it seemed inevitable that Gladstone should be chosen for these reasons:

(i) The older members of the Whig Party—the aristocratic landlords—approved of him because he had received their sort of education, was a member of their church and had once served under Peel (Unit 12). These old Whigs would never have approved of a middle-class leader, such as Cobden (Sections 13.5 and 13.6) or Bright (Section 28.1(c)).

(ii) The newer members of the Whig Party—the middle-class merchants and industrialists—approved of his policies on trade and taxation (Sections 12.6 and 19.1), and had themselves opposed Palmerston's bullying foreign policy (Section 14.4). They would not have followed a Whig of the old party.

(iii) MPs and peers of varying descriptions admired the evident ability of this man who had held office more or less for thirty years, and had proved his fitness for high office throughout that period. They would not have been happy about following a leader without such wide experience.

(iv) Men admired Gladstone's idealism and his willingness to sacrifice office to principle (Section 19.1). They believed that such strength of character fitted a man to be the leader of a great political party.

19.3   First Clash with Disraeli, 1866–7

As leader of the House of Commons in 1866 Gladstone was responsible for introducing a Parliamentary Reform Bill (Section 28.1(a), (b)). Some of his own party, led by Robert Lowe, opposed this further extension of democracy (Section 28.1(b)). Disraeli, leader of the Conservative Opposition, supported Lowe and his followers and together they defeated the government, which was forced to resign. A minority Tory government was then formed under Lord Derby, who was soon succeeded as Prime Minister by Disraeli. Disraeli then introduced his own Parliamentary Reform Bill in 1867 (Section 28.1(c)) and put Gladstone and his followers into a difficult position. If they opposed the measure they could be accused of being opposed to reform, which they obviously were not because they had themselves introduced a bill in 1866. If, however, they supported Disraeli's bill, they would allow Disraeli to appear—in the eyes of the electorate—as the front-runner in the matter of reform.

Gladstone and his more liberal colleagues (Section 28.1(*a*)) agreed that principle (supporting a needed reform) was more important than expediency (getting Disraeli out and themselves back into office). So a combination of Gladstone's followers plus the majority of Disraeli's followers pushed the Second Reform Bill through the Commons, in spite of the Whigs who followed Lowe, and the disgruntled Conservatives who followed Lord Cranborne (the future Lord Salisbury) in opposing Disraeli (Section 28.1(*c*)). Disraeli then decided to call a general election in the hope that a grateful electorate would return the reforming Conservatives to office. However the electorate did not behave as the politicians expected and in 1868 Gladstone became Prime Minister for the first time.

19.4   Gladstone's First Ministry, 1868–74

Gladstone and his fellow ministers were responsible for a number of very important reforms from 1868 to 1874; indeed, this ministry has been called 'the Great Reforming Ministry'. One reason for this rush of reforming legislation was that Palmerston had not supported movements for reform during his long period in office (Section 14.4), so there was a backlog of things that ought to have been done. Another reason for many of the reforms was that Gladstone appreciated that the middle class had grown in number and importance and deserved a fairer chance than they had had in the past when the aristocracy had governed and made the laws. This explains the reforms in the army, civil service and university entrance. A third reason was that some of the working class had been given the vote in 1867 and they demanded reforms—of trade union law, for example. There was also a pressing need to reform the army after the disasters of the Crimean War (Section 15.7) and to reform the educational system (Section 31.5) so that British industry and commerce could get the trained manpower that they needed if they were to compete with Germany and the USA, the two growing giants of the industrial world (Section 24.1). The Paris Exhibition (1867) had shown that Britain's lead in industry and commerce was slipping.

(*a*)   Forster's Education Act, 1870

See Sections 31.5 and 31.6 for details of this educational reform.

(*b*)   University Entrance, 1871

Until the passing of this Act every student going to Oxford or Cambridge had to be a member of the Anglican church, and attend an Anglican service in the chapel of the college of which he was a member. This meant that the sons of Nonconformists were unable to get a university education, and were therefore unable to offer themselves for posts for which a university degree was an essential qualification. Gladstone, though himself a High Anglican, knew that

Fig. 19.2 Gladstone as 'the Colossus of Words' with his policies of peace, retrenchment and reform

the majority of the people who voted for his party were Nonconformists and he wanted to please them and continue to win their support. He agreed with the argument that this insistence on a religious test was an interference with the freedom of people to do as they wanted. He understood their anger at the way in which the old aristocracy was able to cling to certain privileges and positions because of this insistence on a religious test.

In 1871 the government abolished the religious tests and as a result Methodists, Wesleyans, Calvinists and other Nonconformists as well as Jews and Catholics could go to Oxford or Cambridge, provided that they had enough money to pay the fees and had received the sort of higher education that was required before they could go to university. This abolition immediately benefited the richer middle class and, indirectly and in the long term, has benefited the rest of the community.

(c) Civil Service Reform, 1871

Until the 1850s there was no regular method of entrance into the Civil Service. If anyone wanted a job in the Civil Service he contacted 'someone who knew someone who knew of a vacancy'. Government ministers and MPs were able to use their position to ensure that their friends and relations got all the jobs that were available.

In the 1850s the government had introduced a reform of the Indian Civil Service, insisting that candidates for entry into the service would have to sit an examination and so ensure that the most able people would gain whatever positions were going. In 1871 Gladstone's government imposed the same conditions on the Home Civil Service and also said that not only entry but also promotion within the service would be open to competitive examinations. This reform pleased Gladstone's middle-class supporters whose children would now be able to get jobs in the Civil Service. The reform also pleased people who

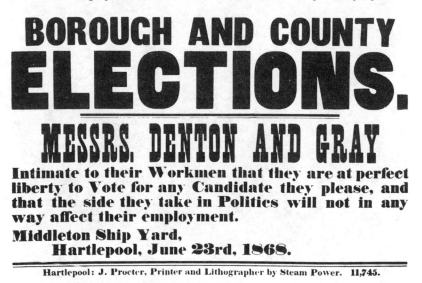

Fig. 19.3 Not all employers were as liberal as Messrs Denton and Gray. Until the passage of the Ballot Act (Fig. 28.3) there were many ways in which employers could influence the way in which employees voted

wanted the government service to become more efficient. The memory of the maladministration which had caused such havoc during the Crimean War (Sections 15.5 and 15.7) was still very vivid.

(d) The Ballot Act, 1872

See Section 28.3 for details of this reform.

(e) Licensing Act, 1872

Until this Act was passed there was no limitation on the number of ale houses or beer shops which could be opened in any town, nor were there any limita-

Fig. 19.4 A beer shop where, at almost any hour of the day or night, anyone, including children, could buy beer or spirits

tions on the hours during which these places could be open. Gladstone's Act set up a *licensing authority* in every town: anyone wishing to open a place in which beer or spirits were to be sold had to apply to the magistrates for a licence. The Act also laid down that there should be fewer such shops than there had been, and many people were refused a licence for shops which they had operated freely in the past. The Act said that the licensing authority would fix certain hours of opening and closing of the licensed premises.

This Act annoyed the brewers, who wanted as many outlets as possible for the sale of their products. It also annoyed the licensees of the licensed premises, who feared that fewer hours of opening would lead to lower profits. The argument over this Act—in every ale house and beershop—made the government very unpopular and was one of the main reasons for its defeat in 1874. 'We have been brought down in a torrent of gin and beer,' said the defeated Gladstone.

(f) Judicature Act, 1873

The government reformed the High Court system in the hope that this would make the legal system more efficient than it had been when Dickens had written 'The law is an ass'. This Act is an example of the government passing an essential, administrative law.

(g) The Army Reforms

The disasters of the Crimean War had shown that a major overhaul of the army was overdue (Sections 15.5 and 15.7). Gladstone asked Cardwell, Secretary of State for War, to take charge of this important aspect of his government's policy. Cardwell's reforms laid down that:

(i) The Commander-in-Chief of the Army would in future be subordinate to the control of the Secretary of State for War.

(ii) The system of purchase of commissions was abolished. In the past a rich young man could buy his way almost to the top of the army tree without having to give any proof of ability. One result of this was that in general the army had been badly led. Cardwell's reforms ensured that, in future, officers would be promoted only on merit.

(iii) To encourage recruitment to the army, Cardwell abolished the old system whereby a man joined 'for life'. In future a man could join for six years on active service, plus six years in the reserve. The British army remained a volunteer one and stayed so until the First World War. France, on the other hand, introduced conscription in 1872.

(iv) As another aid to recruitment Cardwell abolished the old system whereby regiments were known either by the name of the Colonel (e.g. Webb's Regiment) or by a mere number (e.g. 88th of the line). In future, every regiment had to have a county association (e.g. the East Kents, the Gloucesters). This would give the regiment a natural home for its training school, recruiting sergeants and a main barracks for soldiers not on active service.

The opponents of the bill tried to delay its passage. They objected in particular to the abolition of purchase, a system which had allowed the upper classes to get positions for their sons. Some people objected because, having recently bought commissions, they would be unable to recover that money (by re-selling) if this bill became law. The government had to promise to compensate these people, rather as a previous government had compensated the former slave-owners (Section 11.2).

Gladstone was compelled to ask Queen Victoria to play a part in this abolition, as can be seen from the following extract:

> Your Majesty's servants first obtained by Bill the sanction of the House of Commons to the great expenditure involved in the abolition of Purchase, and then sent the Bill to the House of Lords. By that House it was met, not by rejection, but by a dilatory motion. By this motion the Bill was not defeated but delayed, and it became necessary for your Majesty's servants to consider how they could at once put an end to the violation of the law. It appeared to them that the best course was to put an end to Purchase, by cancelling the Royal Warrants. . . .
>
> *Source:* Army Purchase Warrant, Minute of Cabinet (19 July 1871).

(h) Trade Union Acts

See Sections 29.3, 29.4 and 29.5 for details of this legislation.

(i) Ireland

For information about Ireland during this period, see Sections 23.1 and 23.2.

19.5 Foreign Policy

Gladstone's first government was busily involved in domestic affairs as well as in Irish affairs (Sections 23.1 and 23.2). It was less involved in foreign affairs, maybe as a reaction after the long period of Palmerstonian domination, when foreign affairs played such a large part. Also, Gladstone and many other leading Whig–Liberals did not believe that it was right to spend the taxpayers' money on foreign or colonial wars. Finally, the Whig–Liberals believed that other people should be as free as the British to conduct their own affairs without interference from overseas.

Thus when France, under Napoleon III, attacked Prussia, under Bismarck, in 1870, Gladstone's government decided on neutrality, provided that neither country invaded Belgium. Some people saw that a Prussian victory would lead to the creation of a new country, Germany, which would dominate the continent. Gladstone, however, preferred to take the moral line; what France or Prussia did was nothing to do with Britain.

Even more important at the time was the *Alabama* arbitration, the result of the American Civil War (Section 14.4). Gladstone agreed that Britain had offended the USA by allowing a ship called the *Alabama* to be built in Britain and he accepted the decision of an international court of arbitration which pronounced that Britain should pay the USA £3¼ million.

Gladstone did protest, but no more, when Russia decided to break the terms of the Treaty of Paris (Section 15.6) by fortifying her bases and maintaining a navy in the Black Sea. Palmerston might have done more than protest.

19.6 Exhausted Volcanoes

From 1872 Gladstone's government gave the impression of having lost its grip. It had legislated for so many things that it was tired. There was also a sign of division between those Liberals who wanted even more radical legislation and those older Whigs in particular, who thought that Gladstone was in danger of becoming the prisoner of the radical group.

Gladstone himself wanted to resign and make way for a Conservative government. But the ageing Disraeli, now firmly established as the leader of the Conservative Party, was too wily a bird to be caught. He preferred to wait until the government had fallen by its own efforts and had earned a great deal of electoral unpopularity. In 1872 he said:

> As I sat opposite the Treasury Bench, the Ministers reminded me of one of those marine landscapes not very unusual on the coasts of South America. You behold a range of exhausted volcanoes. Not a flame flickers on a single pallid crest. But the situation is still dangerous. There are occasional earthquakes, and ever and anon the dark rumbling of the sea.
>
> *Source:* Speech by Disraeli at the Manchester Free Trade Hall (3 April 1872).

(a) The 1874 Election

When Gladstone finally resigned and called an election, the divisions in the Whig–Liberal Party became clear. The rich middle class, once the backbone of the Gladstonian group, had become discontented with their former hero and they switched their allegiance to Disraeli, with his vague promises of a more vigorous foreign policy and his appeal to imperialism (Sections 20.3 and 20.5). Frederick Harrison, a Radical, noted:

> The real truth is that the middle class has swung round to Conservatism, of a vague and negative kind, for 'leaving well alone'. When we look at the poll in all the centres of middle-class industry, wealth and cultivation, we see that the rich trading class, and the comfortable middle class has grown distinctly Conservative.
>
> *Source: Fortnightly Review,* Vol. 15 (1874).

Gladstone tried to win popular support for his party by promising that if he got back to power he would abolish income tax. But the electorate had had enough of Gladstone, and the Tories won an overall majority in the House of Commons, the first time they had done so since 1841.

(b) Gladstone Gives Up the Leadership

In January 1875 Gladstone, still an MP, decided to give up the leadership of the Liberal Party. He explained his reasons in a letter to Lord Granville, who was his Foreign Secretary from 1870 to 1874, and succeeded Gladstone as leader of the Liberal Party:

> 11 Carlton House Terrace SW January 13, 1875
> My dear Granville,
> I see no advantage in my continuing to act as the leader of the Liberal Party and that at the age of sixty-five, and after forty-two years of a laborious public life, I think myself entitled to retire as the best method of spending the closing years of my life. . . .
> Believe me always sincerely yours,
>
> W. E. GLADSTONE.

> Carlton House Terrace, January 14
> My dear Gladstone,
> I profoundly regret the conclusion at which you have arrived. Your late colleagues share these feelings to the fullest extent.
> We have no doubt that the Liberal Party, in and out of Parliament, will feel as we do on the subject. . . .
> Yours sincerely,
> GRANVILLE.

Source: The Times (15 January 1875).

This, then, seemed to be the end of a great career, and of an era, but it was not to be, as we shall see in Unit 21.

Test Yourself on Unit 19

(a) Document: A critic on the Gladstone Ministry, 1868–74

The Washington Treaty and the *Alabama* arbitration, though Mr Gladstone was in strictness responsible for neither, yet are supposed to have lowered England in its status as a great power. We did not wish to maintain a quarrel with Russia, yet we were sore and resentful when the Treaty of Paris was torn to pieces and flung in our faces. We had no desire to meddle in the French and German War, yet we did not like to see England unconsulted when the map of Europe was remodelled. Internally the ministry made enemies whether they did well or ill. The Irish Land Bill alarmed the owners of property, the Education Bill offended the Dissenters. The abolition of purchase in the army, though welcome in itself to most reasonable persons, yet shocked us all, when the prerogative was called in to overcome the resistance of Parliament. The Licensing Bill exasperated the brewer and the publican. . . . Mr Gladstone himself contributed the last and fatalest blow to his popularity by the suddenness of the Dissolution, which, however he might explain it, resembled rather the coup of a Wall Street speculator than the proud and open display of purpose and policy which Englishmen demand of Ministers in whom they are to place reliance.

In these and other shortcomings of the late Cabinet, we may see some explanation of the fate which has overtaken them. Yet it is not satisfactory or sufficient. Many of Mr Gladstone's crimes were accidents. Mr Disraeli will be fortunate should he remain six years in office, if he escapes worse mischances. . . .

Source: J. A. Froude, written after the general election of 1874.

(b) Questions

1. With which foreign country did Britain arrange the 'Washington Treaty and the *Alabama* arbitration'? Do you think that these arrangements lower 'England in its status as a great power'?
2. When had the Treaty of Paris been signed? By whom was it 'torn to pieces'? Who supported this 'tearing'? How did it affect the position of Britain?
3. In what way was 'the map of Europe . . . remodelled' by the 'French and German War'?
4. Make a list of the enemies which had been made 'internally'.
5. Why was 'the prerogative . . . called in' to deal with the 'abolition of purchase'?
6. Do you think that this is a fair criticism of Gladstone's First Ministry?

(c) Further Reading

Adelman, P.: *The Middle-Class Experience 1830–1914*. Longman (Harlow, 1984).
Feuchtwanger, E. J.: *Democracy and Empire, Britain 1865–1914*. Arnold (London, 1984).
Lane, P.: *Elections*. Batsford (London, 1973).
Lane, P.: *The Liberal Party*. Batsford (London, 1974).
Magnus, Sir Philip: *Gladstone*. John Murray (London, 1979).
Read, D.: *England 1868–1914: The Age of Urban Democracy*. Longman (Harlow, 1979).
Robbins, K.: *The Eclipse of a Great Power: Modern Britain 1870–1975*. Longman (Harlow, 1983).

(d) Documentary

Adelman, P.: *Gladstone, Disraeli and Later Victorian Politics*. Longman (Harlow, 1983).

(e) Exercises

1. Give an account of the career and achievements of Gladstone up to 1874.
2. Explain the part played by Gladstone in the development of free trade.
3. Account for the rise of Gladstone to the leadership of the Liberal Party.
4. Give an account of the main reforms passed during Gladstone's ministry, 1868–74.
5. Why did Gladstone's reforms, 1868–74, arouse a great deal of opposition?
6. Write briefly on (i) Cardwell's Army Reform, (ii) the Forster Education Act, (iii) Robert Lowe and parliamentary reform.
7. How far did Gladstone deserve his image of 'the Grand Old Man'?

Unit Twenty
Disraeli

20.1 Disraeli's Early Career

Benjamin Disraeli was born in 1804, grandson of a Jewish immigrant who had made a small fortune in business and changed the family name from D'Israeli to Disraeli. Isaac, Benjamin's father, inherited the family fortune and sent his children to local private schools where they mixed with other children of the comfortably-off middle classes, were baptized into the Christian faith, and attended the Anglican church for religious services.

Benjamin Disraeli began his career as a novelist—his first book, *Vivian Grey*, was published in 1826. He wrote his two best known works, *Coningsby* (1844) and *Sybil, or the Two Nations* (1845), after he had entered the House of Commons. But this was not something to commend Disraeli to serious men or politicians. Novelists, they thought, were lightweight people, unlike Gladstone with his heavy books on the Church, the Greeks, the Nature of Government, and so on (Section 19.1). In the 1830s and 1840s, serious people also frowned on Disraeli's insistence on dressing up in flamboyant and colourful clothes—yellow waistcoats, red velvet jackets and blue trousers were hardly the sort of dress that one expected from a man who wanted to be taken seriously. But Disraeli did want to be taken seriously and to become a cabinet minister. He tried to enter Parliament several times in the 1830s, once standing as a radical, but he failed each time. Then he met Mrs Wyndham Lewis, whose family controlled a rotten borough at Maidstone (Section 10.5). She persuaded her husband to give this seat to Disraeli in 1837, and so he finally entered Parliament as a Tory, sitting behind Sir Robert Peel. In 1839 he married the widowed Mrs Lewis. Some people accused him of marrying her for her money, but in fact they were very happy together.

20.2 Disraeli and Peel

Peel, as we have seen in Units 12 and 13, carried out policies which pleased the middle classes. Disraeli, on the other hand, had an active hatred for the rising middle class who had gained a share in political power in 1832 (Section 10.5), were well on their way to replacing the aristocracy as the wealthiest people in the country and were making their huge fortunes in dirty industrial towns where the majority of the population lived in insanitary slums and suffered from harsh poverty. It was hardly surprising, then, that Disraeli should have opposed Peel when Peel decided to repeal the Corn Laws (Section 13.6 and Test Yourself on Unit 13, (c)). Most of the leading members of the Conservative Party followed their leader to form the Peelite group (Sections

THE RISING GENERATION—IN PARLIAMENT.

Peel. "WELL, MY LITTLE MAN, WHAT ARE YOU GOING TO DO THIS SESSION, EH?"
D——li (the Juvenile). "WHY—AW—AW—I'VE MADE ARRANGEMENTS—AW—TO SMASH—AW—EVERYBODY.

Fig. 20.1 'Punch' (30 January 1847) shows the young Disraeli telling Peel, whose government he has already smashed, that he will continue to be a wrecker

14.4 and 19.1(*b*)). This was soon assimilated into the Whig Party, with which it formed the Liberal Party under Gladstone (Sections 19.2 and 19.3).

The small number of Conservatives who opposed Peel from 1846 onwards were led in the Commons by Lord George Bentinck and later by Lord Stanley, the son of the Earl of Derby; but these were only the *apparent* leaders. They had the titles, the connexions and the traditional claim to leadership of the landowning party which Disraeli did not have, so he allowed them to appear to lead while, in fact, he controlled the fortunes of the small band of Anti-Peelite Conservatives, or Protectionists, after 1846.

20.3   The Creation of a New Party

Between 1846 and 1874 the Conservative Party held office on only three occasions and for very short periods, usually when the coalition of Whigs and Peelites had squabbled among themselves and could not form a government (Sections 14.4, 19.3 and 28.1(*c*)). The majority of MPs supported one or other of the leading Whigs or Peelites, or Radicals such as Cobden or Bright. The majority of electors gave their votes to well-known politicians and did not trust the candidates put forward by the party which had opposed the repeal of the Corn Laws (Section 13.6 and Test Yourself on Unit 13, (*c*)), appeared not to believe in democracy (Sections 10.2(*b*) and 10.3), and still thought that the days when the landed aristocracy governed were 'the good old days' (Section 10.1(*c*)). And yet between 1874 and 1906 this same Conservative Party held office for over twenty years, and it was the Liberal Party which appeared to be 'out in the cold'. To explain this change we have to understand what Disraeli did during the earlier period, 1846–74. *The Times*, as early as 1860, recognized the value of his work:

> Let the Conservative Party never forget the hopeless state in which they were when fortune sent them Mr Disraeli for a leader. They had grown weary of a chief who was too liberal for their views of national policy, and avenged themselves upon him by an act of renunciation which left them without leaders. They were irretrievably committed to an unpopular cause.
>
> Gradually Mr Disraeli has weaned his party from their most flagrant errors. He has taught them to profess a sympathy for the great body of their countrymen and to recognize the necessity of looking to public opinion for support. When he found the Tory Party they were armed in impenetrable prejudice; under him they have become competitors with the Liberals in the career of progress.
> *Source: The Times* (6 June 1860).

As part of this 'progress' Disraeli 'dished the Whigs' in 1867 by himself proposing a sweeping Reform Bill, having helped defeat Gladstone's more modest measure in 1866 (Sections 19.3 and 28.1(*a*)–(*c*)).

But it would not have been enough to give the party a more attractive image. Disraeli was one of the first politicians to realize that in a more democratic age elections would be won by the party which had the best organization. In the 1870s he appointed his friend, J. A. Gorst, to the task of reorganizing the party machinery. From its headquarters in the Carlton Club in London, instructions were sent to agents in every constituency on how to register electors so that they could vote, how to canvass, to enrol people in the party, to collect money needed to run an election and the party. And to the party faithful and to the electorate at large Disraeli preached a new set of Tory ideals—Tory, and not Conservative, because he disliked the latter name as the

Fig. 20.2 Life in Golden Lane, 1872. Gladstone and the Liberals seemed to care little for the 'condition of the people' in their insanitary and overcrowded houses

one which Peel had used. He summarized these ideals as the maintenance of the nation's institutions—the Church, the Monarchy and the Lords—the upholding of the Empire, and the concern for the condition of the people which he promised to improve by social reforms. In a speech in Manchester, Disraeli dealt with this question of the condition of the people:

> I think public attention as regards these matters ought to be concentrated upon sanitary legislation. Pure air, pure water, the inspection of unhealthy habitations, the adulteration of food, these and many kindred matters may be legitimately dealt with by the legislature. . . . It is impossible to over-rate the importance of the subject. After all, the first consideration of a minister should be the health of the people. . . .
> Source: Benjamin Disraeli, speech at Manchester (April 1872).

20.4   Was Disraeli a Social Reformer?

In his novels and in many of his speeches Disraeli had drawn attention to the shocking conditions in which millions of people lived. He demanded that the government should take firm action to put an end to these evils, and he even went so far as to suggest definite lines along which government policy should go. And yet, when he finally became Prime Minister in 1874, what policy did he follow? He appointed R. A. Cross as Home Secretary to carry out social reforms. But Cross himself wrote:

> When the Cabinet came to discuss the Queen's Speech, I was, I confess, disappointed at the want of originality shown by the Prime Minister. From all his speeches I had quite expected that his mind was full of legislative schemes, but such did not prove to be the case; on the contrary, he had to rely on the various suggestions of his colleagues, and as they themselves had only just come into office, and that suddenly, there was some difficulty in framing the Queen's Speech.
> Source: Cross, Viscount, A Political History, quoted in Adelman, P., Gladstone, Disraeli and Later Victorian Politics. Longman (London, 1970).

There is a good deal of evidence that most of the social reforms passed during the Disraeli ministry, 1874–80, were in fact proposed by the civil service and would have been passed whichever party had won the 1874 election. Certainly there is no evidence that Disraeli was the author of the great number of reforms which were passed in this period.

(a) The Artisans' Dwellings Act, 1875

This Act recognized that large parts of Britain's industrial towns were slums in which ill-health, early death and poverty were commonplace. The 1875 Act allowed local councils to take action:

> Where the local Authority decides that any houses are unfit for human habitation, or that diseases have been from time to time prevalent in a certain area the local Authority shall pass a resolution to the effect that such area is an unhealthy area, and that an improvement scheme ought to be made in respect of such area, and after

Fig. 20.3 Disraeli with some members of his Cabinet. From left to right: Earl Derby, Lord Cairns, Sir Stafford Northcote, Disraeli, Gathorne Hardy, the Marquess of Salisbury

passing such a resolution shall forthwith proceed to make a scheme for the improvement of such area.
Source: The Artisans' Dwellings Act (1875).

This Act, like so many of the Acts passed during this period, was *permissive* in that it gave councils permission to do certain things, but did not insist that they had to do them. When it was proposed that social legislation should be *compulsory*—forcing councils to do certain things—Disraeli replied:

> Permissive legislation is the character of a free people. It is easy to adopt compulsory legislation when you have to deal with those who only exist to obey; but in a free country, and especially in a country like England, you must trust to persuasion and example as the two great elements, if you wish to effect any considerable changes in the manners of the people.

(b) The Public Health Act, 1875

The first Public Health Act had been passed in 1848 (Section 12.4). Since then there had been a large number of Health Acts, most of them dealing with only one aspect of the problem. Thus there had been Nuisance Removal Acts, Burial Acts, Refuse Disposal Acts and so on. It had become necessary to collect all these Acts together into one comprehensive Act to which councils could refer whenever they wished to take action. So Disraeli's government was handed a set of proposals by civil servants, and the 1875 Act was the result. Contrary to the policy outlined above, the Act *compelled* local authorities to appoint a Medical Officer of Health and also *compelled* the authorities to take action to improve the sanitary conditions in their districts:

> It shall be the duty of every local authority to cause to be made from time to time inspections of their district, with a view to ascertain what nuisances exist calling for abatement under the powers of this Act, and to enforce the provisions of this Act in order to abate the same. . . .
> *Source:* Section 92 of the Public Health Act (1875).

(c) Other Reforms

The Disraeli government acted as the agents for essential reforms—essential since existing laws had been shown to be inefficient and civil servants were anxious to tighten things up.

(i) **Factory Act, 1875.** Previous Factory Acts had referred to specific types of factories—textile mills, coal mines and so on (Section 11.3). In 1875 all the existing legislation relating to factories was codified and brought together in one major Act—a Consolidating Act—the provisions of which applied to all places of work employing more than twenty people.

(ii) **Pure Food and Drugs Act, 1875.** In this case, Disraeli's government was asked to amend an Act which had been passed during Gladstone's ministry by extending it to more shops and to more food and drugs.

(*iii*) **Merchant Shipping Act, 1875.** Samuel Plimsoll, a backbench MP, campaigned for the introduction of legislation to protect merchant seamen who were sent to sea in ships that were not seaworthy by shipowners who collected insurance if the ships sank. Plimsoll's campaign led to the introduction of the Merchant Shipping Act. This required a maximum load-line, known as the *Plimsoll line*, to be marked on every ship.

(*iv*) **Education Act, 1876.** The state had begun to take an interest in the education of the nation's children in the 1830s. Since then there had been a number of Education Acts and Disraeli's Education Act was merely one of the series (Section 31.5).

(*v*) **'Climbing Boys' Act, 1875.** This Act made it illegal to employ boys as chimney sweeps in the huge chimneys of the Victorian houses, where they had often been suffocated or burnt. A number of Acts had been passed previously to try to stop this employment. Disraeli's Act was the last of that series. The fact that children were compelled to go to school made it easier to ensure that this Act was obeyed.

(*d*) **Trade Unions**

See Section 29.5 for information about trade unions in this period.

20.5   An Imperialist

It may be arguable whether Disraeli was or was not a social reformer, but there can be little doubt that he was actively interested in imperial affairs and the development of the British Empire. He no longer regarded colonies as 'millstones around our necks' as he had in 1852 (and as Gladstone did) nor as huge markets or sources of raw materials as did later imperialists such as Chamberlain (Unit 24). He simply thought that Britain needed, or deserved, a large Empire.

(*a*) **Popular Opinion**

In this Disraeli shared the views of the majority of British people who had supported Palmerston's blustering (Sections 14.3(*b*) and 14.4) and had resented Gladstone's more moral attitude towards foreign powers (Section 19.5). It was during Disraeli's ministry that the word *jingoism* was coined, from a popular song of the time:

> We don't want to fight but by jingo if we do,
> We've got the ships, we've got the men,
> We've got the money too.
> We've fought the bear before, and while we're Britons true
> The Russians shall not have Constantinople.

Source: Music Hall Song, composed by G. W. Hunt and sung by G. H. MacDermott (1877).

Critics of Disraeli's active and warlike policy christened it *jingoism*, and his supporters became known as *jingoists*. The writer of that popular song had, by his choice of a word, earned a place in the history books.

(b) Intellectual Opinion

This desire for overseas expansion was not only popular, it was also one which the cleverest of men revealed in their writings and speeches. Edward Dicey was a leading political scientist. In 1877 he wrote:

> So long as Englishmen retain their passion for independence, and their impatience of foreign rule, they are bound by a manifest destiny to found empires abroad, to make themselves the dominant race in the foreign countries to which they wander.
> *Source:* Dicey, E., *The Nineteenth Century* (1877).

(c) Suez Canal Shares, 1875

The Suez Canal had been built by a Frenchman, de Lesseps, the money being provided by a Suez Canal Company which was owned partly by French shareholders and partly by the Khedive (or ruler) of Egypt. The canal had been opened in 1869. Its main purpose was commercial but Britain, which had at first been hostile to the idea of the canal, had come to realize its value in strategic terms, for it provided a shorter route to India than the old route around the Cape. In 1875 the Khedive wished to sell his shares because he needed money to pay other debts. Disraeli heard about this and, without consulting Parliament, went to the banker, Rothschild, and asked for a loan of £4 million to buy the shares. Disraeli wrote to a friend:

> After a fortnight of the most unceasing labour and anxiety, I (for between ourselves, and ourselves only, I may be egotistical in this matter)—I have purchased for England, the Khedive of Egypt's interest in the Suez Canal. We have given the Khedive 4 millions sterling for his interest. The Faery [Disraeli's name for Queen Victoria (Section 11.8)] is in ecstasies about 'this great and important event'.
> *Source:* Letter to Lady Bradford (25 November 1875).

This acquisition eventually gave Britain control over the canal which became 'the lifeline of the Empire', particularly when steamships provided a quick method of communication with India, Malaya, Australia and New Zealand.

(d) Wars

Empires are not won merely by financial transactions or by the singing of music-hall songs. In 1877 Disraeli took over the Boer Republic of the Transvaal (Sections 17.3 and 25.7) claiming that he was doing this to protect the Boers from the danger of an attack by Zulu warriors. But some people began to doubt the wisdom of Disraeli's policy of expansion when the British became involved in a war with the Zulus. The Zulus were defeated in 1879 at

Fig. 20.4 'Punch' (11 December 1875) congratulates Disraeli on the acquisition of the shares in the Suez Canal Company

Ulundi, and the Boers then demanded the restoration of their independence. The British delayed and the first Boer War broke out. The British, after a defeat at Majuba Hill (1881), decided to withdraw from the Transvaal. By this time Gladstone was back in power and earned the unpopularity which went with this withdrawal (Section 21.3(c)(iv)).

Disraeli also sent an expeditionary force into Afghanistan (1878) to support a puppet king when the country seemed threatened by the Russians. General (later Lord) Roberts led the army into Afghanistan when these warriors refused to accept the British nominee, but once again Gladstone withdrew the force when he came to power in 1880 (Sections 21.1 and 21.3(c)(iii)).

(e) Queen Victoria

(See also Section 11.8.)

Disraeli's nickname for Queen Victoria was *the Faery*, a title taken from the poet Spenser's *Faery Queen*. We cannot imagine Gladstone giving her such a familiar nickname, nor can we imagine the Queen being delighted with much that Gladstone did. 'He treats me as if I were a public meeting,' she said. But she had a great liking for Disraeli. He was allowed to sit in her presence, not stand (because of his gout); he wrote her long, chatty letters about parliamentary business, he showed deep sympathy for her feelings for her dead husband and, in 1876, persuaded her to take the title of Empress of India as a sign that Britain was a great imperial power. The Queen rewarded him with the title of Earl of Beaconsfield.

20.6 Retirement

After his success at the Congress of Berlin (Section 22.7) the ageing Disraeli took less interest in public affairs, and his defeat in the 1880 election may have come as a relief. He died in 1881 and left to his successor, Lord Salisbury (Unit 25), a party which was well organized, appealed to British patriotism and seemed to be 'the Queen's Party'. It was not Disraeli's fault if Salisbury chose to concentrate only on foreign and imperial affairs and tended to ignore the condition of the people.

Test Yourself on Unit 20

(a) Document: Tory Democracy

Gentlemen, some years ago the Tory party experienced a great overthrow. I am here to admit that in my opinion it was deserved. A long course of power and prosperity had induced it to sink into a state of apathy and indifference. . . . Instead of the principles professed by Mr Pitt and Lord Grenville, the Tory system had degenerated into a policy which found an adequate basis on the principles of exclusiveness and restriction. Gentlemen, the Tory party, unless it is a national party is nothing. It is not a confederacy of nobles, it is not a democratic multitude; it is a party formed from all the numerous classes in the realm. . . .

Now, I have always been of opinion that the Tory party has three great objects. The first is to maintain the institutions of the country. . . . The discontent upon the subject of representation . . . was terminated by the Act of Parliamentary Reform of 1867–8. That Act was founded on a confidence that the great body of the people of this country were

'Conservative'. When I say 'Conservative', I use the word in its purest and loftiest sense. I mean that the people of England, and especially the working classes of England, are proud of belonging to a great country . . . that they believe, on the whole, that the greatness and the empire of England are to be attributed to the ancient institutions of the land. . . .

Gentlemen, there is another and second great object of the Tory party—to uphold the Empire of England. . . . Another great object of the Tory party is the elevation of the condition of the people. I ventured to say that the health of the people was the most important question for a statesman. It involves the state of the dwellings of the poor. It involves their enjoyment of some of the chief elements of nature—air, light and water. It involves the regulation of their industry, the inspection of their toil. It involves the purity of their provisions. A leading member of the Liberal party described this the other day as 'the policy of sewage'. Well, it may be the 'policy of sewage' to a Liberal member of Parliament. But to one of the labouring population of England . . . it is not a 'policy of sewage', but a question of life and death. . . .

Source: Disraeli's speech at Crystal Palace (June 1872).

(b) Questions

1. When and why had the Tory Party experienced 'a great overthrow'? What part had Disraeli played in that 'overthrow'?
2. 'A long course of power . . .' How long had the Tories been in power? Who were their leaders during that period of power?
3. List the 'three great objects' which the Tory Party should have.
4. What part had Disraeli played in the passage of the Act of Parliamentary Reform, 1867–8? What were the main aims of that bill?
5. Which, do you think, was more important to Disraeli—the Empire or the condition of the people? Give reasons for your answer.
6. Why did a leading Liberal describe Disraeli's policy as a 'policy of sewage'? Why did Disraeli call it 'a question of life and death'?

(c) Further Reading

Adelman, P.: *The Middle-Class Experience 1830–1914.* Longman (Harlow, 1984).

Blake, R.: *Disraeli.* Methuen (London, 1969).

Feuchtwanger, E. J.: *Democracy and Empire, Britain 1865–1914.* Arnold (London, 1984).

Lane, P.: *Elections.* Batsford (London, 1973).

Lane, P.: *The Conservative Party.* Batsford (London, 1974).

Read, D.: *England 1868–1914: The Age of Urban Democracy.* Longman (Harlow, 1979).

Robbins, K.: *The Eclipse of a Great Power: Modern Britain 1870–1975.* Longman (Harlow, 1983).

Stewart, R. M.: *The Foundation of the Conservative Party 1830–1867.* Longman (Harlow, 1978).

(d) Documentary

Adelman, P.: *Gladstone, Disraeli and Later Victorian Politics.* Longman (Harlow, 1983).

Grinter, R.: *Disraeli and Conservatism.* Arnold (London, 1972).

(e) **Exercises**

1. Give an account of Disraeli's career up to 1874. How far was he successful in giving the Conservative Party a 'new image' by 1874?

2. What were the main reforms affecting the working classes passed during Disraeli's ministry, 1874–80?

3. How had Disraeli tried to make the Conservative Party more popular between 1866 and 1880?

4. Write briefly on (i) Richard Cross, (ii) the Suez Canal Company, (iii) the Plimsoll line.

5. Give an account of Disraeli's achievements in imperial policy.

6. 'The most colourful of Victorian politicians.' What aspects of Disraeli's personality and career support this opinion?

7. Describe Disraeli's policy towards *two* of the following: (i) Egypt; (ii) the Russo-Turkish War, 1877–8; (iii) South Africa.

Gladstone, 1880–94

21.1 Out of Retirement

In Section 19.6(*b*) we saw that Gladstone had decided to retire early in 1875. However, the Grand Old Man was unable to remain silent when he saw the policies which his chief opponent, Disraeli, was following. He was disgusted when Disraeli sided with the Turks at the Congress of Berlin (Sections 22.6 and 22.8) and in a pamphlet on 'The Bulgarian Horrors' Gladstone called for the removal 'bag and baggage' of the Turks from Europe (Test Yourself on Unit 21(*a*)). This pamphlet became a best-seller and drew Gladstone, once again, into the thick of the political fight.

As Disraeli's imperial policy unfolded, with its wars in the Transvaal and Afghanistan (Section 20.5(*d*)), Gladstone's anger grew. Whereas Disraeli's course of action in both foreign and imperial affairs was based on the consideration, 'What would be best for Britain?', Gladstone tended to regard issues from a moral standpoint. In 1879 and 1880 he went on a long and arduous tour of Midlothian during the course of which he delivered a number of long speeches attacking Disraeli. Typical of these was the speech he made at Dalkeith on 26 November 1879:

> Go from South Africa to the mountains of Central Asia. Go into the lofty hills of Afghanistan and what do we see there? I fear a yet sadder sight than was to be seen in the land of the Zulus. . . . Villages burned, women and children driven forth to perish in the snows of winter, in the name of England. Remember the rights of the savage, as we call him. Remember that the happiness of his humble home, remember that the sanctity of life in the hill villages of Afghanistan among the winter snows, is as inviolable in the eye of Almighty God as can be your own.
>
> *Source:* Speech at the Foresters Hall, Dalkeith (26 November 1879). From Gladstone, W. E., *Political Speeches in Scotland, November and December 1879* (1880).

21.2 Back in Power

In 1880 Disraeli called a general election as a result of which the Liberals found themselves once again the largest party in the Commons. Hartington, who had led the party since Gladstone's 'retirement' and the later retirement of Grenville (Section 19.6(*b*)), asked him whether he would accept a post in a Liberal government; Gladstone argued that while he had no wish to serve at all, he simply could not take a junior position: he had either to be the Prime Minister or he would be nothing. It was impossible to imagine a Liberal government without him—after all, it was his Midlothian Campaign which had done most to rouse Liberals throughout the country against the alleged evils of Disraeli's expansionist policies.

THE GRAND OLD HAND AND THE YOUNG 'UNS.

Fig. 21.1 'Punch' (30 January 1886) shows one view of Gladstone. Many of the young'uns were more radical than the Grand Old Man and were not always willing to follow his advice

Thus Gladstone came back to power in 1880, at the age of seventy-one. With hindsight we can see that it was probably a mistake for him to take up the cudgels again at such an age. He was out of touch with the times—people were calling for a vigorous attack on a number of social problems such as housing, poverty, unemployment and education, while Gladstone was still very much the Peelite who believed that 'good government was less government', and that inferference by government was an evil to be avoided.

21.3   The Ministry of All the Troubles, 1880–5

Gladstone's ministry of 1868–74 is remembered as 'the Ministry of Great Reforms', but his ministry of 1880–5 was, and is, remembered as one in which disaster followed disaster. An underlying reason for this state of affairs was that Gladstone did not fully appreciate how much times had changed, nor did he understand that new problems required new solutions. But apart from this general explanation of the troubles that beset this ministry, there are a number of specific reasons for them.

(a) A Divided Party

In the 1868 ministry, Gladstone had been the dominant politician in his Cabinet, but by 1880 his position was less secure. On one side of the party there was a group of Whigs led by Lord Hartington. They had remained loyal to the Liberal leadership in spite of what they considered to be radical policies. We have seen that many members of the richer classes deserted the Liberals in the 1874 election, an indication of the dissatisfaction many of them felt with Gladstone's policies (Section 19.6(*a*)). Hartington and his group of Whig MPs did not feel able to desert the camp and to follow Disraelian Toryism, but they were, quite obviously, less than happy in Gladstone's company.

On the other side was a small, but vociferous, group of Radical Liberals led by Joseph Chamberlain and Sir Charles Dilke. These men were younger and in tune with the age, and they demanded a more vigorous policy of social reform than Gladstone was willing to pursue. Chamberlain spoke for this group when he said:

> We have to account for and to grapple with the mass of misery in our midst. Now that we have a Government of the people by the people, we will go on and make it the Government for the people, in which all shall cooperate in order to secure to every man his natural rights, his right to existence, and to a fair enjoyment of it. I shall be told tomorrow that this is Socialism. Of course it is Socialism. The Poor Law is Socialism; the Education Act is Socialism; the greater part of the municipal work is Socialism; and every kindly act of legislation, by which the community has sought to discharge its responsibilities and its obligations to the poor is Socialism. Our object is the elevation of the poor—a levelling up—to remove the excessive inequality in social life. . . .
>
> Source: Speech at Warrington (8 September 1885) from Lucy H. W. (ed.), Speeches of Right Hon Joseph Chamberlain MP (1885).

Gladstone was incapable of following the sort of policies which would have pleased Chamberlain who, in anger, described the venerable (and venerated) Gladstone as 'a Rip Van Winkle come down from the mountain' (Section 27.1). But Gladstone did, at least, give Chamberlain and Dilke posts in the government, which seemed to Hartington and his followers an indication that Gladstone was swinging to the side of the Radical 'socialists'. Hartington and his followers became less easy in Gladstone's party.

(b) The Fourth Party

In the Commons there were three distinct parties. There were the *Liberals*, now again the government party, the *Irish Nationalists* under the leadership of Parnell (Sections 23.3 and 23.4), and the *Conservatives* (or Tories), now the Opposition party and led in the Commons by Sir Stafford Northcote. (The leader of the party was Lord Salisbury who sat in the Lords (Section 20.6).) Northcote proved to be a weak leader of the Opposition, unable to match Gladstone's ability, or to offer a sufficient challenge to the Grand Old Man.

In the Tory ranks were a number of younger MPs who had hoped that the party would revive Disraeli's philosophy of Empire, a vigorous foreign policy and social reform. In this group sat A. J. Balfour, nephew of Lord Salisbury, Gorst, who had done so much to reorganize the Tory Party in the 1870s (Section 20.3) and Lord Randolph Churchill, a younger son of the Duke of Marlborough, who was soon regarded as its leader. Gorst and Churchill developed the theme of *Tory Democracy* with its Disraelian idea that the upper class should look after the interests of the lower classes—by social reform, for example (Test Yourself on Unit 20(*a*)). In return, they claimed, the lower classes would vote for upper-class Tory candidates because both the upper and lower classes had a common enemy in the middle-class indu-strialist–employer.

'Trust the People,' said Lord Randolph in one famous speech in which he tried to persuade his party's leaders to pursue the Disraelian path. But neither Salisbury (Section 25.1) nor Northcote was a democrat, nor were they much interested in following in Disraeli's footsteps, except in his imperialism and in his policy of upholding British interests abroad. Churchill and his small band of colleagues became dissatisfied both with the general tendency of the party —away from Disraeli's new Toryism and with the particular failure of Northcote in the House of Commons. They therefore decided to work together to provide a more vigorous opposition to Gladstone than was being offered by Northcote, and to propound the Disraelian philosophy. So much did they act together that they became known as the *Fourth Party* to distin-guish them from the three larger parties. Their aim was to create problems for Gladstone. This was made easier by Gladstone's own temper and by a number of issues which seemed ready-made to embarrass the government.

(*i*) **Gladstone's temper.** Gladstone had grown used to dominating his own party and the House of Commons. He had, indeed, become a little autocratic and resentful of criticism. Churchill and his Fourth Party, by provoking Gladstone to lose his temper, created the impression that he was less in con-trol of affairs then he really was.

(*ii*) **The Bradlaugh affair.** Charles Bradlaugh was an atheist who had toured the country preaching that there was no God and that all religions were a mumbo-jumbo of humbug. These speeches had angered the majority of people of all classes, and Bradlaugh had been stoned, thrown into ponds, chased out of towns and otherwise attacked for his troubles. But in the 1880s he was elected MP for Northampton and went to Westminster to claim his seat. When he appeared before the Speaker he refused to swear the customary oath of allegiance to the Queen on the Bible. How could he do so when he did not believe in God, much less in God's Bible? The House of Commons, therefore, voted to exclude him from the House, whereupon Churchill and others at-tacked Gladstone as being illiberal in his attitude. After all, they claimed, Bradlaugh had been elected to represent a constituency. Was the government claiming the right to tell a constituency who its MP was or was not to be? The debate on the Bradlaugh affair dragged on for months; there were new elec-tions in Northampton and again Bradlaugh was elected. Again the argument went on, until finally the government decided that MPs need not swear an oath on the Bible but could merely *affirm*—without using the Bible—their loyalty and allegiance. Churchill and his group then attacked the government for being in league with the forces of atheism, an attack which was more damaging in the God-fearing days of Queen Victoria than might be the case today.

(c) **Colonial Issues**

Gladstone had come to power in 1880 largely because of his attack on Disraeli's colonial policy (Section 20.5), but he inherited a number of problems resulting from his predecessor's policy. And, in attempting to solve these problems, Gladstone presented Churchill and other critics with plenty of ammunition. It seemed that he was bound to lose no matter what policy he adopted.

(i) **Egypt, 1881–2.** Disraeli had bought the Khedive's shares in the Suez Canal Company (Section 20.5) with the result that the British and French governments were dragged into Egyptian affairs in order to ensure that the company's shareholders received their annual dividends. In 1881 an Egyptian nationalist leader, *Arabi Pasha*, led anti-foreign riots. Gladstone, unwillingly, sent in an army under Sir Garnet Wolseley to restore order, which defeated the Egyptians at the Battle of Tel-el-Kebir in 1882.

One should feel a certain sympathy for Gladstone. If he had not acted to protect British interests he would, rightly, have been accused of allowing foreigners to break the financial agreements which their own rulers had made. But by interfering he was merely imitating the policy of Disraeli, which he had attacked as recently as 1879. Many of his own Liberal followers were disturbed by his actions in Egypt, and Churchill and the Fourth Party saw to it that Gladstone's own dilemma was exposed to the public.

(ii) **The Sudan** was a dependency of Egypt. Gladstone reluctantly agreed to accept responsibility for maintaining order in Egypt but he refused, at first, to accept responsibility for the Egyptian Sudan. While British civil servants and a British army took control of affairs in Egypt, a Moslem fanatic, the *Mahdi*, roused the Sudan when he preached a holy war against the British infidels and their Egyptian officials. The majority of the Sudanese followed this 'holy man' and formed a formidable army which attacked Egyptian-held ports and towns in the Sudan. Britain was responsible for Egypt, which it was well on the way to governing in 1883 and 1884. But were the Egyptian civil servants and garrisons in the Sudan employees of the British government?

In 1884 Gladstone gave in to the Opposition and agreed to send a British force to the Sudan, under the leadership of General Charles Gordon, to bring the Egyptian officials and their families back to safety in British-controlled Egypt. Gordon might have done this if he had acted promptly, but he seemed to want to defeat the Mahdi first, a task which had not been given him by Gladstone. By May 1884 Gordon's force found itself besieged in the capital of the Sudan, Khartoum, by a strong army led by the Mahdi. Gladstone, angry with Gordon, refused for some time to send a force to relieve Khartoum and rescue Gordon. Once again, public pressure built up and finally, but reluctantly, Gladstone ordered a force to be sent. But this, again, was too late and the news of the fall of Khartoum and the death of Gordon in January 1885

Fig. 21.2 Gordon's last stand at Khartoum, as seen in Madame Tussaud's Waxworks in London

roused a great deal of public anger against Gladstone. His former nickname of Grand Old Man (GOM) was altered to another GOM—Gordon's Own Murderer.

(*iii*) **Afghanistan.** Gladstone ordered the withdrawal of General Roberts's force from Afghanistan (Section 20.5), and the Russians took advantage of this to send in their army, which defeated the Afghans at Penjdeh in 1885. It seemed that this independent country on the North-West Frontier of British India would fall under the domination of the hated Russians. The British regarded India as 'the biggest jewel in the British Crown', and Gladstone seemed to be placing this jewel in some danger.

(*iv*) **Transvaal.** Disraeli had annexed the Boer Republic of Transvaal in 1877 (Section 20.5); Gladstone had condemned this action and declared that the Boers had every right to their independence. However, he delayed the restoration of this independence and in 1881 the Boers attacked and defeated a British army at Majuba Hill. Gladstone's reaction to this blot on the British name was not to send a larger army to seek revenge but to invite the Boers to a conference which was concluded by the Convention of London (1884) and which gave them back their independence.

(d) Ireland

Throughout the whole of this ministry Ireland presented Gladstone with a series of complex problems which we shall consider in detail in Sections 23.4 and 23.5.

21.4   Reforms

While the ministry was a long period of almost ceaseless troubles for an ageing Gladstone, it did pass several important reforms.

(a) The Married Women's Property Act, 1882

Until this Act was passed a married woman's property was controlled by her husband. No matter whether she was given the property as a gift by a living relative or whether she inherited the property on the death of her parents, the woman's property became that of her husband. She had no legal rights over it at all. Gladstone's Act was a concession to the growing number of women who were campaigning for equal treatment with men, for it allowed married women to own property.

(b) The Corrupt Practices Act, 1883

This Act was a small step along the road of parliamentary reform. It limited the amount of money which candidates could spend during an election campaign, made certain practices such as 'treating' or buying food and drink or other presents for electors illegal, and in so doing lessened the influence which rich people could exercise during an election.

(c) Parliamentary Reform, 1884 and 1885

This will be considered in detail in Section 28.1. Here we have to notice that the 1884 Act extended the vote to millions of men living in the county constituencies, who in future would have the same rights as voters in borough constituencies. The total electorate became 5 million with qualification for voting in the counties being the same as it was in the boroughs. The 1885 Act involved the redistribution of constituencies (Section 28.2), which meant the redrawing of constituency boundaries, and it also required the compilation of new electoral registers for the changed constituencies. This task would take a long time—and this was very important in the light of events in 1885 and 1886.

21.5   Political Uncertainty, 1885–6

In June 1885 Gladstone's government was defeated by a combination of Irish Nationalists (Sections 23.3 and 23.4) and Conservatives. A major reason for the defeat was that in the crucial vote about 70 Liberal MPs abstained from voting. This 'rebellion' by Hartington and others was not surprising, but its effect was devastating. Gladstone resigned but he was unable to ask the Queen to call an election because the electoral registers were not yet prepared. The Queen therefore invited Lord Salisbury to form a government, even though the Conservatives did not have the largest number of MPs in the House of Commons. Gladstone hoped that this minority government, which was being supported by the Irish Nationalists, would try to solve the Irish problem. Lord Randolph Churchill, now a member of the Cabinet, indicated to Parnell, the leader of the Irish Nationalists, that the Conservatives would try to produce a workable and acceptable answer to the Irish demand for Home Rule (Sections 23.3–23.5). However, no solution had been produced by the time the electoral registers were ready and Salisbury could ask the Queen to call an election.

In the election of November 1885 the electorate was offered a variety of programmes. There were the official policies put forward by *Gladstone*, who talked about lowering income tax, extending education and creating a situation in which working class people could help themselves to the better life. There was the *unofficial programme*, put forward by Chamberlain and his Radical colleagues who preached the need for more social reform. The *Conservatives* under Salisbury promised to restore British influence abroad, while the *Irish* demanded Home Rule. The result of the 1885 election was inconclusive: Liberals 335, Conservatives 249, Irish 86.

The House of Commons would, in one sense, be controlled by the Irish. If they voted with the Conservatives, Gladstone and the Liberals would be overwhelmed, whereas if Gladstone could persuade them to support the Liberals, he would again be able to form a government. On 17 December 1885 he announced that he had come to the conclusion that the only solution to the Irish problem lay in granting Home Rule to that island. When Parliament reassembled in January 1886 a combination of Liberal and Irish votes defeated the Salisbury government (Section 23.5), and in February 1886 Gladstone formed his Third Ministry.

21.6 The Liberal Party Splits

(a) Hartington and the Whigs

Hartington and the Whigs had become increasingly convinced that Chamberlain and the 'socialist' Liberals would come to dominate the party, particularly since the larger electorate created by the reforms of 1867 and 1884 would demand social reforms of one sort or another. In January 1886 Hartington and his followers ceased to support Gladstone and were swallowed up in the Conservative Party under Salisbury.

(b) Chamberlain and the Liberal Unionists

Chamberlain could claim, with some truth, that his unofficial programme was a cause of the Liberal victory in the 1885 election. He resented Gladstone's announcement on Home Rule because he believed that to pursue such a policy would tend to take up the time of the House of Commons, so that it would be unable to deal with the social programme which Chamberlain believed to be essential. He also resented the autocratic way in which the Prime Minister had acted in this matter without consulting any of his colleagues. Finally, he may have hoped that his resignation would force Gladstone into final retirement and leave the leadership of the party open, perhaps for Chamberlain himself. In March 1886 he and over forty colleagues in the House announced their opposition to Gladstone and declared themselves to be *Liberal Unionists*, indicating that they still wished to lay claim to being Liberal while at the same time wishing to uphold the Union between Britain and Ireland.

Fig. 21.3 The Central Lobby of the House of Commons, 1886. From left to right: Inspector Denning, Hillman (a clerk), John Bright, Sir William Harcourt, Gosset (Deputy Sergeant), Labouchere, Bradlaugh, Chamberlain, Parnell, Gladstone, Lord Randolph Churchill, Hartington, Chaplin, Leveson-Gower, Spencer, Lord Hill, Mr Hansard

(c) The Defeat of the Home Rule Bill

In June 1886 the Home Rule Bill was defeated by a combination of Tories and 96 followers of Hartington and Chamberlain (Section 23.5). Gladstone resigned to make way for Salisbury, whose Conservative Party was victorious in the general election of July 1886 when the electors returned Conservatives 316, Liberal 191, Liberal Unionists 78, Irish 85.

Salisbury held office until 1892, when the Liberals were once more returned to power, still led by Gladstone, now eighty-three years old and a Grand Old Man indeed. He held to his belief that Ireland would be given its independence and in 1893 he introduced his Second Home Rule Bill (Section 23.7). This passed through the Commons but was rejected in the Lords. Gladstone wanted to ask the Queen to call an election on this issue of Ireland but his Cabinet refused to agree, and in 1894 Gladstone resigned, to be succeeded as Prime Minister by Lord Rosebery.

Test Yourself on Unit 21

(a) Document: Gladstone on the Bulgarian Horrors

We know that there have been perpetrated, under the authority of Turkey to which all the time we have been giving the strongest moral and material support, outrages, so vast in scale as to exceed all modern example. These are the Bulgarian horrors. What can be done to punish, or to brand, or to prevent?

Twenty years ago, France and England determined to try a great experiment in remodelling the administrative system of Turkey, with the hope of curing its intolerable vices, and of making good its not less intolerable deficiencies. A vast expenditure of French and English life and treasure, gave to Turkey twenty years of repose. The insurrections of 1875 have disclosed the total failure of the Porte to fulfil the engagements which she had contracted. Even these miserable insurrections she had not the ability to put down. . . . A lurid glare is thrown over the whole case by the Bulgarian horrors.

I entreat my countrymen to insist that our Government shall apply all its vigour to obtain the extinction of the Turkish power in Bulgaria. Let the Turks now carry away their abuses by carrying off themselves. Their Pashas, one and all, bag and baggage, shall, I hope, clear out.

Source: Gladstone, W. E., *The Bulgarian Horrors and the Question of the East* (1876).

(b) Questions

1. What did Gladstone mean by 'the Bulgarian horrors'? When had they taken place? Which government was responsible for these atrocities?
2. What had happened 'twenty years ago'?
3. What was the attitude of Russia towards these atrocities? What action did the Russians take? Why?
4. Who was Prime Minister at this time? What was his attitude to (i) the atrocities, (ii) the Russian action?
5. Which Treaty followed these atrocities? What action did the British government take when it heard about this Treaty?
6. What was the significance of this pamphlet in Gladstone's political future?
7. Do you think that Gladstone is arguing on (i) moral *or* (ii) practical grounds? Do you consider this a sign of strength or weakness in a party leader? Give reasons for your answer with examples from other periods of history you have studied.

(c) Further Reading

See reading for Unit 19.

(d) Exercises

1. Compare the imperial policies of Disraeli and Gladstone.
2. What were the main problems facing Gladstone between 1880 and 1885?
3. Account for the break-up of the Liberal Party in 1886.
4. Write briefly on (i) Majuba, (ii) Khartoum, (iii) the unofficial programme, (iv) the Fourth Party.

The Eastern Question, 1870–1914

22.1 Definition of the Eastern Question

We have already seen that the Eastern Question had three main components (Section 15.1).

(a) The Weakness of Turkey

The once great and efficiently run Turkish Empire was governed by a succession of weak rulers who proved incapable of handling its complex affairs. Sultans had had, for example, to ask for the help of a vassal, Mehemet Ali, during the Greek rebellion of the 1820s (Section 9.8), and had been obliged to ask for outside help when Mehemet Ali himself had rebelled in 1839 (Section 15.2). As very often happens with individuals and governments who are unable to control people over whom they are supposed to exercise authority, the weak Turkish government tried, from time to time, to assert its authority. It organized massacres of its Christian subjects in the Balkans, for example, or at least did nothing to stop its soldiers and officials from organizing such massacres.

(b) The Growing Nationalism among the Subject Races

The Greeks had won their independence in 1830 (Section 9.8). Serbia (1856), Roumania (1856) and part of Bulgaria had been granted self-government within the Turkish Empire, but they were all anxious to gain their complete independence from the Turkish yoke.

(c) The Interests of the Great Powers

It is possible that the Turks and their subject nations might have worked out their problems, perhaps peacefully, perhaps after a series of nationalist wars. But the Great Powers were unwilling or, indeed, incapable, of allowing either of the two parties to decide things for themselves. The Russians, for example, were anxious to gain territory for themselves or influence in whatever independent nations might emerge if Turkey should crumble (Sections 15.1(c) and 15.4). Britain was quite determined that Russia should not advance on Constantinople or gain undue influence in the Balkan area as a whole, because this would threaten the now vital Suez Canal route to India (Section 20.5). So while Russia was anxious to see 'the sick man' die, Britain was almost compelled to act as a guardian of the Turk, and appear as the opponent of nationalism because of her fear of Russia.

Increasingly in the latter half of the century Austria also began to take an interest in Balkan affairs, for she had no wish to see a strong, independent Serbia emerge from the wreck of the Turkish Empire. If such a nation-state did gain its independence it might well wish to incorporate within its borders the Slavs who lived in the Hungarian Kingdom, which was part of the Austro-Hungarian Empire. The emergence of Serbia might also encourage other racial minorities in that Empire—Poles, Czechs and others—to seek their independence and so lead to the break-up of the Austro-Hungarian Empire.

22.2   Pan Slavism

For more than a century Russia had been trying to gain influence and territory in the Balkans (Sections 15.1(c), 15.2 and 15.4). Her reasons for this were simple. She needed a warm water port through which, all the year round, she could export her grain from the Ukraine and import the goods she needed from overseas. Her northern ports were ice-bound and closed for about nine months in the year, while her far eastern port of Vladivostok was too far away to be of much use. So she wanted to get a port on the Aegean Sea, or access to such a port through the territory of an independent country which would be friendly to her.

Russia had tried to achieve this end in various ways, with little success (Sections 15.1(c), 15.2 and 15.4), so in the 1860s and 1870s Russian writers and politicians developed the theory of *Pan Slavism*. This pointed to the fact that there was a large number of Slavonic peoples—in Serbia, Bosnia-Herzegovina—all of whom were under Turkish sovereignty and all sharing, with Russia, a common adherence to the Orthodox church. There were also the Czechs and others—known as the northern Slavs—in the Austro-Hungarian Empire, and, largest of all, there was Russia. What was more logical, said they, than that Russia should encourage the development of the Slavonic spirit, the development of Slavonic nationhood in the Balkans, in Austria and Hungary, and indicate that she was prepared to act as the champion for the less fortunate Slavs still subject to foreign rule?

22.3   Slav Rebellions, 1875

The peoples of Bosnia-Herzegovina rose in rebellion in 1875 against their corrupt Turkish masters who refused to grant them the same degree of independence that had already been granted to Serbia. Russia, Germany and Austria acted together in urging the Turkish government to give way, to grant the reforms which were demanded and so put an end to the rebellions. Disraeli, Prime Minister after 1874, refused to join with the other powers. He was afraid of weakening Turkish power, believing that this would allow Russia to gain increased influence.

22.4   The Bulgarian Massacres, 1876

In 1876 the world was horrified to hear of brutal atrocities that took place after further rebellions in Bulgaria, Serbia and Montenegro (Test Yourself on Unit 21(a)). Russia, acting the part of the Protector of the Slavs, decided to invade Turkey, to take revenge for the massacres and to win independence for the subject races. The Russian army advanced through the Dobruja, defeated the Turks at the Battle of Plevna (December 1877) and raced on to Adrianople by 20 January 1878.

While this was going on the British Cabinet was considering what to do. Lord Barrington recorded a summary of a conversation he had with the Prime Minister, who had been made Earl of Beaconsfield in 1876 (Section 20.5(e)):

> Lord Beaconsfield has great hopes of being able to settle this great question. Supposing the Russians [were] to enter Bulgaria, said I. That, he answered, would be an entirely new phase of the question. He is evidently quite determined that the Russians shall not have Constantinople. Many in England say, Why not? England has taken Egypt to secure our highway to India. But the answer is obvious, said Lord B. If the Russians had Constantinople, they could at any time march their Army through Syria to the mouth of the Nile, and then what would be the use of our holding Egypt? Constantinople is the key to India, and not Egypt and the Suez Canal. The Russians say: 'We do not wish to hold Constantinople.' Perhaps not, but for all that their game is to have someone there who is more or less dependent on them. . . .
> Source: quoted in Moneypenny, W. F. and Buckle, G. E., The Life of Benjamin Disraeli (1929).

But Russia had invaded Bulgaria while Britain was talking, and having got to Adrianople, forced the Turks to sit down and make a peace treaty.

22.5   The Treaty of San Stefano, March 1878

By this treaty Russia appeared to have gained most of what she had been seeking.

(a) Bulgaria

A large section of the former Turkish Empire was to be established as a new and independent Kingdom of Bulgaria, and it was of particular significance that this new state would have the Aegean Sea as part of its southern boundary. Bulgaria would be able to establish ports through which trade could pass. Russia must have hoped—and certainly Britain feared—that the new kingdom would become a vassal state of Russia so that these Aegean ports would be open to Russian trade and Russian navies and hence become avenues for Russian expansion into the Mediterranean.

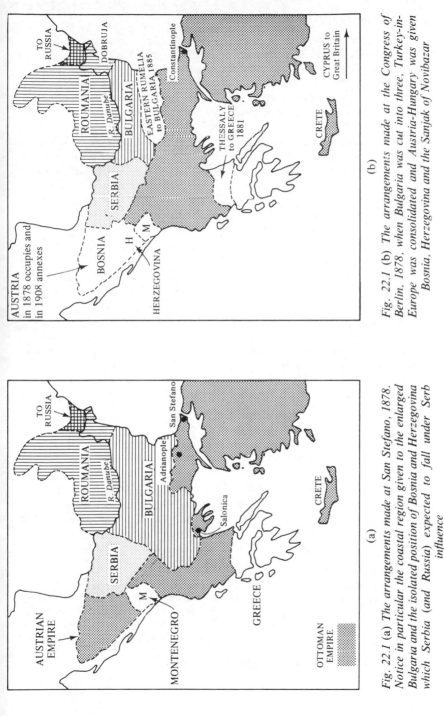

(a)

Fig. 22.1 (a) The arrangements made at San Stefano, 1878. Notice in particular the coastal region given to the enlarged Bulgaria and the isolated position of Bosnia and Herzegovina which Serbia (and Russia) expected to fall under Serb influence

(b)

Fig. 22.1 (b) The arrangements made at the Congress of Berlin, 1878, when Bulgaria was cut into three, Turkey-in-Europe was consolidated and Austria-Hungary was given Bosnia, Herzegovina and the Sanjak of Novibazar

(b) **Turkey**

Turkey also had to concede some territory to Serbia and Russia, but was allowed to retain the outlying parts of the old Empire. Yet even in these areas she had to promise reforms, and it must have seemed obvious that if Turkey had been unable to control her Empire efficiently when she had a free run of the whole of the Balkans, she would be even less capable of controlling these outlying areas, cut off as they would be from the Turkish heartland. And this Turkish heartland, or at least Turkey-in-Europe, was to be reduced to a small region around Constantinople itself. To the Turks who looked at the map as drawn at San Stefano, it must have seemed that the Russians and their new allies, the Bulgarians, were encroaching on the capital, Constantinople, which —it appeared—would one day fall.

22.6   The Great Powers Intervene

(a) **Britain**

Disraeli had been a member of the House of Lords since 1876, when he had become Earl of Beaconsfield (Sections 20.5(*e*) and 22.4). He was outraged by the Treaty of San Stefano, and as Prime Minister, expressed his anger in a speech to his fellow peers:

> The Treaty of San Stefano abolishes the dominion of the Ottoman Empire in Europe; it creates a larger Bulgaria inhabited by many races not Bulgarians. This goes to the shores of the Black Sea and seizes the ports of that sea; it extends to the coast of the Aegean and appropriates the ports of that coast. The Treaty provides for the government of this new Bulgaria, under a prince who is to be selected by Russia; its administration is to be organized by a commissary of Russia; and this new State is to be garrisoned by Russia.
>
> The Sultan of Turkey is reduced to a state of absolute subjection to Russia. We protest against an arrangement which would place at the command of Russia, and Russia alone, the Straits.
>
> *Source:* quoted in Moneypenny, W. F. and Buckle, G. E., *The Life of Benjamin Disraeli* (1929).

And he was prepared to go to war if that were required. His Foreign Secretary, Lord Derby, was the son of Disraeli's 'old chief' (Sections 14.4, 19.3, 20.2, 28.1(*c*) and Test Yourself on Unit 15(*a*)). When it seemed that Beaconsfield—as Disraeli was known after becoming an earl in 1876—was prepared to go to war against Russia, Derby resigned. His successor at the Foreign Office was Lord Salisbury, to whom Derby wrote:

> I know our chief of old, and from various things that have dropped from him I am fully convinced—not indeed that he wants a war—but that he has made up his mind to large military preparations, to an extremely warlike speech, to an agitation in favour of armed intervention (recollect that he said in Cabinet: 'The country is asleep and I want to wake it up'), and if possible to an expedition that shall occupy Constantinople or Gallipoli. . . .
>
> *Source:* quoted in Blake, R., *Disraeli*. Methuen (London, 1969).

Meanwhile, Gladstone was campaigning throughout the country, attacking the Turks for the Bulgarian Massacres and demanding that far from helping Turkey, Britain ought to help drive them 'bag and baggage' out of Europe (Test Yourself on Unit 21(*a*)).

(*b*) Austria

The Austrian government was unwilling to stand by and see the re-drawing of the map of an area which bordered on its Empire and in which it wished to take an interest. Until the 1860s Austrian interest had been concentrated on Italy and the Confederation of German States. But since 1860 Italy had been united and Austria had been driven out, and since 1866 she had also been driven out of the German Confederation by Bismarck's Prussia. Having been forcibly turned out of two territories where she had exercised power, Austria now wished to try to exercise influence in the Balkans. She saw herself as replacing the declining Turkey as the dominant power, and could not, therefore, accept what had happened at San Stefano.

(*c*) Germany

Otto von Bismarck, the Chancellor of the newly-unified Germany, had no interest in the Balkans himself. He had enough to do inside the new country he had created between 1864 and 1871, but he felt that he had to support Austria in this matter. He hoped that Austria would remain friendly to Germany, forget that she had once been the dominant power in the Germanic Federation and not seek an alliance with fellow-Catholic France against the new Germany. Bismarck therefore invited the powers to come to Berlin to discuss the Treaty of San Stefano and to try to work out a new set of territorial arrangements.

22.7 The Congress of Berlin, 1878

At the Congress of Berlin the map of the Balkans was re-drawn again.

(*a*) Bulgaria

The large Bulgaria of San Stefano was cut into three. The southern portion (Macedonia), with its Aegean coast, was handed back to Turkey in return for a promise of reforms. The centre portion was established as a separate State of Rumelia. Only the northern portion remained as an independent Bulgaria. In doing this the British, represented by Salisbury and the ageing Disraeli (as the Earl of Beaconsfield was still better known), hoped that they had made it easier for Turkey to exercise control over the remainder of her European Empire, while at the same time cutting down Russia's sphere of influence and the danger to Constantinople.

(*b*) **Britain**

Britain acquired Cyprus from Turkey, and in return agreed to defend Turkey against Russia, in the Balkans.

(*c*) **Austria**

Austria had supported Britain's campaign against Turkey and at Berlin she was allowed to occupy the Slav territories of Bosnia-Herzegovina—territories which she incorporated into her Empire in 1908 (Sections 26.7 and 26.8). This acquisition had two effects:

(i) Russian hostility to Austria was ensured. Why should Austria have been allowed to take, without any fighting, territories which belonged to the Slavonic peoples? Was this not, said Russia, evidence of Austrian determination to push her way into the Balkans?

(ii) Serbian hostility to Austria was increased. The Serbs regarded these territories as almost 'naturally' theirs. The peoples were Slavs, they—like the Serbs—had suffered under the Turks. What more natural than that together they should establish a large, independent Slav Kingdom? Austria's acquisition of these territories angered the Serbs, who also feared that if Austria had really set out on a southward-facing path, they might be the next to be taken over by the encroaching Austrians.

22.8   The Failure of the Congress of Berlin

Disraeli came back claiming that he was bringing 'peace with honour'. His Foreign Secretary, Salisbury, later Prime Minister, was to admit in 1885 that 'We had backed the wrong horse' when they backed Turkey. The Turks, after 1878, as before that date, proved incapable of efficient government or of carrying out the reforms that they promised to undertake, so that the subject races continued to rebel. Even more to the point, Britain had to agree to Rumelia and Bulgaria uniting to form a new, larger kingdom, in 1885, while from 1894 to 1896 Salisbury had to stand by while the Turks carried out another bloodletting in the Armenian Massacres (Section 25.3(*b*)).

22.9   The Eastern Crisis, 1911–13

(*a*) **The First Balkan War**

The Balkan powers were alarmed by the continuation of Turkish misrule, and decided to unite for their own self-defence and to protect their fellow Christians in Turkey. Serbia, Greece, Bulgaria and Montenegro formed the *Balkan League*, which attacked and defeated Turkey in 1912.

In 1913, Sir Edward Grey, Foreign Secretary in the Liberal government (Section 26.8), called the warring powers to a conference in London. He hoped that territorial arrangements could be made which would satisfy both

A BLAZE OF TRIUMPH!

Fig. 22.2 'Punch' (27 July 1878) greets Disraeli's success at the Congress of Berlin. The Turkish rider's inability to reform proved fatal to the long-term stability of the Balkans

the members of the League and the interests of the Great Powers. But though the Balkan League countries had united to defeat Turkey—whose European territory was reduced to a mere strip around Constantinople—they disagreed over the division of the spoils.

In particular, the League was split over the future of Macedonia, the former Turkish territory stretching along the Aegean coast from Greece to the remnant of European Turkey. The inhabitants of Macedonia were Bulgars, Serbs and Greeks, so it was difficult—if not impossible—to suggest frontiers that would satisfy the three nations. Serbia wanted part of either Macedonia or Albania, because she was a landlocked country and one of these new territories would provide her with a port. But both Montenegro and Italy also wanted Albania. Italy was looking for some overseas possessions to satisfy her imperial dreams, and her claim was supported by Austria, which was determined to prevent the growth of Serbia. The outcome was the creation of an independent kingdom of Albania—a decision which strengthened Serbia's resolve to gain control of Macedonia. The Bulgarians had been given large parts of Macedonia in the Treaty of San Stefano (Section 22.5), but had lost them under the arrangements made at the Congress of Berlin (Section 22.7). So Bulgaria believed that if Macedonia was going to be divided in 1913, she had the prior right to at least a section of it. The Greeks also claimed part of the territory—in particular Salonika, the coastal strip lying to the east of Greece, and inhabited, they said, mainly by Greek nationals. Bulgaria had provided most of the men and money for the war against Turkey, and argued that this gave her the right to a major portion of the spoils. Serbia and Greece were not prepared to accept Bulgaria's claims, and in 1913, a second Balkan War broke out.

(b) The Second Balkan War

This time Bulgaria was the aggressor, and Serbia, Montenegro, Greece and Roumania—a newcomer to the fray—were the countries attacked. Turkey saw an opportunity to regain some of her former territory, and joined in. Not surprisingly, Bulgaria was defeated, and she was forced to accept the terms of the *Treaty of Bucharest* (1913), under which:

  (i) Bulgaria lost Thrace to Turkey and a strip of Dubruja to Rumania.
  (ii) Serbia gained Northern Macedonia, but no coastal region, so that she was still without a port.
  (iii) Greece gained Southern Macedonia, including Salonika.
  (iv) Montenegro was enlarged.

This settlement increased Serbia's ambitions. If she could help in the almost complete dismemberment of the decaying Turkey, why should she not do the same to the Austro-Hungarian Empire, where millions of Slavs were waiting to be rescued from the Hungarian yoke and, so Serbia claimed, incorporated into an even larger Slavonic Kingdom? On the other hand, Austria became even more resentful of Serb growth and ambition, and even more hostile to the national feelings of the racial minorities inside the Empire.

However, this crisis had shown that problems could be solved by international conferences. Big powers, it seemed, were governed by rational people who would not willingly go to war, but could be relied upon to settle their differences around the conference table. Or at least, that is what people believed.

Test Yourself on Unit 22

(a) Document: Occupation of Cyprus, 1878

Now you will at once see that it is very important that England should be able to protect the road to India. Your map will very likely have the British Possessions all over the world coloured RED. Then you will see that, along that road to India, England has four small but important colonies. These are: Gibraltar, at the entrance of the Mediterranean; Malta, in the middle; Cyprus, at the east end; and Aden, at the entrance to the Red Sea. . . .

The circumstances attending the acquisition of Cyprus were these: a war between Russia and Turkey had just concluded, in which Russia had been victorious, and had taken from Turkey considerable territory in Asia Minor. Now there are various reasons why England would be very sorry to see Russia all-powerful in Asia Minor. So the English Government made an agreement with Turkey, by which Turkey gave up to England the Island of Cyprus; and England in return undertook to defend Turkey against Russia in Asia Minor. . . . Cyprus . . . was taken possession of on the 22nd July 1878, by Sir Garnet Wolseley as Lord High Commissioner.

Source: Taylor, T. S., *First Principles of Modern History, 1815–79 (c.* 1890).

(b) Questions

1. What had Disraeli persuaded Queen Victoria to become in order to stress that India was 'very important' to England (line 1)?
2. Do you agree that Russia 'had taken from Turkey considerable territory in Asia Minor' (line 9)? Which territory was the author thinking of? Why was Russia anxious to make Turkey give up this territory?
3. Which two statesmen represented Britain in the negotiations which led up to the acquisition of Cyprus? Where were the negotiations conducted?
4. What was the treaty in which (i) Russia forced Turkey to give up 'considerable territory in Asia Minor', (ii) Britain acquired Cyprus?
5. Which European powers were represented at the negotiations at which 'Turkey gave up to England the Island of Cyprus'? Which European powers (i) lost influence, (ii) gained influence in the Balkans because of these negotiations?

(c) Further Reading

Blake, R.: *Disraeli.* Methuen (London, 1969).
Feuchtwanger, E. J.: *Democracy and Empire, Britain 1865–1914.* Arnold (London, 1984).

Joll, J.: *The Origins of the First World War*. Longman (Harlow, 1984).

Taylor, A. J. P.: *The Struggle for Mastery in Europe 1848–1918*. Oxford University Press (Oxford, 1971).

Turner, L. C. F.: *The Origins of the First World War*. Arnold (London, 1970).

(*d*) Documentary

Joll, J. (ed.): *Britain and Europe: Pitt to Churchill 1789–1940*. Oxford University Press (Oxford, 1967).

Stacey, F. W.: *Britain and Russia from the Crimean to the Second World War*. Arnold (London, 1979).

(*e*) Exercises

1. What part did Britain play in the Eastern Question from 1875 to 1878?
2. Do you agree that Disraeli brought back 'peace with honour' from Berlin in 1878?

Unit Twenty-Three
Ireland, 1860–1914

23.1 Irish Problems

Although the Young Ireland movement failed to rouse the Irish people to a revolution in 1848 (Section 16.5(c)), Ireland continued to be the scene of frequent outbreaks of violence throughout the 1850s and 1860s. This violence was, in large part, inspired by the *Fenians*, who received money and advice from Irish emigrants now living in the USA. They had carried with them a hatred of England and of the English domination of their country. The

Fig. 23.1 The interior of Mountjoy Prison, Dublin, where the Fenians were confined

Fenians were able to count on some support from the Irish peasantry because of the inability or the unwillingness of British politicians to deal with the problems which, taken together, made up 'the Irish problem'.

(a) The Land

See Section 16.1(d).

(b) Religion

The vast majority of the Irish were Catholics, as we saw in Unit 16, and yet they lived in a country in which the Established, or state-supported, church was the Protestant church of Ireland. The religious problem increased the impact of the land problem, since it was the Protestant landowners who were in a position of privilege while the Catholic tenants were the ones who suffered.

(c) Politics

Since 1801 the Irish had sent MPs to Westminster (Section 16.3), where they sat alongside MPs representing English, Welsh and Scottish constituencies. Since 1829 Catholics had been allowed to sit in Parliament (Section 16.4) and under O'Connell they had campaigned, peacefully, for some measure of self-government for Ireland (Section 16.5). The British had granted this privilege—and more—to Canada (Section 17.4) and would show themselves quite willing to do the same for Australia and New Zealand. But no English politician was yet willing to concede Home Rule to Ireland.

However, in recognition of the fact that Ireland was different from Wales, Scotland and England, the British government had set up a separate form of government there. From the Viceregal Lodge in Dublin's Phoenix Park, the Lord Lieutenant, aided by a Chief Secretary, supervised the administration of English law throughout Ireland. The English army, with its headquarters in the Curragh, was under his control, as was the Royal Irish Constabulary, which was modelled on the Peelite Metropolitan Police (Section 8.3(b)). But the Irish, and in particular the Catholic Irish, wanted a far greater degree of self-government and, as we shall see, they increased their demands in the 1870s and 1880s.

23.2   Gladstone's First Ministry, 1868–74

When Gladstone came to power in 1868 he said, 'My mission is to pacify Ireland', and while his government was busy with many reforms (Sections 19.4–19.6), he still found time to legislate for Ireland.

(a) The Church

In 1869 Gladstone disestablished the Protestant church in Ireland, which meant that the Anglican church was no longer the official church in Ireland, and it had to give up most of the wealth which it had inherited from the Catholic past. This move was intended to please the Irish Catholics, but the solution was too late to be really effective. By 1869, centuries of bitterness had been built up and the Catholic Irish were not placated, nor did Gladstone please the English by his action. Opinion saw it as a betrayal of the Church of England and as a concession to the rebellious Irish by a weak Prime Minister.

(b) The First Land Act, 1870

In this Act Gladstone tried to deal with the most serious of Ireland's problems. The Act said:

(i) No tenant could be evicted provided he paid his rent on time.

(ii) When a tenant gave up his farm—at the end of a lease—the landlord had to pay the tenant for whatever improvements the tenant might have made in the farm—by adding buildings, drainage and roads.

However, there was a major loophole in this Act, because the landlord was still permitted to raise the rent-level at the end of a lease and, if the tenant would not pay the new rent, the landlord could evict him. While the Act said that landlords had to pay for improvements that had been made, there were many examples of landlords refusing to do so until the tenant had fought an expensive lawsuit to get the courts to decide that the landlord was, in fact, bound by the terms of the Act. By 1870 the land problem had existed for two centuries or more and this Act came too late to provide an acceptable solution. The Act was one more example of the kind of solution which offered 'too little, too late'.

23.3   The Land League (1879) and the Appearance of Parnell

Gladstone's ministry came to an end in 1874. Disraeli's government ignored the Irish problem, partly because of its preoccupation with foreign affairs and partly because of the Tories' bitter opposition to Home Rule. One effect of Irish disappointment with the weakness of Gladstone's legislation and the failure of the Disraeli government was the appearance of the *Land League*, founded in 1879 by Michael Davitt. This League had as its main aim the solution of the land problem in a way that would be acceptable to the majority of the leading tenant farmers.

If such a solution had been found, however, we might have seen the appearance in Ireland of a prosperous Catholic farm-owning community, and this would have diverted attention from the main issue of political control. One man who understood this was Charles Stewart Parnell, himself a Protestant landowner and, from 1875, an Irish MP at Westminster. When Parnell went to Parliament he found the Irish MPs under the amiable leadership of a lawyer, Isaac Butt, who appeared content to voice Ireland's grievances in a moderate way and to wait for the English to hand out whatever solutions seemed appropriate to them. Parnell decided to adopt a more vigorous policy, to draw attention to Ireland's problems by making Parliament sit up and take notice, by making Parliament unworkable—if need be—until Ireland's grievances had been satisfied.

For Parnell there was only one solution—Home Rule. To pass Land Acts, Disestablishment Acts, Education Acts or whatever, might provide a slight easing of one or other of the many separate grievances, but it would merely be tinkering with the main problem. It was Home Rule alone which could provide the Irish with the opportunity to deal with their own problems. The Land League appeared to present Parnell with a strong rival: would the Irish peasants support the Land League, with its simple and immediate aims of solving the land problem, or would they support the Home Rule Movement, which had long-term aims and appeared to offer no immediate easing of the land problem? So Parnell used his position, as leader of the Home Rule Movement and Ireland's leading spokesman, to get himself elected President of the Land League. He then proceeded to use it as he wished, and not as Davitt had originally intended:

> I wish to affirm the opinion which I have expressed ever since I first stood upon an Irish platform, that until we obtain for the majority of the people of this country the right of making their own laws we shall never be able and we can never hope to see the laws in Ireland in accordance with the wishes of the people of Ireland. And I would always desire to impress upon my fellow countrymen that their first duty and their first object is to obtain for our country the right of making her own laws upon Irish soil.
>
> *Source:* Charles Stuart Parnell, speech as President of National League (1882).

23.4   Gladstone's Second Ministry, 1880–5

We have already seen that this ministry was that of 'All the Troubles' (Sections 21.3–21.6), and Ireland provided Gladstone with its own load of troubles during this period.

(a) Coercion Act

When Gladstone came to power in 1880, Parnell and his Land Leaguers were conducting a violent campaign against the workings of the 1870 Land Act. This involved tenants refusing to pay their rents, resisting evictions and attacking the agents who tried to insist on the payment of rent or tried to organize evictions. English-owned farms were burnt, animals maimed and English people attacked. Gladstone's first action was to impose a *Coercion Act* which allowed the authorities to arrest people and hold them in gaol without trial. This illiberal Act provided Gladstone's opponents with the opportunity to accuse him of being a dictator, and caused many of his more radical supporters to become lukewarm in their support for the Grand Old Man.

(b) Second Land Act, 1881

Gladstone appreciated that coercion offered no solution to the Irish problem. He therefore tackled the land problem by means of another Land Act:

(i) *Fair* rents would be fixed by judges appointed by the government.

(ii) *Fixed* tenancies would have to be agreed between tenants and land-owners, so putting to an end the harrowing scenes of eviction.

(iii) *Free* sale of his lease would be permitted to a tenant who wished to give up farming.

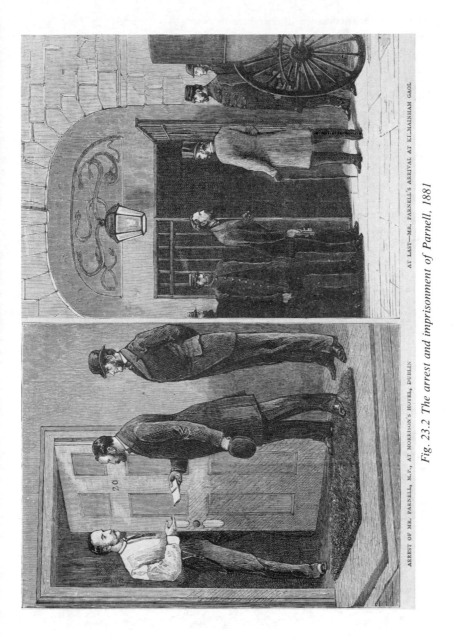

ARREST OF MR. PARNELL, M.P., AT MORRISON'S HOTEL, DUBLIN

AT LAST—MR. PARNELL'S ARRIVAL AT KILMAINHAM GAOL

Fig. 23.2 The arrest and imprisonment of Parnell, 1881

(c) Parnell's Tactics

This Act gave the Irish the *three Fs* which the Land League had been demanding, but Parnell saw to it that this Act was yet another in the 'too little, too late' clause. He continued to campaign among the tenants, advising them not to pay their rents and to resist the activities of landlords' agents and the police. Gladstone had little alternative but to arrest Parnell under the terms of the Coercion Act and put him in Kilmainham Gaol.

This harsh treatment gave Parnell the chance of appearing a martyr for the Irish cause, and it gained him increased support among the Irish voters. In 1882 Chamberlain, President of the Board of Trade in Gladstone's government, went to Kilmainham Gaol to meet Parnell. Parnell agreed, in the so-called Kilmainham Treaty, that in return for his release he would order his followers to halt their violent campaign. However, a short time after his release, the newly-appointed Secretary, Cavendish, and his assistant, Burke, were murdered while walking in the grounds of Phoenix Park. This led Gladstone to pass an even more severe Coercion Act almost immediately.

Meanwhile, at Westminster, Parnell and his Irish Nationalists were using the House of Commons to try to compel the government to consider Irish affairs. They obstructed the ordinary work of Parliament by talking for many hours on end—and one after the other—on whatever issue was being debated.

Fig. 23.3 Parnell and his Irish Parliamentary party, April 1886. Sitting at the opposite end of the table from Parnell is Timothy Healy (wearing glasses)

This obstructionism prevented the government conducting its ordinary business and led, on one occasion, to the removal of Irish MPs from the Commons. Finally the government was compelled to introduce the *closure* or *guillotine*, by means of which it announces before a debate begins that, come what may, the vote on the issue under debate will be taken at such and such a time.

23.5   Gladstone's Home Rule Bill, 1886

Gladstone hoped that Salisbury and the Conservatives, in power during the winter of 1885–6 (Section 21.5), would take this opportunity to make their own proposals for a measure of Irish self-government. If proposals had come from the Conservatives they would have been more acceptable to the House of Lords than if they came from Gladstone and the Liberals. But Salisbury offered no solution to the Irish problem, although Parnell hoped that one might be forthcoming.

On 17 December 1885 Gladstone announced that he now believed that Home Rule was the only solution to the Irish problem. When Parliament reassembled in January 1886, Parnell and his 85 Irish MPs voted with the Liberals to overthrow Salisbury, and in March 1886 Gladstone introduced a Home Rule Bill. This proposed:

(i) To establish a separate Parliament in Dublin to deal with Irish affairs.

(ii) To end the representation of Ireland at Westminster.

(iii) To leave control of foreign affairs, defence and external trade in the hands of the British government.

Chamberlain led the Liberals who opposed this move (Section 21.6), while Churchill led the Tory attack:

> This design for the separation of Ireland from Britain is clothed in the loftiest lan-
> guage but is a tissue of absurdities. For the sake of this nonsense all business other
> than that is to be impeded and suspended . . . all useful and deserved reforms are to be
> indefinitely postponed, the British Constitution is to be torn up, the Liberal Party
> shivered into fragments. And why? For this reason and no other: to gratify the
> ambition of an old man in a hurry.
> *Source:* Lord Randolph Churchill's address to the electors of South Paddington
>   (1886).

Gladstone tried to explain the issues facing Ireland and Britain when he campaigned during the election in June 1886:

> Two plans are before the World. There is the plan of the government; and there is the
> plan of Lord Salisbury. Our plan is that Ireland should transact her own affairs. His
> plan is to ask Parliament for new repressive laws, and to enforce them resolutely for
> twenty years. . . .
> *Source:* Gladstone's address to the electors of Midlothian, June 1886.

Fig. 23.4 Gladstone introducing his First Home Rule Bill in the House of Commons, 1886

23.6   The Conservative Solution

Chamberlain had split the Liberal Party and the Home Rule Bill had been rejected by the House of Commons (Section 21.6). Gladstone's government had had to resign and call an election in June 1886. In this the Conservatives, led by Salisbury, won a majority of the seats in the Commons (Section 21.6). Salisbury tried to deal with the problem of Ireland by a policy of 'whips and carrots'.

(a) 'Whips'

(i) **Coercion Acts.** Throughout the long period of Conservative rule (1886–92 and 1895–1906), the government imposed a series of Coercion Acts which allowed the arrest of suspected lawbreakers and proposers of violence, and their imprisonment without trial.

(ii) **The attempted destruction of Parnell.** The Conservative government tried to destroy Parnell's reputation with the Irish people and British politicians. In 1887 *The Times* published a series of letters, allegedly written by Parnell, which indicated that he had been responsible for the Phoenix Park murders of 1882. However, in 1889, Parnell brought a libel case against *The Times* and during the hearing of the case a journalist, Piggott, admitted that he had forged the letters. *The Times* was found guilty of libel, Parnell was cleared— and his reputation rose even higher than it had been before.

The opposition was not finished. In 1890 Chamberlain, now a Liberal Unionist and well on his way to being a member of the Conservative government, sought out a member of Parnell's own party, Captain O'Shea. O'Shea and Chamberlain knew that Parnell was living with Mrs O'Shea. They had known this for some years, but neither of them had done anything about the affair until 1890, when O'Shea brought a divorce case against his wife, naming Parnell as the co-respondent. Parnell offered no evidence during the case and the O'Shea lawyers were allowed to make whatever allegations they wished without being questioned by lawyers who might have been used to represent Parnell. Parnell's reputation was torn to shreds and the Nonconformist conscience of English Liberals, who had been moving towards support for Home Rule, was outraged at the conduct of the Irish leader. Gladstone indicated that he would no longer be able to work with Parnell; the Irish Catholic bishops, totally opposed to divorce and realizing that there would be no solution to the Irish problem while Parnell remained as leader, campaigned against him; and his own party was split between those who supported him as 'the Master of the party' and those led by the waspish Timothy Healy who opposed him and Kitty O'Shea, 'the Mistress of the party'.

(b) 'Carrots'

The Conservative government did not use 'whips' alone; it also used 'carrots' in the shape of a series of *Land Purchase Acts*. The British government provided about £200 million which tenants could borrow in order to buy their own farms. This, it was hoped, would slowly bring to an end the dominant position of the absentee English landowners. It would also create a strong, prosperous farm-owning group of Irish Catholics who might provide an alternative leadership to the Catholic community, leading it down the road of peaceful co-operation with the dominant partner in the Union. It was sometimes referred to as a policy of 'killing Home Rule by kindness'.

23.7   The Second Home Rule Bill, 1893

In 1892 Gladstone was back in power and brought in his Second Home Rule Bill. This differed from the first in that, while giving Ireland its own parliament, it also said that eighty Irish MPs should sit in the British House of Commons. (This, in fact, is the arrangement that was later to be made for Ulster.) The bill was rejected in the House of Lords after a successful passage through the Commons, but Gladstone failed to persuade his fellow-Liberals that they should fight another election on the issue. His resignation followed this opposition (Section 21.6).

23.8   Ulster

While the majority of people in Ireland were Catholics, there was a large minority in the north-east who were, and are, Protestants. Ireland is traditionally divided into four provinces—Leinster, around Dublin, Connaught, in the west, Munster, in the south, and Ulster, nine counties in the north. In four of these counties the Protestants formed a majority of the population. They feared that 'Home Rule would mean Rome Rule' and they were vigorously opposed to Gladstone's proposals.

After Parnell's death the Irish Party was led by John Redmond but, in spite of his demands for Home Rule, English politicians ignored Irish affairs until the Parliamentary crisis of 1910 gave the Irish another opportunity to dominate the British parliament.

23.9   1910–12

In Section 27.5 we shall see that the House of Lords rejected Lloyd George's budget in 1909. This led to the calling of an election in January 1910 on the issue of the Peers versus the People. In this election the Liberals gained 275 seats to the 273 gained by the Conservatives, leaving the Irish, with their 82 seats, in a dominant position. Asquith, the Liberal Prime Minister, asked the Irish for their support. The Irish Nationalists, realizing that they could not hope for Home Rule from the Conservatives, promised to support the Liberals on condition that, in return, the Liberals would agree to bring in a Home Rule Bill and a Parliamentary Bill which would prevent the House of Lords using its power to throw out the proposed Home Rule Bill. In 1911 the

Liberals brought in the required Parliament Act (Section 27.6) and in 1912, the Third Home Rule Bill. Because of the terms of the Parliament Act, this Home Rule Bill would become law in August 1914, if the Commons passed it in the Parliamentary sessions of 1913 and 1914, whatever the House of Lords decided to do about it.

The Conservative opposition was led by Bonar Law, himself the son of an Ulsterman. Bonar Law and the Conservatives realized that, if they did nothing, Protestant Ulster would in fact be subjected to rule from Catholic Dublin. Thus, from 1912 until 1914, the Conservatives helped to organize Ulster resistance to the proposed Home Rule Bill. Arms were smuggled in, armies recruited and trained, oaths sworn and papers signed. It seemed that Britain was to witness another civil war, led by the Conservatives who were prepared to deny the right of Parliament to decide what should be done. Bonar Law said:

> While I had still in the party a position of less responsibility than that which I have now, I said that in my opinion if an attempt was made without the clearly expressed will of the people of this country, and as part of a corrupt Parliamentary bargain, to deprive these men of their birthright, they would be justified in resisting by all means in their power including force.

Fig. 23.5 Ulster Volunteers, the militant face of Ulster Protestantism

I can imagine no length of resistance to which Ulster will go in which I shall not be ready to support them and in which they will not be supported by the overwhelming majority of the British people.
Source: Bonar Law, speech at Blenheim (27 July 1912).

On the outbreak of the First World War in August 1914 all parties agreed to suspend application of the Irish Home Rule Bill until the war had been won. The danger of civil war had receded but the Ulster problem had not been solved.

Test Yourself on Unit 23

(a) Document: Irish Home Rule

The national demand, in plain and popular language, is simply this, that the government of every purely Irish affair shall be controlled by the public opinion of Ireland and by that alone. We demand this self-government as a right. For us the Act of Union has no binding moral or legal force. We regard it as our fathers regarded it before us, as a great criminal act of usurpation, carried by violence and by fraud. . . .

Resistance to the Act of Union will always remain for us, so long as that Act lasts, a sacred duty and we declare that no ameliorative reforms, no number of Land Acts, or Labourers' Acts, or Education Acts, no redress of financial grievances, no material improvement or industrial development, can ever satisfy Ireland until Irish laws are made and administered upon Irish soil by Irishmen. . . .

But our claim to self-government does not rest solely upon historic right and title. It rests also, fellow-citizens, upon the failure of the British Government in Ireland for the last 100 years. Take the test of population. While in every civilized country in Europe the population has increased, in Ireland, in the last sixty years, it has diminished by one-half. Take the test of civil liberty. There has been a Coercion Act for every year since the Union was passed; there is today in existence a law which enables the Lord Lieutenant, at his arbitrary discretion, by a stroke of the pen, to suspend trial by jury, personal liberty, freedom of discussion, and the right to public meeting all over Ireland. . . . Take the test of the contentment of the people. There have been since the Union three insurrections, all of them suppressed in blood, with sacrifices untold in the prison cell and upon the scaffold. . . . Take the test of the prosperity of Ireland . . . it is the history of constantly-recurring famines every few years over a large portion of the west and north-west seaboard of the country. Take the question of industrial development. A history of industries deliberately suppressed by British Acts of Parliament, and not one finger lifted in the last hundred years to advance industrial prosperity. . . . Now such a record as that cries aloud for vengeance.
Source: John Redmond's speech, Dublin (4 September 1907).

(b) Questions

1. When was 'the Act of Union' signed? In what ways did it affect (i) the composition of the House of Commons, (ii) the government of Ireland?
2. Which national leader might have spoken or written the words in the first three sentences (i) in the 1830s, (ii) in the 1880s?

3. What Land Acts had been passed by (i) the Liberals, (ii) the Conservatives since 1870? What were the objects of the Land Acts passed by the Conservatives?
4. Why did the British government pass Coercion Acts to help them govern Ireland? Which two Irish leaders had been arrested in (i) the 1840s, (ii) the 1880s?
5. Why did the Nationalists hope that they had a better chance of obtaining a Home Rule Bill after 1906 than they had in the decade before that?
6. Why did political developments in Britain provide an opportunity for the Irish between 1910 and 1912? What two measures did they compel the Liberal government to pass?
7. Why did Ireland not gain Home Rule in 1914 in spite of the passage of the Home Rule Bill?
8. Can you explain why the population had 'diminished by half' in the sixty years before this speech was made?

(c) Further Reading

Adelman, P.: *The Middle-Class Experience 1830–1914.* Longman (Harlow, 1984).
Beckett, J. C.: *The Making of Modern Ireland 1603–1923.* Faber (London, 1981).
Hamer, D. A.: *Liberal Politics in the Age of Gladstone and Rosebery.* Clarendon Press (Oxford, 1973).
Hammond, J. L.: *Gladstone and the Irish Nation.* Frank Cass (London, 1964).
Lyons, F. S. L.: *Charles Stewart Parnell.* Collins (London, 1978).
Magnus, Sir Philip: *Gladstone.* John Murray (London, 1979).
O'Farrell, P.: *England and Ireland since 1800.* Oxford University Press (Oxford, 1975).

(d) Exercises

1. Describe and explain Gladstone's policy in Ireland during his first ministry, 1868–74.
2. Why did Irish affairs present Gladstone with problems between 1880 and 1885?
3. Why did Gladstone introduce a Home Rule Bill in 1886? Why did this not pass through the Commons?
4. Give an account of Parnell's work for Ireland.
5. Explain the impact of the Home Rule Movement on British Parliaments between 1880 and 1914.
6. How did the Conservatives try to deal with the Irish problem after 1886?
7. Explain the significance of the Ulster problem in Irish and British affairs between 1886 and 1914.
8. State the main facts about *three* of the following and explain their importance in Gladstone's dealings with Ireland: (i) the Church Disestablishment Act; (ii) the Irish Land League; (iii) the Kilmainham 'Treaty'; (iv) the Phoenix Park murders; (v) Liberal Unionists; (vi) the Second Home Rule Bill.

Imperialism and Tariff Reform, 1880–1906

24.1 Britain's Industrial Decline

In 1881 a British economist, Edward Sullivan, wrote:

> Thirty years ago England had almost a monopoly of the manufacturing industries of the world; she produced everything in excess of her consumption, other nations comparatively nothing. The world was obliged to buy from her because it could not buy anywhere else. Well, that was thirty years ago; now, France and America and Belgium have got machinery, our machinery and our workmen and our capital, and they are sending us a yearly increasing surplus that is driving our own goods out of our own markets; and every year they are more completely closing their markets to our goods. . . .
> Source: Sullivan, E., 'Isolated Free Trade' in *Nineteenth Century* (1881).

(a) No Longer the Workshop of the World

'Thirty years ago' the confident British middle class had boasted that Britain was the workshop of the world. But Britain's domination was short-lived. How could Germany, the USA, France and other countries have managed to catch Britain up when she had had such a long start in the race?

(*i*) **Larger machinery.** One reason was that some of these countries were able to build much bigger, more efficient machines than the British did, as a Report of the Tariff Commission (1904) showed:

> Manufacturers in this country are blamed by outsiders and often by their own countrymen, because they do not show greater enterprise in laying down large capacity plants, such as are common in the United States, and are now being laid down to some extent in Germany. . . . .
> Some American furnaces, complete with equipment, cost over £200,000 each, whereas the average cost of British furnaces is not probably over £25,000. The average annual production of a pair of Bessemer converters or of an up to date rolling mill in the States will generally exceed that of corresponding plants in this country in the ratio of 3 to 1. The truth is that the British manufacturer would not at present know what to do with such a vast product if he had it. Our own home market does not absorb more than 3 to $3\frac{1}{2}$ million tons of steel a year, whereas the American market consumes nearly 15 million tons, and the German market finds an outlet at home for about 5 million tons.

Manufacturers build factories and install machines only if they can safely hope to sell their products. Britain, with a population of about 45 million, could safely expect to sell only to that population; the American manufacturer had a much larger domestic market and, in addition, very large and accessible

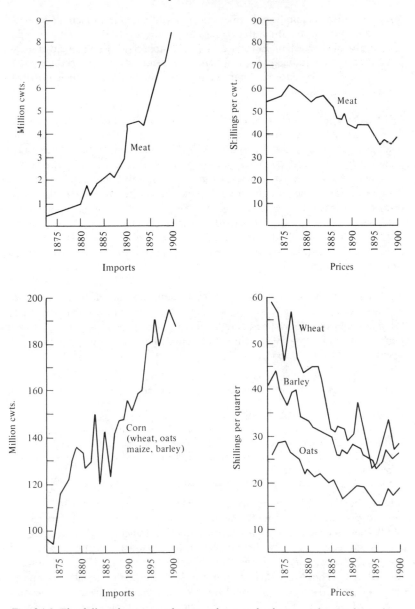

Fig. 24.1 The fall in the prices of meat, wheat and other cereals was due in large part to a massive increase in the level of imports of these products from America, Argentina, Australia and New Zealand. British townspeople welcomed these falls in price which led to improved living standards, but British farmers were unable to compete with these imports and many of them were ruined

markets in Canada and South America. He could plan on a much bigger scale than could British manufacturers. Germany, with a rapidly growing population and with the rest of Europe easily accessible, had a similar advantage. Larger machines and bigger factories enabled manufacturers to produce goods more cheaply—and so foreign manufacturers undercut the less efficient British manufacturers, who sold less.

(*ii*) **Tariffs.** The last line of the extract from Sullivan explains the success of the foreign manufacturer. Foreign governments—in the USA, Europe, the old colonies of Australia, Canada and New Zealand—all helped their own manufacturers by putting taxes on imported goods. Since Britain was the largest seller of goods abroad, these taxes, or *tariffs*, hit the British manufacturer and led to a decline in the amount of goods sold. Britain imposed no such restrictions on imports.

Unrestricted free trade had led to a depression in the British agricultural industry in the early 1870s. Industrialists were finding, in the 1880s, that a combination of British free trade plus foreign tariffs was leading to a depression in British industry.

(*iii*) **Education.** A third major reason for Britain's decline was that the British educational system was less well developed than the educational systems of Germany and the USA. The result of this was reported by a leading British manufacturer, Joseph Swan, who had founded the electric lamp industry. Speaking in October 1903, he said:

> We see one of the evil consequences of our educational deficiencies in the much less rapid progress that we, as a nation, have made, comparatively with our industrial rivals. . . .
> We are still desperately in need of more thorough general education. . . . While we are slowly learning by the painful process of ruinous loss the lesson of our want in this respect, our competitors abroad have long been reaping the benefits of their recognition of the value of knowledge and of the means of acquiring knowledge as a basis of industrial prosperity.
> *Source:* Swan, M. and K., *Sir Joseph William Swan* (1929).

Large numbers of new boarding schools were built in the nineteenth century, to provide education for the sons of successful manufacturers. Rich, middle-class men spent a great deal of money and energy trying to copy the upper-class style of life, and they wanted their sons to be educated at boarding schools in the way in which the sons of the upper classes had traditionally gone away to schools such as Eton and Rugby. But the established boarding schools were fairly small and could not have expanded sufficiently to accommodate all the extra pupils. The heads and governors of these schools were also not prepared to accept the sons of people whom they tended to look down on as being engaged in trade, industry or commerce—occupations which were not as socially acceptable as landowning. Many of the established boarding schools were founded by members of the Anglican church, whereas the new middle class came mainly from Nonconformist sects. So there was a need for new boarding schools, and many were founded—paid for by donations and annual fees—to provide the sons of the middle class with the education which had once been the privilege of upper-class children.

However, the syllabuses and teaching were modelled on those of the old Anglican boarding schools. Most of the day was spent learning Latin, Greek and ancient history, and there was little or no attention paid to subjects such as science, mathematics or modern languages. The result was that when sons inherited businesses from their fathers, they were not equipped to deal with industry or trade. Their fathers had 'learned by doing'; the sons had not received their fathers' practical experience, nor had their education fitted them to run a business or factory.

The education provided for the children of the working class was also deficient. Until 1870, working-class children went—if they attended school at all—to establishments run by religious societies. The majority of these schools were run by Anglicans (Sections 31.2–31.4), although there were some founded by Nonconformists, Catholics and Jews. In 1870 the government stepped in, and passed an Education Act (Section 31.5) which provided for locally-elected school boards. These collected a school-board tax, which paid for the building and maintenance of local schools. The new schools were known as *board schools*—not to be confused with the boarding schools to which the sons of the middle and upper classes were sent. The basis of teaching in both the church and the board schools was religious instruction, aimed at making the children of the lower classes behave respectfully towards their masters, employers and betters. The children also learnt to read (usually from the Bible or some religious books), write and do basic arithmetic, which would enable them to work in shops when they left school. There was little attempt to provide pupils with a rounded education, but this is hardly surprising when we realize that as late as 1898 the school-leaving age was eleven. One result of this lack of basic education was that British workmen were not equipped to cope with the courses which would qualify them in engineering, technical drawing and so on.

The general lack of education had not been a barrier to industrial progress in the eighteenth century, when the machines were simple and men needed brawn rather than brain in the coal-mines, iron-works and shipyards. By the end of the nineteenth century there was a range of new chemical, electrical and engineering industries which needed both highly-trained designers and inventors, and well-educated technicians and workmen. Britain's educational system was not producing enough of either type.

(*iv*) **British industrialists.** In addition to the advantages enjoyed by her foreign competitors, British industry seemed to add to its own problems. Sir Leo Chiozza Money, a leading economist and MP, wrote:

> British employers have been too conservative. They have neglected new processes and inventions, they have relied for success rather on cheap labour than on the utmost

efficiency in organization and in mechanical outfit. Happily a better spirit is [now apparent]. The war has opened the eyes of employers and employed to the inefficiency of the British industries, to the need of progress and to the necessity of vastly increased production per head.

Source: The British Dominions Year Book (1918).

Money was blaming British industrialists for their failure to introduce new methods and to go in for the newer industries and methods.

THROUGH THE BIRMINGHAM LOOKING-GLASS.

OFF TO GLASGOW.

(With Apologies to Sir John Tenniel.)

Fig. 24.2 A cartoon hostile to Chamberlain and his proposals for a British tariff system

(b) Markets Lost

(*i*) **Exports.** What was the result of the failure of the British industrialists and the success of the foreigner? One was the loss of export markets which Britain had previously dominated, as Joseph Chamberlain pointed out in a speech in Glasgow, on 6 October 1903:

If you will compare your trade in 1872, thirty years ago, with the trade of 1902—the export trade—you will find that there has been a moderate increase of £22 000 000.

That, I think, is something like 7½ per cent. Meanwhile, the population has increased 30 per cent. In the same time the increase in [trade of] the United States of America was £110 000 000 and the increase in German exports was £56 000 000. In the United Kingdom our export trade has been practically stagnant for thirty years.
Source: Boyd, C. W., *Mr Chamberlain's Speeches* (1914).

In 1898 *The Times* criticized British exporting firms:

British merchants have failed to adapt themselves to competition. It surprises them to find that the goods they offer, though acknowledged to be superior are not preferred by the foreign purchaser to the inferior goods offered by their upstart rivals. The purchaser humbly suggests that the article they offer is not exactly to his taste. 'Take it or leave it,' they haughtily answer, in the true spirit of the monopolist; 'if you don't know a good British article when you see it, that's your lookout,' and the foreigner too often suits the action to the word—and leaves it. . . .
Source: The Times (14 November 1898).

(*ii*) **Domestic markets.** Foreign trade even invaded the British home market, as this article showed the public in 1896:

You will find that the material of some of your own clothes was probably woven in Germany. Still more probable is it that some of your wife's garments are German importations.
    Roam the house over, and the fateful mark will greet you at every turn, from the piano in your drawing-room to the mug on your kitchen dresser, blazoned though it be with the legend, 'A Present from Margate'. You shall find your very drain-pipes German made. You pick out of the grate the paper wrappings from a book consignment, and they also are 'Made in Germany'. You stuff them into the fire, and reflect that the poker in your hand was forged in Germany.
Source: Williams, E. E., 'Made in Germany', *The New Review* (1896).

(*c*) **Unemployment**

As Britain ceased to be the workshop of the world and as foreign goods drove British goods out of both foreign and home markets, there was a rise in the number of skilled men who were unemployed. These men had once been supporters of the principle of self-help which provided them with seemingly endless rises in living standards (Section 18.5 and Test Yourself On Unit 18 (*a*)). But in the 1880s this rise in standards came to an end for many, and for many more there was the fear that maybe they too would suffer the horror of a long period of unemployment if their employer failed to sell his goods (Section 29.9(*c*)). These workmen had once looked down on the unskilled workers and at their attempts to found a Labour Party. They had never felt the need for state-help; they had always believed in self-help. After the 1890s an increasing number of them became less certain, and the numbers joining the Labour Party grew (Section 30.7).

Fig. 24.3 A demonstration by the unemployed in 1907. The majority of working voters had supported Labour and Liberal candidates in the 1906 Election and had voted against Chamberlain's plan for tariff reform. But free trade had caused their unemployment

(d) Fair Trade

British workmen were not the only ones who began to lose their faith in freedom and self-help. British manufacturers had once had great faith in the virtues of free trade (Sections 4.4, 8.4, 12.6 and 19.1(b)), but by 1881 these same manufacturers were less sure. In *Fair Trade* (1881) the author, W. Farrer Ecroyd, demanded:

> Under these circumstances it has been proposed to establish an import duty of 10 per cent on all foreign manufactures, not for protection, but to regain our power of bargaining with other nations, whose manufactures we buy, to admit ours as freely and fairly as we wish to admit theirs. And, to leave our hands free to do this, it is urged that we ought not to make or renew any commercial treaties but such as either establish free trade in manufactures on both sides or are terminable at a year's notice.
> *Source:* Boyd, C. W., *Mr Chamberlain's Speeches* (1914).

But there were still enough of the old hands left to resist this demand for a change, for the time being.

24.2   Chamberlain and Imperialism

Joseph Chamberlain had taken about 40 Liberal Unionist MPs with him into opposition to Gladstone's Home Rule Bill in 1886 (Sections 21.6 and 23.5). Between 1886 and 1892 he supported the policies of the Salisbury government (Unit 25), and when Salisbury returned to power in 1895, Chamberlain became Colonial Secretary.

(a) Colonial Development (see also Sections 25.4–25.7)

Chamberlain's interest in colonial development was mainly dictated by his belief that a larger Empire would provide increased opportunities for British businessmen and their workers. As he said in 1893, 'We find our profit in the increased prosperity of the people for whose interests we have made ourselves responsible, and in the development of markets.'

He appreciated that these ideas might not appeal to the subordinate races whom Britain was going to conquer and rule. In 1896 he said:

> You cannot make omelettes without breaking eggs. You cannot exercise control over barbarous countries without (occasionally) coming into conflict with their savage rulers, and having to shed some blood.
> Source: Chamberlain, J., Foreign and Colonial Speeches (1897).

But if Britain could gain an economic advantage in Africa and in the older colonies of Australia, New Zealand and Canada, so much the better. He noted:

> I regard many of our colonies as being in the condition of undeveloped estates which can never be developed without Imperial assistance. It is only in such a policy of development that I can see any solution of those great social problems by which we are surrounded. Plenty of employment and a contented people go together, and there is no way of securing plenty of employment except by creating new markets and developing the old ones.
> Source: Chamberlain, J., Foreign and Colonial Speeches (1897).

(b) A United Empire?

The 1887 Golden Jubilee celebrations gave the political leaders of the older colonies an opportunity to meet in London, and Queen Victoria's Diamond Jubilee in 1897 provided another such occasion. Steps were taken to set up some sort of regular meeting between the colonial leaders and British statesmen, and in 1902 Chamberlain invited delegates from the colonies to consider setting up organizations which might lead to the creation of a united Empire:

> Gentlemen, we require your assistance in the administration of the vast Empire which is yours as well as ours. If you are prepared at any time to take any share in the burdens of the Empire, we are prepared to meet you with any proposal for giving to you a corresponding voice in the policy of the Empire. . . .
> Source: Boyd, E. W., Mr Chamberlain's Speeches (1914).

One reason for this particular interest was Chamberlain's experience during the Boer War (Sections 25.7 and 26.2). Britain had started the war against the

Dutch farmers in a confident manner; she had been shocked at the Boers' ability to resist, and Chamberlain was grateful for the contingents of colonial troops who were sent to serve in South Africa. In one of his speeches he said:

> The war has brought the Empire closer together. During that great struggle, Great Britain stood alone, isolated among the greater nations of the world. The splendid, and above all the spontaneous rally of the Colonies to the Mother Country affords no slight compensation even for the sufferings of war. What has brought them to your side even before you called upon them? It is that these peoples for the first time claim their share in the duties and responsibilities as well as in the privilege of Empire. We are advancing steadily, to the realization of that great federation of our race which will inevitably make for peace and liberty.
> *Source:* Boyd, C. W., *Mr Chamberlain's Speeches* (1914).

There was another explanation for this desire to create a united Empire. An Empire might produce an imperial army and navy, fit to face Germany, or France, or Russia or whoever might turn out to be Britain's enemies. Chamberlain, although Colonial Secretary, was actively involved in trying to arrange foreign alliances for the Britain which he appreciated was unable to stand in isolation (Sections 26.3 and 26.4). But underlying military and defence considerations was the *economic* one: Chamberlain believed that in a world of growing foreign competition and increasing unemployment, Britain needed an Empire for commercial reasons.

(c) Imperial Preference

By 1900 Britain had acquired huge areas of Africa and Asia from which she obtained raw materials and to which she exported manufactured goods. These 'tropical' colonies were governed by British civil servants under the control of the Colonial Office in London.

Canada, Australia and New Zealand, on the other hand, had their own independent governments, elected by their white populations. These governments wanted to improve the living standards of their peoples, by developing their own industries and increasing their national wealth. They, like Germany, the USA and other countries, imposed tariffs on imports—including imports from Britain.

Joseph Chamberlain tried to persuade these self-governing colonial governments to put a lower tariff on goods coming from Britain than on similar goods coming from Germany or elsewhere. This *preference* would allow British goods to be sold at a lower price than comparable foreign goods—and so would increase British exports. The colonial governments agreed that this would help Britain, but how would it help them? They exported their food and raw materials to Britain in free and open competition with food and materials from countries outside the Empire. If Britain wanted the colonial countries to give preference (and lower tariffs) to British goods, the colonial countries wanted preferential treatment for their food exports. To achieve this, Britain would have to give up its free trade policy, and impose a tariff on food imports with a lower tariff on food imported from the colonies.

24.3   Chamberlain and Tariff Reform

By 1903 there was a great deal of evidence that free trade was not going to help Britain recover her former position as the workshop of the world. It was also clear that Britain was no longer able to dominate the world's affairs as she had done in Palmerston's time. Germany, in particular, was becoming a possible rival not only in trade but in foreign affairs as well (Section 26.4). This was one of the reasons which inspired Joseph Chamberlain to start his *Tariff Reform Campaign* at the end of 1903. In October he said:

> In the first place, we all desire the maintenance and increase of the national strength and the prosperity of the United Kingdom. Then, in the second place, our object is, or should be, the realization of the greatest ideal which has ever inspired statesmen in any country or in any age—the creation of an Empire such as the world has never seen. . . .
> *Source:* Boyd, C. W., *Mr Chamberlain's Speeches*, Vol. ii (1914).

(a) The Tariff Reform Campaign

Chamberlain opened his campaign with a series of mass meetings throughout the country. He pointed out the failure of British manufacturers to hold their own with foreign manufacturers, and argued that a system of British tariffs would 'gain work for the enormous number of those who are now unemployed'. Chamberlain had once been a Radical Liberal but had resigned from the Liberal Party partly because it had not adopted socialist policies aimed at helping the less well-off (Sections 21.1(a) and 21.6(b)). He had then become Colonial Secretary in the Conservative government in 1895, and was mainly responsible for the attempts to make the Empire in Africa and Asia into an expanding market for British goods.

(b) Opposition to Tariff Reform

The Prime Minister, A. J. Balfour, understood the arguments that Chamberlain was using and saw that if Britain was to recover her lost markets some change was needed along the lines proposed by Chamberlain. However, many other members of the Conservative Cabinet did not share Chamberlain's ideas nor did they see why Balfour should support him. On 16 September 1903 Lord Hamilton resigned. He wrote to a friend:

> As I anticipated we could come to no agreement at our Cabinet on Monday. The Balfour–Chamberlain alliance is an impossible combination for those who are opposed to Joe's protectionist and preferential ideas. Arthur [Balfour] differentiates, poses as a Free Trader, puts forward protectionist principles with limitations, which must disappear if the principles are carried. Chamberlain whilst ready to resign,

Fig. 24.4 Chamberlain speaking at the Bingley Hall, Birmingham in 1904. Holding up a free trade loaf and a tariff reform loaf, Chamberlain asked whether the audience could spot any difference. Logic, however, played little part in the campaign

openly states that he must adhere, whether in office or out of it, to the Preferential scheme, but he adds 'I am not Prime Minister and my colleagues are not necessarily bound by what I say.' But if the Prime Minister will not repudiate his theories we lesser men have no alternative but to go. A. J. [Balfour] cannot afford to part with Chamberlain just now, he may be right, so we mediocrities must go!

Source: Hamilton Papers, A letter to Lord Curzon, Viceroy of India (16 September 1903).

Balfour's predicament was the subject of a poem written by the Canadian Prime Minister, Wilfrid Laurier, in 1904:

I'm not for Free Trade, and I'm not for Protection
I approve of them both, and to both have objection.
In going through life I continually find
It's a terrible business to make up one's mind.
So in spite of all comments, reproach and predictions,
I firmly adhere to Unsettled Convictions.

But unsettled convictions are not the best ones to put before the country in a general election, especially when the Liberal and Labour Parties were united in their opposition to this threat to the system of free trade which had once made Britain 'the workshop of the world'. A divided Cabinet, a Prime Minister of unsettled convictions, a most important issue and a united opposition; such was the background against which the general election of 1906 was fought. The divided Conservatives were swept from office and the Liberals won the greatest number of seats that any single party had ever won in the House of Commons (Section 27.3).

(c) Chamberlain out of Politics

During the 1906 election campaign Chamberlain suffered a stroke which rendered him incapable of going to the Commons or of taking an active part in political affairs. He continued to take an interest in affairs and his son, Austen, wrote him frequent letters which kept his father informed. But the giant was now a shadow of himself and for practical purposes his career was at an end. The man who might once have led both the Liberals *and* the Conservatives was no longer able to play a part on the stage which he had dominated for so long. His death on 2 July 1914 may be taken as the end of an era during which Britain had dominated the world and the Conservative and Liberal Parties had dominated British political life.

Test Yourself on Unit 24

(a) Document: Tariff Reform, 1880–1914

The changes that have taken place, since the adoption of Free Trade nearly sixty years ago in the position of foreign nations, and, above all, in our relations with our Colonies, seem to point to the necessity of a reconsideration of our trading system.

The original object of Mr Cobden and his colleagues was to secure a free exchange of products between the nations of the world at their natural price, but for many years the example of the open door set by the United Kingdom has not been followed by other countries, and hostile tariffs have everywhere interfered with the natural course of trade.

These tariffs, designed to exclude British manufactures, have enabled foreign producers to undersell the British manufacturer in neutral markets and even to attack his home trade. The Free Traders have no remedy to propose for this state of things, which they ascribe to the want of enterprise on the part of our manufacturers or to the action of the Trade Unions. The Tariff Reformers believe that by re-arming ourselves with the weapon of a moderate tariff, we may still defend our home market against unfair competition, and may secure a modification of foreign tariffs which would open the way to a fairer exchange of products than we have hitherto been able to obtain.

But they attach even greater importance to the possibility of securing by arrangements with our Colonies a great development of trade within the Empire. They believe that these objects can be promoted by a slight transfer of existing taxes which will raise the revenue required for defence, while adding greatly to the amount of employment for our ever-growing populace. The questions thus raised, although they interest every class, are more vitally important to working men than to any other, since they alone depend upon the daily employment for their daily subsistence. . . .

Source: 'Imperial Union and Tariff Reform.' Speeches delivered by J. Chamberlain from 15 May to 4 November 1903.

(b) Questions

1. When, according to this, was free trade adopted? Do you agree with this view? Why?
2. In what way had there been a change 'in the position of foreign countries' since free trade was adopted?
3. To which colonies was Chamberlain referring? How was their position different in 1903 from what it had been 'nearly sixty years ago'?
4. Why did foreign countries impose tariffs against British goods in the 1860s and 1870s? How had this affected (i) their own growth, (ii) British exports?
5. What evidence is there that there was widescale unemployment as a result of the 'changes that have taken place'?
6. How would a system of British tariffs help Britain's trading position?
7. How would a system of imperial preference help unite the Empire?
8. Why were these questions 'more vitally important to working men than to any other'? Did working men in general agree with Chamberlain's views?

(c) Further Reading

Browne, H.: *Joseph Chamberlain, Radical and Imperialist.* Longman (Harlow, 1974).
Cottrell, P. L.: *British Overseas Investments in the Nineteenth Century.* Macmillan (Basingstoke, 1975).
Grinter, R.: *Joseph Chamberlain: Democrat, Unionist and Imperialist.* Arnold (London, 1971).
Robbins, K.: *The Eclipse of a Great Power: Modern Britain 1870–1975.* Longman (Harlow, 1983).
Saul, S. B.: *The Myth of the Great Depression in England.* Macmillan (Basingstoke, 1969).

(d) Exercises

1. Why did Chamberlain undertake a tariff reform campaign?
2. How far was the tariff reform campaign responsible for the Conservatives' defeat in the 1906 election? What other factors contributed to this defeat?
3. Why had Britain lost its position of 'the workshop of the world' by 1900?
4. What were the main results of Britain no longer being the world's leading industrial power?
5. Write briefly about (i) the Fair Trade League, (ii) imperial preference, (iii) food taxes.

Salisbury, 1886–1902

25.1 An Anti-democrat

Salisbury became the leader of the Conservative Party when Disraeli (Lord Beaconsfield since 1876) resigned after the 1880 election. He had served in the Derby–Disraeli ministry of 1867—when he had resigned over the issue of parliamentary reform (Sections 19.3 and 28.1(c)). This was one indication of his general attitude towards the lower classes and towards reform in general:

> The Tory party is composed of very varying elements. I think the 'classes and the dependants of class' are the strongest ingredients but we have so to conduct our legislation that we shall give some satisfaction to both classes and masses. This is specially difficult with the classes—because all legislation is rather unwelcome to them, as tending to disturb a state of things with which they are satisfied. It is evident, therefore, that we must work at less speed and at a lower temperature than our opponents. Our Bills must be tentative and cautious, not sweeping and dramatic.
> *Source:* Lord Salisbury to Lord Randolph Churchill (7 November 1886).

In this he was different from Disraeli, but his attitude attracted the Whigs and the older Liberals who, in increasing numbers, deserted the Gladstonian party after 1874 (Section 19.6), and particularly after 1886 (Section 21.6).

25.2 Salisbury's Domestic Policy

Salisbury believed that the government should do as little as possible. His long period of power (1885–6, 1886–92 and 1895–1902) differs from those of his predecessors, Gladstone and Disraeli (Units 19–21) and from the subsequent period of Liberal government (Unit 27) in both of which there was a spate of social reforms.

(a) Local Government

In 1888 Salisbury's government was responsible for a major reform of local government. The 1835 Municipal Reform Act (Section 11.5) had made possible the development of an orderly system of local government in towns and cities. But this Act had done nothing for the vast areas of the country which lay outside the boundaries of the boroughs. Here the local magistrates, or JPs, administered the law, were responsible for administering the Poor Law and were the government's unpaid agents. In 1888 a local government reform Act was responsible for the setting up of county councils, elected, as were borough councils, by the ratepayers. Towns with populations over 50 000 became

Fig. 25.1 The massive form of the dominating Lord Salisbury

county boroughs and had, within their boundaries, the same powers as county councils. The 1888 Act was also responsible for the setting up of the London County Council which, later, was given powers over the twenty-eight London boroughs which were set up in 1899, in matters which concerned the whole of London, such as road building.

(b) Workmen's Compensation

During his third ministry the government passed the Workmen's Compensation Act, 1897, by which some workmen who were injured while at work or caught a disease as a result of their work were allowed to claim compensation from their employers. The Act did not apply to seamen, agricultural workers or domestic servants.

(c) Education

Finally there is the Education Act 1902 (Sections 31.7 and 31.8). This was largely the work of Salisbury's nephew, A. J. Balfour, who replaced his uncle as party leader and Prime Minister in 1902.

25.3   Foreign Affairs

Salisbury was much more interested in foreign than in domestic affairs. The phrase 'splendid isolation' has sometimes been used to describe Salisbury's foreign policy. He himself once used these words as a warning, but an examination of his policy does not show that he followed a path of isolationism, of cutting himself and the country off from the affairs of the world outside. Foreign affairs were very much Salisbury's affairs since, although he was Prime Minister, he was also, until 1900, Foreign Secretary as well.

(a) The Mediterranean Agreement, 1887

Within a year of taking office Salisbury had negotiated this agreement with Italy, by which Britain agreed to support that country in the event of a war with France and promised British support to Italy and Austria in the event of a conflict with Russia in the Balkans.

(b) The Balkans

Salisbury had, as Foreign Secretary, played a major role at Berlin in 1878 (Sections 22.7 and 22.8). However, he was wise enough to see later on that Turkey was incapable of reform, that the nationalist tide could not be held back, that—as he said—'Britain had backed the wrong horse' in 1878. In 1885 he agreed to the reunion of Rumelia with the Kingdom of Bulgaria and in 1895 he tried, but failed, to get the European powers to act together against Turkey after the outrageous Armenian massacres:

> There is one matter which has not passed by, and that is the trouble which afflicts the Turkish Empire. . . . There is a very happy belief in the minds of the British that the Fleet can go anywhere and do anything. But if you desire by force to protect the security of the inhabitants of Turkish provinces, you can only do it by military occupation. No fleet in the world can do it. No fleet in the world can get over the mountains of Taurus to protect the Armenians.

But it may be done by others. I see no course which this country can wisely take except that of adhering to the European Concert. If the European States are willing to act they have means of action which we do not possess. The European Concert means that six Powers act together.

It is said that the Powers are acting on selfish principles, in refusing to enter upon a course which may end in a European war. You have to remember that a war in the Mediterranean will not hurt you very much. But a war in the east of the Mediterranean may spread to the European countries which adjoin the Turkish Empire. You cannot expect nations who are in that position to look upon the problems presented to them with the same spirit with which you, *in your splendid isolation*, are able to examine all the circumstances.

Source: Lord Salisbury's speech at the Lord Mayor's Banquet, Guildhall, *The Times* (10 November 1896).

Perhaps it is fair to say that this was not as 'splendid' as the Disraelian flamboyance. But it was not isolationist.

(c) China

Since the days of the Opium War (Section 14.2) Britain had exercised a great influence in the Chinese trade—and in the internal affairs of China. But by the end of the century this predominance was being challenged, particularly by Russia, eager to expand eastwards if she were not going to be allowed to expand in the Balkans, and by Germany, a growing industrial power which wanted markets for its products and an expansionist power eager to acquire the Empire which, her rulers believed, was a sign of greatness.

In 1897 Germany occupied the district surrounding the port of Kiao-chow; in 1898 the Russians acquired Port Arthur which led the British to acquire Wei-Hai-Wei, midway between the two. Meanwhile, Salisbury obtained from the Chinese government an almost complete monopoly of the trade in the commercially important Yangtze river valley. In order that the European powers should not engage in a series of wars while they struggled to acquire areas of influence in China, Salisbury arranged with Germany, Russia and France that each should have certain areas as spheres of influence.

(d) Burma

Britain had first gone to war in Burma in the 1820s and had further extended its conquest in 1852. Salisbury continued this expansion when, in 1886, the British conquered the remainder of Burma and in 1896 forced the ruler of Siam to grant to Britain spheres of influence in both north and south Siam. The French were also busily engaged in acquiring an empire in this area— taking Saigon in 1859, Cambodia in 1863, Annam in 1884, Tonkin in 1889 and Laos in 1893. Anglo-French rivalry in south-east Asia increased the hostility between the two countries who were opposed to each other in Africa in general and Egypt in particular (Sections 20.5(c), 21.3(c)(i), (ii) and 25.6).

(e) The USA

In 1892 Salisbury agreed to submit to arbitration the dispute which existed between Britain and the USA over the sea fishing rights in the Bering Straits. The tribunal rejected the claims made by the USA and agreed that British seal fishers were entitled to fish in the Straits.

In 1880 the USA had agreed not to build a canal across the isthmus of Panama except as a joint enterprise with Britain. In 1901 Salisbury agreed to surrender British rights under this agreement and in 1901 the USA began to build the Panama Canal.

When in 1895–6 there was a dispute with Venezuela over the boundary between that country and British Guiana, the USA threatened to act as 'big American brother' to 'little' Venezuela. Salisbury, once again, submitted the dispute to international arbitration, and this was settled in Britain's favour in 1899.

In 1898 the USA went to war with Spain over Cuba and Puerto Rico. Salisbury acted as a 'benevolent' neutral in that he prevented France and Germany from going to the aid of Spain.

25.4 Africa

Until the 1870s there had been very little European interest in the interior of Africa, 'the Dark Continent'. The climate was hostile and communication over the deserts and through the jungles was difficult, particularly as the rivers were, in general, not navigable. In spite of the work of great explorers such as Burton and Speke, Park and Livingstone, little was known about the interior except that the native tribes were often hostile. But by 1900 the whole continent, apart from Liberia and Ethiopia, had been divided among the European powers—without a war between any of them. This 'scramble for Africa' may be explained by four factors.

(a) The Work of the Explorers

Explorers charted the rivers, opened up the continent, provided maps and indicated some of the potential wealth that existed.

(b) The Activities of Missionaries

Missionaries brought back tales of millions of 'pagans' who were waiting to be converted to Christianity, and stories of tribal wars, an active slave trade and other evils which, they claimed, Europeans should bring to an end by conquest and the imposition of order.

(c) Economics

There was a growing demand in Europe for some of the products of Africa—rubber and coconut oil, for example—while European merchants saw in

Africa a huge potential market for their products—cotton goods in particular (Section 24.2(*a*)).

(*d*) The Interests of Investors

There was a fall-off in the profits to be made in investing in British industry once the Germans and the Americans had begun to attack Britain's former monopoly of world trade (Section 24.1). British financiers looked elsewhere for a return on their money. Some saw a chance to make a high profit out of investment in Africa. There land was cheap, labour would be both cheap and plentiful, and there were reportedly many sources of raw materials waiting to be exploited.

25.5   Chartered Companies

The British had acquired India because of the activities of the East India Company (Section 17.1). They acquired vast areas of Africa because of the activities of other chartered companies set up by British investors. A number of such companies were formed in the 1880s and 1890s with names which indicate their sphere of interest: the British South African Company was one, the East African Company was another. These companies received their charters from the government which promised to support them if they got into difficulties with native chiefs. Usually they did not do so, managing to make treaties with local chiefs or leaders. The Royal Niger Company issued blank treaty forms to its Company agents:

Form No. 9
Treaty made on the   day of   , 18   , between the Chiefs of
   on the one hand, and the Royal Niger Company (Chartered and Limited), hereinafter called 'the Company' on the other hand.
1. We, the Undersigned Chiefs of   , with the consent of our people, and with the view of bettering their condition, do this day cede to the Company, and their assigns, for ever, the whole of our territory; but the Company shall pay private owners a reasonable amount for any portion of land that the Company may require from time to time.
2. We hereby give to the Company and their assigns, for ever, full jurisdiction of every kind; and we pledge ourselves not to enter into any war with other tribes, without the sanction of the Company.
Source: Herstlet, E. (ed.), *The Map of Africa by Treaty* (1909).

The company was thus guaranteed a monopoly of trade in a certain area, then spent some of its capital on developing the area. Harbours were built, railway lines constructed and forests and jungles cleared. In some places the companies went in for mining, in others for growing rubber or some other product.

25.6 Salisbury and the Scramble for Africa

The British government had refused applications for charters by these companies until after 1887 when Salisbury had become a committed imperialist. After this date Salisbury's government issued charters to several British companies and gave its support to the work of the companies.

The Prime Minister was mainly responsible for the 1890 Conference in which the Great Powers negotiated a settlement defining the distribution of territory between them. France was angered by the control which Britain was exercising in Egypt (Sections 20.5(c) and 21.3(c)(i), (ii)). In 1896 Salisbury had sent a British army to reconquer the Sudan—so avenging the murder of General Gordon (Section 21.3(c)). Kitchener commanded the army which won the Battle of Omdurman in 1898 and then took Khartoum. The French sent an army under Captain Marchand which reached Fashoda where they came into contact with the British army. Salisbury remained firm. Kitchener took no action against the French and they withdrew, acknowledging British supremacy in the Sudan.

25.7 The Boer War

(a) Cecil Rhodes

In Cape Colony and Natal the British had allowed the development of self-governing colonies and from 1890 to 1896 the Prime Minister of the Cape was Cecil Rhodes, the multi-millionaire owner of diamond mines at Kimberley. Rhodes believed that the British were the best of all races and that 'the more of the world we possess, the better it will be for the world'. He had been responsible for the acquisition of the territory to which he gave his name, Rhodesia. He dreamt of a British-controlled Empire running from the Cape to Cairo.

We have seen that the original European settlers in the Cape had been Dutch and that these had left the Cape in 1836 (Sections 9.2 and 11.2(c)), when they founded the new states of the Transvaal and the Orange Free State. We have also seen that Disraeli had ordered the conquest of the Transvaal (Section 20.5) and that Gladstone had handed the state back to its Dutch people (Section 21.3). Rhodes's plan for a Cape-to-Cairo road, railway or Empire, could not be realized without the co-operation or, failing this, the conquest, of these Boer republics.

(b) The Uitlanders

In 1886 gold was discovered at Witwatersrand in the Transvaal and a flood of developers poured in. Most of these came from British South Africa. In the Transvaal they were known as the Uitlanders, or outsiders; they did not speak Dutch or Afrikaans, they did not worship at the Dutch Reformed churches, they were not farmers as were the Boers; they were, in fact, all that the Boers disliked. The President of the Transvaal, Paul Kruger, refused to grant these newcomers the same civil rights as the Boers enjoyed—in voting, and so on. However, Kruger was willing to make use of these newcomers, who were exploiting the wealth of his country. Taxes were arranged to fall most heavily on industry and not on agriculture, to be paid by the British and not the Boers.

One of Rhodes's closest associates was a former Edinburgh doctor, L. S. Jameson. He had gone to South Africa for health reasons, and in 1888 had helped Rhodes reach an agreement with Lobengula whereby the paramount chief of the Matabele people ceded his power, and territory, to Cecil Rhodes. In 1891 Rhodes had appointed Jameson administrator of the new territory (modern Rhodesia) and Jameson was a willing assistant to Rhodes in his attempt to seize the Boer republics. Jameson gathered together an unofficial 'army' which he intended to use to attack the Boers when the time was ripe.

(c) The Jameson Raid

In December 1895 Rhodes arranged with some of the leaders of the Uitlanders that they would organize a rising inside the Transvaal which would give him the excuse of sending in an army to 'protect' British interests. However, the plot misfired; no rising took place, but Jameson, not knowing this, sent in his army—which was defeated. There was an outcry in Britain where Liberal opinion was outraged. Rhodes was forced to resign from his post as Prime Minister although Joseph Chamberlain, Colonial Secetary and, it is thought, one of the architects of the Jameson plot, remained in office.

The German Kaiser sent a telegram congratulating Kruger on his success, which added to the dislike of Germany which was beginning to develop in Britain (Section 26.3). The Boers were even further confirmed in their hatred of the British while the British were angered at the success of the Boers who still stood in the path of a British advance to the north.

(d) The Boer War, 1899–1902

Finally, in 1899, the Uitlanders appealed to the British government for some action to be taken against the oppressive government of the Transvaal. The Boers declared war on the British. The British entered the war rather light-heartedly; they thought it was going to be an easy matter to defeat the Boer farmers who had no regular army at all, and no industrial base from which they could draw a plentiful supply of arms and other material. But the first two years of this war brought nothing but a series of disasters:

> The week which extended from December 10th to December 17th, 1899, was the blackest one known during our generation, and the most disastrous for British arms during the century. We had in the short space of seven days lost three separate actions. No single defeat was of vital importance in itself, but the cumulative effect

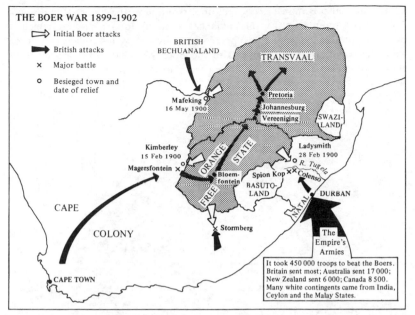

THE BOER WAR 1899–1902

▷ Initial Boer attacks

▶ British attacks

× Major battle

○ Besieged town and date of relief

BRITISH BECHUANALAND

TRANSVAAL

Mafeking ○
16 May 1900

Pretoria ●
Johannesburg
Vereeniging

SWAZI-LAND

Kimberley
15 Feb 1900

Ladysmith
28 Feb 1900
R. Tugela

Magersfontein ×

ORANGE

FREE STATE

Bloem-fontein ○

Spion Kop × × Colenso
BASUTO-LAND

DURBAN

CAPE

COLONY

Stormberg ×

NATAL

CAPE TOWN

The Empire's Armies

It took 450 000 troops to beat the Boers. Britain sent most; Australia sent 17 000; New Zealand sent 6 000; Canada 8 500. Many white contingents came from India, Ceylon and the Malay States.

Fig. 25.2 The Boer War, 1899–1902

occurring as they did to each of the main British forces in South Africa, was very great. The total loss amounted to about three thousand men and twelve guns, while the indirect effects in the way of loss of prestige to ourselves and increased confidence and more . . . recruits to our enemy were incalculable.

Source: Conan Doyle, A., *The Great Boer War* (1900).

The British had to learn the lesson which other countries have had to learn in this century—that a guerrilla force, living among its supporters, cannot easily be defeated. However, by 1902 the Boers had been defeated.

(e) The Settlement of South Africa

In 1902, by the Peace of Vereeniging, the British government—which had created two self-governing colonies in the Cape and Natal—took over the Transvaal and the Orange Free State as crown colonies. However in 1907, the Liberals granted self-government to the Transvaal (1906) and the Orange Free State (1907) and in 1909 approved the formation of the Union of South Africa.

25.8 Foreign Alliances

Salisbury had rejected Bismarck's suggestion of a formal alliance between Germany and Britain, although he recognized that Germany's main enemy,

France, was also Britain's main rival in Africa and in the Far East. Salisbury had no wish to enter into formal alliances with any foreign powers, which is probably the reason why some people have described his policy as one of 'splendid isolation'. But the events of the Boer War had shown that Britain could not in fact afford to stand aloof from the system of alliances that was

THE MEDDLESOME BOY.

JOE (*to himself*). "WONDER HOW IT'S GETTING ON!"
LORD S-L-SB-RY (*Head Gardener*). "I DO WISH HE'D LET THINGS ALONE!"

Fig. 25.3 Salisbury and Chamberlain had different views of the need for an active foreign policy

dividing Europe. If Britain had found it hard to defeat a small number of Dutch farmers, what might have been the result if the Kaiser had sent not merely a telegram but a German army? What might happen if Britain were involved in a major war with Russia in the Balkans or China, or with France in the Sudan or Indo-China?

Chamberlain, Salisbury's Colonial Secretary, was anxious to make a formal alliance with Germany, or better still, with Germany and the USA which would have created an Anglo-Saxon alliance. But these overtures were rejected (Section 26.3). Britain therefore signed an alliance with Japan in 1902 which gave Japan a free hand to expand in the Far East and provided Britain with an anti-Russian ally in case of an Anglo-Russian War.

Salisbury had resigned from the post of Foreign Secretary in 1900 but as Prime Minister he supervised the negotiations for this Japanese alliance which was concluded in 1902, after which he resigned. His resignation and the signing of the alliance marked the end of an era. Britain had begun to realize that she was no longer able to impose a *Pax Britannica* on the rest of the world.

See Sections 23.4 and 23.6 for a discussion of Salisbury's policy in Ireland, and Sections 24.1 and 24.2 for a study of imperialism in this period.

Test Yourself on Unit 25

(a) Document

All the grievances of the Outlanders, of which you hear so much, date from the second Convention of 1884. . . . In 1881 when the Convention was being discussed, President Kruger was asked by our representatives what treatment would be given to British subjects in the Transvaal. He said, 'All strangers have now and always will have equal rights and privileges with the burghers of the Transvaal', and yet . . . the majority of the population of the Transvaal, which consists of these same strangers, chiefly British subjects, have no representation, although they have made the prosperity of the State and although they pay five-sixths of the revenue. . . . If we are to maintain our position as a great Power in South Africa, we are bound to show that we are both willing and able to protect British subjects everywhere when they are made to suffer from oppression and injustice. This is especially incumbent upon us in the present case, because equality . . . promised between the two races by President Kruger . . . was the foundation of the negotiations upon which the independence of the Transvaal was conceded . . . and was promised to British subjects in South Africa by Mr Gladstone, the head of the Government which made the Convention. . . . It is a principle which prevails always and everywhere.

Source: Joseph Chamberlain speaking in 1899, quoted in Garvin, J. L. J., *The Life of Joseph Chamberlain*, Macmillan (London, 1932–4).

(b) Questions

1. Who were 'the Outlanders'? Which people had given them this name?
2. Why were the Outlanders interested in the Transvaal after 1884?

3. What was the significance of the date 1881 in the history of the Transvaal?
4. Why was Kruger opposed to the activities of the Outlanders?
5. List the major grievances suffered by the Outlanders.
6. When, and from whom, had Britain acquired 'South Africa'?
7. Which British statesmen took most interest in African affairs between 1895 and 1900?
8. Who was Prime Minister of the Cape Colony in 1895? Why did he wish to acquire the Boer republics?

(c) Further Reading

Browne, H.: *Joseph Chamberlain, Radical and Imperialist*. Longman (Harlow, 1974).
Chamberlain, M. E.: *The New Imperialism*. Historical Association (London, 1970).
Lowe, C. J.: *The Reluctant Imperialists: British Foreign Policy 1878–1902*. Routledge and Kegan Paul (London, 1967).
Pakenham, T.: *The Boer War*. Futura (London, 1982).
Porter, B.: *The Lion's Share: A Short History of British Imperialism 1850–1970*. Longman (Harlow, 1976).
Robbins, K.: *The Eclipse of a Great Power: Modern Britain 1870–1975*. Longman (Harlow, 1983).
Robinson, R. and Gallagher, J.: *Africa and the Victorians*. Macmillan (Basingstoke, 1961).
Shannon, R.: *The Crisis of Imperialism 1865–1915*. Paladin (London, 1979).

(d) Documentary

Gardiner, L. R. and Davidson, J. H.: *British Imperialism in the Late Nineteenth Century*. Arnold (London, 1968).
Grinter, R.: *Joseph Chamberlain: Democrat, Unionist and Imperialist*. Arnold (London, 1971).

(e) Exercises

1. How do you explain the 'scramble for Africa'?
2. Describe the part played by British chartered companies in the colonization of Africa at the end of the nineteenth century.
3. Why did war break out between the Boers and the British in 1899?
4. How far did Salisbury follow a policy of 'splendid isolation'?
5. Give an account of the work of Chamberlain as Colonial Secretary (see also Unit 24).

Ententes and Crises, 1900–14

26.1 Bismarck's System

Before we can understand British foreign policy between 1900 and 1914 we
have to examine the foreign policy of the new German Empire which had been
founded in 1871 after Prussia had defeated France (Section 19.5). Bismarck,
the Chancellor of Germany, had one main aim behind his foreign policy after
1871. This was to try to make sure that no European power became too
friendly with France which would, one day, want revenge for the defeat of
1871. Germany particularly feared a Franco-Russian Alliance, because this
might mean a war on two fronts for Germany. Thus Germany brought Russia
and Austria into a Three Emperors' League (or *Dreikaiserbund*) in 1872 to
make sure that neither became an ally of France. However, it became increasingly difficult to keep Russia and Austria in the same camp, because of their
rivalry in the Balkans. In 1878 Bismarck supported Austria at the Congress of
Berlin (Sections 22.1(*c*), 22.6(*b*), (*c*) and 22.7(*c*)), which led him to form the
Dual Alliance with Catholic Austria, the other major power which Prussia
had defeated (1866) and which might have felt a common anti-Prussian bond
with Catholic, defeated France. Bismarck still persuaded Russia to re-sign the
Three Emperors' League in 1881 and to continue to do so every three years
until 1887 when Germany and Russia signed a Reinsurance Treaty.

In 1882 Bismarck brought Italy into his alliance and the Triple Alliance
brought together Germany, Austria and Italy. He approached Salisbury and
tried to bring Britain into this alliance. Salisbury was, if anything, anti-French
in his policy (Sections 25.3(*a*), 25.6 and 25.8), and signed the Mediterranean
agreement (1887) with Italy and Austria. But he refused to accept Bismarck's
invitation. Bismarck, by this intricate network of alliances, hoped that he had
isolated France and so deterred her from a war of revenge against Germany.

26.2 The Boer War

Towards the end of the nineteenth century Britain had begun to realize that
she was isolated in a world that was growing increasingly unfriendly towards
her. In particular Britain saw the expansion of France into north Africa
(Sections 25.3(*a*), 25.6 and 25.8), German expansion into China and Russian
expansion into China and Manchuria (Section 25.3(*c*)). By 1898 the Salisbury
government was making approaches to Germany with a view to the formation
of an Anglo-German alliance (Section 26.3). It was the events of the Boer War
(1899–1902), however, which compelled the British government to speed up its
efforts to find friends in a hostile world. The inability of the British army,

aided as it was by colonial reinforcements from Australia, New Zealand and Canada, to defeat the Boer farmers, was a great shock to the British who had once looked down on the foreigners who felt the need to find allies. The immediate effect of this was to send the British on a search for just those allies, and in the first instance to sign the alliance with Japan in 1902 (Sections 25.7(a), (d) and 25.8).

26.3   Britain and the Triple Alliance

There were no areas of the world where Britain came into conflict with the members of the Triple Alliance. On the contrary, Britain had, as we have seen, signed a Mediterranean Agreement with Italy and Austria, two of the partners in that alliance.

After Bismarck's fall in 1890 the German Kaiser had refused to renew the Russo-German Reinsurance Treaty, and for various reasons, which do not, for the moment, concern us, France and Russia had become friendly with each other and in 1894 they had signed the *Dual Alliance*. Britain could hardly have been tempted to join that Alliance; Russia was traditionally her enemy in the Balkans and, more recently, in the Far East (Sections 25.3(b), (c)), while France had almost declared war with Britain over the Fashoda crisis of 1898 (Section 25.6).

It is therefore not surprising that Joseph Chamberlain should have sought a treaty of friendship with the Germans and their allies:

> The natural alliance is between ourselves and the great German Empire. . . . We have had our differences with Germany . . . I cannot conceive any point which can arise in the immediate future which would bring ourselves and the Germans into antagonism of interests. On the contrary I can foresee many things which must be a cause of anxiety . . . but in which our interests are clearly the same as the interests of Germany. . . .
>
> *Source:* Joseph Chamberlain, speaking in 1898.

But the price that Germany wanted for an alliance with Britain was that Britain should formally join the Triple Alliance. Britain did not want to run this risk of a war against France.

26.4   Anglo-German Rivalry

However, between 1895 and 1914 the Germans seemed to invite British hostility by a series of actions each of which seemed, to the British, to be deliberately aimed against them.

(a) Navy Bills, 1898–1908

In 1895 the Kiel Canal was opened, linking the Baltic and its German ports with the North Sea. In 1906 a plan was announced for the widening of this canal so that it could take the new, larger battleships.

The Kaiser appointed Admiral Von Tirpitz as his Minister of Marine in 1897. Between 1898 and 1908 Tirpitz persuaded the German Parliament to vote for Navy Bills which were aimed at the creation of a powerful German Navy, 'a fleet so strong that Britain would be unable to challenge it without risk of losses that would jeopardize her position as the world's strongest naval power'.

The British claimed that Germany had no need for a large navy. They agreed that Germany needed a large, powerful army, since Germany might be attacked by the land forces of France, Austria, Russia or Italy. But no one could possibly want to attack Germany by sea, so that Germany did not need a large navy for defensive purposes; nor did she need one to defend her Empire or her merchant navy, both of which were much smaller than Britain's. The only reason for the German navy which the British could imagine was 'to attack Britain, the British Empire or British trade'.

The British were driven—reluctantly, as we can see—to engage in an armaments race with the Germans in an effort to maintain a superiority over the new German navy. As Winston Churchill recalled:

In the spring of 1909, the First Lord of the Admiralty, Mr McKenna, suddenly demanded the construction of no less than six Dreadnought battleships. He based this claim on the rapid growth of the German Fleet and its expansion and acceleration

Fig. 26.1 Britain and Germany indulge in an arms race, and ill-feeling between the two countries is increased

under the new naval law of 1908, which was causing the Admiralty the greatest anxiety. In conjunction with the Chancellor of the Exchequer, I proceeded at once to examine the reasons by which [this scheme] was supported. The conclusions we both reached were that a programme of four ships would sufficiently meet our needs. . . . The dispute in the Cabinet gave rise to a fierce agitation outside. . . . Genuine alarm was excited throughout the country by what was for the first time widely recognized as a German menace. In the end a curious and characteristic solution was reached. The Admiralty had demanded six ships: the economists had offered four; and we finally compromised on eight. . . . In a flamboyant speech at Reval in 1904 the German Emperor had already styled himself 'the Admiral of the Atlantic'. All sorts of sober-minded people in England began to be profoundly disquieted. What did Germany want this great navy for? There was a growing and deep feeling that the Prussians meant mischief, that they envied the splendour of the British Empire, and if they saw a good chance at our expense, they would take full advantage of it.
Source: Sir Winston Churchill, *The World Crisis* (1923).

The Dreadnought was a new battleship, more powerfully armed than existing battleships and the brainchild of Sir John Fisher, the leading Admiral and friend of Winston Churchill, First Lord of the Admiralty after 1909.

(b) The Kruger Telegram, 1896

We have seen that on the failure of the Jameson Raid (Sections 25.7(b), (c)), the German Kaiser sent a telegram of congratulations and offers of friendship to the Boers. This was, in the eyes of the British, an obviously hostile act, indicating German friendship for Britain's enemies.

(c) The Boer War

During the Boer War Germany was unable to send more than sympathy to the Boers. German newspapers, however, maintained a hostile attitude towards Britain, criticizing Rhodes and Chamberlain, whom they blamed for the outbreak of the war.

(d) The Damascus Speech

The German Kaiser visited Damascus and during the visit made a speech in which he invited Muslim peoples throughout the world to look to Germany as their friend, whenever they rose in rebellion against the Great Powers which were then holding them as colonies. This speech angered the French with their Empire in north Africa, and roused great anti-German feeling in Britain whose Empire included Muslims in India. It also opened up the possibilities of hostility between Britain and Germany, for it now seemed that Germany herself was interested in expanding into the Balkans and the Near East.

(e) The Balkans

Traditionally Britain had opposed whichever power had tried to exercise undue influence in the Balkans. Most frequently this involved Britain in adopting an anti-Russian policy since it was Russia which more often than any other power tried to increase her influence in this area.

From 1900 onwards Germany began to play a more active role in this critical area. Indeed, Bismarck, by supporting Austrian ambitions at the Congress of Berlin, had first raised German interest in this area (Sections 22.1(c), 22.6(b), (c) and 22.7(c)). German support for the Austrian annexation of Bosnia and Herzegovina in 1908 (Sections 22.7(c) and 26.7(b)) aroused British suspicion, but more worrying than anything were German proposals for the building of a railway linking Berlin with Baghdad. The Germans may have intended this to be merely a trade link with Persia and other countries of the oil-producing regions of the Middle East. Britain, however, knew that trade links often led to other links. This was how Britain had acquired India (Section 17.1) and large tracts of Africa (Sections 25.4(a), (d) and 25.5–25.7), and she suspected that Germany might be embarking on the same colonial path, via the Balkans. Was Germany going to try to play the part of protector of Turkey, as was suggested by the agreement whereby the Turkish army was to be trained by a resident corps of German officers? If so, would Britain not be forced into an anti-German position, just as she had once been anti-French? Underlying British suspicions of the new Germany was the fact that she was becoming a rival to Britain throughout the world (Section 24.1).

26.5   The French Entente, 1904

The death of Queen Victoria in 1901 and the retirement of Salisbury in 1902 made it easier for Britain to take a new line in foreign policy. King Edward VII was anxious to use whatever influence he had in ensuring that Britain's position in the world was maintained. He was suspicious of his nephew, the German Kaiser, and prepared to lend his influence to the formation of a closer friendship between Britain and her former enemy, France. Salisbury's successor, Lord Lansdowne, brought new ideas to the Foreign Office and had a clearer appreciation than had Salisbury of the British need for friends abroad.

At the same time the French President, Loubet, and Foreign Minister, Delcassé, were anxious to build up closer relationships with as many countries as possible. And so King Edward went on a visit to Paris where he was greeted by cries of 'Vivent les Boers', indicating the strong anti-British sentiment. He helped to break this down during his visit, by the end of which newspapers were commenting on his kind remarks about French culture and beauty and also commenting on the anti-German sentiment which existed in both France and Britain. When the King left Paris the crowds shouted 'Vive le Roi' and 'Vive l'Angleterre', so great a change had been made in public opinion by this visit.

This change had made it easier for the politicians to reach an *Entente* or agreement, to settle issues which had caused misunderstanding for so long. France recognized the British domination of Egypt and the Sudan while Britain recognized the French position in Morocco. The two countries agreed on the revision of the Newfoundland fishing areas so as to avoid the danger of conflict between their fishing fleets. The *Entente* was not a formal alliance and did not say anything about either country providing help in case the other was involved in war.

26.6   Anglo-Russian Entente, 1907

The defeat of Russia in the Russo-Japanese War (1904-5) had shown that Britain had little to fear from her traditional enemy. There was even more need to be aware of the danger of German infiltration into the Balkans. Friendship between the two countries was encouraged because each had a common friend in France.

In 1907 British and Russian politicians worked out an Entente in which they settled their differences over Persia, Afghanistan and Tibet. Once again we have to note that the Entente was not a formal alliance, nor did it have any military clauses.

26.7   International Crises

(a) Crisis Number 1: Algeciras, 1905-6

The German Kaiser was annoyed by the signing of this Entente—which gave at least a suggestion that France, already allied with Russia, was on the way to gaining Britain as an even more powerful ally. He was also annoyed by the way in which the two powers had divided north Africa between themselves without considering whether Germany wanted a sphere of influence there. He also hoped that the new Liberal government (Section 27.3) would be prepared to give up this Conservative-made Entente, particularly if Germany threatened to make war.

The Kaiser demanded an international conference to discuss the French action in forcing the Sultan of Morocco to accept proposals made by France for the reform of the Moroccan government. A Conference was called at Algeciras in 1906 and the result was a series of rebuffs for Germany. France was supported by Britain and the USA, and the Conference agreed that France should have control of the Moroccan police and bank. Far from breaking the Entente, Germany had strengthened it, for it was seen to work. Indeed, because Germany had made threatening noises before the Conference had assembled, the British and French General Staffs—which controlled the Armies of the two countries—started a series of talks in which British and French generals agreed as to how each country would use its forces in the event of a war with Germany. Such conversations would have been unthinkable in, say, 1900 but German action had helped to bring them into being.

(b) Crisis Number 2: Bosnia, 1908

As if in response to the signing of this Entente, Austria seized Bosnia and

Herzegovina in 1908. The Serbs appealed to Russia for assistance against the encroaching giant from the north, but Russia had not yet recovered from the Japanese War. Her ally, France, and new-found friend, Britain, advised caution, and this allowed Austria to retain her new acquisitions, increased Austrian ambition to extend further her influence in the Balkans, incensed the Serbs and ensured Russian determination to prepare for a struggle with Austria.

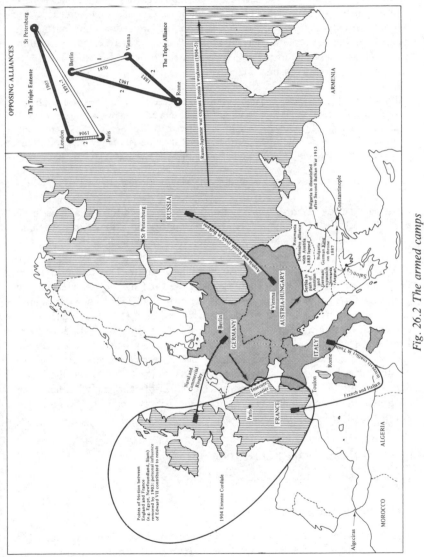

Fig. 26.2 The armed camps

(c) Crisis Number 3: Agadir, 1911

In 1911 some Moroccans rose in rebellion, partly against the way in which France was increasingly controlling the country. French troops moved in to protect French interests. The Kaiser claimed that Germany would protect German interests in Morocco. German colonists in south-east Africa (now Tanzania) were ordered north to provide an excuse for German involvement. Without waiting for them to arrive the Germans sent a gunboat, the *Panther*, and a cruiser, the *Berlin*, to Agadir to indicate German involvement in the Moroccan dispute. The reaction in Britain was immediate and surprising. Soon after the news of the arrival of the *Panther* was received in London, Lloyd George was due to make a speech at the London Mansion House. In the course of this speech he said:

> If a situation were to be forced upon us in which peace could only be preserved by the surrender of the great and beneficent position Britain has won by centuries of heroism and achievement, by allowing Britain to be treated where her interests were vitally affected as if she were of no account in the Cabinet of nations, then I say emphatically that peace at that price would be a humiliation intolerable for a great country like ours to endure.
>
> *Source:* David Lloyd George speaking at the Mansion House (1 July 1911).

If the pacific Lloyd George was prepared to sound so warlike, what must have been the feeling in the country as a whole and in the Cabinet in particular, where other of Lloyd George's colleagues were more inclined to be warlike than he was?

A conference was arranged to settle this latest dispute. The statesmen met in Paris where France gave two small strips of the French Congo to Germany in return for German agreement to French acquisition of Morocco. More significant was the decision to hold Anglo-French naval talks (1912). These led to an agreement that, in the event of a war, the French navy would withdraw from French ports on the Atlantic and English Channel coasts and concentrate on the Mediterranean, while the British Fleet, freed from concern for the Mediterranean, would concentrate its strength in the Channel and the North Sea. As Churchill pointed out, this had the effect of changing what had been an Entente into an Alliance where each country was committed to go to the aid of the other in the event of a war.

(d) Crisis Number 4: the Balkans, 1912–13

For a discussion of this last crisis, see Section 22.9.

26.8   Sarajevo and War, 1914

The ambition of the Serbs to create a large Slavonic Kingdom was supported by the Slavs who lived inside the Austro-Hungarian Empire (Section 22.2).

The ambition of the Austrians to acquire territory in the Balkans was in direct conflict with this Serb ambition and events of 1878 (Section 22.7(c)), 1908 (Section 25.7(b)), and 1912–13 (Section 22.9), had increased hostility between the two countries. The Archduke Franz Ferdinand was the heir to the throne of Austria-Hungary and he had shown in his speeches that he sympathized with the national aspirations of his Slav subjects. On 28 June 1914 he was visiting the small town of Sarajevo, in Bosnia. He and his wife were assassinated by a young Slav student, Gavrilo Princip who, it was claimed, had been trained for his task in Serbia.

The Austrians sent a series of harsh terms in an ultimatum to Serbia and when these were rejected Austria declared war on Serbia on 28 July, almost a month after the assassination. Statesmen still hoped that an international conference could be called to settle this crisis, just as conferences had settled other crises between 1905 and 1913. However, the Austrian declaration of war led Russia to start the long and slow process of mobilizing the Russian army. The Germans asked Russia to stop this but when she did not do so Germany declared war on Russia on 1 August. France was Russia's ally and Germany declared war on her on 3 August and to enable the German army to make its planned attack on Paris, Belgium was invaded.

Britain had no formal treaty with either Russia or France and so was not involved in the various declarations of war which had taken place. Grey, British Foreign Secretary, hoped that a general war could be avoided but the invasion of Belgium forced his hand. The neutrality of Belgium had been guaranteed by the treaty organized by Palmerston in 1839 (Section 14.2(a)). German violation of that treaty led the King of the Belgians to appeal to King George V, and Britain reluctantly declared war on 4 August 1914. Winston Churchill, a member of the Cabinet at the time, noted that British involvement was in doubt until that moment:

> The Cabinet was overwhelmingly pacific. At least three-quarters of its members were determined not to be drawn into a European quarrel, unless Great Britain were herself attacked, which was not likely. Those who were in this mood were inclined to believe first of all that Austria and Serbia would not come to blows; secondly, that if they did that Russia would not intervene; thirdly if Russia intervened, that Germany would not strike; fourthly they hoped ... it ought to be possible for France and Germany mutually to neutralize each other without fighting. They did not believe that if Germany attacked France, she would attack her through Belgium. ... So here were six or seven positions all of which could be wrangled over. It was not until August 3 that the direct appeal from the King of the Belgians for French and British aid raised an issue which united the Ministers and enabled Sir Edward Grey to make his speech to the House of Commons.

Grey wrote:

> The lamps are going out all over Europe; we shall not see them lit again in our lifetime.

It was indeed the end of an era.

Fig. 26.3 12 August 1914 and Britain is at war with Germany because of the invasion of Belgium

Test Yourself on Unit 26

(a) Document: Prelude to the Entente Cordiale, 1903

We arrived at the station in the Bois de Bologne, where we found President Loubet and a large number of officials. We drove in six carriages each drawn by four horses with postilions, and were escorted by a large number of French cavalry. There was an immense crowd in the streets and all along the Champs-Elysees. As regards myself in the last carriage I received anything but a pleasant ovation, for the cheers had become jeers by the time I came, and being in a red coat I was selected by the crowd for witticisms. There were cries of 'Vive Marchand!' and 'Vive Fashoda!', 'Vivent les Boers!' and occasionally 'Vive Jeanne d'Arc!', which seemed to be going back a long way in history. . . .

It was at the Hotel de Ville that the King made a short speech which entirely changed the whole atmosphere and brought all the French round at once. . . . 'Je n'oublierai jamais ma visite à votre charmante ville, et je puis vous assurer que c'est avec le plus grand plaisir que je reviens à Paris, où je me trouve toujours comme si j'étais chez moi.' The last phrase went home, and as he sat down he received a tremendous ovation. He seemed to have captured Paris by storm. From that moment everything was changed wherever he went. Not only the King but all of his suite were received with loud and repeated cheering. It was the most marvellous transformation, and all in three days. The first day distinctly antagonistic, the second cold, and finally frenzied enthusiasm. The visit eventually had far-reaching effects, and it was all very well for Lord Lansdowne to claim afterwards the credit for the Entente Cordiale, but neither he nor the government could ever have got the French people round from hostility to enthusiastic friendship in the way King Edward did. As Paul M. Cambon, the French Ambassador in London, remarked, any clerk at the Foreign Office could draw up a treaty, but there was no one else who could have succeeded in producing the right atmosphere for a rapprochement with France.

Source: Ponsonby, Sir Frederick, *Recollections of Three Reigns* (1951), pp. 169–73.

(b) Questions

1. What was the significance of Fashoda in Anglo-French relations?
2. What is the significance of the cry 'Vivent les Boers'?
3. Who was 'the King'? Do you agree with the author's opinion of the significance of this visit? Why?
4. What position was occupied by Lord Lansdowne? Who was (i) his predecessor, (ii) his successor?
5. What was meant by 'the *Entente Cordiale*'? How did it (i) differ from a formal alliance, (ii) become strengthened by events of 1906 and 1911?

(c) Further Reading

Hinsley, F. H. (ed.): *British Foreign Policy under Sir Edward Grey*. Cambridge University Press (Cambridge, 1977).

Joll, J.: *The Origins of the First World War*. Longman (Harlow, 1984).

Lowe, C. J.: *The Reluctant Imperialists: British Foreign Policy 1878–1902*. Routledge and Kegan Paul (London, 1967).

Magnus, Sir Philip: *King Edward VII*. John Murray (London, 1964).

Robbins, K.: *The Eclipse of a Great Power: Modern Britain 1870–1975*. Longman (Harlow, 1983).

Steiner, Z. S.: *Britain and the Origins of the First World War*. Macmillan (Basingstoke, 1977).

Turner, L. C. F.: *Origins of the First World War*. Arnold (London, 1970).

(d) Exercises

1. What were the main factors in British foreign policy between 1900 and 1914?
2. What were the causes of international tension after 1900?
3. Account for the growth of Anglo-German rivalry after 1900.
4. Explain why Britain signed an Entente with France in 1904.
5. Write briefly on (i) the Dreadnoughts, (ii) Algeciras, (iii) the *Panther*, (iv) Lloyd George's Mansion House Speech, 1911.
6. State the main facts about *three* of the following, and explain their importance in British foreign policy: (i) the Anglo-Japanese Alliance; (ii) the Anglo-French Entente; (iii) the naval rivalry with Germany; (iv) the German invasion of Belgium in 1914.

Unit Twenty-Seven
The Liberals, 1906–14

27.1 Old Liberalism

From 1870 onwards there was an increasing volume of evidence pointing to the failure of the self-help society; Chamberlain certainly doubted whether free trade was an unmixed blessing (Sections 24.1 and 24.3); Forster (Section 31.5) made a strong case for greater government involvement in the education of the working classes; Blatchford argued that self-help only helped the few fortunate and rich (Section 30.3) while it left the masses in poverty. This was what Booth, Rowntree and others were able to prove between 1886 and 1902 (Sections 21.3(*a*), 21.5 and 21.6(*b*)).

The existence of so much poverty and suffering in the midst of so much wealth made many people demand greater government activity in social and economic affairs. The call for such action first came from the Liberals themselves; in 1885 Joseph Chamberlain, then one of the leading Radical Liberals, issued 'an unofficial programme' outlining the social reforms which a future Liberal government should carry out (Sections 21.3(*a*), 21.5 and 21.6(*b*)). But the Liberal Party in 1885 was led by Gladstone who had previously condemned his colleague's proposals:

> There is a disposition to think that the Government ought to do this and that, and that the Government ought to do everything. If the Government takes into its hand that which the man ought to do for himself, it will inflict upon him greater mischiefs than all the benefits he will have received. ... The spirit of self-reliance should be preserved in the minds of the masses of the people, in the minds of every member of that class.
> *Source:* Gladstone, speaking at Edinburgh (September 1884).

Chamberlain's reply was even more violent. He told the ageing Gladstone:

> It is therefore perfectly futile and ridiculous for any political Rip Van Winkle to come down from the mountain on which he has been slumbering, and to tell us that these things are to be excluded from the Liberal programme. ... We have to account for and to grapple with the mass of misery and destitution in our midst. ... I shall be told tomorrow that this is Socialism. Of course, it is Socialism. The greater part of municipal work is Socialism, and every kindly act of legislation by which the community has sought to discharge its responsibilities and its obligations to the poor is Socialism, but it is none the worse for that.
> *Source:* Speech at Warrington (8 September 1885) from Lucy, H. W. (ed.), *Speeches of Rt Hon. Joseph Chamberlain* (1885).

27.2 Socialism Developing

Chamberlain's demand for social action by the government and his admission that this might be called Socialism should remind us that in the 1880s there was a period when a number of Socialist Societies were formed which led ultimately to the creation of the Labour Representation Committee (Sections 30.3 and 30.6). This movement towards Socialism was helped on its way by the work of the great investigators, Booth and Rowntree, and by the onset of the Boer War (1899–1902). When the war against the South African Boers broke out there was a rush of volunteers to join the army; over half of those who volunteered were found to be medically unfit. These were the products of a century of progress and self-help; these were the people on whom depended Britain's industrial future; most importantly, they were the people who would have to fight for King and Country if ever one of the emerging industrial nations, such as Germany, challenged Britain's imperial power (Section 24.1).

Meanwhile in other countries, including Germany, governments had already laid the foundations for their own welfare states. One argument against government interference had been the fear that high taxation and welfare schemes would cripple the country and economy. The evidence from Germany was quite the opposite; Germany had a good welfare state and at the same time was overtaking Britain in the industrial field (Section 24.1).

27.3 The 1906 Election

In March 1894, following Gladstone's resignation, the Earl of Rosebery became leader of the Liberal Party. His government was defeated in June 1895 and in 1896 Rosebery resigned his leadership to be succeeded by Sir Henry Campbell-Bannerman. Rosebery continued to exercise a great influence in the Liberal Party, leading the Old Liberals in their fight to prevent more radical members from gaining too great influence in the party. This split was widened by Rosebery's wholehearted support for the Salisbury government during the Boer War, which Lloyd George and the Radical Liberals denounced. Rosebery's Liberal imperialists attacked the Little Englanders, as they nicknamed Lloyd George and his followers. A party so disunited provided a weak opposition to the Conservatives led, after 1902, by Balfour.

However, a series of events united the various factions in the Liberal Party. All Liberals were united in their denunciation of the 1902 Education Act with its promise to provide Anglican and Catholic schools with money from the rates. 'Rome on the rates' was a rallying cry for the Nonconformists up and down the country (Section 31.8). In 1903 Chamberlain began his Tariff Reform Campaign and this cemented the unity in the Liberal Party, which campaigned vigorously in defence of free trade. We have seen that this same campaign divided the Conservatives (Section 24.3) so that this one issue succeeded in reversing the fortunes of both major parties.

The Liberals also succeeded in making friendly overtures to the infant

Labour Party (Section 30.8) and so increased the chances of Liberal candidates who stood in working-class districts. At the same time the Conservatives, by their failure to listen to trade union arguments after the Taff Vale case (Sections 29.6 and 30.7), only succeeded in alienating working-class voters.

Balfour resigned in December 1905 and the Liberal leader, Campbell-Bannerman, formed a minority government preparatory to calling a general election early in the New Year. The result of that election was a most overwhelming victory for the Liberals, as the figures show: Liberal 377; Conservative 157; Irish 83; Labour 29; Trade Unionists 24.

27.4   Liberal Achievements

In 1906 Sir Henry Campbell-Bannerman formed a Liberal government with Lloyd George at the Board of Trade and Asquith as Chancellor of the Exchequer. When Campbell-Bannerman retired in 1908 owing to ill-health, Asquith became Prime Minister and Lloyd George took over at the Treasury, with Winston Churchill replacing Lloyd George at the Board of Trade. These were the men mainly responsible for the social reforms passed during the five years 1906–11.

(a) Workmen's Compensation, 1906

Under this Act employers were forced to pay compensation to any workman earning less than £250 a year who might have been injured while at work.

(b) Trade Boards Act, 1909

People working in trades and occupations not covered by existing Factory Acts had often been forced to work long hours for low pay in appalling conditions. Tailoring, lace-making and matchbox-making were among the more notorious of these so-called 'sweated trades'. In future there would be government regulations controlling the pay, conditions and hours of work. A board of government officials would be set up to supervise each of the trades involved.

(c) Children

In 1906 the government passed the School Meals Act to help the children of the very poor. It was the teachers who had pointed out that hungry, sick and diseased children were unable to benefit from education. One doctor reported in 1907:

> They seemed to be in a condition of semi-torpor, unable to concentrate on anything. If I told one of these children to open its mouth it would take no notice until the request became a command. Then the mouth would be slowly opened wide, but no effort would be made to close it again, until the child was told to do so; these cases were always associated with bodily starvation, stunted growth, emaciation, rough and

Fig. 27.1 A way of life for many thousands of Britain's working class; clothes and other family goods were taken to the pawnshop on Monday or Tuesday in return for a few shillings needed to buy food during the week. After pay-day the clothes were taken out again for the weekend, only to be 'popped' into pawn again the following week

cold skin. What is the use of educating children whose bodies are absolutely unable to benefit by it?
Source: Arkle, A. S., *The Condition of the Liverpool School Children* (1907).

Under this Act, local authorities were allowed to collect a rate to pay for a school meal service. During the debate on this measure, Sir Henry Clarke, MP said:

The policy of the Bill is a grave social departure . . . the Government are discouraging parents from discharging the most honourable and elevating duty of training their own children. Malnutrition is not always caused by underfeeding; it is caused still more by defective housing, defective clothing, ill-judged feeding and from total absence of knowledge in many households of the most ordinary laws of health.
Source: The Times (7 December 1906).

The Gladstonian opposition to social reform had not yet died out.

In 1907 the government established the Schools Medical Inspection Service. Doctors and nurses visited the nation's schools to inspect all the children each year. In this way, it was hoped, there would be a regular check on the children's health and progress, and some at least of the common diseases would be conquered. The healthier children would then grow into healthier adulthood—and provide the nation with the workers and soldiers it needed. The memories of the ill health of the men who volunteered to serve in the Boer War was a powerful stimulus to this particular piece of social welfare.

Parliament passed a series of Acts which affected children in various ways. The setting up of Juvenile Courts was an important step along the road to a new, more humane way of coping with the problem of young people accused of wrong doing. In the past the young criminal had been sent for trial before an ordinary Court, one in which magistrates and judges were used to dealing with adults accused of crime. The establishment of the new Juvenile Courts provided an opportunity for the magistrates to consider the juvenile criminal in a new light and to consider new ways of dealing with the problem of juvenile delinquency.

Parliament passed an Act limiting the number of hours that a child might be allowed to work in the evening after school or at week-ends. There were also Acts prohibiting the sale of alcohol, tobacco and fireworks to children. The government had decided that freedom for innkeepers and shopkeepers was less important than the danger to the health or safety of children.

The Liberal government also passed an Education Act (1907) which provided opportunities for working-class children to obtain secondary education (Section 31.9).

(d) The Old

Old people formed a large section of those living in poverty as defined by Booth and Rowntree. The Liberals passed the Old Age Pension Act (1908). People aged seventy or over were to receive 5s (25p) a week, payable at the Post Office, provided that they had less than £21 a year from any other sources. The first payments were made on 6 January 1909.

The Woman Worker, one of the radical magazines of the time, showed how one pensioner had spent her first 25p. (In studying the list you should remember that 1p is equal to about $2\frac{1}{2}$ old pennies.)

	s	d
rent	2	3
pint of paraffin		$1\frac{1}{2}$
14 lb of coal		$2\frac{1}{2}$
2 oz tea		1
$\frac{1}{2}$ lb of sugar		$1\frac{1}{2}$
2 lb of potatoes		1
2 lb loin of mutton	1	0
half-bag flour		1
pint of porter (for Sunday's dinner)		$1\frac{3}{4}$
pepper, salt and vinegar		$1\frac{1}{2}$
one loaf		$2\frac{1}{2}$
Total:	4s	$5\frac{1}{4}d$

Source: Wilsher, P., *The Pound in your Pocket* (1970).

The old lady, in typically thriftless manner, said that she intended to have a first-class dinner on Sunday, with perhaps 1d worth of cheese! Later in the week, she would purchase 'a ha'porth of beans' together with a 'penn'orth of onions', and after that, she calculated, she would have enough over to afford '1d for a herring on Friday, and then it will be time to draw my pension again'.

(e) Unemployment Insurance, 1911

Unemployment was a major cause of poverty, since it meant there would be no family income at all if the only wage-earner (usually the father) were thrown out of work. Part 2 of the National Insurance Act, 1911 was planned by William Beveridge, an economist called in to help by Lloyd George. Later on Beveridge recalled:

> The compulsorily insured trades were building construction of works, shipbuilding, mechanical engineering, ironfounding, construction of vehicles and sawmilling. Every workman in those trades had to have an 'unemployment book'. To this book the employer had for each week of employment to affix a 5d insurance stamp, and was entitled to deduct half the value, that is, 2½d, from the workman's wages.
>
> The benefit was 7s a week up to a maximum of fifteen weeks; he claimed and received benefit at an Employment Exchange. He proved his unemployment and his capacity to work by signing an unemployed register there in working hours daily. The contributions were paid into, and the benefits from, an unemployment fund which was meant to be self-supporting. If the fund became exhausted, it could obtain a loan from the Treasury. . . .
>
> Source: Beveridge, W. H., Unemployment (1912).

(f) Labour Exchanges

Closely linked with the insurance scheme was the setting up of a nationwide chain of Labour Exchanges. Beveridge and the politicians wanted the exchanges as places to which the unemployed would go to prove that they were genuinely looking for work; they also hoped that employers looking for labour would send a list of their needs to the Exchange which would then be able to direct the unemployed to a new job. This was welcomed by many workmen who would have shared the experience of Will Crooks, later a Labour MP, who had once been an unskilled unemployed man seeking a job:

> I just went down to the riverside at Shadwell. No work was to be had there. Then I called at another place in Limehouse. No hands wanted. So I looked in at home and got two slices of bread in paper and walked eight miles to a cooper's yard in Tottenham. All in vain. I dragged myself back to Clerkenwell. Still no luck. Then I turned towards home in despair. By the time I reached Stepney I was dead beat, so I called at a friend's in Commercial Road for a little rest. They gave me some Irish stew and twopence to ride home. I managed to walk home and gave the twopence to my wife. . . .
>
> Source: How, G., From Workhouse to Westminster: the Life Story of Will Crooks (1907).

THE PHILANTHROPIC HIGHWAYMAN.

Mr. Lloyd-George. *"I'LL MAKE 'EM PITY THE AGED POOR!"*

*Fig. 27.2 A view of Lloyd George which might have been shared by Liberals
('Robin Hood') and Conservatives ('robbing minister')*

(g) Health Insurance, 1911

Part 1 of the National Insurance Act, 1911, set up a National Health
Insurance Scheme. All manual workers earning less than £160 a year were
forced to become insured under this state scheme. The workman paid 4d into
a fund, his employer paid 3d and the state added 2d. The insured workman

was then entitled to receive free medical attention from a doctor who would be paid out of the fund; he would also receive 10s (50p) per week for up to 26 weeks when off work owing to ill health, after which he could claim a disablement pension of 5s (25p). He would be able, too, to go to a special hospital if he had tuberculosis—then a particularly dangerous disease—while his wife was entitled to claim a maternity benefit of 30s (£1.50) when she was going to have a baby.

(*h*) **Trade Unions**

(i) The Trade Disputes Act (1916) set aside the Taff Vale judgment (Section 29.6) and restored the industrial power of the trade unions.

(ii) The Trade Union Act (1913) set aside the Osborne judgment (Section 29.10 and Test Yourself on Unit 29(*a*)). This restored the political power of the trade unions and secured the financial position of the infant Labour Party (Section 30.10).

27.5   The Budget, 1909

The reforms already introduced by 1909, plus mounting defence costs (Section 26.4(*a*)), called for unusual tax proposals. In the 1909 budget, Lloyd George proposed to collect an extra £16 million in taxation—to pay for these reforms and for the building of new battleships. He proposed an increase in income tax from 1s (5p) in the £ to just under 6p for people who had incomes above £3 000 a year with an additional 6d (2½) in the £ to be paid by those with incomes above £5 000 a year. He also increased death duties and proposed a new form of land tax (which had to be dropped because it was found too difficult to enforce).

The budget and its increased taxation plus the social reforms that these taxes would pay for aroused the anger of the richer classes, and, in particular, of the House of Lords. They threw out the budget when it came to their House, something that had never been done before. This created a political crisis and a general election in January 1910 on the choice between 'Peers or People'.

27.6   The Parliament Act, 1911

The result of the January general election left the Liberals with 275 seats and the Tories with 273. The third largest party in the Commons were the Irish Nationalists led by John Redmond (Section 23.8). Asquith, Lloyd George and Winston Churchill invited the Irish MPs to support them in their struggle with the Lords over the budget, which was passed by the Commons and the Lords early in 1910. In return the Irish demanded that the Liberals give Home Rule to Ireland (Section 23.9 and Test Yourself on Unit 23(*a*)). The Liberals agreed. But the Irish pointed out that a Home Rule Bill might pass the

RICH FARE.

THE GIANT LLOYD-GORGIBUSTER: "FEE, FI, FO, FAT,
I SMELL THE BLOOD OF A PLUTOCRAT;
BE HE ALIVE OR BE HE DEAD,
I'LL GRIND HIS BONES TO MAKE MY BREAD."

Fig. 27.3 A rich man's opinion of the 1909 budget and the Chancellor

Commons and then be thrown out in the Lords, as the budget had been, so in addition to a Home Rule Bill, they also demanded a Bill which would severely curtail the power of the House of Lords.

On 6 May 1910 King George V came to the throne. He invited the leaders of all the political parties to try to solve their differences at a round-table conference to be held at Buckingham Palace. A Constitutional Conference was called and held twenty-one sittings. The Liberals then drafted a Parliament Bill which was aimed at curbing the powers of the House of Lords. It was passed by the House of Commons but rejected by the House of Lords.

This rejection by the Lords led to the calling of a general election in December 1910—the second election in that year. Asquith and the Liberals appealed to the electorate to vote on the issue of The Peers *versus* The People. The result of the election was that the Liberals and the Conservatives each won 272 seats so that the Liberal government was even more dependent on the support of the Irish Nationalist MPs and the smaller number of Labour MPs. Once again the government introduced the Parliament Bill and once again the bill was passed by the House of Commons. Then there took place the struggle inside the House of Lords which was being asked to pass a bill which would curb its own powers. Some members of the Lords wanted to throw the bill out and to challenge the power of the Liberal government, refusing to believe that the King would give his support to Asquith and the Liberals. These were known as the Ditchers, since they appeared to be willing to fight to the last ditch. But a larger number of the Lords were frightened that the King would carry out a promise he had made to Asquith to create, if need be, 500 new peers who could be relied on to vote for the passing of the bill. This, said the opponents of the Ditchers, would lessen the importance of a title, would lead to the King being brought down into the political arena and would in any case end in a Liberal victory. Much better, they said, to give way to the Liberals without such a massive creation of new peers. These were the arguments used by the large number of Lords who earned the nickname of the Hedgers, since they were willing to hedge on their original position of opposition to Asquith. On 9 August 1911 the Lords approved the Parliament Bill by 131 votes to 114 and the Parliament Act became the law of the land.

Part of this Act says:

149 . . . Be it therefore enacted by the King's most excellent Majesty, etc.
  I. (i) If a Money Bill having been passed by the House of Commons . . . is not passed by the House of Lords without amendment within one month . . . the Bill shall be presented to His Majesty and become an Act of Parliament on the Royal Assent being signified . . .
 II. (i) If any Public Bill (other than a Money Bill) . . . passed up to the House of Commons in three successive sessions . . . is rejected by the House of Lords . . . that Bill on its rejection for the third time by the House of Lords . . . be presented to His Majesty and become an Act of Parliament . . .

27.7   A Restless Society

The larger trade unions were more militant after 1910 than they had been (Sections 29.9, 29.10 and 30.7); about this time middle-class women were becoming violently militant in their demands for 'Votes for Women' (Section

Fig. 27.4 Mrs Pankhurst being arrested outside Buckingham Palace in May 1914

28.4); the Lords had created a political crisis over the 1909 budget and the Parliament Bill and now it was the turn of the Conservative Party and the Protestants of Ulster. In 1912 the Liberals brought in their promised Home Rule for Ireland Bill (Section 23.9); because of the Parliament Act, this bill—if it went through the Commons in three successive sessions—would have to become law in August 1914. The Conservatives and the Ulster Protestants were not willing to accept this and were prepared for civil war.

A campaign by the Protestants among army officers led to a crisis within the army, as we can see from this letter written to Bonar Law in March 1914:

> I expect you know everything that I do, but it may still interest you to know that a very large number of officers all over Ireland resigned. It seems that this was effected by the extraordinary action of the Government in calling up the Regiments and in calling upon the officers that had conscientious objection. . . . The Government then got in a panic, and Sir Arthur Paget appealed to most of them with the usual arguments of the Government about strikes, etc., and of course dragging in the King's name. I understand that a large body . . . have consented to remain on, on the condition that they are not expected to act in Ulster, otherwise than in guarding the Government property and stores. I hear now that a large number of non-commissioned officers are saying that nothing will induce them to take sides against Ulster.
>
> *Source:* Letter written by Sir Edward Carson to Bonar Law, 23 March 1914, quoted in Tremlett, T. D., *Documents for History Revision, British History, 1815–1914* (1971).

There was little comfort for the Liberals in all this as they faced the prospect of a civil war in Ulster, a militant suffragette movement, hostile workers in militant trade unions (Sections 29.9, 29.10 and 30.7), and continued splits in their own ranks over the issue of social reform (see Document at end of Unit).

The onset of the war in August 1914 healed the breach between Ulster and the Liberals, at least for a time. This issue was one which had to wait for the return of peace before serious discussions could take place and efforts made to solve the problem. The war also forestalled serious discussion of the matter of women's suffrage (Section 28.4) and of the position of the new and more powerful trade unions (Section 29.10). These issues would have to be left until the war had been won.

Test Yourself on Unit 27

(a) Documents

(i) A Conservative v. New Liberalism

Sir, The strength of this kingdom, in all its past struggles, has been its great reserve of wealth and the sturdy independent character of its people. The measure will destroy both. It will extort the wealth from its possessors by unjust taxation and will sap the character of the people by teaching them to rely, not on their own exertions, but on the State. . . .

Source: C. H. T. Crosthwaite, letter to *The Times* (3 July 1908).

(ii) Old Liberalism v. the New

Sir, Mr Lloyd George while he poses as a Liberal is at heart a Socialist. . . .

It was precisely against the danger of such a bureaucracy as is now growing under Mr Lloyd George that the [voice of the] guide of the Liberal Party 50 years ago was raised in solemn warning. If John Stuart Mill was alive today and could see the things that are being wrought in the name of Liberalism he would assuredly think that the force of irony could go no further.

Source: 'A Liberal of the Old School', letter to *The Times* (December 1911).

(*iii*) New Liberalism *v.* Socialism

Liberalism supplies at once the highest impulse and the practical path. By sentiments of generosity and humanity, by the process of moderation. . . . Liberalism enlists on the side of progress hundreds of thousands whom a militant Socialist party would drive into violent Tory reaction. It is through the agency of the Liberal Party alone that Society will in the course of time slide forward almost painlessly—for the world is changing very fast— on to a more even and a more equal foundation. This is the mission of the Liberal Party. Our cause is the cause of the left out millions. We are all agreed that the State must concern itself with the care of the sick, of the aged, and, above all, of the children. I do not want to limit the vigour of competition, but to mitigate the consequences of failure. . . .

Source: The Times report of a speech by Winston Churchill (1906).

(*b*) Questions

1. Which 'measure' was being attacked in the first extract? Which group of people would not have agreed with the last sentence of this extract? Why?
2. Why was an increase in taxation required to finance the measure referred to in Question 1?
3. Which social class believed that the government was going to 'extort the wealth . . . by unjust taxation'? When and how did they indicate this opposition?
4. What evidence is there in these extracts that there was a split in the Liberal Party?
5. Why, according to Churchill, had the Liberal Party to help 'the left out millions'? Which party did he believe would gain from Liberal failure to do so? Which party, do you think, gained most from the Liberal attempts at social reform?
6. Why should John Stuart Mill have been expected to oppose 'the things that are being done in the name of Liberalism'?
7. By which Acts did the Liberals help (i) the sick, (ii) the aged, (iii) the children (give two Acts affecting children)?

(*c*) Further Reading

Adelman, P.: *The Middle-Class Experience 1830–1914.* Longman (Harlow, 1984).

Clarke, P. F.: *Liberals and Social Democrats.* Cambridge University Press (Cambridge, 1981).

Cook, G.: *A Short History of the Liberal Party 1900–1976.* Macmillan (Basingstoke, 1976).

Feuchtwanger, E. J.: *Democracy and Empire: Britain 1865–1914.* Arnold (London, 1984).

Freeden, M.: *The New Liberalism.* Oxford University Press (Oxford, 1978).

Grigg, J.: *Lloyd George: The People's Champion.* Eyre Methuen (London, 1978).

Hopkins, E.: *A Social History of the English Working Classes 1815–1945.* Arnold (London, 1983).

Murray, B. K.: *The People's Budget 1908–10: Lloyd George and Liberal Politics.* Oxford University Press (Oxford, 1980).

Read, D.: *England 1868–1914: The Age of Urban Democracy.* Longman (Harlow, 1979).
Robbins, K.: *The Eclipse of a Great Power: Modern Britain 1870–1975.* Longman (Harlow, 1983).
Seaman, L. C. B.: *Post-Victorian Britain 1902–51.* Methuen (London, 1966).

(*d*) **Documentary**

Adelman, P.: *The Decline of the Liberal Party 1910–1931.* Longman (Harlow, 1982).

(*e*) **Exercises**

1. Name five people, events or societies which helped to persuade the Liberals to undertake social reform after 1906.
2. Name four social reforms of the Liberal government 1906–14 which led to an increase in taxation. Which political party (i) opposed this increase, (ii) supported it, (iii) wanted even larger increases?
3. The 1911 Insurance Act has been called 'a small step forward'. Make a list of the ways in which Part 1 (on Health) did *not* help the insured worker and his family. Make a similar list of the ways in which Part 2 (on Unemployment) did *not* help the insured worker and his family.
4. Give three reasons for the passing of the Parliament Act, 1911, showing how three different political parties had their own interests in limiting the power of the Lords.
5. How did the Liberal government help the working classes?

Unit Twenty-Eight
Parliamentary Reform, 1860–1914

28.1 Extension of the Franchise, 1867–84

(a) Pressures for Change

(*i*) **A mature working class.** We know that, in the early days of the industrial revolution, the majority of the working class lived in overcrowded and insanitary housing, earned little money and were glad of the small wages that their children could earn in the new factories and mines (Sections 7.2(*a*), (*c*), (*e*) and 11.3). It is all too easy to believe that the underfed, ill-housed, poorly-dressed workers of the 1820s present us with a true picture of the whole of the working class for the whole of the nineteenth century. The truth is that from about 1840 onwards there grew up a small section of the working class which was highly skilled, well-paid and regularly employed; this skilled working class formed the model unions (Section 18.5), saved their surplus money in savings banks or building societies, took out insurance policies with one or other of the new insurance companies such as the Prudential, which was founded in 1848, and created their own self-help social security system by their use of the funds of their unions (Sections 18.5 and 29.1 and Test Yourself on Unit 29 (*a*)).

The first 'immigrants' into Britain's new industrial towns had been country-folk and their children. Their grandchildren, the town dwellers of the 1860s and 1870s, were fully accustomed to living in towns. They knew no other life. They were more sophisticated, mature and educated than their grandparents had been. Henry Mayhew noted this group when he wrote about the working class of London in 1861:

> In passing from the skilled operative of the west-end to the unskilled workman of the eastern quarter of London, the moral and intellectual change is so great, that it seems as if we were in a new land, and among another race. The artisans are almost to a man red-hot politicians. They are sufficiently educated and thoughtful to have a sense of their importance in the State. .... The political character and sentiments of the working classes appear to me to be a distinctive feature of the age, and they are a necessary consequence of the dawning intelligence of the mass. ...
> Source: Mayhew, H., *London Labour and the London Poor* (1861–2).

This confident, urbanized, self-helping working class produced leaders who were quite capable of explaining the demands of the skilled workers—for trade union reform, for more state education and, in this instance, for a share in the political system. In one sense, this class was repeating the arguments that the middle class had used in 1830–2 when they were seeking a share in the system which had once been dominated by the landowning class (Section 10.2

Fig. 28.1 The wives of skilled workers on an outing in the Shirley Hills, Croydon in 1912. Well clothed and well fed, these women reflected the living standards of their well paid husbands

and Test Yourself on Unit 10(*a*)). As a class or a people becomes economically secure and is able to buy for itself the signs of social status (decent housing, clothes, holidays and so on) so that class wishes to acquire political power which will bring their economic, social and political stations into line one with the other.

(*ii*) **Convinced politicians.** Many political leaders had become convinced that this skilled section of the working class had earned the right to a share in the political system. John Bright, an MP from Rochdale, had seen the way that some workers had founded the Rochdale Co-operative Society, the forerunner of the modern, nationwide, co-operative societies. Bright had drawn Gladstone's attention to this new working class, the Lancashire section of which, during the American Civil War, had suffered hardship rather than use slave-grown cotton. Gladstone, the moralist, was impressed by this display of working-class morality. When he introduced a Reform Bill in 1866, Gladstone pointed out:

> And there is not a call which has been made upon the self-improving powers of the working community which has not been fully answered. Take, for instance, the Working Men's Free Libraries and Institutes throughout the country: who are the frequenters of those institutions? I believe that the majority of the careful, honest,

painstaking students who crowd the libraries are men belonging to the working classes. Then again, Sir, we called upon them to save . . . there are now 650 000 depositors in the Post Office savings banks. Parliament has been striving to make the working classes progressively fitter and fitter for the franchise: and can anything be more unwise than to persevere from year to year in this plan, and then to refuse to recognize its legitimate upshot—namely, the increased fitness of the working classes for the exercise of political power?

Source: Gladstone in the House of Commons (12 April 1866).

(b) Proposals for Change, 1866

When Palmerston died it was as if a dam had been breached so that a flood of reform could come pouring out over the country (Section 19.4). Among other reforms which were proposed at this time was that the franchise (or the right to vote) should be extended to a wider section of the population. In Section 10.4 we saw that, after 1832, inhabitants and owners of houses in boroughs which were rated at £10 a year were entitled to vote. In 1866 Gladstone proposed that this should be lowered and that the franchise be granted to inhabitants of houses rated at £5 a year. This would have given the vote to a small number of the better-off workers, and was obviously not a headlong rush into democracy. But even this modest proposal was opposed by the more conservative members of Gladstone's own party. This group was led by Robert Lowe who declared:

> (If the Bill is passed) . . . it is certain that sooner or later we shall see the working classes in the majority in the constituencies. Look what that implies. I shall speak very frankly on this subject . . . let any Gentleman consider the Constituencies he has had the honour to be concerned with. If you want venality, if you want ignorance, if you want drunkenness, and facility for being intimidated; or if, on the other hand, you want impulsive, unreflecting and violent people, where do you look for them in the constituencies? Do you go to the top or to the bottom? . . .
>
> *Source:* Robert Lowe's speech in the House of Commons (13 March 1866).

(c) Disraeli and the 1867 Act

Disraeli led his Conservatives in their opposition to Gladstone's Reform Bill and, with Lowe's assistance, defeated the Whig–Liberal proposals. The Queen then invited Lord Derby to form a government and Disraeli led the government party in the House of Commons. Disraeli had seen that the working class demand for reform was very strong; he realized that sooner or later the franchise would be extended; he decided that he and the Conservatives would bring in a Reform Bill and thereby earn for that party the gratitude of the working class.

In 1867, therefore, the Conservative Cabinet discussed the nature of the proposals they would introduce. In the course of these discussions Disraeli was driven from the point of giving the vote to £5 householders to the extreme point, as some saw it, of giving the vote 'to every adult male householder in

PUNCH, OR THE LONDON CHARIVARI.—MARCH 2, 1867.

A BLOCK ON THE LINE.

SUPERINTENDENT BULL. "COME, LOOK ALIVE! I *MUST* HAVE THE RAIL CLEARED. THERE ARE NO END OF TRAINS DUE."

JOHNNY RUSSELL. "IT'S MY JOB, SIR, IF YOU PLEASE."

JOHN BRIGHT. "*HIS* JOB! BEST LEAVE IT TO ME AND MY MATES."

BEN DIZZY. "OUR GANG'LL MANAGE IT, IF YOU'LL LEND A HAND, BILL GLADSTONE."

Fig. 28.2 Little Lord John Russell, John Bright (with his Quaker's hat), Gladstone and Disraeli (carrying the resolutions) debate the right to bring in parliamentary reform in 1867

the borough'. This very radical proposal was opposed by some in his own Cabinet. In particular, the proposals horrified Lord Cranborne, later Lord Salisbury, who resigned fearing, as he did, the growth of democracy (Sections 19.3 and 25.1). Another critic, Lord Carnarvon, wrote:

> I am convinced that we are in a very critical position. Household suffrage will produce a state of things in many boroughs the results of which I defy anyone to predict. In Leeds, for example, the present number of electors are about 8500. With household suffrage they will become about 35 000.
>
> *Source:* Lord Carnarvon to the Duke of Richmond (11 March 1867).

But Disraeli could afford to let Cranborne go since he knew that he could depend on the support of Gladstone and his followers, who would be unable to oppose a Reform Bill without appearing hypocritical in the eyes of the working class. So Disraeli 'dished the Whigs' and in so doing imitated Peel of whom he had said: 'He caught the Whigs bathing and made off with their clothes.' Disraeli's leader, Lord Derby, called the 1867 Act 'a leap in the dark'. The results of the Act were very important. It doubled the number who were entitled to vote and so was actually a more significant contribution to the growth of democracy than had been the 1832 Act (Section 10.5(*a*)).

(*d*) The 1884 Act

The 1867 Act applied only to the borough constituencies where, from 1867 onwards, the majority of the voters were members of the working class. The Act did not, of course, bring in democracy, even in the towns; only the adult, male householder had the right to vote, plus any lodger who paid a rent of £10 a year for unfurnished lodgings. Notice that the adult sons of a householder did not get the vote, nor did the inhabitants of the blocks of flats where the majority of the working class lived.

However, the 1867 Act did little about the franchise in the county constituencies. The only concession made was that, in addition to those entitled to vote after 1832 (Section 10.5(*a*)) were added all inhabitants of houses rated at £12 a year. Notice the discrepancy between the qualifications in town and county constituencies.

From 1883 onwards there was a campaign to equalize the qualifications between the two types of constituency. This campaign was led by Bright, now an ageing Radical, and Chamberlain (Sections 21.3(*a*), 21.5 and 21.6(*b*)), whom Bright regarded as a young disciple. But the Conservatives, now led by Salisbury—the opponent of Disraeli's Act—were not willing to extend to the county constituencies the same rights as they had once extended to the towns. One reason for this opposition was given at the time:

> So little revolutionary are the householders of cities and towns that it has been possible for Conservatives to enjoy the blessing of office for six years. . . . Now, when Mr Gladstone proposes to extend the principle of the Conservative Government of fifteen years ago, the Conservative Party see in the suggestion a resurrection of all the revolutions which they had falsely prophesied.
>
> *Source: Reynold's Newspaper* (30 March 1884).

When the bill had passed through the Commons it was rejected by the House of Lords. The reason for this is explained in this extract:

> What is there in this to excite the hostility of the peers? This:—that the power of the peers in counties is about to be destroyed. The addition of two million voters to the county register of 1866 means the expulsion of a good many nominees of the aristocracy from the House of Commons; and to give a real representation to the people is just what the peers have most to fear.
> Source: Reynold's Newspaper (20 July 1884).

However, the Lords, led by Salisbury, finally agreed to allow this bill to pass, provided that another bill should be introduced which would redistribute seats (Sections 21.4(c) and 21.5), and so every adult, male householder in both town and county constituencies was given the right to vote.

28.2   Constituency Changes

(a) Reasons for Redrawing Constituency Boundaries

By 1851 over half the population lived in industrial towns and cities: Britain was, for the first time, a predominantly urbanized country. In the second half of the century this process of urbanization went on at a great rate, as we see from the Census Report (1861):

> Three-fourths of the total increase of population has taken place in the towns. . . . The rates of increase varied to a great extent: thus Birkenhead on the south side of the Mersey had 667 inhabitants at the beginning of the century, and 51 649 in 1861. Canterbury had at the same dates 9000 and 21 324 inhabitants. The population of York grew from 16 846 to 40 433: of Bradford from 13 264 to 106 218.
>   In population, next to London stands Liverpool (443 938), and Manchester (357 979) in the north-west: Birmingham (296 076) in the Midland counties: Leeds (207 165), and Sheffield (185 172) in Yorkshire; and Bristol in the west (154 093). . . .

If constituency boundaries had remained as they had been fixed in 1832 (Section 10.5) some constituencies would have consisted of only about 5000 voters while others might have contained about 500 000. This discrepancy would have been intolerable and out of keeping with the democratic spirit which inspired the modest Acts of 1867 and 1884.

(b) The 1867 Act

This Act decided that boroughs with populations under 10 000 should lose one of their two members. This involved forty-five seats. Fifteen of these forty-five seats were given to some new constituencies while Liverpool, Manchester, Birmingham and Leeds were given an extra seat so that each of them sent three MPs to Parliament. The University of London was allowed to return an MP, as the older Universities of Oxford and Cambridge had always done, while twenty-five seats were distributed among those counties where the largest increase in population had taken place since 1832.

(c) The 1885 Act

This Act was passed after the 1884 Reform Act and was a more radical change than anything that had been tried before. Seventy-nine towns which had populations of less than 15 000 lost their representation (and became part of larger constituencies), and thirty-six towns with populations of between 15 000 and 50 000 lost one seat, becoming single-member constituencies. Towns with populations of between 50 000 and 165 000 were given two seats, while the rest of the country, including the larger towns and cities, was divided into single-member constituencies. This is very much like the system that we have today.

28.3   Electoral Practices

In 1872 Gladstone's government passed the Ballot Act (Section 19.4 and Test Yourself on Unit 28(a)) which gave the voter the secret system which we have today. Before this Act, elections had been conducted on the 'open system'. On a set of platforms, or hustings, sat the Recording Officer with the Poll Book in which were written the names of those entitled to vote and the qualifications which entitled them to that privilege. The voter would climb to the platform on which the Returning Officer sat, identify himself to that Officer and then announce, publicly, the name of the candidate or candidates for whom he wished to vote. The Officer then noted in the Poll Book the way in which the vote had been cast, and the voter climbed down into the crowd, to be greeted by the cheers of the supporters of the candidates he had voted for and the boos and worse of his opponents.

This system forced the voter to take account of the wishes of his employer, landlord, government agent or other person who might have been in a position to influence the way in which he voted. The 1872 Act did away with that and ensured a fairer vote. One group which benefited immediately were the Irish Nationalists whose Catholic supporters were able, after 1872, to vote freely for Home Rule candidates without having to worry about any action which the landlord or his agent might be able to take against them (Section 23.3).

In 1883 the Gladstone government brought in the Corrupt Practices Act which limited the amount which candidates could spend during elections and so brought to an end the bribery and vote-buying which had always been features of elections. Robert Lowe had feared that a more democratic style would be a more corrupt one (Section 28.1(b)). In fact, elections before 1867 were often the occasions for great corruption. Contrary to what Lowe had claimed, elections under the more democratic system became more honest. Politicians had to appeal to the voters by offering, not money bribes, but promises of legislation which would please those voters.

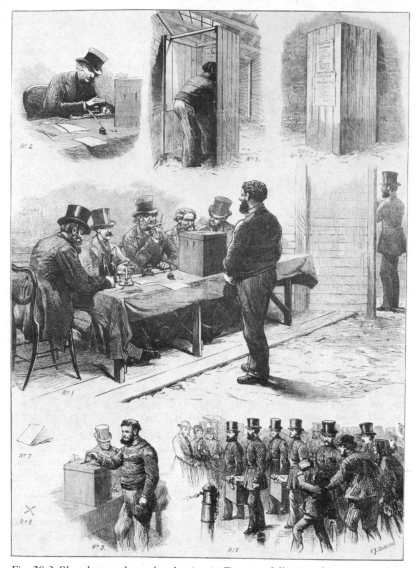

Fig. 28.3 Sketches made at the election in Taunton following the passage of the Ballot Act (1872). For the first time people could vote in secrecy and did not have to fear employers or landlords (Fig. 19.3)

28.4   Women

In all these Reform Acts there was no mention of women. They were considered to be socially inferior to men, not able—until 1882—to be trusted with their own property (Section 21.4). They were also economically inferior to men, not allowed to practise as lawyers, faced with almost intractable hurdles before they could qualify as doctors, and not considered capable of work in offices until the invention of the typewriter and telephone. So, regarded socially and economically as inferior, it is not surprising that they were also put into an inferior position politically.

THE RIGHT DISHONOURABLE DOUBLE-FACE ASQUITH.

VOTES FOR WOMEN

Women's Social and Political Union.

4, Clement's Inn, London, W.C.

Citizen Asq—th: " Down with privilege of birth—up with Democratic rule ! " | *Monseigneur Asq—th:* " The rights of government belong to the aristocrats by birth—men. No liberty or equality for women ! "

Fig. 28.4 Women were denied political equality by the Liberal government which, at the same time, was denouncing the privileged position of the House of Lords

Many middle-class women joined one or other of the many, small societies which were formed to campaign for Equality for Women. However, while they used only peaceful means, few men paid much attention to their pamphlets and speeches. In 1903 Mrs Emmeline Pankhurst founded the Women's Social and Political Union to campaign violently for votes for women. These militants earned the nickname 'suffragettes'. They chained themselves to the railings of Buckingham Palace, set fire to pillar boxes and public buildings, cut telephone wires and interrupted the speeches of politicians and the debates in the House of Commons. When arrested they refused to eat while in gaol and were subjected to the horrors of forced feeding. But in spite of these protests, women had to wait until 1918 before those over the age of thirty were given the right to vote, and until 1928 before they finally achieved political equality with men.

28.5 The House of Lords

It is difficult for us to appreciate the power which the House of Lords once exercised. It was indeed 'the Upper House', superior in almost every respect to the Commons. The Lords had the power to amend, or to reject whatever proposals were made by the Commons. We have seen that they used this power in 1831 (Section 10.3) and again in 1885 (Section 28.1(d)). The Lords had also rejected Gladstone's Second Home Rule Bill (Section 23.7) in 1893, by which time the Lords was a predominantly Conservative House, the majority of the richer classes having gone over to the Conservatives (Section 19.6(a)). This anti-Liberal bias became clearer after the Liberals had won an overwhelming electoral victory in the 1906 election. The Lords rejected or severely amended Liberal proposals on education and licensing laws. The Conservative leader in the Commons, A. J. Balfour, noted that 'no matter which Party sat on those Benches (pointing to the government side), the Unionist Party will always rule the country' through the power of the Lords. He claimed:

> Power is vested in the House of Lords, not to prevent the people of this country having the laws they wished to have, but to see that the laws were not the hasty and ill-considered offspring of one passionate election. . . .
> Source: from a speech by Arthur Balfour (October 1907).

When Lloyd George introduced his radical proposals for establishing the foundations of the Welfare State (Sections 27.4 and 27.5), the Lords rejected the budget in which he had outlined his plans for taxing the rich to provide for the poor. Lloyd George led the Liberal campaign in the election of January 1910, an election which was fought on the issue 'The Peers versus the People'.

The Irish Nationalists had no love for the Lords who had rejected the 1893 Home Rule Bill. When the election of December 1910 ended in a dead heat between the Liberals and the Conservatives, the Irish promised to give their support to the Liberals in the Commons, if they were guaranteed a Home Rule Bill *and*, more significantly, if they were promised a bill which would truncate the power of the Lords. And so, in 1911, there was passed the Parliament Act (Section 27.6). Effectively this Act brought to an end the dominance of the Lords. It was, in a sense, the final, long-term result of the 1832 Reform Act which had set in motion the movements towards a more democratic parliamentary system. In the twentieth century the Commons have dominated affairs—as seems only to be fair in 'the age of the common man'.

Test Yourself on Unit 28

(a) Document: A Quiet Election, 1872

When the poll opened the principal streets of the town were almost as quiet as usual. At the polling booths, thirty-seven in number, there was very little crowding. At each

PUNCH, OR THE LONDON CHARIVARI.—April 6, 1910.

NERVOUS WORK.

Peer (*loq.*). "WELL, I SUPPOSE THEY'LL GO ON MISSING ME AS USUAL ; BUT I MUST SAY
IT'S GETTING RATHER WARM!"

*Fig. 28.5 Attacks on the power of the House of Lords were made by Bright,
Gladstone and Rosebery in the nineteenth century and by Campbell-Bannerman,
Asquith and the Labour Party after 1906. The Irish leader, John Redmond,
helped to deal the death-blow to the Upper House*

polling booth there was erected the compartments prescribed by the Act to secure privacy to the voter while marking his ballot paper. These compartments consisted of an open movable box, with four stalls or recesses, each supplied with a small ledge to serve as a desk, and placed back to back, so that four voters might be engaged in marking his papers at one and the same time.

The Conservatives appeared to be more active with their agents at the various polling booths than the Liberals. The Conservative agents had blue cards fastened in front of their hats, and upon each card there was printed the words 'Conservative agent'. As a rule two of them stood close to the door of egress at each polling booth. A couple of them managed to get into a booth, but being detected by a Liberal were ordered out, and at one of the booths a couple were seen in the backyard within a foot of the door leading out of it, their object being to ask for the ticket of voters as they left the room.

The voting went on rather slowly; four voters were admitted at a time to each booth, and after receiving their papers proceeded to the 'stalls' behind the officials, marked their papers and then returned, putting them into a large sealed tin box, with a narrow slit at the top, as they passed out.

Some of the working men, of the ordinary labouring class, seemed to have no proper idea at all of the Ballot; odd ones of them would ask the constable at the door where they had to tell the name of the candidate they wanted to vote for, and others were very stupid in the folding up of the voting papers.

One or two cases of personations were early reported, but the guilty parties made a clear escape. As the morning advanced the booths became thronged, and at noon the work of vote recording was at its greatest pitch of activity; but the increase in it then in no way deranged the general mechanism adopted.

Cheers and counter cheers have been heard in the streets as the respective candidates and their friends have been seen passing along them. There have been no displays of colours, no bands of music, and even in St John's ward an astonishing degree of order and sobriety have been observable. The Ballot has clearly from today's experience conduced in a striking degree to the general sobriety and order of the people . . .

Source: *The Times* (14 September 1872), News Item.

(b) Questions

1. What is a polling booth? Why does the article note 'thirty-seven in a number'? How did this aspect mark a change from former voting practices?
2. When was this Act passed? Who was Prime Minister at the time?
3. Why was 'privacy' a feature worth mentioning? How did this aspect of elections compare with former methods of voting?
4. Why did this new style of voting provide fewer chances for people to influence the ways in which votes were cast? How had voters been influenced in the past?
5. Why did the Conservatives and Liberals have agents at the doors of the polling booths? Why did this Act lead to political parties becoming more organized?
6. What is meant by 'personation'? Can you suggest who might be 'personated' at a modern election?

(c) Further Reading

Adelman, P.: *The Middle-Class Experience 1830–1914*. Longman (Harlow, 1984).
Blake, R.: *Disraeli*. Methuen (London, 1969).
Briggs, A.: *The Age of Improvement 1783–1867*. Longman (Harlow, 1979).

Feuchtwanger, E. J.: *Democracy and Empire: Britain 1865–1914*. Arnold (London, 1984).

Hopkins, E.: *A Social History of the English Working Classes 1815–1945*. Arnold (London, 1979).

Magnus, Sir Philip: *Gladstone*. John Murray (London, 1979).

Read, D.: *England 1868–1914: The Age of Urban Democracy*. Longman (Harlow, 1979).

Robbins, K.: *The Eclipse of a Great Power: Modern Britain 1870–1975*. Longman (Harlow, 1983).

(d) Documentary

Dawson, K. and Wall, P.: *Parliamentary Representation*. Oxford University Press (Oxford, 1968).

Seaman, R. D. H.: *The Reform of the Lords*. Arnold (London, 1971).

(e) Exercises

1. How was Parliament made more representative of the people by the Acts of 1867 and 1884?
2. Trace the events leading to the Parliament Act, 1911. Give the main terms of that Act.
3. Why was the 1867 Act described as 'surprising in its origins and decisive in its effect'?
4. Write briefly on (i) Robert Lowe and parliamentary reform, (ii) the Ballot Act, (iii) the Suffragettes.
5. Compare the changes made in the system of election and parliamentary representation by the Reform Acts of 1832 and 1867.

Unit Twenty-Nine
Trade Unions, 1860–1914

29.1 The Model Unions

In Section 18.5 we saw that after the failure of the Chartist movement, some working men turned again to the development of a strong trade union movement as the best means of obtaining a higher standard of living. These were the skilled working men whose general behaviour impressed London journalist Henry Mayhew (Section 28.1(a)(i)) and leading politicians such as John Bright and Gladstone (Section 28.1(a)(ii)). The rise of these 'aristocrats of labour' was due to the continuing industrialization of Britain which led to the development of a number of industries in which employers were prepared to pay relatively high wages for the skilled workmen they needed. Engineers and mechanics, carpenters and plumbers, bricklayers and millwrights were able to demand and receive wages of about £2 a week—when, as we will see, unskilled men were lucky if they received 60p.

In 1851 the Amalgamated Society of Engineers was formed (Section 18.5 and Test Yourself on Unit 18(a)) and within a year or two other craftsmen had formed their own trade unions. The General Secretaries and other national officers of these craft, or model, unions made their headquarters in London, which was the centre of the British rail network and from which they could easily get to any of the industrial centres where their presence might be required. Within a short time the various General Secretaries of the leading craft unions were meeting regularly, first on an unofficial, social basis and then on an organized and formal basis. They were given the nickname of the *Junta*, a Spanish word for a group of people who have got themselves into a powerful position.

The Junta used their London base as a means of influencing the leading politicians and other people who helped form public opinion, such as newspaper editors or authors of pamphlets. They tried to persuade such people, and in particular the politicians who made the laws, that trade unionism was not the revolutionary movement which Owen had tried to develop (Section 18.4), but was, in fact, an attempt by working men to do what the middle classes were proud of having done. They were simply trying to help themselves by their own efforts.

They showed how union funds had been used to provide a social security system for the workers (Test Yourself on Unit 18(a)), a development which appealed to the middle classes who approved of thrift. They also showed that when there was a strong trade union there was less danger of a strike or of violence than when there was no trade union. In 1867 William Allen of the ASE was examined by the members of a Royal Commission:

Mr Hughes asked: It is very difficult for a strike to happen in your society, I believe? What measures have the men to take before they can strike in your society?

The witness answered: They have to represent their grievances to the committee of their branch. . . . Then they would require to get the consent of the district committee, and the approval of the executive council. . . .

Mr Hughes: And upon the consent of the executive council being given the men would go out and get their allowance?

Witness: Yes.

Source: The Beehive (11 May 1867), Report on the Trade Union Inquiry.

Union leaders, anxious to use the union's funds for payment of social security benefits, were unwilling to authorize strikes.

29.2   Trades Councils

In a large industrial town there might be a number of branches of the ASE and of each of the other craft unions. The local officials of each of these branches would meet from time to time to consider common grievances and interests. These meetings led to the formation of *trades councils* in almost every industrial town and city. Such councils, representing the skilled working men, would make petitions to local employers, local councils and local MPs whenever they felt such action was needed. They produced evidence of overcrowding, insanitary housing, children's poor education, uncooperative employers and other issues which affected their members.

The Junta dominated the London Trades Council and, as we have seen, used their position to influence national political leaders. Leaders of trades councils in other towns did not welcome this domination of union affairs by a handful of officials in London. There was, and still is, a suspicion that national leaders may 'sell the men down the river', which is one reason why trade union leaders in Britain are still poorly paid compared to their counterparts in other countries.

29.3   The Royal Commission, 1866–7

(a) The Sheffield Outrages

We sometimes forget that the Victorian age was a very violent one. Campaigners for political reform used violent methods to achieve their ends (Sections 7.3(b), 10.3(a), (d), 13.2(c) and 13.3) as did the unemployed. We ought not to be surprised that relations between employers and trade unionists were frequently marred by violence. In 1866 there was a series of very violent incidents in Sheffield connected with local trade unions. The government was forced, by shocked public opinion, to set up a Royal Commission to examine the position of trade unions in general and the Sheffield outrages in particular. We can get some idea of the sort of violence involved from this extract from a Labour newspaper:

Confession of the Murder of Lindley—
Extraordinary Scene in Court
On Wednesday, the Commissioners met and heard evidence of a most startling character. James Hallam, the sawgrinder, had intimated that he was prepared to make a full confession. . . . After confessing to the removal of the tools of workmen who refused to join the union, and the blowing up of Wheatman and Smith's place with gunpowder, he was questioned respecting the murder of a man named Lindley, who had made himself obnoxious to the Union by . . . spoiling the trade by 'filling it with lads'. The witness was evidently frightened. The word 'murder' and a contemplation of the consequences which usually follow the crime, unmanned him. Having confessed to having been seen with a pistol in his pocket shortly before Lindley was shot, he was asked for what purpose he carried that pistol, when he trembled from head to foot. He gave with trying slowness, with downcast eyes, and a distress painful to witness, melancholy details of the murder in which he had taken a leading part. . . .
Source: The Beehive (22 June 1867), Report on the Trade Union Inquiry.

Many people of the 'respectable' classes expected the Commission to come out with a condemnation of trade unionism.

(b) The Hornby–Close Affair

While the Commission was sitting, a court case was heard which showed how fragile the legal position of trade unions was. An Act of 1855 had given friendly societies legal protection by enabling them to bring dishonest officials before the courts. Friendly societies were clubs into which working people paid a weekly subscription which provided the members with social security benefits when they were ill, unemployed or retired. The model unions provided these benefits for their members, and they had registered themselves as friendly societies so that they, too, could have legal protection against dishonest officials (Test Yourself on Unit 18(a)). In 1867 the Boilermakers' Society took legal action against the treasurer of the Bradford branch, who was accused of stealing £24. When the case came to court, the judge decided:

I think, it is impossible to hold that the case is within the Friendly Societies Act, 1855. The purposes of a trade union are not those of a friendly society, and their rules, being in restraint of trade, are by the law of the land illegal and cannot be enforced.
Source: from the Lord Chief Justice Cockburn's Judgment in Hornby v. Close (1867).

Anxious union officials were frightened at the consequences of this judgment, and worried at the possibilities of the Royal Commission producing a report which would condemn trade unionism as a whole because of the Sheffield outrages. The Salford trades council therefore called a meeting of representatives of all trades councils and trades unions—and the Trade Union Congress was born.

29.4 The Commission's Report, 1869

The Junta, representing the London trades council, did not go to that first Congress at Salford. They continued to work at their policy of influencing

[1] *Beehive,* June 13, 1868.

PROPOSED CONGRESS OF TRADES COUNCILS

AND OTHER

Federations of Trades Societies.

MANCHESTER, FEBRUARY 21st, 1868.

FELLOW-UNIONISTS,

The Manchester and Salford Trades Council having recently taken into their serious consideration the present aspect of Trades Unions, and the profound ignorance which prevails in the public mind with reference to their operations and principles, together with the probability of an attempt being made by the Legislature, during the present session of Parliament, to introduce a measure detrimental to the interests of such Societies, beg most respectfully to suggest the propriety of holding in Manchester, as the main centre of industry in the provinces, a Congress of the Representatives of Trades Councils and other similar Federations of Trades Societies. By confining the Congress to such bodies it is conceived that a deal of expense will be saved, as Trades will thus be represented collectively; whilst there will be a better opportunity afforded of selecting the most intelligent and efficient exponents of our principles.

It is proposed that the Congress shall assume the character of the annual meetings of the British Association for the Advancement of Science and the Social Science Association, in the transactions of which Societies the artisan class are almost entirely excluded ; and that papers, previously carefully prepared, shall be laid before the Congress on the various subjects which at the present time affect Trades Societies, each paper to be followed by discussion upon the points advanced, with a view of the merits and demerits of each question being thoroughly ventilated through the medium of the public press. It is further suggested that the subjects treated upon shall include the following :—

1.—Trades Unions an absolute necessity.
2.—Trades Unions and Political Economy.
3.—The Effect of Trades Unions on Foreign Competition.
4.—Regulation of the Hours of Labour.
5.—Limitation of Apprentices.
6.—Technical Education.
7.—Arbitration and Courts of Conciliation.
8.—Co-operation.
9.—The present Inequality of the Law in regard to Conspiracy, Intimidation. Picketing, Coercion, &c.
10.—Factory Acts Extension Bill, 1867: the necessity of Compulsory Inspection, and its application to all places where Women and Children are employed.
11.—The present Royal Commission on Trades Unions : how far worthy of the confidence of the Trades Union interest.
12.—The necessity of an Annual Congress of Trade Representatives from the various centres of industry.

All Trades Councils and other Federations of Trades are respectfully solicited to intimate their adhesion to this project on or before the 6th of April next, together with a notification of the subject of the paper that each body will undertake to prepare ; after which date all information as to place of meeting, &c., will be supplied.

It is also proposed that the Congress be held on the 4th of May next, and that all liabilities in connection therewith shall not extend beyond its sittings.

Communications to be addressed to Mr. W. H. WOOD, Typographical Institute, 29, Water Street, Manchester.

By order of the Manchester and Salford Trades Council,

S. C. NICHOLSON, PRESIDENT.

W. H. WOOD, SECRETARY.

Fig. 29.1 The call to attend the first meeting of what later became known as the TUC

public opinion and gave evidence to the Royal Commission. When the Commission presented its report in 1869 the majority of people were surprised by the way in which this report welcomed the development of trade unions and argued that where strong trade unions existed there was less danger of violence and strikes (Section 29.1). The Report suggested that the legal position of trade unions had to be safeguarded by a new Act.

29.5 Legislation, 1871–5

In 1867 adult male householders in the towns had been given the right to vote (Section 28.1(c)) and politicians had to pay attention to the political demands of these new voters, who outnumbered the middle-class voters.

(a) Gladstone

(i) **The Trade Union Act, 1871** permitted the formation of trade unions and established a system by which unions could register with the registrar of friendly societies. Trade unions were to be allowed to organize strikes and, perhaps most important of all, the officers of a union were to be allowed to:

> ... bring or defend, or cause to be defended, any action, suit, prosecution, or complaint in any court of law or equity, touching or concerning the property, right, or claims to property of the trade union ...
> Source: Trade Union Act (29 June 1871).

(ii) **The Criminal Law Amendment Act, 1871.** On the very same day as Gladstone's government handed unions their charter, it also made their position less secure by a second Act. This said that any person who 'molested' or 'obstructed' any workmen so as to try to prevent them entering a factory or workshop would be liable to imprisonment for three months. So picketing was made illegal and the unions' ability to maintain a strike was severely limited.

(b) Disraeli

(i) **The Conspiracy and Protection of Property Act, 1875.** The Gladstone government had annoyed employers by its first Trade Union Act and had then outraged trade unionists with its second Act. The London Junta called a Trade Union Congress to meet in London in March 1871, when a Parliamentary Committee was set up to watch over all legislative matters affecting trade unionists. From 1871 to 1875 the Committee campaigned for the repeal of the Criminal Law Amendment Act. In the 1874 election every candidate was asked for his opinion on that Act and union members were advised to vote for candidates who promised to support the call for its repeal. Thirteen candidates were put forward by the Committee and two of them, Alexander Macdonald and Thomas Burt (Section 30.2), were successful and became the first working men to sit as MPs. Disraeli, and his Home Secretary

*Fig. 29.2 Riots in London in 1886 when the unemployed clashed with the army,
which had been called in to clear Trafalgar Square of demonstrators. The less
well-off members of the working class were no longer willing to submit to a life
of hardship and want*

Cross (Section 20.4), on the advice of their civil servants, brought in a new Act in 1875 which repealed the hated Act of 1871. Thus, between 1871 and 1875, trade unions had gained legal recognition, the right to organize strikes and, under Disraeli's Act, the right to picket. The law, it seemed, was on the side of the working class.

(*ii*) **The Employers and Workmen Act, 1875.** Disraeli's government gave trade unions and their members more protection by this Act, the second Act affecting trade unions passed in 1875. The main effect of this Act was that it was no longer a criminal offence for workmen (or their employers) to break their contract with each other. Trade unions could now call strikes without fearing a summons to appear before a criminal court, where there was always the possibility of a judge imposing a fine or sentencing someone to a term of imprisonment. After this Act a breach of contract (by a strike) was merely a civil offence and could be taken before a civil court, which has no power to impose fines or send people to prison.

It is not surprising that trade unions and their supporters believed that in the decade 1865–75 they had been granted the right to exist and to exercise their power without being exposed to the danger of legal interference. The fact that a union could be sued before the civil courts was not regarded as a serious menace, and the use of such a court by the Taff Railway Company in 1900 came as a shock to trade unionists and to many lawyers.

29.6   The Taff Vale Case, 1900–1

In 1900 a member of the Amalgamated Society of Railway Servants (now the NUR) came out on unofficial strike against the Taff Railway Company of South Wales. The strike was later made official, but the union was unable to control its members, some of whom destroyed company property, smashed windows and otherwise tried to attain their ends by violent means. When the strike was over the company sued the union for the losses in earnings it had suffered because of the strike. The case went from one court to another until it was finally settled by the Law Lords in the House of Lords, who decided that the company was entitled to £23 000 damages to be paid by the union, which also had to pay £19 000 in legal costs. This was seen as a middle-class attack on the power of unions and an attempt to halt the slow rise of the working class from their position of subservience (notice the name of the union involved in this case) to one where 'Jack was as good as his master'.

This judgment was set aside by the newly elected Liberal government in the Trades Disputes Act, 1906, which said:

> An action against a trade union or against any members or officials thereof in respect of a civil wrong against which damages might normally be claimed shall not be entertained by any court.
> *Source:* from the Trades Dispute Act (1906).

29.7 Unskilled Workers

The model unions represented only a small minority of the working population. In 1888 there were only about 200 000 members in the twenty-three largest unions. None of these unions recruited members from the vast army of unskilled or semi-skilled workers. The craftsmen 'looked after themselves' and saw no reason why they should use their skills and industrial power to improve the lives of the less skilled.

Fig. 29.3 London Dockers (1) *rush for the issue of penny breakfast tickets,* (2) *wait at the railings for a foreman to choose those who will work,* (3) *unload a ship*

One large group of unskilled workers were the labourers in Britain's docks. These men had no regular work but were hired for a few hours at a time whenever a ship had to be loaded or unloaded. Ben Tillett recalled his life as a London docker:

> To obtain employment we are driven into a shed, iron-barred from end to end, outside of which a foreman or contractor walks up and down with the air of a dealer in a cattle market, picking and choosing from a crowd of men, who, in their eagerness to obtain employment, trample each other underfoot, and where like beasts they fight for a day's work.
>
> *Source:* Ben Tillett, *Memories and Reflections* (1931).

If the docker did get a job he knew that it would last for only two or three hours, and he also knew that for this he would receive just over 2p an hour.

Other unskilled workers were equally badly off: millions of working men received less than £1 a week in 1900 when Seebohm Rowntree proved that a family of husband, wife and two children needed at least £1.50 if it were to have enough to maintain physical existence. These were the millions who lived in overcrowded and insanitary houses, got their clothes from pawn shops or from dustbins, scrounged food wherever they could, sent their children to school barefoot and deserved the title given them by an American journalist, 'the people of the Abyss'.

29.8   Unions for Unskilled Workers

No one had thought it possible to organize these lowly paid and unskilled workers into trade unions. How could they afford the weekly subscription of between 5p and 10p? How could they make a strike effective when the employer could recruit the workmen he might need from the army of unemployed and hungry? But in the late 1880s unions were formed among unskilled workpeople. Annie Besant, a middle-class journalist and a friend of Bradlaugh (Section 21.3(c)(ii)), organized the girls at Bryant and May's match factory in Bow, London. These girls had worked a seventy-hour week, for about 1p an hour, in conditions which exposed them to many diseases, including 'phossy-jaw', the name given to the effects of the phosphorus fumes eating away at their skin and bones. Will Thorne organized the stokers at the London Gas Company's works and, merely by threatening a strike, got the employers to agree to a shortening of the working week from seventy to fifty hours. But the most significant union for unskilled workers was formed among the London dock labourers employed at the East and West India Docks, who struck in support of their demand for an increase to bring their pay to 2½p (6d in old money) an hour, the wage being earned by wharf and riverside labourers. Few people expected their strike to succeed, but they were amazed at the response to it. One newspaper reported:

> When the strike was first announced a fortnight ago, the number of men amounted to about 10 000. Soon the figures reached 100 000, and even more. The dockmen themselves had no organization. Had they been left to fight the battle alone, the dream of the capitalist gang at the docks would have been realized, and the pinch of poverty would have driven the men into surrender. But the sympathy of the stevedores was awakened. They protested and joined the dockmen. The gallant example was immediately followed by other riverside employees—shore gangs, carmen, firemen, scalers, ironworkers, coalies, 'lumpers', biscuit-makers, and labourers of every description. As days passed the strike grew in intensity and breadth. . . .
>
> Source: *Reynold's Newspaper* (1 September 1889).

London's docks were brought to a standstill. John Burns, Ben Tillett and Tom Mann organized the strike, collected funds, distributed food among the strikers' families and negotiated with the employers. On 16 September 1889 the employers climbed down, gave the dockers their 'tanner' (2½p), and a notable victory had been achieved.

Fig. 29.4 Ben Tillett, one of the leaders of the 1889 Dockers' Strike, addressing a meeting of strikers on Tower Hill, London, in 1911, the year in which nation-wide strikes by larger, militant unions became a feature of British industrial and social life

29.9   Effects of the Dockers' Victory

(a) On Existing Unions

There was an almost immediate increase in the membership of the older unions. In part this was due to enthusiasm among craftsmen who had not previously joined a union, but their joining was also due to concern at the increase in the level of unemployment in a Britain which was no longer the 'workshop of the world' (Section 24.1). Finally, the increase was due to a change in the rules of the old unions, which allowed the recruitment of unskilled workers into the craft unions whose leaders had no wish to see a rise in the number of unions for unskilled workmen.

(b) On the Formation of New Unions

However, the leaders of the craft unions had waited too long before admitting the less well off into their privileged ranks. The unskilled had seen the unskilled dockers win their own victory. So, in 1889 and 1890, unions were formed for builders' labourers, textile workers, bricklayers' labourers, and even a General Labourers' Union. These unions were unlike the older, more respectable unions. They had no funds, little organization—but a great capacity for militancy.

(c) Militancy

The leaders of the older unions had prided themselves on their ability to limit the number and intensity of strikes (Section 29.1). They preferred to negotiate with employers, using patient argument to achieve their ends. The new unions lacked this patience and had less faith in the reasonableness of employers. They preferred the militant confrontation, the show of strength, to attain their ends. This militancy began to appeal to the younger and more radical members of the older unions particularly when, in the 1890s and 1900s, unemployment was rising, employers succeeded in cutting wage rates—even for skilled men—and negotiations seemed to be getting nowhere.

(d) The Trades Union Congress

The leaders of the unskilled working men went to their first Congress a little in awe of the giants of the older, craft unions. John Burns noted that the leaders of these unions looked like the employers, with their heavy beards, thick overcoats, top hats, watch chains and silver-topped walking sticks. Only the representatives of the unskilled, said Burns, looked like workmen.

Each union leader at a Congress was entitled to a number of votes, in proportion to the number of workers he represented. This 'card' vote gave the leaders of the unskilled workers a strong position since their unions were generally larger than the unions representing the skilled men. While they were afraid to use their power in their first Congresses at the beginning of the 1890s, they soon accustomed themselves to power so that by the end of that decade they were in a position to dominate the affairs of the Congress—and they voted that the trade union movement should help to form a working-class political party (Sections 30.5, 30.6 and 30.7).

29.10   Trade Unionism, 1900–14

We have already seen that the courts tried to limit the ability of the unions to strike (Section 29.6). The courts also tried to limit the ability of the unions to play a part in the political field. In 1908, W. V. Osborne, a branch secretary of the Amalgamated Society of Railway Servants, decided to prosecute his union for giving money to the Labour Party. Once again this union had its case taken from court to court until, once again, the case was finally settled by the Law Lords of the House of Lords. They decided that a trade union was not entitled, in law, to use its funds for political purposes. However, the Trade Union Act 1913 set aside this judgment: the future of the infant Labour Party was assured (Section 30.10).

Test Yourself on Unit 29

(a) Document: Trade Union Act, 1913

The funds of a trade union shall not be applied in the furtherance of the political objects to which this section applies unless the furtherance of these objects has been approved as an object of the union passed on a ballot of the members of the union by a majority of the members voting . . . providing

(*a*) That any payments in the furtherance of these objects are to be made out of a separate fund [in this Act referred to as the political fund of the union] and for the exemption in accordance with this Act of any member of the union from any obligation to contribute to such a fund if he gives notice in accordance with this Act that he objects to contribute.

(*b*) That a member who is exempt from the obligation to contribute to the political fund of the union, shall not be excluded from any benefits of the union . . . by reason of his being so exempt, and that contribution to the political fund shall not be made a condition of admission to the union.

Source: from the Trade Union Act (1913).

(*b*) **Questions**

1. Who provided 'the funds of a trade union'? How, apart from paying small sums to strikers, were these funds used? Why did this make union leaders reluctant to call strikes?
2. Why had unions not had 'a political fund' in, say, the 1860s? Why did some unions have such a fund in the 1890s while others did not?
3. Who (i) paid, and who (ii) did not have to pay into the political fund of his union after 1913?
4. How did the terms of this Act differ from the decision made by the Law Lords in the Osborne judgment?
5. Which political parties (i) supported the Osborne judgment, (ii) brought in the Trade Union Act, 1913 and (iii) gained from this Act?
6. Why did the political situation between 1910 and 1914 favour the passage of such an Act?

(*c*) **Further Reading**

Briggs, A.: *Victorian People: A Reassessment of Persons and Themes 1851–67.* Penguin (Harmondsworth, 1965).
Cook, C. and Taylor, I.: *The Labour Party.* Longman (Harlow, 1980).
Hobsbawm, E. J.: *Industry and Empire.* Penguin (Harmondsworth, 1969).
Lovell, J.: *British Trade Unions 1875–1933.* Macmillan (Basingstoke, 1977).
Pelling, H.: *A History of British Trade Unionism.* Penguin (Harmondsworth, 1976).
Read, D.: *England 1868–1914: The Age of Urban Democracy.* Longman (Harlow, 1979).
Robbins, K.: *The Eclipse of a Great Power: Modern Britain 1870–1975.* Longman (Harlow, 1983).

(*d*) **Documentary**

Browne, H.: *The Rise of British Trade Unions 1825–1914.* Longman (Harlow, 1979).
Evans, L. W.: *British Trade Unionism.* Arnold (London, 1970).
Hay, J. R.: *The Development of the British Welfare State 1880–1975.* Arnold (London, 1978).

(e) Exercises

1. Describe and account for the development of trade unionism between 1860 and 1914.
2. What were the obstacles to trade union development in 1867? How far had these been removed by 1914?
3. Give an account of the London Dockers' Strike, 1889. Why was it of such significance?
4. Write briefly on (i) the Hornby–Close affair, (ii) the Match Girls, (iii) the Taff Vale decision, (iv) the Osborne case.
5. Compare the skilled and unskilled unions in respect of (i) the occupations of their members, (ii) their funds, (iii) their attitudes towards strikes, (iv) their attitudes to the formation of the Labour Party.

The Rise of the Labour Party, 1880–1914

30.1 Social Problems

In the 1860s Britain was the 'workshop of the world' and the richest country there had ever been. Even when Britain no longer dominated the industrial world as she had (Section 24.1), the nation's wealth continued to grow and a section of the population continued to enjoy a very high standard of living. But in the middle of this prosperity and display of wealth there were millions of people who lived in abject poverty, condemned to spend their lives in overcrowded and insanitary houses seemingly incapable of breaking out of the position into which they were born, in which they grew up and in which—at an all too early age—they died (Section 29.7).

The two major political parties seemed unwilling or unable to do much about these conditions. Gladstonian Liberals aimed at reducing income tax (Sections 19.1(b), 21.5, 21.6(b) and 23.7), and providing a Home Rule solution for the Irish problem. It might have been possible for a Liberal Party dominated by the Radical Joe Chamberlain to have produced solutions for the social evils that afflicted the country (Sections 21.3(a) and 27.1), but Chamberlain left the Liberals in 1886 (Sections 21.6 and 23.5), and as he drifted towards his ultimate alliance with the Conservatives he lost his Radicalism. The Salisbury Conservatives were glad to take over Disraeli's interest in Empire and the upholding of British interests abroad, but they paid no attention to the 'social reform' plank in the Disraelian platform. Perhaps the Radical Lord Randolph Churchill might have succeeded in pushing the Tories in the direction of social reform, but he had resigned from the Cabinet in 1886 and died shortly afterwards.

In one sense we may say that the failure of the other parties to deal with the nation's social problems was a major cause of the emergence of a separate Labour Party.

30.2 The Political Opportunity, 1867

The 1867 Reform Act had given the vote to the adult householder in the boroughs (Section 28.1(c)). In 1869 there was formed the Labour Representation League, the first attempt by working men to produce MPs from their own ranks. In 1871 a leaflet declared:

> In the House of Commons there are 658 members, whose business it is to make the laws under which the whole of the people of all classes live. . . . Strange to say, however, every one of the 658 belongs to the middle and upper classes. Labour has not one direct representative—there is not in the House of Commons ONE MAN

whose life has been spent in the workshop in intimate daily experience of the working-man's trials, or who has been engaged in those struggles in connection with labour, upon which he founds his hopes of future regeneration. Working men! We call on you as a paramount and pressing duty, to return qualified men of your own to Parliament.
Source: Address of the Labour Representation League to the Working Men Electors of the United Kingdom (1871).

In 1874 two working men, Alexander Macdonald and Thomas Burt, were elected as MPs. They sat in Parliament with the Liberals and so earned the nickname of Lib-Labs (Section 29.5(c)). Their main aim was to look after trade union interests.

30.3   The Growth of Socialism, 1880–1900

During this period, 1880–1900, a number of societies and individuals produced books, leaflets, pamphlets and newspapers which preached the need for the government to take a more active interest in attacking the nation's social problems. They demanded that the country should have a socialist form of government in which the rich would pay higher taxes, the government would spend these taxes on the eradication of poverty, and the quality of life would improve (Sections 21.3(a), 27.1 and 27.2).

(a) The Social Democratic Federation (SDF), 1881

The first of these societies was formed by a wealthy member of the middle classes, H. M. Hyndman, who had been educated at Eton and Cambridge. Hyndman had read some of the writings of Karl Marx, the German who wrote the *Communist Manifesto* in 1848. The SDF was never a very large society—in the 1880s it had less than seven hundred members—but Hyndman and his colleagues preached the doctrine of Socialism to the working classes wherever they could be reached. Tom Mann was a member of the SDF and he recalled:

I at once [1884] became a member of the [Battersea] branch and a participant in the work, thereof, literature selling and public speaking. I threw myself into the movement with all the energy at my command . . . I found my bearings very quickly on fraternizing with, and listening to the speeches of John Burns, H. M. Hyndman, H. H. Champion, John Williams, James Macdonald, and many other with whom I came into contact. Every weekend I was busy on propaganda work, usually speaking three times on Sunday—twice in the open air and once indoors. Often the round would be near the Bricklayers' Arms, Old Kent Road, at 11 a.m., Victoria Park in the East End, 3.30 p.m., and indoors at some branch meeting or other public gathering in the evening, rarely reaching home before 11 p.m., to be up by five o'clock next morning. No payment of any kind was received for this.
Source: Mann, T., *Memoirs* (1967).

We have to remember that people did not have cinemas or TV to entertain them; a good speaker could attract a large following.

(b) The Socialist League, 1884

William Morris, artist and author, had been a member of the SDF until he quarrelled with Hyndman in 1884, when he left to form his own, small Socialist society. He did not claim to be a Marxist, never having read any of Marx's works. He did claim that the creation of a fairer society was a relatively simple matter:

> As the world is at present there are two classes of society; the one possessing wealth and the instruments of its production, the other producing wealth for the use of the possessing classes.
> What remedy then do we propose? . . .
> All the means of the production of wealth must be declared and treated as the common property of all. Every man will then receive the full value of his labour . . . everyone will have leisure for following intellectual or other pursuits congenial to his nature.
>
> *Source:* quoted in Hobsbawm, E. J. (ed.), *Labour's Turning Point, 1880–1900: Extracts from Contemporary Sources.* Harvester Press (1974).

(c) The Fabians, 1884

In 1884 a small group of essayists and lecturers formed the Fabian Society which hoped that it would be possible to persuade both the Tory and Liberal parties to pass laws which would push the country along a peaceful road to Socialism. In 1889 one of their leaders, Sidney Webb, wrote:

> All students of society realize that important organic changes can only be (1) democratic, and thus acceptable to a majority; (2) gradual, and thus causing no dislocation; (3) not regarded as immoral by the mass of the people; (4) in this country, at any rate, constitutional and peaceful. Socialists may therefore be quite at one with Radicals in their political methods. There is every day a wider consensus that the inevitable outcome of Democracy is the control by the people themselves of the main instruments of wealth production. The economic side of the democratic ideal is, in fact, Socialism itself.
>
> *Source:* Webb, S., *Fabian Essays* (1889).

(d) Robert Blatchford and *The Clarion*

In the 1890s Robert Blatchford edited a newspaper called *The Clarion* which was distributed by members of Clarion cycling clubs to working people, many of whom joined Clarion choirs and attended Clarion Sunday schools. Through these various media Blatchford preached the need for social change so that Merrie England could be recreated. *Merrie England* was the title of the book in which Blatchford reproduced some of the articles he had written in *The Clarion.* It sold one million copies in 1894 and 1895, an indication of the spread of the doctrine preached by Blatchford, who wrote:

I think that the best way to realize Socialism is to make Socialists. . . . My advice to you working men is to return working-men representatives, with definite and imperative instructions, to Parliament and to all other governing bodies.
Source: Blatchford, R., Merrie England (1894).

30.4 Keir Hardie

In 1888 Keir Hardie, a Scottish miner, had tried to get the Liberal Party in mid-Lanark to nominate him as the working-class Lib-Lab candidate (Section 30.2). When they refused and, instead, nominated a wealthy Liberal, Hardie stood as Scottish Labour Party candidate, although he did not actually form his party until he had lost the election. Hardie's example was followed by working men in various parts of Britain and particularly in London, Yorkshire and South Wales. In 1892 several independent Labour candidates stood in the general election. Hardie stood in West Ham, where he declared:

> It is not my fight, men, it is yours. . . . It is you who will lose or win. If you return me to the House of Commons, I will fight for you. I have seen men waiting for work at the dock gate, standing there as they were so many heads of cattle. . . . If the Liberals are prepared to accept our principles, we are prepared to work with them. If they are not prepared to accept our principles they are no more our friends than the Tories.
> Source: quoted in Hughes, E., Keir Hardie. Allen and Unwin (London, 1956).

Hardie won West Ham and another Labour candidate, John Burns, won Battersea. Hardie's appearance in the House of Commons shocked many people. One newspaper report said:

> [Mr Keir Hardie] drove up to the House in a toil-stained working suit with a cloth cap on his head and accompanied by a noisy brass band . . . followed by a noisy and disreputable throng from the dockside slums which included many undesirable foreign elements who should be driven from our shores before they infect our good and sensible working men with their bloodthirsty beliefs. . . .
> Source: quoted in Cockburn, J., The Hungry Heart. Jarrolds (1956).

In January 1893, fresh from the successes of the 1892 election, Hardie organized a conference of representatives of Labour clubs and parties, and some branches of the SDF. This met at Bradford and the Independent Labour Party was formed. But at the 1895 election both Hardie and Burns lost their seats, although the party continued to recruit members.

One of the first members of the ILP was Philip Snowden, the son of Yorkshire textile workers. He was born in 1864 and went to one of the early board schools (Section 31.5). In 1891 he was crippled by a spinal injury, but used his illness as a chance for self-education and obtained a clerical post in a local council office. He admired Gladstone, and in particular was attracted by his financial policies (Sections 19.1, 21.5 and 21.6(b)). Snowden quickly earned a reputation as a 'financial wizard' in the infant ILP, and became a leading figure in the new party. After the First World War he was appointed Chancellor of the Exchequer in the Labour governments of 1924 and 1929—a post which he held in the National government formed in 1931. However, Snowden resigned from this government when it decided to abandon the Gladstonian policy of Free Trade, and he died in 1937. In his autobiography he recalled the early days of the ILP:

> In spite of the disappointment of the Election, the membership of the ILP continued to grow. At the Annual Conference of the Party after the Election it was announced that 77 new branches had been formed during the year, bringing the total number up to 381. These branches were located mainly in the industrial centres of the North. More than half of them were in Yorkshire and Lancashire.
>
> Every one of these branches was an active centre of Socialist propaganda. The movement was something new in politics. It was politics inspired by idealism and religious fervour.
>
> *Source:* Snowden, Viscount, *An Autobiography* (1934).

30.5   The TUC and the ILP, 1895–1900

The Socialist societies, including the ILP, were small—very small compared to the size of the larger trade unions. These societies were also relatively poor, depending as they did on the subscriptions of their small membership. The trade unions, on the other hand, had large funds. The unions also had a well-organized network of branches which might be used as the bases for the formation of politically active groups, and they had leaders who were accustomed to speaking, organizing, negotiating and leading their members.

All of this led Bernard Shaw to call on the TUC to lend its support to the ILP and the other Socialist societies. But when Hardie proposed this at each Annual Conference of the TUC, the leaders of the skilled unions persuaded the Conference to reject the motion—until 1899 (Section 29.9(*d*)). It had taken the leaders of the new unions for unskilled workmen until then to learn how to use their power. By 1899 there was also a new type of man coming to the leadership of some of the skilled unions—men such as George Barnes of the ASE. Barnes and others had begun to realize that Britain was no longer the 'workshop of the world'; they saw that their members were suffering because of the industrial depression which had begun to affect the country (Section 24.1).

In 1899, Hardie once again proposed:

> That this Congress, having regard to the discussions of former years, and with a view to securing a better representation of the interests of Labour in the House of Commons, hereby instructs the Parliamentary Committee to invite the co-operation of all Co-operative, Socialistic, Trade Union and other working-class organizations to jointly co-operate on lines mutually agreed upon in convening a special Congress of representatives from such of the above-named organizations as may be willing to take part to devise ways and means for the securing of an increased number of Labour Members in the next Parliament.
>
> *Source:* quoted in Snowden, Viscount, *An Autobiography* (1934).

A BIT OF A BREEZE.

C.-B. (*Organ Grinder, to* INDEPENDENT LABOUR PARTY). "AIN'T YOU A-GOIN' TO JOIN IN WITH YOUR FRIEND, MISS?" I. L. P. "NOT ME! SHE AIN'T MY CLASS!"

Fig. 30.1 Keir Hardie's ILP refuses to join with the established working class MPs on the Liberal benches of the House of Commons

The resolution was carried by 546 000 votes to 434 000 votes, an indication of the limited size of the TUC in 1899 (today's TUC represents over 10 million workers), and an indication of the strong opposition to Hardie's scheme.

30.6   The Labour Representation Committee, 1900

On 27 February 1900 a Conference took place at the Memorial Hall, Farringdon Street, London between the representatives of those unions who had supported Hardie in 1899, the various Socialist societies and the co-operative societies. The result was the formation of a new party, as Snowden—one of the delegates —recalled:

> It was decided that the name of the new organization should be the Labour Representation Committee. An Executive of twelve was appointed, seven representing the Trade Unions, two the ILP, two the Social Democratic Federation, and one the Fabian Society. The large representation of the Socialist bodies was an unexpected act of generosity on the part of the Trade Unions, who had a membership of over half a million represented at the Conference compared with only twenty-three thousand membership of the three Socialist Societies.
> *Source:* Snowden, Viscount, *An Autobiography* (1934).

30.7   The Skilled Unions Join the LRC, 1902–03

The leaders of the skilled, craft unions had, in general, stayed away from the 1900 Conference, having voted against Hardie's motion in 1899. But the Taff Vale decision (Section 29.6) caused many of them to change their minds. They saw this decision as an attack on the industrial power of their unions; they realized that Parliament would have to pass new laws to restore the rights which their unions had once enjoyed. So, following the Taff Vale decision the richer, better-led, more influential craft unions affiliated to the LRC.

30.8   The Electoral Pact, 1903

In 1903 the Liberals were preparing for a General Election which they knew would have to be called in the near future. Herbert Gladstone, the Liberal Chief Whip, arranged a pact with Ramsay MacDonald, the secretary of the LRC. His reasons were explained in a letter written by Gladstone's secretary:

> What would be the gain and the loss to the party at the General Election, if a working arrangement were arrived at with the L.R.C.?
>   The L.R.C. can directly influence the votes of nearly a million men. They will have a fighting fund of £100,000. Their members are mainly men who have hitherto voted with the Liberal Party. Should they be advised to vote against Liberal candidates, the Liberal party would suffer defeat not only in those constituencies where L.R.C. candidates fought, but also in almost every borough, and in many of the Divisions of Lancashire and Yorkshire. This would be the inevitable result of unfriendly action

Mr. JONES (representing Upholsterers) moved—"That this conference is in favour of the working-class opinion being represented in the House of Commons by members of the working classes, as being the most likely to be sympathetic with the aims and demands of the labour movement."

Mr. PAUL VOGEL (Waiters' Union) seconded.

Mr. GEORGE BARNES moved an amendment in favour of working-class opinion being represented " by men sympathetic with the aims of the labour movement, and whose candidatures are promoted by one or other of the organized movements represented at the conference."

Mr. JOHN BURNS, M.P., in seconding the amendment, said the resolution was narrow, intolerant, and exclusive. He was, he said, getting rather tired of hearing about workmen's boots, workmen's trains, workmen's dwellings, workmen's clothes, and working men candidates for working-class colonies. (Hear, hear.) The time had arrived in the history of the labour movement when they should no longer allow themselves to be prisoners to class phrases. (Laughter and " Hear. hear.") Did they propose to select boiler makers who earned £3 or £4 a week and reject clerks who dressed like dukes on the wages of dustmen ? (Laughter.) A navvy might be elected a Parliamentary representative, and if he became a great contractor would they reject him ?

The amendment was carried by 102 votes against 3.

The Parliamentary Committee submitted a resolution " in favour of establishing a distinct labour group in Parliament, who should have their own Whips and agree upon their policy, which must embrace a readiness to co-operate with any party which for the time being may be engaged in promoting legislation in the direct interest of labour, and be equally ready to associate themselves with any party in opposing measures having an opposite tendency," but in its place

Mr. JAMES MACDONALD moved—" The representatives of the working-class movement in the House of Commons shall form there a distinct party, with a party organization entirely separate from the capitalist parties, based upon a recognition of the class war, and having for its ultimate object the socialization of the means of production, distribution, and exchange : the party shall formulate its own policy for promoting practical legislative measures in the interests of labour, and shall be prepared to co-operate with any party that will support such measures or will assist in opposing measures of an opposite character."

Fig. 30.2 An extract from a report in The Times *describing the meeting which led to the setting up of the LRC*

towards the L.R.C. candidates. They would be defeated, but so also should we be defeated. If there be good-fellowship between us and the L.R.C. the aspect of the future for both will be very bright and encouraging.

Source: Bealey, Frank, quoted in the *Bulletin of the Institute of Historical Research*, Vols. 29/30 (1956).

30.9   The 1906 Election

The LRC changed its name to the Labour Party in time for the general election which was called for 1906. The party put up fifty candidates and in addition there were a number of candidates put forward by the Miners' Federation which had not yet affiliated to the new party. Most Labour candidates were opposed by only a Tory candidate because of the workings of the 1903 pact, and many enjoyed the support of the Local Liberal Association. This helps to explain why twenty-nine Labour MPs were returned, for all except three had had a clear field against the Conservatives. The miners had returned another twenty-four MPs and soon after Parliament met these joined the Labour Party.

One of the new party's first actions was to persuade the Liberal government to remove the threat to the industrial powers of trade unions which had been attacked by the Taff Vale judgment. The Trade Disputes Act, 1906 (Section 29.6) said that, in future, unions were not to be held responsible for any losses which firms might suffer as a result of a strike. The party also supported the Liberal plans for establishing the foundations of the Welfare State (Section 27.4). What was not clear was whether the new party was to be regarded merely as a group representing the interests of the trade union movement, whether it was to be only a radical wing of the Liberal Party or whether it was to be a truly revolutionary party. This uncertainty is reflected in the *Diaries of Beatrice Webb*, a leading Fabian:

> When the conference settled down to business the ILP leaders were painfully at variance. J. R. MacDonald seems almost preparing for his exit from the ILP. I think he would welcome a really conclusive reason for joining the Liberal Party. Snowden is ill, Keir Hardie 'used up', with no real faith left in the Labour Movement as a revolutionary force. Jowett carried his unpractical resolution that Labour Members ought, on all questions and at all times, to vote 'according to the merits' of the particular issue before the House. The rank and file were puzzled and disheartened when Snowden fiercely attacked his colleagues of the Parliamentary Labour Party. The cold truth is that the Labour Members have utterly failed to impress the House of Commons and the constituencies as a live force, and have lost confidence in themselves and each other. The Labour Movement rolls on—the Trade Unions are swelling in membership and funds, more candidates are being put forward; but the faith of politically active members is becoming dim or confused whilst the rank and file become every day more restive. There is little leadership but a great deal of anti-leadership.

Source: Cole, M. (ed.), *Diaries (Webb, B.)*. Longman (London, 1952).

THE PREDOMINANT PARTNER.

LIBERAL PARTY. "YES, I WAS WRONG TO THREATEN HIM WITH THE WHIP. THE DEAR CREATURE MUST BE LED, NOT DRIVEN. STILL—THIS ISN'T QUITE THE WAY I MEANT TO COME!"

Fig. 30.3 Who, in fact, was in charge?

30.10   Moves to Independence

In 1911, after the Parliament Act (Section 27.6), came a law stating that in future MPs were to be paid a salary of £400 a year. This was a great benefit to the working-class MPs who formed the majority in the new Labour Party. Very few of them had been able to earn any money while they served as MPs—unlike the journalists, lawyers and financiers who sat as Liberal and

Conservative members. They had had to depend on the funds of the Labour Party or payments made them by their unions (where the members was supported by a union). From these payments they had had to maintain their own homes as well as pay for rooms and meals in London. The £400 salary represented a major step forward in the lives of the working-class MP.

Fig. 30.4 Labour MPs in the House of Commons, 1910

However, in 1911 the Liberal government passed the National Insurance Act by which working people were compelled to pay contributions to the Insurance Fund (Sections 27.4(*e*), (*g*)). The majority of working-class MPs opposed this 'tax on wages', believing that the Insurance Fund should be derived from the taxes collected by the Chancellor of the Exchequer. This disagreement between the Liberal government and the Labour Party confirmed that the new party was, indeed, an independent one and was not just the radical wing of the older party.

In 1913 the Liberals passed the Trade Union Act (Section 29.10 and Test Yourself on Unit 29(*a*)) which permitted trade unions to collect money from their members to form a political fund, from which the unions would contribute to the work of the Labour Party. This financial backing was essential if the party was to grow, and the passing of the Act marked another step in the movement towards independence from the Liberal Party. The First World War (1914–18) was to confirm this independence, but it split the Liberal Party, so that in the 1918 election the Labour Party became the second largest party in the Commons.

Test Yourself on Unit 30

(a) Documents:

(i) Trade Unions

Mr Hodge said the progress of their movement was shown by the fact that when they met last year, at Birmingham, the numbers affiliated to the LRC were 456 531, and today the numbers were 751 570, an increase of more than 300 000. During the last few weeks the textile workers had come in, making the figures more like 852 000, an increase of about 100 per cent. He believed it would go on more and more as the workers began to realize that the politically made Judges for partisan political services had been placing themselves above and beyond the legislature. The more they realized that these politically made Judges had been taking upon themselves powers it was never intended they should have, the more they realized that they had been subverting the laws of the land, the more would their movement grow in strength.

Source: Report on the Annual Conference of the LRC in *Reynold's Newspaper* (22 February 1903).

(ii) Progress 1903–10

Between the General Elections of 1900 and 1906 three remarkable victories were obtained: Mr Shackleton was returned unopposed for Clitheroe; Mr Will Crooks won Woolwich; and I had the pleasure of beating both the Tory and Liberal candidates at Barnard Castle. In 1906 the Party promoted fifty candidates at the General Election and twenty-nine of them were successful; in January 1910, seventy-eight candidates ran and forty were returned; in December 1910, fifty-six candidates were nominated and forty-two returned. In Parliament these members formed a separate and independent group.

Source: Henderson, A., *The Aims of Labour* (1918).

(b) Questions

1. How many Annual Conferences had the LRC held before the one recorded in Document 1 above?
2. Can you suggest how the LRC benefited when more people affiliated to the Committee?
3. What was the significance of the reference to 'politically made judges'? Which legal decision did the speaker have in mind?
4. Which parties (i) had the opportunity to do something about that decision—and ignored the opportunity, (ii) set the decision aside by passing a Trade Union Act?
5. In what ways did (i) Socialist societies, and (ii) trade unions differ in their expectations of the LRC? Was this difference a source of strength or of weakness?
6. Can you suggest any link between the increase in the number of people affiliating to the LRC and the increase in the number of Labour MPs (Document *ii*)?
7. Which one single explanation would you offer to account for the success of the LRC in the 1906 election?
8. Arthur Henderson (Document *ii*) suggests that the party increased its number of MPs from twenty-nine (in 1906) to forty (in 1910). Why is this an inaccurate picture of the development of the party between 1906 and 1910?

(c) Further Reading

Adelman, P.: *Gladstone, Disraeli and Later Victorian Politics*. Longman (Harlow, 1970).

Cook, C. and Taylor, I.: *The Labour Party*. Longman (Harlow, 1980).

Feuchtwanger, E. J.: *Democracy and Empire: Britain 1865–1914*. Arnold (London, 1984).

Hobsbawm, E. J.: *Industry and Empire*. Penguin (Harmondsworth, 1969).

Hopkins, E.: *A Social History of the English Working Classes 1815–1945*. Arnold (London, 1979).

Lane, P.: *The Labour Party*. Batsford (London, 1973).

Pelling, H.: *The Origins of the Labour Party 1880–1900*. Oxford University Press (Oxford, 1965).

Read, D.: *England 1868–1914: The Age of Urban Democracy*. Longman (Harlow, 1979).

Robbins, K.: *The Eclipse of a Great Power: Modern Britain 1870–1975*. Longman (Harlow, 1983).

(d) Documentary

Adelman, P.: *The Rise of the Labour Party 1880–1945*. Longman (Harlow, 1972).

Hay, J. R.: *The Development of the British Welfare State 1880–1975*. Arnold (London, 1978).

(e) Exercises

1. Account for the growth of the Labour Party after 1880.
2. Trace the development of the Labour Party from 1888 to 1906.
3. Write briefly on (i) the Fabian Society, (ii) Keir Hardie, (iii) the 1903 Electoral Pact, (iv) the Lib-Labs.

The Development of State Education, 1760–1914

31.1 Social Class and Education, 1760

Until very recently Britain was a country in which the future of a child depended almost entirely on the social class into which he or she had been born. Writing in 1961, an American noted:

> It would be a gross exaggeration to say that class distinctions in England no longer exist—but it is nowhere nearly so important as it was. Before the war if a boy's father was a coal miner the chances were that the youngster would follow him; only exceptionally gifted, aggressive or lucky people emerged from their environment. But today young men and women climb out of their backgrounds with comparative ease. . . .
> Source: Gunther, J., Inside Europe Today. Hamish Hamilton (1961).

Over a hundred years before a hymn-writer had written:

> The rich man in his castle,
> The poor man at his gate,
> God made them, high or lowly,
> And order'd their estate.
> Source: from a hymn by Cecil Frances Alexander (1848).

In this apparently God-made society each person was supposed to remain in that class into which he had been born, and to receive the education which would fit him to carry out the work required of someone in that class.

(a) The Rich

In the eighteenth and nineteenth centuries the sons of the landed aristocracy—the old upper class—received their education at home with a private tutor, or at one of the nine great schools: Charterhouse, Eton, Harrow, Merchant Taylor's, Rugby, St Paul's, Shrewsbury, Westminster or Winchester. Many of them then went to Oxford or Cambridge, looking on a university as a sort of finishing school where they would meet the people with whom they would associate later in their political and social lives.

At school and university they were taught Latin, Greek and ancient history and, until the schools were reformed by the work of great headmasters such as Arnold of Rugby, they were places where bullies among the staff and pupils alike made life miserable for younger and weaker people. You can get an idea of what these schools were like in Thomas Hughes' *Tom Brown's Schooldays*, which is an account of life at Rugby School.

The girls of these aristocratic families were taught at home, either by a governess or by their mothers. It was not thought 'proper' to educate girls in

Fig. 31.1 Rugby School, 1891, one of the schools to which the rich sent their sons

the same way as their brothers. The well-brought-up lady was said to require sewing, embroidery, riding, perhaps a little French, dancing and music.

(b) The Middle Classes

Some of the sons of the landed aristocracy went to the local, fee-paying, grammar schools where many of the sons of the local middle class were taught. These schools had been built with money provided by various people in the past—sometimes the money had been left by an individual, sometimes it had come from the funds of a trading company or a guild; some of the schools were founded after the destruction of the monasteries during the Reformation, and were named after King Edward VI or Queen Elizabeth I. Some of these schools provided boarding facilities for boys from outlying districts, but most of the pupils were day-boys. With the development of the railway system (Section 12.5), it was possible for boys to travel from much further afield, and the new middle-class parents were prepared to pay for their sons to have the boarding-school education which was once the privilege of the upper class (Section 31.1(*a*)). Some headmasters—aided by the school governors—changed their grammar schools into boarding schools. Very many of these schools then had no room for the local boys unless their parents, too, were able to afford the high fees.

We have to remember that Britain was a mainly agricultural country in 1760 and that its people lived in small towns or villages. The grammar schools had been built to provide schooling for small numbers—the sons of the merchants, traders, professional men and small landowners of the locality. Samuel

Bamford went to Manchester Grammar School at the beginning of the nine-teenth century. He recalled:

> The school was a large room of an oblong form, extending north and south, and well lighted by large windows. At the northern end was a fireplace, with a red cheerful fire glowing in the grate. The master's custom was to sit in an armed chair with his right side towards the fire and his left arm resting on a square oaken table, on which lay a newspaper or two, a magazine or other publication, a couple of canes with the ends split, and a medley of boys' playthings, such as tops, whips, marbles, apple-scrapers, nut-crackers, dragon-binding, and such like articles.
> Source: Bamford, S., Early Days (1849).

(c) The Skilled Working-Class

Even in the years before the industrial revolution, there were hundreds of skilled craftsmen in Britain. They made the clocks, steel, ships, looms, spin-ning-wheels, glassware and other goods for which the country was famous. These craftsmen were proud of their skill, which separated them from the unskilled workers. They wanted their children to have some sort of schooling

Fig. 31.2 A Dame School, painted by T. Webster (1800–86)

which would mark them off from the children of the poor. Some of them went to the local grammar school—if the parents could afford the £2 or £3 which had to be paid each term. Many others went along with children from the middle class to private schools, most of which were kept by old ladies so that these schools were known as *dame schools*. The children learnt very little from the untrained widows or spinsters who tried to run these schools in their own homes.

(*d*) **The Poor**

The vast majority of the children of the poor had little chance of getting to a school at all. Some of them lived in parishes where the local Anglican church paid for a *charity school*, the money being provided by the better-off parishioners. Other children might have lived in a district where the Methodists or one of Robert Raikes' imitators had founded a *Sunday school* (Test Yourself on Unit 31(*a*)(*i*)). By 1795 there were nearly 250 000 children registered at Sunday schools, Sunday being the only day when these children were not at work.

31.2   The Monitorial Schools

The continued growth of the population after 1760—that is, in the number of children being born—proved too much for the churches and the old methods of providing some sort of schooling for the children of the poor. However, Joseph Lancaster, a former Quaker, and Dr Andrew Bell, an Anglican vicar, both—but quite separately—hit on a new idea in the 1790s. They founded schools in which a teacher would train older pupils to act as helpers or monitors. These monitors would teach the younger children, and in this way one teacher could cope with 500 or more children at a time. Lancaster explained his system in 1803:

> My school is attended by 300 scholars. The *whole* system of tuition is almost entirely conducted by boys. . . . The school is divided into classes, to each of these a lad is appointed as monitor; he is responsible for the morals, improvement, good order, and cleanliness of the whole class. It is his duty to make a daily, weekly, and monthly report of progress, specifying the number of lessons performed, boys present, absent, etc. As we naturally expect the boys who teach the other boys to read, to leave school when their education is complete, and do not wish that they should neglect their own improvement in other studies, they are instructed to train other lads as assistants, who, in future may supply their place, and in the meantime leave them to improve in other branches of learning. To be a monitor is coveted by the whole school, it being an office at once honourable and productive of emolument.
>
> *Source:* Lancaster, J., *Improvements in Education* (1803).

Lancaster and Bell depended on well-off people giving them money to pay for the building of the schools and the small salary paid to the teacher.

31.3   The Beginnings of State Education

After 1814 Lancaster's schools were run by the British and Foreign Schools Society; Bell's schools, where the Anglican catechism was taught, were run by the National Society, formed as a rival organization in 1814. In 1833 the government made a grant to these societies:

> That a Sum, not exceeding £20 000 be granted to His Majesty, to be issued in aid of Private Subscriptions for the Erection of School Houses, for the Education of the Children of the Poorer Classes in Great Britain, to the 31st day of March 1834: and

that the said sum be issued and paid without any fee or other deduction whatsoever.
Source: House of Commons resolution, August 1833, quoted in Dawson, K. and Wall, P., *Education* (1969).

The grant would only be made if half the cost of school buildings had previously been supplied by private subscriptions, which did nothing to help the poorest districts of the new industrial towns where local subscriptions could not be raised from among the poor and frequently unemployed workers.

In 1837 a Parliamentary Committee showed how little was really being done. It reported:

The general result of all these towns is, that about one in 12 receives some sort of daily instruction, but only about one in 24 an education likely to be useful. In Leeds, only one in 41; in Birmingham, one in 38; in Manchester one in 35.
Source: Report of the Select Committee on Education in Large Towns (1837).

In 1839 the government increased its annual grant to £30 000 and set up a Committee of the Privy Council to supervise the spending of this sum. Dr Kay (later Kay-Shuttleworth) was the influential Secretary of this Committee which appointed one inspector to supervise the working of the schools run by the Anglican National Schools' Society, and another to supervise the work of the schools run by the British and Foreign Schools Society.

31.4   Payment by Results

In the 1850s there was a demand that the government should reduce its spending. Gladstone was anxious to abolish income tax (Sections 19.1(*b*), 21.5 and 21.6(*b*)) while the cost of the Crimean War (Sections 13.5 and 13.7) had to be met. In 1856 the former Committee of the Privy Council became the Education Department, with its Vice-President being an MP who had to answer questions on spending on education. The first Vice-President was Robert Lowe, an opponent of increased government spending and of the extension of the franchise to the working class (Section 28.1(*b*)). In 1858 a Royal Commission was set up under the chairmanship of the Duke of Newcastle:

To inquire into the present state of Popular Education in England, and to consider and report what Measures, if any, are required for the extension of sound and cheap elementary instruction to all classes of the people.

In 1861 the Commission presented its Report to Parliament which then approved a Revised Code, of which Lowe said:

I cannot promise the House that this system will be an economical one and I cannot promise that it will be an efficient one, but I can promise that it will be one or the other. If it is not cheap it shall be efficient: if it is not efficient, it shall be cheap.
Source: Robert Lowe, speech in the House of Commons (1861).

In place of the old system of grants, the Revised Code brought in a system of payment by results:

The Managers of Schools may claim at the end of each year

(a) the sum of 4s per scholar at morning and afternoon meetings of their school and 2s 6d per school, at the evening meetings of their school;

(b) for every scholar who has attended more than 200 morning and afternoon meetings of their school

(i) If more than six years of age 8s *subject to examination*.

(ii) If under six years of age 6s 6d *subject to a report by the inspector* that such children are instructed suitably to their age, and in a manner not to interfere with the instruction of the older children.

(c) For every scholar who has attended more than 24 evening meetings of their school 5s *subject to examination*.

Source: The Revised Code (1862).

Grants could be claimed for children who passed an examination set by a visiting inspector, which led to a good deal of learning by rote and caused teachers and pupils to regard the inspector as an enemy. This system was not abolished until 1897.

31.5   The Forster Act, 1870

In 1867 the second Reform Act gave the vote to millions of workers (Section 28.1(c)). Robert Lowe had opposed the extension of the franchise (Section 28.1(b)), but after it had been passed, speaking as Vice-President of the Education Department, he said:

I suppose it will be absolutely necessary to educate our masters. I was before this opposed to centralization (of education); I am now ready to accept centralization. I was opposed to an education rate: I am now ready to accept one. . . . From the moment you entrust the masses with power, their education becomes an imperative necessity. You have placed the government of this country in the hands of the masses and you must therefore give them an education.

Source: Robert Lowe, speech on education and the franchise (1867).

The demand for an extension of the provision of education for the working classes led to the formation of the Manchester Education Aid Society in 1864 and, in 1869, the Birmingham Education League, led by Joseph Chamberlain (Section 21.3(a)). In 1868 Gladstone appointed W. E. Forster as Vice-President of the Education Department. Forster showed that Britain was falling behind other industrialized countries, largely because of the failure to provide enough education for the majority of the children of the working class (Section 24.1(a)(iii)). He said:

We must not delay. Upon the speedy provision of elementary education depends our industrial prosperity. It is of no use trying to give technical teaching to our artisans without elementary education . . . if we leave our workfolk any longer unskilled, notwithstanding their strong sinews and determined energy, they will become over-matched in the competition of the world. . . .

Source: W. E. Forster, speech introducing the Education Bill (17 February 1870).

In 1870 Parliament approved the Education Act which divided the country into about 2 500 School Districts. In each District the ratepayers were to elect a *School Board* of between five and fifteen members. The School Board could impose a school rate and acquire land on which to build new *board schools* if there were not enough places in the existing schools for all the children in the District. These board schools, like the monitorial schools, were meant for the children of the poor. Children of the skilled working class went, wherever possible, to some form of fee-paying private school, leaving the board school with its elementary education for the less well-off. In board schools religious instruction was to be taught either as the first or the last lesson, so allowing parents to withdraw their children from these lessons if they wished. The School Board was allowed to impose a school fee (about 3p qr 4p per week), but could allow children to attend school without paying fees if the parents could not afford to pay. The Boards were also allowed to make attendance compulsory. The London School Board made attendance compulsory for children between the ages of five and thirteen.

This Act marked the first major step by the state into the field of education. Previously the state had relied on the activities of the various voluntary societies to provide the schools. Now, for the first time, the state paid for the building, equipping and maintenance of the government-controlled schools. The voluntary societies continued to depend on the government for their grants; the board schools were paid for out of the local rate.

Following this Act the government increased its interest in popular education: in 1880 the Mundella Act made schooling compulsory and in 1891 parents were given the right to demand free education. In 1893 the school-leaving age was fixed at eleven, in 1899 at twelve, and in 1918 at fourteen, where it remained until 1947.

31.6 Problems Following the 1870 Act

(a) The Voluntary Schools

In a report published in 1890 it was shown that the various religious bodies educated more children than did the board schools. But these voluntary schools found it very difficult to match the board schools in the matter of buildings and equipment. The board schools had the vast resources of the ratepayers of a district to support them; the voluntary schools had to depend on subscriptions and on the grants they received from the system of payment by results (Section 31.4). It is not surprising that these schools found it very difficult to provide the same facilities—workshops, domestic science kitchens, art rooms and so on—as were found in the better board schools.

(b) Higher Classes

In many School Board Districts there was a tendency for some children to be kept at school after the official age for school leaving. Sometimes this was

Fig. 31.3 Elizabeth Garrett Anderson, a champion of women's right to receive the same education as their brothers, and to be allowed to gain professional qualifications. She qualified as a doctor, and when the London School Board was set up she was elected to serve as a member of that Board

because ambitious working-class parents wanted to provide a chance for their clever children to study more advanced subjects, such as technical drawing, which would fit them for a better job when they left school. Sometimes it was an enterprising teacher or headteacher who encouraged the parents to make a sacrifice of the money they could get from sending the child to work at eleven or twelve years of age, to leave him at school for another two or three years so that he could take one or other of the many examinations which were becoming available for fifteen-year-old children.

But the School Boards were only legally entitled to collect a rate to provide money for elementary education. In 1898 a government official told the London School Board that its members would have to pay out of their own pockets all the money which the Board had spent on its 'illegal' higher classes. The issue was taken to court and the judge upheld the official's decision. This meant that all the higher classes in board schools up and down the country were in danger. The government was forced to take action.

(c) Various Authorities

In 1870 the Forster Act had set up School Boards to provide elementary education. The government's Education Department supervised the work of these Boards and of the various voluntary schools. The Science and Art Department, with its headquarters in the Great Exhibition buildings in Kensington, gave grants to schools and classes where pupils were taught technical subjects, provided that the children reached a standard laid down by the inspectors of that Science and Art Department. After the establishment of county councils (Section 25.2), they were made responsible for the provision of technical education in the counties. In addition to these different bodies there were the Charity Commission, the Board of Agriculture and the War Office, each of which played some part in the education of some working-class children.

31.7   Tidying Up the Education System

We have seen that one of Gladstone's main reforms was the opening up of the civil service to the most able sons of the new middle class (Sections 19.4(b), (c)). By the end of the century these highly educated civil servants had reached the top of the tree and were running various government departments. One of the most important of these officials was Robert Morant. In 1898 he was a junior official in the Education Department. It was Morant who forced the government to take a stand over the 'illegal' higher classes. Morant was offended by the way in which the law was being broken. He was also offended by the untidy mess which he saw when he looked at the education scene.

The government had tried to do something about this in 1896 when it proposed to make the county and county borough councils the only local authorities for all the schools in their districts. This bill was dropped because

Fig. 31.4 'Left in charge' in a classroom of 1891

of violent opposition from the politically important School Boards. In 1899 the government set up the Board of Education as a new central authority— but the Board did not meet and all the work was done by the President of the Board, a junior member of the government and not a member of the Cabinet.

Morant, Permanent Secretary of the Board of Education, was the man responsible for the 1902 Education Act, which was intended to tidy things up, to make a link between elementary and secondary education and to increase the government's involvement in popular education.

31.8   The 1902 Education Act

The 1902 Act abolished the 2 500 School Boards and created 140 Local Education Authorities (LEAs) which were to be run by county and county borough councils. Each LEA was to be responsible not only for elementary education but also for providing secondary (grammar) schools, technical and teacher-training colleges as well as adult education colleges.

The old board schools became *council schools* while the voluntary schools became voluntary-aided schools, receiving their support from the local rates. The LEAs were allowed to build their own county secondary (grammar) schools and could also give money to the older grammar schools. However, for most of the country's children education consisted of the period they attended the board, or council, school which they left at the age of thirteen, when they started work. Only the children of the better-off could hope to attend the secondary (grammar) schools where fees had to be paid, books bought, uniforms provided and other expenses met.

31.9   The 1907 Education Act

Morant had hoped to make a link between the elementary schools and the established grammar schools. However, the first definite link was provided by an Act passed by the Liberal government (Section 27.4(c)). In 1907 it was

Fig. 31.5 Children at Snowsfield Board School, 1894. The poverty of the parents is revealed by the children's clothes and general appearance

decided that every secondary school which received money from the LEA had to keep one-quarter of its places as free places available for the children who had attended elementary schools, built and maintained by School Boards until 1902 and by the new LEAs after 1902. In 1907 there were 47 000 such free places; the number rose to 60 000 in 1913 and to 143 000 in 1927, evidence of the building of more secondary schools by enterprising LEAs and the taking-over of more of the older grammar schools. For the first time many of the clever children of the working class could hope to gain a place at the middle-class grammar school, qualify for a better job than their fathers had enjoyed and so move out of that social class to which, it had once been believed, God had appointed them.

Test Yourself on Unit 31

(a) Documents

(i) The foundation of Sunday schools in Gloucester, 1780

Robert Raikes was a well-to-do master printer in Gloucester. . . . One day, in the year 1780, Mr Raikes chanced to go into the lower part of the town in search of a gardener. The man was not in, and Mr Raikes was waiting about. Near by, in the street, a swarm of boys were playing 'chuck'. The noise was deafening, the oaths were terrible! Mr Raikes was amazed. Turning to a decent-looking woman in a doorway he expressed his surprise and pain at what he had heard and seen. She replied: 'Ah, Sir, that's nothing! We have it so every day. But on Sunday it's worse. Sundays, the pin factory yonder isn't working, and so there's more children in the streets, and Sir, then it's like hell!' These words came as a shock to the good Sabbath-keeping heart of Robert Raikes, and the facts before his eyes were a vivid illustration of the words. 'Something must be done,' said this practical man to himself. But what? Pondering a little he hit upon a new idea— new to him, at any rate: and new to the world at large, as it turned out. The idea was to gather these and such like children into schools on Sundays—on the day when they made 'hell' in the streets. . . . Raikes' first four Sunday schools, opened in Gloucester in 1780, contained about 80 scholars and four teachers. . .
Source: Wright, J. J., The Sunday School: its Origin and Growth (1900).

(ii) Opposition to educating the poor, 1807

David Giddy . . . giving education to the labouring classes of the poor, would, in effect, be found to be prejudicial to their morals and happiness; it would lead them to despise their lot in life, instead of making them good servants in agriculture and other laborious employments to which their rank in society had destined them; instead of teaching them subordination it would render them factious and refractory, as was evident in the manufacturing counties; it would enable them to read seditious pamphlets, vicious books, and publications against Christianity; it would render them insolent to their superiors. Besides, if the Bill were to pass into law, it would go to burden the country with a most enormous and incalculable expense, and to load the industrious orders of society with still heavier imposts. . . .
Mr Rose . . . had no doubt that the poor ought to be taught to read; as to writing, he had some doubt, because those who had learnt to write well, were not willing to abide at the plough, but looked to a situation in some counting house. . . .
Source: Debate on Whitbread's Parochial Schools Bill (July and August 1807)

(b) Questions

1. What occupations did most of the children follow during the week? Why were they free on Sunday?
2. Did Raikes found a Sunday school for these children because of concern for (i) the children, (ii) other people's property, (iii) to help the children to get better jobs?
3. Why might people have supported Raikes's plans but have opposed an expansion of education for the poor?
4. What did David Giddy expect the poor to do with their lives? Do you agree with him that educating the poor would make them discontented?
5. What dangers did Giddy foresee from educating the poor? Why might current affairs in Europe have affected his opinion?

6. Why would an extension of education lead to an increase in taxation? Which of the following said much the same thing in the 1860s (i) Arnold, (ii) Lowe, (iii) Forster, (iv) Morant?

(c) Further Reading

Dures, A.: *Schools.* Batsford (London, 1971).

Hopkins, E.: *A Social History of the English Working Classes 1815–1945.* Arnold (London, 1983)

Lawson, J. and Silver, H.: *A Social History of Education in England.* Methuen (London, 1977).

Musgrave, P. W.: *Society and Education in England since 1800.* Methuen (London, 1968).

Read, D.: *England 1868–1914: The Age of Urban Democracy.* Longman (Harlow, 1979).

(d) Documentary

Maclure, J. S.: *Education Documents: England and Wales, 1816 to the present day.* Methuen (London, 1979).

Midwinter, E.: *Nineteenth Century Education.* Longman (Harlow, 1970).

(e) Exercises

1. What was the importance of the work of Lancaster and Bell?
2. Show how the government played an increasing role in the education of the working classes between 1833 and 1914.
3. Why was an Education Act required in 1870? How did this Act affect the development of the state education system?
4. Why was an Education Act required in 1902? How did it affect the development of the state education system?
5. Write briefly on (i) payment by results, (ii) Dame Schools, (iii) Robert Raikes and Sunday schools, (iv) higher grade classes.

Index